The FIRE,
the REVELATION
& the FALL

Reader Comments

This book might have changed my entire life. I hope [it] will change the lives of many more people, and help them find a deeper relationship with Jesus Christ just like it did for me.

—**Stephen Holden,** 11, 5th grade, Fellowship Christian School, Roswell, GA

Jenny L. Cote has outdone herself once again with *The Fire, the Revelation, and the Fall*. The book showed me about Paul and his impact on the early church and the persecution of believers during this time. Another appearance of the Antonius family will keep you reading on! This book truly takes the biscuit!

—**Lara Murdock,** 11, 6th grade, Colby Middle School, Colby, KS

With the perfect blend of historical, biblical, and fiction, Jenny is able to bring you into *The Fire, the Revelation, and the Fall* with her relatable, fun characters and direct Bible quotes. Jenny can make you laugh and cry all in one chapter.

—**Lindsay Marcus,** 15, 9th grade, Kellam High School, Virginia Beach, VA

I really enjoyed this book and found it very hard to put down. I love how Mrs. Cote describes biblical characters and stories in so much detail. *The Fire, The Revelation, and The Fall* taught me the importance of being ready for Heaven. I think this book will have an impact on anyone who reads it.

—**Madeline Owens,** 11, Acacia International School, Kampala, Uganda, Africa

The Fire, the Revelation, and the Fall has easily become a favorite of mine. I especially loved seeing the history behind Paul's letters come alive. I can understand them in a whole new light when I know the context of what happened to Paul when he wrote them. Teenagers shouldn't overlook these books as simply children's stories, for they contain wisdom that adds to your understanding of Scripture.

—**Gracie McBride,** 16, Homeschooled, Kennesaw, GA

Another amazing tale of adventure and intrigue that had us reading aloud for hours on end! You will not be disappointed as you dive into the horrors and heroics of the first century, especially the gladiators.

—**Jordan Tenk (and mom Marcie),** 9, Homeschooled, Aylmer, Ontario, Canada

For the last four years I've been devouring Jenny L. Cote's novels. I've learned more about history and the Bible than I ever would have learned otherwise. I'm also amazed at what the early Christians were willing to go through for Christ; giving me strength to live for Christ myself.

—**Leila Soliman,** 12, 7th grade, Homeschooled, Osceola, IN

I somewhat foolishly picked my favorite of Jenny L. Cote's books and decided to declare it "the best," but I was so wrong. *The Fire, the Revelation, and the Fall* surpasses the rest! Whether it's the long-awaited Animalympics, the madman Emperor Nero, Paul's many travels and letters, or John's Revelation, this book will change your view of the early Christian church forever. The Epic Order of the Seven has never been more EPIC!

—**Kenzie R. Hanna,** 15, 10th grade, Stanford Online High School, Des Moines, IA

I love everything about the Epic Order of the Seven® series, but one of my favorite things in all of the books has been the Antonius family. I was so excited to see how involved they were in *The Fire, the Revelation, and the Fall!* I have been reading these books since 3ʳᵈ grade, and I love them as much now as I did then.

—**Victoria Cox,** 15, 10th grade, Coronado High School, El Paso, TX

Ever since we picked up Jenny L. Cote's first Max and Liz adventure, we have been true fans of her books. In *The Fire, the Revelation, and the Fall*, Jenny does an excellent job of showing all the thoughts and feelings Paul is going through during his journey. Cote makes you feel like you are right there with Paul while he is composing his letters. All of her books have a very special place in our home and we enjoy sharing them with our friends.

—**The Keefler Family (Alan 12 and Anna 8),** Homeschooled, Queen Creek, AZ

The Fire, the Revelation, and the Fall captures the reader and reveals the story of the New Testament and the early Church on a whole new level. It challenged and encouraged me to stand up for my faith no matter what, because "to live is Christ and to die is gain."

—**Scarlett Cuvelier,** 17, 12th grade, Homeschooled, Alpha Omega Academy, Woodbridge, VA

This book meant so much to me during one of the most difficult times of my life. It arrived exactly 24 hours before I was scheduled for major surgery and gave me something to not only keep my mind off things, but inspire me and give me strength. Your writing and the teachings of Christ were the last thing I remember before surgery and it was truly epic!

—**Lauren Slaven,** 20, Ball State University, Muncie, IN

This wonderful, biblically-based piece of art is a fantastic way for kids to learn about God in a fun and engaging way. I loved how the animals created the "Animalympics," and Paul really inspired me to keep sharing the Gospel.

—**Maya Allen,** 12, Year 7, Covenant Christian School, Sydney, NSW, Australia

The book was totally EPIC!!! I love how the Antonius family is weaved into the whole Jesus and now Acts story. Leonitus is my favorite character. The other animal characters are cool too, especially Noah and Nate. Whenever I read about them I can't help thinking about the kids they're based on. This is an awesome read, and I recommend it to anyone who likes Christian fiction.

—**Leia Guillen Lagos,** 15, Homeschooled, Otelu Rosu, Romania

A super fantastic and incredible read by Jenny L. Cote! I really enjoy the way the book brings to life the later events of Acts, including the many adventures of both the epic order and the apostles. *The Fire, the Revelation, and the Fall* is an exciting book that any serious bookworm should have on their shelf!

—**Nadia Guillen Lagos,** 17, Homeschooled, Otelu Rosu, Romania

I really loved this story. It really inspired me to write my own stories. I read *The Ark, the Reed, and the Fire Cloud* in 2013 and have been reading this series ever since. It is almost as good as the Bible, but nothing compares to the Word of our God.

—**Samuel Kajewski,** 12, 8th grade, Christian Outreach College Toowoomba, Queensland, Australia

These books have helped me expand on my knowledge of the Bible and imagine what it was truly like during those times. Jenny L. Cote's books help truly bring the Bible to life. I've seriously learned more about the Bible via her books and Adventures in Odyssey than any Sunday School class or sermon!

—**Kirren Siewert,** 20, Evangel University, Springfield, MO

The Epic Order of the Seven® is ready for their toughest mission yet: project New Testament and the launch of the Church. *The Fire, the Revelation, and the Fall* is another outstanding tale of adventure and amazing grace. Mrs. Cote's writing keeps getting better and better.

—**Claire Roberts Foltz,** Cup of Cold Water for Women: Conference Speaker, Author and Storyteller, Atlanta, GA

The Fire, the Revelation, and the Fall is truly an amazing book. Before this book, when I would read the New Testament, I couldn't see the story behind it. Now I will read the New Testament in a new light of how, when, and why Paul wrote to the churches.

—**Hannah Patterson,** 14, Homeschooled, West Sunbury, PA

Even though you've read the Bible and know the story, the writing is so vivid you feel like you're there and don't know what is going to happen next! *The Fire, the Revelation, and the Fall* is the best book ever!

—**Hannah Wohlever,** 10, 4th grade, The Master's Academy, Orlando, FLA

I love reading about Max, Liz, and the rest of the Order of the Seven. Their adventures in *The Fire, the Revelation, and the Fall* have been some of my favorites so far. Jenny's storytelling abilities never cease to amaze me, the way she weaves church history in fiction is my favorite thing about her books.

—**Ruth Anne Crews,** 23, Graduate Student, Southeastern Baptist Theological Seminary, Wake Forest, NC

This story had me laughing and crying. It was so amazing to see the line of Antonius throughout history from the time of Herod and baby Jesus, to Jesus' cross, onto Paul and then to the end with John and his Revelation. This book was one of the best yet.

—**Declan Cole,** 10, 6th grade, Homeschooled, Boydton, VA

C'est magnifique! Mrs. Cote continues to take the biscuit as the Antonius family legend continues in this amazing masterpiece. Jolly good show! Sure, an' keep it up, Lassie!

—**Carissa Boll,** 14, 9th grade, Clover Hill High School, Midlothian, VA

Jenny's stories always strengthen my relationship with God, and I always look forward to reading her books. I would encourage everyone to read *The Fire, the Revelation, and the Fall.* You won't be able to put it down, and I am sure you'll have quite an adventure.

—**Soleil Bourdon,** 15, Homeschooled, Lynchburg, VA

This is an incredible book! It's amazing how it comes to life as you read it. I love how the excitement builds up. It has a lot of spiritual truth and a lot of things you can learn from it. Keep up the good work, Jenny!

—**Savvy Bourdon,** 12, Homeschooled, Lynchburg, VA

As usual, Jenny's characters are delightful, humorous, and informative, using witty dialogue to clarify potentially confusing issues in history and making it relevant to everyday life. Jenny L. Cote masterfully combines history with fiction to make an exciting and suspenseful book.

—**Faith McColl,** 17, 11th grade, Sprayberry High School, Marietta, GA

I quickly discovered that when I was told to put the book away and go to bed, asking to finish a chapter didn't help, because the chapter endings are cliff hangers. I didn't want to put the book down!

—**Jessie Brunson,** 13, 7th grade, Ridgeview Charter School, Sandy Springs, GA

This book was so amazing, and I couldn't put it down. It felt like I was with Paul going on his adventures to Rome! I love all the animals and how [Mrs. Cote] puts so much research into [her] books!

—**Rebecca Dworkin,** 11, 5th grade, Mount Pisgah Christian School, Johns Creek, GA

I loved *The Fire, the Revelation, and the Fall!* I always was a fan of Nigel (British mice are so stylish!), but in this book Al really grew on me. I loved the humor, biblical truth, and action. You can never go wrong with an Epic Order of the Seven® book.

—**Matthew Dworkin,** 11, 5th grade, Mount Pisgah Christian School, John's Creek, GA

It really helped me understand the life of Christ in a new way. I love all of the letters about Him.

—**Logan Frazier,** 10, 4th grade, Barbra Bush Elementary, The Woodlands, TX

The book is amazing! It has the perfect mix of adventure, mystery, and biblical truth. Mrs. Cote does a wonderful job of insuring that younger readers like me are interested while keeping on track with the story the book was intended to tell. Talk about a great book!

—**Paris Bingham,** 10, 5th grade, Johnson Ferry Christian Academy, Marietta, GA

I literally couldn't put this book down! *The Fire, the Revelation, and the Fall* gives great insight into the founding of the church, the martyrs who died for it, and the first Christian emperor. The history is amazing and the story is awesome! Truly epic!

—**Ethan Nunn,** 12, Homeschooled, 7th grade, Brandon, FL

The Fire, the Revelation, and the Fall is a gripping book that is full of danger, courage, and adventure, and is hard to put down. This book, along with all her others, allows the Bible to come to life in a fun and interesting way. Max is definitely my favorite character. He is brave, daring, and is always looking out for others.

—**Nate Kuhlman,** 15, 9th grade, Calvary Christian High School, Clearwater, FL

In *The Fire, the Revelation, and the Fall*, Max and Liz, along with the rest of their animal friends, bring a unique and powerful perspective, one that made me feel as if I had never been told this amazing story before. This inspiring book is definitely one that will have a permanent place in my heart—and on my bookshelf.

—**Mary Donaldson,** 13, 8th grade, Homeschooled, Union Bridge, MD

The Fire, the Revelation, and the Fall was easy to grasp and understand. I didn't want to put the book down.

—**John Carter,** 11, Year Seven, Guildford Grammar School, Perth, Western Australia

Jenny Cote's portrayal of the apostle Paul gives us a glimpse of the passion and love he had for reaching people for Christ. We use the Epic Order of the Seven® books in our homeschool history lessons, and I can't wait to share this one with the kids.

—**Andrea Rodman,** Children's Ministry Director / Homeschool Mom, Gary, IN

If you've picked up this book, get excited because it's AMAZING! There are pages upon pages of stunning insight into the New Testament, such as a beautiful discussion about the armor Paul wrote about in Ephesians. Thank you God, for giving us your Word, and thank you Jenny, for writing such an exciting fictional account of it!

—**Sarah Fritsche,** 16, 10th grade, Erie High School, Erie, CO

I LOVE IT!!! So many details, plots and intricate descriptions! It is such an amazing book and has fueled my desire to read more of the New Testament!

—**Madison Camp,** 15, 9th grade, Artios Academies, Lawrenceville, GA

I love it! The plot just dragged me in and made me lose contact with the world around me. It was so detailed and made me feel like I was in the book, along with the characters.

—**Madeleine Kelly,** 13, 8th grade, Carmel Middle School, Charlotte, NC

The excitement for working for the Lord, the trials and tribulations of Paul, and the cultures of Rome have never been more alive than they are in Cote's new book, *The Fire, the Revelation, and the Fall*.

—**Tiffanie L. White,** 15, 10th grade, Branford High School, Branford, FLA

Jenny L. Cote has the amazing ability to masterfully weave biblical insights and historical events into her stories. Her books have helped me tremendously in many areas of my life. I really hope their legacy lives on in her books to come.

—**Jessica Jones,** 15, 9th grade, Homeschooled, Leesburg VA

Jenny L. Cote has rapidly become my favorite author of all time! Packed with hidden truths straight from the Bible that you might not quickly find, her books are perfect for any age and really bring the Bible to life.

—**Taylor Rose Henceroth,** 14, 8th grade, Homeschooled, Greer, SC

Once again, Jenny has woven a beautiful masterpiece of a story that will change the hearts and lives of all who read it! [It] makes me want to live my life more boldly for Christ. The amount of research that went into this book is incredible. Now I want to visit Rome and the other sites from this book.

—**Hannah Woods,** 10, 5th grade, Homeschooled, Midway, NC

As a homeschool mom, I have read many, many books to my kids—from Dr. Seuss to C. S. Lewis, but none have impacted my family's lives like Jenny L. Cote's books. Every one of Jenny's books has inspired us to live our faith in strong and vibrant ways . . . [just like] Paul and the early church leaders in *The Fire, the Revelation, and the Fall*.

—**Beth Woods,** Curriculum Developer, Homeschool Mom, Midway, NC

Whether you are 72 like me or 10–12 like most readers, anyone can enjoy these books. After allowing our imaginations to work overtime, Jenny always brings us back to the creator and the reality of God's word. No matter the battle that happens to be going on as I read, I know the author will show us that God's truth wins in the end.

—**Sondra McCarty,** 72, Retired Radio Producer, Palm Beach Gardens, FLA

Jenny L. Cote's latest book is a whirlwind of fun, sorrow, mystery, and the Truth. Our furry friends are as lovable as ever, and this inside view of the apostles and their writings will give you a whole new perspective of the Gospel.

—**Avery Jainniney,** 11, 6th grade, Curtis Baptist School, Augusta, GA

I have been reading the Epic books since I was 10 years old. I absolutely couldn't wait to read this latest one, and it was better than I could have imagined! I felt as if

I was right there with the apostles as they went throughout the world to spread the gospel.

—**Sophie Wenz,** 14, 9th grade, Homeschooled, Myrtle Beach, SC

Mrs. Cote is a talented author! I love how she describes everything. She makes history come alive and helps me tie everything together. She inspires me, too. I had the perfect picture of everything in my head as I was reading.

—**Kenna Hartian,** 12, 6th grade, Homeschooled, Inverness, IL

This book was AWESOME! Ever since I read the first book, I have flown through the rest. My favorite character is Max, and I enjoy finding out what will happen next.

—**Eliana Hartian,** 10, 5th grade, Homeschooled, Inverness, IL

EPIC ORDER OF THE SEVEN

The FIRE,
the REVELATION
& the FALL

JENNY L. COTE

LIVING
INK
BOOKS
Writing Worth Reading

Epic Order of the Seven®
The Fire, The Revelation & the Fall

Copyright © 2015 by Jenny L. Cote

Published by Living Ink Books, an imprint of AMG Publishers, Chattanooga, Tennessee (www.LivingInkBooks.com).

Print Edition	ISBN 13: 978-0-89957-794-4
ePUB Edition	ISBN 13: 978-1-61715-443-0
Mobi Edition	ISBN 13: 978-1-61715-444-7
ePDF Edition	ISBN 13: 978-1-61715-445-4

Scripture taken from *The Message*. Copyright © 1993, 1994, 1995, 1996, 2000, 2001, 2002. Used by permission of NavPress Publishing Group. • Scripture quotations are taken from the New American Standard Bible®, Copyright © 1960, 1962, 1963, 1968, 1971, 1972, 1973, 1975, 1977, 1995 by The Lockman Foundation. Used by permission. (www.Lockman.org) • Scripture quotations are taken from the HOLY BIBLE, NEW INTERNATIONAL VERSION®. Copyright © 1973, 1978, 1984, 2011 by Biblica®. Used by permission of Biblica®. All rights reserved worldwide. "NIV" and "New International Version" are trademarks registered in the United States Patent and Trademark Office by Biblica®. Use of either trademark requires the permission of Biblica. • Scripture quotations are taken from the *Holy Bible*, New Living Translation, copyright ©1996, 2004, 2007, 2013 by Tyndale House Foundation. Used by permission of Tyndale House Publishers, Inc., Carol Stream, Illinois 60188. All rights reserved. • Scripture quotations are taken from The Living Bible copyright © 1971. Used by permission of Tyndale House Publishers, Inc., Carol Stream, Illinois 60188. All rights reserved. • Scripture quotations are taken from The Holy Bible, English Standard Version® (ESV®), copyright © 2001 by Crossway, a publishing ministry of Good News Publishers. Used by permission. All rights reserved. • Scripture quotations are taken from *J. B. Phillips: The New Testament in Modern English,* Revised Edition. © J. B. Phillips 1958, 1960, 1972. Used by permission of MacMillan Publishing Co., Inc. • Scripture quotations are taken from the *Good News Bible* © 1994 published by the Bible Societies/HarperCollins Publishers Ltd UK, *Good News Bible* © American Bible Society 1966, 1971, 1976, 1992. Used with permission. • Scripture taken from the New King James Version®. Copyright © 1982 by Thomas Nelson. Used by permission. All rights reserved. • Scripture quotations are taken from The Authorized (King James) Version, which is in the Public Domain.

First AMG Printing—March 2015

EPIC ORDER OF THE SEVEN is a trademark of Jenny L. Cote.

Cover and internal illustrations by Rob Moffitt, Chicago, Illinois. • Interior design by theDESKonline.com. • Editing and proofreading by Rich Cairnes and Rick Steele

Printed in Canada

15 16 17 18 19 - MAR - 7 6 5 4 3 2 1

To Max

If it hadn't been for you, there would have been no books.
Thank you for being my brave-hearted muse,
not only in my pages,
but in your real life's journey as well.

Much love, me wee lad.

This book contains fact, fiction, fantasy, allegory, and truth.

For the entire true story, read the Acts of the Apostles and the rest of the New Testament.

. . . he marked out their appointed times in history . . .
—Acts 17:26

Contents

ACKNOWLEDGMENTS

My Trinitarian Boss

Thank you, God, Jesus, and Holy Spirit for moving my pen to write this book. Your little dictation girl prays she heard you accurately and that you are pleased with the end result.

Max

If it hadn't been for you, there would have been no books. This thought struck me deeply when Max was diagnosed with cancer in 2014. It has been a heartbreaking journey to watch Max endure the rigors of chemotherapy and the effects of dealing with this terrible disease. At the same time, I've watched this wee lad muster the same bravery and determination as he does in the pages of my books, and that has warmed my heart. Adults and children across the world have lifted Max up in prayer, and sent him get-well cards, pictures and even toys. That, too, has warmed my heart. And I know it has warmed the Maker's heart as well. For now we are enjoying each and every day with the real Maximillian Braveheart the Bruce, and take comfort in knowing that we will be able to forever visit him anytime in the pages of my books.

Family, Critique Team, Prayer Warriors

Thank you for your love and for support while I play the juggling game of author, speaker, traveler and researcher: Casey and Alex Cote, Paul and Janice Mims, Claire Roberts Foltz, Lisa Hockman, Lori Marett, Faith McColl. Laura Brunson, thank you for keeping the Epic Bookstore running smoothly and for being my one and only "Gerle." Max and Liz, much love, me wee ones.

The Wise Guys

If you marvel at the deep spiritual insights in my books, please know it certainly isn't all me! Believe me, I *wish* I was that wise! I am deeply indebted to the amazing Bible commentators and authors whose biographies give me invaluable insight and understanding to bring my characters alive. I weave those insights into the dialogue of my characters and the historical background of my stories. I always list my resources in the bibliographies of my books, so if you wish to study in greater detail the characters and the history in my books, please seek out these wonderful works.

I'm also not an expert on ancient military warfare, gladiators, or riding horses, so for numerous instances in this book I've relied heavily on my technical advisor and friend, military historian Mark Schneider. Thank you for lending your keen mind to this book, Mark. You've saved my pen from writing like a girl.

Publishing Team

An EPIC thank you to the people who take what comes out of my pen and turn it into something so beautiful to hold and read! Illustrator Rob Moffitt, Editor Rich Cairnes, Interior Designer Katherine Lloyd, Literary Agent Paul Shepherd, and the AMG Publishers Team: Dale Anderson, Rick Steele, Trevor Overcash, Mike Oldham, Amanda Jenkins, Donna Coker, and the support staff.

Readers

You are truly EPIC! Thank you for your prayers, encouraging notes, letters, pictures, cards, e-mails, and Facebook posts. They make me smile, and you encourage this author's heart more than you could ever know. I'm honored that you love the books and that they inspire you to pursue God and dig into the Bible to discover the true stories behind mine (and to make sure I get things right.) I welcome your feedback on this book at jenny@epicorderoftheseven.com. I'll keep writing as long as you keep reading!

With Epic Love,

xvi

Main Character Profiles

ORDER OF THE SEVEN

Max: a Scottish Terrier from (where else?) Scotland. Full name is Maximillian Braveheart the Bruce. Short, black with a large head, always ready to take on the bad guys. Faithful leader of the team who started with their first mission on Noah's Ark in *The Ark, the Reed, and the Fire Cloud.* Loves to mess with Al, "encouraging" him to work on his bravery. Immortal.

Liz: a petite, French black cat from Normandy. Full name is Lizette Brilliante Aloysius. Brilliant, refined, and strategic leader of the team, beginning with Noah's Ark. Loves the study of history, science, the written word, cultures, and languages. Prides herself on knowing the meanings of names and simply adores gardens. Immortal.

Al: a well-fed, Irish orange cat. Full name is Albert Aloysius, also called "Big Al" by his close friends. Hopelessly in love with his mate, Liz, since Noah's Ark. Simple-minded, but often holds the key to gaining access to impossible places and figuring out things everyone else misses, including deep spiritual truths. Lives to eat and sleep. Afraid of everything. Immortal.

Kate: a white West Highland Terrier, also from Scotland. The love of Max's life ever since they "wed" on the way to the Ark. Has a sweetness that disarms everyone she meets. Is also a fiery lass, unafraid to speak her mind. Always sees the good in others and sticks up for the underdog. Immortal.

Nigel: a jolly, British white mouse with impeccable manners and speech. Wears spectacles and is on the same intellectual level as Liz, joining her in the thrill of discovery. An expert Egyptologist who joined the team on their mission to Egypt with Joseph in *The Dreamer, the Schemer, and the Robe.* Taught Liz all about Egypt, giving her the affectionate term "my pet"—the mouse was the teacher and the cat was his pet. Able to travel quickly and easily via carrier pigeon. Does spying to help carry out missions. Immortal.

Gillamon: a wise, kind mountain goat from Switzerland. Moved to Scotland, where he raised Max (an orphan) and served as his mentor. Died before the Flood, but serves as a spiritual being who delivers mission assignments from the Maker to the team. Can take any shape or form and shows up when least expected.

Clarie: a sweet little lamb from Judea. Shepherds gave her to Mary and Joseph as a gift for Baby Jesus in *The Prophet, the Shepherd, and the Star.* Died enabling the family to escape to Egypt without harm and joined Gillamon as a spiritual being member of the team. Serves as all-knowing guide in the IAMISPHERE when the team goes back in time to observe historical events. Can take any shape or form.

xviii

Open your ears to what I am saying,
for I will speak to you in a parable.

I will teach you hidden lessons from our past—
stories we have heard and known,

stories our ancestors handed down to us.

We will not hide these truths from our children
but will tell the next generation about the glorious deeds of the
LORD. We will tell of his power and the mighty miracles he did.
PSALM 78:1–4 (NLT)

PROLOGUE

THE WRITER'S PEN

CONSTANTINOPLE, AD 403

THE QUICK BROWN FOX JUMPS OVER THE LAZY DOG

Al wrinkled his forehead as he read the freshly inked parchment, the corner of his mouth drawn up in a confused expression as he cocked his head to the side. "Sure, and I think our little monk may be goin' off the deep end, Lass."

"Whatever do you mean, Albert?" Liz replied, jumping from a wooden stool onto the writing desk next to the window. A wooden triangular stand held the parchment, blank except for those words written vertically in the margin. Liz turned her head sideways to see what Al was reading.

The plump Irish cat pointed to the scribbled text with his outstretched paw. "Even *I* know these words ain't in the Bible. Should I tear it up with me iron claw before he gets too far then?"

The sleek black cat giggled, nudging her mate playfully. "No, *mon cher.*" She placed her dainty paw on Al's and lowered it to an opened copy of the Bible sitting on the desk. "You are right that these words are not in the Bible. But our little monk has merely written an abecedarian sentence."

Al quickly raised his paw back up in the air, exposing his pointer claw and sending a fluff of orange fur rising to the ceiling, passing through a beam of sunlight pouring in through the open window. "That's exactly what I were afraid o', Lass! We don't need any more bad writers tryin' to mess up the Bible that ye and Mousie worked so hard to put together! I didn't know this monk were one o' them . . . them . . . *Ab . . . Abracadabraians!* Stand back while I save the world from his fake Bible!"

Al was ready to shred the parchment when Liz got right in his face with her none-too-pleased expression. Her tail was twitching wildly back and forth and her beautiful golden eyes flashed a penetrating warning. "ALBERT, STOP THIS MINUTE!"

"But, Lassie!" Al protested, putting his ears back and drawing his pointer claw up against his chest. "Don't ye need me to rescue the written word from certain heresy . . . and against dogs, at that? I know Max would if he were here!"

Liz's expression softened. She smiled as she considered the zealous braveness of her usually fearful yet lovable mate. The arena was one place to show bravery. A monk's workspace was quite another. "*Abecedarian*. It simply means to practice writing the letters of the alphabet by writing every letter out in one sentence. Our monk must spend long hours each day copying the Bible word for word, letter for letter, and mark for mark. I admire your passion, *cher* Albert, but no rescue is needed. Our little monk is simply getting his handwriting warmed up for the day. His scribbles in the margins are not meant to be part of the written word." Liz giggled and put her paw up on the manuscript to flip it back a few pages. "Sometimes he scribbles comments about his work."

Al leaned in to read what Liz pointed to.

AS THE HARBOR IS WELCOME TO THE SAILOR, SO IS THE LAST LINE TO THE SCRIBE.

Liz flipped to another page. "Or about his working conditions."

OH, MY HAND.

WHILE I WROTE I FROZE, AND WHAT I COULD NOT WRITE BY THE BEAMS OF THE SUN I FINISHED BY CANDLELIGHT.

She flipped to yet another page. "Or even about the effects of his animal companions, no?" Liz teased as Al's fluff of fur landed on the monk's desk.

THE PARCHMENT IS HAIRY.

A sheepish grin spread across Al's face and he popped his pointer claw back into his paw. He gave a nervous chuckle. "Hee-hee. False alarm then, Lass. I'm glad violence were averted here today."

They heard the flutter of wings followed by a pigeon landing on the windowsill. A tiny white mouse wearing golden spectacles jumped off the back of the cooing bird. "Thank you, my dear. I shall see you later this afternoon. Enjoy your friends at the fountain," he said, giving the bird a tender pet. He proceeded to scurry along the windowsill to the corner of the desk, making his way to where Liz and Al sat.

"*Bonjour,* Nige." Liz greeted the British mouse with a smile, extending her paw.

Nigel gracefully kissed her paw and nodded a greeting to Al. "Splendid morning to you both! I say, am I late? I was inspecting a newly arrived shipment of the most *exquisite* tapestries. Ever the bustling commerce down at the docks of Constantinople, you know!"

"Aye, well o' course it is, bein' the eastern Roman 'capital' and all," Al replied. His eyes lit up. "Mousie, did the fisher laddies arrive at the docks with the catch o' the day yet?"

Nigel gave a jolly chuckle and patted Al's growling belly. "Endless basketfuls, old boy."

Al's mouth began to water. "As the harbor be welcome to the sailor, so be the fish to the kitty!"

Nigel raised his eyebrows. "Jolly good. I see you're waxing poetic today."

"I was just showing Albert some of our monk's scribbles," Liz explained. "You're not late, *mon ami.* He had to go refill his inkpot."

Nigel looked up at the parchment, adjusting his spectacles. "And how is our jolly little Telemachus today?"

"Happy as ever. And if the lad brings back some fish for breakfast, I will be, too," Al reported, jumping to the floor to stretch, extending his back foot. "Telemachus, Telemachus, Telemachus. Sure be a funny name. And it's fun to say."

"He may have been named for Telemachus, son of Odysseus in Homer's *Odyssey,*" Nigel explained, clasping his paws behind his back and rolling up on the balls of his feet with a noticeable grin. "One of my favorite pieces of classic mythological literature."

"Hmm, but his existence as a hermit is far from the meaning of his name or of that mythological character's quest," Liz added, thinking this through. One of the intelligent French cat's hobbies was studying the meaning of names. "*Telemachus* means 'decisive' battle.'"

"And the character laddie's quest?" Al wanted to know, rolling onto his back.

"So glad you asked, old boy! I'm thrilled to relay the tale," Nigel enthused, clasping his paws together behind him. "Right, now Telemachus was the son of Odysseus and Penelope. Odysseus was sent off to fight in the Trojan War when Telemachus was an infant. So the young lad set out on a quest to find his father, whom many presumed dead after twenty years. The lad's valiant quest led to many adventures, and once he returned home, our hero was quite the self-confident and assertive young man." Nigel grew animated as he wielded an imaginary bow and arrow and acted out the scene of his narrative. "Happily, Telemachus was indeed proved correct upon the discovery of his disguised father Odysseus, who had also returned home." The little mouse now pretended to wield a sword in the air. "Together, father and son joined forces to slaughter their foes and stood up to their outraged relatives in the final scene of Homer's brilliant work, the *Odyssey.*"

Al and Liz locked eyes. Liz muffled a soft giggle as she applauded while Nigel took a bow. Al smiled a goofy grin. "I forgot how excited ye got with yer mythology then, Mousie."

Suddenly they heard heavy footsteps coming down the hall, and the happy humming of Telemachus nearing the room.

"*Il est ici!* Hide, *mon ami!*" Liz exclaimed, prodding Nigel to jump off the desk.

"Cheerio!" Nigel exclaimed, quickly hiding behind a stack of books. "May our scribe's pen be swift today," the mouse whispered, peeking his head out.

A short, chubby middle-aged man wearing a simple brown robe and sandals entered the room. He carried a small basket in one hand and a black inkpot in the other. His round ruddy face broke out into a big smile when he saw Liz sitting on his desk. The monk's kind hazel eyes seemingly disappeared behind his cherublike cheeks. "Right where I left you." He placed the inkpot in the slender groove attached to his desk next to the red, blue, and yellow inkpots. "My inkpot is full of black ink, just like you, my little black beauty." The happy little man tickled Liz under the chin while holding the basket by his side.

Al meowed as the contents of the basket hovered over his head. Telemachus gave a jolly laugh. "And *you* will soon be full, too, my fluffy orange friend. I didn't forget." He lowered the basket onto the floor, revealing several small fish inside. "I've already blessed it."

"AYE! THANKS, LAD! HAPPY WRITIN' THEN. I'LL LEAVE YE TO IT," Al meowed, grabbing one of the fish, ready to enjoy his breakfast.

Liz winked at Nigel and shook her head at her predictable mate.

"Now then," Telemachus exclaimed with a grunt as he situated himself onto the stool that creaked under his weight. His short brown hair was neatly combed and looked like a bowl. He started humming his happy tune and picked up a small knife with his left hand that he used for scraping mistakes off his parchment, or for sharpening his quill. He picked up his quill and examined it closely. The monk then began to trim the tip so he could resume his work. "Where were we?"

He looked up and noticed that the page was now turned to the twenty-third chapter of Acts. "Odd. I was just starting Romans," Telemachus remembered. He gazed out the window to the beautiful blue sky and the brilliant sunshine now pouring into the room. "The breeze must have turned the pages." He leaned in to get eye to eye with Liz, holding up his quill with a chuckle. "Unless you were reading to make sure I penned every word correctly, eh?"

"If you only knew, Monsieur," Liz meowed in reply.

Suddenly the monk's gaze landed on a verse that seemed to jump off the page and into his heart.

THAT NIGHT THE LORD STOOD BY PAUL AND SAID, "DON'T BE AFRAID! YOU HAVE GIVEN YOUR WITNESS FOR ME HERE IN JERUSALEM, AND YOU MUST ALSO DO THE SAME IN ROME."

A fragrant breeze blew into the room, gently lifting the corner of the page, making it seem alive. Telemachus set the knife and quill down and placed his hand over his heart as a revelation entered his mind. "Paul had often longed to go to Rome." He leaned over to the opened Bible on his desk that he was copying onto the fresh parchment. He read aloud from the first chapter of Romans:

YOU MUST REMEMBER, MY FRIENDS, THAT MANY TIMES I HAVE PLANNED TO VISIT YOU, BUT SOMETHING HAS ALWAYS KEPT ME FROM DOING SO. I WANT TO WIN CONVERTS AMONG YOU ALSO, AS I HAVE AMONG OTHER GENTILES.

Telemachus scratched his beardless chin. "There's more about Rome!" he muttered excitedly, turning the pages back to the nineteenth chapter of Acts. Liz stole a glance with Nigel, who shrugged his little shoulders. They recognized the inspiration of the Holy Spirit when they saw it. Something was happening here.

AFTER THESE THINGS HAD HAPPENED, PAUL MADE UP HIS MIND TO TRAVEL THROUGH MACEDONIA AND ACHAIA

AND GO ON TO JERUSALEM. "AFTER I GO THERE," HE SAID, "I MUST ALSO SEE ROME."

"Hmmm," the monk mumbled, turning the pages once again to Romans, to the fifteenth chapter. He read the verses out loud:

PRAY THAT I MAY BE KEPT SAFE FROM THE UNBELIEV-ERS IN JUDEA AND THAT THE CONTRIBUTION I TAKE TO JERUSALEM MAY BE FAVORABLY RECEIVED BY THE LORD'S PEOPLE THERE, SO THAT I MAY COME TO YOU WITH JOY, BY GOD'S WILL, AND IN YOUR COMPANY BE REFRESHED.

"Paul didn't know if he would get away from Jerusalem alive," Telemachus realized aloud. "So he asked the Romans to pray for him so he could reach them." The monk turned his gaze back to the open parchment and began to stroke Liz. Again he read:

THAT NIGHT THE LORD STOOD BY PAUL AND SAID, "DON'T BE AFRAID! YOU HAVE GIVEN YOUR WITNESS FOR ME HERE IN JERUSALEM, AND YOU MUST ALSO DO THE SAME IN ROME."

The monk's eyebrows lifted and tears of emotion welled up in his eyes. "But from then on, Paul was *sure*. He had no doubt. Jesus himself had told him to go to Rome, so Paul knew he would make it there alive." His face quickly fell. "Jesus didn't promise him protection once he arrived in Rome, but he at least promised him a safe delivery there."

Another gust of wind blew into the room and the fur on Liz, Al, and Nigel stood on end. This was no ordinary Wind.

Telemachus closed his eyes and shook his head slowly side to side, once again with a hand on his heart.

"*GO TO ROME,*" a Voice spoke into his heart.

The monk quickly opened his eyes. "Go to Rome? But why?" he muttered aloud.

"*GO TO ROME,*" the Voice repeated.

While Telemachus leaned over the desk and rested his face in his hands, Nigel mouthed to Liz, "It's the Maker!"

"*Oui,*" Liz meowed. She leaned over, purring, and meowed in the monk's ear. *"Do not be afraid,* mon ami. *If the Maker is calling you, he has a purpose only you can fulfill."*

Telemachus raised his head and smiled at the meowing cat. He petted her while he once more read the words Jesus was speaking to Paul, this time seeing them written directly for *his* heart:

"DON'T BE AFRAID! YOU HAVE GIVEN YOUR WITNESS FOR ME HERE IN JERUSALEM, AND YOU MUST ALSO DO THE SAME IN ROME."

The gentle little monk sat a long while in silence, praying and petting Liz. Finally, he let go a deep breath and opened his eyes. "Very well, my Lord. I don't understand why you wish me to leave my 'Jerusalem' and go to Rome, but if you are calling me there, I will do as you say."

Tears welled up in Liz's eyes as she remembered the Maker calling her to go to an unknown destination when he called the animals to Noah's Ark. She remembered the uncertainty and the fear. She remembered the unanswered questions. She remembered that she had had to immediately obey, once the Voice had spoken to her heart. She looked with love at this dear little monk and rubbed her cheek on his face. She knew how Telemachus felt, right now in this moment. Liz meowed, *"You will not travel alone,* cher *Telemachus. Just as we went with Paul to Rome, we will also go with you."*

Telemachus kissed the little cat who showed him such affection. "I think it is time for me to lay down my quill, my little black beauty. We are off to Rome." The monk looked around his humble workspace at the volumes of books he had so faithfully penned over the years, and somehow knew that his scribal work had come to an end. He knew he would leave this copy of the New Testament incomplete, but it didn't matter. Someone would take his place and finish it.

He picked up the quill and dipped it into the ink. "Just a few more words." Telemachus proceeded to carefully write several lines in the margin as Liz looked on. When he was finished, he took a deep breath and set down his quill. He nodded to himself, muttered an "Amen," picked up a burlap satchel, and went out the door.

"So we're headed back to Rome?" Al asked from the floor, picking his teeth with a fish bone. "I'd better pack." He gathered up the remaining fish in his arms. "Okay, I'm ready," the cat announced with a goofy grin. "Looks like our Telemachus will have *his own* Odyssey after all, huh, Mousie?"

"Indeed, it appears so." Nigel hurried out from behind the books to join Liz on the desk. "What did he write, my dear?"

Liz couldn't speak, but wiped her eyes as Nigel read aloud:

O, LITTLE BOOK! A DAY WILL COME IN TRUTH WHEN SOMEONE OVER YOUR PAGE WILL SAY, "THE HAND THAT WROTE IT IS NO MORE."

Nigel paused and shared a teary look with Liz. "If his Odyssey ends in Rome, I wonder if he will live up to his name."

"Decisive battle," Liz softly restated.

The little mouse swallowed the lump in his throat and read the monk's last words:

LET THE READER'S VOICE HONOR THE WRITER'S PEN.

PART ONE

MANY ADVERSARIES

Seven Wonders

NOVEMBER AD 52

I 've been wonderin' somethin'," Max said as they walked behind Paul on the dusty road. The Scottish terrier wrinkled his brow. "Why weren't Paul driven out fr-r-rom the synagogue in Ephesus when we were here the last time? The Jewish lads even asked him ta *keep* speakin'. That were not the usual way of things. Everywhere the lad's been it were always the same." Max bobbed his head side to side. "Pr-r-reach in the synagogue, get kicked out, pr-r-reach ta the Gentiles, then tr-r-rouble comes callin' until he's finally r-r-run out of town," he growled. "I wonder if things might be different here for a change."

"I have wondered the same thing, no? Of course, Paul was only here in Ephesus for a week before we left for Jerusalem. It will be interesting to see what has happened with Aquila and Priscilla here the past eight months. They sought to make friends and get their tent-making business thriving for Paul's return after his furlough." Liz curled the tip of her skinny black tail into a question mark as she walked along next to Max. "I'm happy we were able to see Kate for just a little while in Jerusalem. But I wonder when we will see my Albert again."

Max stole a sad look from Liz. "I'm sorry Peter weren't there so ye could see yer Al, Lass. That fisherman has moved on from Jerusalem ta spr-r-read the Good News around the region. But I'm sure that kitty be keepin' the lad near cities where there's fish."

"Of that I have no doubt, *mon ami!*" Liz smiled. "Your Kate is very happy with John and Mary. What an honor for her to share in John's assignment to care for Jesus' mother. I wonder if they will ever leave Jerusalem."

Nigel sat up straight on Max's back as an incredible sight came into view. "And *I* wonder why Antipater had to choose such a dark and dastardly place as this for the Seventh Wonder of the World."

"I thought *we* were the seven wonders of the world," Max quipped. "Who's Antipater?"

"Antipater of Sidon, old boy. He was a poet who lived two hundred years ago. His poem listed nearly all the Seven Wonders of the World," Nigel replied. He cleared his throat to recite Antipater: *I have gazed on the walls of impregnable Babylon along which chariots may race, and on the Zeus by the banks of the Alpheus, I have seen the hanging gardens, and the Colossus of the Helios, the great man-made mountains of the lofty pyramids, and the gigantic tomb of Mausolus; but when I saw the sacred house of Artemis that towers to the clouds, the others were placed in the shade, for the Sun himself has never looked upon its equal outside Olympus.*

"But Antipater left the Lighthouse of Alexandria off his poetic list. Other esteemed writers have listed it in their guidebooks for tourists," Liz added. "Of course, we have seen all of these wonders in our travels to Babylon, Egypt, and Greece. The hanging gardens were one of my favorites when we were with Daniel in Babylon."

"And I, of course, love Egypt's pyramids," Nigel chimed in.

"Aye, we've seen it all," Max noted. "But that Antipater lad forgot one of the gr-r-randest wonders there be: Noah's Ark. At 450 feet long, 54 feet high, an' 75 feet wide, that's a wonder ye don't want ta miss."

"Indeed you're right. But it seems most humans can't find the Ark. It is in a rather difficult place to reach," Nigel replied. "I am most grateful that you took me to see it. It must have been extraordinary to be aboard that vessel!"

Liz smiled as she remembered the incredible year on that first fateful mission with Noah. They didn't meet Nigel until their second mission in Egypt with Joseph, so had taken the curious mouse to see the abandoned Ark high in the Mountains of Ararat. "If we had not been successful in that mission, there would be no other worldly wonders here today." The black cat frowned as she heard the sounds of merchants

4

selling their wares at this bustling site. "The humans have once again turned to darkness just as they did before the Flood."

"It is extraordinary that this Temple of Artemis is larger than Noah's Ark, and took twice as long to build." Nigel grimaced at the growing crowd of people as they neared the Temple area. Merchants displayed their wares on rugs around the perimeter, holding up silver and terracotta images of the goddess Artemis, along with amulets and charms for sale. Visitors traveled home with souvenirs, and Ephesus swelled with money from the tourist trade. "Antipater considered the Temple the most radiant wonder of them all, but I submit that it is the darkest place on Earth."

Paul stopped in his tracks and stared at the massive staircase leading up to the imposing Temple of Artemis. This was not only the nerve center of idol worship in Ephesus, but for all of Asia Minor. Several hundred thousand people came here annually to pay tribute to the mother goddess. Paul had been to the Parthenon in Athens, but this building was four times as large and had taken 220 years to build. It was 425 feet long, 225 feet wide, and 60 feet high. No expense was spared for this house of Artemis. It was lined with 127 Ionic marble columns weighing fifteen tons each, and each the gift of a king. Built with monies provided by pagans throughout Asia, this temple was adorned with richly colored frescoes and gold-glittered sculptures of humans giving homage to the goddess. Fires lit up massive cauldrons at the base of the staircase, and eerie music played as people wailed and danced outside.

"I wonder wha' the big deal be aboot this false goddess." Max scowled. "There sure be a lot of humans here ta see her."

"I wonder as well, *cher* Max. Artemis is the goddess of fertility, but is quite grotesque in her appearance," Liz offered. "More than six thousand priestesses work here to honor her with their despicable rituals of sacrifice."

"The humans sadly think that Artemis fell from Jupiter in the heavens and chose Ephesus as her earthly dwelling," Nigel added with a frown. "What these pitiful creatures do not understand is that a meteor simply landed here! They actually sculpted that black meteorite into the form of the goddess."

"*Oui*, they set up her idol in the spot where she supposedly landed, and built this complex outside the city. The humans wanted it to be visible from far away," Liz explained. "Although we are more than a mile from the city, ships arriving in the harbor can easily see this temple and believe that Artemis watches their arrival."

Max shook his head in disbelief. "Let me get this str-r-raight. A big black r-r-rock comes flyin' out of the sky an' lands in a cr-r-rater. So the humans turn that chunk of r-r-rock inta an idol an' build this big temple ta worship it? They must all be daft!"

Nigel pointed to his head. "Remember the deluded state of these pagans, old boy. They are as lost in the dark as one could possibly be, yet Ephesus is known as the 'Light of Asia.' This is because it is here in this tolerant city where new ideas are launched. If an idea makes it in Ephesus, it will easily spread to the entire region of Asia Minor."

"Which is why Ephesus is a brilliant place for Paul to establish a ministry base for all of Asia Minor," Liz offered. She looked at Paul, whose face wore the grief of watching thousands of lost people wallowing in evil. Paul had just met twelve men on the road here who believed in God but didn't understand that Jesus was Messiah. He easily shared the Good News and baptized them on the spot, and they experienced the coming of the Holy Spirit. It was an encouraging moment as he got ready to enter Ephesus, but he wondered if the dark souls of this city would embrace Christ as readily. Liz went on, "If Paul, Aquila, and Priscilla can make the gospel take hold here at Ephesus, they'll prove it can take hold anywhere. Even in Rome."

Max's eyes widened. "Now THAT would be the *eighth* wonder of the world then, Lassie!"

A merchant holding small rolls of paper in his hand came running up to Paul. "Buy an Ephesian letter! It will bring you good fortune for love and business! You will have guaranteed safety in travel!"

Paul placed his hand on the shoulder of the eager young man and looked deeply into his brown eyes. "My friend, I do not need a good luck charm. I have something better. I have the love of God with me at all times. He protects me and gives me his favor. I would love to tell you about him."

The merchant looked puzzled at first, then smiled. "You have the love of a god? How is that possible?" He turned and looked behind him at the Temple of Artemis. The only love he knew was an empty, worldly love that was required by the goddess. But the goddess didn't love *him*.

The idea of a god loving him was intriguing. "What is your god's name?"

"His name is Jesus," Paul said warmly. "And what is your name?"

"Epaphras," the young man replied.

"And I'm Paul. Why don't you come with me, Epaphras, and I'll tell you all about Jesus."

With that the young merchant started walking with Paul the mile and a half into the heart of Ephesus.

☧

Ephesus was filled seemingly to bursting with 250,000 people from all walks of life. It followed Rome, Alexandria, and Antioch as the fourth greatest city in the world. But it was one of the most important military strongholds of the Roman Empire. Caesar Augustus placed his proconsul here to govern all of Asia Minor, He reported directly to the emperor and the Roman Senate. Soldiers and sailors filled the streets of Ephesus to ensure the proconsul's security, keeping places of ill repute, the amphitheater, and the stadium packed.

Since the Romans did not discriminate against any culture, all races were welcomed in Ephesus. When Cleopatra and Mark Antony wintered here in 33 BC, a large population of Egyptians came here and brought their gods with them. The Egyptians built ornate temples to the goddess Isis and her husband, Serapis. When Cleopatra was warring with her siblings over the throne of Egypt, Julius Caesar had Cleopatra's sister Arsinoe brought to Ephesus, where she was kept prisoner. For a while Arsinoe took refuge in the Temple of Artemis, seeking the protection of the goddess. Eventually she was executed on the steps of the Temple of Artemis by order of Mark Antony, and her tomb was built in the heart of the city.

Ephesus sat on a huge harbor of the Cayster River, five miles from the Aegean Sea. As ships arrived in the massive harbor, they saw the Temple of Artemis in the distance and the Harbor Bath House just off the docks. It was customary for new arrivals to bathe before entering the city so as not to bring sickness and filth inside. As they approached the city entrance there stood one of the largest slave markets in the world. A huge population of slaves filled this city of decadence, serving the needs of the wealthy masses here.

Visitors would then walk through the impressive Harbor Gate, the official entry point of Ephesus. There before them stretched an immense white marble boulevard lined with two hundred columns on either side. The main street stretched 1,800 feet long and 35 feet wide. Pedestrians walked along the lavish, colorful mosaic sidewalks, where statues of gods and notable citizens proudly stood on pedestals all along the route. These statues were painted in vibrant colors to make their clothes, and even their hair, look lifelike. Hundreds of shops, restaurants, and businesses lined the streets under terracotta-tiled rooftop colonnades, and at night the street was lit up by two rows of torches. Ephesus was a city that never slept.

The main street dead-ended with an intersection of decision. If one wanted entertainment, one walked straight ahead up the steps and into the Great Theater of Ephesus. Here twenty-four thousand people attended plays, comedies, musicals, speeches, and occasional fights. If one wanted the educational heart of the city, he turned right onto Marble Street to head to Philosopher's Square. Here the city buzzed with students, philosophers, and men of commerce, as the school of philosophy was located off the Central Market, the main *agora* of Ephesus. And if one wanted bloodshed, one turned left onto the street named Plateia in Coressus, which led to the Stadium where gladiators fought to the death. This street eventually led out to the Temple of Artemis, past the massive graveyard where defeated gladiators were taken for burial outside the Stadium.

The Central Market area included the Central Bath House, public toilets, restaurants, inns, and shops. From the Central Market one could venture north into the wealthiest part of the city onto Curetes Street. Here were richly terraced homes filled with theater rooms, courtyards, kitchens, running water, indoor toilets, and ventilation to keep the wealthy cool in the summer and warm in the winter. A luxurious upper bath house and gymnasium was located in this area, as well as the Basilica, which was the administrative heart of Ephesus. Temples to various gods and goddesses abounded here, with an upper marketplace for the wealthiest patrons to buy goods from all over the world.

"Wha's an Ephesian letter anyway?" Max asked as they walked along Marble Street toward the Central Market. Paul still talked to the merchant who carried the Ephesian letters in his hand.

"It's a good luck charm, a letter with spells to cast off evil spirits," Liz explained.

Nigel shuddered. "Humans wear these *abracadabras* next to their skin for greatest effect. Ironically, it's dreadfully evil."

"But one day, the term 'Ephesian letter' will take on an entirely new meaning," came a voice from behind them.

The animals quickly turned to see throngs of people passing by in their colorful garments embroidered with gold. Some women laughed as they walked by in their heavy makeup and elaborate jewelry, followed by slaves carrying packages. A group of men strolled along discussing the latest plans for enlarging one of the terraced houses. Another group of men gathered for a heated political debate. Two soldiers clutching round shields and spears walked by, almost tripping over Max, who had stopped there in the middle of the street.

"Who said that?" Max asked, looking around.

"Over here," came the voice.

Liz scanned the street lined with painted statues of gods and heroes, but her gaze landed in the center of the Central Marketplace. She caught her breath as she saw the imposing statue of the Emperor Claudius wink at her. The statue depicted the bare-chested emperor as the chief Roman god Jupiter, with a lavish garment draped over his left shoulder and a laurel crown on his head. In his left hand he held Jupiter's signature lightning bolt, and by his feet was the Roman army's most coveted symbol, the eagle. Despite the throngs of people milling about, no human was paying attention to the statue.

"The Emperor is calling!" Liz announced, running over to the statue.

Max grinned and trotted behind her with Nigel on his back. "Aye, I thought so."

"*Bonjour,* Gillamon!" Liz said, gazing up at the statue.

"I'm glad to see you all made it safely to Ephesus," the statue replied with a smile. Gillamon was the spiritual head of the Order of the Seven and could take any shape or form to communicate with the team. He appeared in his natural form of a majestic mountain goat in the IAM-ISPHERE, where the team met with him to get assignments and to travel through time or space. But outside that vehicle, Gillamon could show up as an animal, a human, the words of a scroll, or, as now, the likeness of a statue.

"Splendid to see you, old chap!" Nigel cheered. "You've switched Emperor statues since we saw you last."

"Yes, from Caesar Augustus to Emperor Claudius," Gillamon chuckled, looking down at the eagle that now turned its head to gaze at them. "And this time I have my sidekick."

"I told Gillamon I wanted to try marble on for size," the eagle announced.

Max's eyes widened. "Clarie? Is that ye, Lass?"

The eagle moved its wings slightly and smiled. "Hello, Max. It's me indeed."

Clarie was the other spiritual member of the Order of the Seven. She was a lamb who gave up her life in order for Joseph, Mary, and Baby Jesus to escape that horrible night of the Slaughter of the Innocents in Bethlehem. Like Gillamon, she could take any shape or form. When members of the team traveled back in time, Clarie served as their guide to help them return to the present.

"I am so happy to see you like this, *chère amie!*" Liz said, head-butting the eagle. "I wondered when you would show up again."

"Paul took you on quite the reunion route with his churches in Galatia," Gillamon said. "The infant churches are taking root, but you will see Paul's greatest achievement here in Ephesus."

Max smiled broadly. "That's gr-r-rand news, Gillamon! I were jest sayin' I hoped it would be different here this time."

"Somewhat different, yes, but still the same in many respects," Gillamon replied. "You'll soon see. But the opposition here will be fierce, so prepare yourselves for that."

"We shall be ready for the dreaded Adversary!" Nigel proclaimed with his tiny fist raised in the air.

"Gillamon, you mentioned a new Ephesian letter. Might I presume that the pattern of Paul writing to the churches he has started will continue with a new church here in Ephesus?" Liz asked.

The statue nodded. "Indeed, Liz. Yet from this ministry base will come six other key churches. Together, these seven churches will become the recipients of letters that will contain some of the most important words ever penned, because of the Pen that will write them. Ephesus is known as the 'Light of Asia,' yet even this pagan city's reputation will take on new meaning and spread to the other churches. Those candles will outshine the Seven Wonders of the World."

Liz clasped her paws together. *"C'est magnifique!"*

"Your continuing mission of bringing a New Testament into being is progressing nicely," the eagle assured them. "You'll be pleased to know that Matthew and Mark continue to refine their work."

"Indeed! So far we have assisted Paul with a letter to the Galatians and two to the Thessalonians," Nigel reported.

"And Nigel had the privilege of assisting James with his letter while in Jerusalem," Liz reminded them.

Nigel straightened his spectacles and grinned broadly. "Ah, yes, from the pens of James and 'Anonymouse.'" The mouse chuckled. "That was a splendid letter indeed."

"Clarie, did those cr-r-razy cr-r-ritters Noah an' Nate get that second letter ta the Thessalonians like they were supposed ta?" Max asked with a serious look. "When they went off floatin' in the gourd, I wondered if Paul's wr-r-ritin' would ever make it."

"Of course! They delivered the letter safe and sound," the eagle replied, ruffling its feathers. "Who do you think secretly escorted them to Thessalonica to make sure it arrived?"

Max winked at the eagle. "That's a good lass. That monkey an' lizard had me worried."

"Noah and Nate were ecstatic about delivering the letter. While Nate was strategizing about how to slip it into the humans' house without being seen, Noah swung by his tail from the rafters and through a window before Nate knew what was happening, grabbing a banana from the table on his way out." The eagle smiled. "From there they set off on their quest to tell animals everywhere about the coming Animalympics in Rome."

"*Bon!* I've wondered when we will make it to Rome to organize that event," Liz said. "Gillamon, might we know so we can map out the details?"

"Of course you might, with time," Gillamon teased. He never told them everything that would happen in their missions. "Paul's writing will pick up speed, so for now you will be quite busy with keeping his pen moving and seeing those letters safely delivered. The games can wait."

"An' wha' aboot me keepin' Paul safe?" Max asked.

The statue sighed. "One thing that will not be different here is persecution, Max. Paul will continue to suffer, and you will not always

11

get to protect him. But rest assured, you will know when you must intervene, my friend. I know it is difficult for you, but Paul's suffering is fueling his pen to impact believers for generations to come. And it serves as a catalyst to raise up more believers to stand strong in the faith when tyrants seek to silence them."

The statue looked at Liz, whose face looked sad. "You're missing your Albert, aren't you, Little One?"

Liz nodded silently and the eagle put her wing around the cat's shoulders.

"We'll see if we can arrange a reunion soon," the statue offered.

Liz's eyes brightened. *"Merci."*

"Faith? Gabriel? Where are you?" came Paul's voice coming down the street, using the names he had given to Liz and Max.

"Time to go," the eagle said, turning its gaze once more up to the statue.

"A final word," the statue said, resuming its sculpted form. "Find the real Tyrant."

Max, Liz, and Nigel looked at one another and then up to the statue, wondering what Gillamon meant.

"There you are!" Paul squatted down to pet the animals and noticed them gazing up at the statue. "You must be wondering who this is. Never mind Claudius. He's just the latest tyrant of Rome. Come, let's get to Aquila and Priscilla's house."

As Paul walked away, Nigel tapped his chin thoughtfully. "I wonder exactly which real Tyrant we are supposed to find."

Max trotted after Paul. "Aye, an' wha' are we supposed ta do once we find him, I wonder?"

THE SLAVE AND HIS MASTER

H E'S BACK, PRISCILLA!" Aquila exclaimed, opening the door for Paul. The tall, burly man enveloped Paul with a fierce bear hug, lifting him off the ground. "Praise God you've returned safely to Ephesus, my friend!"

Paul chuckled at Aquila's dancing brown eyes behind his bushy eyebrows. Aquila's curly, wild hair and blackish-brown beard were full of tent fibers. "I see you've been working hard at making tents," Paul said, pulling out a strip of leather cord stuck in Aquila's hair.

"Uh, yes, I'm a bit of a mess," Aquila laughed. "Come in, come in! And I see your faithful traveling companions are with you. Hello there, Gabriel." The big man squatted down to muss Max's fur and to pick up Liz for an embrace. "Hello, little Faith." Liz almost disappeared into the man's large arms, meowing a muffled *"Bonjour."*

"Paul! Welcome!" Priscilla exclaimed, wiping her hands on an apron. "I'm just making supper so you're right on time." She hurried over to give Paul a warm hug. Her long brown hair was pulled back with a colorful headband, and her beautiful olive complexion glistened.

"It's wonderful to see you both again," Paul told them with a big smile. "I've got so much to tell you, and I can't wait to hear about how things are going here in Ephesus."

"Have a seat and tell us about your journey," Aquila said, putting

Liz down with a thump on a pillow on the floor next to the low table. He took a basin of water and washed Paul's feet.

Priscilla poured a cup of water and placed some dates on the table. "Yes, and what is the news from Jerusalem?"

Paul took a big gulp of water and wiped his mouth with the back of his hand. "I didn't realize how thirsty I was. Thank you. Everyone in Jerusalem sends their regards. James still leads the church there, and John remains in the city with Mary. The rest of Jesus' original disciples have dispersed to spread the gospel throughout the world as he commanded. James occasionally gets reports from some of them. Matthew is traveling around the Caspian Sea, Andrew is in Scythia, and Thomas has gone as far as India."

Priscilla set more food on the table. "It is exciting to see the church begin to grow on its own now, with new bodies of believers scattered everywhere."

"Indeed, but the Jerusalem church is in great need of support from believers far and wide," Paul said as he reached for some bread. "They don't have many Gentiles in the city to give practical aid for the sick and aged. I shared with James an idea to support the Jerusalem church with an offering from churches everywhere. If Christ's church as a whole prays and supports the church in Jerusalem, it will unite us all in a joint effort, honor the city of Jesus' death, and it can even help fund missionaries to go east, just as I've gone west."

Priscilla clasped her hands with joy. "What a wonderful idea! I think believers will be happy to help."

"Indeed. As I went back to Antioch and through all the churches we started on the first two journeys—Galatia, Derbe, Lystra, Iconium, Pisidian Antioch—support was unanimous. I already have a large sum to send to Jerusalem."

"If pagans far and wide raised money to pay for the Temple of Artemis here, Christians far and wide can raise money to support the church of Jerusalem there," Aquila noted.

"Yes, and speaking of which, I met a young man named Epaphras by the Temple on my way into town and he has embraced Jesus. He'll join us at the synagogue tomorrow and said he would bring some friends along. Tell me about other believers here."

"We've had only a few as we're full-time tentmakers, but we did

14

already send one named Apollos to help the church in Corinth," Aquila explained. "He's zealous but was a bit misguided. He didn't understand about Jesus as Messiah and only knew of John's baptism. So we helped him understand the truths of Christ, and before long he was eager to go help the Corinthians."

"We think he'll be a dynamic force there," Priscilla shared. She placed her hand on Paul's arm and smiled. "And we asked him to tell Timothy to join us when he can."

Paul smiled at the thought of being with his adopted son, Timothy. "I can't wait to see him again!"

Max, Liz, and Nigel sat in the corner and listened to the three friends getting caught up on all things happening in Ephesus. They shared how they attended the synagogue where Paul had briefly preached. The Jews were much more open-minded than in Thessalonica and Corinth, so things looked promising.

"Sounds like the stage is set for their work to begin immediately," Nigel noted.

"Aye, but I wonder where the Tyrant will show up," Max said.

Liz's tail curled slowly up and down as she listened and pondered. "According to Gillamon, it is *we* who must find *him.*"

THREE MONTHS LATER

The sound of whips cracking on stone echoed in the air. Voices shouted in the marketplace as the bidding for slaves began. Max, Liz, and Nigel stood in the back of the crowd and stared at the sad sight of slaves up for sale on the auction block. A row of young men stood defiantly on stone pedestals as potential buyers forced open their mouths to inspect their teeth. If a slave's teeth were good, it meant he was likely in good health and would be able to do strong manual labor. It also made the slave more expensive.

"I shall never get used to seeing human beings treated this way," Liz lamented. "I am reminded of Joseph being offered on the auction block in Egypt and how cruelly they treated him."

"Aye, but me an' Mousie helped save the day for the lad when ye got Potiphar ta notice him then," Max reminded her.

"But only after our loud camel friend Osahar prevented another

15

buyer from purchasing Joseph," Nigel added. "Camel spit is utterly revolting but, in Joseph's case, saved the day."

Liz smiled as she remembered that scene in the slave market of Egypt and how they had arranged for Joseph to go to a good position in the wealthy home of Potiphar. "How I wish we could rescue another slave here today. *Quel dommage,* just look at them. Such a sad existence for slaves."

"How do these lads an' lassies even get ta this point as slaves?" Max asked with a furrowed brow.

"Right, well, most Roman slaves are born into slavery or become slaves through any number of circumstances," Nigel explained, crossing his arms over his chest. "Some need to escape punishment for crimes, others to pay off debts, so they sell themselves into slavery. But Rome's primary source of slaves is from military conquests in foreign lands. The Romans despise manual labor, so the majority of slaves are male and can better handle hard physical tasks. The Roman Empire has public slaves to work on its many construction projects, but also private slaves that belong to its citizens. Slaves are also used as gladiators in the arenas to provide entertainment for the masses. Simply dreadful."

"Do you see those scrolls tied around their necks?" Liz pointed out to Max. "Those scrolls provide the slave's name, nationality, character, and a guarantee from the slavemaster that the slave will not steal or run away. If the slave proves defective, the buyer can return the scroll for a refund within six months."

"Do the poor lads have any hope then?" Max asked sadly.

"Slaves are interestingly given two 'freedoms' if you will," Nigel replied, straightening his spectacles. "They are allowed to worship the god of their choosing, and they can earn a small wage to save. If they earn enough money, they may attempt to buy their freedom, but their owners of course must be willing to release them."

"OOOOOOOHHHH!" moaned a slave who was knocked to the ground by a cruel slavemaster.

"Speaking of why we are here," Nigel interjected, "if there is any place to find a tyrant, it must be here where slavedrivers abound."

"Aye, do ye think we need ta find such a tyr-r-rant in order ta save some slave?" Max growled, looking around at the hard men driving the slaves. The fur rose on his back.

"You've picked a good place to search for the real Tyrant," came a voice of a man standing next to them.

"Clarie?" Liz asked.

"Yes," the man replied with a wink. "We were hoping you'd come here today. You need to be witness to a transaction getting ready to occur."

"I daresay I shall never get used to seeing such a genteel lamb dressed in human clothing, much less in a *man's* clothing!" Nigel chuckled. "My dear, can you please help clarify what 'real Tyrant' means? I'm afraid we're simply at a loss."

"Aye, we've been searchin' for thr-r-ree months, an' haven't found him," Max added.

"*Oui,* we've looked everywhere," Liz echoed.

"Yes, after this," Clarie replied, pointing at the slaves on the auction block. "The stage is being set right here for another book in the New Testament. Look."

A slender, wealthy merchant approached a slave and looked him over, walking around the pedestal. His deep blue cloak matched his eyes and his no-nonsense approach. He was freshly bathed and clean, having visited the Harbor Bath House after departing his ship. "I come from Colossae and need a strong slave to work in my wool business. I wish to read this slave's scroll."

"You've come to the right place, sir," the grimy slavemaster replied eagerly. He slapped the slave's back to make him stand up straight. "This slave is young, strong, and in excellent health." He grabbed the scroll from the slave's neck and handed it to the merchant.

The merchant read aloud, "Name: Onesimus. From: Rome. Status: Recently sold himself to pay off a debt." He glanced back up and studied the slave, locking eyes with the young man who looked at him with shockingly deep green eyes. "He wasn't born into slavery so he's not conditioned for it mentally. Hmmm. Could be a risk. How much?"

"I assure you that if this slave runs away you will get your money back," the slave master explained. "Because I see you are a man of serious business who doesn't waste time, let's agree on six hundred denarii and be done with this deal."

The merchant's eyes narrowed as he continued to study the slave. "I am Philemon and I must attend to a business matter before leaving

17

Ephesus in three days. When I return from the Temple of Artemis, I will take Onesimus with me. Because I see him as a flight risk, make it five hundred denarii and we have a deal. I will pay you half now, and half when I pick him up."

"Sold! Very well, Philemon, sir, I will have Onesimus here waiting for you," the slavemaster agreed.

"Clean him up," Philemon ordered, handing the coins over to the slimy slavemaster, who snapped for his clerk to make note of the transaction. Philemon looked the slave squarely in the eye. "Three days, Onesimus. And we'll have no trouble from you, understand?"

Onesimus nodded sadly as the slavemaster grabbed him by the arm to pull him off the display pedestal. "He'll be ready!" the slavemaster called after Philemon.

"Je ne comprends pas," Liz said, shaking her head sadly. "How can this be part of the coming New Testament?"

"Yes, and is Philemon the real Tyrant we were to find?" Nigel wondered.

"Do you know where the word 'redemption' comes from?" Clarie asked.

"Bien sûr," Liz answered quickly. It comes from the Greek word *agoridzo,* which evolved from *agora,* the Greek word for the marketplace like this where slaves are purchased."

Clarie nodded. "Paul wrote to the Galatians, *'There is neither Jew nor Gentile, neither slave nor free, nor is there male and female, for you are all one in Christ Jesus.'"* She pointed to Philemon, who walked down the colorful mosaic sidewalk into Ephesus. "Someday Philemon will know this, too. And he'll understand what 'redemption' really means." She turned to follow him down the street. "But he is not the real Tyrant you seek. Come with me."

18

THE TYRANT

Never had the Jewish leaders seen such a large crowd on a Sabbath. The people of Ephesus poured into the synagogue to hear Paul, word having spread about his teaching. Each week the crowds grew to the point that now there was standing room only. Epaphras had become one of Paul's most ardent students, bringing new friends every week to hear him preach.

Clarie slipped in the back door, with Max, Liz, and Nigel under her cloak so they wouldn't be seen. "Listen," she whispered to them.

Paul stood in the front of the synagogue, expounding on Isaiah's prophesies about Messiah and how Jesus fulfilled every single one. "The Kingdom of God is here now, in our hearts!"

"I don't like this," one of the Jewish leaders named Simeon muttered under his breath. "Paul is getting too much exposure with his teaching here."

"Yes, but the crowds," Joash replied. "Look at them! The offerings have steadily increased."

"But at what price? Are you listening to what Paul is espousing about Messiah?" Simeon argued. "That Messiah was crucified like a common criminal?! I know we've been open to hearing Paul's theories, but I am at the end of my tolerance. And will you just look at the number of unclean *Gentiles* and slaves who have filled our halls?"

Joash looked around. Gentiles, slave and free, filled the synagogue in rapt attention to Paul's message on grace. They were coming not to hear about the Jewish faith. They were coming to hear about Jesus. "What do you wish to do?"

"I wish to end this blasphemy," stormed Simeon, walking to the front of the synagogue. He held his hands up to draw the attention of the crowd. "We have heard this argument for three months now. We here in Ephesus are open to ideas, but you are trampling on our laws, which are the very foundation of our faith!"

A gasp rippled through the crowd as all eyes focused on Paul for his response. Paul calmly turned to face the angry Jew. "I must disagree on all fronts, Simeon. Jesus said he came not to abolish the law but to fulfill it. Just so, we who follow him seek to do the same. I am a law-abiding Jew and love my heritage. But there is no salvation from keeping the law. Salvation comes through grace alone. Grace from the blood of Christ shed for you and for me."

"Blasphemy!" Joash shouted, ganging up on Paul. "A crucified criminal may be the savior for the followers of The Way, but he is not the savior for Jews!"

Simeon wouldn't hear any of it and pointed his finger in Paul's face. "I've heard that you followers of The Way make anyone who believes in this Jesus as Messiah go through unspeakable rituals!"

Paul cocked his head to the side, seeing how the attacks were finally coming in this Jewish synagogue. He was surprised that they had allowed him to speak here for as long as he had. His heart grieved for his obstinate Jewish brothers. He knew this opportunity was coming to an end.

"Come now, Simeon," Paul objected. "There are no 'unspeakable rituals' required for followers of The Way."

"I will not have you defy me in such a matter!" Simeon shouted. He then turned to the attentive crowd. "If you consider yourself a God-fearing believer, you are welcome here. But if you consider yourself part of this rebellious Way movement, there is no welcome here for you."

Paul looked around as the people wore looks of confusion upon hearing the Jews speak against The Way. What were they to do?

"That sounds like a tyr-r-rant ta me!" Max hoarsely whispered. "Ye mean he's been here the whole time?"

"Shh, come, let's go," Clarie whispered, quickly slipping out the door. Once outside, she walked ahead of them down the steps. "Nigel, do you remember explaining about slaves who purchased their freedom?"

20

"Indeed I do, but shouldn't we wait to see what happens with Paul and the tyrant?" Nigel asked, looking back to the synagogue.

Clarie stopped and turned to face the bewildered animals. "That Jew isn't the Tyrant. As you may have guessed, Paul will soon be driven out of the synagogue, so the need for you to find the real Tyrant is at hand. Paul needs him. And he needs Paul."

"*Mon amie,* you and Gillamon keep referring to this individual as the *real* Tyrant," Liz said. "I must believe that therein lies a clue as to his identity. *Real.*"

"Indeed, Liz. So I shall leave you one more clue before I go," Clarie said. "Nigel, lead Max and Liz to the gate of freedom. Once you're on the other side, Liz, do what you always do with names. That should lead you directly to your answer."

Suddenly the doors flung open, and the animals turned to see people pouring out of the synagogue. Paul led a procession of people who didn't quite know what to think. When Max, Liz, and Nigel turned back around, Clarie was gone.

"This be one confusin' morn!" Max grumbled. "I know Clarie an' Gillamon cannot tell us ever'thin' but this r-r-riddle be makin' me br-r-rain hurt!"

"Quickly, Nigel! Where is this gate of freedom?" Liz asked.

"Right! She must mean the Gate of Mazeus and Mithridates," Nigel exclaimed, his eyes widening with understanding. "Follow me!" Nigel ran ahead of Max and Liz down the street, darting in and out of the crowds until he stood before a magnificent gate that stood at the edge of the Central Marketplace. Max and Liz ran up next to the mouse as he further explained where they stood. "Mazeus and Mithridates were two slaves who had belonged to none other than Caesar Augustus and his wife, Livia. They built and dedicated this triple-arched gate to the Emperor in gratitude for granting their purchased freedom."

"So an emperor let the lads go fr-r-ree?" Max asked in surprise. "I woulda thought that no tyr-r-rant would do such a thing. Besides, Caesar be a dead tyrant. He can't be the r-r-real one we need ta find."

"Real Tyrant, real Tyrant, real Tyrant," Liz repeated to herself as she walked through the gate to the other side. She quickly scanned her surroundings and realized she had crossed into Philosopher's Square. "Think, Liz, think." The brilliant cat's mind was swirling.

Suddenly she noticed some students walking down a flight of steps next to her. "This is a place of learning. What time is it?"

Max gazed up at the angle of the sun. "Looks ta me like it's aboot 11. Why?"

Liz's tail whipped back and forth. "They're letting out of school." She ran up the steps.

Max and Nigel looked at one another and shrugged their shoulders, then followed her up the steps. When they reached the top, there was a large open air portico. Liz was sitting there with her tail curled around her legs and a coy grin on her face. *"Mes amis,* I give you the 'real Tyrant.'" She pointed to a sign:

SCHOOL OF TYRANNUS

Nigel put a paw to his spectacles as he read the sign. "School of Tyrannus?"

"It is so obvious, I cannot believe I've missed it the whole time," Liz said. "Tyrannus literally means 'tyrant'! That is what Gillamon meant. The real meaning of his *name,* not his character."

"So wha' do this tyrant have ta do with Paul?" Max asked. "An' wha' if he lives up ta his name?"

"Tyrannus operates this school in the morning and evening hours. It is closed from 11 to 4—during the heat of the day when Ephesus shuts down," Liz explained. "Don't you see?"

"By Jove, I see where you're going with this!" Nigel cheered. "Paul has been forced out of the synagogue and needs a place to teach. This school offers a spacious place where a large crowd could gather, and it goes unused five hours a day. Even slaves would be free to attend Paul's teaching during that time! Brilliant!"

Just then a squatty man with cropped gray hair dressed in a white tunic walked across the portico carrying a stack of scrolls. Behind him came a lanky teenage boy. The man plopped the scrolls down and pointed to a bench. "Have a seat, Aristarchus. You will write these sentences until you get them right! No student of mine is going to fail grammar. So I suggest you get busy!" he huffed, tapping the boy's writing tablet. He then softened and got right in the boy's ear. "You're better than this, I *know* it."

"Yes, Sir," Aristarchus said with a respectful tone as he leaned over his writing tablet to get to work.

22

Tyrannus nodded with his hands on his hips. "I'll be back in five hours. And I expect your work to be finished." He turned and headed out of the courtyard.

Liz and Nigel beamed at one another with delighted grins. Max growled. "Figures the Tyr-r-rant were a teacher. Poor lad."

"It appears our *real* Tyrant lives up to his name, at least for that young chap," Nigel chuckled. "But in this case, his motives are to *help* the student with this tyrannical teaching."

"Aye, I guess ye're r-r-right, Mousie," Max agreed. "So now we need ta get Paul an' the Tyr-r-rant ta meet."

Liz started walking daintily over to the student with her tail curled up in the air. "And I know exactly how to make their introduction."

"HEY, CAT!" cried Aristarchus, lunging for Liz. "Come back with that! Stop!"

Liz bolted out of the portico and down the steps of the School of Tyrannus. In her mouth she carried the boy's parchment containing four hours of hard work. The young boy went blazing after her as fast as his feet would take him.

Max grinned wide. "I guess the Tyr-r-rant wouldn't believe the lad if he said a dog ate his homework."

"Jolly good joke, old boy!" Nigel quipped, grooming his whiskers. "I say we stay here and wait for our educational Tyrant and until Liz accomplishes her mission."

Liz darted around people who were once again filling the streets of Ephesus as the heat of the day subsided. She glanced back to see the boy close at her heels.

"That's my paper!" Aristarchus shouted after her.

Liz smiled through her teeth as she reached the tentmaker's shop of Aquila and Priscilla. As she predicted, Paul was gathered there with his friends and several believers who had followed them from the synagogue. She bounded in the open doorway and right up to Paul, dropping the parchment at his feet.

Everyone looked up as the young boy arrived, breathless, at the doorway. "Please! Stop that cat!"

Paul looked at the boy and then down at Liz, who sat there innocent as could be, smiling up at him with her tail curled around her feet. Paul picked up the parchment and recognized that it was school work. "What are you up to, Faith?" He gave her a playful frown and stood to greet the young boy. "Welcome. I'm Paul. And I see you've met my cat, Faith. Is this yours?" Paul held up the parchment.

Aristarchus put his hands on his knees to catch his breath. "Yes, Sir, it is. May I have it, please? My teacher will kill me if I don't have it when he returns."

Paul smiled and handed him the parchment. "So you are a student. Who is your teacher?"

"Tyrannus. I attend his school in Philosopher's Square," the boy explained, holding the paper to his chest in relief, closing his eyes. "Thank you. I'm Aristarchus."

"I'm sorry my cat took your paper." Paul grinned at Liz. "She's been known to act this way, but something good has always come from it."

Liz blinked her eyes affectionately at Paul, meowing, "Bien sûr, mon ami. I always have a reason, no?"

"Tell me, did my cat come to your school? Is that where she took your paper?" Paul asked him.

"Yes, sir. I was working there alone during the school day break, and she just showed up out of nowhere," Aristarchus explained. "She kept playing with the scrolls, unrolling them, and playing with my pen. She did lead me to some things I might have overlooked, so even though she took my paper, she actually made it better."

Liz meowed that the boy was welcome for her assistance, "Je vous en prie."

Aristarchus scratched her on the ear with a smile. "Tyrannus is coming back and I was supposed to have finished this work. I really need to get back before he returns."

"Let me go with you," Paul insisted, putting his hand on the boy's back. "If there are any problems, I want to make sure your teacher knows it wasn't your fault."

Aristarchus smiled at the fifty-something, balding man with the long nose and the bandy legs. "Thank you, Sir. That would help me greatly."

"Very well, let's go see Tyrannus," Paul told him with a smile.

Liz followed along behind them all the way to the school, thrilled with the outcome. Paul found out all about the boy and his life. By the time they reached the school, Paul had already told him he was looking for a place to hold gatherings where he could teach.

"You could teach here!" Aristarchus said as he bounded up the steps. "This school sits empty for five hours every day. Well, that is, except for today. I'm sure you could arrange something with Tyrannus."

Paul saw Max and Nigel sitting there waiting on them as he reached the top of the steps. He shook his head good-humoredly and leaned over to pet Max. "That is most kind of you. I would like to talk to your teacher about it." He whispered in Max's ear, "Well done, little ones."

"I hope you have a good excuse, Aristarchus!" bellowed Tyrannus, meeting them across the portico.

The boy's face fell as he realized he didn't beat his teacher back. "I can explain, Sir."

Paul stepped up in front of him. "It's entirely my fault, Tyrannus. I'm afraid my cat slipped away with your student's paper. So I returned here with him so you would not hold him accountable."

Tyrannus put his hands on his hips in disbelief. "Your cat?!"

"Yes, Sir," Aristarchus replied, handing his teacher the parchment. "Here is my work. Complete as you requested."

Tyrannus took the paper and studied it closely as he rubbed his chin. His frown melted and he raised his eyebrows as he liked what he read. "This is some of your best work. Did this man help you?"

"No, Sir! I did it all on my own," Aristarchus insisted, stealing a glance at Liz. *He'd never believe that a cat helped me.* "Only the cat was here with me." Liz sauntered in and wrapped her tail around Tyrannus. "That's her."

"That's *she,*" Tyrannus corrected him as he reached down to scratch Liz under the chin. "So you're the little feline professor, eh? What are you trying to do? Take over my school?" The brusque man started chuckling.

"*Precisely, Monsieur,*" Liz meowed in reply.

"I hope all is well with Aristarchus's work. Please allow me to introduce myself. I'm Paul." He reached out his hand in greeting. "I was schooled in the law in Tarsus and Jerusalem."

"Tarsus, you say? I've met many fine professors from there," Tyrannus replied. "What are you doing in Ephesus?"

25

"I'm here to teach, actually . . ." Paul began.

"But he needs a place to teach!" Aristarchus interrupted. "Can't he use your school during the day when we're closed?"

Tyrannus raised his eyebrows. "What exactly are you teaching that students would endure the heat of the day to hear?"

"He walked r-r-right inta that one," Max whispered to Nigel.

"Indeed!" Nigel whispered back.

"I teach about the way to have joy, forgiveness, and hope in this life, and salvation for eternity," Paul replied. "I teach about faith in Jesus."

"Jesus? I haven't heard of him," Tyrannus replied, curious. "Come, sit and tell me about him."

"Nothing would please me more." Paul shared a broad smile with Aristarchus and sat down. He caught Liz's eye and gave her a wink.

Liz sauntered over to Max and Nigel, grinning with her tail up in the air.

"Good show, my dear!" Nigel cheered. "Clarie was right. It appears Paul and the Tyrant needed each other."

"Aye, Lass!" Max agreed, nudging Liz. "Yer plan worked then!"

"The real Tyrant was lost," surmised Liz, looking back at Tyrannus, who was listening intently to Paul. "And by this evening, he will no doubt be found."

THE NAME

Philemon's bed was drenched with sweat. He tossed and turned, moaning gibberish. Fever consumed him. Several Ephesian letters lay scattered around his bed, the ink on them bleeding all over the parchment from the moisture.

The slavemaster stood in the doorway, speaking in hushed tones with the innkeeper. "I was expecting him in three days, but now it's been three *months*. I can't release the slave Onesimus to him until I have full payment, and by the looks of things, Philemon is not in his right mind to conduct business."

"I see your dilemma," the innkeeper replied. "I can tell you that Philemon owns a large amount of land in Colossae and has a great deal of money. I'm sure he will make good on the debt for the slave when he's well."

"IF he gets well," the slavemaster interjected, crossing his arms. "What if he dies?"

The innkeeper frowned and shook his head. "I've known Philemon for years. When I heard he was staying at one of those noisy inns by the stadium, I brought him here where it's quieter so he could rest easier."

"He's from Colossae?" Epaphras asked, overhearing the men talking in the hallway. "I'm from Colossae, too."

The slavemaster looked the young man over. "Is this your new servant? The one who wants to learn the inn business?"

The innkeeper patted him on the back and smiled. "Yes, this is Epaphras: He keeps the inn clean and runs all my market errands.

He's a hard worker and one of the most honest servants I've ever had."

Epaphras bowed humbly. "Thank you, Sir. I don't wish to pry, but I know someone who might be able to help Philemon. His name is Paul, and he is a strong man of faith. Perhaps if he can come to see Philemon, he could pray for his healing."

"It couldn't hurt. Although, none of the Ephesian letters I've brought to him have worked," the innkeeper said.

Epaphras winced at the thought that he used to sell these exact same Ephesian letters filled with foolish words and false hope. He used to live in such darkness, but had found Jesus. He had found light and a new way to live. He soaked up Paul's teaching like a sponge and tried to put all he learned into practice. "Let me go see if I can bring him this afternoon."

"Very well, go," the innkeeper instructed him, looking at Philemon and his pitiful condition. "I'm sure he would be willing to try any magic trick at this point."

28

☧

"Be always humble, gentle, and patient," Paul said with the warmth of his smile. "Show your love by being tolerant with one another."

Epaphras slipped into the back of the portico at the School of Tyrannus, where Paul was teaching a huge crowd. Word had spread about his dynamic ideas, and people flocked to hear him, with many believing in Jesus. Students took notes from Paul's lectures, including Epaphras. He tried to come every day when he had a break from his duties at the inn, and he frequently brought friends. His faith was quickly maturing.

Paul nodded a silent "hello" to him as he saw the young man take a seat in the back. Next to him sat Aristarchus, who now frequently stayed after Tyrannus's lectures so he could listen to Paul. Tyrannus himself even stayed many days to learn about this new life in Christ.

"You yourselves used to be in the darkness, but since you have become the Lord's people, you are in the light. So you must live like people who belong to the light, for it is the light that brings a rich harvest of every kind of goodness, righteousness, and truth."

"I see our young Epaphras has arrived," Nigel noted from his hiding place next to Max and Liz.

Liz smiled at the young man. "I am happy we were there the day

Paul met him at the Temple of Artemis. It is wonderful to see his life completely changed, no?"

"So as you go home tonight I want you to think about how you can make a difference in this world where you live and work. Try to learn what pleases the Lord," Paul encouraged the people. "Be careful how you live. Don't live like ignorant people, but like wise people. Make good use of every opportunity you have, because these are evil days. Don't be fools, then, but try to find out what the Lord wants you to do. Have nothing to do with the worthless things people do, things that belong to the darkness. Instead, bring them out to the light. Go with God. I'll see you tomorrow."

A murmuring of understanding from nodding heads rippled through the portico as people stood to leave. Epaphras made his way quickly to Paul. "Thank you for your words of encouragement. I think I know what the Lord wants me to do to make a difference. A man named Philemon is staying at the inn where I now live and work. He's a wealthy businessman from Colossae and has been very ill here for some time. I asked the innkeeper if I could bring you to him."

"Of course I'll come with you," Paul agreed. "I promised Aquila I would be back to help him finish a tent tonight, but we can go see this man first."

Epaphras's face lit up. "Thank you, Paul!"

"Philemon? The man we saw at the slave market?" Liz remembered. "He is still in Ephesus?"

"Sure sounds like it," Max replied. "I'm thinkin' this meetin' with Paul will be important then."

"Undoubtedly," Nigel agreed. "Perhaps this is when Philemon will learn about grace."

"*Oui*, and I wish to be there when he does," stated Liz, following the men out of the school.

☧

Paul stood at Philemon's bedside and gathered the Ephesian letters, handing them to Epaphras. "Get rid of these, will you?"

"Gladly," the young man said, taking the parchments and balling them up to discard in the fire.

Philemon was delirious and shivering with fever. Paul placed his

29

hand on Philemon's forehead and closed his eyes. "I ask for healing on behalf of this one who suffers in body and spirit, in the name of our Lord Jesus Christ."

The innkeeper stood at the doorway with Epaphras, waiting to see what would happen. Liz crept up to stand by their feet. Suddenly Philemon grew very still and he took in a deep breath. Paul smiled as he sensed the fever leaving the man's body. Philemon's eyes fluttered open and he saw Paul smiling over him. He blinked a few times and slowly sat up. "Are you a doctor? I suddenly feel fine."

"You've been healed by the Great Physician," Paul told him. "His name is Jesus."

"Then I would very much like to meet him, so I can thank him," announced Philemon, rubbing his face.

Paul turned to Epaphras and smiled. "Please bring some water and food so Philemon can regain his strength." He then sat down on the floor next to Philemon's bed. "Let me tell you all about Jesus, who has saved your life . . . twice."

The innkeeper's eyes widened and his jaw dropped. He grabbed Epaphras by the arm. "Paul uses the name of Jesus, and Philemon is healed? Just like that? I've got to tell some people about this!"

As the innkeeper hurried off, Liz sat there watching Paul share Jesus with Philemon. While she was thrilled with the wonderful thing that had just happened for this man, she couldn't help but wonder what the effect would be as word spread of Paul's healing miracle. In the name of Jesus.

☧

Paul stepped out into the warm sunshine and stretched his back, closing his eyes as he took in a deep breath. He had been working hard since dawn on a tent that Aquila hoped to deliver to a customer by noon. He untied the sweat rag that was tied around his head and wiped his face and neck with it.

"There he is! That's the man I told you about!" a woman cried to her husband, who struggled to hold on to an unruly young girl who looked as if she was having a seizure. Her hair was a mess and her wild eyes darted back and forth. She was out of control.

"NO-O-O-O-O-O-O! LET ME GO-O-O-O-O-O-O-O-O!" the young girl screeched. "I-I-I-E-E-E-E-E-E-E-E-E-E!"

A small group of people began to gather in the street, wondering what was happening.

Paul immediately snapped to attention as he saw the commotion with these people headed right toward him. He could tell in an instant that the young girl was possessed by an evil spirit, and prayed for divine protection and intervention. The look of despair in her parents' eyes broke Paul's heart. "Please, help us!" they cried in unison.

As Paul held out his hand to the girl, the sweat rag that was still in his hand grazed the girl's cheek. Before Paul had the chance to utter a single word, the evil spirit came out of the girl and she became calm and limp. She fell into her father's arms, completely quiet and at peace. Her father gazed into her eyes and she turned to him and smiled. "Father?"

The father and mother looked at one another and then at Paul, who stood in stunned silence. They saw his eyes fall on the sweat rag still in his hand. "Just the touch of your cloth healed her! Thank you! Oh, thank you for healing her!"

"It was the Lord Jesus who healed her, not my rag!" Paul protested as they held the young girl between them in a tight embrace, then turned to walk away.

31

The crowd erupted in awe and celebration. People ran down the street, telling everyone what had just happened. Word spread like wildfire through the shops all the way down to the harbor, that Paul's sweat rag and the name of Jesus had more power than any abracadabra on an Ephesian letter.

☧

Paul shook his head. He continued to protest as Liz and Nigel sat on a low stone wall next to Aquila's shop. Liz's gaze fell on a dark-looking man in a strangely adorned robe who had seven young men with him. They walked slowly down the street, whispering among themselves.

Paul held the sweat rag up to study it and voiced his thoughts. "Jesus, you healed the woman who touched the hem of your garment. It wasn't your garment that healed her, but her faith in you. And it is my faith in you that has healed this girl. The very same power that raised Jesus from the dead indwells me now with your Holy Spirit." Paul watched the family rejoicing in the distance. "Perhaps these people who have been so immersed in their pagan ways still need the crutch of tangible physical evidence to believe. Please, I pray you let this miracle serve for your glory alone." He frowned and gripped the sweat rag tightly as he walked back inside to continue his work.

"The Maker has given Paul the extraordinary ability to perform miracles here in Ephesus," Nigel remarked in awe. "If he has been given this gift at such a time and in such a place, it must serve a high purpose. Of course, Paul would not relish having such a gift, but will faithfully abide by whatever tools the Lord gives him to reach such a dark people."

"*Oui,* I do not worry about how Paul will handle this ability." Liz frowned, her tail slowly curling up and down as she watched the group of eight men walking down the street. "Once pagans hear about what happened here today, it's only a matter of time before they'll want to buy up Paul's sweat rags as eagerly as images of Artemis."

"Or worse," Nigel echoed gravely.

TWO MONTHS LATER

The sounds of tambourines, drums, and clashing cymbals echoed off the marble columns on Curetes Street. A procession of Curetes priests wailed loudly and danced in a trance-like state, screeching and playing high-pitched flutes as they went down the road. They twirled around and jerked their bodies in unnatural movements as their deafening noise filled the air.

"Do ye think they could be ANY more obnoxious!?" growled Max. He lay on his stomach and covered his ears. "These daft humans be dr-r-rivin' me mad!"

"It IS madness!" Liz put her paws up to her ears and squinted as the horrible noise passed by. Nigel stood there, apparently unfazed, arms crossed over his chest. "Doesn't this noise bother you, too, *mon ami?*"

Nigel didn't respond. Liz and Max shared a confused look. "Check his ears, Lass!" Max suggested.

Liz looked closely and noticed that Nigel had stuffed his ears with scraps of tent cloth. She poked Nigel to get his attention. He quickly turned and smiled at her. "YES, MY DEAR?" he shouted. She motioned for him to unplug his ears.

"AH!" Nigel shouted, reaching up to remove the cloth. His eyes widened at the loudness of the noise. "Simply dreadful racket! I knew we were coming up here on festival day so I took the liberty of bringing what I like to call 'ear plugs.'"

"They appear to work," Liz observed, still grimacing from the pain in her ears. "When Clarie told us to meet her up here, I wish I had thought to bring a pair myself."

Nigel replaced the ear plugs. "MUCH BETTER!" he shouted. "IF THESE HUMANS ONLY KNEW HOW UTTERLY RIDICULOUS THEY LOOKED WITH THEIR FRENZIED NOISEMAKING." The mouse shook his head in disgust.

"Lass, why do these laddies act like this anyway?" Max wanted to know.

"The Curetes are priests of Artemis charged with guarding the goddess, and this ritual stems from her birth," Liz explained. "The myth goes that the goddess Leto was pregnant with Apollo and Artemis by the god Zeus. Because the goddess Hera was jealous, Leto had to keep the birth of her babies a secret. So, she hired demigods called 'Curetes' to create a symphony of noise to conceal their birth. The Curetes banged swords and shields and played loud musical instruments to drown out the sound of the crying newborns, Apollo and Artemis."

33

"An' the cr-r-razy humans have been bangin' dr-r-rums an' scr-r-re-echin' like this ever since?" Max asked sarcastically.

Liz rubbed her temples to soothe the headache the noise was creating. "This group of priests continue the ritual of protecting the goddess, calling themselves Curetes. This street is named for them, as it is from here they lead the masses out to the Temple of Artemis."

Max shook his head vigorously. "Don't even the people of Ephesus hate all this r-r-racket?"

"*Oui,* but they endure it because they believe it will not only protect the goddess but keep the people safe from evil forces," Liz explained.

"I can't think of anythin' more evil than all this c-r-razy noise!" Max protested.

Max and Liz stopped talking and just covered their ears. Nigel continued to stand there in his muffled bliss. After a while, the processional started leaving the area as it trailed off down Curetes Street out to the Temple of Artemis.

Nigel pulled the ear plugs out and wiped back his whiskers. "I say, these items came in rather handy. I shall remember to use them more often."

"Aye, an' next time, br-r-ring me a pair," Max added, taking his paws down from his ears.

"Oh, what a dark and dastardly place this is," Nigel said, looking around. "The very evil these humans try to dispel, they actually invite to their door."

Liz took her paws down from her ears. "Speaking of which." She looked up and saw the group of seven men she had seen in the street with the dark man. "There they are. The sons of Sceva."

"Who be Sceva?" Max asked.

"A scoundrel of the most loathsome sort, old boy," Nigel spat. "He professes to be a Jewish high priest but only his robe has any resemblance to that notion. He practices rituals forbidden by the Old Testament and has slipped deeply into paganism, bringing his seven sons with him in order to operate a thriving business of evil deceit. They are paid to drive out evil spirits."

"Sceva means 'left-handed, untrustworthy scoundrel,'" Liz added.

"Now *there's* a lad who's livin' up ta his name," Max grumbled.

"Word is that they've added Jesus' name to their set of spells after seeing Paul's success. They actually speak to evil spirits and say, '*I command you in the name of Jesus, whom Paul preaches*,'" Nigel reported in a grave voice.

Max's fur rose in anger. "Seven means complete, so these seven must be complete *fools* ta tr-r-ry an' use Jesus' name for evil!"

"I know, Max," Liz agreed, "but of course they have not yet accomplished anything by doing this. They have no idea with whom they are truly dealing."

"They will soon," a blue butterfly said, landing on Max's nose. "Good, Max. I see you brought one of Paul's sweat rags." It was draped around his neck.

"Aye, Clarie, Lass," Max greeted her, looking cross-eyed at her atop his nose. "Jest like ye asked."

The seven sons went up to a house located right there on Curetes Street and knocked on the door. They wore crimson robes made from the finest silk and adorned with ornately stitched symbols. On their heads they wore elaborate turbans. "You sent for us?" one of the young men asked. "May we come in?"

A harried-looking woman answered the door of her opulent house on a terraced hillside in this wealthy part of Ephesus. Her eyes were

34

filled with fear and despair. "Yes, please." She opened the door wide and stood aside as the men filed into the house.

"Hurry, come with me," Clarie instructed Max, Liz, and Nigel, flying over to the open doorway so they could witness what was happening inside.

A man was dressed in rags and sat on the floor. He gurgled an eerie sound from the back of his throat, and foam dripped from the corner of his mouth. His stringy hair was stuck to his face, and his long fingernails dug into the mat on which he sat. His eyes were sunken into his face, and his was a countenance of evil. His body twitched involuntarily and his eyes darted back and forth as the seven men encircled him.

Six men held up their hands as one man took out their spell book, nodding to them once he found the page. In one chorus they began their incantation: "I command you by Jesus whom Paul preaches . . ."

But before they could utter another word, the demon-possessed man jumped up and slapped the book out of the hand of the young man. The seven sons jumped back as the man now stood above them and spoke with an unnatural voice. "Jesus I know. Paul I know about," he said, turning in a circle as his beady eyes stared each one of them down, "but *who are you?*"

The fur rose on Max, Liz, and Nigel as they felt the demonic volcano getting ready to erupt in the room. Suddenly the possessed man leaped on the men, jumping from one to another and overpowering them all. He tore off their robes, and his claw-like nails tore into their skin while he roared like a wild animal. The woman went screaming out of the house, followed by each of the seven men who ran out naked and bleeding, also screaming at the top of their lungs. They ran down the street, and the crowds erupted in mayhem at this spectacle. The seven sons of Sceva were not only terrified, they were humiliated for all of Ephesus to see.

"Quickly now, Max, bring Paul's rag," Clarie instructed as she flew into the house.

Max, Liz, and Nigel crept into the house and saw the man writhing in the corner, his face to the wall. Suddenly Clarie transformed into a young man and quickly removed the rag from Max's neck. As she approached the possessed man he turned to face her, but before he

35

could move she tossed the rag at him, exclaiming, "In the name of Jesus, come out of him!"

The rag grazed his skin, and the man cried out in anguish when the demon left him. His writhing ceased and a look of calm swept over his face before he passed out. Clarie knelt down and used the rag to wipe away the spittle on his chin. "Now, dear one, you are free."

Max, Liz, and Nigel stood in silent awe at seeing the power of the Name free this man from the forces of evil. And of having seen Clarie do something they had never before witnessed any member of the Order of the Seven do.

Clarie looked over at her speechless friends. "When he wakes, I will tell him that I brought Paul's rag, but it was the power of Jesus who freed him, not those charlatans who dared to invoke the Name without his authority."

"And if he asks who you are?" Liz asked softly.

"I'll tell him the truth." Clarie smiled. "I'll tell him I'm just a lamb who was also touched by the Good Shepherd: Jesus."

"Good show, my dear!" Nigel cheered with his tiny fist raised high.

Max wagged his tail. "Aye! We certainly don't want those seven scoundr-r-rels gettin' credit."

"They won't. While the seven sons of Sceva are driven out of town for their failure, the name of Jesus will be elevated to an entirely new level here in Ephesus." Clarie looked down at the now quiet man. "He sent me personally to help this hurting man. Jesus couldn't leave him as he was."

"Jesus lives up to his name, no? 'The Lord is Salvation.'" Tears of joy welled up in Liz's eyes. "The Name that is above every name is too good to leave anyone as they were."

Playing with Fire

Sniff. Sniff. Sniff. The smell of smoke tickled Max's cold black nose as he slept. He wriggled it back and forth but kept his eyes shut.

Max's paws twitched wildly. He was running through the mist of Scotland, trotting across the soft green moss of his beloved homeland. He was so happy to be home!

"Over here! Bring them over here!" came muffled voices in the distance. The Scottie didn't want to come out of his deep sleep.

"Wake up!" Something was now pushing against Max's shoulder, trying to shake him out of his dream. "Wake up, *mon ami!*"

The animals had fallen asleep with full tummies after enjoying the festive meal here at the School of Tyrannus. The students wanted to celebrate Paul's birthday, surprising him with gifts of food following his afternoon lecture. Priscilla had arranged everything, and Paul's heart was warmed by the outpouring of love shown him. But the greatest surprise had come when Timothy showed up after finally arriving in Ephesus. Paul cried tears of joy as they embraced, rocking his son in the faith back and forth in his arms.

"Blast it all, let me handle this!" Nigel's muffled voice exclaimed. He climbed onto Max's head, pulled out the ear plugs, and shouted, "FIRE!"

Max's eyes shot straight open and he jumped to his feet, sending Nigel flying through the air. The mouse landed in a bowl of fruit with his spectacles askew on his face. He held up the scraps of tent cloth still in his paw. "I say, I'm delighted Max wished to try these ear plugs.

37

I believe I've just had an idea. I believe these could come in handy for high-altitude flying. Strange how the oddest situations bring forth new ideas."

"*Merci,* Nigel," Liz said, quickly turning to the now wide-awake Scottie. "Maximillian, there is a fire in Philosopher's Square! We must hurry and see what is happening! The humans have all left the portico!"

"Aye!" Max exclaimed, shaking from head to tail to come alive. "Those ear plugs work too good, Mousie. They be dangerous if a fire br-r-reaks out!"

Nigel crawled out of the fruit and scurried over to Max and Liz. "Well noted, old boy. Now, let's crack on, shall we?"

The three animals ran outside and down the steps. There before them was a massive bonfire in the square. People were running to the fire with armloads of books and throwing them into the fire, sending sparks and flames dancing up into the night sky. In the midst of the chaos, Liz spotted Paul, Priscilla, Aquila, Timothy, and Tyrannus on the far side of the bonfire. She trotted over to where they stood, with Max and Nigel close behind.

"I'm telling you, that incident with the sons of Sceva shook Ephesus to its core!" Tyrannus exclaimed. "These people have the fear of God in them."

"The name of Jesus is respected and revered in Ephesus now," Priscilla said.

Aquila put his hand on Paul's shoulder. "And so is yours, my friend. That demon actually confessed belief in Jesus and recognized that our Lord's power flows through you."

"But it wasn't about to give up ground to those seven men who held no power over it," Tyrannus added with a finger raised.

Paul shook his head slowly, in awe of what they were witnessing. "Praise God that darkness is being consumed by light tonight! Even some of our believers are burning their old books, coming totally clean from their past of dabbling in magic."

"*C'est magnifique!*" Liz exclaimed. Her golden cat eyes glowed as the firelight bounced off them. "Look at all these books burning!"

Max looked at her with surprise. "I cannot believe me ears! I thought ye of all lassies would be upset at seein' books go up in smoke."

"Not *these* books, old boy!" Nigel chimed in. "These are books of

38

magic spells that the people are destroying. Ephesus has been so consumed with darkness that it eats, drinks, and breathes magic. But after word spread across the city of what happened with the sons of Sceva, these people wish to extinguish that dark magic in these flames and in public for all to see."

"*Oui.* It is said that the potency of spells is bound up in its secrecy, so once it is divulged it becomes ineffective," Liz explained. She smiled as she saw Epaphras throw the last of the innkeeper's Ephesian letters onto the fire. "These people are breaking their ties with darkness by renouncing the spells and the secrecy once and for all. The Enemy is losing his grip on Ephesus with this fire!"

"You sure do know how to light up a birthday party, Priscilla," Paul said with a broad smile, hugging his sister in Christ. "Did you arrange this, too?"

Priscilla threw her head back laughing. "No! But I think you can give credit to your sweat rag!"

"It wasn't my rag that freed that man!" Paul protested.

"We know, we know, my friend," Priscilla replied with a grin.

"We know it was Jesus who healed that man. And so does all of Ephesus," Timothy said. The young man bent down to pick up a scroll that had rolled away from the fire. He quickly handed it to Paul, trying not to burn himself. "Happy Birthday, Paul."

Paul took the burning scroll and studied it for a moment. "Greater is he that is in us, than he that is in this place." He boldly threw it into the fire while everyone cheered.

As the friends hugged and praised God for the change overtaking Ephesus, another set of glowing cat eyes appeared in the shadows.

"So you wish to play with fire?" The lion growled. "You call this a fire? I'll show you a *fire.*" He glared at the happy people now turning their backs on evil. "And when you play with *my* fire, you're sure to get burned."

The thunderous shouts of the crowd attending the day's gladiatorial games at the Stadium of Ephesus could be heard all over the city. Thousands of spectators filled the seats to see blood spill from men and beasts engaged in mortal combat. The thrill of the kill excited the crowd as two gladiators drew swords to determine who would leave the stadium a hero, and who would leave a corpse. The foot-stomping against stone rows coupled with shouting voices reverberated off the marble streets and buildings of Ephesus, echoing down to the harbor. The noise built to a deafening crescendo until suddenly a collective gasp of horror silenced the crowd. While they awaited the thumbs up or thumbs down from the host of the games, suspense kept the crowd quiet. Within moments, voices of elation and applause once again erupted as one gladiator plunged his sword into his unfortunate opponent. While the victorious gladiator walked around with arms raised to his adoring crowd, slaves cleared away the dead gladiator, leaving his blood to be soaked up by the sand on the stadium floor. And the crowd was just getting warmed up. They were thirsty for more and couldn't wait for the animal combat to come.

It was against this cacophony of background noise that three Jewish leaders discussed the events surrounding Paul and the bonfire.

40

"Fifty thousand silver drachmes." The Jewish leader Simeon paced the floor of this private meeting room in the synagogue with his hands clasped behind his back. "That's the estimated value of the magic books burned last night, all because of these new Christian beliefs."

"Yes, this is good news!" Joash exclaimed. "The evil pagans saw a fortune in spells slip through their hands last night."

"It may be good news to see the pagans losing so much money," said a man counting coins while working on a ledger. "But by the looks of things, the Christians are costing *us* a fortune as well."

Joash and Simeon looked over in alarm at the treasurer named Alexander. Simeon walked over and scooped up the parchment to look at the figures. "What do you mean?"

Alexander tapped his pen on the underside of the parchment, which Simeon held close to his face. "Not only are tax revenues down in our synagogue, they're down throughout all of Asia Minor. I've been watching the numbers steadily decrease over the past two years as this Way movement has spread and taken hold."

Joash looked over Simeon's shoulder at the parchment. His eyes widened. "I thought we would lose some money as we forced out the Jews who decided to become Christians, but I didn't think it would amount to *this* much."

Simeon snapped his wrist and handed the parchment back to Alexander. "Evidently Paul has encouraged his new followers to abandon their Jewish heritage of paying the Temple tax." He fumed and clenched his jaw as he resumed pacing around the room.

Long ago Caesar Augustus had made a decree giving the Jews imperial protection for monies raised by synagogues for supporting the Temple in Jerusalem. While voluntary, all Jews across the Roman Empire were expected to pay the Temple tax, and Ephesus was the collection center for all monies raised in Asia Minor.

"I don't know if Paul encouraged them *not* to pay the Temple tax. From what I've heard, that's not the way he operates," Alexander disagreed. He used the parchment to punctuate the air. "What I *do* know is that he started an effort to raise money for the poor in Jerusalem, taking up collections at these new Christian churches popping up everywhere."

Simeon gripped the back of a chair as he thought this through. "There has to be a way to stop him. To stop these *Christians!*"

"Well, Gallio's decision in Corinth prevented the Jewish leaders from trying to stop Paul and the Christians there," Joash reminded them. "He ruled they were not starting a new cult, but that this Christian movement was just an offshoot of the Jewish faith, so Rome would not get involved in what they saw as an internal Jewish dispute. That one decision paved the way for Paul and his Jesus-followers to have the protection of Rome."

"Yes, and Paul is a Roman citizen, so he also has Rome's protection as its citizen," Simeon grumbled through clenched teeth.

Suddenly they all heard the unmistakable roar of a lion coming from the stadium. The afternoon entertainment had begun. Criminals were placed in the center of the stadium while wild animals were released to hunt them down and devour them.

Alexander sat back in his chair to resume his counting. "Rome has protected these Christians so far. But there may be a loophole."

Simeon and Joash shared a quick glance and then sat down with Alexander. Simeon's eyes narrowed. "We're listening."

"Anyone found to be tampering with these Temple tax funds—even a Roman official—could be charged with the same penalties as anyone committing sacrilege against a pagan temple," Alexander explained. "It's a very serious crime, resulting in death if convicted."

Joash raised his eyebrows. "So if we can make a case before Proconsul Silanus for Temple robbery . . ." he started to say, when a blood-chilling roar echoed in the distance.

"Paul may find himself convicted of a felony," Simeon interjected with a dark grin, "and facing half-starved lions in the Stadium of Ephesus."

An Inside Job

Marcus Junius Silanus Torquatus walked along the walls painted with frescoes of military victories and scenes of gladiators fighting wild beasts lining the hallway of the Proconsul Palace. He headed toward the sunlit atrium where fountains flowed and huge green plants grew out of massive urns. At the sound of his approaching footsteps echoing off the richly colored tile, servants scurried around an ornately carved desk to make sure the Proconsul had everything he needed for the day's business: a fresh pitcher of water, the day's mail, untouched parchment, pen and ink, a burning oil lamp, and wax for the imperial seal of Rome.

His assistant, a man by the name of Gracilis, waited for Silanus to arrive so he could bring an especially urgent matter to his attention. He stood by the desk that bore the Roman emblem of an eagle and read over the petition once more. He clearly wanted to understand the situation in order to explain it to the proconsul. He looked up with a broad smile as Silanus entered the room. "Good morning, Proconsul. I trust you rested well."

Silanus walked across the center of the atrium where a huge circular mosaic of vibrant colors depicted the scene of Hercules defeating the serpent-like Hydra. Nine snake-like heads lay on the ground around the headless beast while the mighty Greek demigod dipped his arrows in the poisonous blood of the defeated serpent. Hercules would use the poison of one enemy to kill the next. Silanus quickly eyeballed the powerful image as he reached his desk. "Good morning, Gracilis. Yes, thank the gods, it appears I needed rest to tackle this stack of business today."

"Indeed. In addition to what is on your desk, I have another urgent matter to discuss," Gracilis informed him, holding up the parchment.

Silanus took a seat in the claw-foot chair behind his desk, flipping his crimson sash out of his way. He held out his tanned muscular arm to receive the document. The signet ring on his hand reminded everyone of his power. As cousin of Emperor Claudius, he was part of the Imperial Family and served as the imperial arm for all of Asia Minor. He was fair-minded and firm in his decisions, and always took his time to ensure that those decisions were wise ones.

"What does this concern?" Silanus asked, scanning the petition. His brown eyes, square jaw, and tanned face made him quite the handsome man, not yet forty years old. His dark cropped hair was offset by hints of gray above his ears.

"It is a formal accusation from the Jewish leaders of Ephesus against a man by the name of Paul. They claim he is guilty of temple robbery, misappropriating funds meant for their Temple in Jerusalem," Gracilis explained.

Silanus's eyes darted up quickly and a frown appeared on his face. "That is quite a serious charge. What proof do they have?"

Gracilis pointed to some figures on the petition. "The treasurer for Asia Minor by the name of Alexander has provided numbers showing the drop in Temple tax collections compared with the previous year. He claims that this Paul started a new fundraising effort with bodies of believers from his religious movement called The Way, and is using the Temple tax monies for that purpose."

"I've heard of this movement. Come to think of it, I've also heard of Paul. Gallio in Corinth ruled in his favor when the Jews there brought their complaints to him." Silanus frowned and rubbed his chin as he leaned forward to put his elbows on the desk. "This will need to be backed up by proof from the various districts listed here." He took a fresh piece of parchment and wrote out his orders. "Very well. Send this directive to the districts to report back to me." He dripped melted wax onto the document, pressed his ring's imperial seal into it, and handed it to Gracilis. He took another piece of parchment and looked up before he began writing. "What is Paul's business here in Ephesus?"

"He is a tentmaker and a teacher, using the School of Tyrannus for instruction," Gracilis replied. "I understand he is also a Roman citizen."

Silanus raised his eyebrows. "Well, let's hope this tent-making teacher is not guilty of the charges against him. He seems to make regular appearances before Roman governors." He began to write out his instructions concerning Paul. "Have him taken into custody and confined in a room of the Praetorian guard until I have seen evidence from the region and reach a verdict. He is allowed to go about the city under light chain, and may teach on a limited basis." The wax sizzled on the paper as he pressed his seal into it. He handed the paper to Gracilis. "But his tent-making days are over for now."

☧

"Ar-r-rested?!" Max growled. "Why?"

Liz placed her paw on Max's back. "Steady, Max."

Clarie, now in the form of a messenger of Rome, sat with the animals on a hillside terrace overlooking the city. "Trumped up charges of Temple robbery by the Jewish leaders. They've seen their tax revenues decrease as scores of Jews have left the synagogues here in Ephesus and across Asia Minor. They are grasping at the chance to blame Paul. Silanus has ordered him kept in custody until proof is gathered. I will conveniently be one of the official couriers to gather this information, and will ensure that only factual reports are made by the churches and synagogues."

"Oh, dear, will he be kept in dreadful conditions?" Nigel worried. "This will most certainly take months for Silanus to reach a verdict. I hate to think of Paul locked away in a foul dungeon."

"Will the Maker send another earthquake jailbr-r-reak like in Philippi?" Max asked hopefully. "Or like with Peter an' the disciples in Jer-r-rusalem?"

"Not this time. Paul is being kept in the Proconsul Palace, yet will be allowed to move about the city under light guard," Clarie assured them. "His accommodations will not be dreadful."

"That is good news at least," Liz said somberly. "But I am curious as to why he will be allowed to stay in prison."

Clarie smiled at her friends. "The Maker has Paul right where he needs him. Nigel, you won't want to miss what happens in Paul's jail cell. Max and Liz, comfort Paul when you see him, and, of course, take

45

care of Timothy and the others who will be sick with worry."

"If Paul will not be released, should we be worried as well?" Nigel wanted to know. "These are serious charges, my dear, carrying the death penalty if proved true."

"DEATH PENALTY?" Max's fur rose on end. "Maybe the Maker needs ta r-r-rethink this. I say we br-r-reak him out!"

"You seem to be forgetting who is really behind all this, Max," Clarie stated firmly. "Nothing happens unless the Maker allows it to happen, no matter how scary it may be at the moment."

"Aye, but ye never know when the Enemy will send lies flyin' all aboot," Max protested.

"*Oui, mon ami,*" Liz agreed. "It looks like the Enemy has arranged this, but we know all things are working together for Paul's good."

"And that is exactly what Paul needs to learn for himself, so he can write words like that with bold confidence," Clarie explained.

"Fine, so no jailbr-r-reak," Max pouted. "I can't stand not ta be able ta do anythin'. Waitin' isn't me str-r-rong suit."

Clarie scratched Max behind the ears. "Would it help to give you a riddle to solve while you wait? When you solve it, you will understand the Maker's new strategy."

Max lifted his gaze. "Aye, it would then."

"Very well," Clarie said with a knowing grin, looking at Max, Liz, and Nigel as she started walking backward away from them. "Three of you there be, so discover ye these things three: an inside job, a captive audience, and the means to protect and compete. When soldiers greet soldiers, the inside job is complete." She turned and melted into the crowded street before they could ask her anything more.

"Jolly good fun!" Nigel exclaimed, clasping his paws together and rubbing them eagerly. "How I love a challenge of the riddle sort. It gets the cranial juices flowing!"

"*Moi aussi,*" Liz agreed happily. "If we keep our keen eyes open we can figure this out. Any ideas before we begin our quest?"

Max wrinkled his brow and Nigel crossed his arms over his chest, tapping his mouth with his fingers as the three of them thought about the riddle.

"An inside job could mean something Paul would do in prison like Joseph when he worked for the jailer in Egypt," pondered Liz.

"True, and a captive audience could mean his fellow prisoners like those who heard Paul and Silas singing in the Philippian jail at midnight," Nigel added.

"Hmmm. The means ta pr-r-rotect an' compete sounds like somethin' I should be able ta figure out, but I got nothin'," Max admitted, trotting down the street toward the School of Tyrannus. "I plan ta figure it out before I go daft."

☧

The Jewish leaders Simeon, Joash, and Alexander stood in the doorway of the synagogue, wearing smug expressions as they watched Paul being led down the street attached by a chain to a Roman soldier.

"It's good to see Rome taking our side for once," Simeon said. "Silanus acted on our petition immediately, but I would have preferred Paul kept in complete confinement while we await his verdict."

"Be grateful for small blessings," Joash noted, pointing to Paul's chains. "At least he's not free to do as he pleases."

Alexander frowned. "From the look of things, he's pleased at the moment anyway."

Paul and the Roman soldier were enjoying conversation and started laughing as they walked down the street. Simeon fumed at the sight of the Roman oppressor engaged in lighthearted discussion with the very man who threatened their religious power. "That man is relentless! I can only hope that our people report the blame that's due him before Paul befriends the entire Praetorian Guard." He turned and stomped off inside.

☧

"Your brother actually *dared* you to jump off the aqueduct?" Paul asked in disbelief. "Don't tell me you did, Ovidius!"

The Roman soldier made a diving motion with his hand. "Right off the top into the Gardon River. I couldn't let my big brother make me into a coward!" He laughed. "That aqueduct bridge has three arched tiers, and he didn't think I would dive off the top tier." The young soldier grinned at Paul, happy to tell the story of his bold leap. His deep brown eyes shone from beneath the Roman helmet strapped under his chin. "Have you ever traveled to Gaul?"

"No, but I would love to. I understand it to be a beautiful place," answered Paul, walking down the street and catching a glimpse of Liz, who was now walking beside him. "And you came from the south of Gaul? Tell me about your family."

The Roman was amazed that this man in his custody cared to know anything about him. "Yes, my family lives in Nemausus near the aqueduct. I have one brother, Daedalos, and he is a legionnaire stationed in Macedonia."

"Really, where?" Paul inquired, smiling at Liz. "My friends and I have been all over that region."

"Philippi," Ovidius replied. "At least that's where he was the last I heard from him."

Paul smiled broadly. "I have many, many friends in Philippi! In fact, we started a church there and one of our strongest members actually oversees the jail. He was in the Roman army for decades. Arcadius is his name. He's a good man."

Ovidius's eyes widened. "A Roman jailer is part of your church? I thought you were a Jew. A Roman soldier—and a jailer at that—actually follows your beliefs?" Paul could see the confusion on the young Roman's face. "What do you believe exactly?"

"I'm glad you asked," Paul replied, pointing up to the School of Tyrannus, which now stood before them. "Let's go inside and you'll be able to hear all about it."

Max and Nigel caught up to Liz, who sat there grinning as she watched Paul and Ovidius walking up the steps into the school. Timothy met them at the top of the stairs, and Paul quickly introduced him to the Roman soldier.

"*C'est extraordinaire!* This Roman soldier is from the south of France, and his brother is stationed in Philippi," Liz reported. "But the most amazing thing is that on the short walk from the palace, this soldier has already asked Paul about his beliefs. Paul simply showed genuine interest in the man's life and began to share how Arcadius is part of the church in Philippi."

"I say, our Roman jailer?" Nigel asked. "Brilliant! I'm sure Paul will have quite the story to tell him on the way home."

"Do you think he'll tell the lad aboot the jailbr-r-reak?" Max wondered. "It's not the sort of thing ye want ta be tellin' yer current jailer. Or is it?"

"Well, since Paul and Silas did not run when the earthquake opened the prison doors, it wasn't a jailbreak per se." Liz smiled, slowly curling her tail up and down. "But as soon as Ovidius asks why Paul didn't run, Paul will have him right where he wants him."

THREE MONTHS LATER

Ovidius peered into the jail cell where Paul sat praying audibly. He watched his fellow soldier, Justus, listening intently to what Paul was saying, amazed anew to see Paul praying for the soldier and his needs. Justus closed his eyes and bowed his head. Ovidius smiled and shook his head. He could not believe the transformation that had taken place in the Praetorian Palace ever since Paul's arrival. Ovidius was the first to become a believer, followed by a slew of other soldiers who sat listening to Paul pray and read Scripture from the scrolls his friends brought him.

Prisoners here in the palace awaiting trial were allowed to have visitors, and Paul had a steady stream of them. One of them had even volunteered to be Paul's servant, staying in these rough quarters where Paul was confined. Epaphroditus was his name. He was from Paul's church in Philippi, and he brought news and gifts to Paul from the people there—money, food, clothes. A prisoner was expected to pay for his own lodging even if he could no longer earn wages, so this gift from Philippi was timely for Paul. Paul had left Luke in charge to oversee the church when he had to leave Philippi, following his miraculous release from prison there. Luke had been Paul's personal physician, but Paul was more concerned about having him care for the infant church in Philippi.

Ovidius also heard firsthand messages from Arcadius the jailer. Arcadius had helped several Roman soldiers come to faith in Jesus, engaging them in conversation at the fountain when they brought prisoners to his jail. He sent word to Paul that he purposely offered the soldiers there a fresh cup of water so he could share with them about the living water of Christ. Ovidius was surprised at the stories from the Philippian jailer and the Roman soldiers there. Arcadius sounded like someone he could easily call friend.

When Epaphroditus fell ill in the prison, Paul immediately reversed roles to care for the young man. He requested a messenger from the church in Ephesus to send urgent word about him back to the church

49

in Philippi so they could pray for him. At the time Paul worried that the young man would not make it. Thankfully, after much prayer Epaphroditus made a turnaround and regained his health. Paul and his friends were so happy to see their friend made well again.

There was something different about Paul's friends. *My friends now*, Ovidius thought to himself joyfully. Timothy, Aquila, Priscilla, Epaphras, Aristarchus, Tyrannus, and now Epaphroditus had followed Paul's lead and befriended each and every Roman soldier they met here, modeling the love of Christ. Paul showed no resentment, was courteous, never complained, and had inexplicable peace and patience while he waited for word from Silanus. He laughed, slept, ate the food provided with gratitude, and personally engaged each and every soldier on the duty roster, getting to know them well. Paul spent long stretches of time praying for all of his churches in Galatia, Thessalonica, Corinth, and Philippi, and for the believers in Jerusalem, Antioch, and every other place he could name.

50

"Amen," Paul said, finally opening his eyes. He smiled at the Roman soldier who was getting ready to change shifts with Ovidius. "Thank you for allowing me to pray for you, Justus."

"Thank you for praying, Paul. It's hard not to worry about my family back home," Justus said, rubbing his hand through his hair. "I wish I could be as peaceful about life as you are."

Paul placed his hand on the Roman's arm. "Listen, *don't worry about anything;* instead, *pray about everything.* Tell God what you need, and thank him for all he has done. *Then* you will experience God's peace." Paul looked around the jail cell. "Look at where I am. I'm sitting in a prison, not knowing if I'll walk out of here a free man or into the stadium of Ephesus to face the lions." He got right in the soldier's face. "Live in Christ Jesus, Justus, and I promise you, God's peace will exceed *anything* you can even begin to understand. *His* peace will guard your heart and mind."

Justus nodded and clenched his jaw. "Thank you, Paul. You've given me much to think about. And pray about."

"I'm glad, my friend," Paul said with an affirming pat on the soldier's back. "Press on—you can make it. And remember, the Lord has a purpose in all he is allowing in your life. Look at me! What has happened to me has already served to advance the gospel!"

Justus smiled, fastened his helmet, and nodded at Ovidius that he was ready to change the guard. "You're right. See you later, Paul. See you, Epaphroditus." He walked out the door as Ovidius jingled the keys against the metal lock to open it. The two soldiers shared a knowing smile. Justus spoke in hushed tones. "That man is not guilty, Ovidius! He is not here because of temple robbery. He is here for his faith in Christ."

"Yes, and the whole guard and even the proconsular court know it," Ovidius whispered back, handing Justus the key ring. "There are now Christians here in the palace besides us soldiers. We need to keep praying for Paul and for the truth to prevail in his case."

Nigel sat in a crook in the wall, having spent the whole morning listening in on this encounter with Justus, and now with Ovidius. Suddenly he raised his eyebrows as he figured out part of the riddle. "By Jove, I think I've got it. An inside job! Paul is converting Caesar's palace, one soldier at a time, and he's doing it from inside a jail cell." His whiskers quivered with excitement. "Brilliant!"

51

THE HAPPIEST
OF LETTERS

Max sat outside the Praetorium, watching Roman soldiers and officials walk in and out of the palace. He frequently studied exactly who belonged here and who did not. Where Paul's safety was concerned, Max kept a keen eye on the apostle's surroundings. The Roman soldiers were now used to Max following Paul to the School of Tyrannus to teach, even calling him "Gabriel," as did Paul.

All of a sudden the crescendo of shouting voices and stomping feet coming from the stadium filled the air. "More gladiator fightin' today," Max muttered to himself. "Those poor laddies have ta compete whether they want ta fight or not, fightin' ta stay alive."

Compete. Suddenly Max remembered that word from Clarie's riddle. "The means ta protect an' compete." The Scottie mulled this over in his mind. "Wha' pr-r-rotects gladiators?" Just then he saw Paul emerge from the building attached by chain to the Roman soldier Justus. Max wagged his tail and broke out in a huge grin. "The same thing that pr-r-rotects soldiers."

Liz basked in the sunshine on the stone wall at the base of the steps leading into the School of Tyrannus. Her tail slowly curled up and down as she closed her eyes from the cozy warmth of the sun kissing her shiny black fur. Like Nigel and Max, she had been contemplating Clarie's riddle. *An inside job, a captive audience, and the means to protect and compete. When soldiers greet soldiers, the inside job is complete. Hmmm. A captive audience. A captive can mean many things, no? A prisoner of war, one gripped by strong emotions, a slave, one kept under control, one who is restrained by circumstances or entranced by beauty.* Liz opened her eyes and saw Paul walking toward her, chained up to Justus.

Paul smiled and scratched Liz under the chin. "Good morning, little Faith. I'm happy to see you here today. Are you going to join my friend, Justus, here to hear today's lecture?"

Liz purred and meowed, "Bonjour, Paul. Of course I shall join you." Paul chuckled and Justus smiled at her as they walked up the steps. As Liz studied the lightweight chain swaying between soldier and prisoner, a thought struck the intelligent cat. *An audience is someone who is paying attention to a presenter. Of course! Paul and his fellow prisoners aren't the captive audience!*

Just then Max came running up to Liz. "I figured out me part, Lass!"

Nigel came swooping in on a pigeon to land next to them. "I bring enlightening news! I've discovered part of the riddle!"

Liz's eyes sparkled with anticipation. *"Bon!* And so have I, *mes amis."*

Nigel held out his paw to Liz. "Ladies first, of course."

"The captive audience is not the prisoners. It is the *soldiers*!" Liz explained. "They are the ones chained up to Paul and must listen to his prayers, Scripture reading, lectures, and speaking—whether they wish to or not!"

"Thrilling observation, my pet! And it goes along with the other part of the riddle. The inside job is what is happening at the palace," Nigel informed them. "Paul's 'captive audience' of soldiers are putting their faith in Jesus! Not all of them, of course, but as they leave his prison cell they discuss this with others in the palace. Even non-soldiers have accepted Christ now, *ergo* the 'inside job.' There's no other way Jesus could have penetrated the Proconsular Palace of Ephesus than by having Paul imprisoned there!"

"Aye, an' me part of the r-r-riddle has ta do with the soldiers, too. The means ta compete an' pr-r-rotect has ta do with the armor that soldiers an' gladiators wear," Max added. "How that ties in with all this, I'm not quite sure then. But armor be the answer."

"Splendid work, team," Nigel cheered, punching the air with his

53

tiny paw. "So all that remains is for 'soldiers to greet soldiers, and the inside job is complete.' But I wonder what this means exactly."

"I do not believe it refers to simply when they see one another in the palace, even if they do discuss Jesus," Liz surmised, thinking with a wrinkled brow.

"Don't Paul send gr-r-reetin's when he wr-r-rites his letters?" Max asked.

"*C'est ça!*" Liz jumped off the stone wall. "Timothy said he would be accompanying Paul back to the prison this afternoon. Paul requested he pen a letter thanking the Philippians for sending their gifts with Epaphroditus, and letting them know that the young man was now well. Nigel, you must be sure to return to the prison with Paul and Timothy. 'The inside job' may end today!"

As Liz, Max, and Nigel ran joyfully up the steps into the school, a pair of red eyes narrowed from a darkened doorway. The rat had listened in on their conversation as instructed by the lion. He looked at the scroll rolled up in its paw and laughed coldly. "Just wait until they see *this* inside job."

54

☧

As was his habit, Paul stood in order to dictate the letter to Timothy. He always thought better when he paced. Timothy sat poised to write down every word, and Epaphroditus was excited that he could leave right away to deliver this letter. When Ovidius and Justus heard what Paul was getting ready to do, they both remained in the cell. They wanted to hear Paul's words to the Philippians as much as anyone, including Nigel, who sat in his hiding spot high up in the wall.

"Very well, let us begin," Paul said happily. "From Paul and Timothy, servants of Christ Jesus—To all God's people in Philippi who are in union with Christ Jesus, including the church leaders and helpers. May God our Father and the Lord Jesus Christ give you grace and peace." Paul paused to allow Timothy to get it all down. When Timothy gave him the nod to proceed, Paul clasped his hands together and began to pace again.

"I thank my God for you every time I think of you; and every time I pray for you all, I pray with joy because of the way in which you have helped me in the work of the gospel from the very first day until now.

And so I am sure that God, who began this good work in you, will carry it on until it is finished on the Day of Christ Jesus." He paused again, and tears of joy began filling his eyes as he thought about the love and encouragement these people had given him. "You are always in my heart! And so it is only right for me to feel as I do about you. For you have all shared with me in this privilege that God has given me, both now that I am in prison and also while I was free to defend the gospel and establish it firmly. God is my witness that I tell the truth when I say that my deep feeling for you all comes from the heart of Christ Jesus himself."

Nigel adjusted his spectacles as he listened to Paul. "What a simply delightful beginning."

Paul smiled as he locked eyes with Ovidius and Justus. "I want you to know, my friends, that the things that have happened to me have really helped the progress of the gospel. As a result, the whole palace guard and all the others here know that I am in prison because I am a servant of Christ. And my being in prison has given most of the believers more confidence in the Lord, so they grow bolder all the time to preach the message fearlessly."

Nigel grinned as Paul continued to dictate. "An inside job. Bravo."

"I will continue to be happy, because I know that by means of your prayers and the help which comes from the Spirit of Jesus Christ I shall be set free. My deep desire and hope is that I shall never fail in my duty, but that at all times, and especially right now . . ." Paul paused and swallowed as he thought about his predicament as they awaited the verdict in his case. ". . . I shall be full of courage, so that with my whole being I shall bring honor to Christ, whether I live or die."

Timothy looked up at Paul and clenched his jaw. To think of this man of God dying at the hands of false accusers, and potentially in the jaws of lions, made his stomach churn. Timothy shook it off, blinked back tears, cleared the lump in his throat, and kept writing.

"For what is life?" Paul continued. "To me, it is Christ. Death, then, will bring more. But if by continuing to live I can do more worthwhile work, then I am not sure which I should choose. I am pulled in two directions. I want very much to leave this life and be with Christ, which is a far better thing; but for your sake it is much more important that I remain alive. I am sure of this, and so I know that I will stay. I will stay on with you all, to add to your progress and joy in the faith, so that when I am with you again, you will have even more reason to be proud of me in your life in union with Christ Jesus."

Ovidius and Justus were in awe of Paul's courage at the prospect of facing death. His one concern was not his life. He was most concerned about failing Christ in the face of death. Never had they seen a man like this.

"Don't be afraid of your enemies; always be courageous, and this will prove to them that they will lose and that you will win, because it is God who gives you the victory. For you have been given the privilege of serving Christ, not only by believing in him, but also by suffering for him. Now you can take part with me in the battle. It is the same battle you saw me fighting in the past, and as you hear, the one I am fighting still."

Nigel also marveled in stunned silence at hearing these words of bold encouragement. Paul then addressed practical affairs and urged the Philippians to live in ways that honored the Lord. "Don't do anything from selfish ambition or from a cheap desire to boast, but be humble toward one another, always considering others better than yourselves. And look out for one another's interests, not just for your own."

Timothy wrote as fast as his pen would allow, jotting down page after page of encouragement, wisdom, and instruction from Paul. "Do everything without complaining or arguing, so that you may be innocent and pure as God's perfect children, who live in a world of corrupt and sinful people. You must shine among them like stars lighting up the sky, as you offer them the message of life. If you do so, I shall have reason to be proud of you on the Day of Christ, because it will show that all my effort and work have not been wasted."

Paul placed his hands on Timothy's shoulders, rubbing to loosen them up as he leaned over to dictate this happy news. "If it is the Lord's will, I hope that I will be able to send Timothy to you soon, so that I may be encouraged by news about you."

Nigel took off his spectacles and rubbed his eyes as Paul continued to relay the account of his past life and how worthless it was compared with knowing Christ. It was unthinkable that at one time this man who had been called Saul had sought to persecute and kill Christians. Everything he boasted about then was now worthless. Nigel shook his head in wonder and awe at this transformed life. At the beginning of this mission, Gillamon told the Order of the Seven team that they would witness the transformation of a murderer into the model of what a true Christ-follower should be. Gillamon kept showing up in statues as a reminder of how the Maker could sculpt anyone into a new creation with his chisel. This was never more evident than with the living statue of Paul.

"All I want is to know Christ and to experience the power of his resurrection, to share in his sufferings and become like him in his death, in the hope that I myself will be raised from death to life," Paul continued. He thought back to the Isthmian Games in Corinth, and how Aquila took him through the athletic complex, explaining how the athletes trained and the prize they sought. He knew he had come a long way from his days as Saul, but still had so far to go. His race was far from over. *What a perfect analogy,* he thought to himself. "I do not claim that I have already succeeded or have already become perfect. I keep striving to win the prize for which Christ Jesus has already won me to himself. Of course, my friends, I really do not think that I have already won it; the one thing I do, however, is to forget what is behind me and do my best to reach what is ahead. So I run straight toward the goal in order to win the prize, which is God's call through Christ Jesus to the life above."

Timothy had to stop and grab another piece of parchment. He stretched his arms high above his head and worked out the kink in his neck. Paul waited patiently, discussing a matter of dispute between some members of the church that Epaphroditus brought to his attention. When Timothy was ready to resume writing, Paul addressed the dispute and encouraged them to work things out. How he hated to see discord among fellow believers! He wanted them to know joy! Real joy!

"Always be full of joy in the Lord. I say it again—rejoice! Let everyone see that you are considerate in all you do. Remember, the Lord is coming soon. Don't worry about anything; instead, pray about everything. Tell God what you need, and thank him for all he has done. Then you will experience God's peace, which exceeds anything we can understand. His peace will guard your hearts and minds as you live in Christ Jesus." Paul paused as he gathered his thoughts for the conclusion of this letter, and to allow Timothy to catch up.

57

Timothy nodded to Paul. "And now, dear brothers and sisters, one final thing. Fix your thoughts on what is true, and honorable, and right, and pure, and lovely, and admirable. Think about things that are excellent and worthy of praise. Keep putting into practice all you learned and received from me—everything you heard from me and saw me doing. Then the God of peace will be with you."

Paul looked at Epaphroditus, grateful to the Philippians for sending him with their gifts of love. "How I praise the Lord that you are concerned about me again. I know you have always been concerned for me, but you didn't have the chance to help me. Not that I was ever in need, for I have learned how to be content with whatever I have. I know how to live on almost nothing or with everything. I have learned the secret of living in every situation, whether it is with a full stomach or empty, with plenty or little. For I can do everything through Christ, who gives me strength."

Nigel stood up and couldn't help but applaud Paul's words. "Bravo! Bravo! I daresay this happy letter to the Philippians simply *must* make it into the New Testament! These are truths that will help believers throughout time."

Paul thought he heard something squeaking and turned his gaze up to spy Nigel tucked into a hole in the wall. He grinned as he realized the little mouse had followed him here. Nothing surprised Paul about these animals anymore. He shook his head slowly, grateful to God for all of his companions. He leaned down to read over Timothy's shoulder. It was time to end this letter.

"Give our regards to every follower of Jesus you meet. Our friends here say hello." Paul paused and looked over at Ovidius and Justus, who pointed to themselves playfully so they wouldn't be left out.

"Don't forget us!" Ovidius exclaimed, standing to tighten his belt, which securely held all his armor. "Remember us to Arcadius and the others." Ovidius turned to Epaphroditus. "If you see my brother Daedalos in Philippi, please tell him about me. Tell him I now follow Christ, and I hope he will do the same."

"I promise I will," Epaphroditus assured him.

Paul smiled broadly at the two soldiers who had become such strong believers and, indeed, his friends. A thought struck him. *Look at their armor. That belt is like truth that holds everything together. Hmmm.* "All the Christians here, *especially* the believers who work in the palace of Caesar, want to be remembered to you."

"When soldiers greet soldiers, the inside job is complete," recited Nigel, remembering the end of Clarie's riddle. Nigel preened his whiskers expectantly. "Jolly good! Now all that remains is word of Paul's release, and we'll be able to finally crack on from this cell. I must go give Max and Liz the happy news and report on this, the happiest of letters!"

Timothy blew to dry the ink on the parchment and then handed Paul the letter so he could read it over before signing the last line in his own hand. Epaphroditus stood and packed his knapsack, ready to depart with the letter, along with Timothy, who would leave Paul to rest for a while. Ovidius and Justus gathered their pieces of armor and made their way to open the cell door.

Once he saw that everyone was preparing to depart, Nigel scurried to his exit in the wall and made his way out of the building. He failed to notice that a new soldier had arrived in the Praetorium and stood at the end of the darkened hall.

And in his hand he held a letter of his own.

ROMAN JUSTICE

O h, Nigel! I look forward to reading the letter myself," Liz said cheerfully. "'I can do all things through Christ who gives me strength.' Such hopeful words, no?"

"Indeed, my dear," Nigel replied. "I'm telling you, it was by far the most positive, joy-filled letter Paul has written to date. That jail cell was practically illuminated with joy!"

Liz's big smile faded as she saw Max flying down the street straight toward them, a look of panic on his face. "What is it?" Liz exclaimed as he reached them.

"It has ta be a mistake! I've got ta get ta Aquila! No time ta lose!" Max blurted out as he gasped for breath.

"What, old boy?" Nigel asked in alarm. "What is a mistake?"

"Paul!" Max shouted. "He's been taken ta the arena! I were standin' outside the palace like always when I saw a R-r-roman soldier I never seen before takin' Paul in the other dir-r-rection with a heavy chain. I followed them as far as the stadium an' realized wha' were happenin'. I'm goin' ta gr-r-rab Aquila ta take him back there."

"How can this be?" Liz asked in disbelief.

"I dunno but ye best get there an' see if ye can do anythin' while I get Aquila," Max replied quickly.

"Agreed—on our way!" Nigel exclaimed as he and Liz ran in one direction and Max in the other. Blood drained from their faces with the enormity of the situation. "Oh dear, may Paul's words give us strength to help him now!"

☧

Aquila adjusted the heavy tent cloth that was draped across his lap. He was almost finished with sewing on a piece of edging to reinforce the trim. Priscilla handed him a cup of water, which he quickly drank so he could resume his work. He wiped the sweat from his brow and picked up the needle and thread to finish the job. Max came bolting into the shop, barking at a frenzied pitch.

Priscilla and Aquila looked at the little dog in alarm. "Gabriel? What is it, boy?" Aquila asked, putting his needle down.

"Come with me! Paul's been taken ta the arena! Ye must do somethin'!" Max barked over and over, running to the door so they would follow him. *"Hurry! There's no time ta waste!"*

"I've never seen him act this way," Priscilla shouted over Max's barking.

Aquila stood up. "Neither have I."

"I'm tellin' ye, ye must come with me NOW!" Max yelped, now running over to the tent Aquila was working on. He grabbed the trim that Aquila had almost finished sewing onto the tent and pulled it completely off, as he yanked it roughly out of Aquila's hands. He ran back to the door. *"HURRY!"*

"He wants us to follow him," Priscilla suggested urgently, stepping forward.

"AYE! NOW!" Max barked and whined, running up to them and back to the door again.

Aquila stepped over the tent and looked at Priscilla. "Let's see where he leads us."

"FINALLY!" Max barked, running out the door with Aquila and Priscilla close on his heels.

☧

Paul could hear the spectators stomping their feet and cheering for more blood. Dust drifted through the narrow shafts of light coming from the stadium floor above his holding cell. Typical to all Roman stadiums, a series of tunnels and underground passageways ran beneath the arena floor. A maze of cells held both humans and wild beasts awaiting their turn to make an entrance for the viewing pleasure of the spectators. Caged ramps led to trapdoors where lions, bears, leopards, tigers, boars, or wild dogs would be released to the terror of unprotected victims—and to the thrill of the crowds.

Paul was still reeling with shock, and his heart was beating out of his chest. Evidently Silanus had ruled against him, as orders had come for him to be executed in the arena. When Paul asked to see the orders, the Roman soldier handed him the scroll. There it was—the Imperial Seal of Rome and a messy signature belonging to Marcus Junius Silanus Torquatus. Because this soldier did not know Paul, he felt no emotion about the fate of his prisoner. Paul was just another despicable criminal who would allow Rome to carry out justice while entertaining the blood-thirsty crowds of Ephesus. Paul leaned on the cell wall and slowly slid to the floor, dropping the scroll.

The roar of a lion made the hair on the back of Paul's neck rise. Fear began to consume him as the reality of his situation started to sink in. He heard the screams of a criminal who was facing the attacking lion. His terrified voice was joined by the cheers of excitement from the crowd in this sickening spectacle. Beads of sweat poured off Paul's face. "I can do all things through Christ," Paul whispered to himself, closing his eyes, "who gives me strength."

☧

Liz and Nigel darted into one of the stadium entrances undetected and ran up to see the crowds standing to their feet, applauding the demise of another victim. "This can't be happening! It just can't be!" Liz cried, her voice cracking in a panic. "Either Silanus determined Paul was guilty and this is actually happening . . . or a grave mistake is getting ready to unfold."

Nigel was just as panicked as she, but he attempted to keep a calm head. "Steady, my dear. Let us see who the officiating patron is for today's games. The more we know, the better we can take measures to halt this travesty."

Together Liz and Nigel scanned the crowd until they found the spectator box belonging to the patron, or sponsor, of the games. People of wealth and power would pay for an event in order to gain the favor of the masses. If the Proconsul or even the Emperor himself were in attendance, they would sit in the main box. If they were not in attendance, a private citizen could choose to be the patron. Suddenly their eyes locked on today's patron: Proconsul Silanus himself.

"We must find out how Paul got here," Nigel said. "If Silanus did in fact sign the orders, there is nothing we can do."

"But if he did *not* sign the orders, we must find a way to let Silanus know," Liz answered, trying to get her mind in control over her emotions so she could think this through. "First we have to find those orders Quickly, to the lower level of the arena!"

Aquila and Priscilla raced through the streets of Ephesus, trying to keep up with Max. As they turned the corner and saw that the little dog was heading straight for the stadium, they gasped and felt sick with fear. "This can't be!" Priscilla cried out breathlessly.

Aquila placed his hand behind his wife's back as they ran, willing her to press on. "We'll get to the bottom of this. Hurry!"

Together they bolted into the stadium and up to the spectator stands and witnessed the disgusting show of afternoon "entertainment." Helpless victims were being hunted while laughing spectators looked on. The couple scanned the faces of the victims. "He's not here," Priscilla said hopefully, putting her hand over her heart.

Suddenly a new group of prisoners was ushered into the arena from a side gate. The two quickly scanned their terrified faces. "He's not here . . . yet," Aquila remarked gravely.

Max growled and ran off to find the passageway to the lower level, leaving Aquila and Priscilla in the impossible situation of figuring out what to do if Paul appeared on the already blood-drenched sandy floor of the arena.

Liz and Nigel reached the lower level and frantically ran down the dingy passageway looking for Paul. Organized chaos echoed off the cold stone walls of this rat-infested place. The beastmaster was shouting orders to the slaves, who used spears to prod the wild animals into position up the caged ramps. Prisoners cowered in the corners of their cells, hoping they would somehow become invisible to the beastmaster. He used an

63

iron rod to bang on the cell doors of designated victims, shouting orders to the slaves to move them into the corral and out to the arena.

Suddenly Liz spotted Paul, who sat calmly in his cell with his back against the wall. He was praying. Nigel and Liz arrived at his cell just as Max came from the other direction. "There he is! See if the orders are in his cell!" Liz cried above the din of humans shouting and animals roaring.

"Hide!" Max shouted, shoving Liz behind a crate before the humans saw them.

Nigel sneaked in through the bars of Paul's cell to search for the scroll of Roman orders. But just as he spotted it, there came the deafening clang of the iron rod against the bars of Paul's cell. "This one next!"

Paul slowly rose to his feet as the door to his cell swung open. Two slaves entered and roughly grabbed him to push him out of the cell and down the passageway. Nigel ran over to the scroll, shouting, "The scroll is here!" Max and Liz darted into the cell and quickly unrolled the orders.

Nigel scanned the document. "It is a generic dispatch with Paul's name scribbled at the top, yet no charges are listed! Look at the messy attempt to forge Silanus's signature!"

"And the Roman seal was hastily pressed *upside down*," Liz added, turning to lock eyes with Nigel as they both exclaimed, "This is a forgery!"

"We've got ta get this ta Aquila!" Max shouted, grabbing the orders in his mouth and darting out of the cell.

☧

Silanus sat slouched in the plush viewing box filled with purple silk reclining pillows, platters of rich food, and amphorae filled with wine. All around him guests lounged, ate, laughed, and lifted their glasses to toast the glory of Rome. The proconsul rubbed his imperial signet ring, fuming at the carelessness of his chamber servant who had paid the price with his life when it was discovered missing. After a frantic search in the palace, the ring was recovered, lying strangely on the tile floor mosaic of Hercules, in front of Silanus's desk. From that point on, Silanus trusted no one, and did not remove his ring for any reason. He watched the spectacle of criminals paying the price for their crimes, but even Roman justice would not allay his seething anger at whoever could have taken his ring.

Just then the north gate of the arena opened and Paul was ushered into the venue of his assured death. He calmly stood there as the gate slammed behind him. "To live is Christ," Paul muttered to himself, scanning the arena. The lions were occupied with other victims at the opposite end of the arena. "To die is gain."

"Proconsul! Please! Proconsul!" came the shout of a burly man waving a scroll in the air. Silanus turned his gaze as he saw two Roman guards grab the man, and a woman then dare to grab one of the Roman guards by the arm, pleading with him to stop. He sat up and waved the guards forward. For two citizens to rush the Proconsul's box and to touch Roman guards was a dangerous move, yet this man and woman were not concerned about the consequences while they sought his attention.

"What is this about?" Silanus demanded to know.

Aquila stretched out his hand and cried with a broken voice as he saw Paul standing in the arena. "Please! This is a mistake! That man Paul down there has been put here by mistake! No charges are on these orders."

"Paul, the Christian?" Silanus asked, raising his eyebrows in alarm and scanning the arena floor. He quickly spotted a lone man standing at the end of the arena.

"You have not yet ruled in his case, Proconsul," Gracilis reminded him. He clapped his hands at the guard. "Let me see those orders!"

The guard grabbed the scroll from Aquila and handed it to Gracilis, who quickly read its contents and passed it to Silanus in disbelief. Silanus clenched his jaw and rose to his feet as he read the document. "This is a forgery!" He pointed to Paul and then spotted a lion who had finally noticed him standing there. "Get that man out of there immediately!"

Gracilis snapped to attention and ordered the guards to release Aquila and Priscilla. "MOVE!" he ordered them to rescue the innocent prisoner immediately.

Priscilla dropped to her knees, as did Aquila, who grabbed her as they clung to one another to watch what was happening, praying fervently for God to intervene in time. As the lion began to slowly trot in Paul's direction, the gate behind Paul opened. The lion growled and

65

began to pick up speed, yet Paul stood there calmly, not attempting to run. Suddenly two slaves grabbed Paul by the arms and pulled him back to the safety of the gate just as the lion reached them. As the gate slammed in the lion's face, it let out a blood-curdling roar of defeat.

Max, Liz, and Nigel collapsed in a heap together, breathing heavily and flooded with relief. They were exhausted from the physical stress and emotional turmoil of the past hour and Paul's narrow escape.

"We did it! Paul is safe!" Nigel cheered with both of his fists raised in victory.

Liz placed her paw on Max's shoulder. "Well done, Maximillian. Your watchful eye saved the day."

"Aye. That were a close one." Max heaved a sigh of relief. "So it looks as if there were two inside jobs then. One were Paul's an' one were the forged orders inside the palace."

"Indeed, so it appears," Nigel agreed. "It may very well be that your unknown Roman soldier was completely innocent and was simply carrying out orders, albeit false ones."

"Yet someone got to Silanus's signet ring," Liz noted. "Someone who knows to use it, but not how to use it correctly, since it was used upside down."

The three animals turned to see the lion slinking around the stadium. It was staring right at them. "Do ye think it could be . . . who we think it is?" Max wondered with a growl.

"By the looks of things, I would not doubt it," Nigel answered.

Just then Liz looked up to see a Roman messenger arrive at Proconsul Silanus's viewing box carrying a scroll. The messenger handed the scroll to Gracilis, who read it and whispered in Silanus's ear. Silanus stood and stormed out of the box. The messenger turned around and looked right at them. Liz's eyes filled with joyful tears. "Clarie!"

Silanus, seated at his desk, snatched the newly delivered scroll from Gracilis's hand, still fuming over Paul's narrow escape from the arena. The corners of his mouth were downturned as he scanned the long-awaited evidence coming in from the province. He slowly started to nod. "Just as I expected." When he reached the end of the document, he tossed the scroll onto his desk and grabbed a piece of parchment to write out his decision. "There is *no* proof that Paul tampered in any way with the Temple tax. If the Jews in Asia Minor prefer to give money for Paul's Jerusalem relief effort over the voluntary Temple tax, it is *not* Temple robbery." He dripped the wax and pressed the imperial Roman seal into the document. "Paul is innocent of the charges. Release him completely—from the arena *and* from the prison!"

Gracilis took the document and bowed respectfully. "Yes, Proconsul. I'll see he is released immediately." He hurriedly left the atrium to see to the full release of the prisoner.

Silanus folded his arms and watched Gracilis walk away, wondering about his loyalty. He leaned over his desk, shaking his head at the absurdity of Paul's entire situation. Whoever forged the orders to send Paul to the arena did so with his imperial ring, and they had done so right here at his desk, hastily pressing the wax and dropping the ring onto the floor. Silanus realized that whoever had done this was close to him. It was an inside job. His paranoia grew as he considered the fact that anyone close to him could be guilty of parading as the proconsul. But why? What was so threatening about this tent-making Christian that someone would take such extreme measures to ensure his death? Silanus slammed his fist on the desk in anger. He would get to the bottom of this. Meanwhile, Roman justice had been served and Paul was safe.

Silanus's gaze drifted down to the mosaic of Hercules dipping his arrows in the poisonous blood of his defeated adversary, preparing to kill a second foe from the remains of the first. A pair of glowing red eyes stared at Silanus from the shadows. Little did Silanus know that his decision to release Paul would put the apostle in fresh danger in ways he could never anticipate, flying in with the poisonous arrows of Rome.

67

A Deadly Delicacy

The merchant held up a cluster of vine-ripened tomatoes, calling out his produce for sale in the bustling marketplace of Rome. "Fresh vegetables! You will find none better!" He dipped his hand into a bowl of olives and scooped them up for a potential customer passing by. He could tell she had a lot of money, as her gold-trimmed clothes were made of the finest silk, and she was followed by a well-dressed slave. Her sky-blue scarf was pulled over her hair, which was piled high with endless braids and curls, partially covering her face from view. "The richest olives in Italy!" the merchant called again.

The woman held up her hand and shook her head. She was clearly not interested and started to walk away. The merchant reached for a wooden bowl, desperate to make a sale. "Mushrooms, perhaps?"

The woman stopped in the street and turned back to the merchant. Her eyes narrowed as she stared at the merchant who jiggled the bowl to entice his potential customer. "The finest porcini mushrooms to be found in Italy! Their nutty flavor makes any dish to die for."

A sly grin grew on the woman's face and she reached up to clutch the unusual glass ornament hanging from her necklace. "Yes, I think mushrooms are exactly what I'm searching for. They are his favorite. I'll take the lot." She nodded to her slave to purchase the vegetables.

"Excellent!" the merchant said excitedly.

Al sat a few feet away on the cobblestone street watching this vegetable transaction, his mouth watering at all the merchant's offerings. "Sure, I'd be happy with it all, especially the olives." He waited for the humans to drop some produce in the street, as they invariably did, so he could quickly snatch it up. As the merchant eagerly poured the entire bowl of mushrooms into the slave's basket, some spilled over the side and Al went in for the kill.

"Ari? Where are you?" Peter called out, looking for the scavenging cat.

Al popped his face out from beneath the merchant's table to respond to Peter, his cheeks full of mushrooms. *"Over here,"* he meowed in muffled tones with his mouth full. He chewed quickly and swallowed so he could better answer Peter. *"OVER HERE, LAD!"* he meowed, stepping out from under the legs of the humans. *"Jest keepin' the streets o' Rome clean and tidy."*

Mark pointed at the rotund cat. "There he is, Peter. We should have known." He smiled as he caught a glimpse of the wealthy woman walking away. His smile faded as he dug into his pouch and pulled out a coin. He then looked back at the woman walking away, studying her distinctive hair and dress. "Do you know who I think that is?"

Peter scooped up Al in his arms, mussing the cat's fur. "No, who?"

"I think it might be Agrippina, the wife of Emperor Claudius," Mark replied, showing Peter a coin with her face etched in it. "I've heard she sometimes likes to shop quietly among the common people."

Peter raised his eyebrows. "Interesting. I wonder if she longs to get away from the palace and her unhappy life. Even with all that wealth and power, it must be a miserable, paranoid existence to be in that twisted family."

"Indeed. The Emperor may have conquered Britain, but not the women in his life," Mark agreed, handing the coin to the merchant. "Olives, please."

"I LOVE YOU," Al meowed as Mark bought the olives. Peter set Al back down on the street. The hungry cat stayed right under Mark's feet, hoping he would drop an olive on purpose.

Peter watched the woman and her slave walk away. "We may hate the decadent way they live, but we must show proper respect to everyone, and even honor the Emperor."

Agrippina was the fourth wife and niece of Emperor Claudius and

69

twenty-five years younger than he. Both of them were great-grand-children of Caesar Augustus and both had children from previous marriages. Claudius had one son, Brittanicus, but had adopted Agrippina's older son, Nero, when she insisted that he be named as heir to the throne. Claudius had done her bidding and even promised his daughter Octavia in marriage to Nero. Claudius found it impossible to say "no" to the beautiful, power-hungry Agrippina, who was determined to have her way. Despite his repeated warnings, she did as she wished, going about the city with only a slave so she would blend in with the masses.

"Well, so far the Emperor has allowed Christians to live in peace here in Rome and throughout the empire," Mark said as he and Peter made their way through the marketplace near the Roman Forum. "Gallio's ruling in Paul's favor at Corinth made us all breathe easier. Rome itself has given the church its protection."

"Amen! And Gallio's brother, Seneca, is a friend and close advisor of Claudius. Seneca also tutors young Nero," Peter replied. "Let's hope the favor of Rome continues when Nero takes the throne. The church here is beginning to grow." Peter gave Mark a hearty pat on the back as they discussed the infant Church of Rome and their recent arrival here to help it along. "I'm so glad you've accompanied me here, Mark. I expect great things to happen for the Lord!"

"Psst!" came a voice that tickled Al's ears. "Al!"

Al stopped and looked around to see who was calling him. A pair of beautiful blue eyes greeted him atop his nose. A goofy grin appeared on Al's face as he stared at the butterfly. "Top o' the mornin' to ye, Clarie."

The blue butterfly flittered up and landed on a statue of Hercules wearing a lion skin, holding a club over his shoulder. The statue suddenly blinked its eyes and smiled down at Al. "Welcome to Rome, Al. We wanted to check in with you."

"Gillamon? I think I've gotten used to ye showin' up all statuey," Al said, gazing up at the sculpture. "Who are ye supposed to be now?"

"Hercules," Gillamon answered quickly before growing silent as a pair of Roman soldiers walked by. Everyone froze.

Once the humans had passed Clarie opened and closed her delicate wings. "How do you like the city so far?"

"I LOVE IT!" Al replied happily. "The food be especially grand.

Aye, I think I'm goin' to do well in Rome. But how's me lass, Liz? I miss her badly."

"She's doing very well. She, Max, and Nigel are traveling to Corinth at the moment for a quick visit," Clarie replied. She didn't want to alarm him with the news of recent events in Ephesus. She knew the simple-minded cat would soon be upset with the coming changes in the empire. "Paul wanted to revisit Corinth briefly. Liz misses you terribly and sends her love."

Al stuck out his lip. "Aye. I miss her, too. When will I be able to see her again?"

"Well, you're going to be staying put in Rome now, so the good news is that we just need to arrange for Liz to come visit you here," Gillamon informed him. "I will tell you that you will get to see her face very soon."

Al brightened. "Hooray! And no more travelin' for endless mile after mile after mile after mile after mile after mile after mile . . ."

"We get it, Al! No more traveling," Clarie interrupted him. "Peter and Mark will be here to get the church well established in Rome. How do you think Peter and Mark are doing?"

"I be keepin' them safe and happy," Al reported, "and they be keepin' me well fed."

"I see that," giggled Clarie. "But Al, you'll need to get in shape for when the Animalympics come here to Rome. Remember I've told you all about Liz's idea to hold an event for animals, just like the humans do with their Olympic Games."

"Aye! I'll be in great shape, Lass!" Al informed her, patting his belly. "When will the games happen?"

"Well, it will be a while yet, but we have a mission for you since you are the first of the team to settle in Rome," Gillamon said. "We need you to get to know this city like the back of your paw. You need to know every side street, every back alley, every merchant, every home, every entertainment venue, everything. Do you think you can do that?"

Al suavely wiped back the fur on top of his head. "I'll be the Rome expert by the time me love arrives so I can show her around the city then. Aye, I can do it! This will be easy. And since we're stayin' put in Rome, I guess I don't have to worry aboot anythin' happenin' to Peter and Mark out on the road. Now *that's* a relief!"

Clarie smiled weakly. "Yes . . . yes, that's true," she started to say.

"Ari! Where are you?" came Peter's voice.

"You'll be happy to know you get to see a familiar statue tomorrow, but we'll let that be a surprise," Gillamon said.

"I love surprises!" Al cheered, clapping his front paws together.

"Come here, you crazy cat!" Mark called, his and Peter's voices getting closer.

Al looked up and stood to leave. "Gotta go, Gillamon, and little Clarie. Don't worry aboot Rome. This kitty has it well in paw." He winked at them and trotted off after Peter and Mark.

They indeed knew that Peter and Mark would no longer be in danger from travels as they spread the gospel. Gillamon looked up at the Imperial Palace on Palatine Hill. "They are preparing for tonight's banquet."

Clarie lifted off the statue's shoulder. "On my way." She flew high above the Forum, where Peter, Mark, and Al now walked below. No, the danger would not come to them out on the road. She glanced ahead to the Palace. The danger would come to them right here in Rome.

☧

"More wine!" Agrippina ordered, clapping her hands. She scanned the room, studying the faces of their guests lounging on their elbows around the table. She made sure platters of exotic food kept coming, and amphorae of wine kept pouring.

Claudius took a sip and set his cup down with great satisfaction. "My dear, you have outdone yourself. This is a splendid banquet."

"I'm glad you approve, Claudius," Agrippina replied smugly, spying the servants now entering the room carrying new platters of food. "I have a surprise for you."

"Oh? What might that be?" the aging man replied happily, delighted at his wife's sudden desire to please him.

"I found one of your favorite delicacies and had it prepared just the way you like it," she replied, waving over the servant. He carried a special dish full of the mushrooms sautéed in a rich sauce.

Claudius's eyes lit up and he kissed his wife on the cheek. "I do love porcini mushrooms! Thank you, my dear." He waved his eunuch over and handed him a fork. "Halotus, taste these quickly so I can eat them all."

The servant bowed and did as ordered, taking a mushroom to test not for taste, but for poison. He sampled everything that Claudius ate to protect the emperor from harm. He swallowed, nodded, and smiled, indicating that all was well. As Halotus stepped back to stand in the shadows behind the banquet table, Agrippina held the dish of mushrooms up playfully to Claudius. "I expect you to eat them all like you promised, but may I please have a few?"

"Of course, my dear! Enjoy!" Claudius said, taking the dish of mushrooms and putting several on Agrippina's plate. He then proceeded to pop one in his mouth, moaning with delight. "Delicious." He quickly gobbled up the plate, enjoying every bite.

Suddenly a group of musicians entered the room to entertain the guests. "Marvelous," Agrippina exclaimed as she lifted her cup in approval.

While everyone was watching the musicians, Clarie, from her perch high above the banquet table, was watching Agrippina. As her guests reclined to enjoy the music, the emperor's wife fiddled with the glass vial that hung from her necklace, hiding it behind a silk napkin. She slowly poured the poison from the vial onto her plate, covering the mushrooms. Before the song was finished, Agrippina had made her move, setting the napkin aside.

"Bravo!" she shouted, placing her hand on Claudius's back and smiling at his empty plate. "I believe I'm too full to finish these after all. Would you like them?"

"If you insist," Claudius said with a wink, reaching over with his fork to take the mushrooms from Agrippina's plate.

"Of course," Agrippina smiled coolly. "I most certainly insist."

Clarie frowned gravely. "So it begins."

"Let me encourage you now to rid yourselves of all malice and all deceit, hypocrisy, envy, and slander of every kind," Peter shared with the group of believers in this Christian home. He looked around the courtyard at his new friends gathered to hear the Good News. Their hostess, Bella, slowly walked behind the group, bouncing a baby in her arms to give a young mother a break so she could hear Peter.

Peter looked at Bella and smiled. He marveled at the turn of events that had brought him directly to the house of Bella Antonius, a Roman Christ-follower here in Rome. He had known her husband, Armandus, and had the privilege of leading him to faith in Jesus at the home of a Roman named Cornelius back in Caesarea many years ago. But Armandus had not been just any Roman soldier. He had been the centurion in charge the day that Jesus was crucified in Jerusalem. And his father, Marcus Antonius, was also a centurion, who had been ordered to lead the Slaughter of the Innocents the night Herod sought the murder of all the baby boys two years old and younger in and around Bethlehem. Jesus' parents had befriended Marcus and Julia Antonius, so Jesus and Armandus had met as very young children. Marcus had willfully disobeyed orders, turning a blind eye to allow Mary and Joseph to escape with baby Jesus that night. Of course, Marcus didn't know who Jesus was. And neither did Armandus for a long while. It wasn't until Jesus was dying on the cross that Armandus recognized who he was, and the grief was more than he could bear. Peter was blessed beyond measure to help Armandus understand why Jesus had to die. He also helped him understand that Jesus' blood was on the hands of all mankind, not just on Armandus.

74

When Bella came to Rome with their two boys, Theophilus and Julius, Armandus had stayed behind in Caesarea. One afternoon Cornelius called Peter to come to his house. It was the very first gathering of Gentiles to hear the good news of Jesus. Armandus stood in the back of the group gathered that day, and when he accepted the grace and forgiveness of Christ, wept openly with Peter. Peter rejoiced as Armandus was baptized along with all of Cornelius's household that day. Sadly, Armandus died without getting to Rome, and Bella was left to raise their boys the best she could. Armandus had written to Bella about his faith in Christ, and she also became a believer. But the loss of their father, coupled with the influence of the pagan culture of Rome, caused the boys to doubt Christianity. Theophilus was lukewarm about this Christian religion, not fully embracing it, and left his mind open to all religions Rome had to offer. Julius, on the other hand, grew resentful to Christianity when he learned the details of his father's death.

Bella longed for her sons to embrace Jesus as she and Armandus had done, but knew they must find their own way and make their faith journey themselves. So she continued to love and pray for them, but ultimately left them in the hands of Jesus—she knew he had to. Julius had followed in his father's and grandfather's footsteps to become a legionnaire, and grew extremely close to Marcus, who became the dominant father figure in his life. Theophilus pursued another path, preferring a scholarly route, studying law after fulfilling his duty of military service.

When Peter and Mark arrived in Rome, they were delighted to learn that Bella opened her spacious home for believers to meet. As usual, Al trotted along behind them, and his jaw dropped when he saw whose home it was. When they entered the courtyard of this wealthy Roman home, there in the center of their garden stood the statue of Libertas, goddess of liberty. And at the statue's feet was a liberty-loving cat, in the exact likeness of Liz. Al ran up to wrap his chubby arms around the marble figure. "Oh, me love, at least I get to see yer face then!"

This statue of Libertas had been sculpted long ago in Jerusalem, in the garden where Armandus chased Al as a child. Armandus's mother, Julia, had posed for the image of the goddess, and Liz had posed for the image of the cat. Neither Armandus nor Bella believed in false gods such as Libertas, but saw this statue as a likeness of Armandus's mother, nothing more. When his family moved back to Rome, Armandus arranged to send this statue back with them. To him it was simply a beautiful piece of art and a tribute to his beloved mother.

The baby that Bella held began to cry. She tried to shush him, but knew he was hungry. She smiled and handed him to his mother.

Peter lifted his hand to the baby. "Like newborn babies, crave pure spiritual milk, so that by it you may grow up in your salvation, now that you have tasted that the Lord is good."

Suddenly a young man came bursting into the courtyard. His face was ashen. "Emperor Claudius is dead. Nero has already been escorted to the Praetorian barracks and hailed as Imperator."

"How did he die?" Bella asked in disbelief, putting her hand to her face.

"Poison is suspected, but they have no proof other than his symptoms," the young man answered, looking around at the people in the garden. "One of the guards told me they suspect he was poisoned last night at dinner, as he became suddenly ill after eating some mushrooms."

Peter and Mark shot glances at one another. "We saw his wife

Agrippina buying mushrooms in the market yesterday," Mark explained.

Al's eyes got as big as tomatoes. He put his paws up to his neck in horror. "I ate them mushrooms!" he muttered to himself, falling over in full dramatic form next to the Liz statue.

"The strange part is that Claudius's slave tasted the mushrooms before Claudius ate them, so they are not sure how he was poisoned," the young man reported.

"Nero is only seventeen years old!" Bella exclaimed in disbelief. "How is he supposed to rule Rome?"

"His mother will likely be the power behind the throne, along with her select advisors," the young man explained. "Of course it remains to be seen if anyone will challenge Nero's rightful place in the imperial bloodline to be emperor."

Peter frowned and felt a pang of worry. "If this indeed was murder, then any friends or blood relatives of Claudius better take note. These imperial Roman murders have a tendency to spill over to anyone seen as a threat to the new regime."

"He weren't me friend! He weren't me friend!" Al gripped his throat and mumbled, still worried about the mushrooms. "And I KNOW we weren't related. I be Irish! Irish, I say!"

"Steady, Big Al," came Clarie's comforting voice as she alighted on Liz's marble head. "The mushrooms you ate weren't poisonous. They didn't become poisonous until they were tampered with at dinner."

"Aye, still, this makes me want ta watch what I eat from now on," Al worried, relaxing his grip but remaining fearful.

"That's a good thing you should do anyway." Clarie encouraged Al with a smile. "Don't worry, Al. You're in good hands here. Nothing to worry about. At least not for a while." She flapped her wings to get ready to leave.

"That's a relief," Al sighed, putting his paw over his heart. "Where're ye goin'?"

"Let's just say I have to get to another banquet," Clarie offered gravely. "Agrippina isn't finished serving up her deadly delicacy just yet."

Six Lamps to Light

The brisk October wind whipped around Paul's ankles as he and Sosthenes escorted Timothy to the outskirts of Ephesus. Paul pulled his cloak up around his shoulders to ward off the chill, coughing.

"Are you sure you should be heading to the upcountry now, Paul? Winter will be here soon. You could wait until spring," Timothy suggested with a pained expression. "I'm sure Sosthenes, Aristarchus, and Gaius would agree with me that you all should wait to make this Asian tour, at least until you're well."

Paul waved his hand to dismiss the idea. "It's just a cough. If things get worse upcountry then we'll settle somewhere, but I have put off this trip for far too long. That quick jaunt over to Corinth interrupted my plans to head up there in September." He stopped and put his hand on the back of Sosthenes. "But I'm glad we gained you, Sosthenes, to return to Ephesus with us. It was worth that trip to have you here. You are a testament to the change that can happen between men when Christ enters their relationship."

Sosthenes lowered his gaze humbly and nodded. It pained him to think that he had been the leader of the synagogue in Corinth who had Paul arrested and brought up on charges before Roman Proconsul Gallio. When Gallio ruled in Paul's favor, the unruly mob turned their anger on Sosthenes and beat him right there in the street while a disinterested Gallio turned a blind eye. After that he was ministered to by Crispus, his predecessor at the synagogue, who had resigned his post to follow Jesus. Sosthenes soon became an active follower of the movement known as The Way in Corinth. When word reached Paul of the trouble brewing in the church there, he hurried over for a hasty visit. Sosthenes was the first to greet him with an embrace, asking Paul's forgiveness. Paul immediately extended grace to his new brother in Christ, and even asked Sosthenes to accompany him back to Ephesus.

While Sosthenes might have been useful in Corinth, Paul realized he would be of far greater help as they visited the upcountry of Asia. Something in his spirit felt a sense of urgency to get to six particular cities and establish churches. He knew the tour would be fraught with opposition, and he wanted some of his most wise, reliable companions at his side for the various gifts they brought to his ministry.

"I'll do whatever you wish, Paul," Sosthenes said. "If you want to press on now, I'm with you. If you want to wait, then I'll minister with you here until a better time."

Paul smiled. "Thank you, my friend. I think we would be waiting until eternity for a better time. These wicked days make me want to press on as quickly as possible to reach the lost." He turned to Timothy. "So, you have the letter for the Corinthians?"

Timothy held up a scroll. "Right here. I'll get it to Corinth after I stop by Philippi. I can't wait to hear how the Philippians received our letter. I know they must have been overjoyed by your words." He looked at the scroll in his hand and shook it in mid-air. "This one, however, will be received as if by a child who doesn't wish to be punished."

"Step aside!" came a brusque voice from a Roman soldier approaching on horseback. He was clearly a knight in the upper echelons of the Roman military. Behind him was another man on horseback in imperial attire. Both men were in a hurry to enter the city of Ephesus.

Timothy, Paul, and Sosthenes stepped out of their way to the side of the road. Once they had passed, Paul put a hand to Timothy's shoulder. "Thank you for being the bearer of tough news. I only wish these words could be as happy as those you penned for me to the Philippians. But Corinth is in need of quite a bit of discipline. And I fear the bad reports from them have just begun." He paused and studied Timothy's kind face. He hated to be parted from his dear friend. "Go with God. I will plan to see you in Macedonia."

Timothy embraced his spiritual father, mentor, and friend, choking back tears of concern for his safety. "Until Macedonia. God be with you." He let go, cleared his throat, and pulled his knapsack higher onto his shoulder. Timothy then grinned and pointed to Paul. "Sosthenes, keep him out of trouble."

Sosthenes laughed. "You ask for the impossible, I'm afraid. Farewell, Timothy. Godspeed."

With that, Timothy turned to take the road leading out of Ephesus. Paul watched his young protégé for a moment before turning to head back into Ephesus with Sosthenes. "Let's get ready to be on our way as well, my friend."

☧

Max, Liz, and Nigel sat on a hillside that had a magnificent view overlooking Ephesus. Clarie was with them in her natural form as a lamb, enjoying being herself for a change. She gave her friends the full report of events transpiring in Rome. They were shocked by the assassination of Emperor Claudius yet thrilled by Peter's connection with Bella and the infant church in Rome. And, of course, Liz was especially happy to hear of Al's love messages sent for her.

Liz updated Clarie on the letter Paul had written to the church in Corinth, giving them advice as they sought to combat the snares of the wicked city in which they lived. Timothy would carry it to Corinth after he went through Philippi as promised earlier by Paul. While the animals watched Timothy leaving Paul and Sosthenes, Clarie's gaze was on the two horsemen who had just passed them on the road. Liz took note of Clarie's gaze, as she was prone to do.

"Who are those men, *mon amie?*" inquired Liz, now staring at them.

"One is a knight named Publius Celer, and with him is a freedman named Helius," Clarie replied with a serious look. "They are controllers of the Emperor's personal property in Asia."

"I take it we must soon be ready to depart with Paul," Nigel surmised, pointing at Paul and Sosthenes making their way back into town.

Clarie broke her gaze from the men to address the animals. "Yes, and this will be a tough journey ahead. Be prepared for intense opposition and danger to come as you travel about."

"We'll be r-r-ready, Lass," stated Max resolutely.

"That's a good boy. Keep your keen eye about you, just as you've done here in Ephesus," Clarie commended him. "Do you remember Gillamon telling you that from this ministry base of Ephesus would come six other key churches?"

"*Oui,* and these seven churches of light will receive letters that contain some of the most important words ever penned," Liz recalled. "Gillamon said these letters would be important because of *who* would write them. Will someone other than Paul be the one to write these letters?"

"There is a mark of destiny about these new churches to come. The Enemy will strike at Paul in an attempt to destroy them before they are established," Clarie replied, not answering Liz's question. "When you leave Ephesus, you will visit Smyrna, Pergamum, Thyatira, Sardis, Laodicea, and Philadelphia. Then you will return here."

"Understood," Nigel nodded, clasping his paws behind his back. "Shall we see you on this coming journey?"

Clarie smiled with her twinkling blue eyes. "Time will tell. It always does." She walked around a rock and transformed into a servant dressed in the attire of those in the Proconsul Palace. "But for now, I must go witness things unfolding." She looked at each of the animals gravely. "The upcountry danger will begin here. And it will begin tonight."

"Why? Where're ye goin', Lass?" Max wanted to know.

"To a banquet," Clarie replied, walking down the hill toward the palace.

☧

"Murdered?!" Paul exclaimed in alarm. "Where? How?"

"At a palace banquet last night," Aquila reported. "Silanus was poisoned in a rather obvious way, and by the very guests he had invited to the banquet. Publius Celer and Helius have seized control of the province, pending the arrival of a new proconsul."

"But why? Silanus was an effective administrator," stated Priscilla with a worried look as she prepared bags of food provisions for Paul and the others.

"Yes, he was *too* effective an administrator," Aquila agreed. "And he had just as much right to the throne as Nero."

"I see," Paul said, wide-eyed with this news. "So just as Agrippina wanted Nero to be emperor, she must have been concerned that her cousin Silanus might plot to avenge the death of Claudius and seize the throne."

"Agrippina wanted to kill Silanus before he eliminated her and Nero," Priscilla realized. "So Silanus is the first victim of Nero's reign."

"And he won't be the last," Aquila added. "Paul, a word of warning. Because Silanus ruled favorably in your case, there is danger. Celer and Helius will immediately begin to take out any potential enemies, and that includes anyone who was protected by Silanus."

Paul stuffed his scrolls into his satchel. "Then all the more reason for me to clear out of Ephesus for a time. While we go upcountry things will hopefully settle down here."

Sosthenes spoke up. "We must assume that while we are traveling through Asia, nowhere in the province will be safe from Celer's henchmen, who will immediately send word to be on the lookout for anyone loyal to Silanus."

"That may be, but all I know is that the Lord's work must continue, threat or no threat," Paul replied determinedly. "Let's get the others. Time to go."

As Paul finished gathering his supplies, Liz, Max, and Nigel stared at one another in disbelief.

81

"I see what Clarie meant," Nigel said gravely. "This murderous game of thrones will become a shadowy menace on the upcountry journey."

"Aye, an' jest look at the timin' of it," Max pointed out with a frown. "Jest as the lad be r-r-ready ta go set up them new churches."

"We will enter dark places where six new lamps must be lit," stressed Liz with heaviness in her voice. She looked over at Paul, who had already suffered so much in his three missionary journeys. She let go a heavy sigh. "And the Enemy will continue to try to snuff out the one bringing the light."

PHILADELPHIA, FEBRUARY AD 55

Paul sat with his eyes closed and his back against a tree, wincing from the recent beating he had received in Laodicea. His body was exhausted from this upcountry tour, but they had finally seen calmer days in this city of Philadelphia, where they decided to rest for a while. On this unusually warm winter day it was a welcome relief to simply sit in the sunshine. As he had anticipated, their team of missionaries suffered hardships as they traveled from city to city. Opposition came at them from all sides: spiteful Jews in synagogues, angry pagan worshippers of Artemis, and frightened local officials eager to make an obvious break with anyone loyal to Silanus as Emperor Nero came to power. They went hungry and thirsty, they were clothed in rags. They were beaten and all the while worked hard to support themselves. Still, they blessed those who cursed them, enduring their insults and responding only with kindness. It paid off. Although many rejected them, some listened and new doors were opened, especially in this city bearing the name of 'brotherly love.' Six tiny flames were lit across six cities.

They had received more disturbing news from Corinth when Apollos joined them in Philadelphia. He shared about the wicked behavior of a church member, but how the church turned a blind eye and did nothing. Paul saw the heathen environment of Corinth strangling the church, and his heart grew heavy for them. Other members of the Corinthian church, Stephanas, Fortunatus, and Achaicus, had also caught up with Paul here. They brought a letter from the elders of Corinth, asking for clarification about the letter Timothy had delivered in October.

82

Apollos and Sosthenes shared looks of concern as Paul shook his head sadly, the letter from Corinth in his hand. He opened his eyes and leaned forward to wrap his arms around his knees, clearly thinking about a great many things as he tapped the letter on his shins. "Our work here upcountry is finished for now," he finally shared. "We need to return to Ephesus. I have a long letter to write to the Corinthians." His eyes brimmed with tears. "My love and daily concern for all the churches never ends, and this," he told them, holding up the letter, "cannot go unanswered for long. I wish to return to Corinth, but I need to give them much to think about before I arrive."

Paul grunted as he struggled to stand up, and his friends jumped to their feet to help the weary apostle. Together they went to inform the others it was time to go home.

Max stood with a stiffened spine, feeling protective of Paul yet knowing there was little he could do for now other than remain his steady companion. "The lad will never stop. Others would have quit long ago."

Nigel nodded and preened his whiskers as he watched Paul. "His determination stems from an endless supply of supernatural strength."

Tears welled up in Liz's eyes, thinking about Paul's vision that she and

Max had been privileged to witness so many years ago. Seeing Jesus face to face, sitting in the glory of heaven, had given the apostle the motivation he needed to carry out his weighty assignment. "Jesus' piercing look of love has stayed in the forefront of Paul's heart and mind," Liz replied. "And the thorn in Paul's flesh keeps him close to that source. The supreme love of Jesus—*agape* love—will not fail him, no matter what comes."

"Indeed," Nigel agreed. "I for one will be glad to return to the church of Ephesus. But at least we were jolly well able to end this upcountry tour in Philadelphia."

"The 'city of brotherly love,'" Liz replied. "I very much like the name of this city. It is quite an unusual name to live up to, no? Hmmm . . . *phileo* love." Liz began thinking through the various kinds of love as defined by the Greeks.

"Let's get back ta Ephesus then," announced Max, squatting down for Nigel. "Time ta go."

Nigel jumped onto Max's back and rubbed his paws together excitedly. "Right! And by the sound of things, Paul shall be writing quite the voluminous letter to the Corinthians. I'm eager to see if his new work might be a candidate for our growing New Testament."

"*Oui,* I am sure Paul will write words of hard truth, but spoken in love," Liz predicted. Suddenly a thought dawned on her. "*L'amour! C'est ça!* That is the root of Corinth's problem!"

"Wha' do ye mean, Lass?" inquired Max as they began trotting behind the humans.

"It's love, old boy," Nigel interjected, interpreting Liz's French. "I believe I see where you're going with this, my dear. The Corinthians are struggling to break free of a culture that is consumed by the lowest level of worldly love, *eros* love. So if they could truly understand the highest love, which Paul taps into as his source of strength, they could break free of their snares."

Liz's golden eyes lit up with excitement. "*Oui, mon ami!*" She kissed Nigel on the cheek, happy that he understood her reasoning. "Exactly!" She ran to get underfoot of Paul, hoping to listen in on any thoughts he might express about his upcoming letter to the Corinthians.

"Love," Max chuckled, watching Liz wrap her tail around Paul with affection. "Leave it ta the Fr-r-rench ta figure that out."

83

The Greatest of These, *C'est L'amour*

J ust when we thought it couldn't get any worse!" Nigel lamented, pacing the floor. "This is intolerable! Those dreadful Corinthians have become a thorn in *my* side!"

"Steady, Mousie," Max offered with a paw on the tiny mouse's back.

"Shh, I am trying to hear," Liz shushed them.

The animals sat listening to yet another report from the church in Corinth, this time brought by friends of a church member there named Chloe. Paul and his team had no sooner arrived back in Ephesus when they found these people waiting for them at Aquila and Priscilla's house. Paul sat with a furrowed brow as he listened to the latest account of problems with this wayward church.

"The quarrelling never ends. Believers are suing each other in pagan courts. There are even three groups boasting that they are in exclusive camps," Paris explained, lifting a hand as he rattled them off with a satirical tone. "'I'm in Paul's party,' or 'We are Peter's men,' or 'Our loyalties lie with Apollos.' It's insane, Paul."

"Yes, and with all this bickering has come an arrogant attitude among others," Linos reported. "Some actually think that God sees them as superior to any apostle, and they welcome the praise of men for the great thoughts they share in the church."

Liz watched as Paul was clearly heartbroken to hear such vitriol coming from Christians. Tears welled up in his eyes and he slowly shook his head in disbelief. When Paris and Linos had given him their full report, listing problem after problem, he held up his hand. "Is there anything else you can think of? I want to be thorough in my reply and wish to address each and every issue that exists."

Paris and Linos looked at one another and shrugged their shoulders. "I think we have covered everything," Paris replied.

"Thank heaven," Nigel sighed. "Paul can finally crack on with his response."

Paul stood up and put his hands on the shoulders of each young man. "Thank you for bringing this news in person, my friends. Chloe was most kind to send you to me. Please, stay with us as long as you like." He turned to face the others gathered there: Aquila, Priscilla, Apollos, Sosthenes, Aristarchus, Gaius, Stephanas, Fortunatus, and Achaicus. He took a deep breath and began to pace. "Let me summarize the things I must address with the church in Corinth in this next letter to them. All these issues have come from hearing the many reports from you all, and from the letter sent by the elders."

He cleared his throat and held out his hands to number the issues on his fingers as he rattled them off. "They are challenging my authority as an apostle, they are abusing our Lord's Supper, they are concerned about eating meat sacrificed to idols, they are dragging one another into court, they remain silent over immorality inside the church, some are denying the Resurrection, others are arguing about marriage, they are acting like arrogant Greeks who boast over their superior wisdom, and still others have questions about spiritual gifts and abilities." Paul stopped and looked around the room. "Does that about cover it?"

Nigel planted his face into his paw, shaking his head at the Corinthian mess.

Everyone looked at each other to gauge the opinions of the group in reaching a consensus. "I think you've stated everything exactly, Paul." Priscilla got up quickly. "While you dictate, I better get busy making food. This letter is going to take a while."

As she headed to the kitchen, Paul clasped his hands behind his neck and let out a long breath. "I hope she has a lot of food. This is

85

going to take days. Sosthenes, would you do me the honor of writing the letter?"

Sosthenes nodded humbly. "The honor is *mine* to do so. Thank you for asking me, Paul," he answered, making his way to a table that held an empty scroll of fresh parchment, pens, and ink. He picked up a pen and looked at Paul. "I'm ready when you are."

"Very well, let's begin," Paul said, closing his eyes. "Heavenly Father, please give me the words your people need to hear. Let those words be firm but kind, and always from a heart full of love for them. Amen." He began pacing once more.

"From Paul, who was called by the will of God to be an apostle of Christ Jesus, and from our brother Sosthenes, to the church of God which is in Corinth, to all who are called to be God's holy people, who belong to him in union with Christ Jesus, together with all people everywhere who worship our Lord Jesus Christ, their Lord and ours: May God our Father and the Lord Jesus Christ give you grace and peace." He paused to allow Sosthenes to catch up.

Paul continued as Priscilla brought bowls of bread and fruit into the room and set them down on the table. Everyone gathered to listen to what would be Paul's longest letter to date. She then leaned over to the animals and placed a dish of scraps for them as well. "We must all keep our strength up," she told them with a smile and a scratch behind Max's ears. Liz didn't bother looking at the food. She was enthralled by Paul's arguments.

"I have a serious concern to bring up with you, my friends, using the authority of Jesus, our Master," Paul continued. "I'll put it as urgently as I can: You must get along with each other. You must learn to be considerate of one another, cultivating a life in common. I bring this up because some from Chloe's family brought a most disturbing report to my attention—that you're fighting among yourselves! I'll tell you exactly what I was told: You're all picking sides, going around saying, 'I'm on Paul's side,' or 'I'm for Apollos,' or 'Peter is my man,' or 'I'm in the Messiah group.' I ask you, Has the Messiah been chopped up in little pieces so we can each have a relic all our own? Was Paul crucified for you? Was a single one of you baptized in Paul's name?"

"Hear, hear!" Nigel cheered. "Sheer eloquence is rolling off his tongue!"

"For the message about Christ's death on the cross is nonsense to those who are being lost; but for us who are being saved it is God's power. The Scripture says,

'I will destroy the wisdom of the wise and set aside the understanding of the scholars.'

"So then, where does that leave the wise? or the scholars? or the skillful debaters of this world? God has shown that this world's wisdom is foolishness! For God in his wisdom made it impossible for people to know him by means of their own wisdom. Instead, by means of the so-called "foolish" message we preach, God decided to save those who believe."

Liz and Nigel shared a big grin. "Do you realize he just quoted our dear Isaiah?" Nigel whispered in her ear.

Liz nodded, a lump in her throat. She and Nigel had sat on Isaiah's desk as he penned those very words. *"Oui,* it is surreal to hear Isaiah's words now quoted by Paul."

"Wha' do he mean by that?" Max wondered aloud.

"Paul is explaining that no one can discover the Maker with intellect alone. I had to learn this myself, back on our first mission to Noah's Ark," Liz replied. "The Maker does not seek out the *minds* of the wise or the foolish, but is after the *hearts* of all. The world sees those with weaker minds as foolish and undesirable, but the Maker wants the very ones whom the world rejects, no? Most of the followers of Jesus are honestly from the ordinary, uneducated classes of people. They are servants, slaves, and the poor, not the intellectual, wealthy elite. Look at Jesus' disciples whom he hand-picked. He did not call scholars and the wealthy who depend on their own resources. He called those who knew they must depend on a higher power to make it in life. Their hearts are more open to accept the truth of Jesus while the intellectuals try to reason something that cannot be explained."

"Well put, my dear," Nigel encouraged her. "And even those intellectuals who do accept the truth came to it only after the Maker took extreme measures to reach them. Just look at Paul! He was the intellectual Saul, Christian killer extraordinaire! He had to be blinded and stripped of his self-important intellect before he would bend his will."

"Aye, jest like Moses, too," Max added. "The Maker had ta humble the lad by tendin' sheep for forty years ta get his heart r-r-right. Those

87

whose heads have ta catch up ta their hearts be slower ta get it. So while the world thinks Christians be fools, Paul says the Maker will use them ta turn the world upside down."

"Couldn't have said it better myself, old boy," Nigel cheered with a fist jab into Max's shoulder.

Paul continued, "No, the wisdom we speak of is the mystery of God—his plan that was previously hidden, even though he made it for our ultimate glory before the world began. But the rulers of this world have not understood it; if they had, they would not have crucified our glorious Lord. That is what the Scriptures mean when they say, 'No eye has seen, no ear has heard, and no mind has imagined what God has prepared for those who love him.'" Paul paused to let Sosthenes catch up.

Nigel leaned over to Liz. "My dear, I believe we have already helped Paul write this letter, by helping Isaiah write these words, more than seven hundred years ago."

"*Seven,*" Liz emphasized with a smile. "We could never have imagined it back then, *mon ami.*" She looked affectionately at Paul. "Now we must help Paul further by leading him to write about *l'amour.*"

☧

Days passed. Paul took his time. He wanted to make sure he thoroughly addressed each and every issue. He and Sosthenes worked through the list of problems, stopping when either of them was tired. It was emotionally, mentally, as well as spiritually, draining for Paul.

At night when the humans had gone to bed, Liz and Nigel pored over the letter to review the things Paul had dictated throughout the day. Sitting on the table where Sosthenes worked were scrolls of Scripture. Liz and Nigel took the liberty of unrolling them to other passages for Paul to consider when he arrived to begin work the next day. Paul pulled more passages from Isaiah, Jeremiah, Job, Psalms, Deuteronomy, Genesis, Exodus, and Hosea.

"I'm most pleased," Nigel beamed, adjusting his spectacles as he read through one of his favorite entries. "*Surely you know that many runners take part in a race, but only one of them wins the prize. Run, then, in such a way as to win the prize. Every athlete in training submits to strict discipline, in order to be crowned with a wreath that will not last; but we do it for one that will last forever. That is why I run straight for the finish line; that is why I am like a boxer who does not waste his punches. I harden my body with blows and bring it under complete control, to keep myself from being disqualified after having called others to the contest."* Nigel stopped reading and looked up at Liz. "It was simply brilliant of you to leave that wilted celery for Paul to find!"

Liz smiled shyly. *"Merci.* I remembered how much Paul studied the athletes and how hard they trained when we were in Corinth for the Isthmian Games in 51. He held a wilted celery crown and commented to Aquila that those athletes compete for a crown that doesn't last. I simply reminded him."

"Well, those Corinthians should get the analogy perfectly, as the Isthmian Games were held there again just last year," Nigel added.

"I wonder if Noah and Nate attended the games to do more research," Liz thought out loud, referring to their monkey and lizard friends. "I cannot wait to hear their report of the animals they've talked to about the Animalympics in Rome."

Nigel gave a jolly chuckle. "I have no doubt they will be full of stories. I can see Noah holding up his hands in a frame to explain his ideas. 'Picture this!'" Nigel closed one eye and stuck out his tongue from the corner of his mouth, mimicking Noah. "Ah, what a splendidly funny monkey!"

Liz giggled. "And Nate is our serious athlete. I am sure he has dragged Noah to each game of the Olympiad—the Olympics, the Isthmian Games, the Pythian Games, the Nemean Games. I so look forward to when we will all be together in Rome to compete!"

"And your Albert will no doubt be ready for the fish-eating contest," Nigel quipped.

Liz held up her paw as she scanned the scroll to another of Paul's words to the Corinthians. "Albert needs to read this letter himself to control his eating. 'The temptations in your life are no different from what others experience. And God is faithful. He will not allow the temptation to be more than you can stand. When you are tempted, he will show you a way out so that you can endure.'"

"Indeed, there are nuggets in this brilliant letter for everyone," Nigel agreed. "Have you figured out how you shall lead Paul to focus on love?"

Liz thought a moment, curling her tail slowly up and down. "I know

89

it has something to do with Paul's vision, but I have not yet figured out how to bring him to think of it."

"Hmmm. Well, you said he was left with a thorn in his side after that experience as a reminder," Nigel recalled for her.

Liz's eyes widened. *"C'est ça! Merci, mon ami!"* She immediately jumped off the table and ran out the door, leaving Nigel wondering what Liz was thinking and where she was going at this time of night.

Paul rose early, unable to sleep. He didn't wish to wake the house, so very quietly lit an oil lamp so he could read. He made his way to the table where sat his letter in progress. As the light from the oil lamp slowly brightened the room, there on the table sat something that caught him by surprise. He placed the oil lamp on the table and stared at the object as he slowly took his seat. His finger cautiously ran across the object, and he wondered who could have placed it there. It was a branch of thorns.

Paul spoke to the Lord as if he were seated next to him at the table. "Oh, my Lord. When they mocked and scourged you, they placed a crown of thorns on your head." He began to softly weep. "What kind of love would possess you to allow our sin-sick race to do such a thing to you?"

As Paul closed his eyes to picture Jesus' face beneath a crown of thorns, Jesus softly whispered to his heart, *"There is no greater love than to lay down one's life for one's friends."*

Suddenly Paul's heart burst with a realization. "Oh, Jesus, my Savior! You gave me a thorn to also bear! How did I not see this before? Yours was a thorn of love! Of supreme love! And so is mine, because it came from you. This is what the Corinthians have been missing all along with *their* thorn in the flesh that is *not* from you, their selfish, *eros* love. Their problems can ultimately be answered by how you showed us how to love with your supreme, selfless, *agape* love. Perfect love. Nothing of what I have advised them so far is worth anything if they don't grasp this love."

Tears were streaming down his cheeks as the insights exploded in his heart. Liz's golden eyes glowed from the soft lamp light, and they, too, filled with tears. She jumped up on the table next to Paul. *"You see now the many meanings of thorns,"* she meowed.

90

Paul looked up and smiled through his tears at Liz. "Oh, little Faith. God has given me such a fresh understanding of his love. I must share this with the Corinthians." He gently stroked Liz's fur while his mind raced. *"Faith."* Paul studied her beautiful eyes. "Faith. Hope. Love. They are the only things that last, aren't they?"

"Oui, *and the greatest of these,* c'est l'amour," she meowed.

Paul decided he couldn't wait until sunup. He went and woke Sosthenes so he could capture these thoughts while they were fresh. Sosthenes rubbed his eyes and shook his head to wake up. "I'll be right there."

When Sosthenes entered the room, Paul was already pacing back and forth, mumbling. "Thank you for getting up so early, my friend. I feel this just could not wait. After writing so many hard things, my heart was gladdened to have something as happy and joyous to give them as this."

"I look forward to hearing it, Paul," Sosthenes replied, getting things in order on the desk. He looked curiously at the thorns. Paul smiled and quickly picked them up and out of his way.

"Let's begin," Paul said, staring at the thorns and praying a silent prayer of thanks.

Liz was curled up watching while Max and Nigel continued to sleep. Her heart was as full as Paul's.

"If I speak in the tongues of men or of angels, but do not have love, I am only a resounding gong or a clanging cymbal. If I have the gift of prophecy and can fathom all mysteries and all knowledge, and if I have a faith that can move mountains, but do not have love, I am nothing. If I give all I possess to the poor and give over my body to hardship that I may boast, but do not have love, I gain nothing." Paul paused while Sosthenes captured every word.

Paul stared at the thorns and thought about Jesus and his character. He considered how Jesus lived out perfect love. The image of Jesus wearing the crown of thorns filled his mind. From there it was easy to help the Corinthians grasp what *agape* love really looked like. Paul simply described Jesus. "Love is patient, love is kind. It does not envy, it does not boast, it is not proud. It does not dishonor others, it is not self-seeking, it is not easily angered, it keeps no record of wrongs. Love does not delight in evil but rejoices with the truth. It always protects, always trusts, always hopes, always perseveres. Love never fails."

Sosthenes shook his head in amazement as his pen flew across the parchment. "This is incredible, Paul! The people are going to be able to grasp this so well. Even a child will be able to understand this definition of love."

Suddenly a memory stirred in Paul's mind of two Roman boys he had encountered on the docks of Caesarea years ago. They were fighting over a red marble. An older brother was teasing his younger brother by keeping the treasure out of arm's reach. *I've said these words before!* Paul remembered. *The red marble lesson. When I was a child, I thought like a child.* He marveled at how the Lord had prepared his words so long ago when he had no idea they would be written down for the Corinthians.

Paul placed his hand on the scroll of Isaiah that sat on the desk, pondering the analogies that kept rolling around in his mind like that red marble. *Isaiah didn't know that his words would also someday be written down for the Corinthians. All prophecy will eventually be fulfilled, and those who write words of wisdom will themselves pass from this earth. Isaiah has already reached heaven and must understand so much more than he did here on Earth.*

"Ready, Paul," said Sosthenes, dipping his pen in the ink.

Paul started pacing again. "But where there are prophecies, they will cease; where there are tongues, they will be stilled; where there is knowledge, it will pass away. For we know in part and we prophesy in part, but when completeness comes, what is in part disappears. When I was a child, I talked like a child, I thought like a child, I reasoned like a child. When I became a man, I put the ways of childhood behind me. For now we see only a reflection as in a mirror; then we shall see face to face. Now I know in part; then I shall know fully, even as I am fully known.

"And now these three remain." Paul looked over at Liz and smiled. "Faith, hope, and love. But the greatest of these is love."

No Small
Disturbance

And why do you think I keep risking my neck in this dangerous work? I look death in the face practically every day I live. Do you think I'd do this if I wasn't convinced of your resurrection and mine as guaranteed by the resurrected Messiah Jesus? Do you think I was just trying to act heroic when I fought the wild beasts at Ephesus, hoping it wouldn't be the end of me? Not on your life!" Paul exclaimed, slapping the back of his hand into his other palm. "It's resurrection, resurrection, always resurrection, that undergirds what I do and say, the way I live. If there's no resurrection, 'We eat, we drink, the next day we die,' and that's all there is to it. But don't fool yourselves. Don't let yourselves be poisoned by this anti-resurrection loose talk. 'Bad company ruins good manners.'"

"He's on quite a r-r-roll, ain't he?" Max whispered to Nigel as Paul continued to spill out these powerful truths.

"I would say that is an understatement, old boy," Nigel whispered back. "He is determined to get these Corinthians to understand why he does what he does, and to get it through their thick skulls that unless Jesus was resurrected, there is no point to Christianity."

"But let me reveal to you a wonderful secret," Paul said, putting his folded hands up to his chin for a moment, closing his eyes briefly as he pictured what he was about to say. "We will not all die, but we will all be transformed!" He opened his eyes and snapped his fingers. "It will happen in a moment, in the blink of an eye, when the last trumpet is blown. For when the trumpet sounds, those who have died will be raised to live forever. And we who are living will also be transformed. For our dying bodies must be transformed into bodies that will never die; our mortal bodies must be transformed into immortal bodies.

Then, when our dying bodies have been transformed into bodies that will never die, this Scripture will be fulfilled: 'Death is swallowed up in victory. O death, where is your victory? O death, where is your sting?'

"For sin is the sting that results in death, and the law gives sin its power. But thank God! He gives us victory over sin and death through our Lord Jesus Christ."

"Didn't Isaiah say that aboot death?" Max remembered.

Nigel's eyes lit up with delight. "How keen of you to remember, old boy! Indeed he did. Paul has quoted our dear prophet several times, betwixt his own words of wisdom to the Corinthians."

Max looked at Liz, who was curled up sound asleep. "Looks like the lass were up late. She's been sleepin' all mornin'."

"Yes, she went out searching for a branch of thorns last night to inspire Paul's writings," Nigel explained. "Her knowledge of plants and flowers has served her well throughout our missions. She somehow always finds a way to use her love for flora. She was up when Paul began work early this morning."

Paul took a sip of water and continued. "But I will remain in Ephesus until Pentecost; for a wide door for effective service has opened to me, and there are many adversaries."

"Did ye hear that? Looks like we'll be headin' out of Ephesus soon," Max whispered.

Nigel nodded while he cleaned off his spectacles and placed them back on his nose. "We've been here three years, the longest of any place Paul has stayed. But it is time to move on. He speaks true. Many doors have opened here, but there remain many adversaries."

"Aye, too many ta count," agreed Max with a frown. "But the lad still be standin'."

Paul leaned over Sosthenes's shoulder, reviewing what he had just written. "Be on your guard; stand firm in the faith; be courageous; be strong. Do everything in love."

Liz began to stir and stretched out long as her eyes fluttered open. "What have I missed?"

"Good morning, my dear," Nigel greeted her. "You've missed several pages, but never fear. We can review them as the ink dries this evening."

Paul took the pen from Sosthenes to write his closing remarks to the Corinthians in his own hand, as had become his custom following the forged letters that showed up in Thessalonica. Since that time he always wanted the churches to know when he had actually written the letters they received.

"Paul said we'd be leavin' Ephesus ta go ta Macedonia after Pentecost," Max told Liz as she took her place next to him.

"So this means we'll be leaving after the Artemisia festival as well," Liz added, her tail curling up and down as she considered their spring calendar. "Ephesus will be flooded with pagans coming to celebrate Artemis, and with Christians coming to celebrate Pentecost."

"If the Jews complained about the drop in monies to the Temple treasury, I expect the pagans will be next in line to complain about the drop in the number of idols they sell at their biggest festival of the year," Nigel realized, wrinkling his brow. "We best keep a steady eye in the weeks to come. I expect Paul's many adversaries will not take their loss of income lightly."

"Humans yell loudest when their pockets be hit." Max scowled. "Always follow the money."

EPHESUS, APRIL, AD 55

"Take the image of our great Artemis home with you!" the vendor called out to a group of people passing by his stand on the road in front of the Temple of Artemis. On his rugs were spread more than a hundred carved idols. He had sold only half of what he had been given to sell during the festival. He held a silver statue of the beloved goddess in each hand, waving them to the prospective customers. "Finest silver in all of Asia! I will give you a special price!"

The group of men and women smiled but didn't make a move toward the vendor. One man held up his hand to decline the offer. "No, thank you, friend. We no longer worship Artemis."

"Yes, and we no longer have need of such relics," added a woman by his side.

95

"How can you no longer worship Artemis?" The vendor frowned and lowered the idols to his side. His expression soured. "Whom do you worship?"

"We're followers of The Way," the man explained. "We worship Jesus."

"Yes, we're coming to celebrate Pentecost with Paul and other believers here in Ephesus," the woman offered with a warm smile.

"We welcome you to join us," Gaius said. He and Aristarchus had come out here to meet this group of men and women who had just arrived in Ephesus.

"My place is here," the vendor scowled, turning from them to go after prospective customers with more potential. He was desperate for a sale before he had to report back to his employer, Demetrius.

And he wasn't the only one. There were thousands of vendors in Ephesus, all coming up short.

☧

The sun glinted off the rings adorning the hands of Demetrius. He stood with his hands on his broad hips and a frown on his tanned face as his assistant gave a report for the sales so far during the festival of Artemisia. The report wasn't good. He was one of the wealthiest merchants in Ephesus, having amassed his fortune as a silversmith. He conducted a brisk trade in the manufacture of shrines to the goddess Artemis, employing a number of artisans. But as his assistant finished reporting the numbers, his blood boiled and he clenched his jaw in fresh anger.

"It's those Christians!" Demetrius spat, looking out from his colonnaded storefront headquarters. Throngs of people—some pagan, some Christian—milled about the marble streets of Ephesus. The city was packed to overflowing with people buying wares in the marketplace, yet activity in the booths belonging to his vendors both here and out at the Temple of Artemis was markedly slow. "Ever since those followers of The Way started invading this city and the region, our sales are down. This is our prime season! We cannot afford this steady decline."

"Yes, Demetrius, it's true. Your employees have reported the same story over and over again," the assistant noted. "The goddess must be very displeased at how those Christians are causing her worshippers to turn away from their duties to protect her."

Demetrius slammed his fist against a column. "Go get my employees. Now!"

The assistant stood up. "Sir? Which ones? Do you need me to get the ones out at the Temple, or . . ."

"ALL of them! Get the ones here on the main market road and send a messenger to the others out by the Temple!" he shouted. "DO IT NOW!"

As the assistant hurried off to round up the employees, Demetrius stared at the massive stadium of Ephesus at the end of the wide marble avenue lined with columns and statues. Not only was the stadium used for the bawdy entertainment of the Roman masses, but it was the place where every male in the city might attend the monthly Popular Assembly. It was also where the citizens would instinctively run if an emergency befell the great city.

"Oh we're in the middle of an emergency," Demetrius mumbled to himself. "The people of Ephesus just don't realize it . . . yet."

✗

97

Aristarchus and Gaius walked along the marble boulevard, thrilled with the number of new believers who had come to celebrate Pentecost with the church in Ephesus. Paul asked them to go to the market for more bread and wine to observe the Lord's Supper, so their arms were full of provisions. They smiled and laughed as they walked along, happy about everything the Lord was doing through Paul's ministry.

"I think Paul was brilliant to purposely wait to head to Macedonia until both Pentecost and Artemisia were over," shared Gaius.

"I agree. We've been able to reach far more people this way," Aristarchus said, trying to rearrange the amphorae in his arms to better carry them. "I wish we could return home to Macedonia with Paul, but our hands will be full with keeping the church going here."

"Literally!" Gaius quipped, struggling to hold up his arms laden with a heavy basket of communion bread.

The two saw a large group of men assembled in the street ahead, partially blocking the road. "What do you suppose is going on there?" Aristarchus wondered.

"Let's go see," Gaius answered as he and Aristarchus neared the crowd.

☧

Liz and Nigel strolled along the marble boulevard, observing the goings-on of the day. They had followed Gaius and Aristarchus to the market.

"I must say that I don't blame Max for staying behind with Paul," Nigel opined. "His protective instincts have never failed him."

Liz jumped up onto the base of a statue of Caesar Augustus to get a better view of the marketplace. She gazed up at the outstretched hand of this, the most famous of emperor statues placed throughout the Roman Empire. His image reminded everyone of the authority of Rome, regardless of which emperor was currently on the throne. *"Oui,* Max does not wish to be very far from Paul these days," she replied, studying the statue. "Not with the threat of Nero's henchmen keeping an eye out for anyone who might come against the new Emperor."

"No doubt there will soon be statues of Nero coming here to Ephesus and every city in the empire," Nigel predicted. "I do wonder what type of ruler the young lad will prove to be."

"He stepped up to the throne through the murder of Claudius, so he already has blood on his hands, no?" Liz pointed out with a frown. "We shall see which will triumph with Nero's reign—Roman justice or the personal ambitions of a single ruler."

From where they sat they could see the growing crowd of men blocking the street. Nigel spotted Gaius and Aristarchus walking up to the back of the crowd. He then spotted the Jewish leaders who had brought Paul up on charges of Temple robbery. "Curious. The Jewish leaders seem keen on listening in to whatever these pagans are saying. Something tells me we should get over there, my dear."

Liz jumped off the statue base. "My thoughts exactly, *mon ami."*

Demetrius scanned the faces of his employees. There was fear and frustration in their eyes, and they chatted among themselves about their poor sales. Their employer held up his hands to get their attention. "Men, you well know we have a good thing going here—and you've seen how Paul has barged in and discredited what we're doing by telling people there's no such thing as a god made with hands. A lot of people are going along with him, not only here in Ephesus but all through Asia province."

The crowd nodded and murmured in agreement.

Gaius and Aristarchus looked at one another with concern. "This isn't good," Aristarchus muttered under his breath.

Simeon, Joash, and Alexander looked at one another with delight. "So now Paul has hurt the pagan pocketbook as well," Alexander exclaimed, folding his arms smugly over his chest. "We tried to warn the Romans, but they didn't listen, did they? Serves them right."

"Not only is our little business in danger of falling apart, but the temple of our famous goddess Artemis will certainly end up a pile of rubble as her glorious reputation fades to nothing," Demetrius continued. "And this is no mere local matter—the whole world worships our Artemis!"

"Wait for it," Liz warned, watching the fists of the crowd clenched in anger. Her fur bristled along her spine, anticipating the reaction of the men.

"Great is Artemis of the Ephesians!" someone yelled from the crowd. Suddenly the group erupted into a frenzied mob. Voices joined the chant, the crowd raising their angry fists into the air, echoing the praise, "Great is Artemis of the Ephesians! Great is Artemis of the Ephesians!" They immediately turned and ran into the street yelling, "Great is Artemis of the Ephesians!"

Demetrius smiled as the whole city was instantly caught in an uproar, stampeding through the streets. "Follow me!" he shouted, pointing to the stadium.

The vendor who had tried to sell his idols the day Gaius and Aristarchus walked by recognized the two men standing there watching things unfold. "Those men are followers of Paul!" he yelled, pointing. "Get them!"

Immediately Gaius and Aristarchus were grabbed by the angry men. The amphorae of wine and basket of bread fell into the street, trampled underfoot as the mob carried Gaius and Aristarchus along to the stadium.

Liz and Nigel ran past the spilled wine running in the street, casting glances of alarm at each other. "Oh dear, I pray it shall not be their blood on the street next!" Nigel shouted breathlessly.

Thousands of people were now running from every direction and up the steps into the great stadium of Ephesus. Most of them had no idea what was going on. They simply dropped what they were doing, thinking some great danger had hit the city.

"This is madness!" Nigel shouted above the din of people. "Some are yelling one thing, some another!"

"Most of them do not know why they are even here!" Liz shouted as she and Nigel made their way as close to the stage as they could. She spied the Jews pushing Alexander to the front to try to gain control of the mob. "But look who is going to try to give them a unified reason."

"The Romans wouldn't listen to us before. Let's see if they'll listen to us now! Explain what has happened to us with Paul and his followers," Simeon shouted into Alexander's ear, pushing the treasurer forward to take his place on the stage.

"And tell them we're not part of that Way movement!" Joash added.

Alexander looked up at the crowd of twenty thousand people and felt a sense of excitement. All eyes were on him as he quieted the mob with an impressive sweep of his arms. "Citizens of Ephesus!" he exclaimed, holding up his hands to begin his speech.

100

But the moment he opened his mouth, they yelled all the louder to drown him out: "Great is Artemis of the Ephesians! Great is Artemis of the Ephesians!"

"The people know that Alexander is a Jew!" Liz shouted.

"Indeed! They still think Christians are part of the Jewish sect, so they don't want to hear what he has to say!" Nigel shouted back.

The frenzied crowd rocked the stadium, stomping their feet and shouting over and over, "Great is Artemis of the Ephesians!" Demetrius and his men stood on the stage floor, leading the chant and pushing Gaius and Aristarchus to their knees as the cry of the people echoed across the city and throughout the harbor of Ephesus.

☧

"Two hours?" Paul asked in alarm, setting aside his scroll to walk toward the Roman soldier bringing him the report at the School of Tyrannus. "I heard a crowd but assumed it was some regular event taking place."

Ovidius nodded. "Yes, they've been shouting, 'Great is Artemis of the Ephesians!' for two hours. The stadium is completely full. People are even spilling out into the streets now, eager to get a glimpse of what is going on inside." He hesitated a moment. "They dragged Gaius and Aristarchus inside with them."

Paul frowned. "I must get down there now." As he took a step forward he felt a tug on his robe.

Max had clamped his jaws around the hem of Paul's robe, pulling and sitting on his hind legs, growling, *"Not if I have anythin' ta do with it!"*

"You must not get involved with that mob, Paul," Tyrannus cautioned, putting his hand on Paul's shoulder. "Even your dog knows you shouldn't go."

Aquila stood in Paul's way. "He's right. You could be killed in the chaos."

At that moment, the Roman soldier Justus arrived at the school. "I've been sent to deliver a message from the Asiarchs at the palace. Paul, they are warning you not to get involved with what is happening at the stadium. They act as liaisons between the people and the emperor of Rome, and even they say you must not go. You earned their respect from the time you were imprisoned at the palace, so please heed their warnings."

101

"Even non-believers are warning you, Paul," Tyrannus exclaimed. "You must not go."

"Fr-r-riends be there ta help ye not make bad decisions!" Max growled, his teeth still pulling back on Paul's robe. *"Listen ta them, Lad!"*

Justus and Ovidius stepped up to surround Paul. "They also think we should keep you safe from anyone sent by that mob that would try to drag you there," Ovidius told him. "If we have to take you into protective custody, we will."

Paul pursed his lips tightly, nodding in agreement. He looked down at Max, still holding tightly to his robe. "Very well. I won't go to the stadium."

"Now ye're talkin' sense," Max barked after letting go of his robe.

"This is madness!" Nigel fumed, holding his paws over his ears. "This incessant shouting has gone on for long enough. Why haven't the Roman officials stepped in yet? They object to *any* irregular assembly, much less a riot like this! Where is that town clerk?"

The town clerk was the highest position held by a citizen of any local Roman province. It was his job to both interpret and enforce Roman law, seeing that order was maintained at all costs. If a Roman city did not abide by Rome's laws designed to keep civic order, it could be stripped of any of its self-governing privileges. The town clerk was the only official who was authorized to oversee the business of a Popular Assembly.

"Steady, *mon ami*." Liz's tail whipped back and forth impatiently, angry at how Gaius and Aristarchus were still kept against their will on the stage. Suddenly she brightened as she saw the town clerk making his way to the front of the stadium. "He is here! Let us see if Roman justice will show up as well."

As the town clerk reached the stage and lifted his hands, a hush fell over the mob. "Fellow citizens, is there anyone anywhere who doesn't know that our dear city Ephesus is protector of glorious Artemis and her sacred stone image that fell straight out of heaven? Since this is beyond contradiction, you had better get hold of yourselves. This is conduct unworthy of Artemis."

Nigel planted his face into his paw, shaking his head.

102

The clerk pointed at Gaius and Aristarchus. "These men you've dragged in here have done nothing to harm either our temple or our goddess. So if Demetrius and his guild of artisans have a complaint, they can take it to court and make all the accusations they want. If anything else is bothering you, bring it to the regularly scheduled town meeting and let it be settled there."

Nigel lifted his gaze. "Now he's speaking truth!" The tiny mouse raised his fist with a cheer. "Hear, hear!"

The clerk scanned the crowd and put his hands on his hips. "There is no excuse for what's happened today. We're putting our city in serious danger. Rome, remember, does not look kindly on rioters. Go home. This assembly is over."

Slowly at first, the people looked at one another quietly and did as the clerk demanded. As they filed out of the stadium, Gaius and Aristarchus got to their feet and hugged in triumph, leaving Demetrius and his employees standing there humiliated and defeated.

"*C'est bon!*" Liz exclaimed happily. "It appears that Roman justice is still working in Ephesus, for now anyway."

"Bravo! Indeed, my dear! Let's go report back to Max and give him the good word," Nigel exulted. "Then perhaps we'll finally be able to leave Ephesus and crack on!"

The lion's gaze narrowed as he looked from the hilltop down into the stadium, now emptying of its once-crazed mob. The rat at his feet looked on and shook his head. "What a shame. I really thought you had them with that crowd. But those two Christians didn't even have to say a word in their defense. Rome was on their side again, huh?"

The lion snarled and swatted at the rat, sending him flying into a rock with a thud. "Defense is something they will no longer have, once I get Rome where it belongs—on MY side."

103

LE DOCTEUR ET
LE HIBOU

"How splendid to return to Europe and our 'little Rome'!" Nigel
exclaimed happily.

Traveling along the Via Egnatia they neared the six-mile-long
wall surrounding the Roman city of Philippi. Named for the father of
Alexander the Great, wealth flowed through this thriving city established
in close proximity to gold mines. The *acropolis*, or elevated citadel, was
positioned on a hillside looking down upon the city. The *agora*, or public square, was filled with buildings for trade and commerce, and like
other Roman cities there was a huge open-air theater and bathhouse.
Luxury abounded at every turn. Two temples stood on the northern
corners of the agora, and in the center was the *bema*, or court, where
trials were conducted and where people held public debates.

The little mouse chuckled. "I shall never forget the look of relief on
the faces of those officials when we departed their fair city six years ago.
I wonder if they shall organize a welcome party when they hear Paul has
returned."

"Aye, the dumb lads," Max added. "They couldn't wait for Paul ta
leave."

"*Duumviri,*" Liz corrected him. "Hopefully, they will not allow any
trouble for Paul while we are here. What a relief to think of coming to a
city where nothing bad happens, no?"

Philippi was a self-governing province with two military officers, called *duumviri,* appointed by Rome to govern the city. Like the town clerk in Ephesus, they were careful to follow the letter of the law to maintain their status with Rome. But when Paul and Silas healed a fortune-telling demon-possessed girl here, her owners brought them before the *bema* where the *duumviri* had Paul and Silas illegally beaten and thrown into prison for the night. That's when the Lord sent an earthquake to release Paul and Silas as they sang their midnight hymns of praise. When their chains fell off and the prison doors opened, the two men stayed put and did not run. This is how Paul and Silas ended up leading the tough jailer named Arcadius and his entire family to salvation. When it was discovered the next morning that Paul was a Roman citizen who had been so grossly mistreated, the *duumviri* apologized profusely and begged him to leave the city so as not to stir up any more trouble. Paul left them with a stern word that he had many friends in Philippi and would hear of it if they were mistreated. He was hopeful that the infant church of Philippi might be therefore left alone to get established, without interference or opposition.

105

"Perhaps they will hide from Paul in the jail," Nigel quipped.

"Not if Scarface still r-r-runs the place," Max replied with a laugh. Arcadius was a tough old Roman soldier with a scar running from his right eye to his chin. Even though he maintained a gruff personality, he became one of Philippi's most ardent Christ-followers. He had even asked Luke to come give medical aid to his ill prisoners.

Liz's eyes brightened as they entered the city limits and began walking through the marketplace. "I cannot wait to see what has happened with Luke and his medical ministry here. *Le docteur* stayed behind not only to help Lydia and Arcadius get the church going, but also to help the sick. I will be so happy to see him again!" She spied the various stalls selling everything from food to souvenirs. "I wish I had a gift to bring to him."

"After swiping his medicine right from under his nose so he would follow you, I am sure he would be delighted if you actually *brought* him something, my dear," Nigel teased.

"It was the only way to introduce Luke to Paul, no?" Liz replied with an innocent smile. "I had to take the berry branch from his desk."

"Do ye think he'll be comin' with us when we leave Philippi this time?" Max asked. "I thought he were supposed ta wr-r-rite aboot Paul's adventures?"

"Whooooooo else could write them?" came a voice close to their ears. Max stopped in his tracks. "Who said that?"

"Whooooo else?" came the voice again. "Look up, little ones."

Max, Liz, and Nigel shot quick glances up to a table selling pottery. Bowls, vases, amphorae, oil lamps, and terra cotta items of all kinds were spread out for sale. Liz spied a small jar carved in the shape of an owl. Suddenly, it winked at her.

"*Le hibou est*, Gillamon?" Liz asked in delight as she studied the carved and colorfully painted little owl. "This is the smallest form you have taken as a carved object, no?"

"This time I shall be a mobile 'statue,' so I needed to be small," Gillamon replied with another wink. "Welcome back to Philippi. How are you, my friends?"

"Brilliant!" Nigel jumped onto the table next to the owl figurine. He chuckled and gave it a tender pat. "I daresay I might even be larger than you this time, old boy!"

"Mousie's r-r-right, me old friend," Max agreed, wagging his tail. "Why are ye dressed like an owl?"

"Not just *any* owl," Gillamon replied, pointing his wing to his tiny feet mounted on a pedestal. Below his feet was a hole with a string running through it. "I will be Liz's desired gift for Luke. And I will also help Paul write an important part of his next letter to the Corinthians."

Max cocked his head to the side. "I don't get it, Gillamon."

Liz put her face up to the owl. It was small enough to carry in her mouth by the string. "*Bon!* I am very happy about this, *mon ami!* Luke can use this owl for medicine." She turned to Max. "Gillamon has taken the form of an *aryballos*. This is a jar used to hold oil or perfume, and this particular style was first developed by the Corinthians, who carved them in whimsical animal shapes. It has a string so it can be carried around the wrist and hung up anywhere. Athletes use these *aryballoi* to carry oil to the gymnasium, and ladies use them to carry perfume to the baths."

"But shan't we be accused of stealing if we remove you from this merchant's table?" Nigel posited, looking around with a worried expression. "I see you are his last specimen."

"No, I do not belong to this merchant. I am one of a kind. I simply used his table until you all arrived," Gillamon explained. "Now then, after Paul has written his second letter to the Corinthians, Liz, you will go with Luke and Titus to deliver it, while Paul visits his other churches here in Macedonia. Max and Nigel, you can remain with Paul until you all meet up in Corinth. Our doctor will indeed now be with Paul until he reaches Rome."

"Understood," Nigel nodded. "Jolly good! Our doctor, the scribe, shall finally be able to record Paul's journeys."

Max furrowed his brow. "I still don't understand how ye're supposed ta help Paul with his letter."

"You'll see," the owl winked. "Paul is headed to Lydia's house, where Luke has his own room next to the garden. Liz, you may carry me to his desk. We'll let Luke worry about where you got me." The owl smiled and fluttered his wings. "Go now. I shall see you all soon."

"*Merci!*" Liz exclaimed happily. She carefully reached over to grab the owl by the string. Once it was swinging under her chin, Max started sniffing it.

"Looks like he's gone then," observed Max with a wrinkled brow. "He's r-r-right aboot one thing. He's definitely one of a kind. An' sometimes str-r-range. A clay owl?"

Nigel jumped onto Max's back as he and Liz started walking to catch up with Paul. "I guess you could say that now he's a *strange bird.*" The little mouse held his belly while he chuckled.

Max rolled his eyes, muttering under his breath. "Goats actin' like owls an' mice makin' jokes. Never a dull moment."

☧

"Paul! You're back!" Lydia held her arms out in a welcome embrace. Her deep green eyes widened and her beautiful purple tunic flowed as she raced to the door. She ran a large, successful business, selling purple dye and cloth. And she was Paul's very first convert here in Philippi, making her the very first believer in Europe.

Paul smiled broadly and hugged her. "How are you, dear sister? It's been so long."

"*Too* long," Lydia scolded him, shaking him by the shoulders. "Ah, but you're here now. Come, let me get you something to eat. You must be exhausted after your journey." She went into action, clapping her hands for her servants to bring a bowl of water and a towel, and ordering up food. She was clearly an assertive woman who took charge of things. "Luke has a room out back, and I know he will be glad to see you. He was mending a little girl's broken arm before you arrived."

Paul took a seat and frowned. "Then let's not disturb him. I'm sorry about the little girl. Will she be all right?"

"Luke said it wasn't a serious break, so she will be fine," Lydia replied, taking off Paul's sandals to wash his dusty feet. It was then she saw Max come up to her, wagging his tail. "Gabriel! I'm happy to see you! And where is little Faith?" she asked, looking around for Liz. Nigel usually stayed out of sight from all humans except Paul.

Paul looked around but didn't see Liz. "I'm sure she's around somewhere. Maybe she went to see the doctor at work."

☧

"There, now. Do as I say, and your arm will heal in no time," instructed Luke with a comforting smile to the little girl as he secured the cloth sling around her neck. "No more climbing trees for a while."

"Yes, Sir," the little girl answered, wincing from the pain as she looked at her arm. "How do you know how to fix broken arms?"

"Lots of practice," Luke answered, tapping her nose playfully with his finger. He turned to the little girl's mother. "She'll be fine. Make sure she gets a lot of rest and stays still while this arm heals."

"We can't thank you enough, Dr. Luke," the mother replied, handing him a small package. "I hope you will enjoy the raisin cakes. I know it's not much."

"Thank you, I will enjoy them. And I plan to share them," Luke replied, seeing the mother and daughter to the door. "I hope you, your husband, and Sarah will be able to join our church gathering at Lydia's house when Sarah feels better. We will be praying for her healing."

"We will, we will! Thank you again."

Luke stood in the doorway and watched the mother and daughter walking away through the garden, praying over them. He turned and went to his desk, placing the raisin cakes there while he picked up a piece of string to tie back his thick, curly black hair. One strand of hair escaped to hang down his cheek as he opened his journal and reached for his pen. He leaned over his desk and got right to work.

Liz peeked in the door and smiled to see Luke writing his meticulous medical notes. He wrote down everything that happened, both with his patients and with life in general. When he first met Paul, he took down extensive notes about Jesus and the stories of his healing miracles. Liz quietly walked over to the desk and jumped up, startling him. She set the owl jar down on his desk and meowed, "Pour vous. Bonjour, Docteur Luke."

"Little Faith?" Luke asked, his light blue eyes dancing with delight to see her. "Is it you? And what have you brought me?" He picked up the owl jar and studied it curiously before rubbing her under the chin. "You are indeed a mysterious cat. But at least you have brought something *to* me this time. Thank you." He laughed softly as Liz head-butted him. Suddenly it dawned on him. *Faith is here. Paul must be back!* He jumped up from his desk and ran out the door, not thinking too much about the fact that a cat had just brought him a gift.

"Je vous en prie," Liz said with a smile, looking around Luke's desk. The owl was delivered to the doctor. Now she couldn't wait to see how Gillamon would help Paul write his letter.

109

Luke and Paul shared an emotional reunion and spent hours catching up. Luke gave Paul a full checkup, concerned at hearing his report of numerous beatings and physical challenges on his journeys. All the while he listened intently to what had happened to his dear friend over the past six years. Meanwhile, Lydia sent word that Paul had returned to Philippi and prepared a bountiful feast for people from the church to welcome him back. Timothy ran to Lydia's house when he got word, and he and Paul shared a huge embrace. Arcadius the jailer brought his family, and Paul was delighted to see how the children had grown. Luke and Lydia got Paul caught up about the church. They shared how Paul's letter had made the people so happy. Paul shared about all his work with believers in Ephesus and Asia Minor, and also about the funds being raised to take to the church in Jerusalem. As usual, the endless generosity of the Philippians made them eager to help. Paul was so happy about Philippi, but he was unsettled about Corinth.

"So, no word from Titus? He hasn't been through?" Paul asked with a sigh. "I was hoping he would beat me here."

"What has you so worried, Paul?" Luke asked. "I know that frown."

"I had to write a tough letter to the Corinthians, and I've been concerned that it was too harsh," Paul explained. "I sent Titus from Ephesus to go check on the church there for me and to report back. I told him to meet me in Troas, but the people said he hadn't arrived there yet. So I proceeded here right away, since I knew he would head up this way through Greece. I'm just worried I've discouraged them. You know I speak the truth plainly and pointedly when I must."

"Just like you told those *duumviri,*" Arcadius chimed in with a wide grin, shaking Paul's shoulder good naturedly. His scar looked like a deep smile line in his cheek. "They were scared for months that you would report them to Rome. I keep praying for them, though. Even invited them to one of our church gatherings, and try to show them kindness when I can."

"Look at what Christ has done in you, my friend," Paul marveled at the jailer whose name meant 'bear.' "From a mean old bear to a kind old soul. You are proof that if any man be in Christ, he is truly a new creation."

110

"I'm sure the people in Corinth took your letter with the love in which you sent it," Timothy affirmed him. "They know your heart, Paul."

Paul took in a deep breath and let it go. "I pray they do. I love them more than my life."

☧

"Someone is going to be quite the exhilarated apostle today," Nigel reported, preening back his whiskers. "Titus just arrived."

"*C'est bon!*" Liz cried. She jumped up from the flower bed in the garden. "Paul will be so relieved. Let's go see him and Titus!"

"No need, my dear, Paul is on his way here to Luke's room," Nigel shared, stopping her. "He wishes to write a letter immediately to the Corinthians."

"Ah, good. Time for Gillamon's owl ta do wha'ever it's goin' ta do," Max said. "I've been one stumped Scottie over this."

Liz's face lit up as she saw Paul, Titus, Timothy, and Luke walking briskly along the garden path to Luke's room, talking a mile a minute. "*Le docteur et le hibou!*" She ran after the men.

"The doctor and the owl, old boy," Nigel translated for Max. "Our girl is just as excited as Paul."

Liz sat eagerly watching Luke clear his desk so Timothy could be Paul's scribe for the second letter to the Corinthians. She wondered why Luke wasn't the one writing, but her heart warmed when she saw Luke grin at the little owl that he lovingly placed back on his desk next to Timothy's parchment and pen.

"I need to be harsh about some things, once again," Paul said with a frown, already pacing. "According to Titus, the Corinthians have had false teachers telling them I need letters from the main church in Jerusalem to prove my worth as an apostle. Some even doubt my authority over them."

Nigel pulled on his whiskers in exasperation. "This is intolerable! How dare they say such things! Paul *founded* the church at Corinth! The church itself *IS* his letter!"

"Steady, Mousie," Max whispered. "We know the truth, an' so does he."

"Seems like I recently read a brilliant letter that said, 'Be anxious for nothing,'" Luke pointed out. "Hmmm, who do you suppose wrote those words?"

Paul smiled, chagrined at hearing his own words. "I did."

"You most certainly did!" Luke exclaimed. "Remember, you are still human like everyone else, in spite of your great faith, Paul. I deal with fragile human bodies all the time, and find it amazing that our Lord would pour himself into such weak vessels." He reached over and picked up the owl, handing it to Paul. "Just like this little Corinthian jar. It holds valuable, precious oil or perfume, but the container itself is fragile. It is okay that you feel hurt and angry by the Corinthians and those counterfeit teachers, especially after all you've suffered. You're human, and most people would have given up by now. But you press on. Just speak your heart. The Holy Spirit will guide your words to set them right."

Paul took the little owl and gripped it with a big smile. "Amen. Thank you, Doctor Luke. You know how to comfort my heart as well as my worn-out body. Very well, let's begin." He studied the little owl jar while he paced and dictated the second letter to the Corinthians.

"I still don't get the owl," Max whispered as Paul got started with his introductory comments.

"You must wait, *mon ami*," Liz replied. "Allow Paul time to think, no?"

"All praise to God, the Father of our Lord Jesus Christ. God is our merciful Father and the source of all comfort. He comforts us in all our troubles so we can comfort others. When they are troubled, we will be able to give them the same comfort God has given us," dictated Paul, smiling at Luke as he paced and continued, stopping now and then to let Timothy catch up.

"We think you ought to know, dear brothers and sisters, about the trouble we went through in the province of Asia. We were crushed and overwhelmed beyond our ability to endure, and we thought we would never live through it," Paul told them with great emotion, remembering times with Aquila, Priscilla, Aristarchus, Gaius, and others. "In fact, we expected to die. But as a result, we stopped relying on ourselves and learned to rely only on God, who raises the dead. And he did rescue us from mortal danger, and he will rescue us again."

Paul then discussed his reasoning for his change of plans in coming to see them right away, the cry of his heart behind his last letter, the forgiveness for the sinner in their church and the need to now affirm him, the proof of them as testimony to Paul's ministry, and the glory of the new covenant and how they must never give up as they preached boldly about Jesus.

"You see, we don't go around preaching about ourselves. We preach that Jesus Christ is Lord, and we ourselves are your servants for Jesus' sake. For God, who said, 'Let there be light in the darkness,' has made this light shine in our hearts so we could know the glory of God that is seen in the face of Jesus Christ. We now have this light shining in our hearts . . ." Paul stopped mid-sentence.

Liz's heart raced as she saw him hold up the little clay owl. *"Now, Paul."*

"But we ourselves are like fragile clay jars containing this great treasure," Paul continued. "This makes it clear that our great power is from God, not from ourselves."

"Aye! I get it now!" Max whispered with a grin. "Well, I'll be. The doctor an' the owl."

"We are pressed on every side by troubles, but we are not crushed. We are perplexed, but not driven to despair. We are hunted down, but never abandoned by God. We get knocked down, but we are not destroyed. Through suffering, our bodies continue to share in the death of Jesus so that the life of Jesus may also be seen in our bodies." Paul grew more confident with every word. "Yes, we live under constant danger of death because we serve Jesus, so that the life of Jesus will be evident in our dying bodies. So we live in the face of death, but this has resulted in eternal life for you."

Luke glanced over at Liz while Paul continued to spill out truths as effortlessly as pouring oil from the little jar. The doctor winked at her. He didn't know how the little cat came by the owl. He reasoned that she had just brought him a gift, just as cats are known to bring dead birds to their masters. Only this bird was made of clay.

Liz batted her eyes affectionately. *Soon we will get your pen moving, Docteur Luke.* Little did he know that once she became his personal writing assistant, he would in turn give a gift to the world.

113

14

MAPPING
THE ROMAN ROAD

More stones!" A Roman soldier instructed the work crew while an engineer took measurements to ensure the solid progress of the road. "Make sure it's filled in evenly. When we're finished with this section we'll erect a milestone."

This detachment of Roman legionnaires was working hard to build a new intersection for a secondary road that turned off this main road leading to Corinth. Nigel was engrossed in what they were doing as he rode on Max's back as they followed Paul.

"We are witnessing Roman engineering at its finest," Nigel exclaimed while adjusting his spectacles. "Rome is dependent on its roads to move its armies as well as provide movement of its civilians and goods. You see what those fine legionnaires are doing? They begin by digging a trench where they lay a base of large stones, followed by a layer of broken stones, pebbles, sand, and cement." The little mouse gestured layering motions with his paws as he described the process. "Next, they add another layer of cement mixed with broken rubbish such as tiles, and place cut paving stones on top to create the surface of the road. Finally, they add edge stones on either side of the road to allow for water to run off as easily as rain off a tortoise shell. Extraordinary!"

"Tortoise shell. Remember when Clarie turned inta one of those beasties?" Max recalled. "That were the mornin' with Jesus on the beach after Peter an' the lads caught the fish. I wonder when and how she'll show up again."

"One never knows," Nigel replied absentmindedly, preoccupied with the road building. "It's simply brilliant how the Romans came up with this system. They build roads as straight as possible, and they build them *well* so they will not need frequent repair. I dare say these roads could last at least a thousand years. Did you know there are more than 50,000 miles of stone-paved Roman roads?"

"That be a lot of stones, Lad," Max replied, eyeing the massive pile of stones next to the soldiers. "I feel like we've walked over half of those r-r-roads with Paul."

Nigel chuckled. "By my calculations we have traveled roughly 7,000 miles with Paul throughout his journeys. That's only fourteen percent of all Roman roads." The little mouse patted Max on the shoulder. "It's an impressive beginning, old boy."

Max harrumphed. "Says the wee passenger."

As they walked along, Paul noticed an old man sitting on the side of the road next to a milestone. He was carving something on a wooden cup. Paul felt drawn to stop and engage the man.

"Good afternoon," Paul greeted him with a smile. "I see you are working hard on something today."

The man didn't look up but kept carving. "Not as hard as those legionnaires back there. Building roads is hard work. But it's worth it. People need to be able to get from one place to another."

"That is very true. I'm grateful for these Roman roads," Paul answered. It was because of these very roads that he was able to travel and spread the gospel. He pointed to the cup. "What are you carving there?"

"An itinerarium," the old man replied. "The soldiers build the roads. I help people follow them." He held up the cup to show Paul. "I list the cities along the road, and the distances between them, from these milestones placed by the Romans. When people want to journey down a road, they need to know how long it will take." He turned to look at Max and Nigel. "And they need to know which road will help them reach the right destination."

Max grinned at the old man and wagged his tail. Nigel was too busy staring at the cup to notice him.

"You are quite right, my friend," Paul said, admiring the artwork on the cup. "I see you have listed the cities leading to Rome."

The old man nodded. "Caesar Augustus set up the *miliarium aureum,* or 'golden milestone,' at the Forum in Rome so all roads would begin there to spread throughout the world. Ever been to Rome?"

"No, but I've longed to go to there," Paul replied, running his finger along the name of the city that was the center of the known world. "My heart eagerly wishes to get to the people of that great city. Lord willing, I will go there soon."

"All roads lead to Rome." The old man pointed to the cup in Paul's hand. "Take the cup. Consider it a gift to help you find your way there. Meanwhile you can plan your journey. I think it's helpful to map out our thoughts as well as our itineraries, don't you?"

"That is most gracious, but I insist on paying you," Paul protested.

The old man smiled at the weary traveler with his striking blue eyes. "You can pay me by delivering a letter for me, since you're going to Rome." He reached into a leather satchel and took out a small piece of parchment bearing a red wax seal. "Take this to Rome and put it in the hands of a man named Theophilus, who practices law at the Forum. Will you do that for me?"

Nigel snapped to attention at hearing this request and now studied the old man's face.

"I would be happy to do so, however, I cannot tell you for certain when I will actually make it there," Paul replied. "You may wish to have someone else take it for you." His eyes narrowed as he studied the old man's face. He seemed familiar. "Have we met?"

The old man stood to his feet and gave Max a pet on the head. "It doesn't matter when you arrive, just as long as you deliver this letter to the Roman." He turned to walk in the other direction, not answering Paul's question. "I think I can trust you. I like your dog."

Paul looked down at Max fondly. "Very well, good Sir. I will deliver the letter. And thank you for the cup."

The man didn't turn around but held up his hand to wave farewell. Paul stood in the middle of the road studying the cup as the man walked away. "Mapping out my thoughts. Hmmm," he muttered out loud, looking back toward the old man. "What a curious encounter."

"Aye, the Epic kind," Max whispered under his breath to Nigel with a grin.

CORINTH, DECEMBER, AD 56

Luke was busy writing medical notes in his journal. Liz sat on his desk, her tail wrapped around her legs as she read what he was writing about his latest herbal discovery. Suddenly there came a knock on the door. Luke stopped writing and immediately got up to see who it was.

"Paul! You made it!" Luke exclaimed, hugging his friend. "We were wondering when you would arrive. I'm the only one here at the moment. Gaius and the others are at the market."

Paul gave Luke a strong pat on the back. "Oh, my friend, it's so good to see you. I'm grateful to Gaius for opening up his home to us." He stepped inside and looked around this spacious home. He set down his satchel and Max ran inside. "How are things here?"

"You'll be pleased to know that things have calmed down with the church here in Corinth," Luke reported, pouring water into a bowl to wash Paul's feet. "They received your second letter with open hearts and minds. I think it was good for you to wait a while to get here. It's given the people time to think, pray, and put your wisdom to work."

Paul's face lit up with joy. "Praise God, that's great news! I was hoping you'd say that. My heart has been burdened for these people for so long. I hope we can simply enjoy time together without turmoil."

"Yes, and I also think you'll be able to finally just catch your breath for a while. Winter is here. Just spend this time to rest your tired bones. Doctor's orders," Luke added, wiping Paul's feet and examining them for callouses. "Stay here. I have a new ointment to put on these feet." Luke walked over and picked up a jar.

"Very well, Doctor," Paul replied, rubbing his face with both hands while Luke applied the ointment. "I can't imagine being able to just rest."

"I'm amazed at how many miles these feet have walked to carry the Good News," shared Luke with a smile. "Those Roman roads must have 'Paul grooves' in them by now."

"Speaking of which, I have something to show you," Paul told the doctor. He reached into his satchel and pulled out the wooden cup and the letter, placing them on the table next to Liz. "Hello, little Faith." Paul gave her a loving rub behind her ears while she head-butted him.

117

Liz immediately spied the seal on the letter and shot a quick glance down to Max and Nigel. Nigel saluted and Max winked.

Luke set the jar of ointment down on the table and picked up the cup. "Looks like directions to Rome. I've seen these. It's an itinerarium."

"That's exactly what it is. I met a man who makes them and he gave this to me with the condition I deliver his letter to a man in Rome. A man by the name of Theophilus," Paul explained. "I told him I didn't know when I would actually make it there, but he said it didn't matter." Paul smiled at Max. "He said he liked Gabriel."

Luke smiled and gave Max a gruff rub along his back. "Of course he did. Everyone likes Gabriel, right, Boy?"

Max wagged his tail and locked eyes with Liz as she mouthed the word, "Clarie?" Max nodded.

"The old man said something that I can't get out of my mind. He said that it's helpful to map out our thoughts as well as our itineraries," Paul recalled, picking up the letter and tapping it on the desk. "If I'm going to go to Rome, I need to introduce myself to the people there and let them know I'm coming. I didn't start the church in Rome, so they don't know me. Peter is there now, but there were believers in Rome before he even arrived, likely who were in Jerusalem on the day of Pentecost. Since Emperor Claudius is no longer in power, Aquila and Priscilla have returned to Rome, leaving Ephesus in good hands with the believers there. They want to now help the church in Rome."

"I know you do not wish to ever build on another's work," Luke added, "so what are you hoping to do in Rome?"

"I feel I must get to the capital of the world and encourage the church there with the gospel. If all roads lead to Rome, then believers traveling out of Rome on those roads can take the gospel to all points on the map," Paul enthused.

Liz jumped down to be on the floor with Max and Nigel. *"Bonjour, mes amis.* What is our Clarie up to? She has given Paul a letter to take to Theophilus? But why?"

"We didn't get ta speak ta her, so we don't know," Max whispered.

"She did indicate that Theophilus practices law there at the Forum," Nigel added. "I can't help but feel simply *giddy* over the fact that Paul and Theo have met before, on the docks of Caesarea when Theo was just a boy."

"Aye, when Theo were teasin' his little brother with the r-r-red mar-ble," Max recalled.

"*Oui,* I remember that day also," Liz agreed with a smile. "But why would Clarie want Paul to meet him now as a Roman attorney?" Liz wondered out loud.

"Luke, think about this with me," Paul said, picking up the cup. "Corinth is now in better shape. In fact, I feel that the regions of Asia Minor and Greece are well in hand with many new churches taking root. But all the territory west of us is just sitting there, so far untouched by the gospel! If we go west, we need a place to be our base of opera-tions, to provide support, just as Antioch provided us in the east."

"Rome?" Luke suggested.

"Exactly," Paul answered, holding the cup in the air.

"Paul is a brilliant strategist!" Nigel whispered. "He reminds me of a military commander with an eye for the layout of new lands to conquer."

"Except this commander plans ta conquer that land for Chr-r-rist," Max replied.

119

"But in order for the church to get behind me and provide the sup-port I need to take the gospel on to Spain and other regions, I feel it is important that the people in Rome know who I am and what I believe." He stood to pace around the room. "I've been thinking that I need to map out my thoughts to them. Since we'll winter here in Corinth, I'll have time to do just that. For once I won't have to write to a church about a crisis or a particular situation. I've followed Jesus now for more than twenty-five years, Luke. I feel the need to put my full understand-ing of the gospel down on paper."

"A letter to the Romans," Luke said, nodding his head slowly as he traced his finger across the letter to Theophilus the Roman.

"A letter to the Romans," Paul replied with a smile.

"Something tells me this letter to the Romans will be a key book in our New Testament," Liz whispered. "So it needs the right scribe—someone who can provide a perfect touch with a Roman quill."

☧

Tertius leaned over his desk, which was covered with multiple scrolls of parchment. Pens were neatly placed in multiple containers, as were vials of ink, wax, and seals. His office was efficient, orderly, and characteristically Roman. He was in his mid-thirties and rather plain-looking with cropped brown hair and hazel eyes. Schooled in Rome, this scribe was meticulous with the attention given to each letter that flowed from his pen. He pushed aside a scroll with his arm to make room for transcribing a document onto a fresh new scroll.

Liz and Nigel sat in the doorway watching Tertius work. "He's perfect, no?" Liz asked the little mouse. "And he is part of the church here in Corinth. He recently became a believer. When I learned he was a scribe I made a point to see where he worked. Now we simply need to bring him to Paul."

"And how do you propose we get him there, my dear?" Nigel asked.

Liz smiled coyly. "I propose that *you* leave him a note on his desk when he leaves."

"Ah, so you first need a much smaller scribe?" Nigel quipped, brushing back his whiskers. "The pen of Anonymouse?"

Liz kissed Nigel on the head. "Precisely."

120

☧

"Tertius, my friend. How good to see you," Gaius greeted him happily. "What brings you here?"

"Good day, Gaius. I received word that Paul was back in Corinth and might need a scribe," Tertius replied.

"Oh, yes, he most certainly does. Come in, come in!" Gaius replied, grabbing him by the arm to lead him inside. Gaius was a stocky little man with a round face and a balding head. His skin was clear and shiny, and always glowed. But he also glowed from the inside out, as the joy of Christ bubbled up from his heart. Gaius had the gift of hospitality and had opened his home not only to Paul, Luke, and Titus, but to the church in Corinth as well. "Paul? Paul? Come here, please. I want you to meet someone," he called out loudly.

Paul came around the corner to the main room. "Yes?"

"Paul, Tertius is a believer in our church, but he also is a scribe from Rome," Gaius gushed. "He heard you might need one. For that letter I heard you discussing with Luke?"

Paul's face lit up as he walked over to meet him. "Wonderful! Hello, Tertius. I am Paul. I was going to ask Luke to transcribe my letter, but if you're from Rome, you could help ensure that my words will resonate with my audience. I plan to write to the believers in Rome."

Tertius smiled broadly. "I would be honored, Paul! I have many friends there in Rome."

Paul clapped his hands together. "Excellent! I imagine this letter will need to be written over the course of many sessions together. When can you start?"

Tertius shrugged his shoulder to reveal a knapsack full of scrolls, pens, and ink. "How about now?"

Liz, Nigel, and Max smiled at one another as they listened in on this conversation.

"All roads may lead to Rome, but only one Way leads Home," Nigel said, preening his whiskers.

"Aye, time for Paul ta make a map of The Way," Max added.

Liz curled her tail up and down expectantly. "One with plenty of milestones."

☧

Paul rolled over onto his side and let go a deep breath, exhausted from the day. He and Tertius had been working for weeks on his letter to the Romans. They were almost finished with it. When Paul discovered that Phoebe, a member of the church here in Corinth, was soon heading to Rome, he wanted to send the letter with her, knowing he could entrust it to be safely delivered by this dependable woman of God. Paul poured his heart into this letter, taking his time to allow his thoughts to come together in a way that would clearly explain the core of the Good News. He felt that if he never made it to Rome, given the constant threats he encountered, then at least he would leave behind a roadmap for others to follow to find Christ. Paul read and reread Tertius's scroll, making sure he was covering everything he felt the Holy Spirit was leading him to capture on paper. He would jot down his thoughts before he would dictate to Tertius, using the idea of mapping out a road. He frequently held the cup in his hand as he paced back and forth, dictating to Tertius. He prayed for God to bless the unknown man who had given him the cup, and the idea to map out his thoughts to the Romans. He wondered if he should just send the old man's letter on to Rome with Phoebe, but decided he would do exactly as he promised and deliver it in person.

While Paul slept, Liz, Nigel, and Max read over the letter as it appeared at this point.

"Utterly extraordinary," Nigel whispered, shaking his head in awe. He removed his spectacles and cleaned them with a cloth Tertius used to clean his pens. "I have read the masters of literature across time, as you well know. Aristotle, Plato, Socrates. But I daresay that this," Nigel placed his paw reverently on the scroll, "this must be one of the most profound works ever written. It is a masterpiece."

"*C'est vrai!*" Liz agreed. "There is so much here. Every sentence is full of deep meaning and insight. If I had to choose one piece of writing to show the full meaning of life in following Jesus, this letter to the Romans would be it."

"Wha' aboot Paul's map in all of this?" Max wanted to know. "Can ye make out a r-r-road for the r-r-reader ta follow?"

Liz and Nigel looked at one another and smiled. "Shall we show him the roadmap, my dear?" Nigel asked.

122

"But of course, *mon ami!*" Liz replied with glowing golden eyes. She looked over to make sure Paul was still asleep. She jumped onto the table and picked up the scroll to bring it to the floor. "Let us roll it all the way out to show Maximillian the milestones along the way."

"Brilliant!" Nigel enthused, running to the front of the scroll. The little mouse nudged it open with his nose and ran against the rolled edge to push it open to reveal the text. "Now then, pay attention, old boy." Nigel stood on his back paws and cleared his throat, growing animated by lifting his front paws to gesture as he gave a summary of Paul's letter. "Paul has constructed a roadmap for humans to find the way from being lost in sin forever to being found in Christ for eternity." He nodded to Liz, who picked up on the summary while he rolled the scroll past Paul's initial greetings to the opening point of the letter.

Liz pointed to the text. "*Oui*, after his greetings, Paul says that man has a problem: sin, which leads to death. But the Maker has the solution: faith in Jesus, which leads to life. If humans accept the Maker's solution, the problem is fixed, and life can be lived in a way to have unending joy no matter what comes. This is the map of this letter, from start to finish."

Max studied the words. "Aye. He starts the journey by sayin' he's not ashamed of the good news of Chr-r-rist. Good lad."

Nigel ran ahead, unrolling the scroll further. "Now, Liz and I have discovered several 'milestones,' if you will, along this road of getting from point A—dangerously lost—to point B—safe and sound. I shall run through the scroll as we point out each one." He scanned the parchment for the verse he sought. "Ah yes, here we are. Milestone Number One: *No One Righteous*:

WELL THEN, SHOULD WE CONCLUDE THAT WE JEWS ARE BETTER THAN OTHERS? NO, NOT AT ALL, FOR WE HAVE ALREADY SHOWN THAT ALL PEOPLE, WHETHER JEWS OR GENTILES, ARE UNDER THE POWER OF SIN. AS THE SCRIPTURES SAY,

"NO ONE IS RIGHTEOUS— NOT EVEN ONE. NO ONE IS TRULY WISE; NO ONE IS SEEKING GOD. ALL HAVE TURNED AWAY; ALL HAVE BECOME USELESS. NO ONE DOES GOOD, NOT A SINGLE ONE."

"Let me stop here and say that Paul has used more than fifteen Psalms and more than twenty passages from Isaiah," Liz observed. "Nigel and I were very happy to see our work from Isaiah's scroll used once again, now in this letter to the Romans."

"That old Isaiah mission be gettin' more important as time goes on then, Lass," Max pointed out with wide eyes. "I'm pr-r-roud of ye an' Mousie."

Nigel scurried down the scroll to point to the next text. "Right, just a few verses down we find Milestone Number Two: *All Have Sinned*:

FOR EVERYONE HAS SINNED; WE ALL FALL SHORT OF GOD'S GLORIOUS STANDARD."

"Paul has made it clear that all have sinned and are without excuse," Liz explained. "Here, then, is man's problem."

Max frowned. "Aye, no lad or lassie can be good enough for what the Maker r-r-requires."

Liz placed her paw on Max's shoulder while Nigel unrolled the scroll further. *"Oui,* but this is what is so hopeful about Milestone Number Three: *Christ Died*:

WHEN WE WERE UTTERLY HELPLESS, CHRIST CAME AT JUST THE RIGHT TIME AND DIED FOR US SINNERS.

NOW, MOST PEOPLE WOULD NOT BE WILLING TO DIE FOR AN UPRIGHT PERSON, THOUGH SOMEONE MIGHT PERHAPS BE WILLING TO DIE FOR A PERSON WHO IS ESPECIALLY GOOD. BUT GOD SHOWED HIS GREAT LOVE FOR US BY SENDING CHRIST TO DIE FOR US WHILE WE WERE STILL SINNERS."

"Aye! No gr-r-reater love than ta die for r-r-rascals who didn't deserve it," Max remarked happily.

"Precisely!" Nigel exclaimed with a finger in the air. "I feel SO remiss by skipping over all of the juicy segments of these parts but we are simply jumping to the highlights." He unrolled the scroll further and scanned it, mumbling to himself. "Right! Now, here Paul brilliantly shows how humans got into this predicament to begin with so they would understand how this dreadful thing started. Milestone Number Four: *Adam and Jesus:*

124

THIS, THEN, IS WHAT HAPPENED. SIN MADE ITS ENTRY INTO THE WORLD THROUGH ONE MAN, AND THROUGH SIN, DEATH. THE ENTAIL OF SIN AND DEATH PASSED ON TO THE WHOLE HUMAN RACE, AND NO ONE COULD BREAK IT FOR NO ONE WAS HIMSELF FREE FROM SIN."

Nigel scurried down the page. "And a little further down, see here:

YES, ADAM'S ONE SIN BRINGS CONDEMNATION FOR EVERYONE, BUT CHRIST'S ONE ACT OF RIGHTEOUS-NESS BRINGS A RIGHT RELATIONSHIP WITH GOD AND NEW LIFE FOR EVERYONE. BECAUSE ONE PERSON DIS-OBEYED GOD, MANY BECAME SINNERS. BUT BECAUSE ONE OTHER PERSON OBEYED GOD, MANY WILL BE MADE RIGHTEOUS."

"Well, I'll be a Scottie's uncle," Max marveled. "Paul made it r-r-real simple. Adam an' Jesus."

Liz went over to a pile of papyrus and pulled out one of Paul's hand-written notes where he mapped out his thoughts. "Look at how Paul came to this conclusion."

ADAM	JESUS
Made in God's image	God in human form
Tried to grasp the prize to be as God	Thought it **not** a prize to be grasped at to be as God
Desired a reputation	Made himself of no reputation
Snubbed the role of God's servant	Became the lowliest of servants
Sought to be like God	Came in the likeness of men
A man of dust, now doomed,	And being found in appearance as a man,
He exalted himself,	He humbled himself,
And became disobedient unto death.	And became obedient to the point of death.
He was condemned and disgraced	God highly exalted him and gave him the name and position of Lord

125

Liz's eyes brimmed with tears of joy. *"C'est magnifique,* our Jesus!"

Nigel scurried ahead to further unroll the letter to the Romans. "Now on to Milestone Number Five: *Sin's Wages, God's Gift:*

FOR THE WAGES OF SIN IS DEATH, BUT THE FREE GIFT OF GOD IS ETERNAL LIFE IN CHRIST JESUS OUR LORD."

"A wage is wha' ye earn," Max noted. "A gift is wha' ye don't."

"Oui, humans have earned death, but the Maker wishes to give them what they have *not* earned instead—life forever!" Liz marveled. "And for *free! Dieu est bon!"*

Nigel proceeded to push and push and roll and roll the scroll until it opened several sections beyond where they were. "Now we come to the part that delivers our reading traveler home to safety. Milestone Number Six: *Confess and Believe:*

IF YOU CONFESS WITH YOUR MOUTH THAT JESUS IS LORD AND BELIEVE IN YOUR HEART THAT GOD RAISED HIM FROM THE DEAD, YOU WILL BE SAVED."

Max, Liz, and Nigel sat there staring at the open letter to the Romans. This one verse was perhaps the most important line Paul had ever written, or would ever write. In this one line was the key to life or death, joy or anguish, for every soul, for all eternity.

"Jesus walked this r-r-road ahead an' alone," uttered Max softly, "so no one would ever have ta feel lost again."

Nigel nodded. "Indeed. I can see Jesus standing there in the middle of this Roman road, holding out his hand, lovingly asking every single man, woman, and child who shall ever read these words to follow him."

"I pray they answer him without delay," Liz added softly, blinking back hopeful tears. "Time waits for no one."

126

☧

Panels of scenes from time past swirled around Gillamon and Clarie as they stood in the IAMISPHERE, gazing at the scene of Liz, Max, and Nigel reading Paul's letter to the Romans.

"Well done, little lamb. Your idea to inspire the map for the Roman road worked beautifully," Gillamon said, his gentle eyes twinkling behind his pure white hair that blew in the heavenly breeze of this time portal.

Clarie wagged her lamb tail happily. "I was just another marker in the road. I look forward to seeing how many people across time follow Jesus from reading this letter."

Gillamon looked up to the dark panel of the future, known to the Maker alone. "Time will tell."

The wise mountain goat turned his gaze and locked eyes with the sweet lamb. They smiled at one another and then said in unison, "It always does."

15

FOREBODING, FALLING, AND FAREWELL

PORT OF CENCHREAE, MARCH AD 57

Max turned his gaze skyward as he heard the cry of seagulls circling the harbor in search of fish. He smiled, remembering his seagull friends from Scotland, Crinan and Bethoo. Those seagulls had accompanied Max and the others to Noah's Ark, and Max held fond memories of their friendship even after all this time. They had helped spread the word with animals who were trying to reach the Ark. They had been there to support Max through his dangerous encounters aboard. And they had been right beside him through that dangerous, dark day when the animals left the Ark. *Friends like that only come along once in a millennium,* Max thought to himself.

Max, Liz, and Nigel sat on the dock watching these Corinthian seagulls dive bomb toward the water with a splash.

"Breakfast is served, no?" Liz noted. "I am certain my Albert would give anything to find fish like this."

"Aye, that he would," Max agreed. "I wonder if he'd dare take a r-r-ride on a bird like ye do, Mousie."

"I believe neither pigeons nor seagulls could lift our lovable large friend," Nigel chuckled fondly. "But I daresay he would ride a pelican in order to scoop up a gullet-load of sardines."

Max, Liz, and Nigel paused a moment to look at one another before bursting out laughing at the image of Al flying on a pelican.

"Anything is possible for he who so desires fish," Nigel quipped, wiping away his tears of laughter.

Suddenly Max's grin faded as he spied the leaders of the synagogue in Corinth talking with a group of shadowy sailors. They were looking over their shoulders, on the lookout for anyone listening in on their conversation. They stood next to the pilgrim ship getting ready to depart for Jerusalem. Paul had arranged passage on this ship that would carry Jews seeking to reach Jerusalem for Passover. He was eager to finally deliver the collection from the churches for Jerusalem's sick and poor, and saw it as perhaps his last chance to show his love for his own people before heading west. Paul had doubts about making it out of Jerusalem alive, and had even asked the Romans in his letter to pray for his safety.

"Wha' kind of schemin' be happenin' now?" Max muttered, walking away from Liz and Nigel. He trotted over to where the men stood to listen in on their conversation.

128

"It's going to be a new moon, so things will be dark," a sailor whispered. "One blow to the head could send him overboard without uttering a word."

The Jewish leaders looked at one another and nodded in agreement. "Very well. See that it's done. We'll have people on board to pay you once you reach Jerusalem—that is, as long as Paul *doesn't* reach Jerusalem."

"Done," agreed the sailor. He slung a coil of rope over his shoulder and walked away from the men.

The Jews made their way hastily down the dock, leaving Max panicked over what he'd heard. He went running back to Liz and Nigel, who still sat watching the seagulls.

"They're goin' ta kill Paul!" Max cried. "Time for ye ta wr-r-rite a warnin' letter!"

☧

Paul's arm dropped to the table, note in hand, as he shook his head sadly. He passed it off to Luke, who took the anonymous note, reading it in disbelief.

"And here you just wrote to the Romans that your heart is filled with bitter sorrow and unending grief for your Jewish brothers and sisters. You said you would be willing to be forever cursed—cut off from Christ!—if that would save them."

"I still feel that way, despite this plot to kill me. They don't know what they're doing," stated Paul, clasping his hands behind his neck. "Well, we'll obviously need to travel on foot and miss the Passover. We'll go through Macedonia and sail over to Troas to rendezvous with the others. From there we can make it to Jerusalem hopefully by Pentecost."

"This is intolerable!" Nigel fumed. He had been too upset to even pen the letter of warning to Paul about the plot, so Liz had done the honors.

"Steady, Mousie," Max consoled him. "At least we learned aboot the plot before it were too late."

"*You* learned about it, *mon ami,*" Liz corrected him. "Thankfully, Paul can now meet up with his faithful friends in Troas, and together they can travel in safety to Jerusalem." She looked over at Paul. His heart was heavy to be so betrayed by the very people he longed to reach with the Good News. "What a blessing to have dependable friends on our darkest days!"

129

Max thought about their seagull friends. "Aye, the lads Paul asked ta go with him ta r-r-represent the churches r-r-remind me of Cr-r-rinan an' Bethoo. They've helped spr-r-read the word, they've been there when Paul were thr-r-reatened, an' they be by his side thr-r-rough this dark time."

"I say, you're right," Nigel agreed. "And how splendid that they represent churches from each of Paul's three missionary journeys to bring this tremendous sojourn to a close! Gaius from Derbe and Timothy from Lystra represent journey number one. Sopater from Berea and Aristarchus and Secundus from Thessalonica represent journey number two. And Tychicus and Trophimus from Ephesus represent journey number three."

"Not to mention Luke who, I'm happy to say, will travel on with Paul to Rome," Liz added. "Paul may have many adversaries, but the Maker has given him many faithful friends throughout these three missionary journeys."

"Not ta mention a faithful dog, cat, an' mouse," Max added. "An' I don't plan ta let the lad out of our sight fr-r-rom here on out. Somethin' tells me there's more tr-r-rouble ta come."

TROAS, APRIL AD 57

The teenage boy watched a stream of oily smoke curl and rise into the air from a lamp next to where Paul sat. This third-floor room was packed with sweaty people, and the air grew hot, stale, and stuffy. Eutychus had climbed up to sit on this narrow windowsill to reach some cooler, fresher air. Paul had been preaching all evening following a light meal on this Sunday night where the believers of Troas had gathered for the Lord's Day. They knew it was Paul's last time to be with them. He had so much to tell them! And they had so much to ask him.

Since they had just observed the Passover and celebrated the death and resurrection of Jesus, Paul focused on the mystery of the Resurrection. The people asked questions to try to capture the full meaning of this new and growing faith in their risen Lord. Before they knew it, Paul had talked way past midnight. No one wanted to leave. And although Eutychus was interested in what Paul had to say, he struggled to keep his eyes open and his head up. So he stared at the curl of oily smoke, following its path up to the ceiling. But the smoke had a hypnotic effect on him. He had worked hard all day in the marketplace for his non-believing employer, who didn't recognize a Sabbath rest.

No one noticed when Eutychus's head repeatedly bobbed up and down, and his chin came to rest on his chest. Paul's voice drifted in and out of his conscious mind until finally, the tired young man drifted off to sleep.

"AAAAH! Help!" came screams from the street below. Everyone in the room turned to look toward the open window and the sound of the shouting voice. Eutychus was no longer sitting there. Someone jumped up to look out the window, and there in the darkened street fifteen feet below lay Eutychus. "Eutychus! He fell into the street!"

Luke was the first one on his feet to rush down the stairs, followed by the boy's family and friends. Luke dropped to his knees and leaned over the boy, testing for signs of life. Although the fall was not far, his head evidently hit the hard stone pavement at a vulnerable spot. As Luke felt for a pulse, the boy's father and mother knelt down next to their son, sick with worry.

"I'm sorry," Luke said softly, putting his hand on the father's shoulder. "He's gone."

130

"NO!" the mother cried, burying her head in her husband's chest.

The crowd quickly parted for Paul, who made his way to the sad scene. He knelt down next to Eutychus and looked at Luke, who tightened his lips sadly and shook his head, letting Paul know the boy was dead.

Max, Liz, and Nigel stood on the other side of the crowd, watching from the curb. "Oh, the poor boy!" Liz cried. Nigel patted her gently.

"Steady, Lass," Max advised her as Paul lay across the boy, praying softly. "Paul be doin' somethin'."

"This reminds me of Elisha," Nigel whispered hopefully, "and Elijah for that matter."

Suddenly Paul sat up and smiled. "Don't worry, he's alive!"

Gasps of awe and relief rippled through the crowd. Immediately Eutychus opened his eyes and looked into the faces of his parents peering over him. Tears streamed down their faces as they enveloped him in their arms. Luke stood up with wide eyes and his hands on his hips, not believing what he was seeing.

"He was *dead*, Paul. I'm a doctor, so I know for certain he was dead!" Luke insisted, clearly awestruck from his medical perspective.

Paul smiled, nodded, and put his hand on Luke's shoulder. "You're right, Doctor, he was." The parents gathered their son into their arms to take him home, smothering him with kisses. "And thanks to the Great Physician, now he's alive." Paul lifted his hands and exclaimed to the crowd, "Jesus IS the resurrection and the life! Come, let us celebrate our Lord's Supper."

The believers erupted in praise and joyful cheers as they followed Paul and Luke back upstairs to the room.

"Elijah, Elisha, Jesus, Peter, and now Paul. They are the only ones to have raised people from the dead!" Nigel marveled.

"Aye, but Jesus still holds the r-r-record," Max noted happily.

Liz smiled. *"Oui.* And don't forget us. Max, we know exactly how Eutychus feels at this moment, don't we?"

"Aye, Lass, that we do," confirmed Max, wagging his tail. "Come on, let's go celebr-r-rate another mir-r-racle."

The animals trotted back up the stairs to join the humans where they would stay the rest of the night. If no one wanted to leave before, they truly did not want to leave now. The presence of the Holy Spirit

131

filled the room, and everyone soon forgot about stuffy air and a long-winded preacher. The people wanted him to never stop. So he didn't. Paul preached all the way until daylight, and then decided to walk twenty miles to their next destination. Alone.

Paul had had a sense of foreboding ever since the plot against his life in Cenchreae near Corinth. At every stop along the way until they reached Troas, the Christian leaders in Athens, Berea, Thessalonica, and Philippi had expressed the same feeling of warning. Jerusalem would not end well. They all feared for his safety.

After Eutychus's fall and death experience, Paul felt his own mortality. What if he fell to his death with a push off a ship or from a high wall in Jerusalem and no one was there to bring him back to life? What if his ministry was cut short? What if the Enemy's plans finally prevailed and he never reached Rome? Should he venture on to Jerusalem after all? Or should he send the men on to Jerusalem with the collection while he boarded another ship bound for Rome? Was he being stubborn and not heeding the warnings the Lord was giving his fellow believers? Paul decided a full day of walking twenty miles would help him think, pray, and work through each and every question. By the time he reached Assos, he would also reach a decision about his future. And that future would immediately lead either directly to Jerusalem or Rome.

☧

Luke gripped the railing of the ship in the harbor of Assos, scanning the docks and streets of the bustling port. He raised his gaze up to the great block of granite overlooking the city for any sign of Paul. The sun was dropping into the sea, but the light of the sun's rays shone off the rock of Assos like a large white curtain on the hillside.

"I should have gone with him," Luke fumed, pacing back and forth on the deck of the ship. "Not only has there been one attempt on his life at the outset of this journey, he was up all last night and then *insisted* on walking twenty miles today while we sailed ahead!" Luke pulled his curly dark hair behind him, tying it out of his face as he grumbled at himself.

Timothy joined Luke at the railing. "He's stubborn, I'll give him that. He is determined to reach Jerusalem, regardless of what everyone has told him. I think he just needed time to think things through and to make sure he is making the right move. He's still human, after all."

132

"Exactly," Luke emphasized, pointing a finger at Timothy. "And as his friend and physician, I will feel responsible if something happens to him today."

Timothy crossed his arms and grinned. There in the distance against the gleaming white backdrop of the granite rock, he detected a tiny black dog running along the edge of the cliff face. Then he saw a black cat. Then he saw Paul. "I think you can stop worrying now, good Doctor. There's your stubborn patient now." Timothy lifted his hand to point to them.

Luke snapped his head in that direction, and his stubborn wisp of hair fell down his cheek. "Finally. Now he can get some rest." Luke let go a deep breath. "And so can I."

When Paul reached the dock and boarded their ship, his face looked tired, but at peace. Luke and Timothy knew immediately. His decision was made.

☧

Liz, Max, and Nigel stood in the prow of the ship as it sliced through the emerald green waters of the Aegean Sea. Liz loved to stand at the very tip of the ship, holding her paws up behind her like the wings of her favorite statue, Winged Victory of Samothrace. The northern summer wind always kicked up in the early morning hours and died away by late afternoon until it reached a dead calm by sunset. The ship traveled through several ports, anchoring each night when the wind blew itself out. Today they neared the port of Miletus where they would remain for a few days while the captain resupplied the ship.

"What a splendid nautical tour of ports this little cruise has been, seeing where some of the world's greatest minds were born!" Nigel exclaimed, breathing in the salt air and closing his eyes. "Kios, the birthplace of Homer. Samos, the birthplace of Pythagoras. Brilliant minds, simply brilliant!"

"Pythagoras?" Max asked. "Who's he?"

Nigel opened his eyes in shock. "Why, the founder of *math*, old boy! Surely you jest!" The little mouse chuckled. "Who doesn't know Pythagoras?"

Max sat there emotionless, just staring at the mouse. "Me an' math don't always see eye ta eye."

"Apparently neither do you and grammar," Nigel indignantly muttered under his breath.

"Well, I do hope the men of Ephesus will see eye to eye with Paul," Liz interjected. "I heard Paul say he wants the leaders to come meet him here at Miletus. Someone will have to jump on a horse and race thirty miles to Ephesus to bring the leaders back here to see Paul before the ship sets sail again."

"Why didn't we jest stop over in Ephesus?" Max wanted to know.

"Paul is resolute in his destination, and wishes to waste no time. A stop in Ephesus could end up taking weeks," Liz answered. She sighed. "He wishes to give the Ephesian elders his 'swan song' here."

Max wrinkled his forehead and looked at Liz and then to Nigel. Nigel planted his palm in his face and shook his head before looking up to answer the confused dog. "In his brilliant work, 'The Swan Mistaken for a Goose,' Aesop relayed the Greek belief that a swan will not sing until it is about to die. Ergo, *swan song* has become a metaphor meaning 'a final gesture, effort, or performance given just before death.'" Nigel's eyes widened. "Before his death! Liz, my dear, what is Paul thinking?"

Liz didn't answer as her eyes were affixed on the two massive stone lions that guarded the harbor entrance to Miletus. As the ship glided past them, the lion looked right at her and nodded. "I do not know, but Gillamon is here, so Paul must be right where he is supposed to be."

"I am sure you know how I have lived among you ever since I first set foot in Asia. You know how I served the Lord most humbly and what tears I have shed over the trials that have come to me through the plots of the Jews," Paul preached in a resounding voice choked off suddenly with emotion. He fought back the tears. "You know I have never shrunk from telling you anything that was for your good, nor from teaching you in public or in your own homes. On the contrary I have most emphatically urged upon both Jews and Greeks repentance toward God and faith in our Lord Jesus. And now here I am, compelled by the Spirit to go to Jerusalem. I do not know what may happen to me there, except that the Holy Spirit warns me that imprisonment and persecution await me in every city I visit. But, frankly, I do not consider my own life valuable to me so long as I can finish my course and complete the ministry the Lord Jesus has given me in declaring the good news of the grace of God. Now I know well enough that not one of you among whom I have moved as I preached the kingdom of God will ever see my face again."

The Ephesian elders looked at one another as a collective gasp rippled through the small group assembled on the grassy hillside above the harbor. Their hearts were heavy to hear Paul speak this way. Max, Liz, and Nigel sat next to Luke, who held his journal to capture every word Paul was saying. He maintained a frown as he wrote.

"The doctor is concerned," Nigel whispered.

"As well he should be," Liz answered. "We are pressing on to Jerusalem."

"That is why I must tell you solemnly today that my conscience is clear as far as any of you is concerned, for I have never shrunk from declaring to you the complete will of God. Now be on your guard for yourselves and for every flock of which the Holy Spirit has made you guardians—you are to be shepherds to the Church of God, which he won at the cost of his own blood. I know that after my departure savage wolves will come in among you without mercy for the flock. Yes, and even among you men will arise speaking perversions of the truth, trying to draw away the disciples and make them followers of themselves. This is why I tell you to keep on the alert, remembering that for three years I never failed night and day to warn every one of you, even with tears in my eyes. Now I commend you to the Lord and to the message of his grace which can build you up and give you your place among all those who are consecrated to God. I have never coveted anybody's gold or silver or clothing. You know well enough that these hands of mine have provided for my own needs and for those of my companions. In everything I have shown you that by such hard work, we must help the weak and must remember the words of the Lord Jesus when he said, 'To give is happier than to receive.'"

"He has spoken fearlessly, lived independently, and faced the future gallantly," Nigel said. "Paul is by far greater than Homer, Pythagoras, or Aesop could ever have hoped to be in this stellar farewell address."

"If that's wha' a swan sounds like when it sings, it makes some beautiful music," Max added.

Liz wiped the tears from her eyes as she watched Luke put aside his

135

pen and kneel down with Paul and the others to pray. They were all in tears and threw their arms around Paul's neck before walking with him back down to the ship. The entire group of men wanted to spend up to the last second with Paul, waving and clinging to each other as the ship raised its sails.

"What saddened them most of all was Paul saying they would never see his face again," Liz observed as they once again glided out of the harbor and past the massive stone lions.

"No turning back from here on out," came Gillamon's voice from one of the lions. "Into the lion's mouth you go."

136

PART TWO

INTO THE LION'S MOUTH

16

ON TO JERUSALEM

MAY AD 57

The sailors slowly lowered the sails of the ship while the captain ordered their final turn into the port of Caesarea. Max, Liz, and Nigel sat on the bow of the ship as it sliced through the aquamarine waters, eyeing the docks where long ago Paul had boarded a ship to return to Tarsus and await further instructions from the Jerusalem church. Memories crashed into their minds at seeing this place where journeys ended as well as began. The massive white stone wall that encircled the grand harbor held a wide promenade where sailors and passengers walked along, loading and unloading cargo from the numerous Roman ships tied to the docks. It was here on these docks Max and Liz had stowed away on Paul's ship to follow him to Tarsus. And it was here on these docks Paul had a chance encounter with two Roman boys playing with a red marble: Julius and Theophilus, sons of the Roman Centurion Armandus Antonius.

Along the harbor wall rose enormous statues, a lighthouse, and two large towers guarding the entrance to the harbor. The animals looked up at the massive statue of Caesar Augustus, welcoming them to this, the largest seaport in the Mediterranean, which bore his name—Caesarea. Liz looked for any sign of Gillamon in this statue, but Caesar remained unmoved with his outstretched arm. Gillamon was not there this time.

Rising from the pier was a broad flight of steps leading to the Temple of Augustus, another reminder of the city's namesake. Herod the Great had spared no expense at making this Roman capital city of the Judean

Province the most elaborate, beautiful city on the coast, second only to Jerusalem in its grandeur. Two aqueducts brought water into the city of Caesarea from the springs below Mount Carmel ten miles away. The repeating arch structure filled the city with fresh water, and served to remind residents and visitors of the architectural marvels provided by awesome Roman engineering. Caesarea enjoyed the typical constructions of a Roman city, including entertainment facilities—a theater, amphitheater, and hippodrome, where chariot races thrilled the crowds. Pink columns of imported Aswan Egyptian granite lined the entrance to the amphitheater, giving the four thousand spectators an exquisite view of contrasting colors, with the crystal blue sea behind them.

Dotted all along the harbor were houses made of white stone. There were paved streets lined with hundreds of columns. But the grandest house of all was the Procurator's Palace, built by Herod on a natural promontory that jutted out into the sea. Luxury abounded throughout this palace of elaborately tiled floors depicting scenes of animals and fish. A freshwater swimming pool sat at the end of the palace so bathers could enjoy fresh water while they gazed into the salty blue waters of the Mediterranean.

Several Roman governors had occupied this palace, including Pontius Pilate. He lived here when he traveled to Jerusalem for that fateful Passover when he washed his hands of Jesus' fate. He had returned from Jerusalem to this seaside palace, greatly disturbed and seeking solace. Pilate roamed the hallways lined with white gauzy curtains blowing in the sea breeze, reliving every bit of his decision-making process in the matter of that mysterious "criminal." He hoped for relief from the haunting events surrounding the death of Jesus of Nazareth, but not even the beauty of this place could give him peace. Despite the fact that he washed his hands in front of those who accused Jesus, declaring that Jesus' blood was on their hands, all he saw when he gazed at his own hands was the blood of the scourged and crucified Nazarene.

Pilate was replaced by other Roman governors here in Caesarea as time went on. The current governor was a tough ruler by the name of Antonius Felix. His reputation for greed was well known. He was born a slave but had risen to power with the help of his freedman brother named Pallas, who had been a favorite ally of Emperor Claudius. Felix had zero tolerance for political unrest and brutally suppressed any signs of Jewish revolt. He had even arranged for an ex-priest named Jonathan to be murdered right in the Temple of Jerusalem. Felix's brutality only fanned the flames of Jewish pride and anti-Gentile sentiments among his Jewish subjects, including Jewish Christians who still clung to their Jewish heritage.

"Well, we done sailed fr-r-rom Tyre ta Ptolemais an' now ta Caesarea," Max noted as the sailors made ready to dock the ship. "I wonder if Paul's friends will keep warnin' him here like they did at those other places. Did ye hear we be stayin' with Philip?"

"Yes, and I am thrilled to see Philip again!" Nigel cheered. "I shall never forget the day I saw him help that Ethiopian eunuch understand the scroll of Isaiah as he rode along in his colorful chariot. Philip was whisked away after he baptized the jolly fellow, leaving the new believer quite puzzled. But Philip's work spread all the way into Africa as a result of that encounter. Simply brilliant chap, that Philip!"

"*Oui,* he was a perfect choice for one of the seven to serve when the church first began in Jerusalem. So much has happened since then," Liz marveled, shaking her head. "As Saul, Paul *ensured* the death of Stephen, another one of the seven. Now Philip will *welcome* Paul into his home—the man who murdered his good friend. *C'est incredible!*"

"I understand that Philip now has four unmarried daughters, all of whom have the gift of prophecy," Nigel noted. "I wonder if they'll prophesy over Paul. I daresay we are in for many incredible things if they do."

Luke sat with his back against the wall and Liz on his lap, gently stroking her as he watched Philip and Paul enjoying a lively conversation. They discussed the amazing works the Lord had done, not only in their individual lives, but throughout the world as the Good News took hold. Jesus had given them the Great Commission to take his message of hope throughout the lost world, and they celebrated his faithfulness as they obeyed that call. Philip shared about Pentecost and the early days of the church's beginning, including how Saul's (Paul's) persecution drove him to deliver the Good News to Samaria, and then to the Ethiopian eunuch. Paul's eyes filled with tears to see how God had used even his wicked behavior for the good of spreading the gospel. Luke listened and mentally took notes of all he heard.

But it was all Luke could do to hold his peace. He and the other men who had accompanied Paul on this voyage to Jerusalem had heard the repeated warnings that Paul should not continue on to the Holy City. But those warnings fell on deaf ears, for Paul would not listen. Like Jesus, his face was set as flint as they neared Jerusalem. Luke wondered if Paul would suffer the same fate, not of crucifixion since he was a Roman citizen, but some other form of death. But Paul was insistent. He wanted to personally deliver the collection to the church in Jerusalem. He still carried the memory of knowing he had persecuted the church so many years ago and wanted to make amends in a tangible way. But his motives primarily included a desire to unify the Jewish and Gentile believers, and this collection was a key to building that bridge of unity.

Luke looked over at Philip's four daughters, who were busy serving the group around the dinner table. They had the gift of prophecy, but had remained silent about Paul's future ever since Paul and the group had arrived here a few days earlier. "Why won't they say anything?" Luke muttered softly under his breath.

142

Liz heard him and nodded as she thought, *I wonder the same thing, cher Docteur.*

Suddenly the group turned to see a new guest arrive. Philip and Paul both stood as the famous prophet Agabus joined them.

"Agabus! Welcome, my friend," Philip greeted him.

But the prophet's gaze was on Paul alone. He nodded at Philip but walked right over to Paul. He was a stout man with large brown eyes under bushy gray eyebrows. Agabus locked eyes with Paul and reached down to loosen the tasseled cord tied around Paul's waist. Paul held up his hands and didn't interfere with the prophet as he sat on the floor. Agabus proceeded to take Paul's belt and tied his own hands and feet together. He said, "This is what the Holy Spirit says: The Jews in Jerusalem are going to tie up the man who owns this belt just like this and hand him over to godless unbelievers."

Luke set Liz on the floor and jumped to his feet, unable to remain silent. "You see, Paul? It is clear now with this word from Agabus. Please stop being so stubborn! You must not go to Jerusalem!" Tears filled his eyes and he clenched his jaw.

Timothy and the others murmured their agreement, also swept up with emotion. "Luke's right. Listen to what Agabus just said, Paul. You will be captured by the Jews! Let us take the collection while you stay here with Philip. Then we'll rejoin you and make passage to Rome on one of the ships here in Caesarea."

Philip's daughters chimed in, echoing what Agabus had predicted. And Philip placed his hand on Paul's arm with caution. "Listen to them, Paul. Please don't feel as if you must go in order to right some wrong by throwing away your own life. The collection will be delivered as promised. Stay here with us."

Paul looked into the faces of everyone now encircling him and shook his head sadly. Tears welled up in his eyes and he gripped the front of his garment. "Why all this hysteria? Why do you insist on making a scene and making it even harder for me? You're looking at this backward." He paused and looked Philip in the eye. "The issue in Jerusalem is not what they do to me, whether arrest or murder, but what the Master Jesus does through my obedience. Can't you see that?"

"Paul's not budgin'," Max grumbled. "It makes ye wonder if he's ignorin' words sent from the Maker thr-r-rough Paul's friends."

"Agabus has given a *prediction,* not a warning, as have the others," Nigel answered seriously, clasping his paws behind his back. "So while this new word is rather grave, Paul has known since the road to Assos that Jesus is calling him to Jerusalem. Perhaps the Maker is using these friends to test his resolve, or even to prepare him for what lies ahead."

Liz sighed. "He knows his friends are saying these things out of love for him, but Paul knows he must answer to the One whose higher love he must follow."

Luke put his hands on his hips and cast his gaze to the floor. He slowly shook his head but finally looked up. "Very well, Paul." He let go a long sigh. "It's in God's hands now." He closed his eyes while the others standing about finally gave in and agreed to go with Paul. "The Lord's will be done."

"On to Jerusalem," Nigel said, looking at Max and Liz. They each remembered the last time they approached Jerusalem like this, knowing full well the warnings of the Jews that would come against Jesus. Now they would come against Paul.

☧

"I cannot help but feel a sense of *déjà vu,*" Liz lamented as they entered the gates of Jerusalem.

"Steady, Lass," Max comforted her, nudging her gently as they walked along the bustling streets packed with people who were there to celebrate Pentecost. But Max also swallowed a lump in his throat. Too many difficult memories of the traumatic experience with Jesus lingered in these streets. He had been forbidden to protect Jesus, and now wondered if he would be forbidden to protect Paul. He tried to think happier thoughts. "I wonder if I'll get ta see me lass Kate here with John."

"Oh, I do hope so, *mon ami!*" Liz exclaimed. "I would love to see our dear Kate, too."

The group had traveled the sixty-plus miles from Caesarea, with pack mules carrying the heavy money bags of the collection for the church. Some of the disciples from Caesarea came with them and made arrangements for them to stay in the home of Mnason. A native of Cyprus, he had been among the earliest disciples, and his background made him sympathetic to the ex-pagan Christians who were in Paul's party from Greece and Asia. He was the perfect host for this group, and he eagerly opened his home to them.

144

"Welcome, everyone!" Mnason greeted them with outstretched hands. "Please make yourselves at home here. You are my brothers, and my home is yours."

"You are most gracious, my friend," Paul replied, clasping forearms with Mnason. "Thank you for having no barriers here for my friends. They are eager to see the sights of Jerusalem."

Mnason raised his eyebrows. "Ah, of course, of course! They have never seen the Holy City? Well, you must show them everything, Paul! And you must, of course, show them where our Lord was crucified."

Luke set down his pack and took out his journal, placing it under his arm while he took out his pen. "Yes, please, Paul. I wish to see the Place of the Skull."

Tears welled up in Paul's eyes to think of visiting that holy ground. "We will, Luke, right away. Once everyone has put away their things, we'll go out."

"We're ready," Timothy announced, the other men gathered around him. The young men who had never been to Jerusalem were eager to see the city, for it was here Jesus had taught, had died, and had been resurrected. Jerusalem was the epicenter of their faith, and they yearned to see where it all began.

Max trotted after them as they headed out the door. *"I'm not missin' this."*

"I am coming, too!" Liz exclaimed.

"Tally ho!" Nigel exulted, falling in line behind them.

☧

Paul led the group of men in the footsteps of Jesus, taking them to the Garden of Gethsemane, through the Kidron Valley, through the lower city to the upper city where Jesus was taken to trial in the Praetorium, and outside the city walls to the place of the Skull. At each place they prayed, and rejoiced over all Jesus had done at each place. But when they reached Golgotha, they dropped to their knees and wept.

Paul finally led them to the Temple area to show them the jewel of the Jewish heritage, but explained that only Timothy was allowed to go beyond the Temple's Court of the Gentiles. The others could not step past the wall of partition. To do so could mean death.

"How could death come ta Gentiles jest for bein' in the Temple?" Max protested after hearing Paul discuss the barrier.

"When King Herod rebuilt the Temple he enclosed the outer court with colonnades," Nigel explained, pointing to the area. "Because Gentiles were considered unworthy to enter the main Temple area lest they defile it, a large open courtyard known as the 'Court of the Gentiles' was created to separate them. Gentiles are permitted to enter this area but are forbidden to go any farther than the outer court."

Liz walked up to a large stone block sign and pointed. "Gentiles are excluded from entering any of the inner courts and must read this warning:

NO FOREIGNER
IS TO GO BEYOND THE BALUSTRADE
AND THE PLAZA OF THE TEMPLE ZONE.
WHOEVER IS CAUGHT DOING SO
WILL HAVE HIMSELF TO BLAME
FOR HIS DEATH
WHICH WILL FOLLOW.

Liz shook her head. "The penalty for passing this barrier is death. The Romans allow the Jewish authorities to carry out the death penalty for this offense, even if the offender is a Roman citizen."

145

"And this angered Jesus, who saw how the Gentiles were kept from reaching the heart of God," came a voice from behind them. There stood a teenage Jewish boy with striking blue eyes.

"Clarie?" Liz whispered hopefully.

"It's me. Welcome to Jerusalem," the boy greeted them with a wink. "Max, I wanted you to know that Kate and John are not here at the moment. They are visiting family in Nazareth. I'm sorry you will miss her, but you'll get to see her very soon."

Max frowned and nodded. "Aye. Thanks for tellin' me, Lass."

"My dear, we have all been on edge, wondering what is to become of Paul," Nigel offered. "He has ignored repeated warnings to stay away from Jerusalem."

"*Oui*, and the prophet Agabus even predicted that Paul would be captured by the Jews and handed over to the Romans," Liz added.

"Jesus knew that the only way to remove this barrier for the Gentiles was to give up his own life." The boy walked up to the stone barrier sign and ran his fingers along the words. "When the Maker tore the veil in the Temple from top to bottom, it meant no one would ever be kept from reaching him again. Unfortunately, that meaning was lost on the Jews. This very sign will be Paul's undoing here in Jerusalem."

"Wha' are we supposed ta do then, Lass?" Max implored. "Can we stop somethin' fr-r-rom happenin'?"

"Just as Jesus willingly gave himself up to the Jews when a snap of his fingers could have turned them into dust, so too must Paul allow himself to be given up to the Jews," Clarie explained. "It's the only way to get Paul in front of the most powerful man in the world."

Liz and Nigel stared at one another with open mouths before exclaiming at the same time, "The Emperor?"

"Paul has wanted to go to Rome, and I've told you all along you would indeed make it to the capital of the world," Clarie replied, nodding. "That journey begins right here."

"But why does it have to be this way? Why couldn't Paul just go directly to Rome and avoid the trouble with the Jews?" Liz wanted to know.

"You know the Maker never wastes anything," Clarie answered with a big grin. "He has multiple connecting points along every road he asks you to travel. The journey is always the destination."

146

"Aye, but while we're walkin' it, can we DO anythin' ta help Paul?" Max wondered.

Clarie squatted and got down in Max's large, square face. "You, my friend, are going to help arrange a family reunion for Paul." She patted him on the head and stood to leave. "I'll tell you more soon. Keep a lookout for me and be ready to act fast." With that the boy blended into the sea of people walking along the street and was lost to them.

"A family r-r-reunion?" Max wondered.

Liz furrowed her brow. "But his family long ago rejected him. What can this mean?"

"The plot thickens!" Nigel exclaimed. "Let's catch up with Paul, and keep an eye out."

☧

As they walked along the outer wall, Paul was pointing out various sights to the young men with him. Trophimus was especially eager to hear what Paul had to say and got right next to him.

147

Simeon and Joash, the Jewish leaders from the synagogue in Ephesus, had come to Jerusalem for the festival and were walking in the same area when they spotted Paul.

"Look who is here!" Simeon exclaimed, hitting Joash in the chest with the back of his hand. "It's that blaspheming Paul who gave us such grief in Ephesus." He spat on the ground.

"And look who he dares to bring to the Temple," Joash added. "Gentiles!"

The two men looked at one another at first in alarm and disgust, but slowly that feeling turned to one of expectant opportunity.

"We weren't able to see to Paul's end in Ephesus, but perhaps he'll make it easy for us here in Jerusalem," Simeon suggested with a sinister smile.

Joash looked at Paul as he engaged the young men around him. "By all means, Paul. Bring the Gentiles to the Temple. Bring them all the way in. Be our guest."

No Mean City

Up and at 'em, old boy!" Nigel enthused, swatting Max on the nose to awaken him.

Max quickly came awake and stared down his nose at Nigel, standing there excitedly with his gold-rimmed glasses and a happy grin. "Why? Where we goin'?"

"To see *James,* of course," Nigel replied. "Jesus' brother! Time for Paul and his delegates from all the churches to deliver the collection and give their reports to the elders of the Jerusalem church. It shall be a splendid occasion!"

Max yawned and stretched. "Aye, Lad. Okay, I be up."

"Bonjour, Max," Liz greeted him happily. "A wonderful day is ahead of us, no?"

Max yawned again and shook out his fur from head to toe. "Aye. So I've heard."

"Right, the humans are filing out now. Let's make haste!" Nigel urged, running after them.

"He jest can't help hisself, can he?" Max asked Liz.

Liz giggled. "Not when it comes to such grand assemblies and reunions."

As Liz and Max followed Nigel and the humans out the door, Max's thoughts returned to what Clarie had told him yesterday. *A family r-r-re-union for Paul. Wha' could that mean?*

James and Paul heartily greeted each other, embracing and then gripping one another's forearms, so happy to be reunited after so long. The first order of business was formal introductions. James introduced the seventy elders from the Jerusalem church, and Paul presented Luke and his team of church delegates: Gaius, Timothy, Sopater, Aristarchus, Secundus, Tychicus, and Trophimus. As Paul called each of their names, each man stepped up carrying a money bag of donations to present to the elders, while Paul gave details of how God had moved in each ministry to the Gentiles.

Max, Liz, and Nigel stayed out of the way in the inner courtyard of this spacious home where the church leaders congregated. Liz studied the faces of the elders as each of Paul's team presented his gift. While they nodded, smiled, and gave thanks to God, something was missing in their response.

"They do not seem overly enthusiastic or warm toward these Gentiles," Liz noticed, her tail slapping the cool tile floor while she frowned. "Paul is implying that the Jerusalem church can use this money to help the sick and poor as well as send out other missionaries like these men to spread the gospel."

149

"Aye, his idea of one flock under one Shepherd seems ta not be hittin' home with these Jewish lads," Max echoed.

"They *are* giving appropriate praise to the Maker," Nigel added with reservation. "But not as I would have hoped." Nigel propped up his cheeks with his paws as he leaned his elbows on the railing where they sat.

"So much for *this* happy r-r-reunion." Max furrowed his brow.

"And just look at what's been happening here—thousands upon thousands of God-fearing Jews have become believers in Jesus!" James offered before one of the elders interrupted him.

The elder turned to look at Paul. "But there's also a problem because they are more zealous than ever in observing the laws of Moses. They've been told that you advise believing Jews who live surrounded by unbelieving outsiders to go light on Moses, telling them they don't need to circumcise their sons or keep up the old traditions. This isn't sitting at all well with the Jews."

"We're worried about what will happen when they discover you're in town," another elder offered. "There's bound to be trouble."

Another elder stepped up and put out his hands. "So here is what we want you to do. There are four men from our company who have taken a vow involving ritual purification, but have no money to pay the expenses. Join these men in their vows and pay their expenses. Then it will become obvious to everyone that there is nothing to the rumors going around about you, and that you are, in fact, scrupulous in your reverence for the laws of Moses."

James put his hand on Paul's arm. "In asking you to do this, we're not going back on our agreement regarding non-Jews who have become believers. We continue to hold fast to what we wrote in that letter."

"The letter that *I* helped them write to clear up all this Gentiles-not-needing-to-become-Jews-first business!" Nigel fumed. "This is intolerable! How can these elders ask Paul to play this 'keeping up appearances' game?"

"Steady, Nigel," Liz calmed him, with her paw on his shoulder. She hated to see Nigel so disappointed. But as she studied Paul's face, she saw how disappointed the apostle was. "Paul's heart could not be more crushed. He knows the elders wish him to show the Jewish believers that he keeps the law, when in fact he no longer does. While he *honors* the Jewish law and tradition, he knows he has been liberated from those practices."

"Precisely! Blast it all, can't they let him be himself and not go through this exercise in futility?" Nigel continued to rant.

Paul sighed and looked into the faces of the elders, pausing before he replied. "Very well. I will put myself under the Law to win them, although I know I am not subject to it."

"He's bein' a Jew ta the Jews," Max muttered. "Such be his love for his people."

James nodded and gave a weak smile. "Thank you, Paul. You can join the four men in the Temple courts tomorrow. Please pay for their sacrifices, and join their fast for the last two days of their ritual. From there you can depart Jerusalem and be on your way to Rome."

Paul looked at James with sad eyes. Both of them knew that the elders were asking a lot of him. They were asking him to go through the motions of a ritual he knew was unnecessary for himself. But he was willing to do it if it would win more for Christ. He was willing to be a Jew to reach Jews. But Paul knew that for those two days, he would be just as vulnerable as when he faced the lion in the arena.

✗

Max, Liz, and Nigel kept their distance but stayed in the Temple's outer court area to keep an eye on Paul. He had left Mnason's home in order to live here in the Temple with the four Jewish men, until their required ritual was complete. Paul's mind kept replaying the prophetic warnings of what would happen to him here, and he stayed on the alert as well.

Jerusalem's crowd of pilgrims kept the city buzzing with activity and nationalistic Jewish pride. The Roman soldiers roamed the rooftops of the Antonia Fortress, keeping an eye on things in the Temple below. Jewish festivals were frequently marked by unrest, and this powder keg of people was getting ready to explode. But the Romans weren't the only ones keeping watch.

Simeon and Joash, the Jewish leaders from Ephesus, had kept an eye out for Paul ever since they had spotted him showing the men the sights of the city the day he arrived. But with the thousands upon thousands of similarly dressed men milling about, it was like looking for a needle in a haystack. They also were looking for him in the Court of the Gentiles, waiting to catch him crossing the barrier with his Gentile friends.

"He's just not here," Joash lamented as he and Simeon milled about the courtyard. "Perhaps he knows he's being watched."

"Agreed. Let's go to the Inner Court," Simeon suggested. "No use wasting any more time out here with these pagans."

As the two Jewish leaders crossed the barrier warning sign forbidding Gentiles to enter the area, Joash immediately spotted Paul. "Look!" he exclaimed, pointing a finger in Paul's direction. "He's with four men here in the Inner Court! They must be the same men. Doesn't one of them look like the Ephesian Trophimus?"

"Now's our chance. MOVE!" Simeon exclaimed, pulling up his robes and rushing over to Paul.

"Men of Israel, help! This is the man who is teaching everybody everywhere to despise our people, our Law, and this place. Why, he has even brought Greeks into the Temple, and he has defiled this holy place!"

"Wha's happenin'?!" Max shouted, immediately getting to his feet. "Those Gentile lads never set foot past the bar-r-rier!"

"The prophecy is unfolding," Liz answered, her heart racing. A mob gathered around Paul.

"A convenient case of mistaken identity," Nigel added. "Those Jewish leaders must have seen Paul with Trophimus and the others earlier in the week and naturally assumed they were the same men with him now here in the Inner Court."

"Quickly, Max, come with me," came Clarie's voice behind him. "Liz and Nigel, you follow the crowd to the fortress."

"Understood," Nigel answered as Max trotted off with Clarie, and he and Liz took off after the crowd.

The mob seized Paul and dragged him outside the Temple. A Temple guard slammed the doors behind him. There would be no bloodshed to defile the Temple grounds, but outside of the gate, Paul was fair game. The mob immediately began to pummel Paul, hitting him with their fists and dragging him through the streets. People were screaming as their zealous pride and anti-Gentile hatred boiled over. Soon Paul's lip was bleeding, and his face, arms, and legs were covered with red marks that would quickly bruise. Someone was twisting his arm behind his back as he cried out in pain, falling onto the cold stone street.

A Roman guard immediately spotted the trouble and signaled the alarm. Suddenly the sound of clanking metal filled the air as two hundred Roman soldiers rushed across the roof of the fortress and down the two flights of stairs on the northern and western sides of the Temple. The garrison commander, Claudius Lysias, took charge of the situation and the people immediately backed off when they saw him stomping toward them with his blood-red cape billowing behind him. He had a thousand legionnaires at his command. In the last riot, thousands of resisting Jews were trampled to death in the streets.

"Double-chained irons on this man!" Lysias ordered when he identified Paul as the source of the riot. Containment first, answers next. He placed a hand on his hip and pointed at Paul as he addressed the crowd. The sun gleamed off his silver helmet cropped with red plumage. "Who is this man and what has he done to cause this uprising?"

The crowd answered back as if in one garbled, chaotic voice. Lysias quickly grew irritated with this unruly crowd and knew he would not get anywhere by questioning them like this. He called over one of his centurions. "Get this man to the fortress. We'll question him there and get to the bottom of this. I think he's that Egyptian rebel who caused that other riot three years ago."

152

As Lysias turned to lead the Roman contingent back up the stairs to the fortress with Paul in custody, the crowd exploded when they realized they had lost their victim. "KILL HIM! KILL HIM!" the people shouted. They pressed against the Roman soldiers, screaming as the legionnaires pushed back with spears and shields. When they reached the first few steps of the tall staircase leading up to the fortress, the soldiers realized that the force of the crowd was growing too violent. They suddenly picked Paul up and carried him on their shoulders to protect him from the hysterical people. Together they struggled to reach the top of the stairs, where they finally set Paul back on his feet.

As Paul was about to be taken inside, he said to the commander, "May I have a word with you?"

Lysias was startled to hear Paul. Although panting and out of breath, he spoke perfect Greek to the Roman soldier. "Do you know Greek? Aren't you the Egyptian who led a rebellion some time ago and took four thousand members of the Assassins out into the desert?"

"No," Paul replied, "I am a Jew and a citizen of Tarsus in Cilicia, which is no mean city. Please, let me talk to these people."

Now he quotes Euripides? Lysias thought to himself at Paul's description of Tarsus. *He must be a scholar, for even after a severe beating he retains such wit.* The Roman commander cocked his head to the side and studied Paul's bleeding lip and swollen eye, surprised to hear such an articulate Greek-speaking Jew. His curiosity was aroused. "Very well." He held his hand out for Paul to address the crowd.

Paul stood at the top of the stairs and raised his bruised, manacled hand for the people to be quiet. Amazingly, a deep silence enveloped the crowd. "Brothers and esteemed fathers," Paul said, "listen to me as I offer my defense."

Liz and Nigel darted in and out among the legs of the people to get close to Paul. "He's speaking in Aramaic," Nigel realized. "He's picked the language of the Jewish people and non-Greek speakers who are here from much of the Roman world. However I doubt his Roman guards will understand a word he says."

"Stephen began with these same words at the opening of his defense! And look where he is standing!" Liz exclaimed. "In the identical spot where Pilate condemned Jesus. *Déjà vu.*"

Paul looked out over the crowd even as his swollen left eye began to

153

shut. "I am a Jew, born in Tarsus, a city in Cilicia, and I was brought up and educated here in Jerusalem under Gamaliel. As his student, I was carefully trained in our Jewish laws and customs. I became very zealous to honor God in everything I did, just like all of you today." He paused to catch his breath as he held his hand out to the crowd. "And I persecuted the followers of the Way, hounding some to death, arresting both men and women and throwing them in prison. The high priest and the whole council of elders can testify that this is so. For I received letters from them to give to our Jewish brothers in Damascus, authorizing me to bring the followers of the Way from there to Jerusalem, in chains, to be punished." He shook the chains attached to his own wrists as he said this.

Liz and Nigel looked at one another, remembering that incredible day on the road to Damascus. It was surreal to see Paul himself bound by chains for some of the very same reasons he had accused Stephen and other followers of the Way.

"As I was on the road, approaching Damascus about noon, a very bright light from heaven suddenly shone down around me. I fell to the ground and heard a voice saying to me, 'Saul, Saul, why are you persecuting me?' 'Who are you, lord?' I asked. And the voice replied, 'I am Jesus the Nazarene, the one you are persecuting.'" Paul paused to see the response of the people to his mysterious revelation.

"The people with me saw the light but didn't understand the voice speaking to me. I asked, 'What should I do, Lord?' And the Lord told me, 'Get up and go into Damascus, and there you will be told everything you are to do.' I was blinded by the intense light and had to be led by the hand to Damascus by my companions. A man named Ananias lived there. He was a godly man, deeply devoted to the law, and well regarded by all the Jews of Damascus. He came and stood beside me and said, 'Brother Saul, regain your sight.' And that very moment I could see him! Then he told me, 'The God of our ancestors has chosen you to know his will and to see the Righteous One and hear him speak. For you are to be his witness, telling everyone what you have seen and heard. What are you waiting for? Get up and be baptized. Have your sins washed away by calling on the name of the Lord.'"

"Brilliant of Paul to tell them about Ananias. He is well respected by the Jews," Nigel noted.

"After I returned to Jerusalem, I was praying in the Temple and fell into a trance. I saw a vision of Jesus saying to me, 'Hurry! Leave Jerusalem, for the people here won't accept your testimony about me.' 'But Lord,' I argued, 'they certainly know that in every synagogue I imprisoned and beat those who believed in you. And I was in complete agreement when your witness Stephen was killed. I stood by and kept the coats they took off when they stoned him.' But the Lord said to me, 'Go, for I will send you far away to the Gentiles!'"

Liz gasped. "Oh dear, he's said the one word that will set this crowd on fire—Gentiles."

Sure enough, the crowd listened until Paul said that word and then stormed the stairway. "Kill him, and rid the earth of such a man! He is not fit to live!" they yelled, throwing off their coats and tossing handfuls of dust into the air.

Lysias, who did not speak Aramaic, had not understood a single word Paul said, and immediately ordered his centurion to seize Paul. "Take him to the dungeon, and interrogate him to find out what he said to make the crowd so furious. Leave a detachment out here until the people calm down and disperse. Keep me informed." With that the commander stormed off to his headquarters while Paul was taken below.

Liz and Nigel looked at one another in fear. "Paul has been beaten with rods three times and whipped by Jews five times, but he's never faced Roman interrogation! Men either die or are crippled for life from the Roman scourge. Remember what happened to Jesus!" Liz cried, frantic now, with tears filling her eyes. "Oh, Nigel, what do we do?"

"Steady, my dear," Nigel said with a comforting embrace. "I'll go follow them and report back to you here. For now, pray. Agabus the prophet's words have come true, but he did not say how this ends."

As Nigel ran off to enter the dark stairwell leading to the underground dungeon, he and Liz thought exactly the same thing. Never in Paul's life had he been closer to death than now, facing interrogation in the Roman torture chamber.

155

Narrow Escapes

Nigel had to let his eyes adjust for a moment after leaving the bright sunlight and entering a dark, narrow stairwell. Torches were placed along the wall of the curving staircase that led to the dungeon. At first all he heard was the crackle from the flames, but as he scurried down the steps he could hear the sound of clanking chains and moans. "Oh dear," the little mouse breathed out, picking up his pace.

Three soldiers attended to this interrogation detail. One soldier removed the chains around Paul's wrists, and the other stripped off his garments. Paul's skin was a mottled mess of bruises, bleeding cuts, and gashes. They made him stand while they clamped a bar to his ankles and tied ropes around his wrists. Then they threw the ropes over a beam that hung slightly forward from and above where Paul stood. Working with the speed of men who had done this numerous times before, they pulled Paul's arms up tight until he leaned forward with his body stretched taut. This standing position allowed the interrogator to get in Paul's face to force answers, while his stretched muscles would feel the most pain.

Paul heard the sound of the dreaded *flagellum,* or Roman scourge, hitting the stone floor behind him as the third soldier prepared to strike. This was no ordinary whip. Its leather straps contained pieces of glass, shards of bone, and jagged pieces of metal. It was designed to grip the skin on contact so the lictor brandishing it could pull down and inflict excruciating pain and damage. The scourge was used to force its victims to give up information, or as punishment before crucifixion, as was the case with Jesus. It often proved fatal, but at the very least left men deformed for life, or out of their minds from unspeakable pain.

Nigel gasped as he saw Paul being positioned for the scourging. "Please, dear Lord, save him!" he prayed under his breath. Suddenly he realized Paul had a way out. He was a Roman citizen! This treatment was illegal! Paul had once before not revealed that he was a Roman citizen in order to endure the beating along with Silas back in Philippi, but this scourging could end his ministry—if not his life—right here and now! Nigel climbed up the stone wall to reach a ledge that was eye level with Paul. He knew Paul would not likely hear him, much less hear anything but the squeaks of a mouse, but he shouted to him anyway. "Paul, Paul! Tell them you are a citizen of Rome! Tell them! You must get out of this so you can live!"

Metal-soled shoes echoed off the stone corridor as they reached this tortuous scene. The Roman centurion assigned by Lysias to oversee Paul's interrogation arrived to see if the prisoner was ready. Paul looked up and saw Nigel waving his paws hysterically, squeaking. *How did he get here?*

"Is the prisoner ready?" the centurion asked.

"He's ready, Sir," the two soldiers answered, stepping back so the lictor could inflict an introductory blow to Paul's back.

Just as the lictor pulled back his arm, Paul coolly asked the centurion, "Is it legal for you to whip a Roman citizen who hasn't even been tried?"

Immediately the lictor froze, and the leather cords dangled in the air next to him. The centurion lifted his eyebrows in shock, and the other two soldiers swallowed hard as they looked at one another in fear. "Wait here." The centurion quickly turned to go report this news to Lysias.

Nigel fell back on his heels, flooded with relief. "Whew, that was too close, old boy!"

Lysias sat at his desk, preparing to write the report about the incident with Paul in the Temple courts when the centurion reached him. He looked up and noticed the look of alarm on his subordinate's face. He motioned for the man to approach him. "Come."

"Sir, I have news about the prisoner," began the centurion, looking around him and lowering his voice so only his commander would hear. "Do you realize what you were about to do? This man is a Roman citizen!"

Lysias's eyes grew wide, and his chair scraped across the stone floor as he hurriedly got up to walk around his desk. "How did this happen?!"

He and the centurion made their way swiftly back to the dungeon where Paul remained, strung up and ready for scourging. Lysias noticed the scars all over Paul's body from previous whippings, which only added to his confusion. He walked right up to Paul's face and urgently asked him, "Tell me, *are* you a Roman citizen?"

"Yes, I am," Paul replied calmly.

Lysias exchanged quick glances with his centurion before continuing with Paul. "It cost me a good deal to get my citizenship."

"Ah," replied Paul, "but I was *born* a citizen."

Lysias felt the blood drain from his face as he barked orders to the soldiers on this detail. "Get this man out of these ropes immediately. Return his clothes, and take him to the detaining cell upstairs—and under light chain." Lysias turned to go to his quarters. He needed to collect his thoughts of what to do next.

"Yes, Sir!" the soldiers quickly answered, moving with lightning speed to release Paul from the iron bar and the ropes. The lictor set down the whip and fled the cell. They all knew if this Roman citizen pressed charges for such illegal treatment, they could be severely punished and even put to death themselves for having been part of this event. They helped Paul dress and darted down the corridor to get away as soon as possible while the centurion escorted Paul upstairs.

"I must let Liz know all is well," Nigel said happily to himself as he scurried back up the winding steps. "Thank you, Rome, for once again saving our Paul!"

☧

Zeeb, Jarib, and Saar, the Pharisees, and Nahshon, the Sadducee, sat huddled together in the Hall of Polished Stones while the members of the Sanhedrin poured into the assembly. These four elder members of the Sanhedrin had priority seating, given their seniority in this prestigious assembly. They had been present at many assemblies these past three decades, including the assemblies called to condemn Jesus of Nazareth and Stephen the apostle. Despite their age, they were ever eager to be in the center of the action. They turned to see the presiding officer of their august body, Ananias ben Nedebaeus, enter the hall.

Ananias had been high priest for more than ten years, and was likely one of the most corrupt men ever to hold the office. Five years earlier he was sent to Rome on suspicion of involvement in an outbreak of bloodshed with Jews and Samaritans, but was cleared of all charges and restored by Emperor Claudius. He seized tithes meant for the common priests to line his own pockets, and used his wealth, along with stealth assassinations, to maintain control. His pro-Roman reputation was widely known, which alienated him from the Jews, yet no one could touch him.

"What is this all about?" Jarib wanted to know, trying to hide the sneer on his face at seeing the repulsive high priest.

"All I know is that the military governor of Jerusalem, Claudius Lysias, exercised his right to call an emergency session of the Sanhedrin," Nahshon answered, leaning forward to cough.

Suddenly the doors opened and in walked Lysias, personally escorting Paul into the chamber. Lysias had removed his chains and held Paul's elbow as if to show the respect due a citizen of Rome.

"Saul of Tarsus," Zeeb spat. "So he's the one at the center of this meeting."

"You mean Paul the *Christian,*" Saar corrected him with a scowl.

Lysias walked Paul to the center of the room, where witnesses were placed to address the assembly. He nodded to Ananias, who had received Lysias's request to get to the bottom of the matter with this prisoner. Lysias needed information to explain the riot for his report. He left Paul standing there and walked out, closing the doors behind him, but remained just outside the door. He was not about to leave Paul alone, knowing full well the corruption that took place in that room.

Liz and Nigel were there hiding in an alcove above the assembly. "I wish Max and Clarie were here. Still nothing from either one of them?" Liz asked the mouse.

Nigel shook his head. "Nothing yet." He pointed to Paul. "Look where Paul is standing. On the exact spot where Stephen stood when he faced this assembly."

Liz couldn't take it all in. "And then Paul's place was seated alongside these seventy-one men." She scanned the crowd and spotted Zeeb, Saar, Jarib, and Nahshon. "Those scoundrels are still here, after all this time. First they accused Jesus, then Stephen, and now Paul. *Déjà vu.*"

"What do you have to say for yourself?" the clerk asked Paul, opening the proceedings.

159

Paul surveyed the members of the council with a steady gaze, and then said his piece: "Friends, I've lived with a clear conscience before God all my life, up to this very moment."

That set Chief Priest Ananias off. He motioned to his aides, and one of them jumped up to go slap Paul in the face.

"Outrageous! The rights of defendants are protected by Jewish law!" Nigel fumed. "Paul has not been formally charged, much less found guilty."

Paul put his hand to his mouth and his eyes blazed in anger. "God will slap *you* down! What a fake you are! You sit there and judge me by the Law and then break the Law by ordering me slapped around!"

The aides got to their feet. "How dare you talk to God's Chief Priest like that!"

Paul acted surprised. "How was I to know he was Chief Priest? He doesn't act like a chief priest. You're right, the Scripture does say, 'Don't speak abusively to a ruler of the people.' Sorry."

"He apologized to the *office* of Chief Priest, not to the chief priest himself," Liz noted.

Paul quickly changed tactics. He knew how the Sadducees and Pharisees hated each other, and how they differed on their beliefs. The lawyer in him decided to use this to his advantage. "Friends, I am a stalwart Pharisee from a long line of Pharisees. It's because of my Pharisee convictions—the hope and resurrection of the dead—that I've been hauled into this court."

The moment he said this, the council split right down the middle, Pharisees and Sadducees going at each other in heated argument. Sadducees have nothing to do with a resurrection or angels or even a spirit. If they can't see it, they don't believe it. Pharisees believe it all. And so a huge and noisy quarrel broke out.

"Bravo, Paul!" Nigel cheered, watching the men, especially the older Zeeb, Jarib, Saar, and Nahshon. "Even the fearsome foursome are arguing among themselves!"

Some of the religious scholars on the Pharisee side shouted down the others: "We don't find anything wrong with this man! And what if a spirit has spoken to him? Or maybe an angel? What if it turns out we're fighting against God?"

Lysias heard the roar of voices escalating on the other side of the door. He looked at the brass door ring in alarm. *They might tear Paul limb from limb.* He snapped his fingers at the soldiers standing at attention in the corridor. "Get him out of there and escort him back to the barracks!" Lysias stormed off back down the corridor, shaking his head. *I've still got nothing to report. This is getting out of control.*

✗

Max was covered in dirt, digging with all his might to make a hole large enough under the wall for he and Clarie to slip through. He stopped and breathed heavily, assessing the size of his hole. "I think that aboot has it, Lass. Wha' do ye think? Can ye fit thr-r-rough then?"

Clarie, still in the form of a young lad, sat next to him and leaned her head down into the hole to look under the wall. "Looks good. Go ahead and I'll be right behind you."

Max nodded. "Aye." He jumped into the hole and pushed his way along until he was on the other side of the wall. When he was through he looked around the darkened courtyard where a faint oil lamp burned in the distance. He lowered his voice to a hoarse whisper as he looked back down the hole. "Okay, Lass. Come on thr-r-rough."

"I already have," Clarie answered from behind him.

Max spun around to see her standing there. "How did ye get here?"

"Remember I can take any form, Max. I just flew over as a butterfly while you climbed through," Clarie explained with a smile. "You still needed to dig to make it through yourself, though."

Max shook all over to get the dirt off. "Aye, I shoulda known. Now wha'? I still don't know why we keep followin' these scoundr-r-rels."

"You will. Come on," Clarie told him, making her way quietly across the courtyard to where a group of darkly dressed men sat in a circle. There were forty of them.

"All we need is just a moment of access to him. It won't take long," one of the men said in a low voice.

"There's a window of opportunity if he's taken again from the Antonia Fortress to the Hall of the Sanhedrin," added another man. "We can position ourselves along the route and be ready."

"We'll strike quickly and disperse," another man suggested, gripping a dagger and pretending to slice his throat. He looked around the group of men lit by the single oil lamp in the center of the table. "Some of us will likely be captured by the Romans."

"I would gladly die than allow this blasphemer to defile our Temple and infiltrate our people with his lies!" one of them offered.

"It's settled then," the man with the dagger announced. He pricked the palm of his hand with the dagger and squeezed a fist until blood trickled down onto the ground. "Let us take an oath to neither eat nor drink until we've killed him."

The forty young zealots murmured in agreement with their leader.

"Three of us will go to a secret meeting we've arranged with Ananias and some of his top leaders," the man with the dagger told them. "Remain here and wait for further instructions."

With that, the man and two others left the group and walked off into the night.

Max looked at Clarie. "We've got ta stop those murder-r-rers!"

"Precisely, and now we can finally have that family reunion," Clarie whispered back, backing up slowly to exit the courtyard.

Max trotted away with her, keeping underfoot. "Lass, ye've *got* ta give me more ta go on! Wha' exactly are we doin'?" Max pleaded, exasperated with all the mystery and alarmed for Paul's safety. As they neared the hole Max had dug, Clarie transformed into a butterfly to fly back over the wall. Max grumbled and crawled back through the hole to the other side.

Clarie stood there dressed in the finery of an educated young man from a wealthy Jewish family. "Paul is getting ready to meet his long-lost nephew whom he never got to meet because his family cast him out of the house when he decided to follow Jesus."

Max looked her up and down. "Ye're goin' ta be Paul's nephew?"

Clarie nodded. "And the Romans are going to let me in to the fortress after they are charmed by my unusual dog." Her smile then turned to a frown as she noticed how filthy Max was from digging the hole. "But not until we get you cleaned up. Max, you're a mess!"

"Ye *think?*" Max grumbled, looking back at the hole.

Ananias sat in his chair, slowly stroking his beard as he looked over the zealots. "Well?"

"There are forty of us. We've bound ourselves by a solemn oath to eat nothing until we have killed Paul. But we need your help," the man with the dagger told him. "Send a request from the council to Lysias to bring Paul back so you can investigate the charges in more detail. We'll do the rest. Before he gets anywhere near you, we'll have killed him. You won't be involved."

Ananias calmly looked over at his aides and the religious leaders he had called to this secret meeting. They silently nodded their approval. He motioned for his clerk to take a letter. He turned his gaze back to the men and gave them an icy stare. "Consider it done. Kill him."

Paul endured a long day of sitting in his cell, mulling over what was happening. No one knew what to do with him. He had been unable to reach his fellow Jews despite having an audience with them. Now, he might not reach Rome if the Jews found some devious way to keep him in Jerusalem. Knowing the corruption that flowed through the Sanhedrin, he knew that generating false charges would simply be a matter of enough bribe money changing hands, and he would be carried outside the gates of Jerusalem to suffer Stephen's same fate of being stoned. His thoughts grew darker as did the night sky that he could see through the bars of his prison cell. His body still ached from the mob beating, and he leaned over on his straw mat to find a comfortable position. Soon his heavy eyelids closed and he was breathing deeply, about to get some much-needed sleep.

Suddenly he felt the warmth of someone standing next to him. Startled, he opened his eyes and there stood Jesus.

"Be encouraged, Paul," Jesus greeted him, his body awash in a sublime glow of light. He smiled at the weary apostle. "Just as you have been a witness to me here in Jerusalem, you must preach the Good News in Rome as well."

Paul's eyes filled with tears at the sight of Jesus' face. This face, the brilliance of which had blinded him on the road to Damascus and later appeared in the depths of his depression back in Corinth and at the Temple in Jerusalem, was once again present to strengthen him in mind and spirit with this fourth revelation. Just as suddenly as Jesus appeared, he was gone. Paul sat up and rested on his arm as he looked around the now empty cell.

A grateful tear slipped down Paul's cheek. "Thank you, my Lord. Now

163

I know that this is not the end. Now I know that I will indeed make it to Rome." He lay back down and drifted off into a sound sleep, full of peace.

☧

Two Roman soldiers walked up to the barracks entrance to change shifts with the two other guards, who had been there all night. "It was a quiet night. Nothing to report."

The two new guards nodded and took their positions. The early morning sky began to turn from a pale blue to a soft pink as the light of dawn grew brighter.

"Here we go," Clarie muttered under her breath as she and Max walked toward the barracks. "Run up to the guards and disarm them. Be a good boy."

"Watch it, Lass," Max grumbled, but he did as he was told and ran happily up to the guards, wagging his tail.

The guards saw the young man walking toward them, and this unusual black dog with him. They looked at one another and smiled. "Have you ever seen one of these?" one asked. The other shook his head.

"Good morning," Clarie greeted them in Greek.

"Is this your dog?" one guard asked. "What kind is he?"

"Yes, Sir," Clarie replied. "He's a rare breed, from far north of Roman Britannia."

"You don't say!" one guard said, leaning over to pet Max. "How did you get him?"

"My family has a trading business in Tarsus, so many traders bring exotic goods and animals from all over the world there," Claire replied. "Being Roman citizens, our trading power stretches across the empire."

"State your business here," the other guard demanded.

"My uncle is a prisoner here. His name is Paul. I need to see him immediately," Clarie explained. "I have some vitally important news."

The guard petting Max stood up. "You can't bring him inside."

"I can leave him outside. He won't cause any trouble. He'll simply sit and wait patiently for me," Clarie explained, giving Max a rub on his head. "He's a good boy."

Max rolled his eyes at her.

"Very well, come with me," the other guard instructed her. He motioned for her to lift her arms so he could feel for any hidden weapons.

164

Clarie followed after the guard, who took her to another guard, who led her to Paul's cell.

Paul sat with his back to the wall when the guard reached his cell, jangling the keys as he turned the lock. "You have a visitor."

Paul got to his feet and rubbed his grimy hands on his cloak as Clarie stepped inside. "Do I know you?"

"We've never met. I'm your sister's son," Clarie told him.

Paul's eyes widened and he put his hand to his mouth in surprise. "Rachel's son? Oh, my dear boy!" Paul stepped forward, enveloping the young man in his arms. "My heart is elated to meet you. And equally shocked."

"I know, the family disowned you, Uncle," Clarie began. "But regardless of what has happened in the past, I believe blood is thicker than the religious prejudice of my grandfather. I heard what you said on the steps the other day, and I was deeply moved, Paul. I hope I can bridge the gap with our family, but there is a pressing matter. I've overheard a plot by a large group of zealots to ambush you. It's going to happen this morning. Ananias will request you to return to the Sanhedrin to further explain yourself, and they will lay in wait for you on the way. You must let the commander know."

Paul called to the guard. "Guard! Please ask one of the centurions to come here." He put his hands on the young man's shoulders. "I need you to please give him your report. It will be more credible coming from you. Thank you for coming to my aid."

The centurion arrived at his cell. "What is it?"

Paul led Clarie to the door. "Please take this young man to the captain. He has something important to tell him."

"Very well," the centurion replied, opening the cell door. "Come with me."

As Clarie stepped out, she turned to smile at Paul. "I'm proud of you, Uncle. Go with God."

Paul's eyes welled up to have the affirmation of a blood relative after having been considered dead to them all these years. He never dreamed he could be welcomed back into the family. His heart was full, and he choked back the tears and lifted a hand as he nodded. Once Clarie was gone, Paul had an immediate regret. *I didn't get his name!*

☧

Lysias sat at his desk, staring at the blank piece of parchment with one hand on his forehead and one hand tapping his pen on the desk. He had absolutely no idea what to report to his superiors. He had to give an account of the riot, the treatment of the prisoner who was a Roman citizen, and the chaotic outburst of the Jewish leadership at Paul's appearance before the Sanhedrin. *What am I going to write to Procurator Felix?*

At that moment the centurion reached Lysias's desk and cleared his throat. Lysias looked up and saw a young man standing there with the centurion. "Sir, the prisoner Paul asked me to bring this young man to you. He said he has something urgent to tell you."

Lysias looked Clarie over. He was glad to have any sort of news. He stood up, nodded to dismiss the centurion, took Clarie by the arm and led the young man aside privately. "What is it? What do you have to tell me?"

"The Jews have worked up a plot against Paul," Clarie told him. "They're going to ask you to bring Paul to the council on the pretext of wanting to interrogate him in more detail. But it's a trick to get him out of your safekeeping so they can murder him." Lysias's eyes widened at this news. "Right now there are more than forty men lying in ambush for him. They've all taken a vow to neither eat nor drink until they've killed him. The ambush is set—all they're waiting for is for you to send him over."

Lysias clenched his jaw as his mind raced with what he needed to do. "Thank you for coming. I want you to leave now. Don't breathe a word of this to anyone."

"I won't," Clarie agreed as Lysias escorted her to a guard to see her out of the fortress.

Lysias called up two centurions and walked over to stand behind his desk, pressing his knuckles onto the empty parchment sitting there. "Get two hundred soldiers ready to go immediately to Caesarea. Also prepare seventy cavalry and two hundred spearmen. I want them ready to march by nine o'clock tonight. And you'll need a couple of mules for Paul and his gear. We're going to present this man safe and sound to Governor Felix."

"Sir, yes, Sir!" the centurions replied in unison with a salute.

"Go, I have a letter to write," Lysias ordered them with a wave of his hand. He took his seat and picked up his pen. He finally knew exactly what to say. "Then I'll stall the Sanhedrin."

166

PAUL AND GOLIATH

JUNE AD 57

Nigel flew high above the thunderous hooves and marching soldiers below, gazing in awe at the magnificent sight of a Roman army on the move. There was enough moonlight to reflect off their armor, making them appear as one shimmering giant creeping toward Caesarea. Four hundred pairs of metal-soled shoes, fitted with two-inch spikes, pounding down the road was an intimidating sound. Even before Rome's army invaded a city, the sound of their impending arrival struck fear in the hearts of the people who were warned to clear a path. These soldiers stopped for no one, and would maintain a steady gaze ahead as they trampled anyone or anything that happened to get in their way. Seventy horses galloped in the middle of this army of soldiers, with Paul riding in the center, protected on all sides.

Max and Liz stayed behind with Luke and the others, and would follow along the next day when word reached the humans as to Paul's whereabouts. They decided Nigel could most easily accompany Paul, so the mouse enlisted a pigeon to carry him along the sixty-mile route from Jerusalem to Caesarea. Once the army reached the midway point of Antipatris, they stopped for the night to rest and water the horses.

"I must say, the number of men to protect Paul is quite the overkill. Lysias has outnumbered the Jewish assassins more than ten to one. Jolly good show!" Nigel told his flight pigeon. "Please put us down over there, my dear, where Paul is dismounting from his noble steed."

"Gladly, Nigel," the pigeon replied, flapping her wings as she landed.

The little mouse scurried over to where Paul leaned against a stone as the Roman soldiers built a fire. The Roman centurion named Hector, who was directly responsible for his care, handed him a bronze cup filled with water. Paul drained the cup, wiped his mouth with the back of his hand, and handed the cup back to the soldier. "Thank you. So we're in Antipatris?"

"Yes," Hector replied, returning the cup to his satchel. "We are out of the reach of the assassins. In the morning, I'll send the infantry and spearmen back to Jerusalem while we continue on with the cavalry to Caesarea."

Paul smiled. "Thank you for your protection. I can tell you are an excellent commander."

The centurion nodded in reply, but said nothing. Paul studied the soldier as he removed his helmet to wipe away the sand caked on his face. His gaze drifted from Hector's helmet to his breastplate, belt, shield, sword, lance, and shoes.

"I've always been fascinated by Roman armor," Paul said. "You are protected from head to toe. How much does all that armor weigh?"

"It varies, depending on the physical build of the soldier, but my full armor weighs roughly seventy pounds," Hector explained. "Of course, I'm larger than most soldiers."

Paul nodded. "That is a lot to carry, but it's worth it to keep you safe." He looked out across the darkened landscape. "It was here in Antipatris that the Philistine army defeated the Israelites. But later, on a different battlefield south of here, one unarmed shepherd boy turned that defeat around by slaying a giant named Goliath."

"Sounds like a Roman myth." Hector smirked. "Did the gods give him special powers?"

"No, but the God of Israel gave him courage. Goliath was more than nine feet tall and his armor weighed twice as much as yours. He taunted the Israelites with lies and insults. You haven't heard the account?"

The centurion gave a quick laugh. "Sounds like a story with a lot of exaggeration. How could an unarmed boy kill an armored man that huge?"

Paul paused as he studied the centurion. "Because his armor was on the *inside*. David's armor was spiritual. He fought in the strength of the one true God, and defeated the odds of human warfare." Paul pointed to the centurion's helmet. "May I?"

The centurion nodded, handing him the helmet.

Paul held the helmet and looked into its vacant face. "David's mind was protected by the sure knowledge that the God of Israel was more powerful than any army or any giant. He refused to listen to the taunting lies of the enemy. He believed that God would save him just as he had saved him before, from the attacks of lions and bears. He refused to wear the armor offered by King Saul, and instead put on spiritual armor. He ran out to face the enemy with the tools he knew how to use to protect his sheep: a slingshot and five smooth stones. While the Israelites remained paralyzed, not wanting to make a move, David boldly ran out to face the enemy."

"So what happened to the boy?" The centurion was eager to know.

"David hit Goliath in the forehead with the very first shot and sent the giant crashing to the ground," Paul replied excitedly, using his hands to show Goliath falling to the earth. "Then he took Goliath's own sword and cut off his head. All because David protected *his* head with the saving knowledge of his God. Then the Philistine army surrendered to the Israelite army. True story." He handed the helmet back to the centurion.

Hector flipped his helmet over in his hands. "So the shepherd boy had an unseen helmet to save him?" he asked with a smile as he put the helmet back on securely. "That is a fantastic story, Paul. Just in case, I'll keep my armor on so I'm prepared for any giants we meet on our way to Caesarea." He laughed and rose to his feet.

"Oh, and that shepherd boy eventually became the king of Israel," Paul added. "David was his name. He went on to slay tens of thousands of his enemies to establish his kingdom. True story."

Hector's eyes grew wide. He opened his mouth to speak but stopped himself. He left Paul there while he went to check on his men, his mind racing with the imagery of David and Goliath.

Paul rested his head back onto the rock and gazed at the fire. "Helmet of salvation," he muttered under his breath. His eyelids grew heavy, and he closed them to doze off for a much-needed rest.

Nigel stood in the shadows, having heard this discussion about armor. "As Liz would say, *déjà vu*. 'An inside job, a captive audience, and the means to protect and compete. When soldiers greet soldiers, the inside job is complete.'" He recalled the riddle from when Paul was in prison in Ephesus guarded by the Roman soldiers Ovidius and Justus. Paul had been fascinated by their armor when he spent so much time chained up with them. "Hmmm. Paul seems to be thinking a great deal about armor. But, like David, his armor is on the inside. And, like David, Paul has his own Goliath to face tomorrow."

☧

In the morning the soldiers returned to their barracks in Jerusalem, sending Paul on to Caesarea under guard of the cavalry. The cavalry entered Caesarea and immediately went to the Praetorium. Hector escorted Paul to the palace and arranged for Governor Felix to see him. They were kept waiting a few minutes in the marble-floored hallway.

Paul looked at the spear Hector held in his hand. "How far can you throw that thing?"

Hector held it up and cocked his head. "Far enough and fast enough to stop the enemy before he reaches me." He paused and then asked, "How big was Goliath's spear?"

Paul smiled at the centurion's curiosity. "The staff alone was 17 pounds, and the metal tip was 16 pounds. But he didn't have time to hurl it at David, who moved quickly against him."

As the centurion's eyes widened, the door burst open and a servant greeted them. "Governor Felix will see you now."

"Very well," Hector replied as he cleared his throat and motioned for Paul to walk ahead of him.

Felix sat on his imperial chair and studied Paul as he entered the room. The governor's light gray hair was cut short, and he wore a white tunic fitted with a red sash across his right shoulder. *He's such a small, powerless man. Why all this fuss?* the procurator thought to himself as Paul walked toward him, bandy-legged, balding, and with a scraggly gray beard. Felix suddenly heard the flapping of pigeon wings in the corridor leading outside but kept his gaze on Paul.

"Sir, a letter from my commander," Hector offered, handing the letter over to the governor's assistant, who in turn handed it to Felix. He stood at attention while Felix read the letter.

"FROM CLAUDIUS LYSIAS,

TO HIS EXCELLENCY, GOVERNOR FELIX:

GREETINGS!

THIS MAN WAS SEIZED BY SOME JEWS, AND THEY WERE ABOUT TO KILL HIM WHEN I ARRIVED WITH THE TROOPS. WHEN I LEARNED HE WAS A ROMAN CITIZEN, I REMOVED HIM TO SAFETY. THEN I TOOK HIM TO THEIR HIGH COUNCIL TO TRY TO LEARN THE BASIS OF THE ACCUSATIONS AGAINST HIM. I SOON DISCOVERED THE CHARGE WAS SOMETHING REGARDING THEIR RELIGIOUS LAW—CERTAINLY NOTHING WORTHY OF IMPRISONMENT OR DEATH. BUT WHEN I WAS INFORMED OF A PLOT TO KILL HIM, I IMMEDIATELY SENT HIM ON TO YOU. I HAVE TOLD HIS ACCUSERS TO BRING THEIR CHARGES BEFORE YOU."

171

Felix raised his eyebrows and looked at Paul. "What province are you from?"

"I am from Cilicia," Paul replied, not offering more.

"I'll take up your case when your accusers arrive," Felix announced, handing the letter to his assistant and standing to walk out of the room. "Lock him up until they get here."

The centurion saluted. "Sir, yes, Sir!"

Nigel watched as Paul was escorted out of the room. "I see Lysias conveniently left out the fact that he nearly had Paul scourged. He came off sounding like quite the hero," the little mouse quipped before scurrying off to follow Paul to the prison.

FIVE DAYS LATER

"Chief Pr-r-riest Ananias came himself, along with that cor-r-rupt lawyer of his," Max explained as he and Liz greeted Nigel.

"But Luke, Timothy, and the others are here now, too," Liz pointed out. "They will all be in court to support Paul."

"I'm terribly glad to hear it," Nigel replied. "Not about Ananias, of course, but I know Paul will be relieved to see Luke."

"Nigel, please report back to us, word for word, what happens in that courtroom," Liz instructed the mouse. "I wish we could get inside but better to let you be our ears so we are not seen."

"Always an honor, my dear," Nigel told her, taking her paw and giving it a kiss. "I shall give you a full report when court is adjourned."

"Aye, an' we'll be pr-r-rayin'," Max assured his little friend. "No tellin' wha' the schemin' Jews will do after bein' outwitted by Lysias." He grinned at the thought. "It were fun ta watch those assassin lads get hungr-r-ry. Guess they'll get *r-r-real* skinny if they won't eat until Paul be dead."

The doors flung open wide as Hector escorted Paul into the governor's great hall. The buzz of murmuring voices muffled the sound of their footsteps reverberating off the richly tiled floor. Paul scanned the audience to see who was in the room. He immediately saw Luke and gave his friend an assuring wink.

Luke smiled, swallowed the lump in his throat, and whispered to the others, "He's all right. Praise God!"

The Jews looked down their noses at Paul, putting their heads together as they spewed words of boiling anger to see their prey just out of reach and protected once again by Rome. They were still reeling from having been duped by Lysias, wondering who could have tipped him off about their plans.

Suddenly Felix entered the room, announced by his court assistant. He took a seat and looked at the two groups of men assembled in his court: Jews from the Sanhedrin and Gentiles from who-knows-where. And there stood the little man Paul in the middle, calm and unafraid. He couldn't help but notice the silent rage that poured from the Jews' eyes as they stared at him. He knew they wanted him dead, but Felix was more concerned about his own personal outcome with this court decision—and he loved the power of keeping people guessing.

Tertullus the lawyer cleared his throat and walked over to stand before Felix, bowing respectfully. He was a tall, portly man with curly black hair that peeked out from his puffy hat. He wore a forced smile that looked as sincere as that of a hungry lion licking a wounded beast out of concern.

Hector noticed how big Tertullus was compared with Paul, who stood next to him. *Just like Goliath,* he thought.

Luke, Timothy, Aristarchus, and Philip prayed silently that Paul would have the exact words he needed in this courtroom.

"Most Honorable Felix, we are most grateful in all times and places for your wise and gentle rule. We are much aware that it is because of you and you alone that we enjoy all this peace and gain daily profit from your reforms," Tertullus began. "I'm not going to tire you out with a long speech. I beg your kind indulgence in listening to me. I'll be quite brief."

Nigel rolled his eyes and crossed his arms at the lawyer's flattery. "Please, *do* be brief, you cheeky fellow, if you insist on spewing such laughable flattery upon such a brutal beast."

"We've found this man time and again disturbing the peace, stirring up riots against Jews all over the world, the ringleader of a seditious sect called Nazarenes," Tertullus continued. "We caught him trying to defile our holy Temple and arrested him. You'll be able to verify all these accusations when you examine him yourself."

"Indeed!" the Jews murmured with approving voices. "That's exactly right!"

Felix observed the boisterous reaction of the Jews and then looked over at the Gentiles. Although they shook their heads in disagreement to these allegations against Paul, they maintained respectful self-control in his courtroom. The governor motioned to Paul that it was now his turn.

Paul nodded courteously and started right in on his defense. "I count myself fortunate to be defending myself before you, Governor, knowing how fair-minded you've been in judging us all these years. I've been back in the country only twelve days—you can check out these dates easily enough. I came with the express purpose of worshiping in Jerusalem on Pentecost, and I've been minding my own business the whole time. Nobody can say they saw me arguing in the Temple or working up a crowd in the streets. Not one of their charges can be substantiated with evidence or witnesses."

"Brilliant strategy, old boy! Shifting the focus of their charges to Jerusalem alone," Nigel observed. "The Jews cannot even back up their charges in Jerusalem, much less the *entire world.*"

"But I do freely admit this," Paul went on. "In regard to the Way, which they malign as a dead-end street, I serve and worship the very same God served and worshiped by all our ancestors and embrace everything written in all our Scriptures. And I admit to living in hopeful anticipation that God will raise the dead, both the good and the bad. If that's my crime, my accusers are just as guilty as I am."

173

"Hear, hear!" Nigel cheered.

"Believe me, I do my level best to keep a clear conscience before God and my neighbors in everything I do," Paul continued. "I've been out of the country for a number of years and now I'm back. While I was away, I took up a collection for the poor and brought that with me, along with offerings for the Temple. It was while making those offerings that they found me quietly at my prayers in the Temple. There was no crowd, there was no disturbance. It was some Jews from around Ephesus who started all this trouble . . ." Paul paused and looked around the room, locking eyes with Luke for a brief moment before continuing. ". . . and you'll notice they're not here today. They're cowards, too cowardly to accuse me in front of you."

Hector hung onto every word Paul said as he came after his accusers with shocking boldness and courage. *Just like David.*

"So ask these others what crime they've caught me in. Don't let them hide behind this smooth-talking Tertullus. The only thing they have on me is that one sentence I shouted out in the council: 'It's because I believe in the resurrection that I've been hauled into this court!' Does that sound to you like grounds for a criminal case?"

174

All eyes were on Felix for his response. He knew far more about the Way than he let on, and could have settled the case then and there. But uncertain of his best move politically, he played for time.

"When Captain Lysias comes down, I'll decide your case," Felix announced, standing and calling over the centurion. "Keep Paul under open arrest, but allow his friends to visit as much as they wish, and to bring him whatever he needs."

"Yes, sir," Hector replied. The soldier saluted and took Paul by the arm to lead him out of the room.

Paul glanced at Luke, and they shared a knowing look of confident assurance as he walked by.

Once they had cleared the hallway, Paul looked up at Hector. "How do you think that went?"

A smile crept onto the centurion's face. "I think you hit Tertullus with a smooth stone right in the middle of his forehead."

Max, Liz, and Nigel sat outside the palace next to a fountain while Nigel filled them in on the court proceedings. Inside, Luke, Timothy,

Aristarchus, and Philip met with Paul to discuss the trial and next steps. Hector had arranged for Paul to be kept in an easily accessible room near the palace and not in the dungeon. Philip's daughters sent food and fresh clothes for Paul, and Aristarchus agreed to remain with Paul as a voluntary prisoner to serve Paul in any way he could.

"Well, although Paul is not free, at least he is not in deplorable conditions," observed Liz. "But I am curious about Felix's decision. Did he send for Lysias?"

"Not that I'm aware of," Nigel replied. "I do believe he simply wanted to stall for time."

"Aye, an' the Jews jest r-r-returned ta Jerusalem," Max noted. "But they've got their spies here ta keep 'em informed."

"So do I," came a voice behind them.

The animals looked quickly to see a statue of a woman dressed in a rich toga and ornate sandals. She looked down at them and smiled. "Good morning, everyone."

"Bonjour, Gillamon!" Liz whispered, looking around her at the throngs of people walking by. "Shouldn't you be less conspicuous with all these humans around?"

"Sometimes the best way to hide is in plain sight. I'm simply a statue of a wealthy Roman, not an emperor or a god this time," Gillamon assured her.

"I say, it appears Governor Felix is a bit torn over what do to with Paul," Nigel interjected.

"Yes, Felix and his wife, Drusilla, will call Paul in for repeated private audiences to hear what he has to say," Gillamon explained. "While a side of Felix may be interested in Paul's beliefs, his greedy side will be holding out for a bribe from Paul to rule in his favor."

"Then he'll be waitin' a long time!" Max growled. "Paul would never do such a thing!"

Gillamon nodded. "You're right, Max, he wouldn't. So the plan is unfolding perfectly for Paul to reach Rome, but he will be detained here in Caesarea for a while."

"Wha' are we supposed ta do while we wait then?" Max wanted to know.

"Paul will ask Luke to keep you in his care, so your mission will shift to working again on the New Testament," Gillamon explained.

"Brilliant!" Nigel cheered. "Whose pen shall we inspire now?"

"Luke's," Gillamon replied before freezing, as a man stopped in front of the statue. The man leaned his hand on the base as he dug a rock out of his sandal.

Nigel hid while Max and Liz sat there quietly, pretending to be simple animals. The man smiled and petted Max on the back. "Aren't you an interesting breed of dog."

"If you only knew, monsieur," Liz meowed at the man, drawing a wink from Max.

Once the man walked off, Gillamon continued. "As you know, Matthew and Mark are writing their own accounts of the life of Jesus, each from different perspectives but providing the same truth of Jesus as Messiah. Luke will also write an account, and since he never knew Jesus personally, he must gather research from those who did." He turned to Max. "That means you'll get to be with Kate for a while, my friend."

Max wagged his tail. "Kate? Aye! Can't wait ta see me lass!"

"So we will be with Mary and John! How wonderful, no?" Liz added happily. "Is there anything specific Luke needs to know?"

Gillamon smiled, thinking of what awaited Luke's pen. "Everything."

"Might we arrange any other interviews for Doctor Luke?" Nigel inquired.

"Yes, take him to Zacchaeus and anyone else you think has a story to tell about Jesus," Gillamon replied. "Now go. Time for Luke to fill up his journal."

After the statue became motionless once more, Liz realized that Gillamon had not told them exactly who would be the readers of Luke's letter. "But we do not know Luke's audience."

Nigel adjusted his spectacles as he stared up at the now silent statue. "All he said was for Luke to fill up his *journal,* my dear. Nothing more."

"Aye, before the lad can wr-r-rite anythin' ta anyone, he's got ta know wha' ta wr-r-rite aboot," Max added.

Liz's tail curled up and down as she breathed in the salt-air breeze coming off the Mediterranean Sea, closing her eyes as she thought this through. *"Oui,* and if he needs to know everything, we'll keep our detailed, note-taking doctor quite busy." She opened her eyes and looked at Max and Nigel with a big grin. "And I think he'll need more than one journal."

20

LUKE'S JOURNAL

JERUSALEM, JULY AD 57

Kate sat next to Mary in the cool shade of the early summer morning, resting her head on her front paws. She took a deep breath and sighed. Mary set aside the tunic she was mending and placed her hand on Kate's back, softly rubbing her white fur. Things were relatively quiet here in Jerusalem, aside from the recent ruckus with Paul that John and Mary learned of when they returned from their visit to Nazareth. They all were concerned, and lifted up their friend in prayer while they awaited word of his trial. Meanwhile John stayed busy with James as they served the church and ministered to the sick and needy of the city. Mary was well into her seventies now and did not venture out as much as she used to each day.

"What is it, my little Chava?" Mary asked the small Westie. "Are you wishing you were off on an adventure instead of sitting by an old woman all day?"

Kate lifted her head and smiled at Mary, wagging her tail. *No, Lass. I could have no higher honor than ta stay with Jesus' mum each day,* she thought. *Some days I jest miss me love more than others.*

Mary continued to gently stroke Kate's back, talking to the little dog as if she understood. "John thinks we should go to Ephesus. Now that Paul has left that region where there is so much exciting church growth, he thinks he could be of more use there." Mary looked around at John's courtyard. "I have mixed feelings about leaving Jerusalem. Part of me

177

welcomes it, but part of me wishes to stay. So much has happened here. So much history to leave behind."

"I was hoping you could share some of that history with me," Luke said, overhearing Mary as he entered the courtyard.

Mary turned and saw Max and Liz running toward her, and a tall, handsome Greek man standing there smiling, his hands clasped in front of him. "Good morning, Mary. I'm Luke."

"Luke! Our dear physician!" Mary exclaimed happily. Tears filled her eyes as she saw Max and Kate embrace. Liz climbed up into her lap. "And you've brought these precious little ones!"

"Funny how they look like they're right at home here," commented Luke. "The cat is named 'Faith' and the dog is named 'Gabriel.' They took up with Paul when he was in Damascus and have been his faithful companions ever since. He asked me to watch over them while he is detained."

Mary held Liz to her chest and whispered in her ear, "Hello, Zilla, my little shadow. You've been a busy little one since I saw you last. I didn't know you were with Paul. I'm glad." Mary knew that these were no ordinary animals. Jesus had told her they were on mission for him, but said no more than that. She didn't ask any questions, but simply took it on faith. These animals had been with her from the day she learned she would be the mother of Messiah, giving her comfort and companionship during Jesus' growing-up years and beyond. She had called Liz 'Zilla,' Max 'Tovah,' Kate 'Chava,' and Al 'Ari.' But she didn't let on to Luke that they were anything other than Paul's pets.

Luke came over and sat down next to Mary. "It is an honor to finally meet the mother of our Lord."

The smile lines around Mary's eyes gave her an even greater beauty in her old age. "I've heard so much about you, Luke. James said he met you before Paul's arrest here in Jerusalem. It sounds like you helped to get the gospel off to a strong start in Philippi."

"Just serving however the Lord needs me," Luke replied humbly. "And that includes serving as Paul's physician and traveling companion as of late. He sends his greetings to you and prays you are well."

"How is Paul holding up in Caesarea?" Mary asked, now petting Liz, who sat purring on her lap. "I have heard that Felix is not ruling either way in his case."

"Paul is unstoppable, so, of course, is not discouraged," Luke replied.

"He knows that everything is happening for God's purposes. So, while we wait, I decided to come spend some time doing some research." He pulled a leather scroll from his satchel.

"Oh?" Mary asked, scratching Liz under the chin.

"I wish to learn all I can about Jesus, and I plan to take extensive notes. Since I'm a Gentile, I don't have the full historical perspective of the people of Israel about their Messiah. And while I'm learning more and more about Jesus, I know there are many Gentiles like me who need to understand the details of his life. Would you allow me the honor of spending time with you and asking you questions?" Luke asked, preparing his pen.

"It would be our joy to have you stay here, and my joy to help you, Luke," Mary replied happily. "What would you like to know?"

Luke breathed in deeply and smiled, throwing up his hand and shaking his head playfully. "Everything."

"Then we need to start at the very beginning," Mary replied, smiling as her mind raced back to the days of her youth. Her dimples were still as noticeable as they were when she was a young teenage girl. "Heaven had been quiet for more than four hundred years. And when the time came to break heaven's silence—before Jesus, and before me—that silence was broken with a message to a Jewish priest named Zechariah."

Kate nuzzled Max, her heart racing with joy. "Oh, me love! I were jest thinkin' aboot how much I've missed ye then."

"Aye, Lass. I'm here now," Max replied, kissing her. "We get ta spend some time together while Luke visits Jerusalem."

Liz smiled to see Max and Kate's sweet reunion. She knew this process with Luke and Mary would take a long time. She climbed off Mary's lap as Mary began relaying the story of Gabriel appearing to Zechariah in the Temple. Luke's pen was flying across the parchment as he listened intently to the miraculous account.

"*Bonjour, mon amie,*" Liz told Kate, head-butting her friend. "I am so very happy to see you."

Kate's tail wagged furiously and tears filled her eyes. "Aye, Liz! Ta see me mate an' me best friend after so long makes me cry happy tears!"

Liz looked over at Mary and Luke. "I anticipate we will be here for quite a long time, so we will be able to catch up. Why don't you and Max go enjoy yourselves? I'll keep an eye on things here."

179

"Thanks, Lass," Kate replied happily. "But where's Nigel? Isn't he with you?"

"He decided to catch a flight and will join us here later," Liz explained. "Go on. You two have a lot of catching up to do. Go enjoy the day."

"Let's go, Kate," Max nudged her, grinning wide.

Liz smiled as the pair of dogs trotted off. *Now to find Mary's journal,* she thought.

☧

Later that evening, John and Luke embraced like brothers when John returned home. Although he had heard all about Luke, they had never met in person. Mary took her time preparing dinner to allow the two men to get acquainted. Luke got John up to speed on all that had transpired with Paul in Caesarea, and John filled Luke in about the Jerusalem church and how they were able to use the donation monies he and Paul had brought them.

"So you wish to research Jesus in detail while you're here?" John asked. "You'll have to spend time with James as well. Not only can he give you insights as Jesus' brother, but he can also give you his perspective on Jesus' teachings."

"Yes, I will meet with James, of course. But I also need to interview you at length. You were one of the twelve!" Luke enthused. "I can't imagine having that experience of being with Jesus day in and day out for three years. What was it like?"

John gazed at the oil lamp on the table and gently shook his head in wonder. "It was like . . . being continually enveloped by light." Tears filled John's eyes. "I'll never forget that first day with him in our fishing boats. Peter was so frustrated at first!" John wiped his eyes as he chuckled over Peter's stubbornness. "Jesus asked to sit in Peter's boat so he could better speak to the crowd on the shore. Then he told Peter to take the boats out to go fishing. I'll never forget the sour attitude Peter gave Jesus, telling him how we'd fished all night and caught nothing. Jesus had this irresistible grin on his face and said nothing. He just sat and stared at Peter. Peter finally relented, doing as Jesus asked. Soon the nets were full of fish and started to tear."

Luke jotted down notes as John relayed the story. "How did Peter react to that miraculous catch?"

John leaned forward and rested his elbows on the table. "He dropped to his knees in front of Jesus and said, 'Oh, Lord, please leave me—I'm too much of a sinner to be around you.' Jesus put his hand on Peter's shoulder and told him, 'Don't be afraid! From now on you'll be fishing for people!'"

Luke marveled at hearing John's firsthand account of Jesus and Peter. "And now he is. And so are you."

John nodded and smiled. "We walked away from the biggest catch of our lives that day to follow Jesus. But we didn't truly understand everything Jesus taught and showed us while we were with him. I don't know if we were just too blind or if Jesus was just too large to comprehend. Much of it I didn't grasp until Resurrection morning."

"We have a lot of ground to cover, my friend," Luke said with a smile. "I can't wait to hear every word you can remember Jesus saying."

"Oh!" came Mary's voice, followed by a crash. "Faith, what are you doing up there?!"

John jumped up from the table. "What is it, Mary?"

Mary picked up a wooden bowl that had fallen to the floor, scattering some dried beans everywhere. "Faith was up on that shelf exploring and knocked over this bowl," Mary explained. As she reached to straighten the now messy shelf, her hand rested on a leather scroll. She picked it up and smiled. "I forgot I put this up here."

"What did you find?" John wanted to know as he gathered the spilled beans.

Liz sat on the floor, beaming at Mary. At that moment, Nigel scurried into the room and gave her a salute as he darted behind a basket.

"My journal," Mary answered, rubbing her hand tenderly across its aged form. She looked over at Luke. "This will help you, Luke." She carried the scroll over to the table and unrolled it to reveal a treasure of entries she had made over the years. "When I went to live with Zechariah and Elizabeth, he and I were the only two people Gabriel had appeared to in more than four hundred years, so we were anxious to communicate with one another. Because he couldn't speak after doubting Gabriel's message that Elizabeth would give birth to John, Zechariah could only communicate by writing on a tablet until the baby was born. He taught me how to read and write so we could talk. One day, a gift was left on their doorstep with a note, thanking me for coming to take care of Elizabeth during her pregnancy. That gift was this fine journal, with pens and ink bricks."

"Who left the note with such a gift?" Luke asked. "The quality of this journal looks like something belonging to royalty."

"Someone named Nigelas," Mary answered.

Liz and Nigel shared a big grin. Nigel preened his whiskers proudly.

"I didn't know him but happily took the journal to start writing down my thoughts." Mary smiled, unrolling the scroll to her first entry. Tears quickened in her eyes. "I wrote notes to Jesus before he was even born." She unrolled it further. "I told him about his cousin John's birth, and about how hard it was for me to feel Joseph's doubt that I was expecting a child before we had been married." She shook her head as she remembered the pain. "But then, happily, Gabriel appeared to Joseph and he believed me. Later came the journey to Bethlehem, the amazing visit of the shepherds, the bright star. It's all here, Luke. You may borrow this to read it, if it will help you with your research."

Luke took Mary's journal into his hands with reverence. "It will be such a privilege to read this, Mary. Thank you."

Mary put her hand on Luke's shoulder. "Joseph and I shared this journal with Jesus the day we told him who he really was. If it helped Jesus, I'm sure it will help you, too."

Luke's eyes widened as he gazed at this priceless scroll. "That makes it an even greater treasure."

"I think you'll see other things in there to help you. Joseph wrote out Jesus' lineage all the way back to Adam," Mary explained. "And when Jesus returned the journal to me before he left, he had even added a note. But I'll let you find it for yourself."

John leaned over Luke's shoulder. "I wish to see that myself!"

"After I'm finished," Luke said, clutching the journal to his chest with a grin.

"Luke, please just do me the favor of not writing about this scroll. I know people would want to come see it, and I don't wish to make this object out to be more than it is—just a thing. But still it is special to my heart as something I shared with Jesus alone," Mary reminisced with her hand over her heart.

Luke nodded. "Understood, Mary. This journal is your personal possession, and while I appreciate you sharing it with me, I will not share it with the world. You have my word."

"Thank you, Luke. Some things are better left as 'Jesus secrets.' Peter can tell you about that as well," shared Mary with a smile. "Well, both of you please clear the table so we can eat." She walked off to get their food for the evening meal.

"You know, much of Jesus' ministry happened at meals," John told Luke. "Let me tell you about a particular meal that happened at the home of a Pharisee named Simon. An unexpected guest arrived at the end of that meal."

"Who was it?" Luke asked, setting the scrolls aside as Mary had requested.

"A woman with an alabaster jar," John remembered with a smile.

SIX MONTHS LATER

Liz and Nigel pored over Luke's notes to see how his research was progressing. Max and Kate snuggled close on the floor.

"I'm quite pleased," Nigel noted, adjusting his spectacles. "His meticulous notes are extraordinary! Just look at this specific record of Jesus' teachings to the crowds as well as to his disciples. He's capturing it word for word, as if he were there himself."

183

"I am sure he is a bit overwhelmed with all he is learning, and John and Mary give him stories as they come to mind, in no particular order," Liz added. "But this is not important now. Our orderly doctor will see to that later. Look how he is organizing his thoughts:

> *Jesus is the perfect human. He is accessible to everyone, Jew and Gentile alike. He is the Savior for all the world, no matter a person's wealth, race, or status in life.*
>
> *Jesus gave value to women, and they were important to his ministry—Mary chosen by God to be mother of Messiah, Anna (with Simeon), Mary and Martha, Joanna, Susanna, other followers, Mary Magdalene, Jairus's daughter raised from the dead, woman who bled for twelve years, woman with the alabaster jar, widow in Nain (Jesus raised her son from the dead), persistent widow, widow who gave her last mite, women at the cross, women at the tomb. Jesus was tender-hearted toward women who had made mistakes.*

"Lassie power!" Kate exclaimed with her perky grin. "Jesus always treated the lassies with more respect than do the men of this day. I'm glad Luke sees that aboot Jesus."

"*Oui*, Kate. I am especially happy to see this," Liz agreed with bright eyes. "I still bristle when I think of the Jewish morning prayer where a man will actually thank God that he was not made 'a Gentile, a slave, or a woman!' PFFT! So it appears Luke will bring women out in a favorable light with Jesus."

"Look here, he also grasps the fact that Jesus gave value to children," Nigel pointed out.

To welcome a child was to welcome someone with no status, yet Jesus gave a child a status equal to his own. Amazing!

"*Bon!* He also has captured how important prayer was to Jesus," Liz pointed out.

Prayer was a driving force in Jesus' life. He frequently went away to pray alone. He prayed in front of others. He prayed at every great moment: his baptism, choosing the twelve, Transfiguration, feeding 5,000, garden, cross, Peter's restoration.

"Wha' aboot the outcasts like Matthew?" Max asked. "An' the parable of the Good Samaritan?"

Nigel hummed as he rolled out the scroll with his nose. "Ah yes, he has made note of the running theme of Jesus' kindness to the weak, the suffering, the outcasts, the failed, and the lost."

Lost Sheep, Lost Coin, Prodigal Son, ten Lepers (the one who returned was a Samaritan), repentant thief on the cross, Pharisee vs. Tax Collector, Matthew (tax collector turned disciple), Zacchaeus (meeting with him)

"Luke meets with Zacchaeus next," Max noted. "Mousie were able ta locate Zacchaeus livin' in the same house where Jesus ate with him."

"Right! And I'm thrilled to report he is a happy old man," Nigel exclaimed. "I'm sure he will inspire Luke's pen with a touch of special drama and emotion. Simply splendid story of our wee little chap."

Liz wrinkled her forehead as she searched the scroll. "But he's not here," she mumbled under her breath.

184

"Who, my dear?" Nigel asked.

"Armandus," Liz replied. "Luke needs to capture the story of Jesus healing Armandus's servant in Capernaum, and then the story of him as the centurion at the foot of the cross."

"How will you arrange that, Liz?" Kate asked.

"I'll think of something," Liz replied. "I simply will not have him left out of Luke's account."

JERICHO

Luke smiled as he followed Zacchaeus down the street outside his beautiful home. John had told him he was small, but Luke had no idea *how* small. They passed a row of sycamore trees and Zacchaeus stopped and pointed up at one. "That's where he found me. When I heard Jesus was coming into town, I was eager to get a look at him. Since I couldn't see over the crowd, I climbed up there."

Luke ran his hand along the trunk of the tree, trying to imagine the scene. "What happened when he found you?"

185

The little man ran his fingers through his curly white hair. His joyful gray eyes spoke volumes as windows to his soul. "He called me by name, even though we had never met. And he told me he *must* eat at my house that day. So I quickly made my way down to the ground." Suddenly tears welled up in his eyes. "Everyone was staring at Jesus in disbelief. They couldn't believe he was talking to me, the most despicable man in town," related Zacchaeus, placing his hands on his chest. His lip quivered as he told Luke, "But Jesus didn't care what they thought. He just smiled and kept his gaze on me. All he cared about was *me.*"

Tears quickened in Luke's eyes as Zacchaeus shared his story. "As we walked to my house, Jesus introduced me to Matthew. He was a tax collector, too, and his life turned around when he met Jesus," Zacchaeus explained. "So within minutes I had two new friends, after having no friends for years. The only people who wanted to be around me wanted me for my money."

"So what happened next?" Luke wanted to know as they started walking toward Zacchaeus's house.

"We ate. Jesus spoke about truth and living a God-honoring life. He told stories that stirred my heart," Zacchaeus shared. "Suddenly I couldn't take it anymore and blurted out that I would give half my possessions to the poor, and if I had cheated anybody I would pay back four times the amount."

Luke raised his eyebrows. "So you gave yourself the maximum retribution to right your wrongs. How did Jesus respond?"

Zacchaeus gave a choked-up sob. "I'm sorry. I have a very tender heart ever since Jesus said these words." He wiped his eyes.

"Take your time," Luke comforted him.

"Jesus said, 'Today salvation has come to this house, because this man, too, is a son of Abraham. For the Son of Man came to seek and to save the lost.'" The little man cleared his throat to regain his composure. "From that moment on, I was welcomed back into the family of God. And I've never been the same since."

Luke nodded with emotion. "That seems to be the common pattern with Jesus. No one who meets him is ever the same again."

186

✗

Nigel and Liz sat on the table with Mary's journal. The house was quiet with everyone sound asleep. A single oil lamp cast a warm glow across the room.

"I do not think Mary will mind that we added the story of Jesus healing Armandus's servant to her journal," Liz told Nigel as she put down the pen and blew on the ink. "It is too important, no?"

"I heartily agree, my pet," concurred Nigel, fiddling with his spectacles as he read what Liz had written. "And since you placed it with Jesus' entry, Mary may simply assume he wrote it himself."

Liz's tail curled slowly up and down, and she cocked her head to the side as she compared the text. "I tried to make my penmanship look like his. And I, too, did not mention Armandus by name."

Nigel softly ran his paw along the words Jesus had written. "These are undoubtedly the most beautiful words ever to grace a page, simply because of their Author."

"*Oui,* but I am glad Luke will honor Mary's request to keep this journal unknown," Liz added. "Jesus secrets."

Nigel preened his whiskers with a smile. "Jesus secrets, indeed."

21

THE ASSIGNMENT OF JULIUS ANTONIUS

I want the grandest one in the world!" Nero exclaimed, clapping his hands eagerly. "Pliny says," he continued, now squinting as he traced his finger down a scroll, *"nothing is more intense than the green of emerald . . . and sight is refreshed and restored by gazing upon this stone."*

"Emeralds are also known to improve memory and eloquence to anyone who owns one," the older man named Seneca added, raising a finger in the air. "Emeralds also supposedly quicken intelligence. As your tutor, I, of course, welcome these virtues."

The twenty-two-year-old emperor rolled his eyes at his tutor and allowed Pliny's scroll of geology to roll out of his hand and onto the floor. He jumped up from the couch and tossed a purple silk pillow playfully at Seneca. "I'm smart enough already. Smarter than my *mother* anyway! She thinks she knows everything. *Augusta* thinks she runs my empire," he spat with a wave of his hand, hating the title given to his mother by the Roman senate. "Not for long," he muttered quietly under his breath as he gazed at the Roman centurion who stood at full attention before him. "I just need help with my vision."

Nero walked around the twenty-nine-year-old soldier, admiring his armor and obviously physically fit condition. The Roman centurion held his silver helmet under his arm, revealing his short brown hair combed forward to frame his handsome face. The soldier's olive complexion and square-cut jaw contrasted with Nero's thick neck and boyish freckles. Nero's dark blond hair was styled like a charioteer, and he swept it back as he lifted his chin to study the much taller Roman. Suddenly Nero's gray eyes widened and a smile spread across his face. *"Your* eyes are the color of emeralds! It must be a sign from the gods! You are *perfect* for this assignment! What is your name?"

"Julius Antonius, Sir. What do you wish of me, my lord?" the soldier replied, keeping his gaze fixed ahead.

"I wish for you to travel to Egypt and bring me back green fire!" Nero replied, spreading his arms wide. He proceeded to turn around in a big circle, smiling broadly.

Julius wrinkled his brow and shot a questioning look at his superior commander and prefect of the Praetorian Guard, Burrus.

"Emperor Nero speaks of an emerald," Burrus explained.

188

"I want you to bring me the largest emerald ever found!" commanded Nero, poking his finger into the soldier's chest. He then cupped his hands to his eyes as if he were peering into a spyglass to stare at Julius. "Seneca said my artisans can make me an emerald spyglass so I can keep a better watch on things. I may even use it when I watch my gladiators fight." The young emperor turned his imaginary spyglass into a sword and pretended to thrust it into the soldier. "While you're at it, bring me back some exotic new gladiators from Egypt."

Burrus cleared his throat. "The mines in Berenike are the empire's only source of emeralds. The city is located in the eastern desert of Egypt, which you will reach by traveling from Alexandria down the Nile River."

"They've found millions of emeralds there!" Nero interjected, walking over to a servant holding a silver tray laden with fruit. He picked up an apple, glared at the servant, and took a voracious bite. Juice dripped down his chin and he wiped it with the back of his hand. "Seneca, tell me about apples. Why don't we squeeze juice from them like we do grapes?" He spun around and held his apple up in the air as his tutor walked over to discuss Nero's impulsive, off-topic question.

"So you will now be in a special Imperial Regiment on assignment for the Emperor," Burrus continued, handing Julius a scroll containing his orders. "Take a dozen men and make passage to Alexandria now that the *mare clausum,* of winter is over."

Julius took his assignment in hand and nodded. "Yes, Sir. Indeed, the seas are no longer closed to navigation. Traveling east to Alexandria will be swift."

"After Alexandria and Berenike, you will travel on to Caesarea, where I will send further orders of imperial business for you there," Burrus added. He leaned over and in a hushed tone said, "I plan to utilize one of my best officers for more than just a treasure hunt while you're in that part of the empire."

"Understood," Julius replied quietly with a nod.

Burrus nodded and raised his voice. "Very well, Julius. May the gods give you safe passage across the seas."

"Sir, yes, Sir!" Julius replied, saluting. "Hail, Caesar!"

Nero lifted his hand apathetically in reply, pointing at Julius with his apple. "Now go get me that emerald and those gladiators, Julius. I'm counting on you."

189

Julius bowed respectfully and turned to exit the emperor's elaborate chambers in this seaside villa overlooking the blue waters of the Mediterranean. As he walked down the marble hallway, the centurion let go a deep breath and gripped his orders in hand. Julius felt the undercurrent of tension in that room with Seneca and Burrus. It was no small thing to be given an assignment by the emperor himself. Failure was not an option. Failure with Nero could be deadly.

Nero was starting to act strangely, exploding now and then with fits of anger, mostly directed at his mother, Agrippina, who had truly ruled Rome since Nero came to power at such a young age. She had put seventeen-year-old Nero on the throne by poisoning her husband Claudius, but Nero had learned her scheming ways far too well. His stepbrother Britannicus, son of Claudius and rightful heir to the throne, had died suddenly at dinner. Everyone suspected that Nero had poisoned him. He had learned from his mother to eliminate anyone who was a threat. And by Nero's off-handed remarks, they wondered if Agrippina herself would be next.

Seneca and Burrus did their best to direct the young, immature emperor, who was more interested in acting, dancing, singing, and writing poetry than he was in ruling. They knew it was only a matter of time before Nero would relish the thrill of power and increasingly make decisions based on his self-centered whims—like sending one of Rome's finest officers on a quest to find a giant emerald.

Julius stopped to put on his red-plumed helmet, tightening his chin strap. He gazed out at the imposing volcanic mountain, Vesuvius, towering over the city of Pompeii below. The Roman soldier shook his head and thought, *Red fire or green fire. Like Vesuvius, Nero is going to erupt when we least expect it.*

190

PREDICTING THE FALL

JERUSALEM, MAY AD 59

James, it's been an honor to spend time with you like this," shared Luke, jotting down notes from their discussion. "Is there anything else you can think of that Jesus would especially want recorded? You've shared many of Jesus' encouraging words. Were there any words of warning, perhaps?"

James rested his head back in his chair as he gazed up at the ceiling, thinking about a reply. "Most of his words of warning were directed at the Pharisees. He warned them of their hypocrisy. In fact, Jesus was always the first one to start an argument with them! Such was his anger at how they added to God's laws to suit their positions of power, burdening the people while keeping themselves above the law."

Luke smiled. "I loved hearing about how they tried to trap Jesus in the Temple with the issue of paying taxes to Caesar, and how he asked for a coin."

James smiled. "Yes, 'Give to Caesar what is Caesar's and give to God what is God's.'" His smile faded as he thought about the Temple. "There was a warning that Jesus gave to the people of Jerusalem, and it grieved his spirit as he did so."

"What was that?" Luke asked, preparing a new area to write.

"As he approached Jerusalem for the last time, he wept over it, as if looking down through time—Peter told me this. Jesus said, 'If you, even you, had only known on this day what would bring you peace—but now it is hidden from your eyes. The days will come upon you when your enemies will build an embankment against you and encircle you and hem you in on every side. They will dash you to the ground, you and the children within your walls. They will not leave one stone on another, because you did not recognize the time of God's coming to you.'"

Luke's face fell. "That sounds like a siege, James. Was Jesus saying that Jerusalem will fall? That the city will be destroyed?"

James nodded somberly. "Yes. Jerusalem will fall, because the people did not accept Jesus as Messiah when he came to them. Jesus was very specific. 'And when you see Jerusalem surrounded by armies, then you will know that the time of its destruction has arrived. Then those in Judea must flee to the hills. Those in Jerusalem must get out, and those out in the country should not return to the city. For those will be days of God's vengeance, and the prophetic words of the Scriptures will be fulfilled. How terrible it will be for pregnant women and for nursing mothers in those days. For there will be disaster in the land and great anger against this people. They will be killed by the sword or sent away as captives to all the nations of the world. And Jerusalem will be trampled down by the Gentiles until the period of the Gentiles comes to an end.'"

"I wonder when that will happen," Luke posed, jotting down Jesus' words.

James held out his hands. "I don't know. So for now we press on, and we keep spreading the Word. He also warned and prepared the disciples that persecution would come. The night Peter and John were arrested the first time, Jesus' words came back to Peter's memory as they sat in jail, wondering what would become of them: '. . . there will be a time of great persecution. You will be dragged into synagogues and prisons, and you will stand trial before kings and governors because you are my followers. But this will be your opportunity to tell them about me. So don't worry in advance about how to answer the charges against you, for I will give you the right words and such wisdom that none of your opponents will be able to reply or refute you!'"

Luke stared wide-eyed at James. "This has already happened to Paul. It still is happening!"

James held up a finger. "Indeed. Jesus also said, 'Even those closest

192

to you—your parents, brothers, relatives, and friends—will betray you. They will even kill some of you. And everyone will hate you because you are my followers. But not a hair of your head will perish! By standing firm, you will win your souls.'"

"Death will come to believers, just as it came to Stephen, John's brother James, and others," Luke realized. "But no man can ever touch one's soul."

"Death eventually comes to all, does it not?" James added. "And what happens after death is up to each and every soul. Keep writing, Luke. And I'll keep teaching. Each life we touch with the Good News matters."

Luke and James shared a silent moment. They could almost feel the physical weight of their task to tell the world about salvation through Jesus alone.

As Luke gathered up his things and said farewell to James, his mind swirled with all he had heard. *Jerusalem will fall?* He pondered this foreboding revelation while walking along one of Jerusalem's side streets. *"They will be killed by the sword or sent away as captives to all the nations of the world. And Jerusalem will be trampled down by the Gentiles until the period of the Gentiles comes to an end."*

A group of Roman soldiers came marching down the street behind Luke, causing the hair on the back of his neck to rise. *Gentiles. Rome. It has to be Rome! The city that killed Jesus will fall to Rome.*

☧

John nodded slowly as Luke relayed what James had shared with him about the fall of Jerusalem. "I must admit when I first heard Jesus say this, I didn't understand why God would allow it. But this side of the cross, I do. Jesus gave the reason, didn't he? I've watched the rejection of Jesus as Messiah by my own people here in the city." He got up and paced around, grieved at the thought of what would come. He stopped and held out his hands. "Pilate washed his hands of responsibility when the people demanded he release Barabbas and crucify Jesus. The people shouted, 'His blood will be on us and our children!'"

Luke furrowed his brow. "And so it shall. I wonder if it will happen in our lifetime."

"Something tells me it will. I feel that taking Mary to Ephesus is the wise thing to do for this reason alone," John replied. "I've often wondered if that's why Jesus entrusted her to me. He knew James would need to remain in Jerusalem whereas I am free to leave."

Luke looked around John's house. "I know it will be hard to leave your home, but I think you are wise. The Romans already rule over the people here, so whatever will cause them to destroy Jerusalem will be an uprising such as we've never seen. Rome has no tolerance for rebellion."

"Yes, and even Governor Felix has been called back to Rome in disgrace for his vicious handling of a dispute between Jews and Syrians in Caesarea." John gripped his fist. "Rome rules with a strong arm, but with a fair one, even over its imperial representatives."

"Yet Felix left Paul in prison. He played up to the Jews and ignored justice to Paul when he could have released him," Luke fumed, crossing his arms. "Oddly enough, Rome has been on Paul's side before now, but it's been two years! I'm glad Felix is being replaced."

"I understand his coming replacement is a solid leader named Porcius Festus," John offered. "I pray he will put an end to this madness with Paul."

Luke nodded. "Perhaps he'll be a good man like the Roman centurion who amazed Jesus with his faith."

Liz beamed and shared a smile with Nigel.

"'I have not found so great a faith even in Israel,'" John recalled Jesus' words. "Isn't it interesting that Jesus said those words? Given what's coming for faithless Israel, even that statement was a revelation of sorts."

Luke picked up his satchel, ready to depart. "You know, John, you should write your own account of Jesus' life someday. Your knowledge, experience, and insights would bless the world."

John smiled and glanced at Liz, who wrapped her tail around his legs, purring in agreement. "I'm not much of a writer. I'm a fisherman, remember?" He looked up and gripped Luke's arm. "You're the educated physician."

"Well, Jesus made you a fisher of men. Perhaps he'll make you a fisher of words as well," guessed Luke with a broad grin. "Godspeed as you travel to Ephesus, my friend. Give Timothy my best, and tell him I'll send word of Paul's situation as soon as I can."

"I will. And let us keep praying for one another," John added, walking Luke to the door.

194

Outside Mary was petting Max. She leaned over and whispered in his ear, "Go with God, my little Tovah. Thank you for letting Chava take care of me as you take care of Paul."

Max nuzzled Mary with his big square head. *It be our honor,* he thought, winking at Kate, who sighed at having to tell him farewell once more. As Mary stood up to tell Luke goodbye, Max kissed Kate on the forehead. "Be br-r-rave, me bonnie lass."

Tears welled up in Kate's eyes. "I'll try." She turned to see Liz. "Time for ye ta see yer love, too. I'm happy ye get ta see Al in Rome."

"Merci, Kate," Liz replied, kissing her friend on the cheek. "I will give him your best, no? We will see you . . . sometime." Liz and Kate shrugged their shoulders and smiled. They never knew what to expect with their missions.

"Mary, thank you for allowing me to stay with you as I've traveled back and forth from Caesarea these past couple of years." Luke placed Mary's journal in her hands. "And thank you especially for sharing this."

"You are most welcome, dear Luke," Mary replied and smiled, clutching the journal to her heart. "Did you find Jesus' note?"

195

Luke smiled. "I did. And I'll make sure the world knows what the centurion said that day at the cross. He must have been special to Jesus."

Mary gave Luke a parting hug and whispered in his ear, "He still is."

"Goodbye, Mary." Luke kissed her on the cheek.

John put his hands on his hips and looked around the courtyard. "I suppose even these walls will come down when Jerusalem falls."

Luke, John, and Mary shared a silent moment as they considered what was coming to their beloved city.

"Restoration comes after brokenness," Mary offered. "If my Jesus can turn broken people into new creations, then why not Jerusalem?"

John put his arm around Mary. "A new Jerusalem? Now that would be amazing to see."

"Indeed," Luke agreed. He looked around for Max and Liz. "Come, Faith and Gabriel. Time to return to Caesarea. Paul needs us."

John and Mary lifted their hands in farewell as Luke walked out of the courtyard. Max gave Kate a parting glance and a wink.

Kate blinked back her tears. *Farewell, me love.*

"I'm glad Kate's headed ta Ephesus. I don't want her ta be here again when Jerusalem falls," Max whispered to Liz. "Once be enough for the lass." He and Kate had been in Jerusalem in 597 BC when it fell to the Babylonians.

"I am certain that at least one of us *will* be here," Liz suggested. She looked sadly at the walls of the beautiful city. "The fall of Jerusalem is the kind of mission that the Order of the Seven simply must attend to."

196

23

I Appeal to Caesar

CAESAREA, JULY AD 59

The foaming surf swirled around Paul's feet as he and Luke walked along the beach, accompanied by Paul's Roman guard, who stayed a few paces behind them. Paul breathed in the salt air and listened as Luke filled him in on his latest research in Jerusalem. *"You will be dragged into synagogues and prisons, and you will stand trial before kings and governors because you are my followers. But this will be your opportunity to tell them about me. So don't worry in advance about how to answer the charges against you, for I will give you the right words and such wisdom that none of your opponents will be able to reply or refute you!* Jesus predicted all that has happened to you, Paul. And he has been faithful to give you the words you have needed so far."

"I have been dragged into synagogues and prisons, and have stood trial before governors, but the only king I have appeared before wanted me dead after I offended him in Petra." Following Paul's three years in the Arabian desert alone with God, his zealous desire to begin sharing Jesus moved him to share the gospel with the first people he encountered. He stood in the great stadium at Petra, where he proceeded to offend the King of the Nabatean people by telling them they were pagans and needed to turn and follow the one true God. Although his words were true, his untested delivery backfired, and he had to escape Petra with his life. By the time he reached Damascus, the king had placed a price on his head, and he had to escape the city by being lowered over the wall in a fish basket.

Paul stopped to look out into the azure blue water of the Mediterranean with its pounding, powerful waves rolling into shore. Those roaring waves were constant and unstoppable, just like the truth of God. He looked down to watch the surf dissolve his footprints. "The charges against me will dissolve into nothing, I know. But how I long for an audience to share Christ the right way with kings! I pray that my words would not dissolve but remain etched on their hearts."

Luke put his hand on Paul's back. "Your words always leave a lasting impression, my friend. And I know you'll soon make such an impression on the new governor. He arrives any day now."

"I wonder," Paul thought out loud. "Perhaps it's time for me to create the opportunity myself."

"For what?" Luke asked.

Paul turned and looked up into Luke's face, smiling and squinting against the bright sunshine. "To stand before kings."

198

JERUSALEM

Nigel sat high in an alcove to watch the first meeting of the Sanhedrin with the new governor of Judea. Festus had arrived in the province three days earlier, but had come straight here to Jerusalem from Caesarea in order to launch his administration on a solid footing with the Jewish leaders of Israel. After the deplorable administration by his predecessor, Felix, Festus wanted to make it clear that *his* administration would be run according to strict adherence to Roman law and order.

The Jewish leaders talked quietly among themselves as they waited for the governor to arrive. "I just wonder what you will wish to discuss with the governor today," Nigel muttered as he looked at the men dressed in their tasseled robes. He spotted the infamous four who had been involved in the unjust trials of Jesus and Stephen: Zeeb, Jarib, Saar, and Nahshon. "What could possibly be on your scheming little minds, hmm?"

Suddenly the doors opened, and a middle-aged man with cropped black hair strode into the hallway, followed by his contingent of personal aides. He wore a brown sculpted leather breastplate over a red tunic, a wide belt, and sandals strapped up his shins. He displayed a muscular physique developed by his strict personal fitness regimen. How he conditioned his body spilled over to how he conducted his affairs—with order, consistency, and excellence. He nodded to the Jewish leaders as he strode by, making intentional, confident eye contact with them. He took a seat in his ornate imperial chair and lifted his hand for his aide to begin the formal greetings and introductions. He then opened the floor to allow the chief priests and the Jewish leaders to bring before him any business or concerns needing his attention.

"Your Excellency, it is an honor to have you as our new governor. We in the Jewish leadership of Israel look forward to a long, mutually beneficial relationship," Zeeb began, bowing respectfully in front of the assembly. "We do have a pressing matter concerning a troublemaker by the name of Paul."

"I clearly did *not* see this coming," Nigel remarked sarcastically.

"We request as a favor, your Excellency, to have Paul transferred here to Jerusalem, so he may answer multiple charges," Zeeb continued.

"So their nasty band of ruffians can *kill* him in an ambush along the way!" Nigel fumed with a fist raised in the air. "Don't fall for their scheme, Festus!"

199

Festus noted the eagerness on their faces. "Paul is being held at Caesarea, and I myself am going there soon. Let some of your leaders come with me, and if the man has done anything wrong, they can press charges against him there."

"Bravo!" Nigel exclaimed. "I like this chap already."

The Jewish leaders looked at one another with disappointment, but they would not rock the boat with their first request.

"Very well, Festus. We will certainly do as you suggest," Zeeb replied.

"Good. Next?" Festus asked, moving on to their next agenda item.

"I must return to let the others know this good news," Nigel said, scurrying out to the window ledge to catch his pigeon back to Caesarea. "Our Paul may finally get a decent hearing and get out of prison!"

Max, Liz, and Nigel managed to sneak into the great hall ahead of time and hide so they could listen in on everything that happened during Paul's trial before Festus. Along the pillared hallway open to the breezes of the Mediterranean, scarlet curtains hung from the high ceiling down to the richly tiled floor. The animals hid behind one of the panels closest to the governor's seat, and Liz sat on the end of the curtain to keep it in place. The room was filled with the Jews who showed up from Jerusalem.

"It appears that pompous Tertullus is not present this time as the official prosecutor," Nigel noted.

"Aye, but those four old windbag scoundr-r-rels be here!" Max growled, seeing Zeeb, Jarib, Saar, and Nahshon make their way to the front of the assembly.

Nigel pulled on his whiskers. "Blast it all! Zeeb was their mouthpiece in Jerusalem as well."

Liz put her dainty paw on Nigel's back. "Steady, Nigel. Evidently the Jewish leadership has returned the reins to the ones who had great success with Jesus and Stephen."

"So wha' happens now?" Max whispered.

"Right." Nigel cleared his throat and preened back his whiskers to regain his composure. "The Romans have a set procedure for bringing the accused and his accusers face to face." Nigel held up his fingers as he walked through the process. "First, charges must be prepared by the prosecutor (the Jews' legal counsel). Second, there must be a formal act of accusation by the interested party (the Jews). And third, the case is to be heard by the 'holder of the *imperium* in person,' who in Paul's case is Festus. Thus the Romans have a splendid system to address issues betwixt parties."

"*Oui,* but the Jews will need to come up with something that will matter to Rome in order for Festus to not simply dismiss the case," Liz interjected. "Years ago in Corinth, Gallio ruled in Paul's favor that the charges of the Jews were strictly questions of internal religious bickering, and therefore Rome would not be bothered. Rome has viewed Christianity as just a subset of Judaism, nothing more."

"On the other hand, that is changing, thanks in large part to Paul's success in spreading the gospel," Nigel noted. "It may very well be that Christianity has come into its own, and is not viewed as part of the Jewish faith any longer. Gallio's protective decision may no longer hold up in court."

Liz looked at Nigel with concern. "If so, then Christianity may indeed be seen as a threat to Rome, with followers worshipping Jesus, whom Rome branded as a criminal for claiming he was the King of the Jews."

200

The doors flung open and Paul was escorted into the chamber, attached to a light chain by the Roman guard, Hector. Luke and Aristarchus were there and locked eyes with Paul as he walked by, nodding their unspoken support with their presence. Meanwhile, Festus entered from the other hallway, and brushed by the curtains where the animals hid. Liz quickly pulled her tail inside the curtain so they wouldn't be noticed. Festus motioned for his aide to begin the formal proceedings, and then he motioned for the Jews to take the floor.

Zeeb took one step forward, gave a smug glance over at Paul and a sickly sweet smile to Festus as he bowed. "Your Excellency, what an honor to stand before you once again, and in this prestigious hall. Thank you for agreeing to hear our charges against this enemy of Israel and Rome." Zeeb lifted a bony, wrinkled finger and pointed it at Paul.

Paul's face remained calm, emotionless, and even disinterested. Festus took note of Paul's demeanor.

"I stand before you, having had a long personal history with troublemakers such as Paul. As shepherds of the people of Israel, it is our divine mandate to protect our people from those who would lead them astray," Zeeb continued. "We bring charges against Paul of violating our Jewish laws, of defiling our holy Temple, and," he paused for effect, "committing treason against the emperor by claiming another King as his sovereign."

"This is intolerable! They have no proof!" Nigel fumed. "LIARS!"

Max put his paw on Nigel. "Steady, Mousie."

"They are going to attempt to use the same angle they used with Jesus," Liz surmised. "They have to spin their religious charges with a political twist to make Rome listen."

Festus listened to Zeeb carry on for a few more moments, even though the Jewish leader offered not one shred of evidence for his claims. Finally, Festus held up his hand for Zeeb to be quiet and motioned to Paul. "You may answer these charges."

Paul gave the impression of one who was weary of fools, and remained unthreatened by Zeeb's words. "I have done nothing wrong against the Jewish law or against the temple or against Caesar."

Festus softly tapped his finger rapidly on the chair, thinking about how to respond. He wished to do the Jews a favor, and perhaps more stalling would help bring things out to help move this along. He sat up and cleared his throat, looking at Paul. "Are you willing to go up to Jerusalem to stand trial before me there on these charges?"

Paul spread out his manacled hands and shook his head. "I'm standing at this moment before Caesar's bar of justice, where I have a perfect right to stand. And I'm going to keep standing here. I've done nothing wrong to the Jews, and you know it as well as I do."

Festus squirmed as fire poured from Paul's eyes, and the truth hit the proconsul in the face. Indeed, he knew Paul was right.

"Hear, hear!" Nigel cheered from behind the curtain. Liz instinctively put her paw on his mouth lest the humans hear him.

"If I've committed a crime and deserve death, name the day. I can face it. But if there's nothing to their accusations—and you know there isn't—nobody can force me to go along with their nonsense. We've fooled around here long enough." He looked over at Luke before returning his gaze to Festus. "I appeal to Caesar."

A collective gasp rippled across the room. Festus raised his eyebrows at this unexpected development. "Remain here, all of you," he instructed, motioning to Paul and the Jews. He stepped off the elevated platform where his chair sat, making his way to just inside the hall where his advisors stood. They kept their voices low as they discussed the situation, but they did so right in front of the curtain where the animals hid.

"Talk to me," Festus demanded, his hands on his hips.

Festus's legal expert spoke up. "Sir, appealing to Caesar is a long-standing right of citizens of Rome, beginning with Octavian who was granted the right to judge on appeal with the *lex Julia de vi publica*. As a Roman citizen, Paul has exercised his right of *provocatio,* which protects him from summary punishment, torture without trial, from private or public arrest, and from actual trial by magistrates outside Italy, until he can indeed have an audience with the emperor."

"So I cannot convict or sentence him without offending Roman law, nor can I release him without offending the Jews," Festus thought out loud, rubbing the back of his neck as he looked up at the ceiling. "Very well. We must do what the prisoner has requested."

As Festus turned to leave, his advisor spoke up. "Sir, in doing so, you must next prepare a *litterae dimissoriae*—an explanatory statement of the charges to give to Emperor Nero."

Festus hesitated a moment as the next issue hit him. He let go an exasperated breath. "Understood. I'll tackle that problem next. For now, I have a ruling to make here."

The room was buzzing with people talking about Paul's outrageous request. Luke leaned over to Aristarchus. "Paul has created an opportunity to stand before kings. He knew he was going to do this today, regardless of what the Jews did."

Aristarchus raised his eyebrows. "Why does he want to stand before the Emperor?"

"Paul knows his only hope for justice rests with the Romans, not the Jews," Luke explained.

Festus stepped back onto the platform and took his seat. A hush fell over the crowd as they eagerly awaited his verdict. He looked right at Paul. "You have appealed to Caesar. To Caesar you will go!"

Paul nodded respectfully and raised his chin confidently as he glanced at Zeeb and the defeated Jews. Hector took him by the arm to escort him out of the hall. Paul winked at Luke as he walked by.

"But if you want to know the real reason he appealed to Caesar," Luke explained to Aristarchus with a smile, "Paul wants to share the gospel with the most powerful man in the world."

☧

"Another Her-r-rod's in the house?" Max asked in alarm. "No one's safe when one of them Her-r-rods be ar-r-round!"

"Nigel, tell us what you know," Liz demanded.

"Right. Well, King Agrippa II and his sister, Queen Bernic, have come here to welcome Festus to his new post as governor," Nigel explained. "They've been doing all of the official folderol that comes with such formal state business, and finally Festus brought up the issue of Paul."

"Gr-r-reat, that's all the lad needs," Max growled. "It were Agr-r-rippa's gr-r-reat gr-r-randfather who had the wee lads killed when he were out ta kill Jesus. An' his father killed James an' tr-r-ried ta kill Peter! We best not let Paul near him!"

"Steady, Maximillian." Liz put her dainty paw on Max's shoulder. "King Agrippa has little power in this case. He rules a respectable region of Judea, but at the authority of the Romans. Festus could topple Agrippa with a snap of his fingers, so Festus is still in charge for Paul's situation." She turned to Nigel. "Tell us about their discussion concerning Paul, *mon ami.*"

"Festus explained the situation with the Jews' charges against Paul, but how they did not accuse him of any of the evil crimes that he thought they would," Nigel relayed. "He said that all they had were 'some arguments with Paul about their own religion and about a man named Jesus, who has died; but Paul claims he is alive.' Festus shared how Paul refused to go to Jerusalem and appealed to Caesar, asking to be kept under guard until he could be sent to Rome."

"So wha' did Agr-r-rippa have ta say aboot it all?" Max wanted to know.

"He wants to hear Paul for himself," Nigel answered. "So Festus has arranged for a big to-do tomorrow, bringing Paul in to see the King and Queen. All the military officers and prominent men of the city will be in attendance. It will be quite the show of royal pomp, I assure you."

"But this will not be a trial, because no further legal proceedings can take place until Paul sees the emperor," Liz realized. "I wonder, though, if Paul will put Agrippa himself on trial."

☧

The sound of trumpets echoed through the marble hallways of the palace. The Roman military officers wore their full dress uniforms with their most elaborate helmets and swords, and saluted as Festus walked by, also dressed in his scarlet formal robe used for state occasions. King Agrippa and Queen Bernice trailed behind in their purple robes and golden crowns of royalty, with chins held high and wearing attitudes as pompous as their robes. Servants waved peacock feathers as the two proceeded to sit in gilded thrones in the great audience hall. The prestigious crowd stood to their feet, dressed in the finery of wealth and power of this Romanized city of Caesarea. Festus took his seat and motioned to the guards for Paul to be brought in.

Luke and Aristarchus sat in the audience, and couldn't help but grin at the contrast of their bandy-legged, aged, shackled friend paraded in front of such worldly prestige. They knew how meaningless the show of the crowd was to Paul. The Roman guard, Hector, led Paul to the front to stand before Festus, the King, and the Queen, and let the chain fall to Paul's side as he took a post next to the wall.

204

Festus looked around the room and then to his honored guests. "King Agrippa and all who are here, this is the man whose death is demanded by all the Jews, both here and in Jerusalem. But in my opinion he has done nothing deserving death. However, since he appealed his case to the emperor, I have decided to send him to Rome." He looked down at Paul and held up his hand in question. "But what shall I write the emperor? For there is no clear charge against him. So I have brought him before all of you, and especially you, King Agrippa, so that after we examine him, I might have something to write. For it makes no sense to send a prisoner to the emperor without specifying the charges against him!"

"Ye *think?!*" Max growled sarcastically. The animals were once again in their secure hiding place to witness this incredible event.

"*Déjà vu.* Like Lysias, Festus does not know what to write about Paul's case," Liz observed.

Agrippa said to Paul, "You have permission to speak on your own behalf."

"Remember Petra, old boy," Nigel muttered. "Please remember Petra!"

Paul stretched out his hand to begin his defense. "King Agrippa! I consider myself fortunate that today I am to defend myself before you from all the things these Jews accuse me of, particularly since you know so well all the Jewish customs and disputes. I ask you, then, to listen to me with patience."

King Agrippa nodded courteously. Nigel placed his hand over his heart. "I believe he learned his lesson at Petra. What a relief to see a good beginning with *this* king."

"All the Jews know how I have lived ever since I was young. They know how I have spent my whole life, at first in my own country and then in Jerusalem. They have always known, if they are willing to testify, that from the very first I have lived as a member of the strictest party of our religion, the Pharisees," Paul continued. "And now I stand here to be tried because of the hope I have in the promise that God made to our ancestors—the very thing that the twelve tribes of our people hope to receive, as they worship God day and night. And it is because of this hope, Your Majesty, that I am being accused by these Jews! Why do you who are here find it impossible to believe that God raises the dead?"

Festus studied the crowd, who murmured among themselves. And he kept an eye on the reaction of the king, who was fully engaged in what Paul was saying.

"I myself thought that I should do everything I could against the cause of Jesus of Nazareth. That is what I did in Jerusalem. I received authority from the chief priests and put many of God's people in prison; and when they were sentenced to death, I also voted against them. Many times I had them punished in the synagogues and tried to make them deny their faith. I was so furious with them that I even went to foreign cities to persecute them."

Festus raised his eyebrows. He did not realize that Paul had been a Christian killer before he himself became a Christian. *He hides nothing about his past,* thought Festus.

"It was for this purpose that I went to Damascus with authority and orders from the chief priests. It was on the road at midday, Your Majesty, that I saw a light much brighter than the sun, coming from the sky and shining around me and the men traveling with me. All of us fell to the ground, and I heard a voice say to me in Hebrew, 'Saul, Saul! Why are you persecuting me? You are hurting yourself by hitting back, like an ox kicking against its owner's stick.'

"'Who are you, Lord?' I asked.

"And the Lord answered, 'I am Jesus, whom you persecute. But get up and stand on your feet. I have appeared to you to appoint you as my servant. You are to tell others what you have seen of me today and what I will show you in the future. I will rescue you from the people of Israel and from the Gentiles to whom I will send you. You are to open their eyes and turn them from the darkness to the light and from the power of Satan to God, so that through their faith in me they will have their sins forgiven and receive their place among God's chosen people.'"

King Agrippa cocked his head to the side and wrinkled his brow at hearing of Paul's miraculous turnaround with his Damascus Road experience.

"And so, King Agrippa, I did not disobey the vision I had from heaven. First in Damascus and in Jerusalem and then in the whole country of Israel and among the Gentiles, I preached that they must repent of their sins and turn to God and do the things that would show they had repented. It was for this reason that these Jews seized me while

206

I was in the Temple, and they tried to kill me. But to this very day I have been helped by God, and so I stand here giving my witness to all, to small and great alike. What I say is the very same thing which the prophets and Moses said was going to happen: that the Messiah must suffer and be the first one to rise from death, to announce the light of salvation to the Jews and to the Gentiles."

He thinks this Jesus actually came back to life again after being crucified by Rome! He stakes his life on such madness! Festus couldn't take it anymore. "You are out of your mind, Paul!" he shouted. "Your great learning is driving you insane."

"I am not insane, most excellent Festus," Paul replied calmly, then turned his gaze to Agrippa. "What I am saying is true and reasonable. The King is familiar with these things, and I can speak freely to him. I am convinced that none of this has escaped his notice, because it was not done in a corner. King Agrippa, do you believe the prophets? I know you do."

A gasp rippled through the court to hear a prisoner address the King with such impertinence. Hector's eyes widened and he clenched his jaw, concerned that Paul would be silenced.

"Oh, dear," Nigel groaned with a paw to his forehead.

"Paul's got him r-r-right where he wants him," Max answered with a grin.

Agrippa squirmed in his seat. "Do you think you can persuade me to become a Christian so quickly?"

Paul lifted his hands and shook his chains in dramatic fashion. "Whether quickly or not, I pray to God that both you and everyone here in this audience might become the same as I am, except for these chains."

The people assembled in the court quickly murmured amongst themselves about what exactly the King meant. Was it meant to be a jest? Was it sarcastic or angry? Or, could it be that the King actually felt convicted and was interested in becoming a follower of the Way?

Festus snapped his attention to King Agrippa, who sat back in his chair for a moment and stared in amazement at this bold prisoner. The King placed his hands on either side of the throne and lifted himself to his feet. He hesitated for a moment, as if he were going to speak, but then stepped down from the throne to leave the room. Festus and the

Queen stood and followed King Agrippa out to the hallway. Everyone in the court immediately rose to their feet out of respect for the King.

Paul slowly lowered his manacled hands and looked over his shoulder to catch Luke's eye. Luke nodded his approval for how Paul conducted himself. "He did what he set out to do. He shared the gospel with a King." Luke realized that this, in fact, was a rehearsal of sorts, before Paul would stand before the emperor of Rome.

"So Paul considers this a great victory," Aristarchus replied. "These rulers heard the gospel!"

Agrippa, Festus, and Bernice stood in the hallway and discussed what had transpired in the court.

"He presented himself as a faithful Jew, a faithful Roman, and a faithful Christian," King Agrippa observed. "He may sound mad, but he truly believes everything he says."

"This man hasn't done anything to deserve death or imprisonment," Queen Bernice insisted.

"I agree," Festus replied.

"Indeed, he hasn't," stated Agrippa, turning to Festus. "He could have been set free if he hadn't appealed to Caesar." The King shook his head and began walking down the breezy hallway back to their plush quarters, followed by the Queen and Festus.

"The only one who is truly free here today is Paul," Liz remarked as they watched the rulers walk away in their finery. "He may have chains of iron on his wrists, but they have chains of unbelief on their hearts."

"Aye, an' this Her-r-rod will be haunted by Paul's words as long as he lives," Max agreed.

"The next time Paul presents words like that, it will be in front of Caesar himself," Nigel said, straightening his spectacles. "Next stop, Rome."

As the animals sneaked outside the palace to get back to Luke, a sinister voice echoed off the now empty marble hallway. "Not if I have anything to do with it."

208

24

FINAL VOYAGE

CAESAREA, AUGUST AD 59

The cry of seagulls overhead made Julius turn his gaze skyward. He studied the birds that seemed to hover in place above the docks, suspended by the strong, westerly sea breeze. The natural world always continued its rhythm despite what happened in the human realm. Sailing with this stiff wind would enable them to make up precious time as they traveled north. Given the news he had received upon arriving in Caesarea, Julius was anxious to make it back to Rome as quickly as possible, hopefully by October. A lump grew in his throat, and he closed his eyes to fight back tears. Suddenly a memory flashed through his mind as he listened to the seagulls.

"Come on, Grandfather! Let's show these seagulls that we Romans own this beach!" He was a young boy wielding a wooden sword, and ran headlong into a flock of seagulls spread out across the sand. Running next to him was his grandfather, who smiled and spread his arms out like a bird. Together they yelled and laughed as the flock of seagulls scattered before them, taking flight and squawking in protest. "Take that, seagulls! Only eagles are allowed on this beach!"

"We showed them, Julius! That's my little soldier," the grandfather cheered, putting his hand on young Julius's back. "You're a natural, just like your father."

"And just like you! I'm going to be the best soldier the Roman army has ever seen! Hail, Caesar!" Julius exclaimed, holding out his

*sword proudly. "Will you teach me to ride a horse, Grandfather? I'm
seven now. I want to be a knight like you!"*

*Marcus Antonius crossed his arms and cocked his head at his
eager grandson, giving him a teasing grin. "You think you're ready?
I'll make a deal with you. When you beat me at marbles, I'll give
you your first riding lesson."*

*Julius's eyes widened with delight. He dropped his sword on the
sand and eagerly dug into the leather pouch tied around his waist.
He held up his prized red marble. "I've got it with me! Let's go play,
Grandfather. I want to win!"*

*Marcus picked up his grandson and swung him around play-
fully on the beach. "You do, do you? Well, you'll have to be a quick
learner to beat the marble champion!"*

"Sir, new orders from Governor Festus," came the voice of Julius's
aide, Ajax, interrupting his happy memory.

Julius opened his eyes, cleared his throat, and snatched the dispatch
from the soldier's hands. As he unrolled it, he asked, "Have the prisoners
been secured below decks? I want to weigh anchor as soon as possible."

"Yes, Sir, forty-five new convicts from Caesarea, in addition to
our six prisoners from Egypt," the soldier replied, pointing to the new
orders. "Plus these three."

Julius read the orders and lifted his gaze to see Hector walking down
the dock toward him with three men in tow. "Paul of Tarsus, prisoner;
Luke of Macedonia, slave; and Aristarchus of Thessalonica, slave." His
gaze drifted back to the orders when he stopped with a frown. "Paul has
appealed to Caesar himself?" He looked at the bandy-legged, balding
man walking toward him in light chains. *He has no idea that he has
appealed to a madman*, he thought to himself. He would never voice
such treacherous sentiments out loud.

"Officer Antonius, I am entrusting these good men to your care for
safe passage to Rome," Hector said. "This is Paul and his two friends,
Luke and Aristarchus, but they are listed as his slaves. I assure you they
are slaves in name only. They simply needed that status in order to
accompany Paul to Rome."

"Entrusting? Good men? It sounds as if you actually care for these
prisoners," Julius said with a laugh.

Hector frowned and leaned in close to lock eyes with Julius. "I *do*. Paul is the finest man I've ever known. He's a good man of God and is not guilty of any crime. You'll soon see the truth for yourself. *And,* Paul is a Roman citizen."

"Not guilty? The charges against him from his accusers in Jerusalem are significant," Julius replied, holding up the orders with the letter to Emperor Nero, detailing the reason for Paul's delivery to Rome. He shot a sideways glance at Paul, who returned his gaze with his magnetic warmth. Julius did a double-take before looking back at Hector.

"Those charges have been fabricated by angry, jealous Jews who disagree with Paul's teachings," Hector protested, shaking his head. "Every Roman court and official has found Paul innocent, including Gallio in Corinth, Lysias in Jerusalem, and Governors Felix and Festus here in Caesarea. Since you hail from Rome, you are likely unaware of this, but the Jewish leaders in Jerusalem are set in their traditions. They forcefully oppose those who threaten their religious power."

On the contrary, this sounds vaguely familiar, Julius thought. *Something to do with my father . . . and that Jesus matter. Something, but what?*

"Paul has taught me a new way to live, and I believe what he says about Jesus, the Christ," Hector added. "I'm a Christian now. And these men are my brothers. Treat them well."

Julius raised his eyebrows to hear a Roman centurion talk this way. *Just like my father.* He looked at Paul and studied the curious little man. "I respect your opinion, Hector, and I will honor your request."

"Thank you, Officer Antonius," Paul said with a warm smile, bowing respectfully. "My traveling companions and I are grateful for your escort, and will try to be of help to you in any way we can. Luke is a physician and can provide medical assistance to anyone during the voyage." Luke bowed his head humbly.

Suddenly another memory haunted Julius as he gazed into Paul's eyes, but this memory was foggy. He couldn't quite put his finger on it, but something about this man was familiar. "Then we shall have a good journey. Welcome aboard the *Adramyttium*. We'll be stopping in seaports of the province of Asia where we'll locate a ship for passage to Rome. Our first stop will be Sidon."

Hector spoke up. "Paul has friends there. Allow him to go ashore and get supplies that he and his friends need." He handed a bag of food to Aristarchus. "Here is food for the journey to Sidon."

"Very well," Julius agreed.

Hector turned to Paul. "Godspeed, my brother. Thank you for leading me to the truth. May our Lord give you safety and the justice you seek as you stand before Caesar."

"Blessings on you, Hector," Paul said, smiling. "I'm going to have to write about your armor after all our discussions these past couple of years."

Hector nodded. "I'll keep my armor on and ready, including the armor I now wear on the *inside.*"

"Good! Farewell, my friend," Paul said, locking forearms with the Roman soldier.

Armor on the inside? Julius stood back, amazed at what he was witnessing with his fellow colleague and this prisoner. He didn't notice the dog, cat, and mouse scurrying on board while the men were saying their goodbyes.

212

☧

The sea spray rose from the bow of the ship as it plunged into another wave, slicing through the blue swells. Max tried to brace himself but kept sliding back and forth on the deck.

"We cannot stay hidden forever," Liz suggested. "Now that we are underway, we should make our presence known, except for you, Nigel. Although the sailors would not be surprised to see a mouse aboard. They are used to seeing rats."

Nigel shuddered and closed his eyes tightly. "Rats. How revolting!"

"All r-r-right then, Lass," Max replied, sliding into a crate. "After ye."

Liz lifted her curly-Q tail high in the air and sauntered onto the open deck from the stack of crates where the animals were hiding. She noticed Paul and Julius standing at the railing and decided to boldly "introduce" herself to the officer in charge. She went right up to the Roman soldier and wrapped her tail around his legs.

Julius was startled and quickly looked down when he felt her soft fur graze his legs. "Where did you come from?" he asked, picking her up and holding her close to his chest.

Paul's eyes filled with joy to see her, followed by Max trotting up behind Julius. "Forgive me, but these are my animals. They must have climbed aboard in Caesarea. They are extremely loyal and never leave my side, no matter how far I travel. I'll make sure they cause you no trouble."

"How unusual," remarked Julius with a curious laugh. "My grandmother Julia loved cats. My grandfather even had a statue of my grandmother carved with a cat at her feet."

Liz's heart jumped and her eyes widened. *You are Julius? Julius Antonius?* she meowed. Little did Julius know that the cat he now held was the very same cat in that statue.

"By Jove, it's Armandus's son, all grown up," Nigel muttered from his hiding spot behind a coil of rope.

Paul smiled and scratched Liz behind the ears. "Her name is Faith. She's very talkative." He squatted down to pet Max. "And this is Gabriel. Never was there a more faithful dog. Hi, boy. I see you and Faith followed me on board."

Max wagged his tail and licked Paul on the face. *Aye, but that's not important r-r-right now! Do ye r-r-realize who ye be talkin' ta, lad?* he barked in reply.

"Strange names for animals," Julius said, putting Liz down on the deck.

"I named them for the two things that have helped me on my life journey: faith and messages from God," Paul explained.

"Faith," Julius remarked with a sneer. "Faith in this Christ of yours? The man who died on a Roman cross?"

"Yes, who then rose from the dead," Paul replied confidently. "He's the Son of God, and he's very much alive. I've seen him."

"The Son . . . of God," Julius repeated slowly, nodding and pursing his lips doubtfully. "I had no idea that's who he was." The Roman wore a cynical smile. "And you've *seen* him? How?"

"He's appeared to me more than once," stated Paul boldly. "The first time was when I was out to kill Christians because I hated them all."

Paul allowed this fact to sink in a moment, for he already recognized the conflict with Christ within this soldier. Surprise and curiosity immediately entered Julius. *He hated Christians enough to kill them?*

"Jesus called me by name and asked me why I persecuted him. He temporarily blinded me on the road to Damascus and told me I was

213

destined to tell the world about him. From that day forward, he had me—mind, body, and spirit."

Julius's eyes widened. "You turned from a Christian-killer to a Christ-follower, just like that? This Jesus forgave you that easily."

"Just like that," Paul answered with a smile. "Love keeps no record of wrongs."

A distant memory stirred in Julius's mind with those words. His hand instinctively reached for his neckline. His eyes narrowed as he looked at Paul. "And you're saying this Jesus actually talks to you?"

"Yes, he does. More so in prayer and in his Word than in those rare visions. He gives me direction, strength, and encouragement," Paul replied. "Do you have someone like that in your life?"

Julius clenched his jaw and turned to place his hands on the ship's railing. He looked out to sea, trying to stifle his emotions. "I had someone."

Paul picked up on the soldier's struggle. He joined Julius at the railing, but allowed a moment of silence to pass. He didn't want to push. He noticed Julius fiddling with something tied around his neck. After a minute, he said, "I'm sorry, Officer Antonius. Did you lose him or her recently?"

Julius nodded slowly. "I received word from my commander when I reached Caesarea that my grandfather had passed away. He left a sealed box for me in Rome. I lost my father to a shipwreck when I was very young, so my grandfather was really more like my father. He was a good man."

"I'm sure he was," Paul replied. "I'm very sorry. I know how difficult it is to lose someone that close to you. You must be anxious to return to Rome."

Julius nodded and straightened up, clearing his throat. "Yes, I am." He slapped his hands on the railing and turned. He was finished with this conversation. He didn't even get started on his anger over his father's faith in Jesus and how it ultimately cost him his life. He wanted answers but now he had other pressing matters. "Excuse me while I consult with the captain on our course headings."

Paul bowed to let him pass. "Of course. Thank you for sharing with me. I'll be praying for you in this."

Julius halted a step but didn't reply. He proceeded down the deck, his red cape flapping in the wind behind him. Liz jumped up onto a crate next to Paul. He reached out to pet her. "Little Faith, we have a soldier to minister to on this voyage. He has the weight of the world on his shoulders with this grief. And he's fighting Jesus in the midst of it."

If you only knew who this soldier is and who he lost, Liz thought, tears welling up in her eyes at this sad news. *He's lost Marcus! And I never knew he lost Armandus as well.*

When Paul went over to Luke and Aristarchus, Liz jumped down to join Max and Nigel.

Nigel's whiskers quivered with excitement. "I say, do you realize the extraordinary reunion that has just taken place betwixt Paul and Julius? They first met on the very same dock in Caesarea, when Julius was but a boy!"

"Aye, when the lads were playin' with the r-r-red marble," Max remembered.

Liz closed her eyes and tried to envision the long-ago scene. "Do you remember when we asked Clarie if Julius and Theophilus would continue the family legacy of playing a key role in the Jesus story?"

"Indeed, I do," Nigel answered. "She gave the elusive 'Time will tell' answer."

"That day Gillamon were in the Libertas statue on their ship," Max added. "Clarie said he were goin' ta R-r-rome ta watch over the boys. Why would he himself go if they weren't supposed ta do somethin' important in the future?"

Liz's tail whipped back and forth as she thought this through. "When Clarie reported to us about Peter meeting in Bella's home in Rome, she didn't mention Armandus. *Quel dommage!* Julius told Paul that his father died in a shipwreck when he was young."

"Armandus was to follow his family to Rome." Nigel frowned. "It appears he never made it."

"How could this be? How could the Maker allow such a tragedy to happen?" Liz lamented. *"Cher* Armandus. *Je ne comprends pas."*

"Aye, we need answers aboot wha' happened. I for one want ta know how 'an' *why* it happened," Max insisted with a growl. "An' wha' if the Enemy wrecked that ship? He's been after the house of Antonius ever since Marcus saved wee baby Jesus."

Nigel raised a finger in the air. "And although the sword of Antonius

215

did indeed find Messiah at the cross as he so threatened, the Enemy now sees that his vengeful scheme played right into the Maker's plan to save the world. I can only imagine how much he desires to destroy the lives of those boys, but what could Armandus's sons possibly do to threaten the Evil One?"

"We must wait for Clarie or Gillamon to appear to answer our many questions, no?" Liz suggested. "One thing we do know, *mes amis*. This was no ordinary meeting for Paul and Julius aboard this ship. Julius has been assigned to escort Paul to Rome. This tells me we are in for no ordinary voyage."

Nigel clasped his paws behind his back and rolled up and down on the balls of his feet. "It indeed has an overwhelming feeling of destiny to it."

"An' anythin' with destiny will have danger as well." Max frowned. "Includin' another shipwr-r-reck. The Enemy might be out ta finally stop the Antonius legacy once an' for all."

216

25

RESCUED AT SEA

The early morning sun glistened off the blue water as they sailed to the north of Cyprus. The animals sat together at the bow of the ship, where Liz most enjoyed the view. She loved catching glimpses of dolphins hugging the ship in the waves below, blowing kisses to them as they surfaced.

"This turquoise sea is simply breathtaking!" Nigel exclaimed.

"The actual name for this intense blue color came from these very waters," Liz noted. "The humans of Turkey use the word *turkuaz* to describe the color of the Mediterranean and Aegean seas, but of course we call it 'turquoise.'"

"Those cr-r-razy turkeys named this land after themselves when we were on our way ta the Ark," Max recalled. "But those birds weren't nearly as pr-r-retty as this sea."

Paul, Luke, and Aristarchus were also near the bow. Liz beamed when she saw Julius walking toward them. "Our Julius has become quite at ease being with these men. He seeks out Paul's company more and more."

Paul closed his eyes and soaked in the sunshine and the salty air. Once more, the ship's crew called out their now familiar strain of commands to shift the mainsail and change direction back toward the coast.

"Why can't we just sail due west? We've been zig-zagging along the coast for almost two weeks now," Aristarchus noted. "It's taking forever to make any distance at all."

"It's these prevailing westerly winds of late summer that are keeping us hugging the shoreline," Paul explained, holding up a piece of string

217

to show the wind's direction. "We have to tack back and forth from the coast to the sea to catch the wind."

"We can't sail west across the open sea from Cyprus like we sailed east along this coast two years ago," Luke added, making a note in his journal.

Aristarchus pointed to the shoreline. "I remember how quickly we sailed past this coast and south of Cyprus on our way to Jerusalem. A lot of water has passed under us since that time."

Julius stood listening to the men discussing their course. "I see you certainly have been at sea before, Paul. You understand a sailor's challenge in navigating these waters."

Paul smiled. "Good morning, Officer Antonius. Yes, I've had my fair share of sailing. This is my twelfth voyage in these seas."

Julius raised his eyebrows. "That's impressive. Well, the captain informs me we should finally make the port of Myra by this afternoon. I will seek out our transfer ship to Rome once we're in port. There should be at least one Alexandrian grain ship available."

"Egypt is Rome's 'bread basket,'" Luke offered. "You speak of a private merchant ship?"

Julius crossed his arms over a bended knee as he rested his foot on a crate. "Yes, Doctor. One that Rome has commissioned for imperial service. Rome receives about twelve hundred shipments of grain each year, that is, during the eight months when sailing is possible. That means roughly five large grain ships arrive in Rome's port of Ostia daily, so I'm certain we can locate one at Myra on its way to Rome from Alexandria."

"I understand you were in Alexandria before coming to Caesarea," mentioned Luke. "I attended to one of your Egyptian prisoners yesterday who said you picked him up in the emerald mines of Berenike. He is recovering from an abscess, but will be fine. He told me he is to become one of Rome's new gladiators."

"Thank you for treating him, Doctor," Julius replied. "Yes, the Emperor sent us to Egypt as part of his Imperial Regiment." He noticed Luke writing in his journal. "What are you writing there?"

"At the moment, details of our voyage," Luke replied.

"The good doctor journals everything," commented Paul with a smile and a pat on Luke's back. "While I was imprisoned in Caesarea, Luke traveled all over Jerusalem and Judea researching the life of Jesus.

He wanted to get eyewitness accounts from people who knew Jesus best, including his mother, Mary."

Luke nodded with a smile. "Mary is an amazing woman. She's been through so much, losing her husband and her son, but she retains her amazing faith."

"I imagine she is near the age of my grandmother, who lived in Jerusalem for a time," Julius remarked sadly, turning his gaze out to sea.

Paul saw the pained expression on Julius's face. "Officer Antonius, would you walk with me? I need to stretch my legs." Julius nodded and he and Paul slowly strolled down the deck.

"Tell me about your family. Are you married?" Paul asked.

"Not to a woman," Julius answered with a smile. "I'm married to the army."

"I understand. I'm married to my work as well," Paul told the younger man with a laugh. "You mentioned your grandmother. Is she still living?"

"Yes, she is. I know that losing Grandfather hit her hard." Julius shook his head. "My mother lives in Rome. And I have one older brother, Theo—Theophilus—who is an attorney there."

Suddenly Paul's memory stirred at hearing the unusual name of Julius's brother. There was something familiar here. "All the more reason for you to reach Rome quickly, to be with your grandmother. She's lost her husband and a son. Mary could relate to her pain." Neither Paul nor Julius knew the even greater connection those two women shared.

The two men were quiet for a moment, listening to the sounds of the sea as they walked along. Julius had grown comfortable with getting to know Paul, whom he found to be incredibly kind, humble, and genuinely interested in individuals. He treated everyone with love and respect, from the lowliest slave to the captain of the ship. There was something about Paul that drew Julius to him. Despite being a prisoner bound for Rome, Paul exuded nothing but joy and unshakeable peace. Julius felt he could finally give expression to questions he had struggled with silently for years.

"I told you I lost my father in a shipwreck. He was on his way back to Rome after having sent our family on ahead from Caesarea. Before he set sail he wrote to my mother that he had become one of you." Julius stopped and looked over at Paul, who returned his gaze with a puzzled expression. "A Christian."

219

Paul smiled and nodded. "I see. Go on."

"He was anxious to get back to Rome and risked sailing late in the season to reach us," Julius continued. He stopped and leaned against the rail. "There were only a few survivors when his ship wrecked off Sicily. One of those survivors was a slave named Eligius." Julius clenched his jaw and frowned. "That slave relayed all of this to my mother in Rome."

Paul studied the struggling soldier. "What happened?"

"A sudden storm came up at night, the ship caught fire, and everyone scattered in the chaos to abandon ship in the lifeboats. Eligius was pinned under some debris," Julius continued. "My father heard his screams and left the safety of the lifeboat to reach him, despite the fact that he himself was injured. By the time my father helped Eligius get free to swim to safety, he must not have had the strength to swim back to the boat. They never saw him again."

Paul lowered his head. "How tragic, Officer Antonius. I'm so sorry your father was lost that night. He was a hero to give his life for another."

220

"He gave his life for a slave! When Eligius asked my father why he came back for him, he told Eligius that he was safe in Christ, but knew that this slave was not," Julius spat. *Safe? He died!* What did he mean? How could my father lay down his life like that? My mother even became a Christian, but I've never understood any of this. My father is dead because he was a Christian."

Paul let Julius give full vent to his grief and anger, and just listened. Finally, he said, "Your father is *alive* because he was a Christian."

Julius looked at Paul in confusion. Paul smiled and calmly explained what he meant. "That is the promise of eternal life through Jesus, who indeed laid down his life so anyone who calls on his name will be saved. God in his *justice* requires that payment for sin be made, because it is so costly. Sin keeps us from his presence. No one is good enough. We all fall short, for all have sinned. God knew we were unable to pay our debts, so he sent his only Son as the perfect sacrifice to pay the penalty for us. You see, at just the right time, when we were still powerless, Christ died for the ungodly. Very rarely will anyone die for a righteous person, though for a good person someone might possibly dare to die, as your father did for Eligius. But God demonstrates his own love for us in this: While we were still sinners, Christ died for us. Jesus in his *goodness* willingly gave his life on that Roman cross to pay the price for our sins, once and for all. No one sent him there. And as I've shared with you, he rose again to conquer sin and death. Through Christ all sins are forgiven, and new life for eternity in heaven awaits those who accept him as Savior and Lord. But joy, hope, peace, love—these are the spoils of war here and now. We are more than conquerors through Christ, both now and for eternity."

Paul allowed a quiet moment to pass between them. He knew this was a lot for this Roman soldier to wrap his mind around.

"The grace of Jesus saved your father. He knew he was saved, but he knew that Eligius faced an eternity apart from God if he drowned that night. Your father had eternity in mind when he made the decision to get back in that water. The fierce love of God compelled him to rescue Eligius. 'Greater love has no one than this, that one lay down his life for his friends.' Jesus himself said that. And your father realized that in Christ, there is no slave or free. Every soul is priceless treasure."

Julius hung his head, shaking it as he processed all this. "My father is alive with this Jesus of yours?"

"Yes, he is," Paul answered simply. "So you have the hope to be with him again someday as well, if you also choose to believe."

"My grandfather also believed in your God. Is he in heaven?" Julius asked, fiddling with the object on the leather cord around his neck.

"I trust that his faith saved him as well. Perhaps we'll learn the answer to that question when we reach Rome." Paul pointed to Julius's neck. "Whenever you speak of your grandfather, you touch that object around your neck. May I ask what it is?"

Julius didn't realize he was touching it, but slowly pulled the leather necklace out from under his tunic. "He gave me this. Someone once told me to never forget the treasure it represents."

"The red marble!" Nigel exclaimed, putting his paw up to his mouth. He had followed them to listen in on their conversation.

Paul wrinkled his brow. "I've seen this before." He shot his gaze up to look Julius in the face. Those emerald green eyes! He could see a woman with the same green eyes calling her two boys as they stood with him on the docks of Caesarea. Now he knew who this soldier was, as the scene of that day flashed clearly across his mind. He smiled. "Love is patient, love is kind. It does not boast, it is not proud. It does not dishonor others, it is not self-seeking, it is not easily angered."

221

Tears quickened in Julius's eyes and a lump filled his throat. "It keeps no record of wrongs," he whispered hoarsely. "The red marble lesson."

"The red marble lesson," Paul echoed warmly. "Hello, Julius."

☧

"I tell you, it was a sublime moment! I felt as if I were in the poetic scene from Homer's *Odyssey* when Father and Son, Odysseus and Telemachus, are reunited after twenty years!" Nigel exulted, lifting his paw to recite the touching ancient scene:

"Straight to the prince he rushed and kissed his face and kissed
his shining eyes, both hands, as the tears rolled down his cheeks.
As a father, brimming with love, welcomes home his darling
only son in a warm embrace—"

The little mouse wrapped his paws around himself. "To see Paul and Julius also embrace after twenty years left me speechless! Quite the Odyssey in and of itself, I assure you."

Liz's eyes filled with happy tears. *"Magnifique!* Look how the Maker set up that encounter long ago, for such a time as this, when Paul can now help Julius with his struggle."

"Do ye think he'll choose ta believe in Jesus then?" Max asked.

"I do not believe Julius is quite ready to make that decision, as Paul has given him much to ponder," Nigel answered. "But his heart is certainly open now."

Liz looked up at the impressive carvings in the rocky cliff face above them here in Myra. Beautiful sculptures, funeral scenes, and depictions of daily life of the deceased were carved into house or temple tombs above the Roman amphitheater and the east side of the necropolis.

"The Lycians believe that the souls of their dead are transported from these tombs to the afterworld. Like the Egyptians, and the Nabateans at Petra, these lost pagan people are obsessed with death, but sadly don't know the truth Paul shared with Julius about eternal life," Liz lamented. "I know Paul hopes the gospel will spread into this place one day."

"It feels gr-r-rand ta stretch me legs on land," Max exclaimed gladly. He wobbled for a moment. "But why do I still feel like I'm goin' ta tip over?"

"Because you still have your sea legs," came a voice as they walked by the stone wall along the dock in Myra. "All four of them."

Max spun around to see a frieze of carved faces at eye level with him. He cautiously walked up to a face carved with puffy cheeks blowing wind. "Hello, Max," the face said with lively, twinkling eyes.

"Gillamon, it's aboot time ye showed up!" Max exclaimed. "I've got a bone ta pick with ye. Why weren't we told aboot Armandus an' the shipwr-r-reck? Wha' happened? Were it the Enemy? Why didn't the Maker stop it? It were Armandus, after all!"

"Steady, Max," Gillamon said softly. "I know the news came as a shock to all of you, but we felt it best that you learned it now, on this voyage with Julius. While it was a difficult thing for his family, you must trust that the Maker allowed it, even if you are not told why. Reasons may ease the pain of tragedy, but more often than not they prevent trust in the Maker if given too soon. We can't always see the large canvas the Maker is painting with the many lives connected in his masterpiece. Sometimes we simply must wait until the picture is complete."

"*Bonjour,* Gillamon. We have been happy to see Julius reunited with Paul," Liz interjected. "Long ago we wondered if Julius and Theophilus would be part of the Antonius legacy to forward the story of Jesus. With Julius escorting Paul to Rome, we can only assume this is so. The Maker is now 'painting' this part of the Antonius canvas, no?"

"You are correct, Liz. The Maker paints such a picture with every human family on Earth," Gillamon explained. "Generation after generation can lead to blessings or curses, depending on how each generation responds to life events and the choice to trust the Maker through it all."

Nigel straightened his spectacles as he studied the carved, blowing face. "Brilliant picture analogy, old boy. But back to the journey at hand, and Max's question. Was the Enemy involved in that horrid shipwreck? And might history be poised to repeat itself on this journey?"

"The schemes of the Enemy are always working against the Maker's plans," Gillamon answered elusively. "But sometimes a rescue at sea can be more powerful than the storm itself. That includes the rescue of people and even items, like Luke's journal."

Suddenly his face froze as a group of humans walked by. When they had passed, Gillamon's smiling eyes once again filled the face. "Max, it's time for you to know the reason behind something Jesus told you long ago. Do you remember when he asked you to walk on the water with him, when you were terrified of the storm?"

"Aye," Max assured him, closing his eyes to remember that stormy night on the Sea of Galilee.

Gillamon recounted Jesus' words for him: *"You need to overcome your fear not only for your own good, but for my purposes. One day you will be in a far worse storm than this, and you will need to encourage one of my greatest servants to be brave."*

Max stood erect and wore a determined look. "So a storm be br-r-re-win'. I'm r-r-ready ta help Paul then."

"It's not Paul you'll need to encourage." The carved face blew into Max's fur as Gillamon's voice trailed off and the blank eyes of the face reappeared. "It's Julius."

Max, Liz, and Nigel looked at one another in stunned silence as they heard the voice of Julius ordering his soldiers to transfer their prisoners to the new ship.

Max looked at the Roman soldier. "Jesus called the lad wha' he isn't yet—one of his gr-r-reatest servants."

224

"Jesus calls things as they will be, for he already sees the complete picture," Liz pointed out. "Perhaps Julius's portrait as his great servant will be painted in the middle of the coming storm."

"And from Gillamon's comment about rescuing Luke's journal, I daresay Luke's pen will write the words to tell the story behind that painting." Nigel shuddered as a stiff north wind suddenly blew over them. "But it may be more than just a storm. Ever since Homer's *Odyssey*, every literary account of a Mediterranean voyage has included a storm *or* a shipwreck. Even Jonah's account is filled with the violence of the tempest in these waters."

As the growing wind blew back his whiskers, Nigel searched the mercurial skies and quoted prose from Homer's *Odyssey* while they walked to their awaiting ship:

Now Zeus who masses the storm clouds hit the fleet with the North Wind—

> *a howling, demonic gale, shrouding over in thunderheads the*
> *earth and sea at once—*
> *and night swept down from the sky and the ships went plunging*
> *headlong on,*
> *our sails slashed to rags by the hurricane's blast!*

26

SEEKING SAFE HARBOR

Have all of our prisoners and soldiers been transferred and accounted for?" Julius asked his aide, Ajax.

"Yes, Sir," Ajax reported. "All seventy passengers are now aboard this ship. Conditions below are tight for the prisoners, but all are secure."

Julius stood with the captain and ship's owner as they prepared to get underway. The captain was an Egyptian by the name of Pelagius and the ship's owner was a Roman by the name of Proteus. They were none too pleased with this additional burden of passengers, but as a ship commissioned by Rome, they had no choice but to abide this military official, who assumed ultimate command of the ship. In an emergency, Julius would have the final say.

The Alexandrian ship was 140 feet long, 36 feet wide, and required a depth of 33 feet in order to float its massive 500-ton cargo of passengers, grain, and other supplies and merchandise for transport to Rome. The bow and the stern were shaped the same, with upward sloping lines, and a carved goose's neck that hung off the back. Its dark blue wooden hull was trimmed with honey-colored decks, railings, and trim. Two massive paddles came out of the stern to steer the ship that had a single mast with mainsail and one square sail rigged off the bow.

"How many are now aboard in all?" Julius asked the captain.

"We had 206 passengers before you boarded," Pelagius replied, handing him the ship's roster: *137 slaves, 23 merchants, 19 civilian passengers (including 4 scholars from the University of Alexandria, retired military, women, and children), 25 crew, captain, owner.*

"So your prisoners are headed to Rome for a 'Roman holiday'?" the ship's owner Proteus asked with a slimy grin. He referred to prisoners being used as lion fodder in the games, providing entertainment for the masses. If they weren't victims themselves, some would be trained as gladiators to fight to the death against those lions or other gladiators. But at least they had a slim chance of survival.

Julius ignored his comment, choosing not to engage in making light of the plight of his prisoners. He was a soldier who followed orders, whether he approved of them or not. "So 276 is our total passenger count. What is your course heading?"

"We'll sail past Rhodes through the archipelagoes of Greece, and across to the strait of Messina to reach Italy," Pelagius answered, looking up at the direction of the stiff wind blowing from the north. "At least that is the plan. We'll have to keep near the mainland for now to catch the offshore breezes."

226

"Very well," Julius replied. "Let's get underway."

Immediately the captain called orders to the crew, who spread out like ants on a disturbed anthill to ready the ship for departure. Max, Liz, and Nigel sat with Paul, Luke, and Aristarchus between midship and the bow, trying to stay out of the way of the sailors who climbed up the rigging to hoist the sails and who released the massive ropes that secured the ship to the dock.

"It's mid-September, but hopefully we will make it to Rome within a month's time," Julius reported to them. "Let me know if you need any provisions in the days ahead."

"Thank you, Julius," Paul replied. "We were able to buy food in Myra. You are welcome to join us to share a meal this evening."

Julius nodded with a smile, watching Luke find a blank section to begin journaling the log of this voyage. "Many thanks. And for your notes, Doctor, we have 276 passengers on board."

Luke held up his pen and smiled. "I'll make a note of that, thank you."

"Make yourselves comfortable." Julius turned to go inspect the conditions below decks.

Max leaned over to Liz and Nigel and whispered, "I wonder how long until the tempest ar-r-rives."

"I hope sooner rather than later, as I do not believe I shall be able to make myself comfortable knowing what is to come," Nigel replied. "I fear I shall remain awake until that first crack of thunder."

"You must try to rest, *mon ami*," Liz encouraged him. "We all must be rested and ready, for when it comes, it will demand every bit of strength we have."

OCTOBER AD 59

We had several days of slow sailing, and after great difficulty we finally neared Cnidus. But the wind was against us, so we sailed across to Crete and along the sheltered coast of the island, past the Cape of Salmone. We struggled along the coast with great difficulty and finally arrived at Fair Havens, near the town of Lasea.

Luke finished his entry and looked up at the blowing clouds that never ceased to spill across the skies in the wrong direction. *Fair Havens . . . safe harbors.* "So much for the captain's originally intended course. These contrary winds have cost us a lot of time. The weather is becoming dangerous for sea travel this late in the fall."

"Will the captain press on to Rome?" Aristarchus asked, looking over at Paul standing with Julius, the captain, and the ship's owner.

"We'll soon find out," Luke said, opening his journal to make some more notes about the meeting taking place.

Julius stood with his arms folded across his chest, listening to the men debate their options. He had invited Paul's opinion, not only for his sound judgment in general, but for his seafaring knowledge.

"There is no way we can make it to Rome at this point," Pelagius concluded. "We've spent too much time just trying to head west with these contrary winds. The crew has had to do nothing but fight these winds without a single day in port. They are exhausted."

"Yes, it's past the Day of Atonement," Paul agreed, noting an understood date on the calendar that marked a period of feasible but risky sailing until early November. That is when the *mare clausum,* or closed sea, began, as overcast skies for days on end had prevented sailors from getting their bearings. It was for this reason, more so than for storm hazards, that shipping ceased for the winter. Captains navigated with rough

227

charts and depended on seeing the sun and stars to keep their bearings. Otherwise, they were sailing blind.

"But Fair Havens is not where we need to remain for the winter. It is too isolated," Proteus suggested. "The passengers and crew would have to go on slim rations to last the winter at anchorage."

"Not only is it isolated, but contrary to its name, Fair Havens is too exposed. All it would take is a heavy gale to drag our anchors and run us aground," Pelagius added. "I suggest we travel on to the port of Phoenix, where we'll be well supplied for winter, and the passengers can actually disembark the ship. I say we risk it. All we need is a brief south wind to take us to Phoenix where we can ride out the winter in better conditions."

Julius turned to Paul. "Phoenix is some forty-odd miles north. What say you, Paul?"

Paul wore a troubled expression as he gazed up at the soaring mountains of Crete, the largest island of Greece. He knew how quickly a violent northeaster could roar down one of those 7,000-foot mountains, following a south wind. "I believe there is trouble ahead if we go on—shipwreck, loss of cargo, and danger to our lives as well."

The captain and ship's owner shook their heads and murmured their objections. Julius put his hands on his hips and looked across the ship at the weary crew and passengers. He scanned the exposed harbor of Fair Havens and knew that Phoenix was a far better harbor with only southwest and northwest exposure.

"Captain! A light wind is blowing from the south!" a sailor called from atop the mast, pointing to the shifting breeze indicated by the strips of linen tied to the rigging. "We can make Phoenix with this wind!"

Julius looked from the captain to Paul and back to the captain. "Weigh anchor, Captain. Let's make for Phoenix."

The captain and owner smiled, and Pelagius immediately gave the order to pull up the anchor. "Sail close to the shore!" he called.

Paul frowned and clasped his hands behind him as he walked back to report the final decision to Luke and Aristarchus. Julius felt unsure of his decision, not because of the sound arguments made by the captain, but because he trusted Paul. He held him in the highest regard ever since the day he realized who he was, and, like Hector, he came to believe he was one of the finest men he had ever met. The centurion looked up at the Cretan mountains and hoped they would be in Phoenix in just a matter of hours. Then they could get some much-needed time on shore and rest from these incessant contrary winds.

Liz's tail whipped back and forth as she listened to Paul relay the plan to the others. "I do not like this. Paul's advice comes from his knowledge, but also the prompting of the internal Wind—the Holy Spirit."

"Oh dear, we might finally be in for our dreaded storm," Nigel shuddered, looking disheveled. He had hardly slept these last two weeks, remaining on edge for the arrival of the tempest.

"Mousie, I never seen ye look such a mess," Max remarked, noting Nigel's crinkled whiskers and hazy spectacles.

Liz jumped up on a crate to study the winds as they left the harbor of Fair Havens, the lifeboat bobbing along behind them. Since they were not sailing far, the crew didn't bother to pull it up to stow on deck. She frowned, a feeling of imminent danger in her spirit. "They should have listened to Paul."

They were no sooner into the gulf than dark clouds began swirling above Mount Ida, the highest point on Crete. "Look there!" Nigel pointed to the quickly growing clouds. "According to Greek mythology, Zeus, father of the gods, was believed to have grown up in a cave on that mountain. I jolly well see where Homer got the idea for Zeus sending that storm."

Max felt it before he heard it. His fur stood on end as the temperature dropped. "Hang on ta yer spectacles, Mousie. I feel it comin'!"

Suddenly the wind changed direction and roared down the mountain, gaining momentum as it raced into the harbor and struck the starboard bow of the ship. The rotating clouds swirled above them and a wall of dark rain cut off the horizon.

"Everyone take shelter!" Julius and his soldiers shouted, trying to get the passengers to go below decks. The people began shouting and hurried down the narrow stairs to the stifling cabin below.

"All hands to the rudders and sails!" the captain cried as sailors attempted to steer the ship into the wind.

Paul, Luke, and Aristarchus remained where they were and prayed for the endurance of the crew as they fought against the sudden storm. It was no use. The sailors couldn't turn the ship into the wind, so they gave up and let it run before the gale.

229

Julius rushed to the captain as fear rippled through the crew. "What can we do to secure the ship?"

"We'll soon be blown along to the sheltered side of a small island named Cauda," Pelagius shouted above the wind, wiping the stinging rain out of his eyes. "There we'll prepare the ship as best we can. We'll pull in the lifeboat and bind the hull with ropes to strengthen it."

Julius turned to see Paul, Luke, and Aristarchus standing behind them. "We're ready to help," Paul offered. Julius regretted not listening to Paul's wisdom, but was grateful there was nothing on Paul's mind other than doing all he could to help them. He and Paul shared a knowing look of mutual support and ran to help the sailors.

Men lined up along the deck to heave on the rope that pulled the lifeboat, which was now full of water. The men shouted and grunted as they strained with all their might to lift the heavy boat from the turbulent water. Some slipped and fell and others felt the burn of the rope in their hands while they were blinded by the pounding rain. Once the lifeboat was aboard, the men turned it face down, and a wall of water spilled onto the deck, running right toward the animals.

"Hang on, Mousie!" Max shouted as he grabbed the little mouse by the scruff of his neck so he wouldn't be washed overboard.

Max and Liz huddled together until the men had tied the lifeboat securely to the deck. Then they squeezed under the overturned boat, which shielded them from the rain. They were able to still glimpse out from underneath the lifeboat to watch as the crew feverishly began to use tackle and put ropes under the hull of the ship.

"Wha' are they doin'?" Max wanted to know, his voice echoing off the inside of the lifeboat.

"They are bracing the timbers of the ship with those ropes," Nigel replied, shaking the water off his fur. "The strain of these winds above and the mammoth waves below could cause the ship to fall apart or leak until the ship founders, meaning it becomes waterlogged."

"Lower the mainsail!" the captain cried. "Set the stormsails and we'll tack on the starboard side!"

"The sailors are terrified of being driven into the shallows off the African coast of Libya," Liz said, shivering as the cold set in to her drenched fur. "It is a graveyard of shipwrecks on those sandbars."

"Ain't that a long way away?" Max asked, shaking from head to tail.

230

"Once we pass Cauda, the only thing out there is the open sea with nothing to stop us from being blown all the way to Africa," Nigel relayed.

"Well, Gillamon were r-r-right. The storm finally came," Max said. "Ye two huddle close ta me an' I'll keep ye safe an' warm."

Liz curled up next to Max, and Nigel climbed up in between them. They all shivered but took comfort from the fact they were together. For now, there was nothing they could do but hang on.

☧

The ship bobbed along like a cork, now enduring the full agony of high waves and howling winds. Everything and everyone was soaking wet from the rain, the sea spray, and the seeping water waterlogging the timbers. No one could move, else they would slip or be thrown down from another jarring wave. They couldn't light a fire to warm themselves or to cook anything. But no one thought of eating in these miserable conditions. Everyone's stomach was seriously upset.

Julius ordered all the prisoners released from their chains, and men took turns at the pump to keep the bilge from causing the ship to sink further than it was already. The crew began throwing the cargo overboard on the second day. The seas filled with bag after bag of Egyptian grain, amphorae of oil and wine, and all other non-essential foodstuffs. On the following day they even took some of the ship's gear and threw it overboard. The terrible storm raged for day after miserable day. The captain had no idea where they were, as the sun and the stars were blotted out. Finally, all hope was gone.

Julius sat with his back to the wall of the damp ship, allowing the tiny flame of his oil lamp to burn just a moment longer. He listened to the whimpering of children, the crying of women, the retching and coughing of sick passengers, the creaking of the tenuous timbers, and the howling of the wind outside. Fear began to grip him in a vise as he realized that the ship could not hold together for long. Cold water swirled around his feet and he felt his mortality. He was going to die at sea as had his father.

Suddenly he felt a cold nose nudge his hand. He looked down and there sat Max, staring at him. In the midst of this miserable situation, Julius actually smiled to see the dog by his side. He lifted his hand to pet

231

Max, who curled up next to him, resting his head on the weary man's thigh and providing some much needed warmth.

Hang on, Laddie, Max thought. *Ye'll make it out of this storm—I promise.*

Julius repositioned a leather satchel to a more comfortable position behind his head. He was careful to ensure that this satchel carrying the huge emerald for Nero was not inadvertently tossed overboard. He kept it nearby, but only revealed its contents in confidence to Paul, when he shared why he was in Caesarea in the first place. He told Paul about his twelve soldiers and their expedition to Berenike for Nero's giant emerald and gladiators. It all seemed so absurd, that he would cling to a green emerald when they might lose their very lives. But Julius knew that if he did survive this storm and arrived in Rome without the jewel, he'd be dead anyway.

Nero's treasure was the emerald. Julius's treasure was the gift of the red marble given to him by his grandfather. And Paul shared with Julius that his treasure was like a safe harbor where he was always protected: *But we have this treasure in jars of clay to show that this all-surpassing power is from God and not from us. We are hard pressed on every side, but not crushed; perplexed, but not in despair; persecuted, but not abandoned; struck down, but not destroyed.*

Julius looked over and noticed Paul curled up with the cat snuggled in his arms, sound asleep. How that little man could have such peace in the middle of the storm amazed Julius. He wanted that peace, both for this moment and for all time. Paul's treasure was the jewel of liberating peace and power of God. Julius wanted the security of knowing that no matter if this ship went down, he would not be destroyed. He would be safe. *Safe like my father.*

"If ever I needed a message of hope, Gabriel, it's now," Julius confided in Max quietly, petting him and blowing out the oil lamp. He closed his tired eyes and uttered the first genuine prayer he had ever made. "God, please help me."

Just as Julius drifted off to sleep, the answer to his prayer showed up.

232

SHIPWRECK

Liz was the first one to feel it. Her fur rose on end and she looked around, catching Max's eyes in the darkness with her sharp night vision. "Max, do you feel it, too?" she whispered softly.

"Aye," Max whispered back. "Somethin's here."

Suddenly a tiny glow of light particles began swirling between Liz and Max. The two of them marveled as the light particles slowly came together to form a beautiful angel. His light caused Liz's eyes to glow. He held a finger to his mouth and smiled. She returned his smile but didn't move. Nigel was curled up in a deep sleep on top of Luke's journal with his back to the angel. Luke had placed the journal on a crate to keep it off the wet floor. The angel reached out a shimmering hand to touch the journal, and for a moment it glowed. Nigel stirred but did not wake up as the angel grazed his fur.

The angel then reached over to softly touch Liz. She immediately felt warmth course through her body, and her fur dried instantly, giving her comfort she had not felt in almost two weeks. She began to purr and blinked her eyes slowly in gratitude. The angel nodded before turning to reach over and touch Max. He, too, felt warmth run from his head to his tail, drying his fur. The angel looked kindly at Julius, who remained asleep, and touched the weary soldier's foot. Max could feel the warmth spread over the soldier's body, drying his clothes. He let go a contented sigh in his sleep.

The angel then reached over and touched Paul, who also felt the comforting warmth for the first time he could recall. His eyes sensed faint light and he slowly opened them to see the angel. He remained motionless, still holding Liz in his arms.

"Don't be afraid, Paul, for you will surely stand trial before Caesar!" the angel said softly with a voice of such beauty it made Paul's heart swell with peace. "What's more, God in his goodness has granted safety to everyone sailing with you."

Tears welled up in Paul's eyes with relief and gratitude at the angel's message. "Thank you," he spoke in a broken whisper. The angel nodded and slowly began to fade as the light particles dispersed until all was dark in the cabin. Paul hugged Liz to his chest as he felt her purring next to him. "We're going to be okay, little Faith," he whispered in the darkness. "God has brought his peace into our storm." He slowly drifted back to sleep.

An' Paul will br-r-ring peace inta Julius's storm tomorrow, Max thought, looking at the sleeping soldier.

Liz and Max smiled at one another in the darkness and closed their eyes, also falling asleep dry, content, and safe.

234

Julius awakened to the sound of sailors walking around up on deck. His eyes fluttered open, and he felt oddly refreshed. He sat up and noticed that his clothes were completely dry. He patted himself all over before spotting Max grinning up at him. "How did I get so dry?" He reached over to muss the fur on Max's head. "Hmmm, you're dry, too. You can sleep next to me anytime, boy," he said with a smile. He reached behind him and pulled the leather satchel to wear across his chest before climbing the stairs to reach the deck. When he lifted the hatch, a gust of wet sea spray blasted him in the face. Julius grunted. *It was nice while it lasted.*

Liz came over to Max with bright eyes. *"Bonjour, mon ami.* I rested well after the angel came. Did you?"

"Aye, Lass, an' so did Julius," Max answered.

"I simply cannot explain this!" Nigel told them, scurrying over and lifting his paws to look at his dry, clean fur. "Am I dreaming?"

"You were last night, *cher* Nigel," Liz answered with a giggle. "An angel appeared to let Paul know that everyone aboard will be saved from this storm. He reached over to touch Luke's journal and you. He touched us as well, and we became dry."

Nigel's eyes widened through his spectacles that were even clean and spotless. "How terribly sad that I slept through an angelic encounter! But why did the angel touch Luke's journal?"

"I dunno, but it glowed for a wee bit," Max shared. "It looked like the scr-r-roll of Matthew's writin' that Gillamon shared with us when he were that Nike statue. It were all shimmery."

"Utterly fascinating! I must go inspect it!" Nigel exclaimed, running back over to the crate.

Paul sat up and stretched, patting himself to feel his dry clothes. "Thank you, Lord," he murmured as he rose to his feet. He leaned over to nudge Luke and Aristarchus to wake up. "You're going to want to hear this," he announced with a big smile. "Come with me to see the crew and Julius."

Luke and Aristarchus rubbed their eyes and yawned, groggily following Paul up to the hatch and out on deck. Max, Liz, and Nigel scurried along as well. The skies were still gray and overcast, the sea spray still blew, and the whitecaps continued to form around them, but the rain had ceased at least for the moment. Any relief from water was welcomed by the exhausted sailors.

Paul greeted the centurion. "Good morning, Julius. I hope you were able to get some sleep."

"Surprisingly I did," Julius replied, "and, strangely enough, I woke up dry."

Paul smiled at Julius. "I think I know why. Can you please call the captain and the crew together? I need to speak with them."

Julius cocked his head curiously, but replied, "Very well." He proceeded to order his men to call the crew and went to get the captain and the ship's owner.

"What is this all about, Paul?" Luke asked.

"Good news, Luke," Paul answered with a wink.

Once they were assembled, Paul looked at the weary men who hadn't eaten in so long, and who had lost all hope. "Men, you should have listened to me in the first place and not left Crete. You would have avoided all this damage and loss."

Pelagius and Proteus folded their arms defensively. Pelagius muttered, "He called us up here to rub salt in our wounds?"

"Shh, listen to what he has to say," Julius snapped back. "He was *right* before, so pay attention to what he has to say now."

235

Paul smiled and lifted his hands. "But take courage! None of you will lose your lives, even though the ship will go down. For last night an angel of the God to whom I belong and whom I serve stood beside me, and he instructed me, 'Don't be afraid, Paul, for you will surely stand trial before Caesar! What's more, God in his goodness has granted safety to everyone sailing with you.' So take courage! For I believe God. It will be just as he said. But we will be shipwrecked on an island."

The crew looked at one another, hesitant to accept this news as truth. Such words seemed too good to be true. They didn't know Paul's God, but were willing to hang on to any shred of hope. Pelagius and Proteus shared a skeptical look, but inside they secretly hoped Paul was right again. The prisoner had amazingly become the captain, as he was the only man of courage left on board this seemingly doomed ship.

Julius walked over to Paul, shaking his head in wonder. "You told me you named your dog 'Gabriel' because God sends you messages, and last night he sent you a *messenger* with those words?"

236

"*They were at their wits' end. Then they cried out to the Lord in their trouble, and he brought them out of their distress.* That's a psalm that God's people have claimed across time, and God is faithful to answer," Paul replied. "Have you prayed for God's help in this storm, Julius?"

The soldier felt a rush of emotion and nodded slowly. "Last night."

"Then it seems your prayers have been answered," Paul commended him with a hand to Julius's back.

Julius smiled. "I didn't know God would actually hear me, much less answer, and so quickly at that."

"He always hears and he always answers," Paul replied. "But not always so quickly. But his answers always come at the perfect time. Just when we need them the most."

"God is in charge of this ship now," Julius affirmed.

"He always *has* been," Paul followed with a smile.

Luke and Aristarchus stood there in their wet clothes and noticed that Paul and Julius were dry. "How?" Luke asked, pointing at them.

"Must have been the touch of the angel," Paul surmised, looking at Julius, whose eyes widened. "But it won't last. We'll all be in the water soon."

"Luke may be wet but his journal is not." Liz raised her eyebrows as an idea struck her. "And I now have a theory as to why."

DAY 14 OF THE STORM

The ship groaned and creaked as the wind kept up its neverending battering. Two sailors on the night watch sat together on the deck, by now accustomed to the misery of being cold and wet, in the darkness of midnight.

"Do you hear that?" one of them asked the other.

The other sailor sat and listened for a moment. It was very faint, but it was there. He jumped up. "I hear breakers! We must be near land!"

"By Jove, he's right!" Nigel cheered. He and Max decided they would take turns staying on watch with the sailors. Nigel had been awake for thirty-six hours, but the sound of approaching land made him perk up from the adrenaline rushing through him.

"Hurry, let's check our depth," the first sailor said, running to get the sounding line stowed near the rudders. It was a thin rope with a lead weight tied to the end, with knots of leather tied at certain known lengths along the rope. As he cast it into the sea, he began to call out the marks by "reading" them as they slid through his hands. "Three . . . five . . . seven . . . ten . . . thirteen . . . fifteen . . . seventeen . . . twenty." Suddenly the weight hit bottom. "Twenty fathoms!"

"So 120 feet deep," the other sailor replied. "Let's take it again in an hour. We'll know soon if we're nearing the shore."

"And those breakers," the other sailor replied.

Nigel paced back and forth, anxiously awaiting the next sounding. Finally the sailor once again threw the leaded rope into the sea and began the count. "Three . . . five . . . seven . . . ten . . . thirteen . . . fifteen fathoms! We're definitely getting closer to shore."

"Yes, 90 feet now!" the other sailor affirmed. "If we're going to wreck on an island as Paul said, I plan to be in that lifeboat. Only a few of us can fit and I'm not going to come this close to shore only to drown."

"Agreed. Let's alert the captain and set the anchors at the stern," the other sailor replied. "Later we'll act like we're setting anchors on the bow and lower the lifeboat instead."

"Why, you salty scoundrels!" Nigel scowled as the two sailors went to inform the captain and the other crew members about the situation.

"I may not be able to sound the alarm, but I know a certain Scottie who can."

It wasn't long before the captain, Julius, the ship's crew, Paul, Luke, and Aristarchus were topside, watching as the sailors secured four anchors off the stern of the ship.

"If we can hold our position until daylight, then we can try to run the ship aground once we know what this land looks like," the captain explained. "We need to watch for shoals and find an optimal spot to beach her. Right now we don't know where we are and we won't until daylight."

"Well, then we'll pray for daylight," Julius replied, drawing a smile from Luke.

Max, Liz, and Nigel stood off to the side discussing the sailors. "Which ones were they, Nigel?" Liz asked.

Nigel pointed to the two sailors who were on the midnight watch. "It was those two cheeky fellows who took the soundings and discussed their dastardly scheme."

"Then I'm not lettin' them out of me sight," Max growled.

"Right! Give them the what-for and all of that!" Nigel cheered with his tiny fist in the air.

After a while the two sailors went over to some of their friends and huddled together, discussing their plan. Together they walked to the front of the ship and acted as if they were getting ready to set anchors from the bow.

Max waited until they lowered the lifeboat, and then sounded the alarm, barking loudly and running to Paul. He pulled on Paul's cloak to follow him.

"What is it, boy?" Paul asked, immediately following Max to the front of the ship. Julius ran after them when he saw what was happening, calling his soldiers to join them.

One of the sailors had his leg over the railing, prepared to climb down a rope net to reach the lifeboat just as Paul, Julius, and Max reached him.

"YOU THERE! STOP!" Julius demanded.

"They're trying to get away with the lifeboat!" Ajax shouted.

Paul turned to Julius and the soldiers. "You will all die unless the sailors stay aboard."

"Cut the ropes," Julius ordered his soldiers, not questioning Paul's judgment for an instant. "No one is going anywhere. We either sink or swim together."

The sailor quickly jumped back on board as Ajax and another Roman soldier named Nemo pushed their way to the front of the ship, swords in hand. The rest of the sailors cleared out of their way as they raised their swords and severed the ropes to the only lifeline they had.

"Sometimes we have to let the lifeboats go." Paul put his hand on Julius's shoulder as they watched the lifeboat drift away into the darkened sea. "Your father would be proud of the fine soldier you've become, Julius. He released his lifeboat to save another. Now you've released yours to save us all."

Julius didn't reply but clenched his jaw and nodded. There was something cathartic about what had just happened and thinking about his father's experience. But instead of a screaming slave, he had heard a barking dog. "One thing I do know, Paul. You named your messenger dog well."

239

☧

No one wanted to go below decks but sat in groups, waiting and praying for morning. The rain had stopped, so the passengers also came up to get some air. A thick fog started to envelop the ship. Their long ordeal was almost over, but the most dangerous part of their journey still awaited them.

The animals huddled together and listened to the sound of the breaking waves rolling into shore out there in the dark night. Liz curled her tail around her legs. "Well done, *mes amis*. Nigel, your night watch and Max, your alarm saved the day."

"Bravo, old boy," Nigel said, nudging his fist into Max's shoulder. "Thank goodness that suspenseful interlude is over." He yawned as suddenly his eyelids grew heavy from sleep deprivation. "I daresay . . . I feel as if I'm once again in the middle of Homer's *Odyssey*." He yawned again and lay back on a waterlogged rope there on the deck. He started slowly reciting a scene from the *Odyssey*, yawning every few words:

"Well, here we landed, and surely a god steered us in through the pitch-black night. (Yawn.) Not that he ever showed himself, with

thick fog swirling around the ships, the moon wrapped in clouds and not a glimmer stealing through that gloom. (Yawn. His speech was now slurred by his grogginess.) *Not one of us glimpsed the island—scanning hard—or the long combers rolling us slowly toward the coast, not till our ships had run their keels ashore. Beaching our vessels smoothly, striking sail, the crews swung out on the low shelving sand and there we fell asleep . . .*

Nigel's mouth hung open and he started snoring.

"*. . . awaiting Dawn's first light,*" Liz finished the line for Nigel.

"I hope we get ta beach *our* ship smoothly," Max told Liz as they heard the sound of the crashing breakers in the dark, moonless night. "Or else we're all in for a r-r-rude awakenin'."

☧

There was a faint ribbon of light on the horizon behind the clouds. Paul looked around at all the people on board and for the first time could truly see how weak and downtrodden they were. He leaned over to Julius. "No one has eaten in so long. These people won't have the strength to swim to shore if it comes to that."

Julius scanned the crowd. "I agree. Now that we are in calmer waters at anchor, the people might actually feel like eating something."

"And we can finally light a fire to bake some bread. Can you please have the crew bring the remaining supply of grain topside? We'll make bread and feed everyone before we attempt any kind of beach landing," Paul decided. "It will boost their spirits as much as their bodies."

Julius looked at Paul with respect. "Even though you are a man of faith and know God has said that no one will perish, you still use your common sense."

Paul smiled. "Faith without works is dead. God intends for us to use the minds he gave us to do all we *can* do, while we trust him with what we *can't* do."

"This God of yours makes more sense to me all the time," Julius replied, getting up and rousing his men. He told the captain to have the crew bring up all the remaining grain and several baking stones, and to make fires.

As the sky grew lighter, the people woke to the smell of bread, and

240

immediately their faces rose with hope. The crew and soldiers passed around baskets of bread.

Paul stood up in the middle of the ship and urged everyone to eat. "You have been so worried that you haven't touched food for two weeks. Please eat something now for your own good. For not a hair of your heads will perish." He took some bread, and raised it as he gave thanks to God before them all. "Lord, we thank you for this bread, and we thank you that you have delivered us safely here to this shore. I thank you for your promise that not one of us will be lost today. Please, strengthen our bodies and our spirits. Amen." He broke off a piece and ate it.

"This scene has a feeling of *déjà vu* to it, no?" Liz pointed out with a grin as she spotted a hungry little boy devouring a piece of bread, smiling for the first time in two weeks. "It is not five thousand to feed, as with Jesus. But watching the men pass out the bread to these 276 hungry people after Paul's blessing brings that day back to me so clearly."

"Aye, except Al ain't here ta gobble up a basket of fish himself," Max laughed.

241

"I recall how Jesus gave Al the very first fish because he had found the little boy with the lunch," Nigel reminded them. "I think an overeating celebration was in order that day." He saw Julius approaching and scurried behind the rope.

Max shook his head, thinking of Al. "He never would've survived this voyage with no food for so long."

Julius walked over to Max and squatted down with a piece of bread. "A fine watchdog such as you needs to have the strength to swim to shore, too." He smiled and put the bread down for Max, mussing his head. "Here's some for you, too, Faith," placing another piece in front of her. He looked at the two animals and shook his head. "Faith and Gabriel. Who would have thought two little animals could be so important?"

"*If you only knew, Monsieur,*" Liz meowed. "*Merci pour le petit déjeuner.*"

Julius stood to go sit with Paul, Luke, and Aristarchus. Luke held a piece of bread in his mouth while he scribbled the morning's events into his journal.

Julius smiled at Luke's relentless pursuit of capturing moments in time, both past and present. Luke finished and closed his journal, setting it aside to reach for more bread. "May I see your journal, Luke? I've watched you write in it these many weeks, and I'm curious as to its contents."

"By all means," Luke agreed gladly, handing Julius the journal.

Paul grinned. "May I suggest one of Luke's earlier entries of his notes from Mary?"

Julius opened the journal to the beginning and began to read.

Two other men, both criminals, were also led out with him to be executed. When they came to the place called the Skull, they crucified him there, along with the criminals—one on his right, the other on his left. Jesus said, "Father, forgive them, for they do not know what they are doing." And they divided up his clothes by casting lots.

The people stood watching, and the rulers even sneered at him. They said, "He saved others; let him save himself if he is God's Messiah, the Chosen One."

242

The soldiers also came up and mocked him. They offered him wine vinegar and said, "If you are the king of the Jews, save yourself."

There was a written notice above him, which read: THIS IS THE KING OF THE JEWS.

One of the criminals who hung there hurled insults at him: "Aren't you the Messiah? Save yourself and us!"

But the other criminal rebuked him. "Don't you fear God," he said, "since you are under the same sentence? We are punished justly, for we are getting what our deeds deserve. But this man has done nothing wrong."

Then he said, "Jesus, remember me when you come into your kingdom."

Jesus answered him, "Truly I tell you, today you will be with me in paradise."

It was now about noon, and darkness came over the whole land until three in the afternoon, for the sun stopped shining. And the curtain of the temple was torn in two. Jesus called out with a loud voice, "Father, into your hands I commit my spirit." When he had said this, he breathed his last.

The centurion, seeing what had happened, praised God and said, "Surely this was a righteous man."

Julius clenched his jaw, moved to his core by what he had just read about Jesus: his miraculous birth, his ministry and miracles, including healing a Roman centurion's servant with a word, his trials before the Sanhedrin, Pilate, and Herod, and his scourging and mocking by the Roman soldiers.

"We are the only ones who know that Julius has just read about his father in Luke's journal," Liz said, wiping her eyes. "Luke only recorded 'the centurion,' not his name: Armandus."

"Terribly moving, I must say," Nigel added. "Do you think we should somehow help Julius discover his father's identity in Luke's journal?"

SPLASH! Julius turned to see the crew lightening the ship further by throwing the cargo of wheat overboard. He handed Luke the journal. "Thank you, Doctor. I wish to read more, but I need to check in with the captain."

Paul had studied Julius as he read the account of Jesus' crucifixion. He felt the soldier was close to embracing Jesus as Lord. The hunger was there. The faith was there. He simply needed to act on what was stirring in his heart. "I'll go with you, Julius."

243

Together Julius and Paul stood and walked over to the captain and the owner of the ship. Liz watched the men walk along the deck, and turned to answer Nigel's question. "Something tells me we won't have to."

"I don't recognize this coastline, but over there is a bay with a beach," reported Pelagius, pointing to a rocky shore with an inlet and a sandy spit of land.

"I think we can get to shore by running the ship aground," Proteus added.

"Agreed. How do we proceed, Captain?" Julius asked.

"We'll cut off the anchors and leave them in the sea. Then we'll lower the rudders, raise the foresail, and head toward shore," Pelagius explained. "If all goes well, we'll slide onto the beach and at least be able to get the people off the ship in an orderly fashion."

Paul nodded. "It's a complex maneuver, but the captain and crew know what they're doing. We certainly couldn't have done this without those sailors."

"Very well," Julius said. "Make it so."

Pelagius gave the orders and the crew hopped to it, cutting the anchors, lowering the rudders, and raising the foresail all at the same time. Julius explained the procedure to his soldiers, and they brought up the chains to be ready to once again bind their prisoners as they waded in to shore.

Everything was set in motion as they started covering the last half-mile to the beach. But all of a sudden the ship lurched unexpectedly forward and people went falling all across the deck.

"We've hit a shoal!" the captain shouted, getting up and running over to the railing. He looked at the water below them and saw a deep brown swirl of mud clouding the water with silt and debris. "The bow is stuck in thick mud!" He pulled his hands through his hair in fear as he looked back at the waves getting ready to crash into the stern. "Everyone, brace yourselves!"

A huge wall of water came crashing into the stern, lifting the ship from behind and once more sending people falling forward across the deck. The soldiers fell into a heap with the iron shackles covering them. They heard a cracking sound as more waves smashed into the weakened hull. It didn't take long before the ship started to break apart. People began to scream and panic, running to the railing as part of the stern gave way.

The soldiers slowly got to their feet, and Ajax spied Paul, Luke, and Aristarchus at the railing with the six gladiator prisoners. He quickly surmised that they were trying to see how to jump overboard without being sucked under the ship.

"The prisoners! If they swim to shore and escape, we'll be held responsible!" Ajax shouted, drawing his sword, running toward them.

"He's going to kill Paul!" Liz cried, reaching her paw out as Ajax raised his sword above Paul's head.

244

Saving Luke,
Saving Julius

Ajax gritted his teeth and readied his sword to strike Paul but suddenly felt the grip of a firm hand on his upper arm, halting the sword's forward progress. "STOP!" Julius shouted as he stepped in between the Roman soldiers and Paul, Luke, and Aristarchus. "Do not slay these prisoners! I alone will be held responsible if they escape."

Ajax and Nemo drew back their swords and looked at one another questioningly. It was sheer instinct from standing orders that any Roman soldier responsible for losing a prisoner would pay with his own life. Yet here was their commanding officer, taking the full blame should that occur. The soldiers nodded and put their swords away.

Paul exhaled in relief. "Thank you, Julius."

Julius nodded and turned to shout orders to everyone on board. "Listen up! All who can swim are to jump overboard first and make for land. The rest of you, hold on to planks or debris floating from the ship. MOVE!"

Immediately everyone scurried over the side as the ship began to break apart from the center. It was a scene of mass hysteria as water enveloped the feet of everyone on deck. Children were screaming as their mothers jumped overboard, holding them tightly. Those who could swim made it quickly for shore. But Paul, Luke, Aristarchus, and Julius took their time, helping others get onto wooden planks so they would be safe.

"Come on, Liz an' Nigel!" Max instructed, pushing a piece of wood over to them as he dog-paddled in the cold water, swimming as if he had always known how. "This will carry ye in ta shore." As Liz and Nigel climbed aboard their raft, Max suddenly spotted two objects floating out to sea. It was Luke's journal and Julius's leather satchel holding Nero's emerald. "Get ta shore!" Max gave them a shove and turned around to swim out to sea.

"Where are you going, old boy?" Nigel shouted back as he and Liz floated on a wave toward shore.

"I've got ta save it!" Max shouted back, spitting salt water out of his mouth.

Julius treaded water and looked around him to make sure everyone who needed help had received it. He didn't see any people left in the water, as everyone had escaped safely to shore. He bumped into some debris, and thought, *But everything aboard is lost.* He remembered that he had been reading Luke's journal before the shipwreck. *Oh, no! Luke's journal!* He then suddenly realized that the satchel carrying Nero's emerald was no longer around his neck. *It must have slipped off when I jumped overboard!*

Out of the corner of his eye, Julius spotted Max swimming out to sea. *Where is he going?* Julius took off swimming after Max. Rain suddenly began to fall, sending sheets of stinging drops blowing across the water and blinding both Julius and Max.

A riptide was pulling Luke's journal and the leather satchel quickly out to sea, and Max was now caught in the center of it. *Which one do I r-r-rescue?* Max pleaded silently in prayer, growing tired as he fought against the riptide that sought to pull him under. *If Luke loses his journal, he'll lose all he wr-r-rote. But if Julius loses his jewel, he'll lose his life! Maker, please tell me wha' ta do! I can't let the laddie die as his father did!*

Julius was also now caught in the riptide, and felt the strong current that grabbed at his ankles to pull him under. He plunged under the water for a moment but fought his way back to the surface, gasping for air. He strained against the blinding rain to look ahead and saw he was getting closer to Max. He pressed on, swimming with the riptide out to sea, figuring the little dog had simply got caught in the powerful current. As he closed in on Max, it was then he saw what the Scottie dog was after. *Luke's journal! He's going after Luke's journal!*

But as Julius saw Max nearing the journal, the little dog turned to the right, heading toward something else. *What is he doing?* A wave lifted another object up briefly for Julius to see what Max was after. It was his leather satchel. *Gabriel is getting my jewel!* He quickly scanned the water for Luke's journal, which was drifting in the other direction. *And I'm going to get the* other *jewel!*

Max took in a mouthful of salt water as he opened wide to clamp his strong jaws onto the leather strap of Julius's satchel. His eyes were stinging from the rain and salt water, but he turned so he could see how far he was out from shore. Suddenly he spotted Julius reaching for the journal. *There's a good lad!* Max started swimming for the centurion.

Julius put the journal inside his sculpted leather breastplate and smiled as he saw Max paddling up to him, pulling the leather satchel through the water. "There's a good boy!" When Max reached him, he released the strap and Julius grabbed it, slipping it securely over his head. "Thank you, Gabriel!" he cried, getting nose to nose with Max in the water. "Now let's get you back to shore."

Aye! Max thought, barely able to stay afloat. He was tired. Julius put his arm out to steady the tired dog.

"I'll help you to land," came a voice from behind them.

Julius turned to see a small fishing boat with an island native reaching his bronzed arm out over the side, smiling. Max turned and instantly noticed that the native had sparkling blue eyes. He winked at Max as Julius pushed the little dog from underneath so the man could take him into the boat. Julius then gripped the railing and pulled himself into the boat as the native helped him. He landed with a grunt to lie back for a moment, catching his breath after that harrowing ordeal. "Thank you. Our ship got caught on the shoals. What island is this?"

The native smiled as he began rowing them quickly into shore. "Malta." He turned and looked at Max, who shook off water from head to tail, but it was now raining heavily. "I didn't know I'd be a fisher of men . . . or dogs . . . today."

Max grinned and barked, *"But it took a journal an' a jewel ta be yer bait then, huh, Clarie?"*

☧

Flames rose from a bonfire the natives of Malta had quickly built for the cold and weary shipwreck survivors. The passengers and crew huddled around the fire to get warm, and the natives scurried around, giving them pieces of cloth to wrap around themselves. The rain began to lessen, and Paul studied the situation. "We need to keep this fire going." He walked off to go collect more wood for the fire.

Ajax stood on the sand, watching Paul. "He always seeks to make himself useful, even in the smallest of tasks."

Nemo wiped back his stringy wet hair. "I'm glad you didn't kill him."

Just then Clarie rowed the fishing boat into shore, and Ajax and Nemo ran over to help, pulling the boat onto the sand. "We're on Malta. That means we were blown almost 500 miles west over the past two weeks," Julius told them, lifting Max onto the beach and climbing out of the boat. "Is everyone accounted for?"

"Yes, including all the prisoners. Everyone is gathered around the fire," Ajax reported.

Julius made his way over to the bonfire, spotting Luke and Aristarchus. Luke turned and smiled. *"Now* we can say that not one was lost, just as the angel told Paul. Welcome ashore."

Julius nodded, grinned, and reached inside his breastplate for Luke's journal. When he pulled it out he wrinkled his brow and handed it to Luke. "Here's your journal, Doctor."

"Praise God, it's safe! Thank you, Julius!" Luke cried, taking it from him.

"What's wrong?" Aristarchus asked, seeing the centurion frowning.

"It's completely dry," Julius replied, shaking his head. He pointed at the journal and started to speak but stopped himself. He cleared his throat. "Excuse me while I find the captain."

Luke and Aristarchus opened the journal and indeed, the parchment was dry. The ink had not bled into the pages, destroying the words Luke had captured. The two men looked at one another with wide-eyed smiles, and hugged over God's goodness.

Clarie and Max walked up to Liz and Nigel on the beach. "Look who fished me out of the sea then," Max greeted them, shaking all over and spraying Nigel's already spotted spectacles.

"I'd love to be *able* to, old boy," Nigel retorted, removing his spectacles as he squinted at the native. "Alas, I have nothing with which to dry my glasses."

"If only you could use Luke's journal," Liz teased. *"Bonjour,* Clarie.

I knew it! I knew the touch of Paul's angel was meant to protect Luke's journal from being ruined in the shipwreck! Well done rescuing it, Max."

"Julius r-r-rescued the journal, Lass," Max explained, scratching behind his ear. "I went after his jewel then."

"It was beautiful to watch you and Julius work as a team to protect both jewels," Clarie shared. "You did the right thing, Max. The journal is what Julius wanted to save."

"*Bon!* Julius saved Luke's research on Jesus and Paul's journeys!" Liz exclaimed happily.

"Might we finally see what shall happen with Luke and his gospel account?" Nigel asked.

"Indeed, here on Malta," Clarie replied with a grin. Her face suddenly fell as she saw Paul walking toward the fire with an armload of sticks. "For now, prepare yourselves. Look."

The animals turned to see Paul start to lay the sticks on the fire. Max was the first to see it. He growled, running over to the bonfire, but it was too late.

The forked tongue of the dark gray viper tasted the air as it stared at Paul from the bundle of sticks. *Go ahead and reach for me, Paul,* it hissed.

Paul reached to grab another stick from the bundle, and the viper sprang into action, sinking its venomous fangs into his hand. Paul dropped the bundle of sticks and held the viper in the air, his eyes wide from the shock of its bite.

The people of the island saw the snake hanging from his hand. "A murderer, no doubt!" a man shouted, pointing at Paul. "Though he escaped the sea, justice will not permit him to live."

As Max reached him, Paul shook off the snake into the fire. Only the animals could hear the cry of the evil beast as the flames consumed it. *You may reach Rome, but there it will end!*

Liz shivered, not from the cold but from the evil encounter. "Was that . . . Charlatan?"

"No, just one of his minions, sent to do his evil bidding," Clarie explained. "But as you can see, Paul is unharmed. Nothing can stop his deliverance to Rome."

Nigel put his hand over his heart. "I say, what an utter relief!"

249

Max wagged his tail, happy to see that Paul was okay. *"Are ye all r-r-right, Lad?"* he barked.

Paul squatted down next to Max, rubbing his hand. "I'm okay, Gabriel. God protected me." Max licked his hand happily.

Liz noticed the natives huddling together, murmuring among themselves as they stared at Paul. "The people are waiting for Paul to swell up or suddenly drop dead."

"No doubt they harken to the Greek tale of the Palatine Anthology," Nigel noted, clearing his throat and folding his arms over his chest. "As you might recall, that literary work tells of a murderer who escaped a storm at sea and was shipwrecked, only to be bitten by a viper. Nemesis, goddess of justice and revenge, arranged his demise."

After a while the people realized Paul wasn't harmed. They decided he was a god and began chanting around the fire.

"Déjà vu! It's just like in Lystra when the people thought Paul and Barnabas were gods! These people are so deceived," Liz lamented.

"The Enemy uses the same tactics over and over to deceive the human mind," Clarie said. "But now that Paul has landed on Malta, the Good News will spread across this land, beginning with the chief official of the island, Publius." She began walking away.

"Where are ye goin', Lass?" Max asked.

Clarie turned and smiled. "Time for me to change into one of Publius's servants so everyone can get off this beach and out of the rain."

"You are most welcome to stay here for a few days," Publius said to Paul with an upraised arm. Paul, Luke, Aristarchus, and Julius were seated around a table of food, now dry and dressed in clean clothes. Max, Liz, and Nigel sat by a wall in the banquet room of this villa, also warm, dry, and well fed. Clarie had seen to their needs quickly.

"When my servant informed me of your horrific shipwreck, I immediately ordered accommodations for your survivors at huts and cottages around my province," Publius continued. "Officer Julius has shared with me that he intends to rent a house in our port of Valetta, but my villa is yours until you can settle there."

"Thank you, Publius," Paul replied with a humble bow of his head.

"May God bless you for your kindness. We do not wish to burden you and your household, but are grateful for your hospitality."

"I echo Paul's gratitude, Publius," Julius added. "I think three days will be sufficient time to secure our lodging elsewhere while we winter here on Malta. I hope to find another Alexandrian ship heading to Rome by February."

Publius swallowed a bite of bread and nodded. "Although February is actually before the shipping season, we do have ships arrive that early, so it is possible. Whatever you need until you secure passage, I am at your service."

Just then, Clarie came into the room and whispered in Publius's ear. She was dressed in the white linen attire of a house manservant. Publius frowned and nodded, clenching his jaw. "Please excuse me. I must check on my father. He is very sick with dysentery and Malta fever. He has been delirious for several days, not knowing where he is nor recognizing even me."

Paul also stood as Publius got to his feet from the table. "May Luke and I go with you to see him?"

251

Publius halted, curious to see such interest for a sick old man. "If you wish, yes."

Paul leaned down and whispered in Luke's ear. "Come, but pray, good Doctor. I wish for the Great Physician to heal him, not man."

Luke nodded. "Understood."

Paul and Luke followed Publius and Clarie as they walked down the elaborately tiled corridor leading to the bedroom of the sick man. Publius's father lay on wet sheets, and sweat beaded up on his feverish head. He was delirious and groaned softly.

Paul boldly walked ahead of Publius and sat down on the bed next to his father. He reached out his hand and gently cupped it on the ill man's forehead. The soft glow from the oil lamp at the bedside illuminated the beautiful scene. No one spoke a word. Paul closed his eyes and prayed a simple prayer. "In the name of Jesus, our Great Physician, we ask you to heal this man who is suffering so. Please touch his body and take away his fever. Heal him in every way, I pray. Amen."

Paul slowly withdrew his hand and stood up. Publius took a step forward in hopeful anticipation. His father blinked his eyes and stared curiously at Paul, who smiled down at him. He then looked over at

Publius and smiled. "Hello, Son. Have I been asleep for long? I'm suddenly quite hungry."

Tears filled Publius's eyes as he rushed to kneel by his father's bed, grasping his hand, and kissing it tenderly. "You've been sick a while, Father." He turned to look at Paul and shared a knowing look of gratitude. "But no longer. This man's God has healed you." He turned and lifted a hand to instruct Clarie. "I will get you something to eat right away."

Publius's father extended his hand to Paul. "Thank you. Who is your God?"

Paul smiled and went over to enfold the man's hand in his. "The God who loves you enough to heal you and do so much more for your life." He motioned for Luke to join him. "I will tell you about him when you have regained your strength. Please allow my physician, Luke, to attend to you now."

Luke came over to check on the man. Paul whispered in Luke's ear. "Get ready, my friend. An open door awaits you to practice medicine and share Jesus here on Malta this winter."

Luke smiled and nodded. "I am the Great Physician's servant. May he heal as I serve these people."

☧

Immediately, news of the healing of Publius's father spread like wildfire throughout the villa and across the island. All the other sick people on the island came to the house that Julius rented in Valetta and were healed. Luke, Paul, and Aristarchus prayed over them as Luke gave practical medical care. The people of Malta showered the men with honors, and were so full of gratitude that they promised to supply them with everything they would need for their voyage to Rome.

Julius stood by in amazement, watching an entire island come to the men for healing, but even more so, come to the men for knowledge of their God. Julius witnessed conversation after conversation, changed life after changed life until a month had passed.

The oil lamp cast a warm glow over the table as Luke, Paul, Aristarchus, and Julius gathered for their evening meal. Paul lifted the bread and gave thanks to God. "Our Lord, we thank you for this food you have supplied, just as you have supplied all our needs here on this island of deliverance. Bless it to our bodies as we seek to minister to those you bring to us. Amen."

"Please! Pray for me now!" Julius cried out suddenly, his eyes filling with tears as a surge of emotion swept over him. "I wish to follow Jesus. I now know he is real. I've listened to your words these many months. I've seen the proof of his power in delivering us here. I've seen the healing miracles taking place. Luke, from your journal I've read about him and what he did here on Earth, dying and rising from the dead for my sin. But I also see HIM, Paul! I see him in *your* life." He turned and looked at Luke and Aristarchus. "And I see him in *your* lives, through the love and peace *you* have. He *must* be real! My father was right. Please, I wish to be a Christian as he was."

Paul, Luke, and Aristarchus erupted in joy and surrounded Julius with their arms as they wept and prayed. "I knew this day would come, my friend," shared Paul happily. "Oh Jesus, our brother Julius believes in you and wishes to invite you into his heart. Please accept him as he confesses his sin and his belief in you as his Savior and Lord. Come into his heart now."

253

Julius blinked back the tears and lifted up his unashamed prayer of petition. "Jesus, forgive me. I am a sinful man. But I believe that you are the Christ who died for me. Please, be the King of my life from this day forward. I am at your command. Amen." He opened his eyes and looked at his friends. "Is that it?"

"That's it!" Aristarchus exclaimed with a squeeze of the man's shoulder.

"Welcome to the family, Julius," Luke said, giving the centurion a smothering embrace.

Julius wiped his eyes and laughed with joy, letting go a deep breath. "I fought this decision for so long. But what a relief! I can't believe it took me so long."

"Rome was not built in a day," Liz suggested through happy tears from the shadows as she, Max, and Nigel celebrated Julius's decision with joyful hugs. "And neither was this Roman's heart!"

"Aye! Now I can r-r-rest, knowin' the lad be safe an' secure!" Max added. "He were saved from the shipwreck but needed ta be saved on land."

"This takes the biscuit!" Nigel exulted. "Our family of Antonius will carry on the Jesus legacy indeed!"

"Please allow me to help you somehow, Paul," Julius implored as gratitude filled his heart. He already wanted to serve his Master. "You are my brother and my friend. There must be something I can do to help you once we get to Rome. Do you have friends in Rome to offer assistance?"

Paul nodded. "Thank you, my friend. Yes, there is a strong church of believers in Rome who will welcome us when we arrive. I know they will wish to care for us."

"Including my mother!" Julius cried. He had suddenly realized he also shared this faith in Christ with *her*. "She is also my *sister* now! I can't wait to tell her." He shook his head in wonder and awe.

"I know her heart will be overjoyed when you tell her," Paul replied with a warm smile.

Julius's mind was racing. *My brother!* "Paul, do you have legal counsel in Rome?"

Paul shook his head. "No. I'm planning to appear before Caesar on my own."

254

Julius's eyes widened. "My brother, Theo, is an attorney! I know I can get him to represent you before Nero, especially when he learns who you are from our childhood encounter. Please, he is one of the most brilliant minds in Rome. Allow him to stand with you before Nero."

"He's right, Paul. Just as God aids me in healing these people with my skills, allow Theo to assist you with his skills as God enables him to represent you," Luke suggested.

"Theo. Theophilus!" Paul suddenly remembered, wide-eyed, and gripped his head in awe. "Not only is Theo your brother from the docks at Caesarea long ago, I met a man on the road into Corinth who asked me to deliver a letter to a man who practiced law in Rome! He must be one and the same!"

Luke pointed at Paul. "I remember this! He gave you the itinerarium cup as a thank-you, and you were then inspired to write your letter to the Romans."

Paul frowned. "Yes, but that letter is long gone in the shipwreck now. I'm sorry I will not be able to deliver it to Theophilus now."

Julius slapped his hand on the table. "I have an idea for a *new* letter that Luke can write to Theophilus! In order for him to represent you, Paul, he needs a thorough background on why you are being brought to trial for heresy against the Jews. He needs to understand Jesus and Christianity!" He turned to Luke. "I've read your journal, Luke. You can write the letter, pulling from your journal. You know how to lay out the facts for a Roman to comprehend. When we arrive in Rome, I'll take you to Theo and we'll give him the letter. He can begin studying and preparing Paul's case while he awaits trial before Caesar."

Paul and Luke shared a nod and a knowing look. "Agreed. Julius, you are already making your fathers proud—both of them."

Julius clenched his jaw and nodded with great emotion. "I pray my brother will come to know Jesus, just as our father tried to share him with us. Theophilus and I were both told about him as young boys, but I went my rebellious soldier route, and Theo went the intellectual route, making faith a difficult thing for us both. Luke, perhaps open your letter to affirm Theo and what he was taught about Jesus, the Christ."

"I will do just that, Julius," Luke answered. "Thank you for suggesting it. It will help me frame the letter. As I think about it, I may need to write two letters. One that tells the full story of Jesus, and one that tells Paul's story."

Paul nodded. "I think that is perfect, Luke. I would prefer two letters, as I do not wish for my journey to be on the same page as that of my Lord. Mine is nothing in comparison with his."

Luke got up from the table and went to his supply of parchment he kept for recording his medical records, and picked out a fresh scroll for the letter to Theophilus. He also picked up his journal and brought it to the table. "Agreed. The life of Jesus and your life, Paul, are journeys with similarities. I think this is the way I should organize both letters. Jesus' journey was from Galilee to Jerusalem as his desired destination. Paul, your journey is from Jerusalem to Rome as your desired destination. Although you and Jesus differ in your ultimate destination and purpose, both of your stories include a determined goal, arrests, trials in Jewish and Roman courts . . ."

"And ultimately death, but resurrection," Paul interjected.

A quiet moment passed between the men as these truths sank in. Luke finally spoke. "My friend, your life is such a mirror of our Lord that I believe it will become an example of how to live for Christ."

"For to me to live is Christ, to die is gain," Paul told them softly. He smiled and got up from the table. "May the Lord fill your pen with

255

divine words, Luke. We'll leave you with it. Come, let's give Luke some time to gather his thoughts and pray as he starts his letter."

Julius and Aristarchus got up from the table and followed Paul to the door. Luke called after the centurion, "Thank you, Julius, for asking me to write this letter. I pray it will be just what Theophilus needs to read, not just for Paul's sake, but for his own sake."

Julius nodded and placed a hand over his breastplate. "Thank *you*, good Doctor."

When the men left, Nigel stayed in the shadows while Max came over to sit at Luke's feet. Liz jumped up on the table to see what he was going to write. As Luke trimmed the tip of his stylus to prepare to write, he winked at Liz. "Are you going to help me write this letter, little Faith? I welcome your company."

"If you only knew what you were about to write, cher Luke. This letter is not just for Theophilus, but for the entire world," Liz meowed. *"I will be here for every word, as I have been from the beginning of his story."*

256   Luke gave Liz a tender scratch under the chin and dipped his stylus in the ink. Out poured a brand new letter—the Gospel of Luke:

Many have undertaken to draw up an account of the things that have been fulfilled among us, just as they were handed down to us by those who from the first were eyewitnesses and servants of the word. With this in mind, since I myself have carefully investigated everything from the beginning, I too decided to write an orderly account for you, most excellent Theophilus, so that you may know the certainty of the things you have been taught.

AND SO WE CAME TO ROME

FEBRUARY AD 60

Julius just made arrangements with the captain! We set sail in the morning!" Nigel reported, giddy with excitement. "His soldiers are making ready by boarding the other prisoners now. And as promised, the islanders are already bringing provisions for the voyage."

"*C'est bon!*" Liz exclaimed happily. "We can finally leave Malta."

"That's gr-r-rand news, Mousie. Wha' kind of a boat is she?" Max asked.

"She is an Alexandrian ship that has also wintered here, with the figurehead of the twin gods Castor and Pollux on her bow. Of course the pagans consider these mythological twins their patrons of navigation. I'm sure you recall Horace's *Ode,* which sailors have echoed since the time of Augustus," related Nigel, clearing his throat and lifting his paw to recite Horace with his dramatic flair:

> *Then through the wild Aegean roar*
> *The breezes and the Brethren Twain*
> *Shall waft my little boat ashore.*

"Mousie loves all that ancient wr-r-ritin', don't he, Lass?" Max whispered to Liz.

Liz giggled and whispered back, *"Oui,* but isn't it nice to have our own little ancient literature expert to provide colorful prose, mythology, and history along our journey?"

"Aye, an' he enjoys it, too," Max whispered with a grin before addressing Nigel. "Thanks for the good news, Mousie."

"Right. Well, I for one am going to bid you all a good night. I plan to be rested for the morning," Nigel announced, scurrying over to curl up in a little ball under Luke's bed.

"Bonne nuit, mon ami," Liz told him. "We'll soon be in Rome."

"So guess who ye get ta see soon?" Max offered with a wink.

"My Albert!" Liz exclaimed happily. "Oh, to be reunited with him after so long! I don't know if I'll be able to sleep tonight."

"Jest dr-r-ream aboot him r-r-runnin' out ta meet ye," Max replied. "Sweet dreams, Lass."

Liz smiled and kissed Max on the cheek. *"Merci,* Max. *Toi aussi."* She went over and curled up next to Nigel.

258

Max stretched his belly out on the floor with his back legs behind him, resting his head on his front paws. He let go a big sigh. *Wherever ye be tonight, Kate, know I be missin' ye.*

We put in at Syracuse and stayed there three days, and from there we tacked round to Rhegium. A day later the south wind sprang up and we sailed to Puteoli, reaching it in only two days.

Luke put down his pen and gazed out at the huge mountain called Vesuvius towering over the city of Pompeii. As they sailed into the Bay of Naples, a faint ribbon of smoke drifted up from the sleeping volcano.

"We've made excellent time," Julius reported, joining Luke, Paul, and Aristarchus as they observed the bustling harbor. "Are you ready to get off this ship? From here it's only 130 miles to Rome. It shouldn't take us more than five days."

Aristarchus smiled. "I am ready! I'll be glad to travel by land from now on."

"How long will we stay here before heading to Rome?" Luke asked.

"I need to report to imperial headquarters here, but it could be a week to re-provision and act on any new orders I receive," Julius replied. "Nero may be in residence here at his villa."

"So you may be able to deliver his emerald," Paul noted.

"Perhaps. I hope to be rid of it soon," Julius replied, gripping the leather satchel secured over his chest. "I'm tired of being burdened with this jewel."

Paul lifted his chain and smiled. "Burdens come in different forms, don't they? But *liberty* is a precious jewel, isn't it?"

"Indeed, and one I hope you will soon have, my friend," Julius replied, staring at Paul's chains, which he was once again required to wear as a prisoner of Rome. "Although I know you already have liberty on the inside."

"There are many Christians here in Puteoli. May we be permitted to see them while we are here?" Luke asked.

"Of course," Julius replied. "Let me get my soldiers situated with the other prisoners while you locate them."

"Thank you, Julius," Paul replied. "I look forward to introducing you to them as your new friends as well."

"That will be a welcome relief, especially if it is after a visit with Nero." 259

☧

"He's back? My handsome green-eyed soldier is back from his quest for my emerald?" Julius heard Nero bellow from out in the hallway. Hearing his lyrical voice made Julius's skin crawl.

Nero came bounding into the room happily, clapping his hands. "Well? Do you have it? Let me see it!"

Julius bowed and held out the jewel that was now wrapped in a silky purple cloth to present to the emperor. "Hail, Caesar! I bring you the largest emerald Egypt has to offer."

Nero's eyes widened and he made an exaggerated "o" with his mouth as he took the jewel in hand. "OOOOOOOOOOOO! Look at it, Seneca! It's gorgeous! And it's so big!" He spun around to show his mentor.

"Indeed, it is a glorious find!" Seneca echoed, marveling at the green jewel. "Our master artisan will cut it into a beautiful spyglass for you, Caesar. Well done, Centurion Antonius. You have surpassed our expectations."

"Yes! And you should be rewarded! What would you like?" Nero asked flippantly. He plopped down on the couch and held the emerald up to his eye to gaze up to the light. "Money? A new title?"

"I have reward enough in that my emperor is pleased with my performance," Julius replied humbly.

Nero paused and looked around the emerald at Julius, surprised to hear such an unselfish reply. A grin crept onto his face and he wagged his finger at the soldier. "I'm sure there's *something* you'd like. So I will give you time to think about it, and when you've decided, you may let me know. Meanwhile, if *I* come up with something special, *I* will let *you* know!"

"Most kind of you, Caesar," Julius replied without emotion, looking straight ahead. "I also selected six strong slaves from Egypt as new gladiators for Rome. After I receive my orders here I will deliver them for training at the Ludus in Rome."

"Splendid! I cannot wait to watch them through my emerald spyglass as they fight at the Circus Maximus!" Nero exclaimed, gazing through the jewel at Julius.

"You have done well on your mission," Burrus affirmed Julius. "I understand you were in a shipwreck."

260

"Thank you, Prefect Burrus," Julius answered. "Yes, we were caught in a storm that lasted for two weeks and blew us five hundred miles off course. Thankfully, we were able to land and winter on Malta."

Nero put his hands up to his face. "Oh, how horrible! Poor *you!* I'm sure it was dreadful! And to think you brought me my emerald through a shipwreck!" Nero got up from the couch and went over to stand in front of Julius, pointing at his chest. "I insist that you have a long furlough when you reach Rome. Hand off your prisoners and take a few months to play. Enjoy yourself!"

Burrus and Julius looked at one another uncomfortably. The two disciplined soldiers were appalled to hear their non-militaristic emperor treat military service so casually.

"Emperor, I will see Antonius out and send him with his orders," Burrus interjected, bowing. He was hoping to get Julius out of the room before Nero had any other bright ideas.

"Very well. I look forward to seeing you in Rome, Antonius," Nero said with a smile as he twirled around to pick up his golden goblet and toast the centurion. "You will be my guest at the games!"

Julius only bowed respectfully and left with Burrus, closing the doors behind them.

Once they were a distance down the corridor, Burrus and Julius looked at one another with knowing glances over the absurdity of Nero's behavior. Burrus waited until they were out of earshot of anyone and turned to Julius.

"You need to know what's happened over the past year. A month after you left Naples, on March 20, Nero gave a banquet for his mother, Agrippina, here at his villa. She was staying at another villa across the bay. After dinner he sent her home in a boat that was rigged to collapse and crush her to death. A secondary rig of levers was in place to open the hull and sink the ship, but neither device worked."

Julius's eyes grew wide. "He tried to kill his mother?"

Burrus held up a hand. "He *did* kill her. Agrippina saved herself by diving off the boat and was rescued by oystermen, but Nero's men waited at her villa and killed her there. He's insane, Julius. And now he's staying out of Rome, out of the public eye. He's terrified of being stoned for murder, so is wandering around southern Italy. Seneca and I are essentially ruling the empire."

Julius couldn't believe what he was hearing. *And this is the man before whom Paul hopes to appeal his case?* "Burrus, I have in my custody a prisoner from Caesarea named Paul who has appealed to Caesar over unfounded charges of a religious nature brought by the Jews in Judea. He was found innocent by Felix and Festus, as well as Herod Agrippa in Caesarea, but, prodded on by the Jews, he appealed to Caesar. I wonder about his case, given Nero's mental state. He is a good man who I believe is completely innocent. And I must report that his quick thinking saved us all in the shipwreck."

Burrus raised his eyebrows in surprise to hear such a glowing report over a prisoner. "Well, there is a backlog of cases piling up with Nero's absence in Rome, but he can't stay down here forever," Burrus replied, clearing his throat. "I suggest this Paul find good legal counsel in Rome. Since he has not committed a serious crime against Rome, he will be under house arrest with a Roman guard, not imprisoned. He can rent a place at his own expense while he awaits trial upon Nero's return." He coughed and cleared his throat again.

"Understood. I've already suggested my brother, Theophilus, as his legal counsel," Julius explained. He hesitated, then added, "I would like to personally take charge of Paul in Rome, if that would be permissible.

261

Rather than 'taking time off to play' as Nero suggests, this is what I would request for my next assignment. If Nero wishes to grant my request, I will drop the prisoners off with the commander at the Castra Praetoria of the Praetorian Guard in Rome, and then personally oversee Paul's custody."

"Very well. I'll see to the orders," Burrus replied. "And if Paul is fortunate, Seneca will sit in for Nero during his day in court."

☧

The long caravan of prisoners, soldiers, and supply carts traveled along the paved Via Appia. Known as the "queen of the long roads," this highway had served Rome's armies for three-and-a-half centuries. The sound of metal wheels grinding across the hand-cut stones sounded like a blacksmith sharpening his blade.

Paul walked along next to Julius, attached by the obligatory chain that Julius hated as much as did his prisoner. Paul was deep in thought as the reality of entering Rome at last filled his mind. When he wrote to the Romans three years earlier, this was not how he envisioned greeting his Christian brothers and sisters—in chains. He had hoped to come to them in full freedom to serve and minister among them. Luke took note of the fact that Paul's spirits were somewhat low. This observation wasn't lost on Julius, either.

"Up ahead is the Forum of Appius," Julius told Paul. "That means we are only forty-three miles from Rome. That should cheer you up. We're almost there."

Paul took his eyes off the cobblestones and lifted them toward the horizon of the tall cypress trees lining the Via Appia. "Forty-three miles. We've come quite far together, haven't we, Julius?"

"Indeed. I never expected my journey a year ago to lead me across your path," Julius replied with a smile. "I'm eternally grateful it did. And by the grace of God, I will be able to watch over your stay in Rome."

"I'm grateful as well, for all things," Paul replied softly.

"Look up ahead!" Aristarchus called out. "A group of people are coming this way. They look as if they are hurrying toward us."

Everyone scanned the road to see some fifteen or so people, smiling and heading straight toward the caravan. "Paul! Paul! Is that you?" one of the men called out.

Paul turned to Julius and smiled before answering. "Yes! I am Paul!"

Julius held up his hand to halt the caravan as the men closed the gap. "We'll rest here briefly for water."

The people rushed up to Paul and put their hands on him, full of smiles and cheers. "Praise God you've arrived! We received word from the believers in Puteoli that you were on your way to Rome. We had to come greet you ourselves!"

Emotion rose in Paul's throat to see such a warm welcome from these, his brothers and sisters in Christ whom he had never even met. "Thank you, my friends. I wasn't expecting such a warm reception."

"We've waited three long years to meet you, Paul," one of the women replied. "Of course we had to come! More people await you at Three Taverns."

Max, Liz, and Nigel smiled at the tender greeting of these dear Christians. It was just what Paul needed.

"I'd say these believers have certainly gone the extra mile to be here for Paul," remarked Nigel.

"Aye, it were a gr-r-rand gesture," Max added.

Max and Nigel looked at Liz, who put her paw over her heart as her eyes filled with tears. A beautiful smile appeared on her face before she took off running down the Via Appia. There in the distance was an orange figure trotting toward her.

"Ah, the splendid reunion at last!" Nigel cheered as he and Max watched the tender scene.

Al was huffing and puffing but when he saw Liz running toward him, he picked up his pace. In moments they collided in the middle of the road, locked in a happy embrace.

"Oh, *mon cher* Albert! You're here! You came to meet me, too!" Liz cried, smothering Al with kisses.

"I'm here, Lass. I couldn't wait another minute without ye," Al gushed, wiping Liz's happy tears away. "Welcome home, me love."

Liz smiled and rubbed her cheek against Al's. "*Oui,* my home is wherever you are."

"Then our home must be really big since I been a lot of places," Al suggested.

Liz giggled. "Come, Albert. Max and Nigel will be happy to see you, too." Together the two cats made their way, walking side by side over to an umbrella pine tree, where Max and Nigel sat in the shade.

263

"Hello, old boy! Brilliant of you to come out and meet your bride on the outskirts of Rome," Nigel cheered.

"Top o' the mornin', Mousie!" greeted Al, scooping Nigel up for a smothering hug.

"Well I'll be a monkey's uncle, Big Al. Ye done made the extra mile ta see yer lass, too," Max noted with a big grin, nudging Al with his big square head.

"Greetin's, Max," Al replied, then added with a puzzled look, "but ye couldn't be a monkey's uncle. Ye're a dog."

"Yeah, but he at least can be a monkey's friend," came a voice from up in the tree. "And I *know* that pretty lady is my friend."

Everyone looked up to see a brown capuchin monkey hanging by his tail upside down with a big-toothed grin. "Hiya, dudes! Long time, no see!"

"Noah! We haven't seen you since Corinth!" Liz cried. "Is Nate with you?"

The capuchin monkey swung up to grab a branch by his long, skinny arms and dangled for a moment, looking both ways down the Appian Way. "He's out training for his marathon, as usual. He'll meet us at the next stop." He swung down to land on the ground in front of Liz, grabbing her paw to kiss it.

"Albert, this is Noah, whom I've told you about. And he is very . . . charming," Liz explained with a grin. "It's his way."

"Hiya, Big Al," chuckled Noah, jabbing Al in the belly. "You've made quite the catch with this pretty little lady. Good on ya!"

"Aye, I know it," agreed Al with a definitive nod.

"I say, Clarie told us of your valiant delivery of Paul's scroll to the Thessalonians after your sea voyage in that hollowed-out gourd of yours," Nigel offered. "Good show."

Noah blew a raspberry. "It was easy! We sneaked into the house and I dropped the scroll and picked up a banana on my way out. Hey, a monkey's gotta eat after all that work."

"So where ye been these past nine years?" Max wanted to know.

Noah rolled his eyes. "Only all over the world! We've been waiting forever on you guys to arrive in Rome," Noah explained. "Nate and I went on our mission to tell animals everywhere about the

Animalympics. Clarie showed up as a zebra when we were in Africa and told us we could start making our way to Rome."

"I'd like to see Clarie's stripes," responded Al with a goofy grin, admiring his orange stripes on his fluffy belly. "She's always a butterfly when *I* see her."

Noah's jaw dropped and his eyes grew big. "A butterfly? Wow, she can do anything! I want her on *my* team! She'd be really convenient, depending on the sport."

"Do tell us the plans you've made to date," Nigel implored.

"Well, Nate knows most of the plans and stuff, so better wait for him," Noah answered, lying back to watch the sun dance through the umbrella pine above. "Look! It's like nighttime with the stars when you look up there just right."

Liz giggled at Noah's penchant for distraction. "You haven't changed a bit, *mon ami.*"

Noah popped back up and winked at Liz as he scurried up the tree. "That's why the ladies love me! Wahoo-hoo-hoo! I'll run ahead and grab Nate. See ya at Three Taverns!"

The animals watched the silly monkey swing from branch to branch, choosing to make his way down the Via Appia from above.

"Cr-r-razy monkey," Max chuckled. "The last thing that monkey needs be one tavern, much less three."

"The name of the next stop is *Tres Tabernae,* or "Three Taverns." But the term 'tavern' is used for any kind of shop, old chap," Nigel explained. "At that first relay station thirty-three miles outside of Rome, there is a general store, a blacksmith, and a house of refreshment, *ergo,* 'Three Taverns.'" The little mouse looked around their current stop and noticed Julius getting the caravan ready to move on. "Of course, despite the warm welcome received by those from Rome, Horace wrote about this Forum of Appius as being 'full of stingy tavernkeepers.' Time to crack on."

"Aye! ONE LAST STOP BEFORE R-R-ROME!" Max exclaimed.

Paul was visibly moved by the crowd of people waiting for him at Three Taverns. Aquila and Priscilla were there, along with others Paul knew from his previous missionary journeys, whom he had greeted in his letter to the Romans.

Julius marveled at seeing the bond between these friends who had been separated for so long, but who remained close at heart. But he wasn't surprised at the outpouring of love for this little sixty-year-old, bandy-legged, balding Jew named Paul. Julius smiled as he watched Paul enveloped by those whose lives he had changed with his tireless message of grace and hope.

Luke came up to Julius and smiled. "Paul's spirits have been lifted by these welcomes."

"Indeed," Julius agreed. "Now let's get him to Rome. The eternal city awaits this amazing man."

"Hmmm, no sign of Nate and Noah here," Liz remarked as they continued down the Via Appia the last thirty-three miles into Rome.

"Why don't I give us all a refresher overview of the 'Eternal City' of Rome before we enter its splendid gates?" Nigel suggested as they walked along. "Right. Now according to legend, Rome was founded on April 21, 753 BC, by the twin brothers Romulus and Remus. Of course you recall they were descendants of the Trojan, Aeneas, who fled to Italy after the fall of Troy."

Al joined in. "Aye, so Romulus decided he wanted to make a wee town on the Palatine hill, and Remus wanted to make a wee town on the Aventine hill. There be SEVEN hills in Rome, just like us, don't ye know?" Al smiled. "But the brothers fought over which hill, so they had a contest to see whose hill would win by lookin' at a flock o' birds. I think they were daft."

"Precisely, old boy," Nigel agreed, clearing his throat. "Alas, a quarrel broke out over the choice of hills for the city. Romulus killed Remus, thereby becoming the sole ruler of the city he named after himself: Rome."

Al leaned over and whispered to Liz and Max, "Didn't surprise me to learn that Romulus acted like such a wild beastie, seein' how he and his brother were raised by a she-wolf."

Max looked at Liz with obvious skepticism to hear the myth of the founding of Rome. "These humans get cr-r-razier the more I learn aboot 'em."

"Oooh, here be the Porta Capena," Al told them as they passed through its cool stone arch. "It be one o' sixteen gates from the old Servian Wall built to keep bad guys out four hundred years ago."

266

Liz's eyes brightened at Al's knowledge of Rome. "Why, Albert! You've learned quite a lot about Rome. I'm so proud of you!" She kissed him on the cheek.

Al wore a goofy grin as he melted under her kiss. "Clarie said me job were to learn every bit aboot Rome, so I did. I know every street and back alley and arch there be."

"Brilliant! I must say I am astounded by your newfound acumen for history *and* tourism," said Nigel.

Al wrinkled his forehead, not quite getting Nigel's compliment. "Aye, but at least I know stuff to show people in Rome now."

As they walked a bit farther, they saw an aqueduct with water flowing atop its 110-foot arches. "Now this be the Claudia aqueduct. Emperor Claudius built it aboot ten years ago," related Al. "But way before him, that Caesar Augustus lad said that when he got here, he 'found a city o' brick' and 'left it built o' marble.'"

"R-r-rome be a gr-r-rand city," observed Max as they entered its bustling streets. "How many humans live here?"

"Aboot a million free humans and aboot a million slaves, give or take a few thousand," Al answered. "Some live in big, pretty villas with gardens, an' some live in high-rise apartments."

Soon they heard the thunderous sound of horses' hooves. "Now *that* be the Circus Maximus where the horsies run around in circles all day!" Al explained as they walked past the incredible track where teams of charioteers raced in front of the roaring crowds.

"Circus *Max*imus?" Max asked. "With a name like that, it must be gr-r-rand!"

"I remember it well when Clarie, Albert, and I were here," Liz recalled. "This is where Marcus gave his lightning fast chariot racehorse Achilles to Armandus."

"And where Clarie gave Marcus the star coin," Al remembered. "The one with the star above Augustus's head."

Liz nodded. "*Oui,* and we saw that star coin change hands from Marcus to Armandus to Zacchaeus to Jesus. The last we saw of the star coin, Jesus had Nigel place it in the widow's basket in Jerusalem."

"It is terribly fascinating to think of that notched coin traveling from hand to hand across time," Nigel added. "I wonder if we shall ever see it again."

Behind the oblong stadium rose the imperial palaces on the Palatine hill. "There be Romulus's hill up there," continued Al, "so that's where all the emperors live."

"I say, have you been inside Nero's palace?" Nigel wanted to know.

"Aye. That laddie be aboot the prissiest decorator I ever seen," Al scoffed with a puff of air. "He jest don't know when to quit. Now he's diggin' a huge lake below his palace."

"And that's where we'll have our water events for the Animalympics," came a little voice running up next to them. It was the green-plumed basilisk lizard.

"*Bonjour,* Nate! I'm so happy to see you!" Liz greeted him.

"Hello, Liz and all," Nate replied. "Noah and I are glad you're finally here. Um, I've been dreaming of the day when we could finally have our Animalympics in Rome!" Nate was a serious athlete, cross training with running and swimming. Ever since they attended the human Isthmian Games when Paul was in Corinth, Nate had dreamed of animals having their own competitive events. He and Noah had done nothing but dream, plan, and talk to animals everywhere about the first-ever games in Rome.

"Gr-r-rand ta see ye, little Nate," Max greeted him. "So water events in Nero's lake? Wha' aboot the other events?"

"Why in the MAX-imus, Max!" Nate replied. "They already bring animals in there for sporting events, so it's the perfect spot for animals to be there without the humans becoming suspicious."

"Brilliant!" Nigel cheered. "And it should make for an easy venue whilst the humans are sleeping, to have events by night."

"Exactly, Nigel," Nate agreed. "So when can we get all this going?"

"Allow us to settle in with Paul, *mon ami,*" Liz suggested. "We'll know more soon, but I'm sure Clarie or Gillamon will give us an idea for when we could hold these events."

"Awesome!" Nate cheered, pumping his fist in excitement. "Okay, we'll see where you end up staying and go from there."

"Where be yer monkey?" Al asked Nate.

"He's up ahead in the Forum," Nate replied. "It's his favorite place to hang out, with all the food stalls and stuff going on. Gotta get his bananas every day."

Al's ears perked up. "Maybe me and that monkey will end up bein' buddies, if he likes bananas as much as me."

Nigel raised his paw as they strolled along behind Julius's caravan. "Ah, now here we enter the Roman Forum on the famed *Via Sacra,* or "Sacred Way," where Rome's victors march with the spoils of war past the throngs of cheering crowds. The Forum is the very heart of the Eternal City, where law, commerce, and power entwine. The *Curia Julia,* or "Senate House," is just down here on our right. As you can see, we have temples, statues, shops, market stalls . . ."

"And platforms for speakers to stay stuff to the crowds!" came Noah's voice as he hung on an iron railing above a marble platform. He jumped down and jabbed a banana in Al's belly. "Here ya go, Dude."

Al's eyes brightened. "Thanks, Lad!" He proceeded to peel and eat his banana as they walked on through the Forum. "Keep 'em comin'."

Paul was astounded with Rome. It was the most incredible city he had ever seen. As they passed by the Temples of Castor and Pollux, of Vesta, of Venus, of Mars, and, ultimately, to the supreme temple of the Roman king god Jupiter, Paul's heart ached. This was the most powerful civilization on Earth, and it was from here, in the center of the Forum, that Rome's power truly emanated. If only that power could be used to transmit the gospel! The possibilities illuminated Paul's mind.

269

Julius pointed to a monument of gilded bronze as they passed the temple of Saturn. "That is the Miliarium Aureum, erected by Caesar Augustus. All roads begin from this monument and all distances to cities in the Roman Empire are measured from this point. You have now reached the heart of Rome, my friend."

"All roads lead to Rome, no?" Liz remarked.

"Aye, Lass, that's wha' ye always say," Max agreed, looking at the cities and distances marked on the Miliarium Aureum.

Suddenly Paul was filled with gratitude as he walked along in his chains that brought him to the Eternal City, and soon to an audience with the most powerful man in the world. Had he entered Rome as a free man, he never could have hoped to stand before the Emperor and share with the house of Caesar the way to reach the true Eternal City.

"And so we came to Rome," Luke said as they exited the Forum on their way to the Praetorian Guard's barracks.

Paul grew excited to fill these streets with the Good News. "Now to make Rome come to us."

PART THREE

FIERY
TRIALS

30

MOST EXCELLENT THEOPHILUS

Julius! You've returned!" Bella exclaimed, running across the garden to her son with open arms. Her silken blue *stola,* or tunic, flowed with her movement. Her brown hair was pinned up by an ornate golden comb, with wisps of curls hanging by her cheeks. Hints of gray appeared at her temples, but she radiated the beauty of her name.

"Hello, Mother," Julius answered, grabbing her by the waist and twirling her around in the courtyard. He set her down gently and looked into her green eyes, now framed with gentle smile lines. "You're looking beautiful as ever."

Bella cupped her son's face with her hand. "And you are as sweet to your mother as ever. I want to hear all about your adventures this past year. When did you return to Italy?"

"About two weeks ago," Julius replied, looking behind him as Paul, Luke, and Aristarchus stood waiting in the colonnade leading to the courtyard. "I will tell you all about it, but first I have someone very special for you to meet."

"Oh?" Bella replied wondering, looking around Julius and seeing Paul with chains on his wrists. She frowned and said in a hushed voice, "You've brought a *prisoner* here?"

"Not just any prisoner, Mother," Julius answered with a wink. He put his hand on the small of her back and led her over to the men. "Mother, meet Paul. Apostle, prisoner, friend, and now, my brother in Christ."

273

Bella smiled and tears quickened in her eyes. She gripped Julius by the arm. "Julius? Are you a Christian?"

"Yes, Mother! Thanks to Paul, for helping me understand what you and Father tried to tell me all these years," Julius answered happily. "And thanks to you for not giving up on me."

"Praise God! I've prayed for this day for so long," Bella cried, hugging Julius. She quickly turned and reached out to embrace Paul. "Thank you for leading my son to the truth! I'm so happy to meet you, but especially with this joyous news."

Paul smiled and gripped Bella by the arms. "God arranged it, my sister. I was blessed to share the Good News with Julius. Please, let me introduce you to Luke and Aristarchus."

"We've traveled all the way from Caesarea with Julius," Aristarchus offered, taking her hand.

"He is a fine soldier and a fine man," Luke added. "You should be very proud."

"Oh, I am!" Bella assured them, wiping away her tears of joy. "I'm delighted to meet you all. And I've heard about you from other believers here in Rome. Paul, your letters are read here often. Welcome to my home."

"That is what we need to discuss with you, Mother. Paul has come to Rome on appeal to Caesar over false charges by the Jews. He was found innocent by Roman courts, but felt the need to appeal to Caesar. I escorted him to Rome and have been given an assignment to guard him until he goes to trial," Julius explained. "Since he is not convicted of violence or crimes against Rome, he is allowed to stay in rented quarters under Roman guard."

"I see. So you are the guard," Bella began, "and he needs a house?"

"If you have room for me to stay, and I must pay for my boarding," Paul added.

"It would be my honor to have you stay here, Paul! I have guest quarters on the other side of the courtyard that you may certainly use," Bella offered. "There is room enough for all three of you, and any other guests you wish to have."

"I knew you would come through, Mother. Thank you!" Julius exulted, kissing her on the cheek. "I'm glad you mentioned guests, because it will get quite busy here with many people coming to see

Paul." He smiled and pointed to the animals, noticing Al for the first time. "He also has these special little ones that I know you will love having around the garden. Looks like you already have a cat."

"I'm used to it," Bella said with a grin, smiling at the animals. "Peter and Mark speak here frequently when believers gather. Yes, Peter's orange cat loves to stay in my garden. He's always sitting by the Libertas statue. You are all welcome here, Paul."

Paul put his hand over his heart and bowed. "You have my undying gratitude, Bella. And I'm anxious to see Peter and Mark."

"I will send for them soon." Bella shook her head in wonder and awe, looking back at her son. "I knew *some* day. Your father would be so happy," she told Julius as she hugged him again. "We have much to discuss." She pulled back with a sad expression. "Did you receive word about your grandfather?"

Julius tightened his lip and nodded. "Yes, while I was in Caesarea. Paul helped me as I worked through my grief."

"He left a box for you," Bella offered, motioning to the villa.

"I look forward to seeing it," Julius answered. "For now, let's get our guests settled." He turned to Paul. "Welcome to the home of Antonius."

As Bella showed the men to the guest quarters, Liz, Al, Max, and Nigel looked around the courtyard. Al ran over to the Libertas statue and pointed. "Look who's here! Remember her?"

Liz smiled and sauntered up to the statue with her carved likeness at its base. "How well I remember this statue, and the courtyard of Antonius in Jerusalem where she first stood! I can hardly believe she is actually here."

"No wonder Big Al likes ta hang out here, seein' how he gets ta see yer face," Max remarked with a wide grin.

"This is utterly mind-boggling! These layers of history coming together with the house of Antonius are simply astounding! Of all the places for Paul and Luke to stay—if they only knew whose home this really was—the centurion from Luke's journal!" Nigel exclaimed, walking around the statue.

"And now from Luke's letter to Most Excellent Theophilus," Liz added. "Now that Paul has a place to stay, it's time for his reunion with the other little boy from the docks of Caesarea."

275

☧

"Hello, Theo," Julius said, knocking on the wall of the entrance to Theophilus's study. His brother was bent over his desk, which was covered with scrolls, reading intently as his lips moved silently.

Theo looked up and smiled. "Well, look who has returned from Egypt!" He stood to his feet and walked over to meet his brother, giving him a vigorous embrace. He was taller than Julius, thinner, with hazel eyes and paler skin. He wore the white wool tunic of a man of learning, and leather sandals belonging not to a soldier, but to a statesman. "Welcome back, Julius! It's good to see you. You're looking well."

"It's good to be back, Theo," Julius replied, stepping inside the study and scanning his desk. "It looks like your law practice continues to keep you busy."

Theo lifted his hand to the scrolls and let it fall to his side as he exhaled. "Neverending cases to prepare for, as always. So how was Egypt? Did you have a big adventure?"

Julius smiled wryly. "You could say that. I have an amazing story to share with you."

Theo was curious and took a seat, motioning for Julius to sit down across from him.

"Do you remember the day we left Caesarea with Mother? You were teasing me about the red marble down on the docks," Julius began. "Do you remember?"

"Of course I do. How could I forget that?" Theo flashed a big grin. "That man gave me likely the kindest scolding I've ever received. I was so worried he would tell Mother, but he promised to keep my secret. What about it?"

Julius smiled and leaned forward in his seat. "He still gives kind scoldings. Wait right here." Julius jumped up from his seat and went out into the hallway. When he returned, he led Paul to Theophilus's doorway.

"Hello, Theophilus," Paul greeted him with a smile. "Your guilty secret is still safe with me."

Theophilus's jaw dropped as he looked from Paul to Julius and back to Paul. "How in the world?" He slowly rose to his feet and walked over to Paul, examining him up and down, noticing his chains. "Sir, it appears that you are the one now guilty."

Julius laughed and pointed to the red marble around his neck. He shook Theo by the shoulder. "Not by the time you finish representing him, big brother. Time for you to return the favor. Allow me to introduce Paul, an innocent Christian who has appealed to Caesar on trumped-up charges from the Jewish leaders in Jerusalem.

"I escorted Paul all the way from Caesarea. We left together from the *same* dock where we met, Theo! *The same dock."*

"If you're guilty of something, you must make it right. That's what you told me that day," Theo reminded Paul, marveling. "I must say I'm taken aback to have this reunion with you, especially under these circumstances. But I'm glad. Your words actually inspired me to want to study law."

"I never knew that, Theo," Julius exclaimed.

Theo shrugged. "You never asked."

Paul's heart warmed to see the two brothers together again. "I'm happy to see you again, and delighted that you've become such a fine man of the law. Julius has done nothing but sing your praises as one of the finest minds in Rome," Paul offered.

"*You* never told *me* that," Theo exclaimed in surprise at hearing this.

Julius shrugged, bantering back with a grin. "You never asked."

"Please, come have a seat," Theo offered. "How can I help?"

Paul and Julius took their seats across from Theo's desk. "Paul is under house arrest, and I have been assigned to guard him. He's renting the guest house at Mother's home."

Theo raised his eyebrows in surprise. "How convenient. Go on."

"I've discussed Paul's case with Burrus," Julius began. "Paul was found not guilty by the Roman courts, with charges that are solely based on complaints concerning Paul's teachings, which the Jews claim are heresy against their faith."

"According to Gallio's ruling, the Christian sect is simply a subset of Judaism and completely allowable by Roman law," Theo stated.

"Exactly," Julius answered quickly.

"So why then are you here?" Theo asked, turning to look at Paul.

Paul took in a deep breath and smiled. "To present the case for Christ before the Emperor himself. I wish to espouse the truths of the Christian faith before the highest court in the empire, once and for all gaining the highest Roman authority for Christians to freely share their faith."

277

Theo rubbed his chin and cocked his head to the side. "That is rather bold of you, Paul. How do you wish me to help?"

Paul reached over and laid a scroll on Theo's desk. "This is a letter written by my colleague, who is also a physician, named Luke. Your brother knew that the doctor had thoroughly researched the origins of Christianity and the life of Jesus Christ. He recommended that Luke write his findings down in this letter to you."

"Yes, I believe it will give you a thorough background of the Christian movement, and you will see that time after time, Rome has been on the side of the Christians," Julius added. "The only opposition to either Christ or Paul has come from the Jews."

"Why this sudden fervor for Christianity, Julius?" Theo asked, calmly lifting the scroll to unroll it. "Have you decided to follow in our father's footsteps?" He chuckled softly.

"Yes, I have," Julius replied confidently. "Father was right. It took me a long time to understand what it all meant, but after meeting Paul and seeing with my own eyes the miracles of Christ, I have surrendered my life to him as Lord."

278

Theo looked up abruptly over the scroll with a frown. "I see. Be careful how and where you say such things, Brother. Despite what you believe, remember that Caesar should be the recipient of your allegiance, especially in public."

"Understood, Theo. I will watch the verbiage I use, so as not to offend my position while remaining loyal to both," Julius confirmed. "I've learned that Nero has slipped into madness. Burrus gave me the report of the murder of Agrippina," reported Julius.

"Yes, murder is the family tradition in the house of Augustus as of late. Agrippina murdered Claudius, and Nero turned around and murdered her," Theo recounted, scanning Luke's letter.

"I worry for Paul's case with such a madman," Julius lamented.

"Your brother pleased Nero by bringing back a large emerald from Egypt, so he is in the good graces of the emperor," Paul offered.

Theo raised his eyebrows. "Well, good for you, little brother. That could come in handy someday."

"So will you help Paul? Will you take his case?" Julius asked.

Theo tapped his finger on the table and continued to read, his lips moving. He cleared his throat and then read out loud, "As it is written in the book of the words of Isaiah the prophet:

A voice of one calling in the wilderness,
  'Prepare the way for the Lord,
  make straight paths for him.'

He closed the scroll and studied Paul and Julius for a moment, resting his chin on the tips of his fingers. "It appears that your Messiah even prepared his case before his arrival, so I shall do the same. But only in gratitude for your kindness on the docks long ago, Paul, and to answer the request of my little brother here. I wouldn't want you accusing me of being a bully to him again." Theo smiled at Paul.

"Thank you, Theophilus," Paul replied humbly, then, smiling, "I would never accuse you of something you aren't guilty of."

"Good, but don't expect me to become a Christian like Julius and my father, and my mother for that matter," Theo replied, leaning his elbows on his desk. "I believe in intellect over faith. Still, I also believe in the liberty to worship however you choose."

Paul looked at Theo intently and wore a look of confident doubt, as if he knew something Theo didn't know. "I look forward to discussing my case with you after you've read Luke's letter. It presents the story of Jesus. He's writing a second letter about the acts of all the apostles, including my journey in the faith."

"Excellent. I'll look forward to reading it, but no rush. We must of course, wait for your accusers to arrive from Judea and for Nero's return," Theo responded. "As your counsel, I advise you to prepare for a long wait until you appear before Caesar."

"How long do you think this could take?" Julius wanted to know.

Theo scanned the caseload on his desk and knew it represented only a fraction of the cases out there waiting on Nero's return for trial. "Two years."

☧

"He's been here only three days, an' he's got all the local Jewish leaders comin' over," Max whispered to Nigel. Al and Liz were off scoping out the Circus Maximus with Noah and Nate.

"Well, he certainly isn't wasting any time," Nigel answered, straightening his spectacles. "Of course, our Paul never sits still for long."

"Aye. An' he's consistent, ye got ta give him that," Max added. "He's in a new city, an' he always goes ta the Jews first. Or in this case, they be comin' ta him."

The courtyard of Bella's home was buzzing with Paul's invited guests, all dressed in their Jewish robes and rabbinical attire. "I wonder how they'll react to seeing the Libertas statue in the middle of the courtyard," Bella whispered to Julius.

Julius shrugged. "I'm sure they won't like it, but they know Paul is renting a house here, so that should get him off the hook."

Paul held up his hand, with the chain still attached, and called them to order. "Brothers, I was arrested in Jerusalem and handed over to the Roman government, even though I had done nothing against our people or the customs of our ancestors. The Romans tried me and wanted to release me, because they found no cause for the death sentence. But when the Jewish leaders protested the decision, I felt it necessary to appeal to Caesar, even though I had no desire to press charges against my own people," recounted Paul, looking around the courtyard and making eye contact with each one of them. "I asked you to come here today so we could get acquainted and so I could explain to you that I am bound with this chain because I believe that the hope of Israel—the Messiah—has already come."

The Jewish leaders looked at one another and murmured among themselves. One of the leaders replied, "We have had no letters from Judea or reports against you from anyone who has come here. But we want to hear what you believe, for the only thing we know about this movement is that it is denounced everywhere."

Paul and Luke shared a look of surprised delight at this news. "Might I suggest that we schedule a time for you to return and bring as many people as would like to hear from Paul?" Luke offered. "He can go into depth about the beliefs of the Christian movement and answer any questions you and your people may have."

"Brilliant suggestion, Luke," Nigel commented to Max. "Perhaps the Jews here in Rome will be more open to Paul than they've been elsewhere."

"We can only hope, Lad," Max replied.

So a time was set, and on that day a large number of people came to Paul's lodging. He explained and testified about the Kingdom of God

280

and tried to persuade them about Jesus from the Scriptures. Using the law of Moses and the books of the prophets, he spoke to them from morning until evening. Some were persuaded by the things he said, but others did not believe. And after they had argued back and forth among themselves, they left with this final word from Paul: "The Holy Spirit was right when he said to your ancestors through Isaiah the prophet,

'Go and say to this people:
When you hear what I say,
you will not understand.
When you see what I do,
you will not comprehend.
For the hearts of these people are hardened,
and their ears cannot hear,
and they have closed their eyes—
so their eyes cannot see,
and their ears cannot hear,
and their hearts cannot understand,
and they cannot turn to me
and let me heal them.'

So I want you to know that this salvation from God has also been offered to the Gentiles, and they will accept it."

Luke frowned and put down his pen. "Once again, the Jews have chosen blindness over Messiah." He blew on the ink as he finished writing the last line of this, his second letter to Theophilus. "I hope the acts of the apostles I've recorded will at least stir Theo's Gentile heart."

Liz watched as Luke stood and stretched out his back. He then leaned over to blow out the oil lamp on his desk. He reached over to scratch Liz under the chin. "Good night, little Faith."

Liz had read Luke's entire scroll and was thrilled to see yet another book that would undoubtedly be placed into the emerging New Testament. *Do not worry, cher Luke. If these acts do not stir Most Excellent Theophilus, they will undoubtedly stir countless others who will read about them throughout time.*

31

GOD OF MESSAGES

"Y ou've waited a long time for this day," commented Paul as he watched Julius sit before the large wooden box his grandfather Marcus had left him. "Ever since the day I met you on the docks of Caesarea."

"You mean the *second* time we met on those docks," Julius corrected him, running his hand across the intricate wooden carving of Roman soldiers on horseback. "Yes, the day I learned that I had lost him." The Roman centurion slowly opened the box and scanned the contents. He smiled as he reached in and picked up a cloth bag sitting right on top. He held it by his ear and shook it. "Marbles. Our favorite game."

Julius set the bag on the table and proceeded to lift out several military decorations, handling them with respect as each item pointed to a long and valiant military career: an *hasta pura,* or a blunt-headed miniature spear for wounding an enemy; an *armilla,* or golden armband for military service; several *phalerae,* or sculpted disks of gold, silver, and bronze worn on breastplates in military parades; and a *corona aurea,* or golden crown, for killing an enemy in hand-to-hand combat while holding the ground until battle's end.

"Oh, his armor," Julius remarked in awe as he removed the items, studying each of them with reverence: his grandfather's breastplate, loinbelt, round ceremonial shield, sword, and shoes. He raised his eyebrows and reached in with both hands to lift out a silver helmet with red plumage. Julius held it for a moment and studied its hollow eyes as images flashed across his mind. As a boy he first remembered seeing his grandfather wear it, overcome with awe as the warrior towered over him, the sun gleaming off his helmet before the imposing centurion winked at him. Julius smiled and set the helmet on the table. He then spotted Marcus's red cape. He picked it up, buried his face in the woolen fabric and breathed in the scent of his grandfather, fighting back tears. After a moment he set the cape aside and cleared his throat, looking for what he had hoped to find. At the bottom of the box he saw a scroll, sealed with an "A" in red wax.

Julius clenched his jaw, and held up the scroll. He looked at Paul, who nodded at him with confident encouragement. "May God give you the message you need in your grandfather's letter," Paul said softly, turning to leave Julius alone to read the letter.

Julius took a deep breath, broke the seal, and began to read.

Dearest Julius,

I hope you will accept my armor and military decorations with pride. Since you are my soldier, I decided you would most appreciate these items. I've given other possessions to Theophilus as well as a letter of his own. It was important that you each receive a personal word from me.

You and your brother have been the joy of my life, ever since I lost my son—your father—Armandus. I pray that in some small way I've been able to take your father's place as a source of wisdom and guidance. I know how hard it has been on you both. You have grown into such fine men, and I could not be more proud. But I wish more for you. I wish for you to have lives full of meaning and eternal hope. I found the secret to this life in my later years, becoming a follower of Jesus Christ, but I have been guilty of more often than not keeping it a secret. I should have been more open to share my faith with you. There were reasons I kept my faith to myself, and now I see they were selfish ones. I should have told you more when you were growing up. Ultimatel, I know that you must find your own way spiritually, so I've prayed that God would lead you to himself when the time was right.

By the time you read this, I will be gone. It is my dying wish to impart to you some things that may be hard to hear, and harder still to believe. Your grandmother knew some of this, and your mother knows some as well, but not all. The only person who knew everything of what I'm about to tell you was your father, Armandus. He was going to tell you

283

some of these things when he joined you in Rome, but he never arrived. I have struggled with the decision to tell you, as I did a despicable thing. I also committed treason ultimately against the Emperor, and I did not wish to put you in a position of knowing, with the difficult decision to act on that knowledge. My fear kept me from sharing with you while I was alive. Forgive me. I pray it is not too late for me to tell you now. You need to know about the things that have happened to our family, for I now know we were chosen by God for these divine encounters. Why? I have no answer. Perhaps the answer will come to you, the third generation of Antonius.

When I was a centurion in the service of Herod the Great, there came to Jerusalem scholars from the East inquiring about a newborn king of the Jews. They had studied prophecies and seen a star that signified the fulfillment of a promise of a newborn Messiah. After their hasty departure, Herod demanded elimination of this threat and ordered all male babies two years and younger in and around Bethlehem to be slain. Those orders fell to me. Herod threatened the life of your father, who was two at the time, if I did not comply. A soldier must sometimes do the unthinkable. So I carried out this horrific act with my men, shutting down my emotions. But I willfully disobeyed the order to slay one particular child whom I allowed to escape, for I knew his parents and could not allow them to lose their only son. Your father had even played with him as a toddler. I grieved for the rest of my life over what my hands had been forced to do to the children of Israel, and I begged forgiveness from their God. I prayed he would somehow at least give me credit for the one life I had saved, but realized that one child couldn't mean much in a sea of children lost to their parents. So I raised your father to be kind to the Jewish people, encouraging him to help them whenever he could.

But your father was more than kind. God gave him a heart to love the Jewish people. He even built them a synagogue in Capernaum. One day his servant was severely injured, and he sought out a man who he had heard was a miracle worker. This man was Jesus of Nazareth. He went to Jesus to ask for healing, and Jesus agreed to come to his home. But your father stopped him and said if Jesus merely gave the word, his servant would be healed. Jesus told his disciples he had not seen more faith anywhere in Israel, and he, indeed, healed the man's servant with a word.

Sadly, a terrible series of events led to a tragic end for Jesus, who was falsely accused by the Jews, and sentenced to die like a common criminal on a Roman cross. Those orders fell to your father. It sickened him to oversee the scourging and crucifixion of this good man who had healed his servant. At the time he didn't know that this was the one he had played with as a child. He didn't realize who Jesus really was until he was about to die, when God revealed it to his mind and his heart. He then knew that Jesus was the Son of God. He carried the grief and guilt for having had to carry out such horrific orders, and, of course, he feared what would become of him for killing the Son of God.

Three days later, Jesus rose from the dead and appeared to many people. One of those people was your father. Jesus came to him and told him he was forgiven and that he need not carry the guilt of what had happened, for Jesus had laid down his life to pay for the sins of mankind. He said his kingdom was not of this world but was a spiritual kingdom to rule the hearts of men, and to offer them a hope and a future. Jesus then gave your father a word for me. He said, "Tell your father that the child he saved has now saved the world."

285

Can you imagine my joy when I received your father's letter? Can you fathom the awe I felt in my heart at reading those words of freedom after thirty years of carrying such a burden? I still feel unworthy that Jesus would care enough to let me know. From that moment I surrendered my heart to the King of the Jews, who is the King of Kings. But my fear kept me quiet all these years. Until now.

I do not understand why both your father and I were chosen to have such personal encounters with our Lord. All I know is that Jesus desires a personal encounter with every soul, for he is alive and well to rule the hearts of men. And every encounter with Jesus is filled with the miraculous. I also do not understand why Jesus would allow your father to die, especially when he was trying to save another in that shipwreck on his homeward voyage. But God only allows things that ultimately work for our good and for the good of others. And I know that your father went immediately into the presence of Jesus, where I will see him again in heaven. Someday the answers will be clear, but for now they are dark.

In recent days I've heard of a man of God named Paul. Your mother allows believers to meet in her home, and they sometimes read his letters, which the churches have started to share with one another. I listened to one of his letters that he wrote to believers in Corinth. He said, "At present we are men looking at puzzling reflections in a mirror. The time will come when we shall see reality whole and face to face! At present all I know is a little fraction of the truth, but the time will come when I shall know it as fully as God now knows me!" I think that's what I'm trying to say to you. We may not understand things as they happen, but, eventually, God will make everything clear. We will fully understand why we were allowed to endure pain, hardship, and suffering. And we will see a purpose behind it all, if we will just trust him.

So, my grandson, I pray that you will trust him so you, too, can discover the secret of a life with Jesus and the answers you seek. But when Jesus comes to you in the way only he can, don't keep it a secret. The world needs to know about him. Tell them. Like the red marble you wear around your neck, Julius, make Jesus visible. Be ready to share with anyone who asks.

Always remember that I love you,
Grandfather Marcus

Julius slowly rolled up the scroll containing the letter. He wiped away tears as emotion rose in his throat. He couldn't speak.

A short while later Paul returned. He looked at Julius and tilted his head as he studied the visible emotion of the Roman soldier. "What did your grandfather have to say?"

Julius stared in disbelief at the miraculous turn of events in the life of his family. He stood and walked over to hand Paul the scroll. "More than I could have ever imagined."

"Sounds like he encountered Jesus," Paul replied with a grin, starting to unroll the scroll.

Julius laughed softly at Paul's supreme understatement. "It evidently runs in the family."

☧

To Peter: Greetings in Christ
Our Lord prepared us for the troubles we would face as we boldly shared the good news of his saving grace to a hostile world. He never promised us that we as the bearers of the good news would be triumphant—only that the gospel itself would be. The Enemy seeks our

destruction, and to keep us from fulfilling the commands of Jesus to take the gospel to the ends of the earth.

You were with me when I lost my brother, James, early on in Jerusalem as the first of the twelve to be martyred for Christ. It grieves me to have to now share with you that your brother, Andrew, has been lost as well. After ministering in the far northern regions of Scythia, he was sentenced to death by the Roman governor of Patras in Achaia. Andrew did not wish to be executed in the same manner as our Lord, and requested a different cross. So they bound him with ropes to a decussate, or X-shaped, cross. He suffered a prolonged dying process but, ultimately, we know he entered paradise with Jesus. I am certain my brother, James, immediately welcomed your brother, Andrew, there.

Please know that the brothers and sisters here in Ephesus are keeping you lifted in prayer as you receive this difficult news. Stay strong, Peter. May our Lord continue to bless you as you faithfully serve him in Rome.

– JOHN

287

Peter sank to his knees and let the parchment fall from his hand onto the floor. He wrapped his arms around himself, weeping bitterly.

The animals walked along the Via Sacra through the Forum, somberly taking in the sights of Rome. Al was most interested in taking in the *tastes* of Rome, picking up tidbits that fell from carts onto the road. He needed comfort food.

"What a sad message! I still cannot believe it," lamented Liz, her eyes glistening with tears. "Andrew is gone. I am glad we were there to give Peter comfort."

"Aye, and now *I* need comfort," Al answered, picking up a pomegranate and biting into it. "I'm not used to seein' Peter the Rock weep so."

"I saw him like that once," Max added. "After he betr-r-rayed Jesus. But this time his weepin' were different. At least Peter has comfort in knowin' that Andrew be with Jesus."

Nigel frowned and clicked his tongue. "Indeed a tragic shock for us all. A terribly sad message in that letter. But I'm grateful we also witnessed the happy message Julius received from Marcus's letter."

"*Oui!* Julius now knows the truth of who his grandfather and father actually were in Luke's account," Liz agreed joyfully. "If Marcus wrote a similar letter to Theophilus, I cannot imagine that he will not be moved to open his life to Jesus."

"Aye, I heard Julius say he plans ta ask Theo all aboot his letter," Max offered. "I can't wait ta see wha' he does when he hears the tr-r-ruth of Jesus fr-r-rom his own gr-r-randfather then."

"One of us, of course, must be there to witness Theo's response," Liz agreed. "But it truly has been a strange week of messages, both happy and sad."

Nigel raised his paw in the air. "I shall volunteer for that mission, my dear. Indeed, life is filled with messages of both happiness and sadness, isn't it?"

"Aye, ye never know what ye're goin' to get when ye unroll one of them scrolls," Al agreed, spitting pomegranate juice on Max's head. The Scottie frowned. "Makes me want to steer clear o' them."

"Then you may need to steer clear of Paul for a while, Al," a voice came behind them. "It's time for him to write several scrolls."

The animals spun around to see a marble statue of the god Mercury, adorned with winged shoes and a winged hat. In his hand he carried the *caduceus*, the staff with two entwined snakes. At his feet was a rooster heralding the start of a new day, a goat symbolizing fertility, and a tortoise symbolizing Mercury's legendary invention of the lyre made from a tortoise shell.

The goat blinked its eyes and the rooster ruffled its feathers. "Good morning, all."

"Gillamon, ye actually look a wee bit like yerself!" Max observed cheerily.

"But Clarie, ye look like Henriette's husband, Jacques," Al noted, leaning in to get eye to eye with the rooster and poking it with his iron claw. "Good thing ye're not Henriette in livin' marble. The last thing we need be that hen bossin' us around."

"Watch it, Al," admonished Clarie, pecking him on the nose with her chiseled marble beak. Al held his paw to his nose and stuck out his lip.

Gillamon chuckled. "I thought you'd enjoy more of a familiar face today."

288

Liz stared at the statue of the god Mercury. "And you have chosen to be with the form of the god Mercury, the god of messages, no? This week has been filled with messages, so might I assume there are more to come?"

"Yes, Liz. The *true* God of messages breaks through with his Word in multiple ways, and it's time for him to send more messages through Paul," Gillamon explained.

Al stared at Mercury, poking the wings on his sandals. "Does Paul have to wear little winged shoes then?"

Clarie pecked at Al again. "OW! I were jest askin'!"

Gillamon chuckled. "Not winged shoes, Al, but he will need a pair of feet to carry his messages. Do you remember what Paul wrote in his letter to the Romans about feet?"

"Of course, old boy!" Nigel piped up, preening his whiskers and clearing his throat to recite the passage. *"How, then, can they call on the one they have not believed in? And how can they believe in the one of whom they have not heard? And how can they hear without someone preaching to them? And how can anyone preach unless they are sent? As it is written: 'How beautiful are the feet of those who bring good news!'* Of course Paul was quoting our dear Isaiah's words in his own text."

"Precisely, Nigel," Gillamon affirmed. "It's important for two pairs of feet to first arrive at Paul's doorstep, and it's up to you to make that happen."

"There's nothin' *but* pairs of dusty sandals pilin' up outside Paul's door," Max reported. "Paul's got more visitors than can fit in his house."

"*Oui*, right now Timothy, Mark, Tychicus, Epaphroditus, Demas, Justus, Luke, Aristarchus, and, of course, Julius are all there," Liz added. "After a wonderful reunion with Paul, Peter has taken some time for himself to get away and grieve for Andrew."

"Paul has quickly turned his confinement into message headquarters for believers to easily find him here in Rome," Clarie noted. "Word has now reached all the churches of Paul's situation here."

"Thanks, I am sure, to a certain rooster who has let all of those churches know about Paul's pending trial," Liz added with a wink.

The rooster cocked its head with a smile. "More like a human courier."

"So whom precisely shall we expect next?" inquired Nigel.

"A runaway slave whom you saw at the slave auction in Ephesus long ago," Gillamon answered.

Nigel and Liz glanced at one another as they tried to remember the name. "Onesimus?" Liz finally recalled. "The slave that Philemon bought? Philemon was worried about him being a flight risk even back then."

"Onesimus is, indeed, the one," Gillamon answered. "And Epaphras needs to run into him here in Rome so he can take him to Paul."

"Oh dear, Onesimus is in a dreadful predicament as a runaway slave," Nigel lamented. "Rebellious slaves are promptly eliminated once caught. At best he'll be branded with an "F" on his forehead for *fugitivus.* And at worst . . ." Nigel paused with a gulp ". . . he'll be crucified."

Al's eyes filled with fear and he placed his paws up to his mouth. "Not that! Why are the Romans so mean to the poor slaves? Shouldn't we hide Onesymouse from the other guy so he won't be caught?"

"O-ne-si-*mus,* old boy," Nigel corrected him. "The Roman Empire has six million slaves who could be dangerous should they become like Spartacus and rise up against Rome. Hence, the drastic measures taken to discourage rebellious behavior."

290   "Albert, Epaphras was a pagan who met Paul on our way into Ephesus," Liz explained. "He was selling wicked Ephesian letters by the Temple of Artemis, but he quickly accepted the good news of Jesus. He attended Paul's teaching there at the School of Tyrannus while working at the inn where Philemon fell ill. Epaphras brought Paul to see Philemon, and Paul prayed for his healing. Philemon owes Paul his very life, no? Epaphras eventually became the first missionary to Colossae. Since he knows Onesimus and Philemon—but, most importantly since he knows *Jesus*—Epaphras can be trusted to help our runaway slave."

"Well, *that's* a relief," Al sighed, wiping his brow.

"So wha' does this have ta do with us?" Max wanted to know.

"Epaphras has traveled from Colossae to see Paul in order to discuss problems arising in the church there," Gillamon explained. "You must arrange an encounter between him and Onesimus. This will ultimately save Onesimus's life, but also lead to another book in our growing New Testament."

Liz and Nigel gaped at this news. Nigel's whiskers quivered with excitement. "How terribly intriguing! I say, a book in the New Testament from a runaway *slave?* Fascinating!"

"They are both in the Forum right now, buying food in the market," Clarie explained. "Find them and bring them to Paul."

Suddenly Gillamon and Clarie turned back to solid stone as a group of senators went walking past them on their way to the *Curia*, or Senate House.

"Remember, the God of messages is ready to fill Paul's pen," came Gillamon's voice.

The animals stood there looking at the now quiet statue. Al went over to the stone tortoise and knocked on its shell.

"Wha' are ye doin', Lad?" Max asked.

"Jest checkin' to make sure Clarie didn't jump from the rooster to the tortoise," Al replied. "If she changed from a fish into a tortoise once, why couldn't she change from a rooster into a tortoise?"

"Fish!" Liz exclaimed. She kissed Al on the cheek. "Perfect, *mon cher!* Come, Albert, time for you to do what you do best. Max and Nigel, you look for Onesimus while Albert and I find Epaphras. Meet us by the central market stalls." She trotted off to the market.

Al looked questioningly at Max and Nigel, who simply shrugged their shoulders. "Better follow yer lass."

"Aye, before she grows wings on her petite feet," Al replied, running after her.

"Blast it all, we didn't get to ask Gillamon about dates for the Animalympics," Nigel complained, snapping his fingers.

Max crouched down for Nigel to climb onto his back to seek out Onesimus. "Well, Mousie, whenever we're supposed ta know aboot that, Gillamon will be sure we get the message."

USELESS TO ARGUE

There he is!" Liz whispered to Al, pointing to Epaphras, who was in the middle of purchasing some fish. "I knew it. Epaphras always loved to eat fish in Ephesus. He would pack it for lunch when he attended the School of Tyrannus."

"Then he's my kind o' human! He sounds like the little boy with the fishy lunch that I found for Andrew," Al recalled, his mouth watering. "Do he like bread, too?"

"I am sure he does," Liz added, suddenly saddened again by the recent news of Andrew's death. It was Andrew who brought the little boy with the lunch to Jesus that day, when Jesus multiplied the loaves and fishes. "You need to take Epaphras on a chase with his fish once we find Onesimus."

"Ye mean I have to run?" Al sighed, gazing over his fluffy belly as he attempted to see his feet.

"It is for the cause, no?" Liz reminded him. "You wish to help our runaway slave, don't you?"

"Aye, Lass. That I do," Al agreed. Then he perked up. *"Déjà vu!* Do ye mean I need to run away with a fish like I did with Barnabas so he would meet Paul in Jerusalem?"

"Oui, Albert, but I do not think you will need to run as far this time," Liz replied, jumping up onto a stone pedestal of a statue, scanning the crowds for any sign of Max and Nigel. She suddenly saw Nigel swinging by a cord, waving his paws wildly in the air, trying to get her attention. He was pointing toward a stall that sold bread. Liz spied

292

Onesimus standing nearby, looking suspicious. "Got him!" She turned her gaze back to Epaphras, who carried the fish wrapped in grape leaves. "Albert, quickly! Go knock that fish out of Epaphras's hand, and run with it to the bread stall. Onesimus is there now. Go!"

"I've got it, Lass!" Al exclaimed, taking off to blaze toward Epaphras.

Liz bounced her gaze between Epaphras and Onesimus. Suddenly she saw the slave move over to the display of bread. He looked as if he didn't intend to buy the bread, but steal it. He looked around him to make sure no one was watching. *Hurry, Albert!* she thought. *If he is caught, it may all be over for him right here and now.*

Al's chubby legs took him down the cobblestone street as he moved his head in and out of human legs to see his way around. Epaphras was walking away from the fish stall, holding the fish down by his side. "Now's me chance!" Al exclaimed, making a running leap for it. He hung in mid-air for a moment, sprung his iron claw and pierced the fish to bring it crashing to the pavement. He hurriedly scooped the fish up in his mouth and made his way to the bread stall.

"Crazy cat!" Epaphras cried as he lunged toward Al, almost toppling over but keeping his balance. He kept up the chase, following Al through the busy Roman marketplace.

Liz frowned as she saw Onesimus slip a loaf off the table into the folds of his cloak. Al was closing in fast, Epaphras right on his heels.

"Are you planning to pay for that, or do I need to alert the soldiers that a thief is at my stall?" the bread merchant asked Onesimus.

The slave didn't realize he had been seen and spun around just as Al came bounding into him, knocking him to the pavement. The fish went flying and the bread went rolling. Epaphras reached out to grab the fish and tripped, grasping at air while he took a dive, landing right on top of Onesimus. Coins flew up into the air from Epaphras's hand.

In the chaos, Onesimus reached out to grab the coins that fell next to him in the street. Epaphras quickly sat up and the two locked eyes, instantly recognizing one another.

"Epaphras?" Onesimus asked with wide-eyed fear.

"Onesimus?" Epaphras answered in shock to see the slave there.

"And I'm Apollo," the bread vendor said, getting in their faces with the bread. "Someone owes me a denarius, and it's useless to argue!"

Epaphras saw his coins in the slave's hand. "He's got the money to

293

pay you," he said, thinking quickly and snatching the bread from Apollo's hand. He shot a convicting glance at Onesimus. "Go ahead and pay the man."

Onesimus sheepishly handed over the coin to Apollo who took it in a huff and left the men sitting in the street. The two got to their feet. Onesimus handed the rest of the coins back to Epaphras. "Thank you," the slave said, looking around him to make sure no one was going to arrest him.

Epaphras put the coins in the bag tied to his waist and looked around for his fish. Al sat in the street, holding it once again in his mouth. He reached down and took the fish from Al, wrinkling his brow at the odd turn of events. "I suppose I should thank you, crazy cat."

"Ye're welcome!" Al meowed.

"I heard you ran from Philemon," Epaphras whispered, taking Onesimus by the elbow and leading him away from listening ears. "So here you are in Rome. This can't be a chance meeting, Onesimus."

294

Al rolled his eyes. *"O' course it weren't! It were planned!"*

Onesimus stared at his feet. "I've been on the run but have nowhere left to go. I have no money, and no one will hire me without papers. I don't know what to do."

Epaphras looked at this scared slave and had compassion on him. "Come with me. I know someone who can help. I'm on my way to see him myself."

"Who?" Onesimus asked, hesitant to go with Epaphras.

Epaphras smiled. "A prisoner by the name of Paul."

"Got ta hand it ta ye, Big Al, ye done good," Max told his feline friend with a big grin.

Al picked his teeth with a fish bone. "Thanks, Lad. I think connectin' humans with loaves and fishes be me specialty."

Liz giggled. "It was kind of Epaphras to offer you some of his fish after you swiped it from him."

Al patted his full belly. "Aye, once he saw how helpful it were after all to find Onesymouse."

"There is no 'mouse' in the name, old chap. O-ne-si-*mus,*" Nigel once again corrected him. "I say, did you hear his harrowing tale?"

"*Oui,* it sounds as if his rebellious spirit saw a slim opening to escape and he took it," Liz answered.

"An' that ain't all he took," Max said with a frown. "Sounds like he made off with some of Philemon's money."

"But none of this seems to matter to Paul," Nigel offered in amazement. "All he sees is a blind, lost, frightened soul. I daresay he views Onesimus as the prodigal son who needs to be found."

Liz studied the tender way Paul spoke with Onesimus, even drawing a smile from the runaway slave's face. "If anyone knows about being lost and blind, it is Paul."

"And if anyone can lead him to being found in the light, it is Paul," Nigel added.

WEEKS LATER

Epaphras pulled his fingers through his hair and let his hands fall into his lap in frustration. "I wish I could return to Colossae, but I have to follow the Lord's lead and do the work the people there and in Laodicea and Hierapolis have sent me to do here in Rome."

295

"If anyone knows the frustration of wishing you could be in another place, it's Paul," Luke noted as he locked eyes with Paul. "I've seen him face blocked paths and closed doors, but God always had his reasons, which he revealed in time."

"The people of Colossae have hearts that are genuinely full of love for the Lord and for other believers," Epaphras continued. "They are steadfast in their faith, but this heresy has been slowly creeping into the church."

"Tell me exactly what this heresy involves," inquired Luke in a serious tone. "I'm sorry I wasn't here when you and Paul were discussing it."

"It is a mix of Jewish, Greek, and Oriental religious views," Epaphras explained. "Some are calling for worship of angels as intermediaries between God and man. Others insist on strict observance of Jewish requirements, like the Pharisees of old."

Paul shook his head sadly. "The Enemy never ceases using tactics to invade the church through false doctrine. So some people are suggesting that Jesus alone is not enough for salvation."

Epaphras nodded slowly. "That's right, Paul. Some believe we can't know God through Jesus alone, and seek to expand the gospel message to include contemporary thought and reason. I've poured out my soul praying for the church, and beg all of you to please lift up Colossae so it can see the light of truth and not lose its way."

"Indeed, we will pray," Luke offered. "Have you seen this heresy spilling over to other churches in the region?"

"I did stop by the church in Ephesus on my way here, and while I do not see such heresy per se, I do think all churches could use a fresh word of remembering who Christ is and whom he embodies," Epaphras replied.

"Christ is the visible likeness of the invisible God," Paul stated plainly. "The only true knowledge of God's character, and the only way *to* God is through Jesus alone."

"They need to remember the incredible love of Jesus," Epaphras suggested. "When you grasp that unconditional love, your heart is unlocked to the truth across all aspects of the Christian life."

Onesimus walked in with a platter full of food, to the delight of everyone there. "I hope you don't mind I took the liberty of preparing some food. It is my area of expertise in service."

Paul clasped his hands together, the chains clanking as he did. "What a delight! Thank you, Onesimus. You have done nothing but tirelessly serve us, and you have tended to my every need. We are so grateful for you."

"It is *I* who am grateful," the slave replied, frowning to see Paul's chains. "You, who are in chains, have shown me the way to be free."

Gratitude had welled up in Paul's heart as he observed the change in Onesimus over the last few weeks. "If any man be in Christ, he is a new creature: old things are passed away; all things are become new."

Onesimus nodded humbly. "I am full of joy to have a new beginning. Old things in me are, indeed, passed away, but I feel I must still set things right with Philemon. I need to return to Colossae."

"But you could be maimed or killed!" Luke protested.

"It's useless to argue, Luke," Onesimus answered. "I need to return to my master."

Julius frowned. "Onesimus is right, and as a Roman officer, I am obligated to see that he is returned to his owner."

Paul clenched his jaw and nodded slowly. "I agree with all of you, as much as I would like to keep Onesimus here. But I will not send him back alone." He looked around the room and locked eyes with Tychicus. "I would like to send a letter to the church at Colossae. Tychicus, would you take the letter and escort Onesimus back to Philemon?"

"It would be my honor and privilege to do so, Paul," Tychicus answered.

Onesimus nodded. "Thank you, Paul. And thank you, Tychicus. I will accept whatever consequences await me there."

"The Lord knows what awaits you there, so let's take this matter before him. Prayer is the greatest protection we can provide as you face this journey," Paul told the slave, getting to his knees. "And then, Timothy, we have a letter to write."

☧

After a time of prayer, Paul stood in preparation for his familiar pacing around the room while he dictated a letter to the Colossians. Paul smiled at everyone gathered there and took a deep breath. "Let us begin." He motioned for Timothy to ready his pen.

297

"Paul, messenger of Jesus Christ by God's will, and brother Timothy send this greeting to all faithful Christians at Colossae: grace and peace be to you from God our Father and the Lord Jesus Christ! I want you to know by this letter that we here are constantly praying for you, and whenever we do we thank God the Father of our Lord Jesus Christ because you believe in Christ Jesus and because you are showing true Christian love towards other Christians. We know that you are showing these qualities because you have grasped the hope reserved for you in Heaven—that hope which first became yours when the truth was brought to you. It is, of course, part of the Gospel itself, which has reached you as it spreads all over the world. Wherever that Gospel goes, it produces Christian character, and develops it, as it had done in your own case from the time you first heard and realized the amazing fact of God's grace."

Paul allowed Timothy to catch up and smiled at Epaphras.

"You learned these things, we understand, from Epaphras who is in the same service as we are. He is a most well-loved minister of Christ, and has your well-being very much at heart. As a matter of fact, it was from him that we heard about your growth in Christian love, so you will understand that since we heard about you we have never missed you in our prayers. We are asking God that you may see things, as it were, from his point of view by being given spiritual insight and understanding. We also pray that your outward lives, which men see, may bring credit to your master's name, and that you may bring joy to his heart by bearing genuine Christian fruit, and that your knowledge of God may grow yet deeper.

"As you live this new life, we pray that you will be strengthened from God's boundless resources, so that you will find yourselves able to pass through any experience and endure it with courage. You will even be able to thank God in the midst of pain and distress because you are privileged to share the lot of those who are living in the light. For we must never forget that he rescued us from the power of darkness, and re-established us in the kingdom of his beloved Son, that is, in the kingdom of light. For it is by his Son alone that we have been redeemed and have had our sins forgiven.

"I myself have been made a minister of this same Gospel, and though it is true at this moment that I am suffering on behalf of you who have heard the Gospel, yet I am far from sorry about it. Indeed, I am glad, because it gives me a chance to complete in my own sufferings something of the untold pains for which Christ suffers on behalf of his body, the Church. For I am a minister of the Church by divine commission, a commission granted to me for your benefit and for a special purpose: that I might fully declare God's word"—Paul looked right at Julius, thinking of Marcus and his letter—"that sacred mystery which up to now has been hidden in every age and every generation, but which is now as clear as daylight to those who love God. They are those to whom God has planned to give a vision of the full wonder and splendor of his secret plan for the sons of men. And the secret is simply this: Christ in you! Yes, Christ in you bringing with him the hope of all glorious things to come."

While Paul continued to dictate for Timothy, addressing the issue of the heresy creeping into the church, Liz studied Onesimus. He was tending to the needs of everyone in the room, out of his heart's desire to serve, not as a slave. "If Onesimus returns to Philemon with Tychicus and this letter alone, I do not believe it will be enough to shield him from severe consequences. Philemon needs to hear from Paul specifically about his runaway slave."

298

"Agreed, my dear," Nigel whispered back. "What do you suggest we do?"

"Hmmm, it shall come to me," Liz responded, her tail curling slowly up and down. "'Useful.' Onesimus's name means 'useful.'"

"Perhaps Paul needs to tell Philemon that Onesimus is now living up to his name," Nigel suggested.

Liz and Nigel sat together, paying close attention to every word as Paul dictated over the next hour. Finally, Liz could tell that Paul was nearing the close of his letter.

"Devote yourselves to prayer, being watchful and thankful. And pray for us, too, that God may open a door for our message, so that we may proclaim the mystery of Christ, for which I am in chains. Pray that I may proclaim it clearly, as I should. Be wise in the way you act toward outsiders; make the most of every opportunity. Let your conversation be always full of grace, seasoned with salt, so that you may know how to answer everyone.

"Tychicus will tell you all the news about me. He is a dear brother, a faithful minister and fellow servant in the Lord. I am sending him to you for the express purpose that you may know about our circumstances and that he may encourage your hearts. He is coming with Onesimus, our faithful and dear brother, who is one of you. They will tell you everything that is happening here."

Liz's eyes lit up. "I have an idea. It is rather drastic, but perhaps it will work." She got up and walked over to where Timothy was writing the letter and jumped onto the table. She sat there a moment, considering her next move.

Paul held his hand out as he referenced each friend in the room. "My fellow prisoner Aristarchus sends you his greetings, as does Mark, the cousin of Barnabas. (You have received instructions about him; if he comes to you, welcome him.) Jesus, who is called Justus, also sends greetings. These are the only Jews among my co-workers for the kingdom of God, and they have proved a comfort to me. Epaphras, who is one of you and a servant of Christ Jesus, sends greetings. He is always wrestling in prayer for you, that you may stand firm in all the will of God, mature and fully assured. I vouch for him that he is working hard for you and for those at Laodicea and Hierapolis. Our dear friend Luke, the doctor, and Demas send greetings. Give my greetings to the brothers

299

and sisters at Laodicea, and to Nympha and the church in her house.

"After this letter has been read to you, see that it is also read in the church of the Laodiceans and that you in turn read the letter from Laodicea. Tell Archippus: 'See to it that you complete the ministry you have received in the Lord.'"

Liz braced herself and took in a quick breath, swishing her tail as she stared at Onesimus. *Follow my lead, Onesimus.* She reached out her paw and knocked over Timothy's bowl of ink, which began to spread all over the table and onto the brass seal used to affix wax to the scrolls. Timothy quickly lifted the scroll and stood to his feet. "Silly cat!"

Immediately Onesimus jumped up and ran over to help clean up the mess. He gently lifted Liz off the table and set her on the floor. "Careful, little Faith. Timothy is writing an important letter for Paul." He proceeded to take a rag and clean up the ink. "Allow me to get you more ink, my friend." He walked hurriedly into the other room while Paul stood by Timothy.

300

"I'll finish it from here, Timothy," Paul offered, taking the pen from Timothy's hand.

"As you wish, Paul," answered Timothy, handing him the scroll also. "I know how you like to authenticate your letters with your own signature."

Onesimus brought in a new bowl of ink and set it down on the table. "Anything else I can get for you, Paul?" He picked up the brass seal and pressed it into the back of his hand to remove the excess ink.

"Thank you, Onesimus. You are ever so helpful to me," Paul answered as he gazed at the mark on Onesimus's hand. He slowly dipped the pen in the ink and wrote his closing remarks on the letter to the Colossians:

I, Paul, write this greeting in my own hand. Remember my chains. Grace be with you.

He leaned back and locked eyes with Onesimus. This runaway slave had come to Rome in defiance of authority, yet had now come to submit to the highest authority of Christ, willing to face the consequences of his actions in order to set things right with Philemon. This slave could be branded or even crucified for his rebellion. While he doubted that Philemon would ever be so severe, he didn't wish for any such harm to come to Onesimus.

Paul thought a moment and tapped the pen on the table. "Timothy, we're not finished. I cannot send Onesimus back to Philemon without a word in his defense." He stood and handed the pen to Timothy. "Please prepare another scroll."

☧

"You are simply brilliant, my pet," Nigel cheered to Liz as Paul began to dictate a letter to Philemon. "It appears Paul shall do your unspoken bidding, and we shall have our most unusual letter for the New Testament."

"Merci, mon ami," Liz answered with a shy smile. "Let us pray that a little spilled ink will help our runaway slave."

"Paul, prisoner for the sake of Jesus Christ, and brother Timothy to Philemon our much-loved fellow-worker, Apphia our sister and Archippus who is with us in the fight; to the church that meets in your house—grace and peace be to you from God our Father and from the Lord Jesus Christ.

"I always thank God for you, Philemon, in my constant prayers for you all, for I have heard how you love and trust both the Lord Jesus himself and those who believe in him. And I pray that those who share your faith may also share your knowledge of all the good things that believing in Jesus Christ can mean to us. It is your love, my brother, that gives us such comfort and happiness, for it cheers the hearts of your fellow Christians.

"And although I could rely on my authority in Christ and dare to order you to do what I consider right, I am not doing that. No, I am appealing to that love of yours, a simple personal appeal from Paul the old man, in prison for Jesus Christ's sake. I am appealing for my child. Yes I have become a father though I have been under lock and key, and the child's name is—Onesimus!"

Paul smiled and held out his hand toward the slave. Onesimus placed his hand over his heart and nodded with humility as tears of gratitude welled up in his eyes. Paul rushed over and hugged the grateful man.

"Oh, I know you have found him pretty useless in the past but he is going to be useful now, to both of us," Paul continued, patting Onesimus on the back. "I am sending him back to you: will you receive him as my son, part of me? I should have dearly loved to have kept him with

301

me: he could have done what you would have done—looked after me here in prison for the Gospel's sake. But I would do nothing without consulting you first, for if you have a favor to give me, let it be spontaneous and not forced from you by circumstances!"

Paul walked behind Timothy and gripped his shoulders. "Thank you, my friend. I will finish the letter now." Timothy nodded and handed the pen to Paul. Paul took a seat and tapped the pen on his chin as he studied Onesimus. How he loved this brother who was once lost, but now found! He smiled and began to write:

> *It occurs to me that there has been a purpose in your losing him. You lost him, a slave, for a time; now you are having him back for good, not merely as a slave, but as a brother-Christian. He is already especially loved by me—how much more will you be able to love him, both as a man and as a fellow-Christian! You and I have so much in common haven't we? Then do welcome him as you would welcome me. If you feel he has wronged or cheated you put it down to my account. I've written this with my own hand: I, Paul, hereby promise to repay you. (Of course I'm not stressing the fact that you might be said to owe me your very soul!) Now do grant me this favor, my brother—such an act of love will do my old heart good. As I send you this letter I know you'll do what I ask—I believe, in fact, you'll do more.*

302

Paul paused and considered his confident hope that God would grant him a favorable outcome with Nero.

> *Will you do something else? Get the guest-room ready for me, for I have great hopes that through your prayers I myself will be returned to you as well!*
>
> *Epaphras, here in prison with me, sends his greetings: so do Mark, Aristarchus, Demas and Luke, all fellow-workers for God. The grace of our Lord Jesus Christ be with your spirit, amen.*
>
> *PAUL*

He placed the pen on the table and leaned back, wrapping his hands behind his neck to stretch out. It had been a long day of writing.

"I'll get these scrolls prepared for you to take with you, Tychicus," Timothy announced, rolling up the letter to the Colossians. He reached over to pick up a stick of wax to hold over the oil lamp in order to place a seal on the letter.

Just then, Julius walked back into the room and nodded his silent greeting. He leaned his spear next to the wall where Marcus's armor was displayed. Julius had put the pieces of armor on an upright stand in order to admire them, and to have a visual reminder of his grandfather. A thought suddenly struck Paul as he thought about the soldiers who had long ago sat with him while he dictated the letter to the Philippians from prison in Ephesus. His thoughts then drifted to Hector and the conversations they had about "armor on the inside." Paul locked eyes with Julius and was once again overwhelmed by the story of the Roman centurions in the family of Antonius.

"Before you leave for Colossae, Tychicus, there's another letter I must write," shared Paul, leaning forward as he studied Marcus's armor. "A letter to the Ephesians."

303

ARMOR UP

Julius yawned, slowly petting Max, who was curled up next to him on the couch. "The hour is late, Paul. Everyone else has turned in. Shouldn't you call it a day and finish tomorrow? You've been working on that letter for days now. Surely one more day won't matter."

Paul held up a finger as he continued to write:

Grace to all who love our Lord Jesus Christ with an undying love.

He put down his pen and blew on the ink. His breath caused the flame in the oil lamp to flicker on the desk. Liz blinked her eyes contentedly at Paul, purring. He rubbed his eyes and petted Liz on her cheek. "I'm finished. I wanted to complete my train of thought so I wouldn't lose it. I've needed to write this letter myself as I pulled my thoughts together." He reached over and studied the ornate Roman helmet that had belonged to Julius's grandfather, Marcus. All of Marcus's armor was now spread out on the floor next to Paul's feet. He had been studying each piece. "I marvel at how the Lord used your grandfather's armor to inspire me. Thank you for allowing me to handle it."

"I'm honored and grateful that it could help you, Paul," Julius replied. "What do you hope this letter will communicate?"

"Although I'm sending this letter first to the believers in Ephesus, I wish for copies to be sent to all the churches, so I have not written personal greetings as I usually do." Paul traced the filigree design etched into the cheek flaps of the helmet. "I hope it will communicate the importance of unity among the churches. I've spent my life teaching Gentiles they can follow Jesus without following the Jewish laws and traditions. While that encourages the Gentiles, it always upsets a faction of Jews, and this continual cycle of discord between the two groups of believers persists. I want Gentiles to stand firm in the liberty of Christ without resentment or prejudice against their Jewish brothers and sisters in Christ." Paul leaned back to stretch. "There is no Jew or Gentile. But the enemy seeks division across other lines, too. I wish for *every* dividing line to be removed. I look at Onesimus and Philemon, and see no slave or free. I look at you and your mother, and I see no male or female. In Christ we are all one." Paul scanned back over the scroll. "Unity is the key to the body of Christ, and living a life that reflects that unity through love."

"You're right, Paul," Julius replied. "Unity is the key. I've seen how division can tear families apart."

"Yes, and I've seen how your Roman army has marched and conquered the world, united as one force," Paul answered, pointing at Marcus's armor. "And every soldier is armed to the teeth. So we as believers can learn a thing or two from you Romans."

305

Julius raised his eyebrows and grinned. "Excuse me, but some of us are Romans *and* believers."

"Of course, forgive me, Julius!" Paul apologized, shaking his head at himself. "The hour is late and I am quite tired."

"I look forward to reading your letter to the Ephesians tomorrow," Julius commented, standing to leave the common area for their sleeping quarters. "Rest well, my friend. We'll send Tychicus and Onesimus on their way, and I'll touch base with Theo about your case."

"Thank you, Julius," Paul replied with a yawn, following Julius with a pat on his back. "I pray Luke's letters have helped your brother."

"I think they've actually caused him a great deal of anxiety," Julius replied with a smile. "And I plan to add to it when I take him grandfather's letter."

As the two men left the room, Nigel scurried up onto the table. "I thought he would never finish. I'm eager to read his latest tome."

"If Julius is taking Marcus's letter to Theo tomorrow, you need to be there when he reads it," Liz suggested.

"You can count on me, my dear," Nigel replied. "For now, shall we explore Paul's letter?"

Liz and Nigel scanned the scroll to read Paul's letter to the Ephesians:

All this energy issues from Christ: God raised him from death and set him on a throne in deep heaven, in charge of running the universe, everything from galaxies to governments, no name and no power exempt from his rule. And not just for the time being, but forever. He is in charge of it all, has the final word on everything. At the center of all this, Christ rules the church. The church, you see, is not peripheral to the world; the world is peripheral to the church. The church is Christ's body, in which he speaks and acts, by which he fills everything with his presence.

"This could be one of his finest letters yet," Liz suggested as she kept her eyes on the scroll. Neither she nor Nigel noticed that Al had jumped up onto the table with them.

306

The Messiah has made things up between us so that we're now together on this, both non-Jewish outsiders and Jewish insiders. He tore down the wall we used to keep each other at a distance. He repealed the law code that had become so clogged with fine print and footnotes that it hindered more than it helped. Then he started over. Instead of continuing with two groups of people separated by centuries of animosity and suspicion, he created a new kind of human being, a fresh start for everybody.

Christ brought us together through his death on the cross. The cross got us to embrace, and that was the end of the hostility. Christ came and preached peace to you outsiders and peace to us insiders. He treated us as equals, and so made us equals. Through him we both share the same Spirit and have equal access to the Father.

That's plain enough, isn't it? You're no longer wandering exiles. This kingdom of faith is now your home country. You're no longer strangers or outsiders. You belong here, with as much right to the name Christian as anyone. God is building a home. He's using us all—irrespective of how we got here—in what he is building. He used the apostles and prophets for the foundation. Now he's using you, fitting you in brick by brick, stone by stone, with Christ Jesus as the cornerstone that holds all the parts together.

✗

"I do believe you're right. This is simply *exquisite* work," Nigel concurred, adjusting his spectacles as he and Liz remained absorbed in reading Paul's letter, oblivious to Al.

Al patted Marcus's helmet, which sat on its side, smiling as it rocked back and forth on the table. He suddenly noticed the sculpted lion's head on the front. It moved.

"C'est magnifique! Paul is using Roman armor to show how a believer can defend against the Evil One," Liz exclaimed. She put her paw on the page and began to read aloud:

"Finally, build up your strength in union with the Lord and by means of his mighty power. Put on all the armor that God gives you, so that you will be able to stand up against the Devil's evil tricks. For we are not fighting against human beings but against the wicked spiritual forces in the heavenly world, the rulers, authorities, and cosmic powers of this dark age. So put on God's armor now!"

Al jumped at Liz's passionate reading, thinking he heard the lion on the helmet roar to give him an order. "Aye!" He cocked his head, leaned over, and stuck his head inside the helmet.

Nigel finished reading the next sentence. "Then when the evil day comes, you will be able to resist the enemy's attacks; and after fighting to the end, you will still hold your ground." Nigel held up a fist of victory in the air. "Good show, Paul! This is brilliant!"

"AHHHH! It's got me!" Al cried, holding his paws up to either side of the helmet.

Liz and Nigel broke from their mesmerized state to see Al wearing Marcus's helmet. Only now, the helmet had shrunk to fit Al's head. Unused to carrying such weight above his shoulders, Al's body tipped from side to side, as he staggered around the table trying to pull the helmet off. Suddenly he neared the edge and toppled off onto the floor.

"Albert!" Liz cried.

"Wha' are ye doin', Kitty?" Max shouted as Al bumped into him on the floor.

"By Jove, Al is wearing Marcus's helmet!" Nigel realized as he and Liz jumped down to where Al ran around on the floor in hysterics, holding his head.

307

"Help! Help! Help!" Al screamed. "The lion's got me! The lion's got me! The lion's got me!"

"Well, this daft kitty ain't standin' *his* gr-r-round!" Max grumbled, chasing Al around the room to try to help him. "Hold still, Lad!"

"Do as he says, Al," came a voice of authority.

Al stopped in his tracks, breathing heavily, his eyes wild with fear. "Aye, Sir!" His lip quivered.

Liz, Max, and Nigel looked at one another in shock. Max crept up to examine the source of the voice. It was coming from the helmet.

"Gillamon?" Max asked cautiously.

"Indeed," Gillamon replied. He had animated the sculpted lion on the helmet. His eyes sparkled and the fur on his mane moved. "What Paul has just written will become one of the most important teaching illustrations for believers across time. In order for you to fully understand the full armor of God, I thought I would give you a demonstration. Do you remember the riddle Clarie gave you long ago in Ephesus?"

Liz's eyes brightened, recounting the riddle. *"Oui!* 'An inside job, a captive audience, and the means to protect and compete. When soldiers greet soldiers, the inside job is complete.'"

"Very good, Liz," replied the lion on Al's helmet. "Nigel, do you remember the conversation Hector had with Paul the night they fled Jerusalem on their way to Caesarea?"

Nigel tapped his paw on his chin and then snapped his fingers. "Right! Paul and Hector discussed the story of David and Goliath, whereby Paul relayed how David's armor was on the *inside."* He thought a moment more, and his mouse eyes widened behind the spectacles. "That night Paul said David wore the helmet of salvation!"

"Looks like this r-r-riddle keeps on r-r-riddlin', Gillamon," Max suggested.

"You are both correct," Gillamon replied. "The riddle wasn't meant just for Ephesus, or for Caesarea. Now its meaning is for Rome."

"Is this because Paul's letter has been written in Rome to send back to Ephesus?" Liz wondered.

"Yes, but there will be more meaning behind the riddle as time unfolds here in Rome," Gillamon shared. "For now, let me help you understand Paul's meaning behind the full armor of God."

"Can I take this off now?" begged Al, continuing to whimper.

308

Gillamon chuckled. "No, Al. You're just getting armored up. Wouldn't you like to know how it feels to wear a complete set of armor, where the Enemy cannot touch you?"

Al blinked his eyes behind the helmet and he stroked his whiskers that stuck out the side. "I never thought aboot it like that. Aye! What do I need to do next?"

"Liz, if you'll read each part of Paul's letter on the armor, your brave mate here will demonstrate while I explain," Gillamon told the group. "Al, walk over to Marcus's armor."

Al did as he was told and moved over by the armor on the floor.

Liz read about the first piece of armor. "So stand ready, with truth as a belt tight around your waist."

"Pick up the belt, Al," Gillamon instructed.

"This should be interestin' ta see if Big Al can tighten that belt around his belly," Max muttered under his breath.

Al cautiously reached over to pick up the leather belt studded with ornate brass plates, buckle, and silver decorations. Seven strips of leather hung down from the center of the belt, each beaded with small silver medallions. On either side of the belt were clips for holding other items. When Al held the belt in his hand, it immediately wrapped around him, shrinking to Al's size and buckling itself. Al threw his paws up in the air and then looked down to see his fur spilling over the front of the belt. He wore a weak grin. "I been meanin' to lose weight."

"Now tell me, would you consider this belt to be the most important piece of armor for a soldier?" Gillamon asked.

"A belt?" Max asked, walking around Al as he stood on his hind legs. "Don't look like it ta me."

"Ah, but it is," Gillamon explained. "A soldier's belt is seemingly the least impressive piece of armor, but it holds the rest of the armor in place. It first helps the soldier by holding up his tunic so it does not hang too low and get caught in his legs when he needs to move. Those clips on the side hold the soldier's shield, sword, and breastplate. Without the belt, the rest of the armor will not work together."

"So the belt is what gives the soldier confidence in the fight," Liz offered.

"Fascinating! Paul likens truth to a belt and says to keep it tight around one's waist," Nigel observed. "What specifically is Paul referring to as 'truth,' Gillamon?"

"Paul means the written Word of God, for it holds everything together for the believer," Gillamon explained. "It is the starting point of armor to equip the soldier for the fight."

"Makes sense to me," Al agreed, trying to look at his belt behind his back. "So what comes next?"

Liz held up her paw and read the next item on Paul's list, "with righteousness as your breastplate."

Al's eyes lit up to behold the muscular sculpted breastplate adorned with an eagle in the center. "Now this should look great on me!" The silver breastplate had two pieces, front and back, that attached with brass rings at the shoulder. Al squatted down and squeezed in between them. Suddenly the breastplate resized and affixed to Al's chest, and he stood up tall and proud. "How do I look?"

"Oh, Albert, you look so handsome!" Liz exclaimed, holding her paws up to her cheeks with admiration.

Max and Nigel rolled their eyes at Al's fake muscles, walking around Al as he put his paws on his hips to show off his now svelte middle.

310

"Now this be the shiniest, most beautiful piece of armor," Max pointed out.

"That's right, and it is what onlookers first notice," Gillamon replied. "Imagine the sun glistening off this breastplate, multiplied by a legion of soldiers marching toward the enemy."

"I say, I believe such bright gleaming metal would blind the dreaded foe," Nigel supposed. "Isaiah wrote, 'Listen to Me, you who know righteousness, the people in whose heart is My instruction: do not fear disgrace by men, and do not be shattered by their taunts.' Ergo, righteousness protects the soldier's heart from the taunting words and lies shouted by a blinded enemy."

"Aye, that r-r-right there gives a soldier cour-r-rage an' confidence!" Max cheered. "No need ta fear wha' the enemy tr-r-ries ta do when yer heart be covered."

"Excellent," Gillamon affirmed them. "Now, for your feet, Al. In your case, your hind legs and paws."

Liz read the next item in Paul's list of armor. "And as your shoes the readiness to announce the good news of peace."

Al looked down at the leather-strapped shoes and touched his paw to the one-inch spikes protruding from the bottom of one of the sandals. "OW!" He pulled his paw back. "Those be deadly!" Sitting next to the sandals were two tube-like pieces, brass greaves that covered the lower part of the leg from the feet to the knees. "Here goes nothin'." He picked them up and placed them on his hind legs as he slipped his paws into the sandals. Immediately they resized and covered his feet and legs. Al lifted up a foot and admired his fierce look.

"He looks like a puss in boots," Max whispered to Nigel.

"Hmmm, puss in boots," Nigel replied. "An interesting concept, old boy."

"Gillamon, what does Paul mean by shoes fitted with peace?" Liz asked.

"Those spikes allow a soldier to stand his ground on the battlefield," Gillamon explained. "He can step with a firm footing of confidence. He has peace in the fact that he will not fall or be moved, getting eye to eye with an enemy who would intimidate him. While chaos swirls around him, the soldier has supernatural peace both mentally and emotionally that he is protected where he stands."

311

"Wha' aboot those leg coverin's?" Max asked.

"Soldiers are called to march through rocky, thorny, and other difficult barriers," Gillamon answered. "The greaves give them peace that they can march into rough territory without fear of being bruised or scratched. They also are protected from broken bones if the enemy tries to kick them in the shins."

"I say, might those deadly shoes also serve to help a man go on the offensive by kicking the stuffing out of the enemy's shins?" Nigel asked, kicking out his leg. "One could really give the enemy the what-for and all of that!"

"Absolutely, Nigel. Paul wrote in his letter to the Romans: 'And the God of peace shall bruise Satan under your feet shortly.' You need to understand what Paul meant by the words he chose," Gillamon told Nigel. "'Bruise' means to squash like a grape. Satan's rightful place is under a believer's feet, completely squashed and subdued, but only with the Maker's power—not in his own strength, which is no match for the Enemy alone. 'Shortly' is the Greek word *tachos*, which is how Roman soldiers march, with very hard, short, heavy steps. The noise of marching soldiers pounding the pavement in those hob-nailed shoes sends a warning they are coming and will stop for no one."

"Sure, so if the enemy don't get out o' his way, a soldier will stomp on him like a bug then," described Al, making a squishing motion with his foot.

Max nodded. "Peace thr-r-rough str-r-rength."

"So a believer has peace from feet firmly planted in the knowledge of the Maker's protective, saving power, and from confidence to march without fear wherever the Maker leads," Liz summarized.

Nigel held up a paw to quote another passage from Isaiah: "You, Lord, give perfect peace to those who keep their purpose firm and put their trust in you."

The lion on Al's helmet nodded and smiled. "Splendid, all of you. Next, Liz?"

"At all times carry faith as a shield; for with it you will be able to put out all the burning arrows shot by the Evil One," Liz read.

Al looked down at the round, ornate shield. As he picked it up, it changed shape into a door-shaped shield that was long and wide. Al peeked his face over the top, revealing only his eyes through the helmet. "I gotta get one o' these!"

"Soldiers have two types of shields. The one Marcus left for Julius was his *aspis,* or ceremonial shield for parades and ceremonies," Gillamon conveyed. "In battle, soldiers use these *thureos*, or long shields, to completely cover themselves. It's made of six layers of thick leather woven together. Nothing can penetrate such a shield, but a soldier must take care of it to keep it that way."

"I have often seen soldiers daily apply oil to their shields to keep them supple," Nigel reported.

"Indeed," Gillamon answered. "It is a soldier's daily responsibility to keep his shield oiled. If it is allowed to get dry, it will become brittle and crack over time. Now when battle comes, a soldier will immerse his shield in water to saturate it."

"Aye, so flamin' ar-r-rows can't set it ablaze," Max finished the thought. "Jest like the Enemy tr-r-ries ta launch flamin' ar-r-rows of lies an' accusations at believers."

"*Oui,* so keeping the shield of faith attached to the belt of truth is like keeping the shield saturated with the Word of God," Liz added.

Gillamon smiled. "Bravo, Liz. Faith in Christ will shield us from anything the Enemy tries to throw at us. Next on the list?"

312

"And accept salvation as a helmet," Liz replied. "Albert, you already have on that handsome piece of armor."

"Aye, I like how fancy it be with ye on me head, Gillamon," Al joked, turning his eyes up at the helmet.

"A soldier's helmet is the most beautiful piece of armor, and many times is more like a piece of art with the intricate carvings and sculptures on pieces like this one," Gillamon replied, spreading his lion arms across the front of the helmet. "The red or white plumes of horse hair or feathers are attached to the helmets not only for public ceremonies but so soldiers can easily identify their commanders on the field of battle."

Max studied Al's head. "A helmet pr-r-rotects a soldier's head. The enemy would like nothin' better than ta knock it clean off!"

"So salvation is the most beautiful, intricate, and elaborate gift the Maker has given," Liz continued, making the spiritual comparison with the helmet.

"And it keeps a believer from losing control of his mind or emotions," Nigel added. "As Paul wrote in his second letter to the Corinthians, 'The weapons we use in our fight are not the world's weapons but God's powerful weapons, which we use to destroy strongholds. We destroy false arguments; we pull down every proud obstacle that is raised against the knowledge of God; we take every thought captive and make it obey Christ.'"

313

"A stronghold is a prison that keeps one in bondage from irrational or fearful thinking. The Enemy loves to suggest to believers that they are failures or will never be able to do what they need to do," Gillamon explained. "He knows that the only way to take a believer captive is through the mind. If he can take control of your mind, he can then take control of your whole person. So remembering that you have eternal salvation from sin and darkness will give you strength to bring all thoughts captive to Christ. He has the final say on what you really can and cannot do."

Al was eyeing Marcus's beautiful sword. "Can I pick that up now?"

Liz smiled, reading the next item of armor on Paul's list. "And the Word of God as the sword which the Spirit gives you."

Al tried to lift the heavy sword, but it wouldn't budge.

"Before you take this sword in hand, allow me to explain about swords," Gillamon suggested. "While a soldier uses many different types of swords, like long swords or daggers, the most common and powerful sword is this two-edged sword called the *machaira*. It is nineteen inches long, and is razor sharp on each side. Again, it must stay attached to a soldier's belt so he has it with him at all times."

"I thought we already heard aboot the Word of God as tr-r-ruth," Max wondered, furrowing his brow.

"That's right, Max. The belt of truth is the *written* Word of God in Scripture," Gillamon explained. "This Word of God is a *spoken* word, or *rhema,* from the Holy Spirit that he will whisper to a believer's heart and mind just when it is needed."

"Right! Just as Jesus told the disciples not to worry about what they would say when they were brought before governors and kings," Nigel said. "Peter and John spoke with confidence as they each wielded their swords before the Sanhedrin!"

"Or when Jesus himself faced the Enemy during his forty days in the desert!" Liz reminded them. "He pulled out his 'It is written' sword to quote verses against Satan."

314

"Indeed, you are both correct. It may also come as a single, simple word of instruction from the Maker," Gillamon added. "Just as the Maker gave a specific word to Noah to build the ark, Abraham to leave his home, Joseph in his two dreams, Moses for his many assignments, Mary to become the mother of Jesus, and Paul to spread the gospel—all of these were short but powerful words of instruction." He looked down at Al, who stood patiently by the sword. "Go ahead, Al. Pick up the sword."

Al grinned and put his paw on the sheath of the sword. It became the perfect size in his grip. He attached the sheath to his belt clip and slowly pulled the sword out to wave in the air. The light from the oil lamp glistened off the blade. Max and Nigel ducked for cover as Al sliced through the air.

"Watch it, Kitty!" Max shouted. "Ye'll kill somebody with that!"

"Only the bad guys, Lad," Al replied confidently, his tongue hanging out the side of his mouth while he fought an imaginary foe.

Liz looked around and saw that Al was wearing every piece of Marcus's armor. "So there are six pieces of armor?"

The lion smiled. "When was six ever a complete number, Liz?" He pointed over to Julius's spear leaning against the wall. "Liz, read the next line in Paul's letter."

"Do all this in prayer, asking for God's help. Pray on every occasion, as the Spirit leads. For this reason keep alert and never give up; pray always for all God's people," Liz read.

"Go ahead, Al. Pick up the spear," Gillamon instructed him. "Paul concludes his armor-of-God instructions with prayer. Although he does not mention it specifically as a spear, there remains this last piece of armor that a soldier must always have for protection. And spears come in all shapes and sizes for a soldier's use."

Al put his sword back in his sheath and walked over to pick up the spear. "Sure, and I could throw this at the enemy long before he reached me."

Nigel lifted his eyebrows in understanding. "Of course! Prayer is an offensive weapon that can be hurled at a distance to cut off the Enemy's advance, like praying on someone's behalf or in advance of something."

"Aye, but there be all sorts of different pr-r-rayers, jest like different types of spears," Max suggested. "Prayers can be short an' quick, like a 'thank ye' or a 'help me' prayer."

"So, we have three weapons of defense: breastplate, shield, and helmet; three weapons of offense: shoes, sword, and spear; and one weapon that is neutral: the belt," Liz summarized.

"Seven pieces!" Al exclaimed, suddenly getting it. "There be seven pieces o' armor! Jest like there be seven o' us!"

"And there are seven hills in this city of Rome," Gillamon reminded them. "All of which will be conquered when Rome falls to an army of soldiers."

Max, Liz, Nigel, and Al looked at one another in disbelief. "You mean that Rome, the most powerful city on Earth, will fall?" Nigel asked in shock.

"Just as Paul speaks of symbolic armor based on real armor, I speak of the symbolic fall of Rome based on a real fall," Gillamon replied. "But the true fall we're after will come from believers armored up like Al here."

Al stood there with his head held high, wearing his belt, breastplate, shoes, shield, helmet, sword, and spear. "Do I look like I'm dressed to kill?"

"Albert, you truly look like my noble, famous warrior now," Liz gushed, running up to embrace her mate.

"Wha' is it aboot uniforms that lassies love?" Max asked Nigel.

"Ah, damsels await their gallant knights in shining armor to fight for them with valor and bravery," Nigel offered.

"And that is how the church sees her ultimate warrior, Jesus, who leads his army to defend his true love," Gillamon told them. "The hour is late, and it is time for me to go. Al, you will need to remove the armor so it can return to its original form before the humans come in the morning."

Al stuck out his lower lip. "But I love wearin' this armor now," he pouted.

"Wear it on the inside from now on, my love," Liz encouraged him, kissing him on the cheek.

"Aye, if ye say so, Lass," Al answered, leaning the spear against the wall.

"One thing before you go, old boy. Might we know when we are to hold the Animalympics?" Nigel asked Gillamon. "Nate and Noah have been most diligent in preparing for the games and wish to know a date."

The lion's face grew serious. "Tell them July 18, 64." The lion then suddenly grew still and Gillamon was gone.

316

"I say, I don't believe we've ever had such a specific answer before," Nigel remarked. "Splendid!"

Liz frowned. *"Oui,* but did you notice his tone? I think there will be something significant about that date besides our games. Whatever it is, I sense foreboding about it."

"Time will tell, Lass," Max interjected, yawning. "Ye can think aboot it tomorrow. Let's all turn in."

As Al removed all the pieces of armor, setting them down where the humans had left them, they miraculously returned to their original state. He looked at the armor and sighed. "I hope I get to wear ye all again for real someday," he whispered to the armor before trotting after the others to go to bed.

"You best armor up for real, Kitty, Kitty, Kitty," came a voice from the shadows when the animals were gone. "You're going to need it."

OF SECRECY AND CLEMENCY

ROME, MAY AD 62

And pray also for me, that God will give me a message when I am ready to speak, so that I may speak boldly and make known the gospel's secret. For the sake of this gospel I am an ambassador, though now I am in prison. Pray that I may be bold in speaking about the gospel as I should.

Julius finished reading Paul's letter to the Ephesians, which Luke had copied for them to keep in Rome. *Make known the gospel's secret,* he repeated to himself. *Grandfather told me not to keep it a secret.* Last week they said their farewells to Tychicus and Onesimus, entrusting Tychicus with Paul's letters to the Colossians, to Philemon, and to the Ephesians. *All Paul does is make known the gospel's secret, in how he speaks, in how he lives, and in what he writes. He desires the whole world to come to the saving grace of Jesus, including Nero himself.* Julius thought about Theo preparing for Paul's appeal before Nero. When Julius went to see Theo, excited to share their grandfather's letter with him, he was saddened by his brother's indifferent response. Theo had not even bothered to read his own letter from their grandfather, which is something Julius could not begin to understand. Julius decided to entrust his letter to Theo, telling him there was information in it that would help Paul's case. *Oh,*

Grandfather, I pray he'll read your letter. I'm trying to make known the gospel's secret, beginning with Theo.

✕

Theo sat with his arms crossed over his chest, staring at the scrolls on his desk. He had just finished reading Luke's first letter yet again. Luke's words had haunted him for weeks, to the point he couldn't sleep. He kept reading the account of Jesus of Nazareth over and over as argumentative questions flooded his mind. *A virgin birth? Not possible. How could a poor, Jewish nobody carpenter suddenly rise up as the long awaited Savior of the world? Why would any god do what this supposed Hebrew God did in sending his Son to die for the sins of mankind? And surviving crucifixion? Impossible! Yet so many eyewitness accounts were given for his resurrection. And what of the miracles this Jesus performed? Too good to be true. And the words he spoke? Also too good to be true. How could anyone love like that?* "Everything about Jesus was simply too good to be true!" he shouted out loud to no one but himself.

318

He put his unanswered questions from Luke's first letter aside to once more study Luke's second letter, hoping he would find answers. All Theo found were answers that led to more questions. *How could the uneducated, poor disciples of Jesus—fishermen, no less!—start such a powerful movement that caught and spread like fire across the Roman Empire? But the greater question was, "Why?" If this Jesus was either a liar or insane, as surely he must have been to claim to be the Son of God, why would his followers seek to follow him after he was gone? Why would they endure beatings and even death to forward such a cause? Why would someone of Paul's upbringing, education, and stature throw it all away to follow a dead man who he claimed spoke to him in a vision? Why was Paul willing to now die over a belief system that he once hated enough to murder its followers? Why had Paul traveled thousands of miles, endured beatings, persecution, rejection, hardship, and shipwrecks, yet pressed on to share about this Jesus Christ? Why did he actually want to stand before Emperor Nero when he could have just walked away a free man in Caesarea had he not appealed to Caesar? WHY?*

Theo pulled his fingers through his hair and buried his face in his hands, unable to deal with all these unanswered questions.

He reached for the scroll Julius had left for him to read, addressed from their grandfather to Julius. Theo had not opened his own box and scroll that he had also received from Marcus. Something had been holding him back. It wasn't that he was just too busy with work. He didn't want to face the reality of death and feel the raw emotion of it all.

When his father Armandus was lost in the shipwreck, as the older son, the weight of responsibility to look after their mother and his younger brother fell on Theo's shoulders. The emotions of loss and death were too overwhelming for the nine-year-old boy. He decided he would pursue an intellectual course to seek logical reasons for how life worked. He would allow his head to rule over his heart from that point on. He chose not to venture far into the emotional realm. It was too painful there. He had no closure with the death of his father. And Theo preferred to keep it that way. He would live life in the realm of law and justice where things were laid out clearly, with order and consistency—where he could make sense of things.

Julius had always been closer to their grandfather than had Theo, not only from an emotional standpoint, but naturally because Julius chose to follow in the Antonius tradition of military service. Marcus was a centurion. Armandus was a centurion. Julius was a centurion. Theophilus was an attorney. So Marcus and Julius had far more in common than Marcus and Theo, including the red marble.

Theo married a beautiful woman from Gaul, and they had a blonde little boy, named Leonitus. While he loved both his wife and his son, Theo always kept his emotions in check, guarding the deepest chamber of his heart. No one was allowed to enter, so he at times came off as distant, even to his own family. Theo met life with his intellect, and it served him well for a while. He became a successful attorney, amassing wealth and prestige in Rome. He was able to maintain control of life, as long as life dealt him no more tragedies. Then his grandfather died. Facing his death would mean venturing into the emotional realm. So he ignored it instead.

Theo picked up Julius's letter and tapped it in his open palm. He didn't want to read it, but Julius had told him that what his grandfather had written would have a huge bearing on Paul's case. If there was anything Theo was willing to do, it was to conduct exhaustive research until he had explored every resource in search of answers to prepare for a trial. Julius would not tell Theo what Marcus had written. He would have

319

to read it for himself. Perhaps his grandfather would somehow shed light on this Christian movement on an intellectual level. He had heard enough about it on an emotional level from his mother and brother. Theo took a deep breath and exhaled loudly. He took his seat, opened the scroll, and began to read.

Nigel sat up high on a shelf filled with scrolls in Theo's study, waiting to see his reaction to Marcus's letter. "Oh, most excellent Theophilus," Nigel muttered, "opposing the case for Christ is one you must lose in order to win."

Nero gazed through his emerald spyglass at Seneca, who stood before him, frowning.

"I'm back in Rome, aren't I?" Nero protested.

"But you must take charge of things in a visible way, Nero," Seneca insisted. "You nearly gave up the empire's rule of Britain in the revolt, you've brought scandal on the house of Caesar by murdering your own mother, now you're divorcing and banishing Claudius's daughter in order to marry that Jewess Poppaea, and your lust for building projects is a continual drain on the resources of Rome. You're already building the new Domus Transitoria Palace between the Palatine and the Esquiline Hills, yet it's not enough."

Nero rolled his eyes at hearing Seneca's list of criticisms. "But I *didn't* lose Britain! That Boudica woman and her followers may have burned Londinium to the ground but my Roman governor Gaius Suetonius . . . what was his last name?"

"Paulinus," Seneca answered drolly.

"Yes! Paulinus! He defeated those rebels, despite being outnumbered, and crushed the rebellion," Nero recounted, pointing the emerald spyglass at his mentor. "So my governors have things under control in my provinces. *Paulinus.* I must reward him."

Nero tossed his spyglass on the couch and went over to some fruit sitting in a cobalt-blue glass bowl. He picked up a bunch of grapes and plucked one to put in his mouth. "So that British problem was solved. As to your other complaints," he retorted as he picked off another grape to squeeze between his teeth, "no one should care what I do in my private life! Did the public call for my death over the incident with my mother, even when they didn't believe me when I framed it as suicide? *Nooooo!* Some even joked about it. I've seen what they wrote on the walls of Rome: *Add the letters in Nero's name, and 'matricide' sums the same."* He gave a shrill laugh and plucked off another grape. "And Octavia bored me. She had to go." He threw the grape across the room.

"As for my building projects," walking over to a model of an elaborate new palace, "a magnificent fortune can only be enjoyed by squandering it. Only tight-fisted, miserly people keep a close account of their spending. Truly fine and superior people scatter their wealth extravagantly. That's why I shower gifts on people and give money away. You know how I long to be loved and popular among the people." He bent over to stare at his future palace. "Besides, Rome owes me. I deserve it."

Nero traced his fingers along the miniature palace still under design. "The Domus Transitoria isn't grand enough. My architects Severus and Celer are creating a gorgeous masterpiece house for me, overlaid with gold and studded with precious stones and mother-of-pearl: my *Domus Aurea*. My "Golden Palace." The dining rooms will have ivory ceilings, and panels will slide back to shower my guests with flowers and perfume!" Nero's voice was giddy with excitement. He squinted and stared into a tiny replica of a circular building. "But my favorite part will be this main dining room. The roof will revolve, day and night, just like the sky! Imagine, Seneca, the stars in the heavens will move at my command!"

321

Seneca scanned the proposed new palace. "It will indeed be a magnificent building to rival anything ever built in Rome," he agreed with a frown. "But where will you build such a large complex? The Senate has already disallowed other building suggestions."

Leave that to me, Nero thought. He waved his hand to dismiss Seneca's practical concern. "My Golden Palace will be the treasure of Rome, and the people will be in awe of its splendor." The delusional ruler smiled and picked up a miniature statue that towered over the model complex of buildings, gardens, and lake. "Especially with this 120-foot golden statue of me, placed at the entrance for all Rome to see!"

"I was speaking of a different kind of public appearance, Caesar," Seneca offered in a flat tone.

Nero picked up his lyre and strummed it, humming as he twirled around the room. "I've been thinking of taking to the stage to perform.

You know how talented I am at singing. The people will love me!"

Seneca's eyes widened at such an embarrassing, ludicrous idea. Only commoners performed on stage for the masses. It was beneath rulers and members of the elite to do so. He cleared his throat. "I was thinking more about you taking up the cases awaiting your ruling, Caesar. There is a backlog of them, and I believe having you appear as ruler of the court will garner fresh respect from the senators and consuls. I know you have previously requested Burrus to oversee such trials, but given his recent death, I believe you should show that you are in charge of administering the law in Rome."

Nero strummed a few more bars and hummed while he turned his back on Seneca. A wicked grin covered his face as he thought about the poison he had sent to Burrus under the guise of "throat medicine" to help with his throat cancer. "Yes, how tragic about our dear Burrus." He wiped the grin off his face and turned to face Seneca. "Very well, I will hold court in the justice hall here at the Palatine Palace."

322

"Before you attend the court, might I advise you to read once more the essay I prepared for you several years ago, 'Of Clemency'?" Seneca offered. "I've taken the liberty of bringing a copy for you to refresh your mind on how and why to show clemency, meaning of course compassion, mercy, or forgiveness when judging." He unrolled the scroll and read from it:

To save men's lives is the privilege of the loftiest station, which never deserves admiration so much as when it is able to act like the gods, by whose kindness good and bad men alike are brought into the world. Thus a prince, imitating the mind of a god, ought to look with pleasure on some of his countrymen because they are useful and good men, while he ought to allow others to remain to fill up the roll; he ought to be pleased with the existence of the former, and to endure that of the latter.

"Very well, Seneca, leave the scroll. You may go and arrange for my day in court." Nero strummed a few more chords and smiled. "I think I will find it rather amusing."

Seneca cringed at Nero's endless desire to be amused, and his flair for the dramatic. He had recently taken to dressing up in animal skins to attack slaves tied to posts, pretending to be a beast hungry for the kill. In the corner sat one of Nero's favorite costumes—a lion skin, with a hollowed out lion's head. Seneca hadn't yet told Nero that he was going to retire. He had had enough and wanted out of this madman's inner circle. He hoped that perhaps the senators and consuls would come to the same conclusion when they saw Nero in court, and stop him before he went too far. He secretly hoped they would take measures to remove Nero from power. Seneca realized that Nero had not only turned his back on wise counsel, but was sinking further into madness that would only spell doom for Rome. He recounted what he had written for Nero in his essay "Of Clemency":

> *Cruel masters are pointed at with disgust in all parts of the city, and are hated and loathed; the wrong-doings of kings are enacted on a wider theatre: their shame and unpopularity endures for ages: yet how far better it would have been never to have been born than to be numbered among those who have been born to do their country harm!*

Seneca bowed and stepped out of the room. He listened to Nero singing and playing his lyre as he walked down the palace corridor. *May the gods have mercy on those awaiting trial before this madman!*

FROM THE LION'S MOUTH

igel wiped his eyes under his spectacles. "I do not believe I
have ever witnessed such a tender moment for a new believer.
To see Theophilus weep and embrace Julius with an overflow
of unrestrained emotion was remarkable! Paul helped him understand
the gospel, and he finally opened his heart to the truth."

"Sure, Theo had to understand Jesus with his heart before he could
understand him with his head," Al noted, drawing looks of amazement
from the others.

Liz's eyes glistened and she smiled. *"Dieu est bon!* Marcus's letter was
the closing argument he needed, no?"

"Indeed, once he read Marcus's letter to Julius, he immediately
opened his own box and read the letter Marcus had left for him as well,"
Nigel reported. "Marcus left Armandus's favorite oil lamp to Theo, the
one etched with Armandus's prize horse, Achilles. Quite a serendipitous
moment, I assure you!"

"The very oil lamp Armandus bought from Clarie's stall at the Circus Maximus long ago!" Liz exclaimed, shaking her head in awe. "I
cannot believe the connecting points between this family of Antonius
and the Order of the Seven!"

"Aye, this be gr-r-rand news!" Max cheered. "So, Mousie, wha'
aboot Paul's appeal?"

"Right, well Theo explained that Nero has agreed to hear Paul's case,"

Nigel answered. "An initial hearing is called the *actio prima* wherein a charge is established and the determination is made whether a trial is needed. The *actio secunda* establishes the accused's guilt or innocence, followed by punishment."

The animals looked at one another while Al gazed up at Marcus's armor. He stared at the lion's head on the front of the helmet. "It almost looks as if the soldier's face sits in the lion's mouth."

Nigel shuddered. "I've heard dastardly rumors about Nero of late, that he dresses up as a lion to stalk his human prey for amusement."

"Now that be a r-r-really sick lad," Max growled.

Liz put her paw up to her face in shock. "Let us pray that Paul is delivered from the lion's mouth."

Al grinned, waving an imaginary sword in the air. "Paul be armored up, and if anyone knows how to handle the sword against lions, it be him."

☧

Nero plopped down on his couch with Seneca's essay on clemency. He respected his mentor, and if he could pick up a helpful thought to make him look good in court tomorrow, it would be worth it. He began to read:

For if, as we may infer from what has been said, you are the soul of the state, and the state is your body, you will perceive, I imagine, how necessary clemency is; for when you appear to spare another, you are really sparing yourself. You ought therefore to spare even blameworthy citizens, just as you spare weakly limbs; and when blood-letting becomes necessary, you must hold your hand, lest you should cut deeper than you need.

Clemency therefore, as I said before, naturally befits all mankind, but more especially rulers, because in their case there is more for it to save, and it is displayed upon a greater scale.

"Oh, such lofty thoughts, my friend," Nero sighed, "but oh, so very boring." He skipped down until the word 'cruelty' caught his eye:

Cruelty is far from being a human vice, and is unworthy of man's gentle mind: it is mere bestial madness to take pleasure in blood and wounds, to cast off humanity and transform oneself into a wild beast of the forest.

Nero's pulse raced as evil coursed through his sick mind. He stared at the lion's head and skin in the corner and smiled wickedly. He slid off the couch and crouched down like a lion on the prowl, making his way over to the skinned beast. He growled face to face with the lion and then broke out laughing hysterically. "Did I scare you?" he asked, patting the stuffed lion head. Nero rolled over and leaned back onto its mane. "Seneca wants me to read about clemency, but I prefer to read about cruelty. Listen to this, king of the beasts:

> The reason why cruelty is the most hateful of all vices is that it goes first beyond the ordinary limits, and then beyond those of humanity; that it devises new kinds of punishments, calls ingenuity to aid it in inventing devices for varying and lengthening men's torture, and takes delight in their sufferings: this accursed disease of the mind reaches its highest pitch of madness when cruelty itself turns into pleasure, and the act of killing a man becomes enjoyment. Such a ruler is soon cast down from his throne; his life is attempted by poison one day and by the sword the next; he is exposed to as many dangers as there are men to whom he is dangerous, and he is sometimes destroyed by the plots of individuals, and at others by a general insurrection."

Nero got face to face again with the lion. "Doesn't that sound exciting?" "READ ME MORE," the lion seemed to say to Nero's mind.

Nero shuddered from the thrill of imagining this lion talking to him. He threw his arm around the lion's mane and gestured as he read Seneca's words of warning in dramatic mockery:

> Ye gods! what a miserable life it is to slaughter and to rage, to delight in the clanking of chains, and to cut off one's countrymen's heads, to cause blood to flow freely wherever one goes, to terrify people, and make them flee away out of one's sight! It is what would happen if bears or lions were our masters, if serpents and all the most venomous creatures were given power over us.

Nero stopped and hugged the lion. "You would like that, wouldn't you?" He laughed.

326

Even these animals, devoid of reason as they are, and accused by us of cruel ferocity, spare their own kind, and wild beasts themselves respect their own likeness: but the fury of tyrants does not even stop short at their own relations, and they treat friends and strangers alike, only becoming more violent the more they indulge their passions. By insensible degrees he proceeds from the slaughter of individuals to the ruin of nations, and thinks it a sign of power to set roofs on fire and to plough up the sites of ancient cities . . .

Nero stopped suddenly and sat up, his eyes transfixed on that last line. "A sign of power to set roofs on fire and to plough up the sites of ancient cities. *Fire.*"

He rolled the scroll back to another section. "Where is it? Where is it?" His finger ran along the parchment until he found it:

If a fire breaks out under one single roof, the family and the neighbors pour water upon it; but a wide conflagration which has consumed many houses must be smothered under the ruins of a whole quarter of a city.

I remember that many great but odious sayings have become part of human life and are familiar in men's mouths, such as that celebrated, "Let them hate me, provided that they fear me," which is like that Greek verse, "When I am dead, let fire consume the earth," . . .

Nero let the scroll fall to the floor and stared at the lion with a wicked smile. He picked up the lion's skin and draped it over his back and ran over to the model of his Golden Palace. "No, it should rather be—while I yet live . . ."

☧

The senators and consuls stood around impatiently in the hall, waiting for Nero to arrive. Julius remained with Paul in a waiting area with other prisoners while Theophilus and other attorneys waited behind a podium. Gripping his scroll of notes, Theo turned and caught Paul's eye. Paul winked at him. Theo grinned slightly and turned his gaze back to his notes. His heart and mind had never felt so free. Once he opened his heart to Jesus, things started to make sense. He finally understood what made this movement of Christianity so powerful in the lives of Jesus' followers. It wasn't a movement of men, *it was a movement of God in the hearts of men.* And despite the evil that came against it, Theo knew the gospel would prevail. His grandfather and father had even been used as pawns in the Enemy's attempt at thwarting Jesus' kingdom here on Earth, but those attempts had failed. Theo felt as if a mantle of responsibility had been placed on his shoulders, like a family baton had now been passed to him to play his part in once again defeating the Enemy for the sake of Christ. But this time, it wouldn't be a military warrior in the field, but a legal warrior in the courtroom.

Suddenly the doors flew open, and Nero strolled past the leaders of Rome, his thick neck and chin lifted in the air and a golden laurel-leaf crown on his head. He climbed a few steps to take a seat and with dramatic flair spilled his robe across the golden throne so everyone could see the intricate thread and gems sewn into the hem. Seneca had followed behind and now stood below him to administer the proceedings. Nero motioned for him to begin, but said nothing. He looked around the room but seemed to gaze over the heads of everyone there, distracted with other thoughts at best and disinterested in these proceedings at worst.

"Caesar has returned to Rome to ensure that order and justice are maintained in his empire," Seneca began, hoping that Nero had read his essay on clemency, and perhaps at least to have momentarily returned to sane thinking. "In his magnanimity he has chosen to personally oversee these cases awaiting his wisdom. We shall begin with the *actio prima* in order of your assigned cases." He motioned, and one of the other attorneys stepped forward to present the charges of his client.

"When do you think they will get to Paul's case?" Liz whispered to Nigel. She, Al, and Nigel were sitting in an alcove high above the hall.

"We shall have to wait and see," Nigel answered, straightening his spectacles. He smiled at Al. "I must commend you, old boy. Good show on getting us into the palace."

Al held up his paw and sprung his iron claw, which he had used to open a series of gates. "I told ye I been in this palace lots o' times. I used to love banquet night until people started droppin' like flies from the food. It's dangerous eatin' here now."

After a time, Seneca motioned for Theophilus to approach the podium. Theo's heart pounded, and he swallowed as he stepped forward. "Hail, Caesar. I am Theophilus Antonius. Thank you for hearing this case." He motioned for Julius to bring Paul to stand before Nero.

Nero lifted a finger lazily in the air. "Proceed." *Antonius?* he thought.

As Julius took Paul by the arm and led him to the front of the courtroom, he hoped that Nero wouldn't notice him. His helmet covered much of his face, and he quickly turned to release Paul's chain. He locked eyes with Paul, nodded, and turned to go stand in the back of the room.

Theophilus motioned toward Paul. "May I present to you a Roman citizen, Paulus from Tarsus. He was schooled in law and comes from a fine upstanding family of business in that trading city. While highly regarded for his knowledge of Jewish law, and respected by his peers for his intelligence, his beliefs differ from those of a group of Jewish leaders in Judea. He stands before you on his own request to appeal to Caesar following a series of trials in Caesarea about this religious dispute."

Nero surveyed Paul's humble appearance as Theo continued to explain the circumstances of Paul's presence in his court. *Paulus. Such a boring little man,* Nero thought. Paul was almost completely bald with a white beard, dressed in a plain beige linen tunic and sandals. He stood with his manacled hands folded in front of his body, and with eyes that projected inexplicable joy and confidence. He kept his gaze on Nero, as if sizing up the emperor.

"So I believe you will see that his Christian beliefs have been held up in Roman courts as a legal outgrowth of Judaism, which of course is protected by Roman law as a *religio licita,* a permitted religion. Paul has proven time and again he is no threat to Rome, and has received repeated favor with Roman officials for the past thirty years, including this landmark ruling," Theo explained, holding up Luke's second scroll. "Paul was placed before a Roman court in Corinth with the identical charges of the Jews that he is charged with here today. I beseech Caesar to hear the outcome of that court's decision." He unrolled it and read that passage:

"If this were a matter of some evil crime or wrong that has been committed, it would be reasonable for me to be patient with you Jews. But since it is an argument about words and names and your own law, you yourselves must settle it. I will not be the judge of such things!"

329

Theo turned and lifted a hand toward Seneca. "Those words were said by none other than Governor Gallio, brother of your esteemed advisor, Seneca."

Nero's eyebrows rose with approval as Seneca bowed his head in grateful acknowledgment.

"Gallio himself knew it was a waste of Rome's time to interfere in matters where no law had been violated," Theo added. "He immediately dismissed the charges as unfounded, and I ask that Caesar in turn does the same, with the same man accused by the same people of the same charges."

"Here's hopin' Nero likes *déjà vu* moments," Al muttered.

"I might add that Paul's accusers have not even come to Rome to stand behind their charges," Theo pointed out, holding his arms up and looking around the courtroom. "Christians are peaceable, responsible citizens of Rome, and their leader even specifically encouraged his followers to honor Caesar by paying their due taxes."

330

Nero smiled broadly. "Well, that is good news. We certainly want Rome's citizens to keep Rome's coffers full." He chuckled at his wit, drawing smiles and polite chuckles from the assembly of senators. He looked at Paul. "You certainly don't sound like a threat to Rome. You don't *look* like a threat either, I might add." More chuckles in the room. "Your counsel has presented you in quite a favorable light. Would you like to say anything for yourself?"

Paul had thought about this moment for two years. He breathed a silent prayer, asking for the Holy Spirit to give him the words Nero needed to hear. He bowed respectfully and smiled. "Thank you, Caesar. It is a privilege to stand before you, and I have looked forward to this day for some time," Paul began. "I believe that you were appointed by God to your post to rule Rome, and I respectfully acknowledge your position. He has established kingdoms and rulers to provide order in this world."

Nero perked up, liking what he heard. "Which god said this?"

"Nero played right into Paul's hand with that one," Nigel commented with a grin.

"I believe in the God of the Jews, who created man in his likeness to have fellowship with him," Paul began. "May I be allowed to tell you the story?"

"Paul knows that Nero has married a woman who recently became a Jew," Liz noted. "He knows exactly what specific references to make as he relays the gospel."

"He also knows that Nero adores dramatic stories," Nigel added.

"By all means," Nero consented with a wave of his hand, sitting back in his throne, eager for a story.

"God created the heavens and the earth and all the creatures that roam the land and fill the seas. But his most prized creation was man. He loved his creation that he gifted with intelligence, talents, skills, and ability, and wished for them to soar in the ecstasy of fellowship with him! He wished for them to enjoy the bounty and the beauty of the earth he gave them," Paul told Nero with a hopeful tone. Then he allowed his face to fall. "But man sought a different path when they broke the one rule he gave them, to not eat of the tree of knowledge of good and evil. Man turned his back on God and chose instead a life of sin. And this broke God's heart." Paul paused for a moment of dramatic silence.

Nero leaned forward in his seat.

331

"God is a God of justice who demands that sin be paid for. But he also is a God of fierce love! His heart broke to lose the fellowship with his children, so he set forth a plan to win back their hearts," shared Paul, gripping his chest. "He even chose to pay for their sins *himself*, by sending his only Son through the Jewish people to die for the sins of mankind. But Jesus rose from the dead. Jesus died so everyone who believes in him and the power of his resurrection may have eternal life. Their sins are paid for and forgotten through grace. And the broken relationship between God and his creation is restored, one heart at a time." Paul looked down at his manacled hands and held them out, allowing the chains to dangle in mid-air. "It is for my belief in Jesus that I am in these chains, Caesar. Yet how grateful I am that my chains have allowed me to stand before you and share the reason for my hope."

Nero sat there for a moment, mesmerized by Paul's words. Silence filled the courtroom. Everyone leaned in, waiting breathlessly to see Nero's reaction to such an unusual speech. Paul did not ask for mercy. He did not ask for his own release. He simply asked to share his faith. Nothing more.

Suddenly Nero applauded rapidly. "Bravo! Bravo! What a wonderful story of tragedy and love! And you tell it so well." He looked at

Theophilus. "I had already decided that I would uphold Gallio's ruling, especially since I know he is brother to the wisest man I know," stated Nero, holding out a hand toward Seneca. He returned his gaze to Paul. "I not only like what you've had to say about this God of yours appointing me, I like your *name*. Another one of my brilliant governors goes by Paulinus. He protected the empire in Britain. My governors like Gallio and Paulinus know what they are doing." He looked out at the assembly of senators and consuls. "What say you, leaders of Rome? Do you agree that I should drop these charges against this Paulus of Tarsus?"

Liz clung to Al who clung to Nigel as they waited for the answer.

A murmuring of the men soon led to nodding heads of approval. "We agree, Caesar."

Nero clapped his hands once. "There you have it. The charges are dropped. Let him go."

"Thank you for your clemency, Caesar," Theophilus told the emperor with a respectful bow. "We are grateful for your thoughtful and wise ruling." He turned and motioned for Julius, who came walking forward, trying to suppress the joy on his face over Nero's decision.

"Indeed, thank you, Caesar," Paul echoed. He looked at Nero sadly. He was grateful for Nero's ruling, but he realized that all Nero had cared to hear was a dramatic story. He was too depraved to hear the truth. Nero was bypassing the opportunity for salvation, swept up in his own corrupt, evil existence. Paul knew he only had the power to share, nothing more. Jesus promised him that he would stand before Caesar, and so he had. God had now granted his release, so he would be free to continue spreading the gospel. His heart lit up at the thought.

Nero suddenly recognized Julius as he removed the shackles from Paul's wrists. "Antonius!"

Theo and Julius both responded at the same time, "Yes, Caesar?" They looked at one another and then back at Nero, who squinted to look at the two men.

"Wait now, are you two brothers?" Nero asked.

Julius swallowed hard, uncertain if this fact would affect Nero's decision in any way. "Yes, my lord, we are brothers."

Nero studied them a moment. Slowly a grin appeared on his face. "Just like Gallio and Seneca!" he laughed. "Paulus, it appears you have been aided by *two* sets of brothers today. I see that as a double confirmation that my judgment is right," he announced happily. He pointed at Julius. "You, my emerald soldier, must join me for the games soon."

"As you wish, my lord," Julius responded, shooting a quick glance at Theo as if to say, *Get me out of this!* Theo shrugged his shoulders with a barely detectable grin.

Seneca stepped forward to keep the court proceedings in motion. "Next case, please." He nodded to Julius, Theo, and Paul to indicate they were dismissed.

Together the three men walked triumphantly out of Nero's courtroom. Paul was a free man.

"The family of Antonius has once again served the Maker's purposes!" Nigel cheered with a fist raised in victory.

"Marcus and Armandus would be so proud of their boys!" Liz cried with tears of joy. "Paul is free!"

"Told ye," Al beamed as he put on his imaginary helmet and held up an imaginary sword. "But it were the Lion o' Liberty that got Paul out o' the lion's mouth today."

333

FAREWELLS
AND FREEDOM

The sunset slowly began to paint pink and orange clouds against what had been an intense blue sky over Rome. Quietly the half-moon and North Star appeared, and they patiently awaited the host of other stars to fill the nighttime canvas. The feeling of gentle relief in the air was as fragrant as the roses in Bella's garden for the group of believers gathered to celebrate Paul's freedom. They cried tears of joy, sang their praises of gratitude to God, and enjoyed a bountiful meal in this house filled with Christian love.

"He actually said, 'Bravo'?" Peter asked in astonishment, handing Al another piece of fish. *"Bravo to your presentation of the gospel?"*

Paul nodded, unconsciously rubbing his shackle-free wrists. "Sadly, he saw it as nothing more than a story. Nero is so deluded, and I think he is possessed of the Enemy, Peter. You can sense the evil pouring out of him."

"We believers may be temporarily afflicted here on Earth but ultimately we are liberated from evil. But once evil men like Nero have done the Enemy's bidding, they themselves are devoured by evil on Earth, and for all time." Al meowed for more fish, and Peter handed him his last piece. "That's all I have, Ari." He wiped off his hands and wrapped them behind his head, gazing at Paul. "Well, Brother, you are finally free. What will you do now?"

Paul motioned over to Luke and Timothy. "We will head back to

Asia and Greece. I wish to visit Titus on Crete to see how the church is faring there. Then we'll go to Ephesus and back through Macedonia. I would like to visit all my start-up churches from ten years ago. What about you?"

"I feel I'm needed here in Rome, so I'll stay until the Lord leads me elsewhere," Peter replied. "But Mark would like to go with you."

"If you'll have me, that is," Mark added quickly. "I'm sorry I left you and Barnabas on that first missionary journey."

Paul smiled and shook his head. "All is forgiven, Mark. You were young and not ready for the call. I'm sorry we parted ways in anger for a time, but all has been redeemed. I see how God even used our disagreement to spread the gospel. We ended up with two teams instead of one. We would be thrilled to have you with us."

"I only wish I could go with you, but I must return to active duty with Rome," Julius lamented. "But I've inquired about a post in southern Gaul so I can get as far away from Nero as I can. I actually love that beautiful region of the empire."

Liz brightened. *"Julius loves France? Bon!"*

"I will miss you, Julius," Paul said sadly. "It has been a joy to meet you and your family, and, of course, to welcome you into the family of Christ. Thank you for all you've done for me. You will have to spread the Good Word in Gaul. Theo, what about you?"

"I shall remain in Rome, of course," Theo offered, smiling and gesturing over to Peter. "Peter and I look forward to working together with the church. Peter, I still cannot believe you were the one to help our father to Christ in Caesarea."

Peter smiled. "Yes, your father Armandus was at the very first Gentile church gathering at the home of Cornelius, and it was my privilege to know him briefly there. I look forward to now getting to know you here in Rome."

Theo nodded, marveling at the tapestry of connections God had weaved with the people seated around this courtyard. "Luke, I have an idea. I would like to publish the two letters you prepared for me. People everywhere need to read your account of Jesus and then about the acts of Paul and the other apostles. Would that be agreeable to you?"

Luke's eyes widened. "Nothing would thrill me more! Of course, Theo!"

335

Theo wagged his index finger. "Most Excellent Theophilus," he teased. "I'm glad you approve. I feel this is how I can do my part to help spread the gospel."

Liz and Nigel grinned at each other. "Two more books for our growing New Testament, taking root in the early church," Nigel cheered. "Brilliant!"

Bella came walking into the courtyard with a young man by her side. "I'm afraid this day must end with sadness after all. This young man brings news from the church in Jerusalem."

Everyone got to their feet in concern. Max, Liz, Al, and Nigel also turned to hear the news.

"My name is Samuel. It is with a heavy heart I tell you that James, the brother of our Lord, has been executed in Jerusalem," the man reported. "Procurator Festus died, and Albinus was appointed the new procurator for Judea, but it took a few months for him to reach Caesarea. The Jewish high priest, Ananus, moved quickly, before Albinus's arrival, to attack the church. He convened the Sanhedrin and brought James and others before them with accusations of transgressing the law. Ananus ordered James to be stoned. Afterward, many residents rose up in protest and contacted King Agrippa II, who removed Ananus as high priest, but, of course, it was too late for James."

Everyone stood in stunned silence. "Another martyr's blood spilled for the cause of Chr-r-rist," Max growled.

"And in this case, one who shared actual family blood with Jesus," Nigel added with a heavy-hearted tone.

Peter finally spoke up, wiping his eyes and clearing his throat. "Does Mary know?"

Samuel sighed deeply. "Mary did not live to hear this news. John recently sent word that Mary died peacefully in her sleep in Ephesus." He turned and looked at the animals. "Mary has been reunited with both her sons in heaven."

Liz's eyes filled with tears and she clung to Al, who also mourned these enormous losses. Max and Nigel fumed at the thought of what happened to James.

Paul hung his head and shook it sadly. "While I grieve for James, I know he is secure with our Lord, and, indeed, with his mother in heaven. My immediate concern is the church in Jerusalem. How are they doing?"

336

"The leaders are in shock, of course, but are holding steady," Samuel reported. "Perhaps you could write to them, Paul. I'm sure you could encourage them, as you have with other churches, to stand steady in the faith."

Paul thought a moment. "I am not very popular in Jerusalem, but perhaps I could send a letter without my name attached to it."

"You wrote to the capital of the Gentile world with your letter to the Romans," Samuel offered. "Now you can write to the capital of the Jewish world with a letter to the Hebrews."

"Very well, I will give this a great deal of prayer as we travel to Crete and Ephesus," Paul promised. "I can send a letter to Jerusalem from there."

"Allow me to take it to Jerusalem, Paul," Mark suggested. "This will allow me a good opportunity to visit my family and the church there."

"Yes, and perhaps you and I can visit Jerusalem after your time in Macedonia," Timothy added.

Paul placed his hands on Mark and Timothy. "Agreed."

"Thank you for bringing this news," Luke told Samuel. "It was my honor to spend time with Mary in Jerusalem before she and John went to Ephesus. My heart grieves to lose this incredible woman of God, but I am relieved she died peacefully."

Samuel nodded and looked again to the animals. "I'm sorry to be the bearer of bad news, but we felt you should all know."

Nigel cocked his head at the man and then smiled when he noticed his eyes.

"I know you must be tired. Please, allow us to serve you a meal," Timothy suggested.

"Yes, we have plenty," Bella added, "and of course you are welcome to stay."

"Thank you," Samuel replied. "I need a place to stay, and must find work here in Rome. I'm a scribe by trade."

Theo raised his eyebrows and lifted his hand. "What a coincidence! I'm going to need someone to help me do a bit of copying work with Luke's letters. Would that interest you?"

Samuel smiled broadly. "What a perfect idea! Yes, thank you."

"Wonderful! We can discuss everything tomorrow," Theo replied, walking behind Bella to the kitchen to get Samuel something to eat.

Peter put his hands on his hips and lifted his gaze to the darkening sky, clenching his jaw. "John's brother, James, my brother Andrew, and now Jesus' brother James. All gone. But I know more martyrs will be added as Christianity spreads. I will likely be added to that list of names at some point. Jesus said, 'When you grow old, you will stretch out your hands and someone else will tie you and carry you where you don't want to go.'"

Paul came over and put his hand on Peter's back and pointed to the stars. "Each one is a point of light in a dark sky. And though you cannot see them in the light of day, they reflect the light of the sun forever, showing the way in the darkness. If the Lord chooses me to light up the darkness with my death by reflecting the Son, I am ready. To live is Christ, to die is gain."

Peter smiled and nodded. "Indeed. Jesus then also said, 'Follow me!' And that is what I plan to do, until the end."

Paul continued to gaze up at the stars. "With a large cloud of witnesses surrounding us, cheering us on."

338

☧

Max, Liz, Al, and Nigel sat in the courtyard after the humans had gone to bed, unable to shake the grief they felt over James and Mary.

"I cannot be sad for *them,* of course," Liz pointed out, wiping her eyes. "They are with Jesus. But I am sad for *us.*"

"I know ye an' Mary were especially close, Lass," Max comforted Liz softly. "She always called ye her 'little shadow.'"

Liz smiled at the thought of Mary's pet name for her as memories raced through her mind. *"Oui,* from the time she was a young girl waiting to marry Joseph. It was a joy to be her little shadow from Jesus' birth to his ascension and then on to Pentecost in Jerusalem."

"You'll always be *my* little shadow," said the statue of Libertas with Liz's own image carved at the base.

Liz looked up and smiled to see the statue smiling at her. *"Bonsoir,* Gillamon."

"Good evening, Liz, and everyone," Gillamon replied. "It has been a day of joy mixed with sadness yet again."

Samuel came walking into the courtyard. "Indeed, it has."

"I thought that was you, my dear," Nigel greeted him. "Good evening, Clarie."

The man went over and sat down with the animals, pulling Liz into his lap to hug her close to his heart. "This is one of the benefits of taking human form. I can better hug you."

"You've all done a stellar job here in Rome. Paul's mission to stand before Nero is complete, but his work is far from over," Gillamon explained. "It's time for you all to split up once again."

Al pouted and climbed up into Clarie's lap with Liz. "Do we have to?"

"This time, Al, you and Liz can stay together with Peter and Theo here in Rome," Gillamon answered. "Not only do you need to assist Theo with publishing Luke's letters, you can prepare for the Animalympics."

"Did ye hear that, me love? Ye get to stay here with me!" Al exclaimed, enveloping Liz in a fluffy embrace.

Liz smiled. *"Oui,* Albert. This is happy news."

"I say, what shall Max and I do next?" Nigel asked.

"Nigel, you will go with Max as he accompanies Paul, Luke, and Timothy on their travels," answered Gillamon. "Paul will have three more letters to write on this journey that we need to capture for the New Testament. And, Max, you finally get to be with Kate for a while. She is anxious to see you."

339

"Aye! I can't wait ta see me bonnie lass!" Max exulted. "It's been too long."

"Clarie already suggested a letter to the Hebrews," Nigel noted. "What other kinds of letters will Paul write?"

"He will write letters of encouragement to help young pastors understand how to lead their churches, namely Titus in Crete and Timothy in Ephesus," Gillamon offered. "As there are no schools to train these young leaders, they need instructions for dealing with false teachers, how to organize their members, and simply how to teach God's Word."

Nigel preened his whiskers. "Brilliant strategy! Might I ask what John is doing while in Ephesus, if not pastoring the church there?"

"John's ministry is broader than just Ephesus, as he acts as bishop to travel among the churches of the region," reported Gillamon. "He gives them instruction and encouragement. Do you remember me telling you that from the ministry base of Ephesus would come six other key churches?"

Liz sat up. *"Oui,* and you said that they would be seven churches of light: Ephesus, Smyrna, Pergamum, Thyatira, Sardis, Laodicea, and Philadelphia. They will receive letters that contain some of the most important words ever penned because of *who* will write them."

"Right! Will Paul also be writing these letters on our next adventurous journey?" Nigel asked.

Gillamon and Clarie shared a knowing look. "Not Paul," Clarie answered.

"John then?" Max asked.

"Yes and no," Gillamon answered. "You will understand with time."

"Speakin' of which, ye said the Animalympics weren't happenin' until July, two years fr-r-rom now," Max realized. "So I guess we'll have ta all say 'farewell' until then."

"Yes, two years," Gillamon answered.

Al climbed out of Clarie's lap and picked up Nigel in a smothering embrace. "I'll miss ye, Mousie!"

"Indeed, parting is such sweet sorrow, old boy," Nigel struggled to say.

"So we'll all meet back here in R-r-rome then?" Max asked.

"All seven of us will be here for the big event," Clarie interjected. "The Order of the Seven will be ready to compete as a team!"

"Splendid!" Nigel cheered as Al set him down. "I say, Liz, can you manage Noah and Nate and the plans here without me?"

"I believe so, *mon ami*," Liz answered. "And, if not, I shall call on you for backup, no?"

"I'll keep everyone informed," Clarie said, "including the animals heading to Rome. Noah and Nate have been spreading the word, but, Liz, it's time I help you with plans around the Circus Maximus. I'll have to see if my old stall is still there to use for a planning base."

Liz rubbed Clarie's legs and purred. "*C'est bon!* I was very happy to hear that Marcus left to Theo the oil lamp he bought for Armandus from your stall at the Circus Maximus long ago."

"Aye, and the lad puts it on his desk when he's workin' late at night. Lights up his whole room," Al added. "It's amazin' what a little bit o' fire can do to light up the place."

Gillamon looked at Al with a somber expression. "Indeed it is. Enjoy this last night together. Max and Nigel, may you have safe journeys with Paul. Liz and Al, enjoy your time in Rome with Theo and Peter."

340

"But won't Paul miss me when he departs and I do not go with him?" Liz asked with concern.

"He will of course miss you, but Max will help him along," Gillamon explained. "Plus he'll have Kate with him soon."

Al studied the Libertas statue, and a thought struck him. "I jest realized somethin'! Paul be free to leave Rome, and here ye been sittin' the whole time where he stayed, bein' the symbol o' freedom and all. Almost like this house o' freedom were planned."

"Almost," Gillamon chuckled as his voice trailed off. "Freedom has always been the plan. And ever will it be so, for those who choose to be free from the mouth of the lion."

341

DO YOU WANT
TO LIVE FOREVER?

The coolness of the nighttime air was a welcome relief after the sizzling hot summer day in Rome. All were asleep, and everything was quiet as Liz slowly walked through Bella's garden. She lifted a rose bloom with her paw and closed her eyes to breathe in the exquisite fragrance. The solitude, beautiful scents, and loveliness of this garden were a welcome relief after the noise, stench, and ugliness she had seen that day. This garden was a haven for her, as it had been for Paul before he was given his freedom. She made her way to the statue of Libertas and gazed up at the image of a beautiful woman with her outstretched hand.

Libertas was the symbol of freedom. Liz's mind raced back to the scene of this statue being sculpted long ago in the garden of Marcus and Julia Antonius back in Jerusalem. She closed her eyes and recalled their conversation on that dark morning following the Slaughter of the Innocents in Bethlehem. Marcus secretly shared that he had chosen to disobey military orders for the first and only time in his life when he allowed Joseph and Mary to escape with their child.

"Joseph was wise to take his family and flee from this place. It won't be safe here for as long as Herod is alive." Marcus held tightly to Julia as he gazed over at Armandus. "Perhaps the Jewish God will grant me mercy for allowing one of his children to live. I know it is just one child—that can't make much of a difference."

Julia leaned back and cupped Marcus's face in her hands. "But it will make a difference to that one family. That child is everything to them, just as Armandus is to us."

Oh, but the one child whom Marcus saved ended up saving the world! Liz opened her eyes and stared at the image of herself carved into the marble, sitting at the feet of Libertas. This statue had remained the same, as the people around it changed. Armandus had grown up from the toddler running around the garden where she was carved to having his own boys who played hide-and-seek in her shadow here in this garden of Rome.

Theophilus and Julius also had grown into men, and Theophilus now had his own little boy, Leonitus, who loved to chase Al around Bella's garden. *"Jest like his grandfather!"* Al would cry as Leonitus tried to grab his tail.

Liz smiled at that image. Four generations of this Roman family had grown up in gardens with Libertas in their midst. "What is it about gardens and freedom?" she wondered out loud.

Suddenly Liz saw a soft red glow appear on the statue, right over the heart of the cat figure. She wrinkled her brow and studied the glow until the distinct form of the seven seal formed. Her gaze drifted to the face of Libertas. "I presume you wish to see me, but not out here as usual." She stuck out her claws and stared at the seven seal. "You prefer to meet me in there." She pulled her claws across the seal, breaking it open.

Immediately Liz was enveloped in a sphere of light reaching seventy stories high. Inside were swirling panels with scenes of people from all walks of life and from all points in time. She was standing in the IAM-ISPHERE, which was the portal into how the Maker saw time—past, present, and future, all happening at once.

"Bonsoir, Liz," came a familiar voice behind her. Liz turned to see Gillamon standing there, smiling with his twinkling blue eyes and his white goatee blowing in the ever present wind inside this mysterious place. "I know you've had a hard day seeing the animals caged up around the Circus Maximus."

Liz rushed up to the team leader of the Order of the Seven, and hugged him, weeping. "Oh, Gillamon, it was such a horrible day. I just didn't understand how bad it really was for the animals until today."

Gillamon placed his front leg around the petite cat's form. "I know, Dear One. I know it broke your heart to see the animals in such bondage."

Liz pulled back and stared up at Gillamon, wiping her eyes. *"Oui,* such *evil* bondage! Here I thought we could have the Animalympics in Rome, and that the animals could enjoy a time of joy and lighthearted competition. But how can we have such an event now, in light of why these animals are in Rome? It was a foolish idea. Noah and Nate did not realize what was happening with these animals. They thought they were here just to perform stunts and to play games . . ."

"But games to provide entertainment for the humans, leading to the animals' slaughter," Gillamon finished her thought.

Liz nodded and wiped her eyes again, sobbing as she spoke. "The lions told me how they were separated from their parents, captured, and brought here as cubs. They are kept in horrible conditions in cages, cruelly treated, and trained to unnaturally want to devour humans."

Gillamon furrowed his brow. "Yes, it is a sad reality. The Romans have turned animal capture into an industry to provide games across the empire. Hunters, captors, transporters, trainers, and handlers are all needed to bring animals by the thousands to Rome and other major cities."

"I just don't understand how this all started," Liz lamented.

"In the Garden, of course," Gillamon responded, walking over to a panel depicting a pristine garden of beauty and splendor. A couple walked through plush greenery, enjoying a menagerie of animal life all around them. Liz watched as the man smiled and dropped to his knees where a lion lazed under a tree. The man reached out to pet the lion, burying his face in the mane of the beast as the lion wrapped its paw playfully around the man. "But then came the Fall." Gillamon reached his hoof over to touch another panel that came into view.

The snake was coiled around the limb of the tree as the woman walked by in the cool shade of the day. Its forked tongue tasted the opportunity for temptation in the air. "Did God really say, 'You must not eat from any tree in the garden'?"

The woman stopped and turned her gaze to stare at the snake. "We may eat fruit from the trees in the garden, but God did say, 'You must

344

not eat fruit from the tree that is in the middle of the garden, and you must not touch it, or you will die.'"

"You will not certainly die," the snake replied with a soft, sarcastic chuckle, as if to dismiss her naive thought. "For God knows that when you eat from it your eyes will be opened, and you will be like God, knowing good and evil." With its triangular head, the serpent nudged the fruit, making it glisten in the sun as it swayed on the branch.

The woman slowly walked closer to the tree of the knowledge of good and evil. She wrinkled her brow as she looked from the snake to the fruit dangling in front of her. She licked her lips as she considered the power behind the tantalizing fruit. She gave a curious smile to the snake and reached up to grasp the fruit, hesitating a moment.

"Go ahead, take it," the snake hoarsely whispered, its eyes smoldering with anticipation.

The woman threw back her head and pulled on the fruit, snapping it off the branch. She slowly brought it to her lips and cast another glance at the snake before biting into it.

345

Gillamon touched another panel that swirled immediately into view. The snake slithered away through the grass as the man and woman fearfully hid behind some bushes, now dressed in animal skins that the Lord had made for them. The lion that Adam had previously played with so harmlessly now growled menacingly and fled the Garden.

"THE MAN HAS NOW BECOME LIKE ONE OF US, KNOWING GOOD AND EVIL. HE MUST NOT BE ALLOWED TO REACH OUT HIS HAND AND TAKE ALSO FROM THE TREE OF LIFE AND EAT, AND LIVE FOREVER."

Once more, Gillamon touched a panel and the scene of Adam and Eve running away from the Garden appeared before them. On the east side of the Garden of Eden stood a cherubim slicing the air with a flaming sword, back and forth, to guard the way to the Tree of Life.

Liz studied the scene. "Humans were given the freedom of choice to follow the Maker's lead, and thus fell from grace when they chose the Enemy's path."

"That's right, Liz. The entire world fell, including the animal kingdom, when Adam and Eve chose to follow the Evil One's lead. All the pain and heartache in this world can be traced to that one decision in the Garden. Humans no longer had peace between themselves. Nor did they have it with the animal kingdom. The Enemy seeks to destroy not only humans, but all of creation, including animals. And if he can do it by pitting humans and animals to destroy each other, then all the better in his evil mind." Gillamon touched the panels to bring several new moments of time into view.

In one panel, a strikingly handsome young soldier with blonde, wavy hair and a ruddy complexion rode a magnificent black horse, leading a massive army of Macedonian warriors with its famous infantry in their phalanx formation and their elite cavalry upon their noble steeds. On his head he wore a helmet shaped like a lion, with the open mouth of the dead lion positioned behind his head, as if it were biting the back of his skull, depicting Hercules in his victory over the lion.

"Do you know who this is?" Gillamon asked.

"But of course, it is Alexander the Great riding his beloved horse Bucephalus," Liz replied. "He was the greatest warrior who has ever lived, no? He conquered the world. I recognize the lion on his helmet."

"Indeed, it is Alexander," Gillamon replied. "Before his birth, his father, King Philip, dreamed that he placed on his wife's body a seal depicting a lion. One of the king's advisors interpreted Philip's dream to mean that the queen was with child—a son who would one day be as stout and courageous as a lion." He pointed to another panel of Alexander outside the gates of Jerusalem.

Alexander bowed before the high priest, who was dressed in a blue and gold robe and wore a headdress adorned with a gold plate inscribed with the name of God. "Do you know what happened when Alexander came to take over Jerusalem? It ties in with your time with Daniel in Babylon."

Liz thought a moment to recall the scenario. Her eyes lit up. *"Oui.* As Alexander approached the city, the high priest Jaddua had a dream in which God told him to take courage and decorate the city with wreaths. The people were to wear white while the priests wore their formal attire, and together they were to march out to meet Alexander and his army." Liz studied Alexander's lion helmet as he bowed before the priest. "When Alexander saw the high priest with God's name on his headdress, he bowed before the Name. Before coming to Jerusalem, he also had a dream about this meeting. In his dream this very priest told him not to delay but to cross over Asia with confidence and take Persia."

"Very good," Gillamon replied, tapping another scene of Alexander sacrificing to God in the temple of Jerusalem. "The Jews showed him the book of Daniel, that prophesied that a Greek would destroy the Persian Empire."

"*Oui,* Daniel wrote about a goat with one large horn between its eyes that would destroy the ram with two horns," Liz recounted Daniel's prophecy. "Greece was the goat and the horn was Alexander. The ram's horns were the Medes and Persians, who joined into one. When Alexander saw that Daniel had prophesied about his victory, he granted favor and honor to the Jews, bringing no harm to them. He moved on to conquer Egypt and eventually did, indeed, conquer Persia, just as Daniel had written he would."

"And then he went to India." Gillamon reached over and touched another panel. Alexander and a group of soldiers stood beside a wall, glancing upward and calling for ladders to be brought to scale the wall to reach the Mallians of India on the other side of the citadel.

"Gillamon, this is very fascinating about Alexander, but I do not see what all this has to do with what is happening here in Rome."

"You will," Gillamon replied, pointing to the scene. "Watch."

Alexander grabbed a ladder from his men and hurriedly placed it against the wall. He immediately began to climb the ladder ahead of his men, using his shield to ward off the arrows of the enemy. Behind him climbed his faithful shield-bearing soldier, Peucestas, and his bodyguard, Leonnatus. On a second ladder climbed Abreas, a loyal soldier ready to fight to the death for Alexander.

Alexander was the first to reach the top of the wall, and, wielding his sword against the defenders and shoving others back with his shield, he soon cleared a section of the wall. Alexander stood on top of the wall in full view of the enemy, but his men below panicked for his safety. Their king was a ready target for the arrows of the enemy, who easily recognized his glorious armor and courageous leadership. In their zeal to reach their king, the soldiers rushed up the ladder. It broke, and they were then unable to reach Alexander. They began calling to him to please jump back down to the safety of his men. Alexander gazed down

347

at his men and smiled. "If you love me, follow me!" He motioned for them to follow him. "Do you want to live forever?"

With that, Alexander leaped down, but on the other side of the wall. He was the first one to stand and face the enemy alone. Peucestas, Leonnatus, and Abreas soon joined him and together with their backs against the wall, they took on the incoming arrows of a vicious enemy. Within moments Alexander's sword found and killed his attackers, but an enemy arrow hit Abreas in the head, killing him instantly. Suddenly an arrow whizzed through the air and found its way through Alexander's breast armor, piercing his lung. Alexander quickly started losing blood, but continued to wield his sword even as he gasped for breath. He soon became dizzy and fainted, falling forward over his shield. As he lay there in a pool of blood, Peucestas and Leonnatus stood by like lions defending their prey. They themselves were covered with bloody wounds, but were determined to protect their king. Death seemed inevitable for the three outnumbered men.

Meanwhile, the Macedonians desperately scaled the wall by taking broken pieces of Alexander's ladder to dig into the clay-like wall, climbing on one another's shoulders, and, finally, with newly arrived ladders they reached their valiant leader. As they crested the top of the wall, their eyes fell on the lifeless body of Alexander. Rage filled the soldiers, who shouted as they jumped to the ground to mercilessly come after the enemy with blood-curdling screams. Some defended Alexander's body while others drove back the enemy, not sparing any of them. Several soldiers carried Alexander on his shield away from the battle, where he roused enough to instruct them to remove the arrow. As they pulled out the arrow, a great rush of blood ensued and once more he fainted.

Gillamon walked in front of the panel and Liz frowned, trying to peek around him. "But what happened next, Gillamon?"

Gillamon smiled and touched another panel. "I'm glad to see you are eager to see the end of this story." He moved away, and it showed a camp of Macedonian soldiers next to the Hydraotes River, grieving over the news Alexander was dead. Suddenly one of the men stood to his feet and pointed to a ship headed toward them. "Look! The king's ship!" The men got to their feet as the canopy was removed from the stern of the ship where Alexander lay. "It's just his dead body," one of the soldiers lamented.

But as the ship neared the bank, they saw Alexander raise his arm to greet the soldiers. They erupted in cheers! He was alive! Some wept, some stretched their hands out to him, and others lifted their arms to the heavens. A group of soldiers brought a stretcher to carry Alexander off the ship, but when they reached him he gave them different orders: "Get my horse." The soldiers looked at one another in disbelief that their nearly mortally wounded king would dare to mount a horse in his condition. "Go!" Alexander instructed them. They immediately obeyed.

The mighty Macedonian army watched in awe as Alexander's horse was brought to him. Their king rose to his feet and mounted his steed. A roar of cheers echoed off the banks of the river as Alexander rode through his men, whose hope was restored to see their brave leader not only alive, but at his post, ready to lead them once more. As he neared his tent, he dismounted his horse so his men could see him walk on his own two feet. They crowded around him in awe, desiring to touch their king whom they had thought was dead. But here he was, walking among them. They reached out to touch his arms and legs, and strained for even just a touch of Alexander's garments. The men called out blessings and showered him with ribbons and flowers.

"We want to live forever!" one of the soldiers shouted out in joy. His head was bandaged from a wound he also had suffered in the battle.

Alexander turned, and a smile crept onto his face at hearing those words. He nodded at his wounded soldier, locking eyes with him and raising his hand in acknowledgment. He then entered his tent while his soldiers proceeded to celebrate on into the night. Their king was alive, and he would lead them to victory over their enemies.

"*C'est magnifique!* I see why Alexander was called 'the Great!'" Liz exulted at watching this amazing scene. "He did grow up to have the courage of a lion. He was a military leader unlike any who ever lived."

"Indeed. He never lost a battle." Gillamon stepped in front of the panel. "Alexander was hungry for glory and he gained it. But he gained it by leading from out in front with unmatched courage. His choices affected not only his men, but the outcome of history. Alexander said, 'Remember, upon the conduct of each depends the fate of all.'"

"Alexander was right, no? One person's conduct can affect the fate of all," Liz offered. She suddenly remembered David's psalm. "'With your help I can advance against a troop; with my God I can scale a wall.'

349

Gillamon, I'm seeing meaning behind Alexander's story that I did not see before."

Gillamon nodded. "The Maker leaves his mark on every page of history, doesn't he? Even on the pages of those who don't follow him. Why do you think it is called HIStory?" The wise old mountain goat chuckled. "What do you think Alexander meant when he asked his men if they wanted to live forever before jumping down over the wall?"

Liz pondered this a moment as she gazed up at the swirling panels showing moments of history. "Perhaps he was asking if they wanted to live by not risking death but miss the glory of fighting valiantly in battle. Or perhaps he was asking if they wanted to live forever from the fame of what they were about to do."

"And how does one live forever from such fame?" Gillamon asked with a knowing smile.

"Well, both in history books and perhaps in the form of statues?" Liz's eyes widened. "Like Libertas! She has stood through four generations of the Antonius family, and she will stand forever in time."

350

"I need to show you another leader whose conduct affected others in the past, but will also affect millions more in the future," Gillamon told Liz, touching another panel. A man stood in the Roman Senate, talking for hours on end. "This is Cato the Younger. He was Julius Caesar's worst enemy."

"His worst enemy?" Liz asked. "But he is dressed in a toga, not in a military uniform."

"Indeed. He opposed the policies of Julius Caesar, fighting to preserve the Roman Republic while Julius positioned himself to take over Rome as dictator. Cato's battlefield was for the freedom of the people, and he led them both in speech and militarily until his back was up against the wall in Utica. In fact, he was so passionate about his battle for freedom, that when surrender to Julius Caesar became unavoidable, he drew a sword and killed himself."

"You mean he chose death if he could not be free?" Liz wondered, shaking her head as a scene of Cato drawing his sword swirled before them.

"Yes, for Cato, it was either liberty . . . or death," Gillamon answered. "Remember what you see here, for just as you've inspired Luke to write down the story of Jesus, you will need to inspire a man by the name of

Plutarch to write down the story of Cato. He will also write about Alexander and many other men in history, and how their conduct affected the fate of all. But, Liz, you must help these characters live forever in the pages of history when it comes time for Plutarch to pick up his pen. The voice of a future leader depends on it."

"Je comprends." Liz curled her tail up and down as she thought about this future assignment. "Gillamon, there is more to this idea of living forever than what you've shown me, isn't there? You've shown me the fall of Adam and Eve in the Garden and how the Maker said they had to leave because of their choice. They lost their freedom from sin and the ability to live forever. But Jesus freely made a choice in the Garden of Gethsemane to die on the Tree of Life to actually redeem the poor choice of men!"

Gillamon smiled. "That's right, Liz. And just like Alexander, Jesus asks those who love him to make a choice. Do they truly want to live forever? If so, they must choose to follow him. He was the first one over the wall of death to face the Enemy, and in so doing, Jesus truly conquered the world. Jesus is the greatest hero of history."

"Because it is HIS story," Liz answered happily. Jesus' words poured into her mind. "'If anyone wants to come with Me, he must deny himself, take up his cross, and follow Me. For whoever wants to save his life will lose it, but whoever loses his life because of Me will find it.'"

Gillamon nodded. "True freedom must always involve choice."

Liz thought of the animals in bondage. "So what do we do about those who are in bondage not by their own choice, but through the poor choices of others?"

"Jesus can reach anyone in bondage and release their spirit, even if they are imprisoned in body," Gillamon replied. "So this finally brings us back to answer your question of how it all started with the slaughtering of animals by Rome. Even when there is forgiveness and the eternal promise of freedom given to all, earthly consequences remain."

"The fate of all was determined by the conduct of Adam and Eve," Liz recounted with a new perspective. "Their choice to disobey the Maker led to the fall of men and the entire animal kingdom."

"Yes, their conduct led to the Fall for all," Gillamon agreed, touching another panel showing a triumphant military parade down the Via Sacra and through the Forum of Rome. "And Alexander's conduct has

351

made every ruler throughout time long to be great just like him, including Nero himself."

"Pfft! Nero? Great? *C'est impossible!*" Liz spat.

"Even so, Rome's generals and emperors like to make a show of greatness by copying how Alexander celebrated his victories through parades of triumph."

Liz watched the scene of hundreds of soldiers marching in formation, with human captives being forced to march ahead of them, and with countless carts carrying the spoils of war. Suddenly she saw a row of caged exotic animals being paraded before the people. And then she saw elephants being herded through the paved heart of Rome. Onlookers gawked, seeing giraffes, hippos, and crocodiles for the first time. Liz heard the roar of lions as four hundred of them were brought through the mass of cheering Romans.

Gillamon pointed to a man dressed in purple wearing a crown of golden laurel leaves, driving a four-horse chariot. "This is Julius Caesar and his famous quadruple triumph to celebrate four victories. One victory was over your beloved France, which the humans, of course, call Gaul. Another victory he celebrated here was over his worst enemy."

"Cato," Liz realized. "*Veni, vidi, vici.*"

Gillamon nodded, interpreting her Latin: "I came, I saw, I conquered."

Liz shook her head in saddened amazement at what she was witnessing with the animals. "So the animals are paraded through Rome before being sent to the arena for the games?"

"Yes, Liz. Although Roman General Pompey before him had also brought hundreds of lions for his triumphant parade, Julius Caesar was the first of Rome's leaders who truly saw how the display of animals and games would lead to power. The more exotic the animals, the greater impression it made on the people. Every new species on display communicated that Rome's empire had spread to conquer a new land, just like Alexander. But parading the animals wasn't enough. They had to be used for entertainment in the games. So men began sponsoring games to win the favor of the people, and they constantly push one another to outdo any games that have been staged before. Consuls, senators, and emperors themselves sponsor games all over the empire. Some sponsors may take two years and spend millions to plan the games, going bankrupt in the process. The price of a single lion equals a year's salary for 250 soldiers."

Gillamon tapped other panels that showed scenes of Roman coliseums and circuses in cities across the territories of Rome. Inside, animals fought against gladiators and against each other. "The most visible part of any Roman city is its coliseum. And the most celebrated way to enjoy being a Roman is to watch the slaughter of men and animals in the games."

Liz's eyes filled with tears to watch animals killed by the thousands. "*C'est tragique!* The Enemy is destroying the Maker's creation. So how can these species possibly expect to live forever?"

"Some will not survive," Gillamon told her. "Lions will someday no longer roam in Greece, and panthers will no longer prowl through Turkey. The Roman games will take their toll on the animal population until they are driven back into remote areas."

"Is there nothing we can do to stop this?" Liz cried.

Gillamon leaned over and looked Liz in the eye. "Not until another fall occurs—the fall of Rome. But for now, you can stop the slaughter of all the animals that are in Rome right now. It's only a small number in the countless sea of animals who will perish in Rome. Surely it can't make that much of a difference—or can it?"

353

"Oh, Gillamon, but it *will* make a difference to those we can save!" Liz cried, thinking of Marcus saving Jesus. "*S'il vous plaît*, tell me how to help!"

Gillamon smiled at seeing renewed hope in Liz's eyes. "Very well, then. Proceed with the Animalympics on July 18, and release them all to enjoy the freedom of your games. But you must be finished by 2:00 AM. Then the animals will be able to leave Rome without the humans stopping them."

Liz wrinkled her brow. "But how is this possible? How will thousands of animals be able to leave Rome? Even though it is the middle of the night, Rome does not sleep. The animals will be seen, just as the animals were seen coming to Noah's Ark."

That twinkle in Gillamon's eyes told Liz he knew more than he let on. "I'm not at liberty to tell you everything, as you know, Liz. But trust me. Everything I've shown you here tonight with Alexander will come into play, so remember what you've seen."

"I shall, *mon ami*, I shall," Liz promised expectantly.

Gillamon touched his hoof to the scene of Bella's garden and the statue of Libertas still standing there in the cool night air. "I will see you there. We will all be there together."

Liz smiled. "But, Gillamon, our games are only two weeks away. How will Max, Kate, and Nigel join us here in Rome?"

The wise leader of the Order of the Seven chuckled and looked around the IAMISPHERE. "Have you forgotten? This portal allows our team to not only travel in time, but also to any place in the blink of an eye."

Liz put a paw to her forehead. *"Bien sûr!* Then I shall look forward to our team gathering together in the Circus Maximus on that night. *Merci,* Gillamon. For everything."

"Bonne nuit, little one." Gillamon smiled as he tapped on the panel to take Liz back to the garden. *"À bientôt."*

Instantly Liz was outside once again in the garden next to Libertas. She smiled and lifted her gaze up to the night sky. There above her was the constellation of Leo. She smiled, remembering that the star announcing Jesus' birth was placed in this cluster of stars resembling a lion.

"REMEMBER THAT THE TRUE LION OF JUDAH IS OVER AND ABOVE ALL THINGS, LIZ. THE ENEMY MAY TRY TO MIMIC MY POWER AS A LION, SEEKING TO DEVOUR WHOEVER HE CAN. BUT WHEN I ROAR, EVEN THE WEAKEST OF HEARTS WILL FIND COURAGE TO FOLLOW ME."

Liz's heart swelled with hope. "And in following you, they will live forever."

354

SETTING
THE STAGE

ROME, JULY 18, AD 64

"Ye can let go now, Lass," Max whispered gently. "Welcome ta R-r-rome."

Kate slowly opened her eyes and blinked a few times, releasing her grip on Max's leg after their trip through the IAMISPHERE. "It's been a while since I've traveled that way. Goin' eight hundred miles in less than a second makes a lass need ta catch her breath." The white Westie looked around her and saw they were outside the Circus Maximus. "Wha' a grand place!"

"It be called the Circus *MAX*-imus," Max told her with a wink.

Kate nudged Max affectionately. "That must be why it's so grand, me love."

"Ah, the Eternal City!" Nigel cheered, wiping off his spectacles. "It's good to be back."

"Paul an' John won't even know we've been gone," Max noted, looking around where they stood in the market stalls of the Circus. "We'll jest have fun at the games an' go back ta the moment we left."

"Mousie!" Al exclaimed, running up to Nigel and enveloping him in a smothering hug.

"Hello, old boy," Nigel uttered in a muffled voice beneath Al's fur.

"Traveling through the IAMISPHERE is the only way to go, no?"

asked Liz as she sauntered up to them. "It is good to see you, *mes amis.*"

"Liz!" Kate cried. Immediately she ran up to Liz and the two old friends locked in a timeless embrace. "How I've missed ye."

Liz's eyes were moist with the joy of reunion. *"Moi aussi.* I am so happy that time apart does not change our friendship, *mon amie."* Liz leaned back and put her paw on Kate's cheek. "I was sorry to hear about Mary. Were you with her when she died?"

Kate nodded. "I were privileged ta be lyin' next ta her, keepin' her warm. Liz, Jesus *himself* came ta take her home. He sat on the bed with me a wee bit an' thanked me for takin' care of his mum all these years. Me heart were full of joy an' sadness at the same time. With every mission me part seems small compared ta the rest of ye, but in that sweet moment with Jesus, he made me feel so valuable an' important. He thanked me for bein' willin' ta serve him in a quiet way, an' said not everyone can do wha' I do. He's taught me that me main part with the Order of the Seven be ta comfort an' encourage others. Even if that's all I ever do, then I be a blessed lass indeed."

Liz's voice cracked with emotion. "I can think of no higher honor than to serve Jesus with such a gift, *chère* Kate. Indeed, many feel that in order to be important, one must be out in front, but Jesus needs selfless servants like you. He needs those whose acts may never be seen by the world, yet are so very important, no? I am so honored to serve with you, *mon amie.* You always comfort *me* with your big heart."

"'Tis a grand thing how he made us all different ta serve him with wha' we each can do best," Kate replied with her perky grin. "Thank ye for bein' out in front, Liz. I look up ta ye an' depend on ye ta lead us."

Liz and Kate put their heads together and exclaimed at the same time, "Lassie power!"

"Wha' aboot the lads then?" Max wanted to know, sitting with Al and Nigel in a row, tapping his paw.

Kate and Liz smiled at one another and went over to embrace their mates. "We'd be nowhere without our strong lads," Kate answered.

"Oui." Liz rubbed her cheek on Al's face and leaned over to kiss Nigel on the head. "Including our valiant Nigel."

Nigel preened his whiskers, straightening them after Al's hug. "I am happy to be of service."

"The Maker is proud of all of you," came a voice from a vendor in the stall next to where they stood. "And tonight, we will all be together. All seven of us."

"Clarie!" Kate cried, running over to the stall, wagging her tail happily. She looked at the stall that sold oil lamps and other souvenirs. Clarie was dressed as a man in an olive green tunic with a brown belt and sandals. "Will ye be dressed like that tonight?"

Clarie smiled. "No, little Kate. Tonight Gillamon and I will be in our true forms with all of you for the Animalympics."

"So wha's the plan for tonight then?" inquired Max.

"Albert and I have been working with Noah and Nate for weeks, getting things ready for the opening ceremonies and events," Liz announced. "Some animals traveled to Rome on their own to be here for the events, but many were brought here by the Romans. Two fun pre-game events are taking place today in Rome involving unique species of size and abilities unto themselves. The frogs are competing in the Lily Pad Leap over in Nero's lake, with Nate overseeing that event."

"Aye, an' the rats be competin' in the Rat Race in Rome's sewers," Al added. "Noah be judgin' that one."

357

Nigel closed his eyes tightly and shuddered. "Rats. How *revolting!*"

"Tonight there will be four athletic events and three artistic events involving multiple species for the main games," Liz continued. "As judges were needed to oversee these main events we felt it would only be fair for the Order of the Seven to serve and not compete."

"Except for the fun ones!" Al quickly added with a goofy smile and his paw up in the air. "Like the Goat Gulp eatin' competition an' the Tug o' War."

"*Oui,* we thought it would be fun if we as the seven judges have a Tug o' War with the seven winners of the main events."

"Brilliant! How may I assist with this endeavor?" Nigel asked happily.

"We chose you to judge what you love most, *mon ami,*" Liz answered with a smile. "You and I will judge the artistic events: Poetry Reading, Singing, and Art."

"Splendid!" Nigel cheered, cupping his mouse ears. "I shall be all ears to judge objectively, my dear. Might I inquire as to who shall be competing?"

"But of course," Liz replied. "For Poetry Reading, a hedgehog named

Glenna, a boar named Dave, and a yak named Earwig. For Singing, a ladybug named Dot, an ostrich named Francine, and a crocodile named Doug. And for Art, we have a painting elephant named Suda, a group of sand sculpting ants who call themselves 'Michelangelart,' and our beloved lizard Nate, who I didn't realize loves to draw. He will compete in both artistic and athletic events."

"I say, this shall prove to be quite the stiff competition!" Nigel predicted. "But I shall judge with fairness, I assure you."

"Wha' aboot me an' Kate?" Max asked.

"You two, of course, will judge the athletic events with Al and Clarie: Foot Race, Javelin Throw, Long Jump, and Wrestling," Liz explained.

Max grinned broadly. "Aye! The Foot R-r-race will be me favorite."

"Nate be in that race, o' course, along with a zebra, a millipede, a rhino, and a sloth," Al told them. "That millipede goes by the name 'Legs.' He's got a lot of foots, so he may have an unfair advantage."

"Feet, Albert," Liz corrected him. She turned to Kate. "I think you will enjoy the Javelin Throw, Kate. Signed up for this event we have a giraffe, a baboon, and a scorpion, but wait until you see the porcupine in action! He is a natural."

"I can't wait!" Kate enthused. "Of course, I'll be wantin' everyone ta win."

Al started jumping around the group. "I get ta judge the Long Jump with all the big cats—lions, tigers, panthers, and cheetahs!"

"And I will judge the Wrestling competition," Clarie offered. "Our entrants include a bear, a hippo, a hyena, and a snake."

"Gillamon will judge the Goat Gulp, since it is obviously named for him, but it will be an event for fun only," Liz announced.

"Who will be tryin' to out-eat me, Lass?" Al wanted to know, rubbing his belly.

"We have an antelope, a civet, a rabbit, and a pig," Liz relayed. "Each must bring an item for the other contestants to eat."

Kate cocked her head. "Wha's a civet, Liz?"

"It is a small mammal with mottled gray shaggy hair and a long tail, and somewhat resembles the raccoon," Liz explained. "And this little fellow is an Asian palm civet. He came from China on one of the ships trading silk and spices with Rome and heard about our competition. His name is 'Bang.'"

"Fascinating! I say, I've always wanted to visit that land full of mystery and intrigue," Nigel told the group. "And they have quite the peculiar language. No telling what he will bring for you to eat, Old Boy."

"Aye, with a name like Bang, ye might get somethin' spicy, Lad," Max joked.

"This belly be ready for anythin'!" Al snorted, gripping his orange fur. "No eye has seen, no ear has heard, and no mouth has tasted the cornucopia o' food this kitty can eat."

"But won't the humans see all of this goin' on?" Kate wondered with a frown.

Max looked up from where they stood. "Me lass has a point. The emperor's palace be r-r-right up there behind the Circus Maximus after all."

"Nero is nearly forty miles away from Rome at his palace in Antium," Clarie assured them. "So the Palatine Palace will be deserted for the most part tonight, as he issued an unusual order for his entire family and servants to accompany him there."

"Curious," Nigel said. "I presume we shall need oil lamps to see the events ourselves."

Clarie lifted her hand to the display of oil lamps behind her in the market stall. "Will this supply do?"

"Brilliant!" Nigel cheered.

"There is more you need to know," Liz added. "Gillamon informed me that we will be releasing the animals from their cages here around the Circus Maximus in order for them to compete in the Animalympics. As you know they have been brought here against their will to compete in Rome's bloody games. But tonight they will be free to compete in our games, and their captivity will be over!"

"They get to leave Rome!" Al cheered, jumping once more around the group.

"Freein' the beasties will be the best part aboot the games!" Kate cheered.

"This takes the biscuit!" Nigel exclaimed with his fists raised in a big cheer. "I say, what could be more splendid than an evening of friendly competition followed by the liberation of our fellow animal kingdom members?"

359

Al patted his fluffy belly. "The Goat Gulp alone comes mighty close, Mousie."

"*Bon!* Noah and Nate will be here soon to prepare for tonight. And just so you know, we've decided to allow Noah to be the emcee of the Animalympics. It was the one thing he begged us to let him do."

Max rolled his eyes. "That cr-r-razy monkey will keep everyone entertained, but we could be here all night listenin' ta his jokes then."

"Gillamon said we must be finished by 2 AM in order for the animals to be able to leave Rome without notice from the humans," Liz informed him.

Nigel tapped his paw on his chin. "As I think about it, I see a dilemma, my dear. How shall the animals be able to leave? Rome certainly does not sleep."

"*Oui,* I asked Gillamon this very thing, *mon ami,*" Liz answered. "He said to trust him and follow his instructions."

"And follow his instructions we shall," stated Clarie, standing to leave. "It's nearly nightfall. I must go meet Gillamon. Max and Kate, you are to meet Noah and Nate down on the track of the Circus. And Liz, Al, and Nigel, you have some animals to set free."

360

☧

The dank smell of sweat, blood, and filth filled the dark corridor. Nigel held his nose as they walked along. The feeling of death was in the air.

"This is intolerable! How can humans be so, so, well, *inhumane?*" Nigel scowled.

"I had a long talk with Gillamon about this, *mon ami,*" Liz answered, proceeding to lead the group down the stone pathway. "It all goes back to the Fall."

Al wrinkled his brow. "Fall? But that's such a pretty time o' year."

"I believe she means the Fall *of man,* Old Boy," Nigel replied.

"We shall discuss this later. For now, let us split up for this liberating mission," Liz directed them. "The key to each holding pen hangs on a nail outside. Albert, please go release the small animals like the snake, boar, and hyena. Then proceed to the panthers, cheetahs, and tigers."

Al held up his paw and sprung his iron claw. "No key needed with this, Lass."

Liz giggled. "Nigel, please head to the large animal stall holding the elephant, hippo, giraffe, and baboon. I will release the others, beginning with the lions."

"Understood, my dear. And we are to follow this corridor through the tunnel leading into the Circus Maximus, correct?"

"*Oui,* and, Nigel, with this animal parade, you will get to see what it looked like when the animals left Noah's Ark," Liz added with a grin.

"Right! No doubt the joy of this exodus will be just as splendid," Nigel replied with a salute. "Cheerio, I shall see you in the Circus." The little mouse scurried off into the darkened corridor.

Al sat there, not moving.

"Albert, is something wrong?"

"I were wonderin' aboot that snake. Do ye think we can trust him?" Al asked nervously. "Ye said it would be like Noah's Ark. And we all know what happened with *that* snake."

Liz placed her dainty paw on Al's shoulder. "I believe he is simply a regular snake, so we can trust him, *mon cher.* But keep an eye on him just to be sure. You are my noble, famous warrior. So if he causes any trouble, I am certain you will be the first to know."

Al stood on all fours and straightened up his tail. "Aye, I'll stay on the alert, Lass."

"*Bon,* Albert. See you in the Circus." Liz kissed Al on the cheek. "And I hope you will win the Goat Gulp competition."

"I'll give ye me crown," Al promised her happily. He then took off down the other darkened corridor.

Liz turned and looked toward the lion cage. She had been so sad here the other day when it was full of lions ready for the human games. She didn't know how many would be left, but she couldn't wait to set them free.

Four lions sat alone in the cage. A piece of raw meat lay untouched in the muddy straw with flies buzzing around it. Liz walked over to the cage and jumped on a stone block above which the key hung by a nail. A torch remained lit on the wall outside the cage, so Liz looked around to make sure no humans were present. When she was convinced they had all returned home for the night, she reached up and lifted the key, inserting it into the lock.

361

"Bonsoir, mes amis. It is time for you to leave this place," Liz told them. The lions stood but did not approach the door as Liz swung it wide open. "What is the matter?"

"My friends are having second thoughts," the largest lion replied, slowly swinging his tail side to side. "One of the lions attempted to escape and was slain before it reached the Circus."

"If we are recaptured by the humans, the beastmaster might kill us, too," a smaller lion added.

"Besides, how can we get our freedom as easily as you say?" the third lion asked. "What's the catch?"

The fourth lion squinted at Liz. "This all seems too good to be true."

These lions had never known anything but cruelty and captivity since they were young cubs. No wonder they found it hard to trust. Liz walked into the cage and stood before the lions that towered over her. "There is no catch. I assure you that you are free to go. Tonight the animals of Rome will celebrate their own games, and then will be free to leave this city and return to their homes."

The lions looked at one another with sad eyes. "We don't have homes to return to."

The large lion stepped forward. "Then we'll make *new* homes! I say we do this. The humans took everything from us, and I say we take it back."

"What are your names?" Liz asked them.

"We don't have names," a smaller lion answered. "We were snatched from our parents when we were too young to learn them."

Liz choked back her emotions and cleared her throat. "No names? Well, names happen to be my specialty. And with your newfound freedom, you will most certainly need names." She smiled and stood before the large lion. "You seem to be the leader of this group."

"He is! He's been the one to lead us and stand up against the humans when they tried to hurt us," a smaller lion said.

Liz studied his blond mane, now matted with grime, but she could tell it would be magnificent when clean and blowing in the breeze. Suddenly an idea struck her. Her eyes lit up. "I have the perfect name for you. Alexander, the name for a great commander."

The large lion lifted his chin and a grin slowly emerged from the corner of his mouth as he said the name: "Alexander."

"He *is* a great commander!" another lion shouted. "We'd follow him anywhere."

"Bon! Then I have the perfect names for the rest of you," Liz replied, walking in front of the other three lions. "Leonnatus, Peucestas, and Abreas," she recited, pointing to each one in turn. "These are names of faithful fighters who follow their commander no matter what."

"Then let's be going." The large lion walked to the open door of their cage. "Do you want to live?"

"Yes, Alexander, I want to live!" Leonnatus answered, stepping forward.

Liz's heart warmed to see Leonnatus, Peucestas, and Abreas fall in line behind Alexander, just like the humans they were named for. These lions wanted to live and be free. And now they finally had the chance.

"Very well, let's get out of here," Alexander told them. "Follow me. The Animalympics await."

363

ANIMALYMPICS

The city of Rome was anything but quiet on this sweltering summer night. Vendors rolled their noisy carts along the cobblestones, going to resupply their stalls with more items to sell at the market come morning. People roamed the streets, visiting inns where food was abundant and where laughter flowed as easily as the wine. Families gathered for their evening meal in the *insulae,* or tightly packed apartments. Neighbors greeted. Strangers argued. Lovers strolled. Thieves robbed. Merchants shouted. Slaves ran. The only things missing from the streets of Rome were animals.

The *Vigiles,* Rome's night watchmen, were occupied with fire and police duties. Nicknamed *Spartoli,* or "little bucket fellows" for the water buckets they carried, these men kept a watchful eye to quickly douse some hundred daily fires that started across the fourteen regions of Rome. They also kept a lookout for runaway slaves and kept the public peace. Busy with their nightly patrol, the *Spartoli* gave little thought to what could be getting ready to take place within the high walls of the Circus Maximus.

"You have waited a long time for this, *mon ami,*" Liz whispered to Nate with a paw on his tiny shoulder. She knew he was preparing himself for the competition. "Are you ready?"

Nate gazed out at Rome from the top row of wooden seats in the Circus Maximus, stretching his legs. He turned around to face Liz and smiled. "I thought this night would never arrive. I'm ready."

"*Bon,* and so are they," Liz replied, extending her paw out to the stadium below.

The Circus Maximus spread out almost 700 yards long and just shy of 160 yards wide. It was situated in a valley between two of Rome's seven hills, the Palatine and the Aventine. Both of the long sides of the oblong arena were built with stands to hold 150,000 spectators, divided into three sections according to social class. At one end were twelve starting gates with iron arches designed to keep chariots and horses at bay until the races began. A marble building resembling a temple rose from the third tier of seats on the Palatine Hill side of the track that housed the emperor's special viewing box. From here, the Emperor could be seen by the people when he attended the races, with his hand raised to drop the *mappa,* or white cloth, to signal the start of a race.

In the middle of the racetrack was the *spina,* or central barrier. Each end was rounded off with turning posts. The *spina* had high stone walls and statues of gods, marble altars, and shrines placed along the middle of the island barrier. At either end were lap counters, with seven dolphins on one end and seven eggs on the other. As the charioteers finished each lap, a dolphin or an egg would drop so the screaming fans as well as the racers would know how many laps remained. In the center of the *spina* was a huge obelisk, towering over the other structures and close to the white finish line.

But tonight, there was no emperor, no chariots, nor cheering crowds of humans. There were only animals filling the stands, from the rats that ran in the sewers below Rome to the birds that flew above, and to all manner of wild animals here for the Animalympics. Plenty of seating was available for each of the seven events spread out across the sandy floor of the Circus. Spectator animals were free to roam and go to whichever event they chose after the opening ceremony. Never had the animal kingdom been so happy to come together for such an event. Their joyful murmuring filled the air with excitement.

"Hurry, Dude! We're getting ready to start!" Noah screeched when he spotted Nate and Liz making their way over to the sand below the Emperor's box. The rest of the Order of the Seven were assembled with each of the animal groups they were going to judge. Several oil lamps were lit around the stage and at each event around the Circus. Noah tripped over one as he headed to the stage. It was sitting right beside the white cloth *mappa* he was to use to open the games.

365

"Careful then, Noah," Kate warned, catching the lamp and righting it. "I know ye're excited but we don't want ta start a fire, do we?"

"No, ma'am! Sorry, Little Lady!" Noah exclaimed with a sheepish grin.

Kate smiled and handed him the *mappa*. "No harm done, Lad. Go on now an' make us all proud."

"Thanks for being so sweet to me!" Noah blew her a kiss and took the *mappa* in hand. He then pointed at Nigel. "And thanks for helping me learn my lines today, little dude."

"My pleasure, old boy," Nigel replied with a rallying fist. "Open the games with grandeur!"

Noah gave one final white-toothed grin to Nate and took the stage. The capuchin monkey looked out at the throngs of animals assembled there and held up his lanky arms. "Citizens of the Animal Kingdom! I welcome you to these games provided for your entertainment by the Order of the Seven, Nate, and me. We dedicate these games to you!" he began in a deep bellowing voice, mimicking the lines that an emperor would say before a race. He stopped and rolled his eyes. "That's not how I talk!" He blew a raspberry and whipped the *mappa* around in the air like a wet rag.

"Woo-hoo-hoo! Welcome to the Animalympics! We're gonna have fun tonight, dudes and dudettes! Who's ready?" He went jumping across the stage as the animals erupted in applause. "Are you ready to see our Animalypians?" More applause. "He-e-e-e-e-e-ere they are!"

"This is not exactly what I had envisioned," Nigel shouted to Liz above the noise.

"Of course it is not," Liz shouted back happily. "Noah is the emcee!"

"Do we have some poetry-lovin', music-listenin', art-appreciatin' critters in the Circus tonight?" Noah shouted, shaking his hands in the air. Cheers went up and Noah pointed at Liz and Nigel. "I give you Ms. Brilliant Liz and Mr. Musical Nigel, your epic judges for the artsy events, whoop-whoop! You can hear a yak yak, a little lady connect the musical dots, and watch an elephant paint with her trunk!"

"Ooooo. Ahhhhh," the animal crowd replied enthusiastically as the artistic contestants strolled by. The hedgehog, boar, and yak walked along, rehearsing their lines under their breath.

Dot the ladybug flew through the air, warming up her vocal chords by running up and down the scales, "La-la-la-la-la-la-la."

Francine the Ostrich also warmed up by stretching her long neck and singing, "Me-me-me-me."

Doug the crocodile held a monotone note like one long chant: "ANNNNNNNNNNNNN."

Suda the elephant held a paint brush in her trunk as she carried the colony of ants on her tail.

"We're just gettin' started, oh yeah, we're gettin' started, oh yeah, we're gettin' started!" Noah sang-shouted as he wiggled his behind backwards across the stage. "We've got a jivin' Javelin Throw, look out! Javelin Judge Kate will see who's great!" He pointed to the giraffe, baboon, scorpion, and porcupine who paraded by with Kate. "Whoa, I gotta catch a ride on that neck up to the treetops, dude!" he hollered to the giraffe.

The animal crowd was now clapping to Noah's chant, making the monkey grow more animated. "Leapin' Lions! Where are my big cats in the Circus?" Noah shouted, holding his hand up to his ear.

Al strutted out in front of the pack of sixteen large cats, his tail high in the air as he led his large cousins in front of the stage. "Here come the kitties! Here come the kitties! Here come the kitties!"

Alexander, Leonnatus, Peucestas, and Abreas smiled at one another and roared, exhilarated to feel the freedom of walking across the sandy stadium floor for fun instead of in fear. Alexander led the lions as they walked in front of the stage, nodding his head nobly to the crowd of animals, who cheered respectfully for the king of the beasts. The tigers, panthers, and cheetahs sauntered along proudly behind them.

"Tigers and panthers and cheetahs will be leapin' with the lions for the Long Jump Team Competition. But don't let me see no cheatin' now!" Noah guffawed. "Get it? Cheatin' from the cheetahs? Get it?"

A ripple of laughter came up from the animal crowd. Max rolled his eyes. "An' here come the painful jokes fr-r-rom the cr-r-razy monkey."

"Okay, now, riddle me this! What do you get when you tie a bear, a hippo, a hyena, and a snake together?" Noah asked as the Wrestling Animals started parading by.

"What?" shouted the enthusiastic crowd.

"Beats me!" Noah snickered. "But you'll find out at the Wrestlin' competition judged by the lovely lamb Clarie!"

Noah started running back and forth across the stage. "What am I doin'? What am I doin'? What am I doin'?"

367

"Running!" the animals shouted back in reply.

"Whoop, yeah, dudes! So that means we got us a foooooooot race led by Maximillian Braveheart the Bruce!" Noah cheered and pointed to Max and the animal contestants. "Just look at all those racin' feet! That millipede must have a million! My best pal, Nate, is the fastest lizard on land *or* water, woo-hoo! He's gonna do a quick draw and race around the track!" Noah winked and shot pointer fingers at Nate, who waved at the crowd. Noah clapped his hands and pointed at each of the other racers. "We got racin' stripes on that zebra, 'ahead by a horn' on that rhino, and . . . and . . . and . . . um . . . just a minute, folks." Noah held up his finger, and his jaw hung open as he watched the sloth creep by. "Really?"

The three-toed sloth reached out his long arms as his claws dug into the sand. He slowly pulled himself forward while his short back legs bunched up behind trying to push off the sand. The animal crowd quieted down as it watched the painfully slow progress of this normally tree-dwelling animal attempting to tackle the ground. Kate ran back to walk next to the sloth to give him support. Max stood by with her. It was as if time had just stopped in the Circus Maximus.

"Wha's yer name?" Kate asked.

The sloth lifted his head and looked up at the animals staring at him. "Name . . . is . . . F-l-a-s-h." He pulled himself forward. "I . . . dream . . . to . . . race."

Kate's heart melted at the sweet sloth's determination. She looked around at the animal crowd staring at him in this awkward moment. "I say Flash be the most courageous beastie at these games!"

"Aye, he's tr-r-ryin' ta compete in somethin' he's not even able ta do," Max agreed.

"We all can learn a lesson from him ta dream big!" Kate cried, looking around at the animals to rally their support. "Let's give a big cheer for our friend, Flash!"

"You heard the little lady!" Noah shouted. "Go, Flash! Go, Flash! Go, Flash! Go, Flash!" he started chanting, clapping his hands to get the animal crowd rallied around the sloth.

As the animals erupted in supporting cheers for the sloth, the little civet ran up to Kate. He had a white mask on his forehead, small white patches under his eyes and beside his nose, with a dark line running

368

between his eyes. "Bang has bang!" he cried with a thick Chinese accent as he smiled and nodded quickly, reaching into a pouch he carried over his shoulder. He held out a handful of berries. "Bang hep Frash!" He set the berries in front of the sloth. "Bang fo Goat Gup! Bang!"

Max and Kate leaned over to sniff the berries as Gillamon came walking up to them. "What do we have here?"

"Bang!" the civet shouted happily.

"It's coffee berries, Gillamon," Kate answered with a grin.

"Bang br-r-rought these for the Goat Gulp competition, an' wants ta help Flash as well," Max explained.

Kate's heart willed Flash to take each step. "I say we let the sloth eat them."

Gillamon chuckled to himself. "Well, as the leader of the Order of the Seven team, and as judge for the Goat Gulp competition, I hereby rule that Flash may have a few berries to help energize him, as he is racing at a severe disadvantage." He turned around and faced the animal crowd. "But to make sure there is no concern about special assistance for the sloth, what do you all say?"

"BANG!" came the shout from the crowd!

Kate wagged her tail happily. "It's unanimous!"

"Give that sloth some java!" Noah declared.

Kate leaned over and whispered in Flash's ear, "Go ahead, my friend. Eat some berries. We're all cheering you on."

Flash turned up his face and gave Kate a precious smile. "O-kay." He proceeded to eat the coffee berries and the animals cheered as Max helped him move on ahead. "Bannnng," he exclaimed slowly as he slightly picked up his pace.

"Thank ye, Bang," Kate told the civet. "That were very kind."

"Bang grad to hep!" The civet bowed repeatedly.

"We've got some fun ahead after the main events, dudes! Who better to judge the Goat Gulp eating competition than a goat?" Noah exclaimed, pretending to stuff his face. "Gillamon will see who can gulp the most grass from the antelope, the most carrots from the rabbit, the most slop from the pig, the most fish from Al, and the most *what* from the civet?" Noah cupped his hand to his ear.

"BANG!" the crowd shouted back.

"Whoop, whoop, yeah!" Noah exclaimed. The animals all clapped and cheered. "Enjoy the events and see you back here for the grand finale of the Animalympics: The Order of the Seven Tug o' War! Let the games begin!" Noah twirled the *mappa* in the air and sent it flying as the animals cheered to quickly disperse to the events around the Circus.

"I must say, it wasn't the most *refined* opening ceremony I've ever attended for an Olympics," Nigel whispered to Liz with an impish grin. "But it certainly was the most *lively.*"

"*Oui*, it was perfectly . . . Noah," Liz giggled. "And besides, these are not the Olympics. They are the *Animalympics!*"

After the animals had spread out, Bang made his way to the stage where Noah sat looking out over the Circus and the excitement of the games. Bang bowed and returned the *mappa* to Noah.

"Hey, Dude, that was a classy move with the sloth!" Noah exclaimed, punching the civet playfully.

Bang bowed rapidly and reached into his pouch. "Bang has diff'lent bang for gland finale!"

370

Noah's eyes widened and a big grin grew across his face. "DUDE! AWESOME! What is it?"

The civet laughed. "BANG!"

40

UP IN FLAMES

"Take yer seats! Take yer seats! Hurry, hurry, hurry!" Al cried, his eyes bulging as large as his belly. He waddled-ran through the crowd of animals making their way to their seats by the emperor box of the Circus. His fur was covered in bits of grass, carrots, slop, and fish. On his head he wore a crooked laurel-wreath crown, and he had another four crowns draped over his arm. "Time for closin' ceremonies, and I don't wanna be late! Hurry, hurry, hurry!"

"He's a mess, Lass!" Kate chuckled. "Looks like he won the Goat Gulp competition. He's wearin' a crown."

"*Oui,* and he also wears the remnants of everything he had to eat to win that crown," Liz added.

Max laughed. "Daft kitty. He smells as nice as he looks. Want me ta thr-r-row him in Nero's lake ta clean up, Lass?"

Gillamon came up behind them. "I must warn you, Liz, that Al will likely not sleep tonight. He ate almost every last one of Bang's coffee berries."

Liz giggled. "I thought he was more hyperactive than usual. Well, at least he enjoyed himself."

"Allllllllllll-righty, dudes, time to present our Animalympics champions with their crowns! Everybody take your seats and we'll get this party started!" Noah shouted from the stage. He looked back behind him and winked at Bang, who gave him the thumbs-up sign. "The Order of the Seven judges will present the winners with their crowns and then each of the two groups will take a side for the Tug O' War. First up, the artsy judges and winners!"

Liz and Nigel walked forward to face the competitors from their artistic events. They held laurel wreaths to crown the victors as they were announced.

"Allow me first of all to congratulate each of you on a job well done," Nigel began. "We had simply splendid talent that made it quite difficult to choose winners. Thank you for your hard work and preparation to compete in the Animalympics." He motioned to Liz to announce the first winner.

"For the singing competition, the winner is . . . Dot the ladybug for her delightful rendition of David's Twenty-Third Psalm!" Liz cheered. "She was the tiniest competitor in these Animalympics!"

Dot flew around happily above them. "Well, heavens be!" she said happily, flying down to the ground. She folded her red and black dotted wings and stood before Nigel and Liz, who exchanged awkward glances. The crown was obviously too large for the ladybug.

Liz smiled and plucked off a single leaf to hand to Dot. *"Félicitations, mon amie!"*

"I am honored!" Dot replied, waving her leaf in the air as the crowd cheered for the tiniest competitor.

"For Poetry Reading, our winner is Dave the boar, but he was anything but a *bore,* I assure you," Nigel quipped. "He gave a riveting recitation from Homer's *Odyssey.*"

Liz placed the laurel leaf crown on Dave's head, and kissed the boar on the cheek. "Well done, *mon ami.*"

"My mother always told me that Pig Latin would come in handy someday," the boar snorted.

"And, finally, we are thrilled to award the crown for Art to our largest contestant of these games, Suda the elephant, for her exquisite painting of sunflowers," Nigel announced.

Tears welled up in the elephant's eyes, as she was immediately over-joyed with her prize. Liz held up the laurel leaf crown and Suda took it with her trunk to place on top of her head. "You have a true gift, Suda. Perhaps you can paint a huge wall mural someday."

"Thank you," the elephant replied shyly. "That would be a dream come true!"

372

"Me next! Me next!" Al shouted, running up to grab the lions to step forward.

"Okay, the Goat Gulp champ will announce the Long Jump champ," announced Noah. "But looks like Al gobbled up all of your bang, Bang!"

Bang chuckled and waved his hand to dismiss the thought. "Bang has other bang! No probrem!"

"The king o' the beasts be the king o' the long jump!" Al shouted, running around the lions. "Here ye go!" He proceeded to throw a laurel leaf crown up onto each of the four lions' heads. "One o' ye choose to be in the Tug o' War! Okay, I'm done, I'm done, I'm done!"

Alexander, Abreas, Leonnatus, and Peucestas laughed at the hyper Al, who continued to run around in circles. "You do it, Alexander," Leonnatus suggested. "We followed you here, so you should have the honor."

"Very well," Alexander replied, straightening his crown. "I'll represent us as the king of the beasts." He let out a victory roar and took his place at the Tug o' War line.

"Next we have the little lady Kate and her jivin' javelin judgment!" Noah cheered.

"The crown goes ta Pinecone the porcupine!" Kate announced. "He be a natural, pullin' out his own javelins for the quick throw!" She put the crown atop the porcupine's quills.

"Never knew I had it in me," stated Pinecone as he looked back at his quills.

"Now let's see if Clarie can answer our Wrestlin' riddle!" Noah shouted as Clarie approached the front. "What did we get with a bear, a hippo, a hyena, and a snake?"

"A laughing hyena crying 'uncle' to squeeze out a winner!" the lamb answered. "Congratulations to our python wrestler, Mabel!" Clarie slipped the crown over the snake's head.

Mabel smiled as the crown slid down her neck. "I could just hug you."

Clarie smiled and backed away. "Thanks, but I think I'd rather not."

Noah held his lanky arms up in the air. "Now the moment *I've* been waiting for! Max, who had the fastest feet in the Foot Race?"

Max trotted up and stood in front of the runners. "This lad has trained every day ta be the best r-r-runner he can be, an' he never gives

373

up," Max exclaimed. He put the wreath over Nate's head. "Nate the lizard be the fastest r-r-runner in these Animalympics!"

"Whoop-whoop! I knew it, Dude!" Noah cheered. "That's my buddy! Nate's great! Nate's great! Nate's great!"

"Um, Max? I can't wear this crown, so I'd like to give it to someone who can. I know he will never give up on his dream," Nate answered, pointing at Flash in the distance who was still crawling slowly along the track to reach everyone. "Flash wins the best dreamer award!"

"That's a gr-r-rand idea, Lad!" Max cheered with a wink. "Come on, let's take it ta him together."

The animals roared in support of Nate's gesture as Max and Nate ran over to meet Flash. Max placed the crown on Flash's head, and Nate held up one of his three-toe hands.

"Flash! Flash! Flash!" Noah started chanting as Nate helped the sloth climb onto Max's back for a victory lap around the track. The crowd chanted his name as the sloth grinned wide, feeling the wind in his face as he never had before.

374

"W-o-w," Flash said. "Thank . . . you . . . Nate. You . . . are . . . my . . . hero."

Nate gave Flash a big hug and whispered in his ear. "Heroes are first champions in the heart, so you're *my* hero, too."

"It just doesn't get any better than this, dudes!" Noah screeched. He was so proud of his friend. "Have these been the best Animalympics ever, or what?"

The animals roared, cheered, squawked, bellowed, and made every sound the animal kingdom knew how to make in celebration of their fun night.

"Nate, I got a special surprise for you! Just you wait, Dude!" Noah said, pointing at him.

Nate wrinkled his brow and shrugged his shoulders. "What?" he mouthed to Noah. He saw Bang up there behind him on the stage. They were doing something. "I know that mischievous look anywhere. What's he up to?" Nate muttered to himself as he got in line for the Tug o' War.

Gillamon whispered in Clarie's ear and she nodded, running up to the stage. "Noah, it's almost 2 AM. Gillamon said we need to hurry so all the animals can get away from Rome."

Noah gave her the thumbs up as she returned to join the Order of the Seven lined up on one end of a long rope, with the seven Animalympics winners lined up on the other end over a line drawn in the sand. A ribbon was tied in the middle of the rope. "Okay, here comes the grand finale, dudes! The Tug o' War! Whichever team gets the ribbon on their side of the line wins. After this, there's a BIG surprise! Then it's time to leave Rome, so here we go!"

Gillamon the anchor-goat was at the back of the Order of the Seven line, followed by Clarie, Max, Kate, Al, Liz, and Nigel. Suda the elephant was at the back of the winner's side, followed by Alexander the lion, Dave the boar, Mabel the snake, Pinecone the porcupine, Nate the lizard, and Dot the ladybug.

"What surprise?" Liz asked Nigel.

"On your mark . . ." Noah started.

"I don't know, my dear," Nigel answered, hanging on to the rope tightly. He glanced up at the stage but couldn't see. "Pass the word back to see if the others know."

"Get set . . ." Noah continued.

Liz turned to Kate. "Do you know about Noah's surprise?"

"Pull!" Noah shouted.

All of the animals on both sides of the rope dug in their heels while the animal crowd cheered.

Kate strained with the rope between her teeth, yanking on it with all her might and punctuating every word. "No . . . I . . . don't!"

Noah turned and ran back to where Bang was busy with an oil lamp on the stage. "This is going to be *awesome,* Dude! What do I do?"

"When ready, right this," Bang instructed the monkey.

"Right this?" Noah asked with a wrinkled brow, looking over at the tug o' war and waving at Nate, who glanced his way with a frown.

"No, *right* this," Bang repeated. "With oir ramp!"

"Ohhhhhhhhhhhhh, *light* this with the *oil lamp!*" Noah repeated back, blowing a raspberry. "Got it!"

Nate looked across the rope and realized he and Dot weren't really doing anything but hanging onto the rope, since they couldn't touch the ground. He looked back up at Noah. "Dot, something tells me I better go see what Noah's up to." He let go and scurried up to the side of the stage and over to Noah and Bang.

Nate's eyes grew wide as Noah held a stick in his hand near an oil lamp. "Um, Noah, what are you doing?" The lizard looked over to see a row of twenty sticks leaning against a stone ledge.

Bang held up his hands and exclaimed, "BANG!"

"Yeah, BANG!" Noah shouted. "Bang brought these sticks from China. He said the humans use them in their celebrations. These sticks light up the sky!"

"Fireworks!" Bang revealed. "BANG!"

"Um, Noah, something tells me this isn't a good idea," Nate cautioned him.

"Why not? It will be fun!" Noah protested, locking Nate in a headlock.

While Nate, Noah, and Bang were debating about lighting the fireworks, they didn't see that something was happening down on the sand of the Circus Maximus. Suddenly all the oil lamps on the track were snuffed out, plunging everyone into darkness. Out of the shadows came a dark figure walking up behind the line of winners. As it reached Suda, it knocked the elephant away with a shove. It then picked off Alexander, Dave, Mabel, Pinecone, and Dot, sending them flying across the sand before they realized what was happening. All the while it hung onto the rope.

"Who turned out the lights?" Al asked as he continued to pull with all his might on the rope.

"Steady," came Gillamon's voice of caution. "Order of the Seven, get ready to move on my mark."

"Come on, Bang! Let's light 'em!" Noah shouted as he and the civet each grabbed an oil lamp and lit the fuses on the row of sticks. Immediately they sizzled and cracked as the fuses caught fire and burned down until the sparks reached the powder charges.

"Get back!" Bang cried, pulling Noah and Nate away from the ignited fireworks. "BANG!"

Suddenly the sticks shot off into the sky in all directions and exploded with colorful, shimmering light like weeping willow trees over the arena. A collective gasp went up from all the animals gathered there in the Circus Maximus. Never had they seen anything like this! Their attention was directed up at the sky so they forgot all about the Tug o' War. Noah, Nate, and Bang stood there with their jaws hanging open and eyes wide at the exploding fireworks above them.

It was then that the Order of the Seven saw what the shadowy figure was—a massive lion.

"Lucifer!" Clarie screamed.

"Care to take me on again, little lamb?" The lion scowled with a wicked laugh. "Time for ME to play GAMES! And I plan to WIN THIS WAR! I TOLD YOU ROME WOULD BE A DEAD END!" He roared and pulled on the rope.

"NOW! LET GO!" Gillamon shouted, letting go of the rope. "Get these animals out of the arena! MOVE!"

Immediately they all let go of the rope and Lucifer went falling backward while the animals split up and sped over to the stands, shouting for the crowd of animals to flee the Circus. Mass chaos and shouting ensued, and the animals began to stampede.

Alexander, stunned when Lucifer hurled him, shook his head to wake himself out of his temporary blackout as he heard the roar of the evil lion. He got to his feet and in turn roared for Abreas, Leonnatus, and Peucestas. The lions saw what was happening and bolted over to pounce on Lucifer. It was a massive brawl of teeth, claws, and blood as the four lions tore into the one evil lion.

Suddenly flames shot up on the outside of the Circus Maximus where the market stalls were located, spreading quickly along the south end of the arena. Noah's eyes filled with fear, and he put his hands up to his face. "What have I done?" he screamed.

"Get everyone out of the Circus!" Nate cried, seeing Max and the others herding the animals out of the gates to safety. He saw a human dart through the crowd to pick up Flash and then run out of the arena to safety. "Hurry!" Nate yelled as he pushed Noah along, who had been staring at the fire in shock. "MOVE!"

"Uh-oh," Bang said. "BAD BANG!" The civet ran off the stage and into the darkness.

"MOVE! R-R-RUN for yer lives!" Max shouted, as did the rest of the Order of the Seven team.

"The fire is spreading!" Liz shouted as she saw the flames leaping quickly outside the walls of the Circus Maximus.

The fire was being fueled by the wooden bleachers at the top of the arena, then jumping from stall to stall and roof to roof of the buildings made with timbers stacked on top of one another. Soon screams of humans were heard as people began to realize what was happening.

Thousands of people now ran through the streets, and the animals split off in every direction to get out of Rome.

Alexander fell back from the lion brawl and saw that the entire Circus Maximus was in flames. It was one oblong inferno. "LEAVE HIM!" he ordered his friends. "RUN!"

Abreas, Leonnatus, and Peucestas released their grips on the evil lion and fell back as Lucifer got to his feet and roared at the top of his lungs. "I AM THE KING OF THE BEASTS!"

Bloody and wounded, the three lions ran off after Alexander, who called to guide them through the flames. "FOLLOW ME! HURRY, BEFORE IT COLLAPSES!" he shouted as he ran to an exit arch.

Just as the four lions reached the exit, the timbers fell, trapping Abreas. Leonnatus and Peucestas cried out, and Alexander shoved them on. "MOVE! GET TO SAFETY! GO!"

As Leonnatus and Peucestas did as instructed and ran off into the night, Alexander struggled to push the fiery timber off his friend whose head was bloody from the fight with Lucifer. Fire singed Alexander's mane but he didn't care.

Abreas coughed and his eyes rolled as he struggled for breath. "Lead the others to safety. Leave me, Alexander."

"ABREAS! NO! This wasn't supposed to happen!" Alexander cried. "You were supposed to LIVE!"

Abreas suddenly grew calm. "But at least I get to die *free*. And for that, I thank you, Alexander."

Another timber started to fall and Alexander jumped out of the way as his friend was lost to a wall of flames. He fell back in anguish, and then shook his head before running off to find the others. He was determined to get them out of Rome alive.

Lucifer slowly walked around the sandy floor of the Circus, reveling in the inferno that encircled him. He smiled when he spotted a discarded laurel leaf crown. He picked it up and placed it on his head with satisfaction. "It's good to be the king." The evil lion's eyes blazed red, reflecting the fire that now was quickly spreading across Rome, lighting up the night sky. He heard the panicked screams of the people and chuckled to himself darkly as he gazed up at the reddened sky.

"Now *that's* what *I* call a fire cloud," Lucifer smirked. "Time to add my own music to this glorious evening."

378

THE FIRE

I can't see anythin'!" Kate shouted, coughing and holding up her paw to shield her eyes from the blinding smoke that filled the streets of Rome.

"Jest stay r-r-right behind me, Lass," Max instructed her. "I'll lead us thr-r-rough!" The Scottie barreled on ahead, darting around panicked humans, raging fire, and falling debris. "Gillamon said ta get ta Ner-r-ro's lake!"

The intense heat was fanned by summer winds that caused new flames to ignite in buildings and objects, before the source fire even reached them. The city of Rome was quickly becoming engulfed in flames. People fled their homes to run from the fire, only to run into another fiery dead end. Destruction reigned in every direction.

"Max!" Al cried as he made out the fire-lit silhouette of Max's pointy ears and distinctive bouncy trot heading towards him. "And Kate's with him!"

"Where?" Nigel pleaded, desperate for a glimpse of their friends. He strained to see them through his filthy spectacles.

"*Merci,* Maker," Liz exclaimed in relief as Max and Kate emerged from a cloud of smoke to reach them. "Are you both alright?"

"Aye, we made it through," Kate answered, trying to catch her breath.

"But there be lots of humans fallin' at every turn," Max reported, coughing from the toxic fumes. "An' the fir-r-re be headin' this way!"

"He knew all along this was going to happen," Liz realized as she gazed on the destruction of Rome. "Gillamon *knew* Rome would burn tonight when he gave us this date two years ago! Why did he have us go through all of the Animalympics?"

"We were able ta save the lives of those animals that would have died in their cages tonight," Kate reminded her. "That be reason enough alone, Lass."

"Aye, but if that daft monkey hadn't set off those fireworks, there wouldn't have been a fire ta save them fr-r-rom!" Max grumbled.

"Then how could the animals have escaped Rome without the humans seein' 'em?" Al wondered.

"There simply must be more to this than we realize," Nigel offered.

"Indeed. The Maker needed you here for what you are about to do together," Clarie told the animals as she walked up behind them, now in human form. "Gillamon knew about the coming fire, but not the extent of it, or everything that would happen as Rome burned. Remember, even he only receives rare glimpses of future events when the Maker deems it necessary. Much is still kept veiled from him." She squatted down with the animals. "We don't have much time."

380

Max, Kate, Nigel, Liz, and Al huddled around Clarie on the bank of this manmade lake while Rome burned behind them. "We're listenin', Lass," Max urged her. "Wha' do we need ta do?"

"You need to save the scrolls of Luke and Acts from Theo's study in the Forum. I've copied them for Theophilus who plans to publish the letters, but the enemy wants them destroyed in the fire. The originals are with Theo at his house, but the fire is headed there, and so am I," Clarie explained. "Gillamon had to get to other parts of Rome to save believers who are in harm's way, which leaves this mission to you."

"Understood," Nigel replied as Clarie turned to leave. "I know the way to Theo's study."

"Rescue those scrolls at all costs and get them to Bella's house. I will meet you there," Clarie answered. "Hurry now, go!"

In an instant she was gone, leaving the animals staring down the Via Sacra that led into the Forum. Flames were already licking at the pagan temple of the six Vestal Virgins who were the supposed guardians of Rome. "I find it ironic that the very temple guarding the sacred fire that is not allowed to go out shall soon be destroyed by fire itself," Nigel remarked, climbing onto Max's back. "Head straight for it, Max. Then turn right at my direction."

"Aye, ever-r-ryone look lively an' stay together," Max instructed them, hearing the roar of the fire consuming another building as voices cried out in despair. "Be r-r-ready for anythin'!"

Together the animals ran towards the Forum just as a wall of fire lit up the heart of Rome.

ANTIUM, JULY 19, AD 64, 5:00 AM

"I bring urgent news for the Emperor!" the Roman legionnaire belted out to the servant at Nero's palace in Antium, pushing his way into the atrium. He held up a scroll. "Where is he?"

"The Emperor is on the veranda," the servant replied, wiping his hands with a towel. "But I cannot tell you if he is awake. There was quite the party here last night."

"This can't wait!" the soldier shouted as he ran down the marble corridor to reach the outside courtyard. There he found Nero and his court sprawled around on the couches of this ornate seaside palace. Platters of half-eaten food and half-full goblets of wine were scattered about. Oil lamps flickered and white gauzy curtains rippled with the sea breeze that wafted through the open-air veranda this early morning hour before sunrise. Nero and the others were sound asleep after their riotous night celebrating Nero's private singing performance. Nero's crown was askew on his head and he hugged his golden lyre as he snored there on the couch.

The soldier grimaced at the mess and condition of the Emperor, but stepped around the others to kneel down next to him. He dared not touch him. He cleared his throat and whispered to try and rouse Nero. "Forgive me, Sir. I bring urgent news from Tigellinus!"

Nero's eyes rolled under his closed eyelids, and he smacked his lips. "Hmmm," he moaned, hugging his lyre to his chest, not waking up.

"Sir, please!" the soldier cried, raising his voice. "Rome burns!"

Immediately Nero's eyes shot open, and he stared at the soldier with a confused look on his face, trying to figure out where he was and who this was kneeling next to him. He blinked and brought a hand up to rub his face, letting his lyre fall to the floor. He slowly rose up on one elbow and felt dizzy from his overindulgence the night before. The room was spinning. "Who sent you?"

"Sir, I come from Tigellinus," the soldier replied, holding out a scroll. Tigellinus was the prefect of the Roman imperial bodyguard, a unit known for its love of ruthless and licentious behavior. He was a close friend of Nero. He had taken the place of Burrus and normally would have accompanied Nero to this palace outside of Rome, but Nero had instructed him to stay behind.

Nero shook his head and snatched the scroll from the soldier, blinking hard as he broke the seal. He held it up to his face while the Roman soldier stood to attention, looking out to sea. The corners of Nero's mouth curved up as he read the report from Rome:

FIRE STARTED IN CIRCUS MAXIMUS. SPREADING RAPIDLY THROUGH PALATINE PALACE, DOMUS TRANSITORIA, AND DOWN TO FORUM. COMPLETE DESTRUCTION LIKELY.

Nero wiped the smile off his face. It was time for him to do what he loved best: to perform. "Oh, what horrific news! I must get to Rome immediately! The people need me," Nero exclaimed in a dramatic voice. He stood up and had to put a hand to his head to steady himself. "Ready my carriage. I must leave within the hour."

"Sir, yes Sir!" the soldier replied in salute. He quickly exited the room.

Nero looked at the sleeping people around him and held the scroll over one of the oil lamps, watching it burn. When it was completely consumed he held his head back with glee. "Well done, Tigellinus!" He laughed and picked up his lyre before staggering out of the room.

THE FORUM, ROME, JULY 19, AD 64, 5 AM

The fire had quickly blazed through the Forum of Julius Caesar and would soon make its way to the adjacent Forum of Augustus. That was the forum where Marcus Antonius received his promotion as Centurion and was sent to Judea for his assignment under Herod the Great. But before the fire reached the Forum of Augustus, it first sought to devour the law office belonging to Marcus's grandson, Theophilus. Lawyers and bankers kept offices in the complex of the Basilica Aemilia, with their financial and legal documents secured behind iron gates.

Nigel pointed through the bars of the gate where the animals huddled. "Theo's study is in that building. But we must get through this gate to reach it!"

"AHHHHHHHH!" Al screamed as flames shot out to singe his backside. He grabbed his tail and held it to his chest, frowning at the smell of burnt fur. "Hurry, let's get the scrolls and get out o' here!"

Max nudged Al. "Get up there an' use that iron claw of yers ta open the gate, Big Al! Then we can get in ta gr-r-rab the scr-r-rolls."

"Aye!" Al hollered, letting go of his tail. He started to climb up the iron bars to reach the lock but had to let go. "OW! Those bars be burnin' up! I can't hold on!"

Liz's eyes glowed against the light of the approaching fire as she studied the gate. "The iron has overheated from the fire! The lock itself might be melted, in which case Albert cannot unlock it. We must find another way!"

Suddenly Noah and Nate came bounding into Max. "We followed you!" Nate shouted.

383

"I'm so sorry! I'm so sorry! This is all my fault!" Noah bawled, wiping away the tears that were streaming down his cheeks. "All those people are dying and losing everything because of me!" He was inconsolable and buried his face in his hands, weeping as he fell onto the ground.

Kate wrapped her paw around Noah. "It were an accident."

Max frowned. "Aye, the biggest accident in histor-r-ry!"

"We do not have time to focus on the cause. We must think about a solution!" Liz exclaimed. She turned to Nate and Noah. "We must find a way in to get Luke's scrolls from Theo's study before they are lost to the fire."

Nigel pointed to the small lizard standing next to him. "Nate and I of course can fit betwixt these narrow bars, but being the smallest animals, we cannot carry the scrolls."

"*Oui*, Max and Kate will need to carry the scrolls," Liz agreed.

"What about me?" Noah begged, holding up his hand. "I can carry them! Please let me help!"

"He's right," Kate said. "An' he can swing over this gate!"

"Yes, Noah and I can get in there, with Nigel leading the way," Nate exclaimed.

Liz studied Noah's monkey hands. "Noah, those iron bars are hot from the fire. Albert could not hold on as he had to wrap his arms around them, but your hands can easily grip them to swing over." Liz explained. "Can you do this?"

"I've got to try!"

"Very well! We will be able to exit on the far side of the building and climb over the wall beyond the Forum of Augustus," Nigel told them. "The fire will not be able to proceed past that point."

"I'll get the r-r-rest of us back a-r-r-round the Forum," Max added. "We'll meet ye back at Bella's house."

"Please be swift and be safe!" Liz said with a paw on Nigel's shoulder.

A huge crashing sound of a collapsed building sent more flames rolling closer to them.

"RIGHT!" Nigel exclaimed. "Noah, get up and over that gate. Nate, you're with me!"

Noah jumped up the bars of the gate, whooping from the scorching heat of the iron. "OW! OW! OW!" he screeched. But he was up and over in no time, running along behind Nigel and Nate.

"The r-r-rest of ye, follow me!" Max shouted and turned to lead the others back down the Via Sacra and out of the Forum.

☧

Nigel led Noah and Nate up a set of marble stairs to Theo's study. "Hurry, look for those scrolls!" he instructed as he darted up onto Theo's desk. "Search for Clarie's copies. There should be two of them."

Noah and Nate split up to scour the study. Noah jumped up onto the shelves, pulling the scrolls out and tossing them onto the floor. "Nope! Nope! Nope! Nope!" he shouted as he tossed the wrong scrolls.

Nate scurried over to a corner where sat a small table. He climbed up the table legs and opened a scroll to read:

> *Many have undertaken to draw up an account of the things that have been fulfilled among us, just as they were handed down to us by those who from the first were eyewitnesses and servants of the word. With this in mind, since I myself have carefully investigated everything from the beginning, I too decided to write an orderly account for you, most excellent Theophilus, so that you may know the certainty of the things you have been taught.*

"I think I found it!" Nate cried. "Doesn't Luke call Theo, 'Most excellent Theophilus'?"

"Indeed, he does!" Nigel exclaimed, jumping off the desk to join Nate on the table. He quickly scanned the scroll. "Brilliant! You've found *Luke!* Now to find *Acts!*" Together Nigel and Nate scanned the other scrolls while Noah searched the upper shelves.

Smoke began to fill the study as fire ignited throughout the Basilica. Flames licked at the doorway.

Nate coughed. "We've got to hurry!"

"It's not here!" Nigel fumed, exasperated. "Where could it be?"

"Looking for something?" came an ominous voice from the doorway.

Noah's eyes grew wide with fear. "I heard that voice in the Circus." He swallowed and slowly turned to see Lucifer blocking their way out.

The lion held up a scroll in his paw.

Clarie battled her way through a collapsed wall of Theo's house, struggling to search for any signs of life while she sought Luke's original scrolls. "Theo! Where are you?" she screamed, holding her arms around her face to protect herself from falling debris. The heat was so intense that she knew if Theo's family were still in this house, they were likely dead. Frantically she ran to the room where Theo kept his documents, including Luke's scrolls. It was a blazing inferno filled with destroyed rubble. "NO!" Clarie cried as she realized that Luke's scrolls had been completely destroyed. There was nothing she could do.

She ran outside to the courtyard, looking for any signs of life. Just as she was about to morph into a bird to take flight she heard the sounds of someone crying. There, huddled under the fountain was a little boy, sobbing with his face buried in his knees, his arms wrapped around his legs, rocking back and forth.

"Leonitus!" she called, running over to the little boy.

Leonitus looked up at Clarie with a dazed look on his face. He was too terrified to speak.

"Let's get you out of here!" she told him as she scooped him up in her arms. "Don't be afraid." With that she took a deep breath and jumped through the fire to reach the only opening she saw to get him out of there alive.

☧

"What a pity," Lucifer boohooed sarcastically. "Now look what you did, Noah. Not only have you destroyed Rome by starting the fire, but the world will never read about the acts of the apostles." He held the scroll over a flame and chuckled as it caught fire. "So much for all those lovely stories written down for all time. Poof. They're gone. Like they never happened." The lion chuckled darkly.

Nigel scanned the room, knowing they had to quickly escape. He spotted the tiny window high above the shelves where smoke billowed outside. While Lucifer continued to taunt them, Nigel whispered under his breath, "Noah, take Nate and Luke's scroll. While I distract him, get up there and escape out that window. I have a rescue plan and will meet you outside. GO!"

Noah didn't reply. He shook with fear and crushing guilt, but did as Nigel told him. Nate climbed onto his back.

"Those stories may be repeated out loud, but I'll make sure they get filled with error," Lucifer continued. "Except for Stephen's stoning. I rather like that part. I'll make sure Christians hear only the stories of death for sharing the Good News. I'll intimidate them until they are afraid to speak. Just like *you*, Noah! Or I'll silence permanently whoever dares to spread the word, like Theo."

Nigel jumped off the table and ran back over to Theo's desk. "What do you mean?"

Lucifer laughed. "Theo's house was one of the first to go. I especially loved fanning the flames to destroy that house. Yes, I'm afraid the original scrolls are gone. And so is Theo. The legacy of the Antonius family ends tonight!"

Nigel's heart sank, but he boldly faced the lion while Noah climbed up the shelves. "Do you really think you can stop the Maker's plans to tell the world the Good News? With every martyr that dies for sharing Christ, ten more rise up in his place!" He slowly walked over to Armandus's oil lamp that Theo kept on his desk.

Lucifer turned to face Nigel as flames shot up the wall to the ceiling. "Just wait until I turn up the heat! You think THIS is a fire?" he roared, swiping his massive paw at the desk and toppling it over.

Noah yelped and scurried up the shelves to jump out the window.

Lucifer tore through the study as he erupted in anger. Nigel was nowhere to be found.

☧

"Where did you find him, Samuel?" Bella asked, holding Leonitus in her arms. Her face was stained with grime and tears. She rocked the little boy back and forth.

"In the courtyard, under the fountain," Clarie answered softly. "Bella, I'm so sorry about Theo and his wife. They were gone before I could reach them."

"I hate lions," Leonitus muttered.

Bella and Clarie looked at one another in confusion. "What about lions?"

"I hate them," Leonitus repeated, his lip trembling. "We couldn't leave. The lion was there."

Bella pressed Leonitus to her chest. "There are no lions here. You are safe now." She looked up at Clarie with a confused look on her face and with her eyes full of tears. "Come, let me put you to bed."

Clarie nodded while Bella carried her grandson to the bedroom. She sighed heavily and shook her head with sadness over the tragedy and loss of this night. She walked outside into the courtyard where the rest of the animals waited for her in Bella's garden.

387

☧

The animals were quiet, exhausted from the trauma of this night, and reeling from the tragic loss of Theo and the scroll of Acts.

"That dear boy lost his parents, and Bella has lost not only her husband, but now her son," Liz wept. "Lucifer has been out to destroy the family of Antonius ever since Jerusalem."

"Aye," Max agreed sadly. "At least Bella an' the lad have each other. An' at least the fire hasn't come ta this house. Not yet anyway."

Nigel staggered into the courtyard, covered in soot. Max didn't even recognize him. "Stop r-r-right there, ye wee r-r-rat!"

"*Rat?!* Max, old boy, you must be suffering from distress!" Nigel argued. "I'm simply covered in soot."

"It IS Mousie!" Al cheered, running over to the little mouse. "Noah and Nate said they lost ye when Theo's office were on fire!"

"I escaped using Armandus's oil lamp over me as a shield. I looked rather like a turtle as I scurried through the flames untouched," Nigel explained.

"Thank goodness!" Nate cheered, embracing the little mouse. "Noah and I thought you were a goner."

Noah sat sobbing on the grass while Kate tried to comfort him. "Look, Noah, Nigel is here now. I told ye he were okay."

Noah looked over and saw Al giving Nigel a big hug. "I'm glad. But I'm so sorry about the others," Noah whimpered. He was beside himself with grief. "I didn't mean to burn down Rome."

"Noah, it's not your fault," Clarie told him as she sat down on the grass next to him. "Yes, you set off the fireworks but this fire was intentionally set."

"Ya hear that, Noah?" Nate exclaimed, wrapping his tiny hands around Noah's cheeks. "The fire isn't your fault!"

"You're just trying to make me feel better," Noah argued. "I destroyed Rome. I saw our fireworks go over the wall and then the flames shoot up into the sky. Lucifer even *told* me it was all my fault!"

388

Clarie stuck her face by Noah's. "Noah, look at me. Lucifer started the fire. But he'd love nothing better than to make you think this fire is your fault so he can heap guilt on you."

"Aye, he be a liar, Lad," Max added. "He'll make ye think things that jest aren't so. Tr-r-rust me, I know."

Noah wrinkled his brow with a confused look. "Really? You're sure? I'm not to blame?"

Clarie shook her head. "No. Nero has wanted a catastrophic fire to wipe out most of Rome so he can proceed with building his new palace. This fire is from his evil, not from your fun."

Noah blinked his eyes and smiled through his tears, wrapping his lanky arms around her neck. "Thank you, sweet lady. I didn't know how I could fix what I broke this time!"

Nate punched Noah in the shoulder. "You still should have listened to me about the fireworks."

"Well, Noah, not only did ye not start the fire, but ye saved Luke's scroll," Kate affirmed him.

"*Oui,* but we've lost Acts," Liz said sadly. "The recorded miracle of Pentecost is gone. Paul's story is gone. The details of his journeys are gone. The story of the birth of the church is gone."

Max growled. "Aye, Paul's other letters won't be able ta help believ-ers understand the cost that were paid ta spr-r-read the gospel."

"Nor will believers grasp the power of the Holy Spirit without understanding how he has worked with the apostles. I suppose we shall have to try and piece it together again and rewrite it as best as we can," Nigel offered.

"No need," Clarie declared.

"But Clarie, we must *try!*" Liz argued.

"Max is right, Noah. The enemy is a liar and a deceiver." Clarie smiled, holding out her hand. "Where is Luke's scroll?"

Nigel and Nate shared a confused look. Noah picked up the scroll they had escaped with out of Theo's burning study. "Here," Noah answered meekly, handing her the scroll.

Clarie proceeded to unroll the scroll. "You didn't read far enough." The animals gathered around to see what she was talking about.

In my former book, Theophilus, I wrote about all that Jesus began to do and to teach until the day he was taken up to heaven, after giving instructions through the Holy Spirit to the apostles he had chosen. After his suffering, he presented himself to them and gave many convincing proofs that he was alive. He appeared to them over a period of forty days and spoke about the kingdom of God.

389

Liz and Nigel exchanged looks of shock before smiles erupted on their faces and they shared a huge embrace.

"Um, what's going on?" Nate wanted to know.

"I must say, you are one clever scribe, my dear!" Nigel exclaimed.

Liz shook her head in happy relief. "Nate, Clarie copied Luke's sec-ond letter of Acts on the same scroll following Luke's first letter about the life of Jesus."

"Lucifer made you *think* he was burning the remaining copied scroll of Acts," Clarie explained.

"So that means we still have both of Luke's books, right?" Nate asked.

"Right!" Liz and Nigel answered at the same time.

The animals erupted in cheers and celebration over this surprising victory. Luke and Acts were safe, having been snatched from the enemy's jaws. "I'll make sure this scroll gets into the right hands for publishing," Clarie assured them, standing to leave.

"Thank goodness!" Noah said, scooping up Nate in his arms. "Did ya hear that, Dude? I didn't burn down Rome, and both of Luke's books are safe!"

"Noah and Nate, you are free to leave Rome now, or what's left of it," Clarie told them. "I've arranged for a ship to leave the port of Ostia. Flash is already aboard, but he could use some friends to help him get somewhere safe. Would you be able help him?"

Nate grinned at the others. "Um, yeah, I'd love to help Flash! Besides, I think Noah and I should be going before anything else happens."

"Yeah, let's go before I almost not destroy something else," Noah agreed.

"*Merci* for all you've done, *mes amis,*" Liz exclaimed, reaching her paws out to give them a farewell embrace.

"Thank you for helping me realize my dream for the Animalympics, Liz," Nate answered shyly.

"Yeah, even though it ended with a BANG!" Noah added, jumping around to hug everyone goodbye.

"Ye may be a daft monkey, but I'll miss ye, Lad," Max said with a grin.

Nigel shook Nate's hand. "We shall never forget you."

"Me, neither," Nate replied with a smile. "Thanks for allowing us to help you with Luke's scroll."

Kate smiled as Noah kissed her on the cheek. "God speed ta ye."

"Here, Lad. One for the road," Al said, handing a banana to Noah.

"For ME? Thanks, Dude," Noah exclaimed with wide eyes, taking the banana and bonking Al on the head. "Come on, Nate. Let's go."

"Give me a minute with my friends, and I'll be right out to take you to the port," Clarie told them.

"Okay, bye everyone," Nate said. "We'll see ya again sometime." Together he and Noah left Bella's garden.

Clarie turned to the other animals. "They need to clear out of Rome, and you need to prepare for what's coming. Far more difficult battles are on the way. Liz and Al, stay here with Bella and Leonitus. You'll be safe here for a while. Gillamon will see you soon, after the fire is out."

"We shall, *mon amie,*" Liz answered her. "How long will the fire burn?"

"I don't know, but so far the humans are unable to contain it," Clarie answered. "Max, Kate, and Nigel, you need to get back to Paul and John. Word of what's happened in Rome will spread quickly to Asia." She pointed to the Seven seal that appeared on the Libertas statue.

"Aye, we'll leave r-r-right away," Max declared as Nigel prepared to break the Seven seal. "An' we'll be r-r-ready ta fight."

"Stay strong, my friends. This battle with the enemy is far from over," Clarie warned them as she turned to leave. "In fact, it's only just begun."

42

NERO'S BLAME

Report, Tigellinus," Nero said casually as he adjusted the neckline of his tragedian costume, making it fit just right. He slowly waved his arms to see the flow of the golden silk fabric as he walked to the balcony. "Tell me about the extent of the damage. And the relief efforts. Are they working?"

Gaius Ofonius Tigellinus wiped his mouth with the back of his hand. He set down his bountiful plate of food and picked up a scroll from the table with a smirk. Tigellinus was a stocky man in his fifties, with silvery hair cropped short and milky gray eyes that contrasted with his black, wiry eyebrows. He scratched the stubble on his chin as he scanned the latest report. "You mean, do the people see you as a hero for coming to their rescue?"

"Of course! I brought you back from Caligula's exile for a reason. You have the gift of gathering intelligence, so tell me what is going on with the people," Nero replied, reaching for his lyre. He turned to gaze out from this Tower of Macenas, overlooking the gardens untouched by fire. He scanned the beautiful grounds filled with pavilions, lovely lanes lined with flowers, shrines, marble fountains, statues, and terraces. He then frowned to see the crowds of homeless and destitute people now encamped all over the place. "I've thrown open the Field of Mars and my own gardens for the fugitive masses. I've brought food from Ostia and cut the price of corn. I had *better* be appreciated for this!"

"Of the fourteen regions of Rome, so far three have been completely leveled, seven are burning, and four remain intact," Tigellinus reported. "But the people are grumbling over this second outbreak that started on my estate after the fire was under control. They may suspect something, Nero."

Nero ignored the report and fixed his gaze on a wall of flames in the distance. He cocked his head as he studied the shape of the fire. "They almost look like flowers springing forth from the earth."

"What does?" Tigellinus asked, tossing the scroll onto the couch. "Did you even hear what I said? Almost *seventy* percent of Rome has been destroyed!"

"The flames. The artist in me sees the beauty of the flames," Nero replied. "The city landscape is scorched and cleared. Therefore, Rome is a blank canvas of a garden! New flowers can spring forth as new buildings and temples and monuments! Especially *golden* ones."

Tigellinus crossed his arms over his chest. "You mean your new golden *palace*. Your Domus Aurea."

Nero smiled and pulled his fingers across the strings of his lyre. "I shall call this new city . . . Neropolis." Ever the dramatist, the Emperor held back his head and feigned great sorrow. "But first we must weep for the fall of Rome! Just like the other great cities that fell, as Troy of old. Oh, the tragedy of it all! I must grieve through song!" He proceeded to fill the room with music as he sang about the fall of Troy.

Lucifer sat in the courtyard below while Nero strolled along the balcony strumming his golden lyre and singing *The Sack of Ilium*.

"Sing, my pitiful minion. Sing it loud for all to hear."

The massive lion laughed to himself and walked toward the base of the Esquiline Hill where the fire had halted. He delighted in watching the shadows of the flames dance along the wall of this building still left standing. "Now to point the blame to Nero, so he'll be forced to place the blame exactly where I want it—on the precious Christians." Lucifer popped out his claw and carved into the wall as the shadowy flames danced around his words:

THOUGH NERO MAY PLUCK THE CORDS OF A LYRE,
AND THE PARTHIAN KING THE STRING OF A BOW,
HE WHO CHANTS TO THE LYRE WITH HEAVENLY FIRE
IS APOLLO AS MUCH AS HIS FAR-DARTING FOE.

The brick-faced Roman Senate House *Curia Julia,* had survived the fire. Senators walked through the still smoldering ruins of the Forum, climbed the single flight of steps and poured in through the tall bronze doors, crossing the ornately tiled floor to enter this hallowed chamber. Many of them had lost their homes as well as loved ones and possessions in the fire. The soaring ceilings echoed with the low murmurs of senators gathering for this potentially explosive meeting while they awaited Nero's arrival. Despite the massive recovery efforts underway these past few weeks, all of Rome was on edge and the arrows of blame were desperate for a target. Surrounding the rows of senators in this chamber, marble statues looked on with fixed gazes, standing as silent witnesses for the proceedings that would determine that exact target of blame. And one of those statues was listening to every word.

"The rumors have spread as quickly as the fire," a senator whispered to another. "The people have even written on the walls of the city about Nero singing while Rome burned."

"It's disgusting," spat the senator in a hushed tone. "How dare he think he can do whatever he so desires! The only thing I wish that had burned was the Emperor himself."

"We must take action soon," the other senator replied.

Suddenly a clerk called the senate to attention, as Nero entered the building. Everyone stood in obligatory respect for the Emperor who strode confidently through their midst, adorned in a purple robe with his golden crown firmly in place. He nodded to the senators as he walked past, and took his seat with confidence, draping his robe across the steps at his feet.

"Tragedy. Sadness. Weeping. Mourning," Nero began dramatically, setting the tone. "We've all been through the fire of sorrow. And the people deserve a new beginning."

"They deserve answers!" shouted a senator.

"The people blame *you,* Nero!" another senator echoed. "The Roman Senate wouldn't approve of your building plans, so they believe you took matters into your own hands to accomplish what *you* wished. Not what Rome decided."

Nero wore a look of shock and deep anguish. He placed his hand over his heart, as if an arrow had pierced him to the core. "Grief causes irrational thinking. The people cry out for answers! Of course they do!"

Nero exclaimed, standing with outstretched arms. "And I shall give it to them, for I know who set the fire. I even have proof from the very lips of the guilty ones."

A buzz of murmuring erupted among the senators as Nero clapped his hands and motioned for Tigellinus to come forward. The Roman prefect wore his ornate armor and impressive red-plumed helmet, portraying the power and might of Rome. He held a scroll and nodded to Nero as he stood in the center of the floor. The governing body of Rome sat with rapt attention for what he had to say.

"I've asked my prefect to read you a report that will provide the answer the people need. Tigellinus is a brilliant intelligence officer as well as a faithful military commander. Listen as he reads the report about the true arsonists of Rome: the *Christians.*" Nero took his seat and motioned for Tigellinus to proceed.

"We have thoroughly examined the motives of the sect who call themselves 'Christians.' The founder of their sect, one Christus, was crucified by Pontius Pilate during the reign of Tiberius," Tigellinus began. "He was quoted to have said, 'I come not to bring peace, but a sword.' Even though this movement was at first thought to be squashed, it erupted again in Judea and even Rome. But it has spread. Repeated reports abound as to the trouble that Christians have caused across the empire. An eyewitness brought us this report about their ring leader, Peter, who rallied three thousand of them in Jerusalem. Listen to the words he told these Christian followers about their God:

> "Even on my servants, both men and women,
>   I will pour out my Spirit in those days.
> I will show wonders in the heavens
>   and on the earth,
>   blood and fire and billows of smoke.
> The sun will be turned to darkness
>   and the moon to blood
>   before the coming of the great and dreadful day of the Lord."

The senators looked around at one another, murmuring over this revelation. Nero studied them to see if they were taking the bait before he spoke. "But this is just a *segment* of prophecy that their leader quoted.

Listen to the larger text where he took those words." He waved his hand over at the prefect who nodded and held up his report to read more. "Continue, Tigellinus."

"Yes, we researched to find the source of Peter's words, and he quoted from a prophet named Joel. It is alarming to say the least. The soldiers of Rome do as our Emperor commands to protect the empire. And these Christians have formed a new kind of army to defend theirs. Listen to what the prophet foretells about the attack of the servants of their God:

> "Let all who live in the land tremble,
>   for the day of the Lord is coming.
> It is close at hand—
>   a day of darkness and gloom,
>   a day of clouds and blackness.
> Like dawn spreading across the mountains
>   a large and mighty army comes,
> such as never was in ancient times
>   nor ever will be in ages to come.
> Before them fire devours,"

Tigellinus stopped and paused for effect, looking around the senate,

> "behind them a flame blazes."

Gillamon in the statue of Caesar cringed. *They're twisting Scripture to make it mean something it does not.*

"We have heard these Christians are a suspicious, strange group of people," a senator offered with a raised hand. "They have a ritual of holding people under water to simulate drowning."

Another senator spoke up. "Yes, and they hold these 'love feasts' where they supposedly eat the body of their Christus and even drink his blood!"

Now they are twisting the observance of Baptism and the Lord's Supper, which they do not understand, Gillamon thought.

"Not to mention they call each other 'brother and sister,' even their own spouses. What does this possibly mean?" another voice cried out.

"Yes, but despite all of this strange behavior, we Romans are tolerant of every religion," an older senator reasoned.

"Except for those who do not sacrifice to Rome's gods for the protection of Rome. Every Roman citizen must do his part to appease the gods," another argued.

"EXACTLY!" Nero exclaimed as he got to his feet. "These Christians are guilty of treason against Rome, not for what they believe, but for what they *don't* believe. They don't believe in Rome's gods, let alone our beliefs! You've heard how their god seeks to devour with fire. So you see, this army of Christians took Judean prophecies into its own hands and decided to show Rome that its god is more powerful by making Rome burn!"

The senate broke out in debate and further murmuring. Nero locked eyes with Tigellinus and had to suppress a grin as he saw some heads nodding around the great hall. Although he had seemingly persuaded a few of them to accept his accusation of the Christians, he only needed a few to deflect blame and make his unilateral decision as Emperor. Finally he raised his hands to dismiss the matter.

"So there you have it, senators. I rule that the Christians are to blame for setting the fire, and from this moment I declare them to be outlaws of Rome, deserving punishment for their crime. Rome must have justice, and I give you my word that justice will be served. I must get back to the business of the people and rebuild their city." Nero stood to leave and noticed the Altar of Victory that was prominent at this end of the hall. Caesar Augustus had erected this statue of Winged Victory who stood on a globe with an outreached hand holding a wreath. She signified Rome's military dominance of the world. And in this moment, she signified for Nero his dominance of this situation. He made the Christians the scapegoat for his blame, so the people would now look elsewhere to point their angry fingers. He smiled to himself as he strode out confidently from the senate floor. *I'll put the Christians up on pedestals for all of Rome to see.*

As Tigellinus escorted Nero down the steps of the senate building, Nero muttered under his breath, "Well done, my friend. Make the Christians the main attraction at the next games over in my circus. The people will be ecstatic to cheer on the lions to devour those accused of setting the fire."

"Yes, the gods spared the Circus of Nero from the fire, so it is a fitting place to put the criminals on display for the people," Tigellinus replied coldly.

397

"It was an especially nice touch with that quote from their ring-leader about the fire and blood moons," Nero said with a finger pointed in the prefect's chest armor. "What was his name again?"

"Peter," Tigellinus replied.

"Hmmm, that's not the right name I'm thinking of. There was someone else the Jews accused of being out in front with spreading all those Christian ideas," Nero replied as he thought a moment. Finally he snapped his fingers. "Paul! Paul was the other ring leader of the Christians, but I let him go free a couple of years ago."

"But we can't have that now, can we, Sir?" Tigellinus asked, leaning in to Nero.

"Indeed not," Nero replied with a grin. "Peter and Paul. Find them and bring them to me. I might play with their followers in the arena, but I need to show the people that I've cut the head off of this Christian sect by killing their leaders." He raised his eyebrows at the thought. "Ooooh, what a splendid idea!"

398

"Pilate crucified their original Christian leader. Perhaps they should suffer the same fate," Tigellinus suggested.

"You know how I like variety," Nero jested with his hand in the air. "I have many creative ideas for how to punish these Christians. Bring Peter and Paul to me. We'll put them on trial, and then I'll decide something spectacular for their demise." Nero's eyes lit up with evil intent. "But first, order more lions for the arena. The people deserve to watch a good kill while they wait for the main event."

CAT O' COMBS

T he enemy has secured the fate of the Christians here in Rome,"
Gillamon relayed quietly. "Peter and the other believers are
not safe. They must find a secret place to gather."

"Then Bella's home is no longer a safe place for believers to meet,"
Liz whispered back to the statue of Libertas.

"Indeed, but all of this will lead to good," Gillamon replied. "It is
time for Peter to pick up his pen." At the sound of human voices, the
statue went still.

Liz turned to see Mark and Silas walking into the garden with Peter
and Bella, speaking in hushed tones. Al came running up to Liz with a
distraught look on his face.

"What is happening, Albert?" Liz asked in alarm.

"Nero be killin' the Christians in his circus and in his gardens in
all sort o' terrible ways!" Al lamented. "Mark and Silas jest arrived in
Rome, and Peter were tellin' them all aboot it. They be tryin' to figure
out what to do."

Liz shook her head sadly. "*Oui,* Gillamon just told me that the
Christians must find a place to meet in safety. But where can they go?"

Al thought a moment and tapped his chin. "Clarie told me long ago
that I needed to learn Rome like the back o' me paw."

Liz placed her paw on Al's shoulder. "Albert, do you know of a place
where Christians could be safe from the eyes of Nero?"

Al looked around the garden as if prying ears were listening in to
what he had to say. He leaned in to whisper to Liz. "I know a secret

spot." He pointed his paw toward the ground. "But I never understood what it were aboot. Some strange thing aboot cats and honey. Oh, and fish. I never could find any o' that, but I bet humans wouldn't be caught dead down there. It be a dark and scary place."

Liz wrinkled her brow. "Down there? Are you saying this place is underground?"

"Aye," Al whispered with a wink. "I can take ye there."

"Then let us go, Albert. We do not have time to lose!" Liz said with urgency as she nudged him out of the garden.

It took a moment for their eyes to adjust from the bright sunlight outside. Al led Liz down a five-foot wide corridor with ceilings eight-feet high. Into the walls on either side of the corridor were several rows of long, hollowed-out recesses. To Al they looked like honeycombs in a beehive.

400

"What kind o' cat do ye think lives down here in these honeycombs, Liz?"

Liz stopped when she noticed that one of the recesses was covered with a marble slab. Fish were carved into the slab, along with writing. She walked over to study the slab. "I do not believe cats live down here at all, Albert."

He walked up next to her and pointed to the fish. "Well, they call this place the cat o' combs, and there's even pictures o' fish, so I jest figured cats lived down here."

"No *cat* resides down here, Albert," Liz answered matter-of-factly. She placed her paw on the marble slab. "But dead humans do." She read the inscription on the slab. *"Being called away, he went in peace."*

"Ye mean to tell me there be dead laddies in these honeycombs!?" Al's eyes widened, and he swallowed hard as he put his paws up to his mouth.

Liz walked farther down the corridor and stopped at another section of slabs with writing. She read one of the inscriptions aloud.

"OSSA NICENIS HIC SITA SUNT. SUPERI, VIVITE, VALETE; INFERI, HAVETE, RECIPITE, NICENEM. *The bones of Nicen are buried here. Ye who live in the upper air, live on, farewell. Ye shades below, hail; receive Nicen,"* Liz translated. "This must be a pagan tomb. Albert, these are the *catacombs*, not the cat o' combs. It is the place where humans bury their dead."

"And I thought humans wouldn't be caught dead down here!" Al cried.

Liz turned to read another inscription. *"Live for the present hour, since we are sure of nothing else."* She looked up to read another. *"I lift my hands against the gods who took me away at the age of twenty though I had done no harm."* She frowned, walking on through a row of tombs. *"Quel dommage.* These pagans have no hope for life after death. Here is another: *Traveler, curse me not as you pass, for I am in darkness and cannot answer."*

"What aboot these pictures, Lass?" Al asked, pointing to a shepherd, an anchor, and a ship with sails heading to a lighthouse. "That one looks like Noah's Ark."

Liz studied the symbols. *"Oui!* These are symbols that believers would use. Listen to what is written here: *Farewell, my dear one, in peace, with the holy souls. Farewell in Christ.* These tombs must belong to believers."

"So that must mean the Christians know aboot these cat o' combs."

Liz tried to peer down the endless corridor. "Albert, how far do these corridors go?"

"They go on for miles, Lass," Al answered with a gulp, thinking of how many humans could be buried down here.

"Perfect!" Liz said excitedly. "Plenty of room then, no?"

Al's eyes widened. "Ye can't be sayin' ye want to fill up these cat o' combs with more Christians, Lass!"

"That is exactly what I am saying, *cher* Albert," Liz answered, sauntering back toward the exit. "But *live* ones."

☧

Leonitus sat alone quietly in the garden, mindlessly jabbing a stick into the ground.

"He looks so sad," Peter told Bella, his heart going out to the little boy.

Bella glanced over at her grandson. "He lost his world in the fire. He doesn't say much. I am worried about him, Peter."

Peter exhaled through his nose and crossed his arms over his chest.

"I'm worried about all of us, but I know the Lord has us in his care. He will strengthen us to get through this ordeal. Jesus told us that we would be persecuted. I once boasted that I would follow him to the grave, yet I denied him and hid as a coward. Now I know I will follow him to the grave, but wish to hide for the sake of serving the church. But I am putting you in harm's way by being here."

"But where will you go?" Bella asked him.

"I don't yet know, but feel I must not leave the believers in Rome with this wave of persecution taking over the city," Peter replied. "You've been gracious to host us here, and I pray that your position as the widow of a Roman centurion will keep you safe for now."

Al walked into the garden and noticed Leonitus sitting there by himself. He frowned to see the little boy so sad and walked over to sit down next to him. Leonitus smiled and held up his stick. *"Want to chase me, Lad?"* Al meowed, pawing at the stick in the boy's hand. Leonitus reached out to grab Al's tail. Al took off running, with the little boy chasing after him, wielding his stick as a sword.

402

Bella smiled. "Ari is the only thing that seems to make Leonitus smile."

Leonitus giggled and ran past them. Al ducked under a shrub. "I'll get you, Lion! You can't hide from me."

Peter grinned to see the little boy playing with his cat. "Leonitus calls Ari a lion. Does he still talk about the lion he saw the night of the fire? I wonder if he imagined it."

"If he speaks about the lion, he always does so in anger. I've wondered about that lion. It could have escaped from the Circus area during the fire," Bella answered. "I don't know which scared Leonitus more that night. The fire or the lion."

"Both seek to devour, don't they? Just like Nero chasing after the Christians," Peter answered with a frown. "We need to find a hiding place like Ari."

"Come out, cat!" Leonitus called, trying to reach Al under the shrub. "Where did you go? CAT! CAT! Where did you go?"

Mark and Silas joined them in the courtyard. "We better get going, Peter," Mark said. "We just received word that more Christians were killed last night. Lions in the arena." He handed Peter a scrap of parchment. "And the note was signed with a strange message, a passage from Job."

Liz sat on a nearby wall in the garden, curling her tail up and down as she listened to their report.

"We can't stay here," Silas urged him as Peter took the note. "But where should we go?"

"If only you would hide me in the grave and conceal me till your anger has passed," Peter furrowed his brow as he read the note with the mysterious Job reference.

Come now, Peter, put this together, Liz meowed. *Think!*

"The Lord will show us. I feel we need to warn other believers that they will be hunted down. There are arenas all across the Roman Empire, and trials and persecution are coming, as long as Nero's anger . . . ," Peter said, stopping short as he watched Leonitus hunt for the cat. *Hunt. Arenas. Lions. Cat. Hide. Grave.* He turned to them. "I think I have an idea."

☧

The oil lamp flickered off the wall of the catacombs on the outskirts of Rome. This place of solemn burial had become a place of sanctuary for the believers who gathered here to pray, worship, and support one another. As long as believers went about their daily lives and did not gather to worship in their homes, they would be at less risk for discovery by Nero's men. Peter knew he would have to lie low and out of sight, but other believers could have some sort of normal life as long as they kept quiet above ground.

Liz and Al sat by, watching Peter and Silas work on a letter for Silas to take to the churches in Asia. "I am relieved that the Christians have a place where Nero's men will not think to look for them. The '*cat o' combs*' was the perfect idea. *Merci* for being you, Albert."

"It comes easy for me, Lass," Al grinned. He looked over and saw Leonitus sitting on the floor next to Bella. "I think I need to go be me for the wee lad." He got up and went over to sit by the boy.

Liz smiled at her sweet mate and then turned her gaze to look at Peter as he leaned over Silas's shoulder, seeing what he had written so far. A lump caught in her throat as she was reminded of all the times she had watched Paul do the same as Silas or Timothy took down letters that he dictated. *Oh, Maker, I know that Peter cannot hide down here forever. And neither can Paul, wherever he is in Asia. The enemy isn't about to give up his fight to hunt them down. But I know your grace will be sufficient for them when the time comes.* Liz smiled at the words that Peter spoke to encourage believers. She already knew that the timelessness of Peter's words would find their way into the coming New Testament with this letter. The enemy would never give up the hunt, and believers throughout time would need to hear these same words from the one Jesus called the "Rock."

"Dear friends, do not be surprised at the fiery ordeal that has come on you to test you, as though something strange were happening to you. But rejoice inasmuch as you participate in the sufferings of Christ, so that you may be overjoyed when his glory is revealed," Peter said, pausing to give Silas a chance to get the words down on parchment. "If you are insulted because of the name of Christ, you are blessed, for the Spirit of glory and of God rests on you. If you suffer, it should not be as a murderer or thief or any other kind of criminal, or even as a meddler. However, if you suffer as a Christian, do not be ashamed, but praise God that you bear that name. So humble yourselves under the mighty power of God, and at the right time he will lift you up in honor. Give all your worries and cares to God, for he cares about you."

404

Peter looked over at Leonitus and considered the impact that terrible night of the fire had had on this little boy. He wondered if that lion he had seen was real or imagined. Either way, Leonitus's story was a picture of what was happening to the church. The enemy wanted to seek out and destroy all the children of God. The hunt wasn't isolated to one boy, or one disciple, or one apostle. It was universal to the entire family of Christians, whether in Rome or throughout the empire. Peter knew they needed an image they could identify with to stay strong.

"Stay alert! Watch out for your great enemy, the devil. He prowls around like a roaring lion, looking for someone to devour. Stand firm against him, and be strong in your faith. Remember that your family of believers all over the world is going through the same kind of suffering you are."

Peter paused and thought of Jesus' words to him that day on the beach long ago, when he restored Peter after his denials. Jesus told him what his earthly future would hold: *I am telling you the truth: when you were young, you used to get ready and go anywhere you wanted to; but when you are old, you will stretch out your hands and someone else will tie you up and take you where you don't want to go.* Peter knew what was coming, but he no longer cared about this earthly future except to serve Christ faithfully until the end.

He ran his hand across the marble slab belonging to a fallen believer here in the catacombs. The picture of a shepherd holding a lamb around his shoulders was etched next to the words, *Victorious in peace and in Christ*. Jesus had also told Peter that morning on the beach, "Feed my sheep." And that is what he planned to do until his last day. Peter realized that what he and the other Christians were experiencing was part of taking up their cross to follow Jesus. In the end, they would follow their Good Shepherd to eternal joy, and the days of these lion hunts would end.

"Are you ready, Peter?" Silas asked, dipping his pen in the ink to continue writing.

"Yes, my friend, I am." Peter smiled and looked around the catacombs before continuing to dictate his message of hope to fearful believers everywhere. "In his kindness God called you to share in his eternal glory by means of Christ Jesus. So after you have suffered a little while, he will restore, support, and strengthen you, and he will place you on a firm foundation. All power to him forever! Amen."

405

44

MAMERTINE

TROAS, MARCH AD 66

A stiff breeze fluttered through the dark blue canopy that shielded the market stalls from the intense Mediterranean sun. Luke meandered through the bustling market of Troas, surveying herbs and lifting them to his nose to smell for their freshness. One of his medical interests involved trying different herbal ointments for healing various conditions. As Paul's personal physician, Luke continually sought to help the apostle maintain good health. During those early years of Paul's repeated beatings on his missionary journeys, Luke formulated an especially soothing salve to assist with lacerations and wounds. He picked up a sprig of orange sea-buckthorn berries and smiled, thinking of the day he first met Paul. *That little black cat was a brilliant thief.*

Liz had followed Luke home from this very market and took the sprig of orange berries from his desk so he would chase her to where Paul was staying. Luke administered ointment from the berries to Paul's wounds, and then Paul shared with him about Jesus. That day changed the course of Luke's life, for not only did he discover Jesus as Savior, he began his new life journey as personal physician, fellow-worker, and scribe for Paul. *Thank you, Lord, for using sea-buckthorn to lead me to Paul. And thank you that I haven't had to use it on Paul in a long time.* These years of freedom since Paul's release in Rome had been relatively peaceful, and Luke was grateful that the aging apostle had been spared the wrath of the whip.

A vendor in a nearby stall spotted Luke roaming the market. His booth displayed numerous idols for sale, but lately potential buyers were scarce. His eyes narrowed and he grumbled under his breath, picking up his hammer to strike forceful blows to a sheet of copper. His racket caught the attention of a group of Roman soldiers who stood in the street next to where he banged away at the metal. One of the soldiers gave a singular laugh and walked over to the vendor.

"You look like you want to murder that copper," the Roman said with a laugh, picking up a tiny idol of Artemis.

The coppersmith clenched his jaw and brought his hammer down hard again. "I wouldn't mind if someone's head were on my anvil instead of this copper, I'll admit."

"Oh, and who might that be?" the soldier asked him.

"That preacher, Paul. When he brought his ideas of worshipping one God to Ephesus, I lost so much business that I had to come here and try to make a living. *Now* he's preaching here, and it's happening all over again," he vented. "He and his followers are bad for business and bad for the economy. Rome certainly is losing taxes on me anyway."

407

The soldier turned to the other soldiers recently arrived to Troas from Rome. "What was the name of that man you were looking for? Was it Paul?"

"Yes, Paul. Why? Is there word of him here in Troas?" the soldier from Rome replied, quickly stepping up to him.

"According to this coppersmith, it sounds like he is causing trouble here," the soldier replied.

"Where can we find Paul?" the soldier from Rome asked with urgency. "We have imperial orders for his arrest."

"Really?" The coppersmith looked from one soldier to the other and smiled. He set down his hammer and pointed over to Luke. "If you follow that man, you'll find Paul. I'm glad you've come to take him away. What are the charges for his arrest?"

"Arson and treason against the divine Emperor Nero," the soldier replied.

The coppersmith raised his eyebrows in surprise. "Arson and treason? That's something I never would have suspected."

The soldier motioned for his soldiers to follow Luke. "The Emperor is grateful for your cooperation. What is your name for our report?"

"Alexander," the coppersmith answered gladly, handing an idol to the soldier. "Take this with my compliments, for good luck on your journey back to Rome. With a man as powerful as Paul, you're going to need it."

"Where are you taking him?" Luke demanded to know as the Roman soldiers slapped the iron shackles around Paul's wrists. Max was barking at the soldiers, asking the same thing.

"By order of Emperor Nero, Paul is hereby charged with encouraging arson against Rome and propagating the outlawed cult of Christianity," the soldier replied gruffly, shoving Max with his foot.

"That is absurd! Arson?" Luke protested. "Paul hasn't been in Rome for four years!"

Paul called over his shoulder as the Roman soldiers dragged him out of the house. "Pray and follow me there, Luke."

408

Luke stopped at the threshold of the house and put his hands up to his head in dismay. "This can't be happening!" He turned and ran back inside. He grabbed a satchel and threw in a few items. Max continued barking at the open doorway, feeling helpless as he watched the Roman soldiers carry Paul away in chains.

"We're going to Rome, Gabriel. May God be merciful to our friend," Luke muttered with a furrowed brow. "Peter was right. The hunt has begun in Asia." The doctor surveyed his medical kit and shook his head. "We must go back to the market before we leave Troas. I fear I'll need that sea-buckthorn after all."

As Luke went to the other room to retrieve some food for their journey, Max and Nigel looked at one another in dismay.

"This is intolerable!" Nigel fumed. "Nero is mad!"

"Aye, mad an' bad, Mousie," Max scowled. "We best be pr-r-repared for the worst when we get ta R-r-rome."

Nigel's face fell. "Indeed. I fear this is Paul's final journey."

Nero held out his arms as Tigellinus read him the disturbing report from Jerusalem. He was being fitted for a new costume, and his tailor worked quietly on his measurements.

"The Jewish revolt started in Caesarea when some Greeks deliberately performed a pagan sacrifice in front of the Jewish synagogue there. A group of Jewish zealots started protesting, but the Roman garrison refused to intercede," Tigellinus explained. "Long-standing tensions between the Greeks and Jews spiraled out of control, and Procurator Florus arrested the Jews. He further ignited the situation by extracting money from the Temple treasury, and ordering his troops to raid the markets in Jerusalem. About thirty-six hundred people were slaughtered, and now the zealots have led the Jews around Judea to take up arms against Rome."

"So what are we doing about this uprising?" Nero wanted to know, more irritated over this interruption than anything. He turned so the tailor could check the back of his garment.

"Herod Agrippa II has sent two thousand riders to help the Jewish leaders located in the upper part of the city, but the lower city is already under rebel control," Tigellinus relayed. "I think we need to keep a close watch on this situation, Nero. Things could get out of control there quickly."

409

Nero dropped his hands to his side and let go an exasperated sigh. "Very well. Keep me posted, but I don't want this Jewish problem interfering with my plans to travel to Greece. I've worked hard to be ready to compete in the Isthmian Games, and come fall I will be there regardless of what is going on in the rest of the world. I plan to return to Rome as a victor and to hold a magnificent celebration at my newly completed palace. Do you hear me?"

Tigellinus rolled up the scroll and tightened the chinstrap of his helmet. "Yes. Sir. Loud and clear."

"What is the latest on the arrest of Paul and Peter? I wish to get all of these nuisances taken care of before I head to Greece so I can focus on my performance at the games."

"Peter was captured this morning, and the contingent of soldiers dispatched to arrest Paul sent word that they have him in custody and should arrive in Rome soon," Tigellinus reported. "Both men will be held in Mamertine Prison until their trials."

Nero clapped his hands. "Wonderful! Then we can finally squash this Christian movement. Well done, Tigellinus!"

The Roman prefect hesitated. "Sir, I must report that there has been some backlash from the public about the treatment of the Christians."

Nero slapped away the hand of the tailor who immediately got up and left the room, knowing the signal that he was dismissed. Nero stepped forward to Tigellinus and squinted at him angrily. "What do you mean? Don't they appreciate how I've punished those who destroyed their city?"

"Although the people have no love lost for the Christians, word is that the people think their suffering is not so much for the good of the state as it is to satisfy the cruelty of an individual," Tigellinus told him. "Even Seneca sympathized with the Christians before you forced him to commit suicide. His words have garnered even more sympathy for them."

Nero picked up a glass bowl and threw it against the wall, shattering it all over the floor. "Seneca!" he spat. "Even *dead* he's causing me grief! What did he write?"

Tigellinus pulled out a piece of parchment and cleared his throat before he read Seneca's words. "In the midst of the flame and the rack, I have seen men not only not groan, that is little: not only not complain, that is little: not only not answer back, that too is little; but I have seen them smile, and smile with a good heart."

"AHHHH!" Nero screamed, closing his eyes and putting his hands over his ears. "Seneca won't even stop lecturing me from the dead! And those Christians are *smiling* over their torture?!" Nero ranted. "Maybe I've been too *gentle* with them!" His eyes darted back and forth as he thought this through.

"Remember the opinions of the people, Nero. If they think you are being too cruel as it is, further types of punishment will do no good," Tigellinus cautioned him.

"Oh, but it *will* do *me* good!" Nero screamed, storming out of the room. "Light up my gardens tonight, and let me know as soon as Paul arrives in Rome!"

☧

"Luke!" Bella cried, running over to embrace the weary traveler. "You look exhausted. Is Paul with you?"

Luke hugged Bella and drew back to look her in the face. "He was arrested in Troas, Bella. He is due to stand trial here in Rome, but I don't know where they've placed him in prison."

Bella put a hand to her forehead in dismay. "Nero has them both now."

"What do you mean? Who?"

"The soldiers arrested Peter and threw him in the Mamertine Prison," Bella explained. "It's a horrific dungeon by the Forum." She sat down on a bench and buried her face in her hands.

Luke rushed to her side and sat down. "That must be where they are taking Paul. What do you know about that place?"

"There is no more foul prison in Rome. Prisoners are lowered through a hole in the floor to reach a cave-like cell. It's a hellish place with no air, no sanitation, and no light except from the hole above. It's filthy, damp, and cold, and infested with rats." Tears rolled down Bella's face, and she looked Luke in the eye. "The only reason people are released from the Mamertine is to be executed."

Luke's eyes grew wide at this news. He and Bella sat in stunned silence as the horror of what was happening to their friends came crashing in on them.

Max, Nigel, Liz, and Al clung together in equally stunned silence, feeling helpless. There was literally nothing they could do. Not since Jesus was arrested and sentenced to death had the animals felt such despair.

☧

Paul felt a searing pain in his shoulder as he landed on the cold stone floor. The Roman soldier had allowed the rope to quickly fall as he lowered Paul into the hole. Paul groaned and slowly rolled over as he tried to catch his breath, only to inhale the smell of waste next to his face. The soldier pulled the rope quickly back through the hole and covered the opening with a metal grate. Paul lay there a moment to try and adjust his eyes to the darkness. He heard a slow, relentless drip of water coming from somewhere, and the sound of another set of chains scraping across the stone floor.

"Are you all right?" came a voice and the sound of shuffling feet.

He knew that voice. "Peter? Is that you?"

"Paul!" came Peter's cry as he reached out to embrace his longtime friend. The two men instantly felt strange comfort to have each other in this hellish pit. "Where did they find you?"

"Troas," Paul answered, sitting up and rubbing his shoulder. "Luke

411

was to follow along behind, but I never saw him." Paul winced. "What has happened to you here in Rome, Peter?"

"Nero sent out an arrest warrant for us both, my friend. I stayed in the catacombs as much as I could with the believers, but I knew I couldn't live the rest of my days underground," Peter explained. "Nero's henchmen captured me when I was in the streets of Rome."

"So now I suppose we shall be put through a trial, but I have no doubt that Nero has already made his ruling," Paul suggested. "The enemy has seen to our chains and our end, but even now I know the Lord will get the glory. And for that I thank him."

"There is still so much work to be done. I had hoped I could do more," Peter lamented. "But it's not up to us. It never has been, has it?"

Paul smiled in the darkness. "God will accomplish his purposes regardless of the people who do or do not do his bidding. Indeed, the gospel is not dependent on us. It is only dependent on the One who is at the heart of it all—Jesus."

412

"Amen," Peter replied. "He will forever call people to fulfill his great commission to spread the good news despite the cost. And he will forever bless them beyond measure when they answer the call."

A rat went scurrying by, grazing Paul's leg. He jumped instinctively.

"Despite the rats." Peter wrapped his arm around Paul's small frame and helped him over to the wall. "Come and lean against the wall. Let's pray. We'll stay close and fight off the rats down here together."

Paul and Peter scooted over and leaned against each other and against the slimy wall. Paul looked up at the dim light coming from the hole. "And God will help us fight off the rats up there."

It seemed like only moments before the sound of clanking iron startled Peter and Paul. Perhaps they had drifted off to sleep, but with the active rats, the cold, and the stench, sleep seemed unattainable in the pit of the Mamertine. A Roman soldier banged an iron bar across the metal grate and shouted for the prisoners to wake.

"Peter! Get up!" the soldier yelled, scraping the grate off the covering and throwing a rope down the hole. "Grab the rope."

Paul put his hand on Peter's arm. "Go with God, my friend. I will pray without ceasing for you."

Peter placed his hand over Paul's. "And I for you. How grateful I am that you are my brother in Christ and that you're here with me."

"Hurry, you scum! Grab the rope!" the soldier commanded him.

Peter stood wearily to his feet. He ached all over. He rubbed his hands on his grimy cloak and wrapped them around the thick, coarse rope. "I've got it."

Slowly two soldiers heaved on the rope and gradually lifted Peter off the floor. Paul watched as Peter was dragged through the hole onto the upper floor and roughly handled by the guards. They replaced the metal grate and carried Peter away, leaving Paul alone in the pit. Paul closed his eyes and began to pray.

☧

Paul lost all track of time, drifting between prayer and sleep and back to prayer. Soon he heard the scuffling of Roman footsteps and chains clanking on the floor above. The metal grate was once more removed and Peter was lowered into the cell. He landed with a thud and moaned.

413

"Peter! I've got you, my friend," Paul exclaimed, hurrying over to his side. "What happened?"

Peter grunted as he sat upright. "Thank you, Paul. I was brought into court, accused of setting fire to Rome, and brought back here. It was a mockery of justice and simply a formality."

"Did you stand before Nero?" Paul asked him.

"No, his prefect, Tigellinus, was present to oversee court," Peter explained. "I am to await sentencing now that my 'guilt' of leading the Christians to burn Rome has been determined. It could be days, weeks, or months. Since you are a citizen of Rome, I presume your court case will be handled with greater respect."

Paul frowned. "I'm sorry, my friend. This is nothing but evil running rampant to crush Christianity with lies."

Peter scooted over to rest his head against the wall and let go a deep breath. "Jesus said, 'You shall know the truth, and the truth shall set you free.' Isn't it amazing that you and I are the ones in this hellish pit, yet we are the ones who are indeed free?"

"Indeed, Nero and those under the enemy's thumb are the ones who are truly in bondage," Paul answered.

"I worry about the church being led astray by the enemy's lies. False teachers are increasingly on the move to distort the gospel."

Paul nodded. "Agreed, and I worry for the young pastors who will need to rise up and lead the church when we're gone. I need to warn Timothy about such things. And I want to strengthen him for the days ahead."

"We must pray for one last opportunity to write out the things we desire to express for those who will carry on the Lord's work," Peter suggested.

Paul looked around them and knew they had nothing. "I was taken so abruptly that I had to leave everything behind—my scrolls and all of my writing materials." He rubbed his upper arms with his hands. "I never thought I would want to wear the sheepskin coat that Philemon gave me in the summertime, but how I long for it now."

"Give Luke time to find us," Peter suggested. "Perhaps they will allow him to bring us what we need."

Paul smiled to think of Luke's care. "I'm sure the good doctor is beside himself with worry that I might need some sea-buckthorn."

"Sea what?" Peter asked.

"Orange berries that Luke uses for ointment," Paul explained. He thought of little Faith and how she had taken the berries from Luke's desk to lead him to the house that first day. "And ones God used to introduce me to the good doctor. If God can provide orange berries when I needed them, I'm certain he can also provide parchment and ink, if he has more for us to say before we depart."

"PAUL!" the soldier shouted from above, dangling the rope. "Grab the rope!"

Peter gripped Paul's arm. "Someone wise once wrote, 'If God is for us, who can be against us?' Remember that."

Paul smiled to hear Peter quote the words that Paul had written to the Romans. "Amen." He rose to his feet and wrapped his hands around the rope. "Yet in all these things we are more than conquerors through him who loved us."

The soldiers heaved and lifted Paul off the floor and up through the hole. At the sound of the metal grate covering the hole, Peter closed his eyes and began to pray.

The bright sunlight was blinding to Paul as he stepped outside. He squinted and lifted his manacled hands to his face. But his arms were quickly jerked back in front of him as the Roman guard started walking down the stone path toward the Forum.

Paul glanced up as they approached the newly refurbished basilica, where court was being held before a large public audience. Senators, consuls, and citizens were packed into the courtroom. Paul smiled sadly as he passed by the area that used to be Theo's office. This time he had no one to represent him in court. He was on his own legally, but he knew he was not alone. Jesus would be with him in that courtroom.

"Nero will soon arrive for court," the Roman soldier informed him. "I would hold my tongue if I were you."

Paul laughed to himself. "That is something I've never mastered, and I don't plan to start today."

LAST WORDS

The newly-hung doors of the reconstructed basilica were opened, and all eyes were on Paul as he was ushered into the courtroom. The Roman citizens, dressed in their finery, turned their noses up at this grimy, white-bearded prisoner being pulled along by a chain. Paul scanned the crowd and didn't see one familiar face. But his heart went out to the people here, for despite all of their finery, all of their worldly power, and all of their wealth, he knew that none of it mattered if they were eternally lost in their own darkness. He began to pray for the words to reach them.

"All hail Nero Claudius Caesar Augustus Germanicus, Divine Emperor," announced the voice of the clerk as Nero came bounding into the courtroom. Everyone bowed as Nero walked past, dressed in a blood-red cape pinned at the shoulder with a gold lion medallion. He wore his gold laurel-leaf crown and proudly lifted his chin as he sat down on the judgment seat. He draped his hands over the armrests and gritted his teeth as he gazed at Paul standing before him.

"Well, here we are again," Nero spat mockingly. "Perhaps if I had not extended such *clemency* the last time you stood before me, Rome would have been spared and we would not all be gathered here now." He turned to the clerk and lifted a finger. "Read the charges."

The court clerk held up a scroll. "Paulus of Tarsus is hereby accused of conspiracy to cause irreparable harm to the city and people of Rome through deliberate acts of arson, and for treason against the

Divine Emperor for propagating an illegal religion called Christianity and refusing to perform the required sacrifices due the gods of Rome."

"Well? How do you answer?" Nero asked Paul.

Paul gave a courteous nod of respect to Nero. "Once again I am honored to stand before you, Emperor, and plead my case. As a citizen of Rome I am also honored to stand before the people gathered here, my fellow citizens."

The people looked at one another in surprise to hear such respect and well-spoken words coming from such a filthy little man, and a wanted criminal at that.

"It has been four years since I was here in Rome, and, needless to say, I was grieved to hear of the horrific fire that tore through this city," Paul continued. "I wept to hear of the loss of life, and I prayed for those who lost everything in the fire. I must answer that I am innocent of the charges against me for arson. Not only was I not here, but such a dastardly crime of intentionally setting fire in the name of God is simply not in my ability to comprehend, much less actually perform. I had nothing to do with the fire. Nor did the Christians who are accused of setting it, for such behavior is foreign to the character and teachings of Jesus whom we worship. I find it far more plausible that the summer winds fanned the flames of an unintentional fire that tragically swept across the city." He turned and looked squarely at Nero. "I can't imagine anyone would actually want to destroy such a magnificent city as Rome."

417

Nero cleared his throat and squirmed in his seat as the people murmured. He scanned the crowd and could see heads nodding at Paul's reasoning. He gripped his fingernails into the arms of the seat where he sat. "I defy your reasoning, Paul. It is not beyond the realm of possibility for anyone to commit such a heinous crime if he is driven by the zeal of his desired purposes."

Paul smiled, and allowed the self-incriminating words of Nero to resonate in the air for a moment. "Indeed, this is true. But such purposes were not mine, nor were they those of my fellow believers. As to your second charge against me, I plead guilty. I am indeed fully responsible for spreading the beliefs of Christianity. I was rescued by the saving grace of Jesus Christ, Messiah, and Son of the Living God, who came to earth to die for the sins of all mankind, and who rose triumphantly from the grave to conquer death. God loved the world so much that he sent Jesus to die for it, rather than watch it destroyed by the fires of sin and destruction. Jesus willingly gave up his life for me, and so I have given up my life for him, to do as he has called me to do in spreading the Good News." He turned to address the crowd gathered there, making as much eye contact with each Gentile as he could. "Jesus lives within me and offers freedom, grace, hope, and eternal life to all who will receive him as Lord." He returned his gaze to Nero. "While I respect all earthly authority such as yours, Emperor, I cannot bend a knee to worship any other than Jesus, my God."

Nero's eyes quickly looked around the room as people murmured among themselves. This time they were frowning, and some were even laughing at Paul's words, thinking them ludicrous. He needed only one of the charges to stick. He shot out his hand at Paul, "There you have it! Paul claims he is *not* guilty of arson but *is* guilty of treason against Rome." He scanned the people and saw their agreement. He then looked down at Paul and grinned wickedly. "And since you so *willingly* wish to give up your life for your God, this *Jesus,* who am I to keep you from doing so? Regardless if your claim of innocence about the fire is true or not, your admission of guilt about refusing to worship Rome's gods is sufficient grounds to condemn you. You will be kept in prison until punishment is determined. Guard, take the prisoner away!"

As the Roman guard walked across the ornate mosaic floor to reach him, Paul's eyes bored into Nero. "For me, to live is Christ, to die is gain. How I pray the same for you."

Nero's mouth twitched to hear such unending compassion pour from this condemned man. He looked around the great hall and saw nothing but respect from the people toward Paul as he was led away. Nero knew respect was something he would never have from the people. They hated him. As Paul was hauled out of the courtroom, Nero's anger was only rekindled, for sitting here as the supreme emperor of Rome, he was jealous of this grimy, bandy-legged, bald, white-bearded prisoner. Despite the fact that he knew he would soon execute Paul, Nero couldn't shake the feeling that Paul had just won today with having the last word.

Luke caught up with the Roman soldier who was escorting Paul back to the prison. "Paul! I just learned about the trial! Forgive me for not being there. I'm sorry you were alone."

Paul smiled, relieved to see the kind face of his friend. "Do not concern yourself, Luke. I wasn't alone. I escaped from the mouth of the lion."

"I am the prisoner's personal physician. I've brought him food and medicine," Luke told the soldier. "May I be permitted to talk with him?"

The soldier looked inside Luke's bag to make sure all was in order. "You better do so before he goes back into the pit."

"Thank you," Luke answered, then turned to Paul as they continued to walk along. "Are you well? How is Peter? I understand he is with you."

"The Lord is with us despite the horrible conditions," Paul relayed. "Can you please bring us writing materials? He and I would like to write some last letters."

Luke swallowed back a lump in his throat at the realization of what was coming. "Right away. I'll go get them now." He handed Paul the bag of food. "Here is food and ointment for any wounds you have. And, Paul, Onesiphorus just arrived from Ephesus. He has been looking for you all over Rome. He is at the prison now."

Paul's eyes welled up to see the care and concern of his friends, after so many had deserted him when the Christian persecution began. He didn't blame them, but his heart was heavy for their fear. "He can deliver my letter when I'm finished. Thank you, good doctor. And give my thanks to our friends."

Luke nodded, realizing that he and Paul couldn't mention Bella's name or any of the other believers here lest they be sought as outlaws. "I'll hurry back with what you need. Stay strong."

Nigel fought against every fiber in his being to climb down that hole. He took a deep breath, straightened his spectacles and gave himself a pep talk. *Come now, old boy. You know there are rats down there. But there are also two princes, and you must be there to stand as a silent sentinel for two letters that shall no doubt become precious jewels to believers across time. You shall press on whilst the revolting rats scurry past. And after the ink of their letters is dry, you shall have been there as a witness to the last*

419

words penned by two of God's most faithful servants. Nigel welled up at the thought. He preened his whiskers and lifted his chin. *Right. Onward!*

From: Simon Peter, a servant and missionary of Jesus Christ.

To: All of you who have our kind of faith. The faith I speak of is the kind that Jesus Christ our God and Savior gives to us. How precious it is, and how just and good he is to give this same faith to each of us.

Do you want more and more of God's kindness and peace? Then learn to know him better and better. For as you know him better, he will give you, through his great power, everything you need for living a truly good life; he even shares his own glory and his own goodness with us! And by that same mighty power he has given us all the other rich and wonderful blessings he promised; for instance, the promise to save us from the lust and rottenness all around us and to give us his own character.

But to obtain these gifts, you need more than faith; you must also work hard to be good, and even that is not enough. For then you must learn to know God better and discover what he wants you to do. Next, learn to put aside your own desires so that you will become patient and godly, gladly letting God have his way with you. This will make possible the next step, which is for you to enjoy other people and to like them, and finally you will grow to love them deeply. The more you go on in this way, the more you will grow strong spiritually and become fruitful and useful to our Lord Jesus Christ. But anyone who fails to go after these additions to faith is blind indeed, or at least very shortsighted and has forgotten that God delivered him from the old life of sin so that now he can live a strong, good life for the Lord.

So, dear brothers, work hard to prove that you really are among those God has called and chosen, and then you will never stumble or fall away. And God will open wide the gates of heaven for you to enter into the eternal kingdom of our Lord and Savior Jesus Christ.

Peter looked over at Paul and knew that whatever he was now penning for Timothy would not only bless that young, unsure pastor, but also bless the church at Ephesus and the church at large, just as his numerous letters had blessed the churches over the years. He smiled, thinking of the legacy that Paul would leave behind. He marveled to think of the radical change that Paul had made all those many years ago on the road to Damascus. Before then, Paul had actually approved the death of the first Christian martyr, Stephen, gladly looking on as he was

420

stoned to death. Paul had been the champion of *squashing* the Christian movement, leading the charge to kill and persecute Christians. Now, here he sat next to Peter, in chains because of championing the *spread* of the Christian movement. Paul was a living example of the radical change a life in Christ could take.

Because I preach the Good News, I suffer, and I am even chained like a criminal. But the word of God is not in chains, and so I endure everything for the sake of God's chosen people, in order that they too may obtain the salvation that comes through Christ Jesus and brings eternal glory.

Paul blew on the ink and held the papyrus close to his face so he could read what he had written in the dim light from the hole above.

Peter smiled at Paul. Oh, what the world would lose when it no longer had preachers like Paul to communicate the gospel! Peter continued to write his letter, warning believers of the false teachers that were already trying to pull them away from the truth of Christ. Finally, he decided to mention Paul as he closed his letter.

421

And so, my friends, as you wait for that Day, do your best to be pure and faultless in God's sight and to be at peace with him. Look on our Lord's patience as the opportunity he is giving you to be saved, just as our dear friend Paul wrote to you, using the wisdom that God gave him. This is what he says in all his letters when he writes on the subject. There are some difficult things in his letters, which ignorant and unstable people explain falsely, as they do with other passages of the Scriptures. So they bring on their own destruction.

But you, my friends, already know this. Be on your guard, then, so that you will not be led away by the errors of lawless people and fall from your safe position. But continue to grow in the grace and knowledge of our Lord and Savior Jesus Christ. To him be the glory, now and forever! Amen.

Peter put down his pen and rubbed his eyes. He breathed in deeply and thanked God for the privilege to finish his letter. He glanced over at Paul who was still going strong writing to Timothy. *Paul always had more words in him than me.* He smiled and prayed for God to give Paul the words he needed to finish his own letter.

But you have followed my teaching, my conduct, and my purpose in life; you have observed my faith, my patience, my love, my endurance, my persecutions, and my sufferings. You know all that happened to me in Antioch, Iconium, and Lystra, the terrible persecutions I endured! But the Lord rescued me from them all. Everyone who wants to live a godly life in union with Christ Jesus will be persecuted; and evil persons and impostors will keep on going from bad to worse, deceiving others and being deceived themselves. But as for you, continue in the truths that you were taught and firmly believe. You know who your teachers were, and you remember that ever since you were a child, you have known the Holy Scriptures, which are able to give you the wisdom that leads to salvation through faith in Christ Jesus. All Scripture is inspired by God and is useful for teaching the truth, rebuking error, correcting faults, and giving instruction for right living, so that the person who serves God may be fully qualified and equipped to do every kind of good deed.

422

In the presence of God and of Christ Jesus, who will judge the living and the dead, and because he is coming to rule as King, I solemnly urge you to preach the message, to insist upon proclaiming it (whether the time is right or not), to convince, reproach, and encourage, as you teach with all patience. The time will come when people will not listen to sound doctrine, but will follow their own desires and will collect for themselves more and more teachers who will tell them what they are itching to hear. They will turn away from listening to the truth and give their attention to legends. But you must keep control of yourself in all circumstances; endure suffering, do the work of a preacher of the Good News, and perform your whole duty as a servant of God.

As for me, the hour has come for me to be sacrificed; the time is here for me to leave this life. I have done my best in the race, I have run the full distance, and I have kept the faith. And now there is waiting for me the victory prize of being put right with God, which the Lord, the righteous Judge, will give me on that Day—and not only to me, but to all those who wait with love for him to appear.

Nigel stayed up with Paul until he finished. Finally, Paul set aside his pen and rested his head on the cold stone wall of this pit, closing his eyes with relief. He was grateful that he had been able to pen some last words to his beloved son in the faith. Nigel read the words of Paul's second letter to Timothy, just as he had done with Peter's second letter to the churches in Asia.

The little mouse stood back and looked at the two condemned servants of God, in awe of not just the words they had written, but the faith with which they had written them. Once enemies, these two men were forever joined together through the blood of Christ. Nothing would ever separate them from the love of Christ, come what may. Nigel wiped his eyes and whispered softly with a broken voice in the darkness of the Mamertine, "Well done, good and faithful servants."

46

THE PRIZE

The mood was solemn in Bella's Garden. Max, Liz, Al, and Nigel hung their heads as Clarie relayed their final assignments with Peter and Paul.

"Today will be hardest on you four," Clarie relayed. "Gillamon and I will, of course, be on the other side of this day. But we know you can do it."

Liz let the tears fall down her cheeks. "If only there was a way to spare them. But I understand that this is how it must be."

"We've tr-r-ravelled a long r-r-road with these lads," Max said sadly. "It's hard ta believe we've got ta let them go."

"Indeed, I shall never forget that first day we met Peter, when Andrew brought him to meet Jesus after those brothers had been to see John the Baptist," Nigel recalled. "Just think of how far Peter has come from those rough-around-the-edges beginnings."

"Aye, from a rough pebble to a smooth polished rock," Al agreed.

"F-r-r-rom a loud-mouthed, temper-flarin' fisherman, ta a Jesus-denyin' coward, ta the leader of the disciples," Max remembered.

"And think of Paul, no?" Liz added. "He went from being the murderous tyrant, Saul, to the model of what a Christ-follower should be, just like Gillamon told us so long ago."

"Gillamon said those words when he first made Libertas come alive in Jerusalem," Clarie reminded them, gazing up at the statue. "Just as a sculptor chips away stone to bring a desired image out of the cold, hard marble, so would the Maker sculpt Saul's cold, hard soul into Paul."

"So I guess the Maker's work be finished with Peter *and* Paul," Al said.

Clarie nodded. "Al, this day will be the hardest on you. Are you up for it?"

Al sat up straight and wore an uncharacteristic look of bravery and confidence. "Jest as I were there for Daniel in the lion's den, I'll be there for Peter in Nero's lion's den. Aye, I'm ready, Lass."

Liz kissed Al on the cheek. "I am so proud of you, *cher* Albert."

"It's time," Clarie said gravely. "We better take our positions. And remember what Gillamon has always told you."

"Know that you are loved and you are able," Nigel quoted for them all.

Clarie nodded with a gentle smile. "Steady hearts, everyone. Let's go."

"PETER! Grab the rope!" came the soldier's voice.

Peter and Paul shared a look of anguish as their stomachs dropped. Peter swallowed hard and looked over at the rope waiting to pull him out of the pit. "This is it, my friend. Let's keep praying for one another." The old disciple slowly rose to his feet.

"Remember Jesus' words, Peter. He will never leave us nor forsake us," Paul encouraged him. "He will be with us every moment of the way."

"I'm grateful for that," Peter replied, nodding as his eyes filled with tears.

The two friends shared one final embrace, not wanting to let each other go.

"HURRY! NOW!" the soldier shouted from up above.

Peter's hands shook as he reached out to take hold of the rope. He looked back at Paul. "Jesus was right. I don't want to go where they are taking me."

"Be strong in the Lord's strength Peter, not your own," Paul told him. "I will see you soon."

Peter closed his eyes and held onto the rope. "Amen."

Paul watched the soldiers hoist Peter up through the hole to take him away. He swallowed back the lump in his throat and closed his eyes to say a prayer for his friend.

"PAUL! Grab the rope!" came the soldier's voice, startling Paul.

He didn't realize that he and Peter would be taken away the same day. He walked over to the rope and looked up into the dimly lit hole. He wrapped his hands around the rope and breathed a silent prayer. "Your grace is sufficient." He called up to the soldier. "I'm ready."

425

☧

The crowds poured into Nero's Circus, filling the stadium for a day of games. The sun was already hot overhead, and people were eager to take their seats, which were not just places to view the entertainment, but places to view each spectator's status in Roman society. Nero's viewing box was covered in gold and filled with comfortable couches of red and purple satin pillows for his family and guests. A green canopy provided him shade, and lush potted foliage created a setting of beauty from which to view the carnage below. Servants brought platters of food and amphorae of wine to keep goblets full during the games. Special seating was provided for Rome's priests and Vestal Virgins down front, as well as for senators and knights who were easily recognizable in their purple-trimmed togas. Citizens wore white woolen togas and were separated from the soldiers. Men were separated from women, married men from single men, and even boys from men. Women and the poor were only allowed to sit in the top rows of the arena, and they wore the drab gray tunics of their station.

426

Like the Circus Maximus, a long *spina* ran through the center of Nero's oblong circus, with an Egyptian obelisk erected in its middle, placed there by Emperor Caligula. While this circus did not boast the same volume of seating as the larger Circus Maximus, the people were nonetheless ready for a variety of entertainment today. Charioteers would race around the track, gladiators would fight animals and each other to the death, and criminals would be executed for the viewing pleasure of the masses. And today, the backdrop for all of this entertainment would be the execution of one of Nero's most despised criminals: Peter.

The cornu sounded, and the people turned their attention to the opening gates of arches where the horses and chariots would line up for the races. Suddenly, cheers rose from the crowd as a single charioteer entered the circus being pulled by four black horses. He lifted his hand in greeting and acclaim while his flowing red cape filled the air as he raced down the track. The people soon realized that it was Emperor Nero himself, making a grand entrance. When he reached the imperial box, he stopped his chariot, and attendants immediately surrounded him to take charge of the horses. He stepped onto a platform and lifted his voice to open the games.

"People of Rome! Welcome to today's games. I have something special for you. You have witnessed the death of the Christians who burned down your city, but today I have arranged for the ringleader of them all to be executed before you! Revel in the justice of Rome!"

Nero stretched out his hand to direct the people's attention to an entry gate. Out walked the executioners to get things ready in the center of the spina. After a moment there appeared a man slowly walking into the arena carrying a crossbeam over his shoulders. "I give you the criminal, Peter!"

Sweat dripped from Peter's brow as his feet shuffled across the hot sand of the arena. He heard the masses cheering and knew they were thirsty for blood. *Lord, let me not dishonor you in any way. Give me strength,* Peter prayed to himself as he made his way to the place of execution.

Nero walked up to his gilded viewing box, surrounded by soldiers who would stand at attention throughout the games and protect him from would-be assassins. Nero plopped down on his cushioned seat and lifted his emerald spyglass to watch as Peter was crucified. He smiled. "Put on a good show for us, Christian."

Peter dropped the crossbeam and stumbled back a step as he tried to catch his breath. The Roman soldiers immediately grabbed him and stripped off his clothes. As they grabbed his wrists, Peter glanced down at the cross and the nine-inch nails. "Please, may I request that I be crucified differently than my Lord?"

The two soldiers looked at one another and grinned. "Do you have a position in mind, scum?" one of the soldiers joked.

"Upside down," Peter answered resolutely.

"That's a new one. Very well," the second soldier replied, grabbing Peter and laying him over the cross. "Have it your way."

Peter cried out as they stretched his arms wide and nailed his hands and feet to the cross. *Jesus, this is what you endured for me? Thank you.* He continued to talk to Jesus throughout the ordeal, keeping his focus on his Lord.

"What are they doing?" Nero wanted to know as he watched the soldiers lift the cross with Peter's feet up in the air. "They're crucifying him upside down?" He removed the emerald spyglass from his face and looked around at his guests seated with him. He broke out in laughter, clapping his hands. "Brilliant! I love it! Bravo!"

Once the soldiers hefted the cross into the hole, they stepped back and saluted Nero.

Nero rose to his feet and lifted his arms in the air. "The criminal, Peter, is in his rightful place, so let the games begin!"

427

The crowds erupted into cheers, as the far gates opened and four teams of chariots came racing down the track.

Peter was in agony and felt the blood rushing to his head. As the horses pounded down the track, the ground vibrated, increasing his pain as the cross shook. *Forgive them, Lord.* Dust flew up into his face as they raced by. After a moment he opened his eyes and couldn't believe what he saw. "Ari?" he uttered weakly.

Nero's attention drifted from the charioteers back to Peter, as he lifted his emerald spyglass up again to check on his prize. "What's this?" He smiled and laughed. "It appears we have a miniature lion running out there to devour our criminal!"

Al trotted out across the sandy floor of the arena and walked right up to Peter's face. His eyes filled with tears to see his friend in this horrific scene, but he knew he needed to be brave for the suffering man. He lifted his paw and wiped away the sweat and blood that dripped into Peter's eyes. He hesitated a moment and then figured it didn't matter anymore.

"I'm here, Lad," Al said, speaking so Peter could understand him. "My real name be Al."

Peter couldn't believe what was happening. "How . . . how can this be?" He gasped for breath and looked into Al's green eyes. "I knew the Master's touch . . . made you special . . . Al." Peter mustered a weak smile.

"He sent me to be with ye all these years," Al explained. He rested his head softly next to Peter's. "And I'll be right here with ye 'til the end."

☧

Paul shuffled along in chains behind the Roman execution squad. The lictors held up their *fasces* of the rod and ax, symbols of Roman justice, but the main executioner held a sword. Together they walked a mile and a half south of Rome along the Ostian Way, passing mile markers until they reached the third milestone. They came up to a tall, marble-covered pyramid that was actually a tomb built for a man named Cestius a decade before Jesus was born. Paul looked up at the imposing pyramid, but his attention was diverted when he noticed movement at the base.

Max and Liz walked around the side of the pyramid into view. Paul wrinkled his brow, shocked to see them way out here. "Gabriel? Faith?"

The animals looked at one another before walking over to follow along after Paul. The executioners kept their gaze ahead, paying no attention to the animals. Nigel scurried up Paul's tunic and climbed onto his shoulder.

"We have come to say farewell," Nigel whispered in his ear. "It has been our honor to be at your side all these many years, Paul."

"We are grateful the Maker allowed us to witness your ministry, *mon ami,*" Liz echoed quietly.

"Aye, ye've been the br-r-ravest lad I've ever known," Max added.

Paul's eyes grew wide. "Those *voices*. I've heard them before," he whispered quietly.

"When you were blind in Damascus," Nigel answered.

"You were the strangers who came to see me in the house on Straight Street?" Paul asked, marveling at this revelation. "And you've been with me all along."

Max nodded. "So we had ta be here with ye now."

"May the Maker remove all fear from your heart, *cher* Paul," Liz voiced quietly.

"Thank you," Paul whispered through tears of sadness mixed with joy. "My angels unaware."

"We're here at the Aquae Salviae," the lead executioner announced. "Tie the prisoner to the post." The sound of gently flowing water was oddly soothing in this moment.

Nigel scurried off Paul's shoulder to the ground. Liz gasped and buried her face in Max's shoulder as the men led Paul over to a stone pillar, tying his arms around the front and tearing away his shirt to leave his neck exposed.

"I do not hold this against you. As Jesus Christ forgave me, so I forgive you," Paul told the men who readied him for execution. "Jesus, take me into your kingdom," he murmured quietly.

Paul leaned his head against the white marble and looked over to see the mysterious little friends who had been his companions all these years. He closed his eyes and took strange comfort in their presence.

The executioner stood over Paul and held up his sword. Max, Liz, and Nigel shut their eyes and braced for impact.

In a split second, and in a flash of light, Paul was in heaven.

☧

Paul breathed in deeply. The air was laced with an exquisite fragrance

429

that filled Paul with instantaneous well-being. The peace was indescribable. Only goodness was here. Evil and death were nonexistent. The love enveloping him instantly removed every shred of pain, sadness, and despair he had ever known. He looked around. The beauty of the landscape and the colors were unlike anything he had ever seen. The sound of music, cheering, and celebration was almost deafening. And the light was blinding.

Paul looked around him and saw that he was surrounded by a great crowd of witnesses. Their faces were radiant with joy and youth and wholeness, and they called his name as one voice. But he immediately recognized those who stood up front on his left, cheering him on. Ananias. James. Mary. Andrew. Thaddeus. *Stephen*—the very first martyr to die because of *him*. It was surreal. Regret and sadness were wiped away in an instant.

All eyes turned, and Paul followed their gaze. Before him was a path of gold and up ahead, with outstretched arms and nail-scarred hands, stood Jesus. Paul ran and fell at his feet, in awe of the splendor of his king. "My Savior and my God!"

"Welcome, dear Paul," Jesus told him. He enveloped Paul in his arms and whispered in his ear, "Well done." Jesus beamed an infinite smile into Paul's heart as he rose to his feet. As he locked eyes with Jesus, everything he had suffered vanished into insignificance. Standing face to face with the One he had suffered for, Paul suddenly realized his thorn was gone.

"Your grace *was* sufficient for me," Paul declared humbly and gratefully.

Jesus nodded. "Receive your prize." He spread his hand across the expanse of the heavens. "This is just the beginning."

Paul gazed out and saw the faces of those who were here in heaven because of him. They spanned all walks of life, and all parts of the globe, from former slaves to wealthy rulers, from Jew to Gentile, Greek to Roman, pagan to godly—thousands of souls were here, safe for eternity. Suddenly Paul's eyes fell on Theophilus, who lifted his hand in joyful greeting. Behind him stood his father Armandus, and his grandfather Marcus. Three generations of the Roman family of Antonius were here, happy and together for all time.

"And now, it's your turn to welcome someone," Jesus whispered in Paul's ear.

Paul turned, and his heart caught in his chest with unspeakable joy.

430

PART FOUR

THE
FALL

47

HIS FINAL ACT

larie smiled as she watched Peter's welcome into heaven. "I wish the others were here to see this." After a joy-filled, tearful reunion with Jesus, Peter gave Paul a huge bear hug, lifting the smaller man up in the air as they celebrated their victory in Christ. Then he was reunited with his brother, Andrew, and the other faithful disciples who had faced martyrdom ahead of him. "All of their pain, sadness, and dealings with evil are gone. And these followers of Jesus get to be reunited! I wish every believer could see this."

Gillamon gazed around at the swirling panels of the IAMISPHERE. "If they could see everything, there would be no need for faith."

"I know, but Max, Liz, Al, and Nigel were so sad to lose these two," Clarie lamented. "If only they could see how happy they are now."

"They will need to trust what they know to be true," Gillamon answered. "And they will need to put their attention on those who still need their watchcare." He directed Clarie's attention to Nero standing in the middle of a large room, giving a performance. "After the Enemy pulls the curtain down on Nero, a whole new play is set to begin."

"It's like one big play to Lucifer, isn't it?" Clarie asked with a frown.

"Yes, the apostles had their acts, and so does the Enemy," Gillamon answered. "For his 'Nero Play,' the Enemy used Nero to start the persecution of Christians, to begin the destruction of Israel, and to once again attempt Lucifer's long-sought destruction of the Antonius family." He pointed to the scene of Leonitus sitting in the courtyard during the fire before Clarie rescued him. "Lucifer's broad-reaching acts affect nations as well as specific to individuals. The evil lion prowls around seeking whom he can devour, large and small. His first act with Leonitus began during the fire."

Clarie looked at Gillamon in alarm. "But I rescued him that night!"

"Yes, but for his 'Leonitus Play' he devoured Leonitus's home with fire, took his parents by blocking their escape, and also instilled in him a fear and hatred of lions," Gillamon explained. "The Enemy set the stage for the boy's destruction with the fire. The boy will need to choose to be one of the Enemy's puppets in a play in the coming acts, or escape the jaws of the lion."

"How are we to help the boy?" Clarie asked urgently.

"Liz and Al will go to Gaul when Bella takes him away from Rome, and what the boy decides will determine what happens next," Gillamon explained. He turned to the panel of Jews being slaughtered in Israel. "Meanwhile, for the Enemy's 'Jerusalem Play,' the warnings Jesus gave the city long ago will finally come to pass. Jerusalem will fall. Max and Nigel are to go there to protect a Jew by the name of Josephus when the Romans invade Jotapata, and remain with him until he is brought to Rome. He will prove to be a vital scribe for the history of these days. You and I will provide as much comfort as we can to the Jews in Jerusalem. Terrible days are ahead."

Clarie nodded somberly. "Understood. And for the end of Nero's Play?"

Gillamon looked at the scene currently taking place of Nero on stage. "The final act is coming."

CORINTH, FALL AD 66

General Titus Flavius Vespasian rested his face in the palm of his hand, his elbow propped up on the arm of the ornately carved chair. Although he had fought sleep for over an hour, the eyelids of the old war horse grew heavy and he dozed off. His head fell forward, and he suddenly awoke to the sound of a loud, singular snore. He looked around the room decorated with plush furnishings and lit with flickering oil lamps. He was embarrassed to see the faces of the elite members of Roman society in this Greek province staring at him. It quickly dawned on him that he was the one who had made that sound. Some faces looked as if they were trying to stifle a laugh. Others expressed fear in their eyes. But one face expressed anger, for Vespasian had fallen asleep during his musical performance. And that angry face belonged to Nero.

Vespasian had commanded Rome's legions in Germania and Britain, and was considered one of Rome's most competent generals. Nero had requested Vespasian to accompany him on his tour of Greece, so, of course, the general had to comply. He had to endure Nero's ludicrous performances in the Olympic and Isthmian games where the insane emperor "won" every event he entered, receiving prizes by the judges who were either bribed or threatened. Nero entered athletic, musical, and dramatic competitions, and sometimes wished to compete honestly. When dropping a scepter on stage during a play he quickly picked it up and was terrified that he would be disqualified, but one of the stagehands assured him that no one saw his foible. He suffered from stage fright like any other actor, but once on stage he came alive as he lived out the fantasy of the mythical character he portrayed.

For an athletic competition, Nero raced a ten-horse chariot but fell onto the sandy floor, as the horses tried to turn around the spina of the arena. He was yet awarded the laurel-leaf crown of victory, for it was reasoned that Nero *would* have won if he had not fallen out of the chariot. Nero threatened other performers and had the statues of previous champions pulled down and dragged away to the public toilets. No one was allowed to leave his performances, so people feigned death to be carried out of the stadium. And no one was allowed to fall asleep. Yet Vespasian had done just that in this private celebration performance. Today had been a spectacular day for Greece in the stadium of Corinth. Nero publicly declared that Greece was free from Roman taxation, and while this was a reason for the Greeks to celebrate, it would soon become a reason for other Roman provinces to revolt. And it would become reason for the Roman Senate to reach the end of their patience.

Nero clenched his jaw and laughed off Vespasian's snore in order to save face. "It seems I have worn out my best general with my extended tour of Greece! Poor you, Vespasian! The hour does grow late, and Nero himself is tired, so I shall lay down my lyre and bid you all goodnight." He took a bow while the intimate audience rose to their feet and wildly applauded him, shouting, "Bravo! Bravo! Nero is great! Nero is merciful! Nero's talent is unmatched! Bravo!"

435

Vespasian bowed and applauded along with the crowd, smiling awkwardly. When Nero finally left the room, the general sat down and rubbed his face in his hands, exhaling in relief that he was spared the wrath of the unstable emperor. But within five minutes, Nero's secretary was whispering in his ear that he was hereby decommissioned, had lost his pension, and would be exiled. He was told to leave the imperial residence before Nero changed his mind and decided not to be merciful.

ROME, JANUARY AD 67

"I don't want to go down there anymore," Leonitus moaned. "Please, Mama, please? Can't we stop going there?"

Bella frowned as she led her grandson by the hand through the streets of Rome. It was dusk as they headed to the catacombs. She leaned down to speak quietly as they walked through the crowds, looking around for listening ears and watchful eyes. "But it's where we get to see our Chr . . . our friends. You know we can't see them up here."

Leonitus dragged his feet and frowned. "I hate it down there."

Bella stopped and faced the boy, rubbing his shoulder. "Tell me why."

"Our friends keep dying," Leonitus muttered. He looked up at her and gritted his teeth. "Bad men keep killing them. And lions keep killing them."

Bella bent over to cup the boy's face in her hands. "My dear boy, that's all the more reason we need to keep meeting our friends, so we can pray for one another and encourage one another. Rome isn't a safe place for us."

"Then we should fight back!" the boy insisted, tossing his sandy brown hair out of his eyes and gripping his fists. "I see Roman soldiers with swords. Maybe I could get one!"

"Your Uncle Julius is a Roman soldier, as was your grandfather Armandus and great-grandfather Marcus before him," Bella reminded him. "And they are Christians . . . or were." She wrinkled her brow. Marcus and Armandus were gone now, and only Julius remained. Even Roman soldiers who professed being Christians could potentially be persecuted, depending on the Roman governor of a province and if they were called out by hatemongers. Bella had been contemplating taking

Leonitus away from Rome to Gaul where she could at least be near her only remaining son. "Remember what Paul told us. We are soldiers for Christ and need to fight with the armor of God. Our sword is the Word of God." She knit her brow, seeing the confusion on Leonitus's face. She understood how defenseless he felt, especially after all he had been through. "Come, you'll feel better after we've been with our friends."

The nine year-old boy frowned and folded his arms across his chest, but followed along as he was told. When they turned a corner, Leonitus noticed a man painting a mural on the side of a building. He halted while Bella walked ahead. His eyes lit up to see the image of a man wearing a helmet with a tall rim and a wide edge, holding a shield in one hand and a sword in the other. He faced another man who wore no helmet but had armor covering his left shoulder, a trident in one hand and a net in the other. The boy stopped and stared at the mural, mesmerized by the images he saw.

"Who are they?" he asked the painter.

"Gladiators, of course," the man replied with a snort, continuing to paint in the details on the mural. He tapped the flat end of his paintbrush on the date announcing the games. "Big match coming up between these two soon." Beneath the date was also listed the venue, the name of the *editor* or organizer of the games, and special food and drink to be offered to the crowd.

Leonitus stepped up and pointed to the man with the helmet. "Who is that?"

"That is Spiculus, a *murmillo* gladiator. He's one of Nero's favorites. The emperor has awarded him riches beyond compare!" He pointed to the second man. "And this is Blandus, a *retiarius*. You can tell by his net and the trident. Different kinds of gladiators make the games more exciting for the crowds."

"They must have a lot of power with those weapons," Leonitus suggested, tracing his finger along the trident. He scanned the wall, and suddenly his eyes locked on another image of a man thrusting a long spear into a lion that leapt toward him. He put his hand up over the image.

"Now that is a *venator*. They specialize in wild animal hunts in the arena," the man told him.

Leonitus turned his gaze up at the man and smiled. "They kill lions?"

"Lions, bears, leopards, even elephants," the man replied. He dipped his paintbrush to keep painting in the details of the mural.

"I'd like to do that someday," Leonitus replied, drawn to the image.

"You think you could be a gladiator? You need to be ruthless and fight with fury." The man looked down at Leonitus and tilted his head. "What's your name, boy?"

"Leonitus! Where are you?" came Bella's frantic voice.

Leonitus took in a quick breath of alarm and looked in her direction. "I need to go," he told the man sheepishly as Bella spotted him.

"Leonitus? That's your name? Hmmm. It means 'lion-like'. You've got the right name for a gladiator, boy," the man said. He leaned over and whispered to him, as Bella hurried over to them. "Sneak by here after the games to see who won. I'll paint a 'V' next to the victor."

Leonitus grinned with excitement. "I will! I can't wait to see who wins."

The man winked at him. "I shall see you later then, Leo."

Bella looked at the mural with uneasiness and pulled her grandson protectively toward her. "Come away from there, Leonitus. Let's be going."

As the boy ran off with his grandmother, the man tossed his paintbrush on the ground and smiled to himself. "Act Two."

GREECE, JANUARY AD 67

"At last, I can live like a human being!" Nero exclaimed as he received the news. "Isn't it wonderful, Sabinus? My golden palace is finally completed, and now I can enjoy it."

Nymphidius Sabinus, who now shared the office of Praetorian Prefect with Tigellinus, was well familiar with Nero's new Domus Aurea. The extravagance of Nero's 150-room palace was despicable, especially in light of the chaos erupting throughout the Roman provinces because of the taxes he imposed on the people to pay for it. But Nero didn't care. He wanted to return to Rome an Olympic champion, albeit in his own eyes, and to his long-awaited palace. Nero was all that mattered to Nero.

"Indeed, it is, but I must return you to the urgent matter at hand. I need your decision about Vespasian," Sabinus told him. "Tigellinus warned you that this situation in Judea could turn explosive, and now it has. The Roman garrison was overrun by rebels in Jerusalem. Cestius Gallus then led the Syrian legion against the rebels, but he lost over six thousand men when they were ambushed by the rebels. Emperor, the legion also lost its *eagle standard!* This does not happen to an army of Rome! You must send Vespasian to squash this Jewish rebellion. He is the most qualified general we have."

Nero made an ugly face at the thought. It still stung him that Vespasian had fallen asleep at his performance, but even he realized that this Jewish revolt was in need of serious attention. "I know Vespasian is your brother, but even *I* must admit he is the best one to stop those Jews. Very well, reinstate the general, and send him to crush this rebellion. That is all." Nero waved Sabinus away. "I must plan my victory parade into Rome. Oh! I think it should lead right to my golden colossal statue. I could have servants drop flowers from the top as if they are coming out of my crown!"

Sabinus replaced his helmet and saluted in disbelief. "Hail, Caesar."

Nero did not respond but giggled as he thought about his return to Rome.

439

Sabinus turned and left Nero to his fantasy world, shaking his head and deciding he would finally withdraw his support from this madman. All the Praetorian Guard of Rome would as well. The Senate was already secretly making moves to get rid of Nero, following his foolish tour of Greece and the public outrage over this palace. Nero had taken one-third of Rome for his own use to build this palace, and the people felt they had been robbed twice. They were robbed by the fire, and now they were robbed by the rebuilder of Rome. Uprisings were coming in Gaul and Spain against Nero's tax policies. Sabinus knew it was only a matter of time before Nero would be removed from power, and he wanted to make sure he was on the right side when a new Emperor arrived.

GALILEE, JUNE 8, AD 67

Vespasian sat on horseback next to his son, Titus, as they gazed out over the Galilean countryside. The general had appointed Titus as his second in command, and the young officer arrived from Alexandria with his legion of soldiers. Together, with the other legions led by

Vespasian and King Agrippa, the Roman force of over sixty thousand heavily armed and trained soldiers stood poised to crush the Jewish revolt. The Jewish leadership in Jerusalem bitterly opposed the rebelling zealots who had gained confidence that they could defeat Rome after routing the smaller Roman military force. Vespasian saw his opportunity of pitting the two factions of Jews against one another.

"We've expelled the leader of the zealots named John from Gadara, so the most radicalized area is coming under our control," Titus reported. "Our men are ready to attack Jotapata. Our scouts inform us that the Jewish commander is a general by the name of Josephus."

Vespasian had a square face, a receding hairline, and four lines across his upper forehead that grew more pronounced when he raised his eyebrows. The old general nodded and pursed his mouth in approval. "Good. We will continue our strategy of crushing this resistance in the north. I will make Caesarea my headquarters, and we will proceed to take every port along the coast. We will wipe out the zealot faction and drive the rebels back to one remaining Jewish stronghold."

440

"Jerusalem," Titus confirmed. "And then?"

Vespasian turned to look at his son. "We'll surround the city and wait."

ROME, JUNE 9, AD 68, MIDNIGHT

Nero tossed and turned until he finally sat up straight in bed, breathing rapidly and covered in sweat. He looked around his luxurious bedchamber and swallowed hard. Shadows from the oil lamps danced around the room and only increased Nero's paranoia that people were hiding behind the gauzy curtains that hung from his high-post bed. He put his feet over the side of the bed and slowly looked around his bedroom, listening. All was silent. He stood up and was startled by his lion head rug sitting in the corner.

Nero got up and walked down the hall. Normally, palace guards stood at attention outside the tall doors leading to his bedchamber, but not one was around. "Guards? Where are you?" No one answered.

"Epaphroditos! Come here!" he cried, calling his personal secretary who came running. "Send word for my friends in the palace chambers to come to me at once!"

"Very well, Emperor," Epaphroditos answered, hurriedly making his way to do as Nero requested.

After a while Epaphroditos returned to find Nero pacing in the dining room where the heavens rotated at his command. "No one has replied, Sir."

Swallowing hard, Nero walked down to the palace chambers belonging to some of his friends but found them abandoned. Panic filled his mind. He suddenly felt like he would be taken away and led where he didn't want to go. "Call for my favorite gladiator, Spiculus! I need someone who is efficient with a sword!"

Epaphroditos's eyes widened, and he sent a servant out into the night with a message for the gladiator.

An hour passed, and no one appeared. Nero was beside himself with panic. "Have I neither friend nor foe?" he cried, running outside. "I'll throw myself into the Tiber River!"

After he had run into the night, he looked up at the night sky and realized he had no control over real stars like he had in his fantasy dining room. He had no control over anything. He didn't have control over his emotions, his thoughts, or his actions at the moment. He returned back to the palace and was met by Epaphroditos and a loyal imperial freedman by the name of Phaon.

"Sir, Phaon has a villa four miles outside of Rome," Epaphroditos told him. "He has offered it as a place of refuge. Let us gather some horses and take you there tonight."

Nero's lip quivered like a little boy, and he nodded silently. "Take me there."

Within half an hour Nero, Epaphroditos, Phaon, and two other men were riding in disguise on horseback to the outskirts of the city. When they arrived, Nero dismounted from his horse and looked around the villa. He pointed to a spot under a tree nearby. "Dig a grave for me there." He ran inside the villa, and the men looked at one another in shock.

They immediately heard the sound of an approaching horse that had followed them to the villa. "Get inside," Epaphroditos told the others. "Let me see who this is." He stepped forward as the rider approached. "Who are you?"

"Sir, I bring a message to the Emperor from the Senate," a

441

courier replied, handing a scroll to Epaphroditos. "He needs to read this immediately."

"Very well, I'll see that he gets it," Epaphroditos replied, dismissing the courier.

"They are right behind me," the courier answered before turning his horse and riding off into the night.

Epaphroditos tapped the scroll in his hand and walked inside. "It's a message from the Senate," he told Nero, handing him the scroll.

Nero pushed it away with his hand that trembled in fear. "You tell me what it says."

Epaphroditos nodded and unrolled the scroll while Nero bit his fingernails. He cleared his throat and read, "The Senate has declared you a public enemy, Nero. They intend to execute you in the Forum by beating you to death." Epaphroditos slowly looked up at the emperor who was now the outlaw. "Armed men are on the way to arrest you now."

Little did any of them know that the Senate was divided on the right course of action, as Nero was the last remaining member of the Julio-Claudian dynasty. Some of the senators wanted to preserve Nero's life until he could have a blood heir and were working through the night to find a solution to the obstacles of keeping Nero in power to save his life. They had to put down the revolt in Spain where the imperial forces were already poised to name the Provincial Roman Governor Galba as Emperor. Here in Rome, Sabinus had incited the Praetorian Guard to transfer their loyalty from Nero to Galba.

"I will not die like a humiliated animal in the Forum!" Nero wailed, grabbing a sword that the men had brought with them. Sweat beaded off Nero's forehead, and he paced around the room. He stopped and studied the sword for a moment. He held his head back in dramatic form and with a broken voice uttered sadly, "What an artist dies in me!"

His palms were sweaty and he panicked. Nero dropped to his knees and cried out. "Please, won't one of you kill yourselves to show me how to do it?" Suddenly they heard the sound of galloping horses coming toward the villa. Nero held the sword up to his neck but his hands trembled. He sighed and shoved the sword toward his secretary. "Epaphroditos, I order you to do it!" he shouted, his eyes wild with fear.

Epaphroditos reluctantly took the sword in hand and swallowed hard, hesitating.

Nero heard the sound of men outside. "DO IT!" he screamed. Epaphroditos jumped and quickly did as he was told, sending Nero falling to the floor.

"Where is the Emperor?" a horseman demanded, barging into the room. He saw Nero lying there and rushed over to put his hands on the wound to stop the bleeding.

Nero looked at the horseman and gasped. "Too late!"

The horseman locked eyes with Epaphroditos and sat back on his knees, realizing it was no use. As they watched Nero take his last breath, a look of horror covered his face.

☧

Complete darkness. Hopeless screams. Nauseating smells. Intense heat. Nero put his hands out in front of him, trying to see where he was. Something hit him, sending shockwaves of excruciating pain through his body. He heard a low, evil laugh that filled him with such fear he thought he would die. But he knew he was already dead. The utter despair and aloneness he felt was indescribable. He lost the ability to breathe except for shallow, quick intakes of air that burned his lungs. He longed for a sip of water, but somehow he knew there was none in this place. He tried to scream but had no voice.

"No, don't speak. Your days of being heard are over," came a growling voice from the darkness. "Well done, my pathetic puppet, for playing your role so well. But I have no further use for you. You chose the *earthly* rewards I gave you, so now you will receive my *eternal* rewards. You will never escape this prison but will be forever tormented by my demons. You will never rest or sleep again. You will hunger and thirst but never eat nor drink again. And for my final act, since you love fire . . ." a blaze of flames lit up the face of the massive lion as he roared, "WELCOME TO HELL!"

443

Is Life So Dear?

According to Clarie, our human shall someday wield as powerful a pen for history as he has a powerful sword for defending the Jews in this war with the Romans," Nigel whispered to Max as they hid among the forty men in a cavern below the Jewish city of Jotapata. The Romans had finally broken through the walls of the city after a long and bloody battle, and were searching for Josephus. "He shall go from being a general to a scribe, and we must pay attention to what he says, sees, and records."

Max studied the slender, dark-haired, thirty-year-old general. "Aye, but a scr-r-ribe for who? The R-r-romans? He seems like he'll fight ta the death against 'em."

Nigel shrugged his shoulders. "I suppose we shall find out as this story unfolds. But he appears to also be a prophet and a dreamer. He told his men that Jotapata would fall in forty-seven days and that he would be taken alive by the Romans."

"An' it's the forty-seventh day. So he's a bit like Isaiah an' Joseph," Max posed. "Josephus. Joseph an' us. Okay, Lad, I'll make sure he's safe an' ye take note of wha' he wr-r-rites then."

"Josephus! It's Nicanor, your friend from Jerusalem," the Roman soldier called from the opening of the cavern above. Josephus had ignored the pleas by two other tribunes sent to seek his surrender, and Nicanor stepped up when he learned that his friend was still alive. The

Romans had discovered Josephus's hiding spot when they captured and interrogated a woman who had been hiding with them. Nicanor and the Jewish scholar-turned-general had befriended one another when he was assigned security near the temple area long before this Jewish rebellion. "Vespasian wishes to offer you protection and asks that you turn yourself in willingly."

"Don't listen to him, Josephus!" the men urged him.

"Nicanor?" Josephus looked up through the hole where he was hiding with the others to see if it was really him. "I'm sorry to see you again in these circumstances, my friend. Why should I give myself up to an enemy that has sought my destruction and has slain so many in this city?"

"Vespasian admires your valor and the way you've brilliantly waged battle against him," Nicanor explained. "He would never have sent a friend for the purpose of deceiving you. He wants to save a brave man."

Some impatient soldiers stood behind Nicanor holding torches. "Enough of this stalling!" one of the soldiers exclaimed, making a move to throw fire into the cavern.

445

"STOP! He must not be harmed!" came the voice of a commander who stopped the soldier.

Josephus suddenly recalled a recurring dream he had where God told him the fate of the Jews and the destinies of the Romans, Vespasian and Titus. He closed his eyes and prayed silently, *Since you have chosen me to announce what is to come, I will consent to live, but I call you to witness that I go, not as a traitor, but as your servant to deliver your message.* He knew that his men would fight to keep him from surrendering.

"Very well, Nicanor," Josephus called out, looking back around the darkened cave. "I'm coming."

Immediately Josephus's men came after him, pointing their swords and threatening to kill him as a traitor if he surrendered. "Is life so dear to you, Josephus, that you would endure to see the light in slavery? Look how quickly you've forgotten who you are! How many of us have you persuaded to die for liberty? And yet here you think you can hope for safety from those we've fought so hard against? We must take care of our country's glory! If you take a sword and die at your hand voluntarily, you will die as a general of the Jews, but if we must slay you, you'll die as a traitor."

Max growled at the men with swords to the general's throat. Josephus knew this situation was about to explode here in the cave, and he sought to calm them down with reason. "Brothers, why be so eager to die? It is honorable to die, I admit, to die in war, but only by the law of war and by the act of the victors. It is foolish to die at our own hands. It is right to die for freedom, but let it be a fair fight, and by the hands of those who would rob us of it." He pointed up the hole of the cavern. "But now they neither meet us in battle, nor slay us. What is it that we dread that we won't surrender to the Romans? Death? So should we inflict upon ourselves that which we fear? Some may say it is noble to destroy oneself, but I say it is far from it! Suicide is sin against God who created us, and nature's law is strong in man and animals—the will to live. God has given our souls this gift of existence in these mortal bodies, and it is not ours to take. If we are to be saved, then, let us be saved."

But the men were beyond reason, having been conditioned to expect death in the brutal fight against the Romans. They charged at Josephus, and a war of words was waged in the cavern. Josephus could see there was no convincing them of surrender. Finally, he held up his hand. "If we must die, let it not be by our own hand, but by each other's hands. Let us draw lots, and the one who draws the first lot will be killed by him who draws the second, and so on, so that no one escapes."

"This is madness!" Nigel shrieked.

"Steady, Mousie," Max told him coolly. "If someone tr-r-ries ta put a sword in Josephus, I'll pull him off."

As the men drew the lots and began killing the others, the circle of men decreased until miraculously, it was only Josephus and one other man left standing. Max stood ready to attack the other man.

"We have no choice but to surrender, for now one of us would need to commit suicide, and that would be the greater sin to God," Josephus reasoned. "Come, let us give ourselves up."

The man nodded and dropped his sword, and Josephus dropped his as well, filled with relief that God had spared him. He looked back up to the top of the cavern. "Nicanor, I will come out now."

Max and Nigel sat back in relief. Nigel looked around at the dead Jews who preferred death over slavery to the enemy. "What a tragic loss."

"Aye, but Josephus were spared," Max said with a heavy sigh. "That were way too close."

Josephus was immediately taken to General Vespasian's tent, and the Roman soldiers gathered around him. Some hurled insults at him, bitter over how hard he had fought against them. Titus, however, was struck by how nobly Josephus handled himself in defeat, offering himself humbly and confidently to the Romans.

"I'm sending you to Nero," Vespasian told him after a debate among his commanders of what to do with the captured Jewish general.

Josephus spoke up boldly. "May I please have a word with you and Titus, alone?"

Titus and Vespasian shared a curious look and ordered all but two other soldiers out of the room. "Very well. What do you have to say?" Vespasian asked him.

Josephus stepped up to where the Roman general sat. "You think, Vespasian, that you have a mere captive in Josephus, but I come to you as a messenger of a greater destiny. Why send me to Nero? Do you think he will remain in office? Who is there to succeed him as emperor? You, Vespasian, will be Caesar," he said, and looking over at Titus. "So will your son, Titus. For you are master not only of me, but of sea and land and of the whole human race."

Vespasian sat with his arms crossed over his chest, head tilted with a doubtful grin.

One of the other soldiers in the tent spoke up. "I'm surprised then that you didn't predict the fall of Jotapata or your own capture! No doubt you wish to save yourself with such flattery."

Josephus answered with confidence. "But I *did* predict the fall of the city, down to the forty-seventh day, and told my men that I would be taken alive by the Romans."

"It's true. He did," the other soldier confirmed, having interrogated other prisoners.

Titus and his father exchanged looks of amazement. Vespasian raised his eyebrows, causing the creases in his forehead to deepen. He then squinted at Josephus, curious as to this revelation. Indeed, Nero had already removed him from exile, and that alone was miraculous. He knew things were unstable in Rome, but there were many others who would seek to be Emperor. "You shall remain in custody, and we shall see what transpires."

Max and Nigel were hiding in the folds of the tent. "Ye mean we be

447

standin' in a tent with two of R-r-rome's future emperors?"

Nigel adusted his spectacles. "If Josephus's revelation is accurate, I believe so, old boy."

"Then I think we know who the lad will be a scr-r-r-ibe for," Max posed. "An' who he'll soon become a tr-r-raitor to."

ARLES, GAUL, JULY AD 68

Beautiful green trees dotted the shoreline as they neared the port of Arles. Leonitus watched the wake of the ship slice through the green waters of the Rhone River. He squinted up at the seagulls trailing along behind them. The gulls had followed the ship from the open sea when they entered the coastal waters off Gaul.

"We're getting ready to dock, Leonitus," Bella told him with a smile. "I know you'll be happy to get on dry land."

"But it won't be Rome," the boy replied with a frown, wrapping his arms over the ship's railing. He strained his eyes toward the wharf up ahead. "Will Uncle Julius meet us?"

Bella scanned the high wall that ran along the river belonging to this city that was to become their new home. "I hope so, Love." She looked around at all of their possessions that they brought from Rome. She was relieved to arrive safely on their voyage across the Mediterranean Sea from the port of Ostia outside of Rome. Her heart ached for her grandson. She knew this was the right decision to leave Rome with its many dangers there, but it was one more loss for Leonitus. He loved the big city. It was his home and was all he had ever known, despite the pain he had suffered there. "We'll make a new beginning in Arles. You'll love it here. You'll see."

Liz sat on a crate of cargo, her eyes beaming with joy to see the shoreline as the ship docked. "Oh, Albert! How happy I am to return to my beloved France!"

Al studied Leonitus. "Aye, I know ye are, Lass, but the wee lad isn't."

Liz looked over at the young boy. "*Oui*, he did not wish to leave Rome. We will need to keep him busy, Albert."

"I be good at that," Al remarked, trotting down the deck of the ship to escape off the gangplank. A fishing boat was unloading next to them on the wharf.

448

Bella spotted the cat making a run for it. "Ari!" She grabbed Leonitus's shoulder and pointed. "You'll have to keep up with Ari!"

Leonitus ran after Al. "I will, Mama!"

Liz ran after him. "And I shall keep up with them both."

Julius Antonius stood on the wharf with one hand on his hip and his helmet under his arm, scanning the harbor. He waved when he saw Bella on the ship. "Mother! Over here!" Bella waved and pointed to Leonitus who was running off the ship after the cat. Julius smiled and nodded, making his way over to the boy.

Al stopped at the baskets of fish being unloaded on the dock. "Sure, and I'm goin' to love it here!"

"Come here, crazy cat!" Leonitus exclaimed, running up to grab Al by the tail.

"Don't tell me he wants some fish," Julius said, walking up behind the boy.

Leonitus spun around, and his eyes widened to see his uncle. He beamed and threw his arms around the centurion. "Uncle Julius!"

449

"Welcome to Gaul. I'm happy to see you," Julius answered, enveloping his nephew in a warm embrace. He pulled the boy back to size him up. "Let me get a look at you."

"I've grown," Leonitus declared. His eyes fell on Julius's silver breastplate, and he immediately zoned in on the lion design. "Look at your armor!"

Julius looked down at his chest as the boy touched the armor with awe. "This belonged to your great-grandfather Marcus. You like it?"

"I *love* it!" Leonitus exclaimed. "I wish I had armor like this."

Julius leaned in and slipped the helmet on the boy's head. "You have indeed grown. I'll let you wear my helmet while we unload your belongings. It has lions on it, too."

Leonitus's face lit up with joy. "Thank you, Uncle Julius! I can really wear this?"

"As long as you guard Ari and Faith while your grandmother and I get things settled," Julius told him.

"Yes, Sir!" Leonitus exclaimed, giving his uncle the traditional Roman salute of a balled fist to his chest, followed by a quickly upraised arm.

Julius returned the salute. "Very well, soldier. Stay here. And make sure Ari doesn't eat that whole basket of fish."

Liz sauntered up to Leonitus and smiled to see the boy wearing the helmet. It was exactly the kind of happy welcome the boy needed upon arriving here. She wrapped her legs around the boy who picked up a fish on the dock and used it like a sword against Al.

"Take that, lion!" Leonitus exclaimed, jabbing the fish into the air.

"Don't mind if I do!" Al replied, with drool coming down his chin. He slapped the fish out of the boy's hand and made Leonitus laugh.

"Julius!" Bella exclaimed, giving her son a big hug. "I'm so happy to see you!"

"I as well, Mother. I'm glad you and Leonitus have come to Gaul," Julius replied, holding his mother as they embraced on the dock. "It's much safer here. How is he doing?"

Bella and Julius glanced over at the boy who continued to play gladiator with the fish and the cat. "He's been through unspeakable pain. There is much sadness and anger in him. I pray he can start a new life here."

Julius fought back tears, thinking of the boy's loss. Leonitus had lost a father, and Julius had lost a brother. Theophilus was lost to both of them. "I pray so, too."

"Where is this going?" a deckhand asked. "My men are ready to unload your cargo."

Bella and Julius turned to answer the man. "I have a cart and horses waiting. Just unload and follow me," he instructed the man. Julius smiled at his mother and pointed. "I see you brought her with you."

"How could I leave her behind? She has the face of your grand-mother," Bella replied with a smile. She nudged her son playfully. "And you are her namesake after all."

"Heave!" the deckhand shouted at his men. "This statue is heavy!"

Liz watched from the dock as the men lifted the statue of Libertas and placed her on a wheeled cart to take her down the gangplank. *From Israel to Italy, and now to France,* she thought. *Libertas is a well-traveled statue. I wonder where she could possibly go next.*

ALEXANDRIA, EGYPT, DECEMBER AD 69

"Extraordinary! This makes four emperors in one year!" Nigel exclaimed. "I dare say, three of them were *dethroned* by the sword, and one was put *on* the throne by a sword."

"So do ye still think the pen be mightier than the sword, Mousie?" Max wanted to know.

Nigel preened his whiskers. "Of course, old boy. Words live on, even when rulers pass from this earth."

They sat in Vespasian's tent, listening in on the conversation with the general and his son. An incredible turn of events had brought them here to Egypt. A tangled web of murder, bribery, and civil war caused control of Rome to shift from one hand to another. Vespasian was preparing to march on Jerusalem when word reached him of Nero's suicide. He decided to wait and see who would be appointed emperor. Galba, the governor of Spain, was proclaimed emperor by the Senate and marched into Rome with the seventh legion, Gemina. But on his march to Rome he destroyed or demanded fines from towns who did not yet embrace him as emperor, angering the masses. Once in Rome, Galba canceled Nero's reforms, and being paranoid like Nero, he executed many powerful men in the Senate without trial. And perhaps most detrimental of all, he refused to pay the Praetorian Guard rewards promised them by Sabinus.

451

Meanwhile, Rome's legions in Germany refused to swear allegiance to Galba and claimed Vitellius as emperor instead. Galba panicked to hear he had lost the Rhine regions of the empire, and appointed Lucinianus as his successor. But this offended many influential men, including Marcus Salvius Otho, who desired the title. Otho bribed the Praetorian Guard, and because they were already against Galba, they readily sided with him. When Galba went to the Forum they murdered him on the spot, and the Senate proclaimed Otho emperor on the same day. Vespasian had sent Titus to Rome to congratulate Galba and to receive the new emperor's orders about Jerusalem. King Agrippa went with Titus, but when they learned of Galba's assassination, they returned back to Vespasian's headquarters in Caesarea.

Although Otho was ambitious, he wasn't cruel, so many expected that he would make a decent emperor. But back in Germany, Vitellius declared himself emperor with the backing of his troops and sent half of them, the finest of all Roman legions, marching toward Rome. Otho did not desire continued civil war and offered a truce to Vitellius. But the greedy general rejected peace and defeated Otho on the battlefield. Rather than retreat, Otho decided to put an end to the unrest and committed suicide, after only three months in power.

The Senate once again met to declare a new emperor upon hearing of Otho's death, and Vitellius marched victoriously into Rome. However, he turned the city into a camp for his seven legions and plundered Rome's own citizens. A glutton and a drunkard, Vitellius spent untold amounts of money on outrageous banquets and triumphal parades that emptied the imperial treasury close to bankruptcy. As Rome incurred debts and money-lenders demanded payment, Vitellius ordered their execution. The violent emperor also murdered anyone thought to be a rival to take the throne.

Now it was the Roman legions in Africa and the Middle East who proclaimed that Vespasian should be emperor. They urged their beloved general to save the empire. Not only was Vespasian a strong leader, he had two sons and a brother to provide heirs to the throne. But Vespasian refused, not desiring to become emperor. His officers pressed him on the matter, and his troops surrounded him, drawing their swords and threatening to kill him if he refused. Vespasian tried to persuade them otherwise, but they would not listen. Finally, he gave in and accepted their demands. He would be Emperor, at the point of a sword.

The governor of Syria, Mucianus, backed Vespasian, and led a legionary force to Rome while Vespasian went to Egypt to cut off Italy's grain supply. They would force the citizens of Italy to make Vitellius surrender, and they would do it or starve to death. The governor of Egypt, Tiberius Alexander, joined his troops and support to Vespasian. Back in Rome, Vespasian's brother, Sabinus, took control of the city but was killed by Vitellius one day before Vespasian's troops reached the city.

Vitellius left one of his palace banquets, stuffed and drunk, and was dragged by the mobs into the streets where he was killed. The people claimed Vespasian emperor, and he was now preparing to sail for Rome.

"Josephus was right, Father," Titus reminded him with a smile. "You are Emperor."

Vespasian's eyebrows lifted as he recalled the prophecy of the Jewish general. "And he is still in chains! Titus, release him immediately."

"I shall, Father, and may I suggest that we not just release him from his chains, but sever them with an ax? This is customary for someone put into chains unjustly," Titus told him.

Vespasian nodded. "Of course, make it so. And take him with you to Jerusalem to act as a translator to talk to the rebels in the city. Make

Josephus a citizen of Rome and give him whatever he desires, including our family name of Flavius. He will be a Roman now."

"Will do, Father. My men are ready to leave for Jerusalem." Titus put on his helmet and locked forearms with his father. "And if the Jews do not submit?"

"If Jerusalem will not surrender," Vespasian said, leaning in close to Titus and balling his fist, "crush them."

JERUSALEM, SEPTEMBER 26, AD 70

Clarie, Max, and Nigel sat on the Mount of Olives, gazing at the streams of smoke rising from the city of Jerusalem. The mood was somber, and the day was dark. Tears rolled freely down their cheeks to see the destruction of the city that had been the heart of the Jewish people for 2,177 years, ever since King David.

"Jesus wept over Jerusalem when he sat here the day he ascended into heaven," Clarie said softly with a broken voice. "He peered down through time and saw this day. It grieved him that his beloved city would someday be destroyed for rejecting him as Messiah."

Nigel cleared his throat. "I had no comprehension of the level of destruction that would come, before the Romans even entered the city. The Jews killed themselves. Titus tried everything he could to save the people and the Temple."

"Aye, but in the end, the Jews chose destr-r-ruction," Max lamented. "An' it all started with a r-r-revolt over Nero's taxes."

"Such a dreadful thing to say, but always follow the money," Nigel stated, shaking his head. "Such horrid waste of life."

Vespasian's strategy had worked. The Romans terrorized towns and villages across Israel, starting in Galilee, sending the rebels fleeing to Jerusalem. Once there, the zealots killed everyone in Jewish leadership that did not agree with their radical beliefs or wished to surrender to Rome. Every moderate Jew died at the hand of another Jew—not at the hand of Rome. A civil war erupted inside the walls of Jerusalem, as the zealots ran rampant in the city, stealing, murdering, and abusing the people. They even destroyed food supplies that could have fed the people for years. Horrors abounded, even in the holy temple area. But then came the famine as Titus's army besieged the city.

The Jews fought to the death, driving back the Romans who repeatedly tried to invade the city through towers, artillery, and troops. Each time, Titus had Josephus plead with the zealots to surrender to Rome. But they spewed venomous hatred for Josephus, whom they considered a traitor, rejecting any talks of surrender or peace. Finally, Titus built a siege wall around the city and starved Jerusalem into submission. Those who tried to escape were captured and crucified, as many as five hundred a day. Jerusalem filled with death.

When the Romans finally broke through the walls and headed to the temple, Titus tried to save it, but in the chaos and bloody fighting, it was set on fire. The Romans plundered and removed everything from the golden menorah to the solid gold candlesticks, tables, bowls, platters, veils, precious stones, to the coffers of coins in the temple treasury. The temple was destroyed on August 30, the very same date it had been destroyed when Babylon marched on Jerusalem over 650 years before.

It took a few more weeks of bloody fighting in Jerusalem to crush the city once and for all. One final outpost of rebels remained in a place called Masada. Titus sent Flavius Silva to take the mountain-top fortress, finally ending the Jewish War with Rome.

In the end, over one million Jews were dead, and one hundred thousand were taken prisoner as slaves. Titus and his legions would now head to Caesarea and then on to Rome with seven hundred of the choicest slaves as trophies to parade through the streets of Rome, including the two zealot leaders from Jerusalem, Simon ar Giora and John of Giscala.

"Gillamon said that the nation of Israel will no longer have a homeland for many centuries to come," Clarie told them. "But the Maker always has his remant, even with the fall of Jerusalem."

"An' Josephus will wr-r-rite all aboot these things," Max added. "Aboot how the Jews chose death over slavery."

Nigel shook his head sadly. "Is life so dear indeed?"

454

49

A COLOSSAL IDEA

ROME, AD 71

Max was awakened by the vibrating ground beneath him. His head shot up, and he looked around to determine what was going on. It wasn't quite yet sunrise, but the sky had a pink hue. He saw Nigel sitting nearby on the base of a statue outside the Temple of Isis. "Wha' am I feelin', Mousie? An earthquake?"

Nigel shook his head. "No, old boy. You are feeling the marching feet of Rome's military legions forming in honor of today's big event: the Triumph parade for Vespasian and Titus."

Max frowned. "Aye, an' the defeat par-r-rade for the poor Jews." He shook from head to tail to wake himself up and walked over to stand next to Nigel. "It's goin' ta be a long day."

The sun peeked up over the horizon, and the sound of thousands of cheering soldiers filled the air. Vespasian and Titus appeared, dressed in their purple regal robes and laurel crowns, and walked up the steps of a massive platform that had been erected for this moment. Vespasian and Titus waved and smiled at the soldiers who lifted their arms as well as their voices in victory. Together the soldiers and these two generals had fought through a long, bloody war with the Jews, and today they would finally celebrate their triumph.

Vespasian held up his hand to quiet the crowd, and after saying a few words and customary prayers to the gods, he sent the procession on its way through the Triumphal Gate of Rome.

"I suppose we should make our way to the Forum to be in position for the grand arrival of the procession," Nigel suggested. "Might I ride on your back so as not to be trampled by the cheering masses of Rome?"

"Jump on, Mousie," Max replied.

The little dog ran through the streets of Rome that were already lined with hundreds of thousands of jubilant people, hoping for a glimpse of Emperor Vespasian, the victorious Titus, and the spoils of war. Vespasian's other younger son, Domitian, would also be part of this grand triumph, having stayed in Rome as a hostage under Nero while General Vespasian went to Judea. The Senate had decreed that each of the Flavian men should receive their own triumph, but the three decided to hold one common triumph. Titus reportedly had refused to accept a wreath of victory, as he claimed that he had not won the victory on his own, but had been the vehicle through which the God of the Jews had manifested his wrath against his people.

When they reached the Forum, Nigel shouted in Max's ear, "Head down the Via Sacra to the Temple of Jupiter. We'll be able to find a good viewing spot there."

Once in place, Max and Nigel prepared themselves for what all of Rome had turned out to see in parade form—the complete domination of Rome and the total annihilation of Israel.

No expense was spared for the display showing the fall of Jerusalem. Massive stages were built on floats that rolled by depicting the scenes of the War with the Jews. Murals and tapestries presented scenes of Israel in its pristine glory and prosperity, followed by scenes of destruction. The proud, high walls of Jerusalem and Israel's cities were shown smashed with the instruments of the Roman war machine. Ramparts were overrun with Roman legionnaires invading the cities. Houses were destroyed, and the mighty temple where the Jewish God resided was destroyed by fire. Surrendering Jews lifted their hands in despair, as they knelt in the streets filled with those who had died from famine or slaughter. On each float Vespasian placed the general of the captured city in the exact position he had been taken, in order to reenact the moment of surrender. Except, of course, for Josephus, who walked with the procession as a citizen of Rome.

Then came the seven hundred choice Jewish captives who were well dressed so as not to tarnish the display. Tears rolled down the faces of some. Anger filled the eyes of others. But defeat covered the faces of all, the human spoils of war presented to Rome. Thousands of other Jews were ushered to holding pens, where they awaited their fates. Other thousands of Jewish slaves had already died in celebratory games that Titus held in the arenas of Caesarea and Alexandria while en route to Rome. After the human spoils of war came unspeakable riches of gold, silver, and ivory in every conceivable form. Tapestries made in Babylon, jewels, golden crowns, and images of gods paraded by. Even exotic animals taken from Israel were included in the parade.

The crowds oohed and aahed at the floats bearing disorganized mounds of treasure taken from the temple in Jerusalem. There before them were items most dear to the Jews: the golden table, the seven-branched menorah, a copy of the Jewish Law, bowls, platters, and even the trumpets from the battle of Jericho.

Finally, a procession of soldiers holding images of victory created out of gold and ivory marched by, followed by Vespasian who drove his own chariot. Behind him Titus drove his chariot while Domitian rode a horse adorned with ornaments of victory and beauty. The parade ended at the Temple of Jupiter, and there they brought forth Simon, the ringleader of the zealots. They executed him, and the crowd erupted in cheers to see the fall of the one who had dared to oppose Rome and lead the Jews in revolt. Rome always made use of visible punishment to drive home its message: no one can defy Rome and live.

457

"I guess Josephus must have mixed feelin's aboot today," Max said. "He's safe as part of the Flavian family now, an' has wealth an' a home here in R-r-rome."

"And the prestigious job of being a historical scribe for the imperial family," Nigel added. "Indeed, he escaped the fate of his countrymen, but I doubt he will ever escape history's label of him as traitor. I wonder which is the lesser of two evils."

"Remember that the Maker can use even a traitor for his purposes," Clarie reminded them, sitting down next to the two, dressed as a young Roman boy. "Jesus needed Judas to fulfill his mission of the cross. Josephus may be viewed as a traitor by the Jews, but God will use him nonetheless."

Max and Nigel surrounded Clarie, climbing into her lap as they watched the Romans cheering the fall of Jerusalem. "So wha' happens now, Lass?" Max wanted to know. "Wha' will happen to all of those poor lads an' lassies that were br-r-rought here as slaves?"

Clarie looked down the Via Sacra at the imposing statue of Nero that stood at the entrance to his Domus Aurea. "They will be used to build what history will forever remember about Rome—the ultimate arena of death."

☧

Vespasian stood behind his two sons, and leaned in to whisper in their ears as they studied the elaborate model in front of them. "With this, the Flavian Dynasty will be forever secured and remembered. With this, we will give Rome back to the people and win their love and favor."

"Panem et circenses," Titus said with a smile as he nodded. "Bread and circuses."

Vespasian slapped Titus and Domitian on their backs with a hearty laugh. "Exactly!" He walked around them to point to the model with one hand and made a fist with the other. "Give food and games to the people, and they will be in your grip forever."

"Father, how is it possible to build something this massive?" Domitian asked. "Walk us through the plan."

Vespasian held out his hands over the model. "I give you the Flavian Amphitheater! As you can see, this is a free standing structure of two amphitheaters placed back to back." He held up four fingers. "There are four keys to making this structure a reality: design, place, money, and labor. For the design, there are two things the engineers realized we must have: arches and *opus caementicium,* simply called *concretus.*"

"What is concretus?" Titus asked, coming over to peer inside the model of the massive amphitheater.

"Concretus is a new form of mortar, and it is much stronger than anything we've ever developed," he explained. "It's one good thing that came from Nero's rebuilding efforts after the great fire. It's a mixture of volcanic dust or *pozzolano,* rubble, sand and lime. We can pour and mold it into any form we desire, including vaulted arches." He pointed to the outside of the model. "Outside there will be a base outer ring wall of eighty arches of columns and stone and two more tiers of arches, making the amphitheater 157 feet high. It will be 615 feet long and 510 feet wide." He then pointed to an open cross section showing the inside. "Look here, and you see that inside, there will be six central rings of vaulted arches made of concrētus. These rings will provide a strong support for the seats."

"This is brilliant!" Domitian exclaimed, peering over the side of the model to the seating design. "How many will the arena hold?"

"At least fifty thousand, but possibly upwards to seventy thousand," Vespasian replied. "Enough for one out of every twenty Romans to be entertained and kept from idleness. And we'll give them tickets for their exact seats." He pointed to the Roman numerals at the top of each entrance arch. "There will be seventy-six numbered entrances for the masses, and four grand entrances for us and the elite of Rome."

"So the people can enter and exit quickly?" Titus asked rhetorically. "What about keeping the people comfortable? Hot crowds are unhappy crowds. And unhappy crowds can easily riot."

Vespasian smiled. "Oh, the crowds will be happy, I assure you. They'll have indoor latrines, 110 marble drinking fountains, vendor booths to buy food, drink, souvenirs, services, and," he paused to point to the spikes protruding from the top of the arena. Elaborate ropes interlaced to the center and were suspended directly over the stadium.

"The *velarium*." Titus finished his sentence.

"Precisely. This retractable awning will cover the seating area to give them shade and shield them from the rain. But it will mainly create a ventilation updraft of a cool breeze for the spectators," Vespasian showed them, bobbing his finger along the spikes at the top. "There are two hundred and forty masts that will be manned by sailors from Rome's navy."

"I bet sailors never thought they would be working in the heart of Rome!" Domitian joked.

Vespasian gave a knowing smile and held up a finger. "Sailors won't just man the velarium. They're going to man ships inside the arena." He pointed to the floor of the arena. "We're going to flood the bottom and have naval battles."

Titus and Domitian looked at one another, wide--eyed and like little boys receiving new toys. "Impossible, Father! How?" Titus wanted to know.

Domitian nodded eagerly, holding out his hand. "And you said another key was the place to put this magnificent arena. By the gods, where will you put this?"

"Come with me," Vespasian told them, gesturing with his pointer finger to follow.

The three Flavians walked down the marble corridor of the Domus Aurea outside to Nero's lake. The water rippled as a breeze blew across the surface. Vespasian walked to the edge of the lake and turned around to face his sons. He smiled, held his hands out wide and exclaimed. "The Flavian Amphitheater will be placed right here! We're going to tear down Nero's beloved Domus Aurea and give this land back to the people of Rome. My architects and engineers have already figured out how to drain this lake by digging a trench around it, filling it with concretus, and building a drainage system that connects to Rome's existing sewers that empty into the Tiber River. This is how we'll be able to flood the floor of the arena. We'll just reverse the process. My engineers think we can transform the arena in a day's time for naval battles."

"Unbelievable!" Titus exclaimed. He held both hands to his head as he gazed across the lake and slowly turned, envisioning the floor of the arena to be right where they stood. "I'm astounded by such a Herculean feat, for that is what it will be."

Domitian placed his hands on his hips, awed by what their father had told them. "Incredible! So you've told us two of the keys: design and place. What about the last two? Money and labor. How are you going to pay for this?"

Vespasian placed his hand on Titus's shoulder. "Your brother has delivered the last two keys to the city of Rome. We'll pay for the amphitheater with the booty from the Jewish temple."

"And the labor?" Domitian asked.

"Our Jewish slaves," Titus answered, crossing his arms as he nodded with an approving smile. "*They* can build it."

"We'll have skilled laborers, of course, but yes, the Jews will do the unskilled, repetitive work. But they'll also work in the mines of Tivoli to produce the two hundred thousand tons of limestone we're going to need," Vespasian answered. "We estimate two hundred carts a day traveling back and forth the twenty miles will take six years for the transport of materials alone. We'll also use slaves to work in brickyards all over Rome to produce the hundreds of thousands of bricks and tiles we'll need."

"But we can also sell some of the slaves to finance this endeavor,

460

Father," Domitian suggested. "Even common Romans can afford one house slave, and we've got thousands to spare."

Vespasian clapped his hands. "Bravo! A slave for every Roman household and a ticket to the games so they can enjoy their newfound leisure! Look at the bounty that the Jews have given us from that little revolt over taxes in Judea. We are now the rulers of the world with me as Emperor and you two as Caesars. And they will finance and build the greatest arena ever built!"

"The fall of Jerusalem is a blessing of the gods on Rome!" Titus cheered. "It was worth it all, Father!"

Domitian pointed to the colossal golden statue of Nero that soared one hundred twenty feet above them. "And what do we do with him?"

Vespasian tilted his head and studied the statue bearing Nero's image. "I'll have artisans give him a spiked crown of sun rays and turn him into the *Colossus Solis,* in honor of our sun god."

"I love it, Father," Titus exclaimed. "He's tall enough to peer into the arena and be pleased with the games. Just think! Gladiators, naval battles, chariot races, animal hunts, executions! How glorious it will be!"

461

"Yes, we shall have opening games the likes of which have never been seen," Vespasian told them. "We will drench the sand with an offering of blood from men and animals that will satisfy all the gods of Rome."

"If any of the Jews live long enough for the arena to be complete, we can use them for the games," Titus suggested.

"Or if we run out of Jews, we can always use Christians," Domitian suggested with a sinister smile.

As the three men continued their lively discussion over their plans for the coming amphitheater, they didn't see the massive lion lurking through Nero's gardens, reveling in all he heard. *Oh, how glorious it will be indeed. Everything is coming together nicely. Nero is dead. Jerusalem and the temple are destroyed, and my enemy's precious, chosen people will build the Colosseum to destroy the Christians. My brilliance is staggering!* The lion slinked off and disappeared into the green trees of Nero's soon to be destroyed gardens.

As the Flavians left the courtyard to set their plans in motion, they didn't notice the tear slip down from the face of Nero's statue. Gillamon had also heard every word.

50

GLADIATOR GLORY

ARLES, AD 74

"Hurry up!" Leonitus whispered, looking around both ways.

"Almost done," Lucius snickered as he finished making his last few marks on the wall. There were drawings and words covering the side of this building. He stepped back, crossed his arms, and read what he had written, admiring his new graffiti.

APOLLOS MANDUCAT RANCENS PISCIBUS

Leonitus shoved his friend. "Apollos eats smelly fish? Come on, Lucius, I can't believe you wasted my time to write that! I want to get to the games before the gladiators march in." He started walking quickly toward the Roman circus of Arles.

"Better not let your grandmother catch you there," Lucius teased him. He turned his voice into a high, mocking tone, "You know we can't attend the games, Leonitus! Christians *die* at the games!"

Leonitus jabbed his friend in the arm. "Be quiet! Let's just get there, alright?" He frowned as he walked along with his friend. *Some friend. All he does is get me in trouble.* He picked up his pace, and Lucius had to take more steps to keep up with him. Leonitus was now sixteen, tall, muscular, and handsome. He tossed back his sandy brown hair from his hazel eyes and smiled when he saw the parade of gladiators getting ready to enter the circus. "There they are! Hurry!"

The two teenage boys went running to where the crowds gathered at the entrance to the arena. There they cheered on the gladiators who were walking by. Leonitus scanned the faces of the gladiators, looking for a famous Thraex gladiator he had seen advertised as coming to the games today.

"Which one is Celadus, the one who is 'the sigh of the girls' in Pompeii?" Lucius asked again in a high-pitched voice, standing at shoulder height with Leonitus, laughing. "Or so the graffiti says about him anyway."

He is really getting on my nerves. Leonitus didn't answer his silly companion but moved down the crowd so he could get a better look. Leading the group of gladiators was their owner, or *lanista.* He was an older man with a hard, leathery face and a pronounced scar above his eyebrow. He wore a deep burgundy toga and brown sandals. Leonitus looked directly behind the lanista and spotted the tattoo on the thigh of the man he was looking for: CEL.

"There he is!" Leonitus shouted, pointing with his left hand to the muscular gladiator who walked with the others. He wore a brown cloth wrapped around his loins and upper thighs, a wide leather belt, tall shin-guards and protective leather armor over his left arm. His helmet was topped with a griffin crest, the distinguishing mark of a Thraex gladiator. Once inside the arena, he would hold a small rectangular shield in one hand and a curved sword in the other. "Celadus! Celadus! Celadus!" Leonitus cheered with his fist pumping in the air. "Victory! Victory! Victory!"

The lanista turned his head in their direction and smiled at the enthusiastic young man. Celadus also smiled and lifted his arm in acknowledgement. Suddenly a swarm of girls started calling out his name, and he winked at them. Leonitus looked on in awe of the reception this gladiator had here in Arles. *Look at how powerful he is! He's adored and invincible.*

"Did you see that?!" Lucius asked. "Everyone *loves* that gladiator! Especially the girls!"

Leonitus rolled his eyes. "Yes, that's *why* we're here, Lucius. He's a star. He's undefeated. Come on, let's get inside. You got the tickets?"

"Yeah, here," Lucius told him, handing him a clay disk. "It wasn't easy to get these. I had to steal them. You owe me."

Leonitus gave a snort. "Hardly. You owe *me.* Have you forgotten you lost our last bet?" He handed the disk to the Roman servant at the gate and hurried inside. They could hear the excited crowds above them. His heart started pounding, and he couldn't wait to get to their seats. But there before them were vendor stalls selling special souvenirs of gladiators. Leonitus stopped and scanned the merchandise. His eyes lit up. He longed to buy something.

"I've got all the best gladiators on this cup!" the eager vendor cried. He held up a green glass that was inscribed with the images of four fighting pairs showing the winner of each match, with a sword or shield held up over the defeated gladiator. "Gamus over Merops, Calamus over Hermes, Tetraites over Prudes, and Spiculus over Columbus. Or, if you want a figurine," he said, putting down the cup and handing Leonitus a colorfully painted clay figurine, "here's the star gladiator of today's game: Celadus!"

Leonitus took the figurine in hand and studied the replica of the gladiator he had seen walking into the circus. His name was painted on the base: CELADUS. "How much?"

"For you, one sestertius," the vendor replied.

"I don't have much money with me." Leonitus frowned and placed the figurine back down. "Maybe later, thanks." He walked away from the vendor. *I'm tired of not having my own money.*

Lucius nudged him. "I bet you'd like *your* name and face on one of those someday."

You know it. Leonitus walked out into the bright sunlight of the arena, ready to watch the carnage of the games. In walked the *bestiarius*, a gladiator trained especially to fight against lions and other wild animals to open the games.

☧

Liz sat at the foot of Bella's bed, watching her toss and turn. Her tail slowly curled up and down, and she wore a frown.

"Is she asleep yet?" Al whispered, putting his paws up onto the side of the bed.

"*Oui,* but she is restless. Her heart is heavy over Leonitus," Liz whispered sadly. "She does not know what to do with him anymore. He continually skips school and hangs around the worst kind of boys. He does not wish to listen about Jesus or Christianity, preferring to practice no faith at all."

"And he goes to the games." Al frowned. "The lad's a rebel, and he's pavin' his own path with bad choices. There's not much more the lass can do for him then, other than pray."

Liz's eyes welled up. "He's a lost, hurting little boy inside." Suddenly they heard a noise from the other room. "Is Leonitus awake?"

"I'll go check, Lass," Al offered, trotting out of the bedroom.

Leonitus was tiptoeing across the tiled floor. In his hands he carried a knapsack, and he looked around the foyer of their house. *This has never been my home.* The young man saw Marcus's helmet sitting on the table. Julius had left it for his mother to hold onto after he received a new one with different plumage for his rank. Leonitus traced the lion etched on the front and hesitated a moment before snatching it up to put in his knapsack. He then went to the secret pottery vase where Bella kept emergency money.

What are ye doin' Lad? Al meowed.

"Shh, Ari!" Leonitus whispered with a finger to his mouth, grimacing at the sound of tumbling coins as he turned the vase over to empty out its contents. The teenager poured the coins into a small leather pouch and replaced the vase. He bent down and gave Al a pat on the head. "I'll miss you, boy. Take care of Mama. I love her, but she'll be happier without me here." With that he crept over to the door and slowly opened it, so as not to make it creak.

As Leonitus slipped into the night, Al slipped out to follow him.

465

A rogue wave slammed into the side of the ship, sending sea spray over the side railing and onto the deck. Leonitus awoke abruptly and sat straight up. As he wiped the sea spray from his face, he heard laughter. "Good morning, boy."

Leonitus turned his gaze and had to shield his eyes from the sun that was already high on the horizon. "Good morning, Sir. I didn't realize it was so late."

The man tilted his head and studied the teenage boy. "What are you doing here? I saw you in the streets of Arles." It was the lanista, the owner of the gladiators.

Leonitus got to his feet and cleared his throat. "I'm following you to Rome, Sir. I want to be a gladiator."

The man raised his eyebrows. "Do you, now?" He looked into the boy's eyes. "Why? You're not a slave or a criminal. That is, not that I know of. And you don't look like a prisoner of war."

"No, Sir. I want to volunteer to go to gladiator school and become the greatest gladiator that has ever lived!" Leonitus answered him excitedly. "Look, I'm left-handed! And I know how to handle a sword. My uncle is a centurion. He taught me how to sword fight and to ride a horse. I've studied all the different types of gladiators! I want to be an *elite* gladiator. I'll bring the crowds to their feet, I know it!"

"You're pretty sure of yourself, aren't you?" the man replied with a low chuckle. "So you have dreams of fame and fortune as an *auctoratus* volunteer? You long for the cheer of the crowd and the adoration of the ladies?" He looked Leonitus up and down slowly. "You're certainly a handsome boy, I'll give you that. And left-handed gladiators are always an attraction. What's your name, boy? How old are you?"

"My name is Leonitus, Sir. And I'm . . . seventeen," he lied.

"Do your parents know you're on a ship bound for Rome to sign your life away to become a gladiator?" the man asked, folding his arms over his chest.

466

"My parents are dead, Sir. They were killed in the great fire of Rome," Leonitus told him. "I'm . . . I'm on my own now. I have nowhere else to go," he lied again. "Please, Sir, what do I have to do to get into the gladiator school? I'll do anything."

The man frowned and rubbed his stubbly chin. "Do you realize that you would need to sign a contract for a designated amount of time where I will *own* you? You must give up your rights as a citizen of Rome and swear an oath to the gods of the underworld that you will accept, without protest, any form of humiliation, including death."

Leonitus flinched slightly at the oath to the gods but lifted his chin in defiance. "Whatever I must do, including death, Sir."

"Hold out your arms, boy." The man walked around Leonitus, examining his height and build, squeezing his biceps and looking in his mouth, inspecting his teeth. "A contract includes how often you will perform, what weapons you will use, and how much you will earn. But nothing happens unless our physician says that you are physically fit after a thorough exam."

"Yes, Sir! I'm in perfect condition," Leonitus exclaimed. "I know your physician will find me fit and ready for the challenge. When can he see me?"

The man pursed his lips and nodded with a grin. "I haven't said I would take you yet."

Leonitus's face fell. He clenched his jaw and could feel the anger boiling inside. He wanted this more than anything. "Test me, Sir, please."

"Oh I will," the man replied. "And if you survive the test, I'll have you examined." He quickly backed away, and Leonitus felt a blow to his lower back.

Leonitus fell to the deck, gasping for breath as he heard the laughter of men surrounding him. The anger rose to his face. He gritted his teeth and spun around to see the gladiator slave who had attacked him from behind. The man was huge, with bulky biceps and braided locks of hair. He looked to be of Egyptian descent.

"AHHHHHHH!" Leonitus screamed as he lunged for the man, swiping his legs out from under him. He and the gladiator began wrestling across the ship's deck. Men gathered round to shout, and some immediately started making bets on who would win. The gladiator held Leonitus in a neck lock and Leonitus struggled to get traction with his feet against the deck. He put his hand down on the deck, reaching for a nearby rope that had a massive knot dipped in pitch to seal the end. Leonitus gripped the rope and slung it at the gladiator's head, hitting him in the temple. The gladiator released his grip, and Leonitus stood up quickly while the man held his head in pain. Leonitus looked around and lifted a dagger from the belt of a man whose back was turned. He put the dagger up to the gladiator's throat and put his knee in his chest. "Do you yield?" he shouted.

The gladiator was caught off guard and held up a finger, using the motion of a gladiator who was ready to surrender on the sand of the arena. Leonitus didn't move a muscle but held the dagger in place and looked around. No one said a word for a moment, shocked by how swift the boy was, and how he had overcome the more powerful gladiator. All of a sudden Leonitus heard the singular clapping of hands from the lanista.

"Well, well, well," the man said, chuckling. He leaned over, putting his hands onto his knees as he got face to face with Leonitus and the gladiator with the dagger to his throat. "It looks like we may have a *novicius* here after all." He put his hand between the two, breaking up the match.

Leonitus slowly stood up and put his hand with the dagger down to his side. His breathing was heavy, and he wiped his face with the back of his arm.

"You've passed the first test, boy," the man told him. His eyes narrowed. "You've got fire in you. Where did that come from?"

467

"From the fire itself, Sir," Leonitus told him, throwing the dagger onto the deck. "I wish to be a *bestiarius*. I want to kill lions, and I'll handle them just like I handled this gladiator."

The man looked down at the gladiator and then back to Leonitus. "You've just beaten the best *bestiarius* in Pompeii, named Atticus." He put his hands on his hips and smiled. "We'll see how you handle yourself with the king of beasts." He reached his hand out to Leonitus. "My name is Spiculus."

Leonitus's eyes grew wide, and the image of graffiti he had seen that night long ago in Rome immediately flooded his mind. Spiculus was the name of the gladiator who he later sneaked back to see had a "V" painted on the wall for his victory. Spiculus was Nero's favorite, and the one who refused to go to him the night Nero took his own life. He swallowed hard and took Spiculus's hand, overcome with awe and respect for one of the greatest gladiators of all time. "It's an honor to meet you, Sir. You were the first gladiator I ever knew about in Rome. Your fame has spread across the empire!"

468

Spiculus got eye to eye with Leonitus and held up the back of his hand that was tattooed with a bee. "My name means 'sting.' And yours means 'lion-like.' Let's see if Rome will come to feel your name as it has mine. Whether you live or die by your name will be up to you, boy."

"Death or glory, Sir," Leonitus replied with a grin. "I plan on glory, like you."

"I like you, boy," Spiculus said with a grin. "I have a feeling you will have your glory as a gladiator. But I will teach you not only how to *live*, but how to *die*. And I will teach you to die with honor, which is the only way any of my gladiators will ever leave this earth standing before the Emperor of Rome."

Al peeked out from the coil of rope where he was hiding throughout this scene on the deck of the ship. He swallowed hard and sadly shook his head to see the path that Leonitus had chosen. The cat looked over and saw the knapsack with Marcus's helmet. "At least he's got the helmet o' salvation with him for the outside. Oh, Maker, please help the laddie find it for the inside." He decided to stay hidden until they reached Rome. Given the violent nature of the men on this ship, he didn't want to take any chances that they didn't like cats.

ROME

"Look at the size of it!" Atticus exclaimed. "I've never seen an arena so huge."

The band of gladiators rode along in a caged cart in front of the Flavian Amphitheater rising from the ground. The lower ring of arches was complete, and scaffolding rose to the second level that was in process.

"It's going to be even bigger than that. I've seen the plans," Spiculus told them from where he sat in front of the cart. "It will be the greatest arena in the entire Roman Empire, so you must train and fight hard so you will be able to fight for the opening games."

"I'll be there," Leonitus declared, drawing sneers and laughs from the veteran gladiators.

"You'll have to prove it, *novicius,*" Celadus challenged him. "You're not even a *tiro* yet."

Novicius was the title given to a prospective gladiator. *Tiro* was a gladiator who had completed his training yet had not competed in the arena.

"When will it be opened, Spiculus?" Atticus asked.

"Years. For now, let your focus be on training and fighting in the smaller arenas around Rome," Spiculus replied.

The gates ahead of them opened and the horses pulled the cart into the courtyard of the gladiator school. Once the back of the caged cart was unlocked, Leonitus and all of the gladiators stepped out onto the cobblestone pavement. Leonitus watched as the gate was closed and locked, leaving them standing in a square courtyard surrounded on all four sides by barracks where the gladiators stayed. In the courtyard were various training areas where gladiators trained with heavy wooden swords: a tall log platform eight feet off the ground, a scaffold that held a massive log suspended by a chain, and a series of crosses or *palus* poles six feet high. Pairs of other gladiators wielded wooden swords and followed the numbered, choreographed movements called out by the *doctores,* or trainers, as if they were learning a dance. Lethal weapons were not allowed in the schools.

Other pairs of gladiators were being trained with a referee who held a long staff or a *rude* to caution or separate opponents during the match. A gladiator on the ground self-acknowledged his defeat with his upraised finger. In a real match, the referee would step in and look to the *editor* of the games to determine the fate of the defeated gladiator. Many times the editor would allow the mood of the crowd to determine if a gladiator would be spared or if he would be killed, and would indicate his decision with a thumb to the throat for death, or a thumb up for life. If a gladiator was to be killed, he had to follow strict rules of conduct. He could never ask for mercy or cry out. A "good death" allowed a gladiator to die with honor and redeemed him from the dishonor of weakness and defeat, providing a noble example to those who looked on. All over the courtyard, gladiators were learning how to fight well and die well.

In two field arenas beyond the courtyard, gladiators known as *equites* trained on white horses in one arena, while gladiators known as *bestiarius* fought against wild animals in another. These were the two types of gladiators that Leonitus longed to be. It was rare to train in more than one gladiatorial style, and that is precisely why Leonitus wanted to be trained in both. He didn't wish to be an *ordinarii*, but an *elite* gladiator. His glory would be in standing out and getting the fame with the crowds by entertaining them in multiple ways.

Equites gladiators rode horses into the arena to open the gladiatorial competition. They only fought with other equites and began each match on horseback, fighting with lances or some kind of short throwing spear. They would then dismount the horses to engage in hand to hand combat with short swords and small round cavalry shields. Equites were lightly armored since they needed to move easily and quickly. An *eques* wore a visored helmet without a crest, but with two large feathers, and an armguard, or *manica*. He also wore a sleeveless tunic belted at the waist that came to his knees. His lower legs were wrapped with protective covering as well.

Spiculus and Leonitus walked through the grounds, while the veteran gladiator explained the life that the young man would experience in this gladiator school. Over one hundred gladiators lived, trained, and fought here. The gladiators were divided by type, each with its own teacher: *murmillo, thraex, hoplomachus, retiarius, secutor, eques,* and *bestiarius.* Gladiators were housed by type and status with separate living quarters, as they would be pitted against one another in battle. The novicius were assigned to a small cell with a bed, whereas gladiators with higher rank such as *primus palus* were afforded larger, more private accommodations.

Gladiators were well fed with a high-energy diet of barley, beans, oatmeal, and dried fruit. They also were expected to have warm baths and massages daily after training. And they received the finest medical care available in Rome. If they were wounded in matches, physicians were excellent at tending broken bones and external wounds. But if the wounds were internal, there was not much they could do.

"After six months you will be tested here to see if you are ready to have a live match in an arena," Spiculus told him. "You will be paid after each match the equivalent of the annual salary of a Roman legionnaire. You will be expected to fight at least three matches per year. When you have won five matches you can earn your freedom, if you so desire it. Otherwise, you will serve for a minimum of five years."

Leonitus grinned broadly and his eyes widened at hearing this news. *So much money!*

"You will train first as an eques, beginning with mastering the skills needed to fight once you dismount from your horse," Spiculus explained. "Then you will move onto the field to learn to fight with the lance. Once you have mastered becoming an eques, you can train to be a bestiarius. Understood?"

471

"Understood, Sir," Leonitus replied.

Spiculus put his hand on the boy's shoulder. "Very well, it is time to take the oath. Once you repeat these words, there is no turning back. Are you ready?"

Leonitus stood before him and put a balled fist over his heart. He held his chin up with confidence. "I am."

"Repeat the *sacramentum gladiatorium* after me," Spiculus instructed him. "URI, VINCIRI, VERBERARI, FERROQUE NECARI."

Leonitus cleared his throat and in a loud voice repeated the sacred oath of gladiators, "I will endure to be burned, to be bound, to be beaten, and to be killed by the sword."

Spiculus grinned. "Welcome, *novicius* Leonitus. Now, you may see the physician while I draw up your contract. He will also give you a tattoo on your thigh: LEO. When you win your first match I will put a lion on your hand."

"Thank you, Sir," Leonitus replied. He grinned back. "Death or glory."

Spiculus nodded. "For your sake, I hope it will be gladiator glory."

51

GATE OF LIFE

ROME, APRIL 25, AD 80, MIDNIGHT

Franciscus dipped his small brush into the vial of white paint to put the finishing touches on the horse figurine. He then held it up and inspected the detail under the light of the oil lamp that hung over the table, wanting to make sure it was perfect. His blue eyes blinked hard against the late hour and the smoky lamp. Franciscus blew on the paint and set it aside. The handsome young entrepreneur got up and stretched out his back, tired from his late night of painting. He didn't mind the work, for it brought him much Roman coin at his booth in the Circus Maximus. Lately he had been considering hiring someone to assist him, for he could hardly keep up with the demand. *If I'm this busy now, I'll be overrun when the new arena opens.*

Franciscus looked around at the crates full of souvenirs ready for sale: oil lamps, knives, and figurines, all bearing the image of the latest star of Rome. His work was so good that he had already been invited to bring his wares to a private banquet the night before the inaugural games of the Flavian Amphitheater. The host wanted each of his guests to have the sought-after souvenirs stamped with the opening date as a memento to celebrate the spectacular event. All he lacked was the date. Franciscus pulled a hand through his black hair and took a large gulp of water. As he set down his cup he smiled at the painted clay eques figurine that would sit atop the white horse he had just painted. He again took his seat and picked up another brush, this time dipping it into black paint while holding the eques figurine in hand. "You, my friend, have brought me fortune while you have amassed fame. May the gods continue to give you favor." He kissed the figurine for luck and then put the final touch on the leg of the gladiator, spelling his nickname chanted by the adoring crowds of Rome: LEO.

☧

"Report," Titus demanded, walking ahead of his entourage of advisors out onto the sandy floor of the arena. He put his hands on his hips as he slowly turned full circle to gaze up at the nearly completed amphitheater.

"Emperor, relief efforts are under way for the displaced citizens near the Capitoline district where the fire burned for three days. Although the damage did spare the insulae, many public structures were destroyed," the secretary reported. "The Temple of Jupiter, the Pantheon, and Pompey's Theatre were badly burned."

"But many more have died from the plague than the fire, Emperor," another advisor noted. "The people do, however, appreciate the relief efforts you have put forth in these twin disasters."

Titus frowned and crossed his arms over his chest, shaking his head in disbelief at the disasters that had befallen the Roman Empire since his father had died June 23, AD 79. "Twin disasters of Pompeii and Herculaneum, wiped out in a single day by the eruption of Mount Vesuvius last August. Now twin disasters of fire and plague in Rome," he recounted. "The people must surely think I have fallen out of favor with the gods." He knelt down and scooped up a handful of sand from the arena floor. "My only hope to escape assassination is the success of this arena. We will drench this sand with blood to appease the gods and to satisfy the people." He cast the sand out and wiped his hands. "My father didn't get to see the completion of this arena, which was his prize project for the people of Rome. I will not allow its opening to be tainted by the shadow of suspicion and doubt over the Flavian Dynasty. I will wait no longer. Announce the opening games for August 1st."

The advisors looked at one another in alarm. "But, Sire, the inside of the arena is nowhere near being ready for the inaugural games!" one of them protested.

Titus rushed up to the man's face and punctuated his words with

473

a finger pointed to the arena floor. "Whoever doesn't accomplish their task to be ready for the games will have their blood spilled here on opening day! Am I clear?"

The advisor swallowed hard and nodded aggressively with an uneasy smile, clutching his easel to his chest. "Very clear, Emperor. It will be done as you say."

Titus held the man's gaze for a moment longer, causing beads of sweat to break out on the frightened man's forehead. "See to it. We will also open the new baths for the people the following week." He turned and looked around the stadium. "One hundred days of games. Nine thousand animals for morning entertainment. A continuous supply of prisoners for execution at midday. And five thousand gladiators for the main attraction in the afternoons. Make it so."

ROME, JULY 21, AD 80

474

Steam rose from the hot water in the giant wooden barrel as Leonitus climbed into it, resting his head back in sheer delight. "Ahhhh, thank the gods for a warm bath."

"Is it to your liking?" a servant asked him, pouring scented oil into the water. "I wish for the water temperature to be perfect for you, Leonitus." Even the servants were star struck by this gladiator who had captured the hearts of Romans across the empire. He was undefeated, showered with money and gifts, adored by women, and sought after by the elite of Roman society to attend their banquets. He had achieved exactly what he set out to win: the glory of Rome.

Leonitus smiled and looked up at the servant. "Perfect as ever, Tycho, just like your name."

The servant bowed humbly and smiled. "When you are finished, I will have your massage table ready."

Leonitus stretched out his hands across the back of the bath and breathed in the aromatic oils. "Thank you, Tycho." He watched the steam rise, but his smile quickly faded as he glanced over at another gladiator sitting in a nearby bath barrel, staring at him. Leonitus grimaced and flicked the water with the back of his fingers to splash the other man in the face. "What are you looking at, Domitius?"

"Nothing, just enjoying the bath like you, Antonius," Domitius replied, resting his head back on the bath. He had learned the family history of Leonitus through many discussions over the past three months, and was the only one that knew he was of the family of Antonius.

"Don't you *ever* call me that, slave lover!" Leonitus shouted, flicking water again. He rested his arms on the edge of the bath, and his lion tattoo glistened from the water on the back of his hand.

Domitius closed his eyes and smiled slightly. "As you wish. I don't mind you calling me slave lover. In fact, I'm proud of it. I've accomplished what I set out to do here, and next week I plan to win my freedom and leave this place. I need only one more victory to attain the *rudis.*"

The *rudis* was a wooden sword given as a symbol of a gladiator's freedom for his having completed the required number of wins. Domitius had volunteered just like Leonitus, but for far different purposes. He did so to get enough money to pay for the release of a friend who was a slave. Domitius was a poor laborer, and his slave friend was a Christian Jew taken from Jerusalem when Titus destroyed the city. Together they worked on the building of the new arena, and over the years the slave had slowly witnessed to Domitius about Jesus. Domitius eventually became a Christ follower. When he realized that his friend would be used as a prisoner for execution in the arena for the opening games, he had to do something. In desperation he signed a contract to be a gladiator, hoping he would not have to take life, but only fight to win three matches and be done with it.

Domitius had once been a soldier for the Roman cavalry and was a master horseman but had lost everything to idleness and a wasted life in the taverns of Rome after he left military service. When he first met Leonitus, he soon discovered that the young gladiator was from the family line of Antonius. Leonitus shared that his uncle was a centurion who had taught him to ride and handle a sword; when Domitius learned that his uncle's name was Julius, he put two and two together that Julius was the centurion who had escorted Paul to Rome, having been shipwrecked on Malta. The gladiator had several scrolls in his possession, and one was Luke's Acts of the Apostles.

When Domitius realized that Leonitus had lost his father, Theophilus, to the great fire, he tried to comfort the young man with words of hope, but Leonitus would have none of it. The prideful gladiator had turned his back on his past—his parents, his family, their faith, and especially their God. Leonitus despised Christians now, for he saw them

475

as weak. He could never reconcile a God who would allow him to lose his parents in a fire, much less Jesus' followers to be slaughtered at the hands of the Romans because of their belief in him. Besides, now that he had attained such earthly success, Leonitius didn't feel the need to deal with spiritual matters. He was young, handsome, talented, adored, successful, and had Rome eating out of the palm of his hand.

"Maybe you'll exit the arena through the Gate of Death next week," Leonitus chided Domitius with a laugh as he climbed out of the bath, wrapping a towel around himself. He referred to one of only two exits for gladiators in the arena. They entered through the Gate of Life into the arena, and if they lived through the match, they exited back out that gate. But if they died, they were carried out through the Gate of Death, where their bodies were prepared for burial.

"Someone once told me that Jesus said he was the gate, and that whoever entered through him would be saved," Domitius replied calmly, also getting out of the water. "He's the only true Gate of Life."

476

"Saved?" Leonitus smirked. "All of this 'Jesus died on the cross for sinners' thinking makes no sense to me. I've seen plenty of crucifixions in the arena of believers who *weren't* saved from that fate. And it all started with their Jesus. Who would actually give up his life that way for someone?"

Domitius smiled and nodded, knotting the towel at his waist. "I know. It is difficult to believe that someone could love so much to be willing to die for someone else. But you're wrong about the believers. Every single one of them who has died in the arena has exited through the Gate of Life."

"Well, *I* will choose when *I* die—no one else!" Leonitus shouted at him. "I must maintain control of my life."

"Jesus also chose when he would die—no one else," Domitius told him. "He is the way, the truth and the life."

"SILENCE! I will not listen to this any longer!" Leonitus shouted, putting his hands to Domitius's throat. "Do you realize you could be used as lion fodder in the arena for being a Christian? It's only because Titus needs so many gladiators for the games that you are allowed to live. And nothing would give me more pleasure than to send you on your way to the afterlife."

Suddenly Spiculus entered the room. "ENOUGH! Let him go, Leonitus."

Leonitus clenched his jaw but did as his lanista ordered. He released Domitius with a shove and walked away to where his masseuse waited. He climbed onto the table on his stomach and closed his eyes as Tycho worked out the knots in his shoulder. But try as he might to relax, all Leonitus could see behind closed eyes was the haunting image of his father hugging him and telling him how much Jesus loved him.

ROME, JULY 30, AD 80

Max, Liz, Al, and Nigel sat together in the ruins of Bella's garden, now gutted by fire but long ago abandoned when she fled for Arles with young Leonitus.

"I just don't see how such a sweet little boy from such a wonderful Christian family could turn out to be a cold-blooded killer," Liz lamented. "Sweet Leonitus is a *gladiator.*"

"Aye, an' not jest an ordinary gladiator, Lass," Max answered. "He's the star of R-r-rome. Ye should hear how the people cheer his name when he enters the arena."

"LEO! LEO! LEO!" Al cheered, giving his rendition of the crowd with his paws raised in the air. "He even wears Marcus's lion helmet when he fights lions. I have to close my eyes when he does that. But I'm always there in case somethin' bad happens to him."

Nigel put his paw on Liz's shoulder. "I know this comes as a great shock, my dear, but our Leonitus has killed many lions as well as other gladiators."

"Now I'm glad Bella didn't know what became of him," Liz said, shaking her head sadly. "At least now she is at peace and with her beloved Armandus and Theophilus in heaven."

Liz had stayed with Bella in Arles all these years, giving her as much comfort as she could after Leonitus ran away. Clarie had made sure that Liz knew where the boy and Al had gone, so Liz held on to the secret as she watched Bella grieve the loss of her prodigal grandson. Julius had been unable to track him down and was angry at the boy for the pain he caused Bella. She finally died peacefully of natural causes, and Liz returned to Rome.

"So the g-g-grand openin' of the games be soon," Max lamented. "Mousie an' I were with those poor lads an' lassies that built the arena. But I don't want ta be inside when it opens."

477

"But you must be there," came a voice. Over in the corner of the courtyard sat a pair of small, charred statues in the form of lions at the base of a staircase. "You need to see what happens with Leonitus that day."

"Gillamon!" Max cried, running over to the statue. "Will somethin' good finally happen ta the lad?"

"There is the *possibility* of something good finally happening to him. As always, what he chooses to do will be up to him," Gillamon replied as the stone lion blinked its eyes. "Glad to see you back in Rome, Liz. Thank you for taking care of Bella all these years."

"It has been my honor to do so," Liz replied.

"Do you mean that we must all attend the opening of the games in the amphitheater?" Nigel asked. "All of that bloodshed is simply dreadful."

"Yes, but before the games, Nigel, I need you to attend a pre-game banquet," Gillamon relayed. "Leonitus will be the guest of honor, and I need for you to make sure someone else is in attendance."

478

"Who?" Max asked.

"Julius. He has briefly returned to Rome," Gillamon explained. "You must get him an invitation to the banquet. It will be his only opportunity to see Leonitus."

"I do not think he will be pleased to see his nephew," Liz said with a wrinkled brow.

The lion statue nodded. "Let us pray that Julius's love will triumph over his anger in that moment, Liz. There is something that Leonitus needs to know, and he can only learn this from Julius. Do you remember how Armandus saved the life of the slave on that shipwreck long ago, and how difficult it was for Julius to understand why his father had given up his life for a slave?"

"*Oui*, Paul helped him to understand this when we were aboard the ship," Liz remembered.

"Leonitus is hostile to a fellow gladiator who he will face in a match during the opening games," Gillamon told them. "That gladiator is none other than the grandson of the slave that Armandus saved. His name is Domitius."

The animals' jaws dropped at this incredible turn of events. "How staggeringly poignant!" Nigel exclaimed.

"Quite so. What is more, Domitius is now a believer, and has been trying to share Christ with Leonitus," Gillamon added. "Leonitus is hostile and wishes to hear none of it. Domitius knows that Leonitus is the son of Theophilus, and the nephew of Julius, as he received a copy of Luke's Acts scroll, compliments of Clarie."

"*C'est magnifique!*" Liz cheered to hear of Luke's work circling back to impact the very son of the one who published it.

"Domitius sold himself as a gladiator in order to release a Jewish Christian from slavery. But even he does not realize the connection he has with Leonitus and their grandfathers," Gillamon continued. "If Julius can make this connection for them at the banquet, both of their lives will be changed."

"Right, so where is the banquet, and where shall I deliver Julius's invitation?" Nigel asked, turning to Liz with a raised paw. "If you would be so kind as to pen it, my dear."

Liz placed her paw on her chest. "*Bien sûr, mon ami!*"

"You don't need an address," Gillamon replied. "The host is none other than Titus himself. The banquet will be held at the imperial palace. You can find Julius at the Praetorian Guard headquarters."

479

"Talk aboot goin' into the lion's den with Julius bein' a Christian and all," Al remarked.

Liz frowned. "Titus is thankfully not as obsessed with persecuting Christians as was Nero."

"Speakin' of lions, will ye know who be lurkin' aboot for the games?" Max asked.

"I am sure he shall be there in one form or another. He has waited for this day longer than anyone," Gillamon replied. "I will be there too."

"Shall you be peering into the arena from Nero's colossal statue perhaps?" Nigel asked. "I know you kept watch from there while the amphitheater was built."

"No, I need to be closer to the action," Gillamon replied. "I'll be wearing Vespasian that day."

Liz furrowed her brow. "What do you need us to do in the arena, Gillamon?"

"Once you arrive in the arena, find a place to watch. And pray for Leonitus and Domitius," Gillamon instructed them. "Look lively, everyone. It will be the day of the lion, with the darkest one of all on the prowl."

THE LION TAMER

ROME, JULY 31, AD 80

Julius could hear the music pouring out of the imperial palace as he turned to walk up the path lined with umbrella pine trees. Tomorrow they would no doubt burn the aromatic pinecones from these trees in bowls to mask the smells coming from the arena. The very word "arena" meant "sand," appropriately named for the thick layer of sand that was used to soak up the blood spilled there.

A group of Rome's elite citizens stood outside laughing as they arrived at the front entrance to the palace. The ladies were dressed in the finest red, green, and blue silk dresses trimmed in gold, and decorative combs pinned up their hair in elaborate styles. Enchanting ringlets of curls cascaded down their rouged cheeks. Their necks were bejeweled with necklaces, and their wrists adorned with golden cuffs. The men wore togas of prominence and rings of power. These were the senators and knights of Rome, invited by the Emperor to this exclusive banquet on the eve of Rome's shining moment of history: the opening of the Flavian Amphitheater.

Julius cleared his throat as he excused himself to pass through the pompous crowd, making his way up the steps and handing his invitation to the servant guarding the entrance. *What am I doing here?* he thought to himself, feeling like a fish out of water. He had no idea why he had been invited to this event and had no desire to be here. But when the Emperor called, a soldier of Rome unquestioningly answered.

Inside the musicians played and the dancers danced. The wine flowed, and numerous servants dressed in pleasing attire circulated the platters of abundant food. Guests lounged around on couches, enjoying the bounty provided by Emperor Titus. Others stood up so they would be seen. Men strategized, women gossiped, and lovers whispered in dimly lit corners. Julius didn't know where to stand, so he remained in the shadows, observing the crowd and taking in the incredible décor of this palace.

Every square inch of this place was filled with beauty. The ceiling and walls were painted red and crowned with thick gold molding. Painted frescoes adorned every wall with delightful scenes of gaiety and celebration. Intricate mosaics covered the floor in a flourish of designs, depicting the gods bestowing favor on the Emperor. Busts of Vespasian, Titus, and Domitian stood around watching the guests, reminding them of the power behind Rome. Massive pots held greenery and eight-foot palm trees. Iron filigree hooks holding oil lamps jutted out from the walls to provide light.

481

Julius heard the sound of coins dropping and turned to see a young lady drop to the floor to pick them up. She stood before a table where a man displayed trinkets and treasures of the gladiators. Julius walked over and scanned the items he had for sale. He saw oil lamps, knives, and figurines depicting the various gladiators: *murmillo, thraex, hoplomachus, retiarius, secutor, bestiarius,* and *eques.* Never had he heard of a common vendor attending an imperial party to sell his wares, but Titus was not a common emperor. He wanted his guests to have such souvenirs without having to leave their elite seats at the arena tomorrow. Julius wondered why the rich emperor didn't just give these souvenirs to his guests, rather than make them buy them there. He laughed to himself at the absurdity of providing the elaborate games to the people for free, yet making them buy the trinkets that would remind them to keep returning to the arena for one hundred days.

Julius smiled at the thought and picked up an *eques* figurine sitting atop a white horse. He studied the detail of the artwork and was impressed with the quality of the piece, noting that it was stamped with the opening date of the amphitheater. He tilted his head as he read the name on the leg of the eques figurine: LEO.

"Ah, I see you have selected the greatest gladiator in all of Rome!"

Franciscus noted eagerly, clasping his hands together in anticipation of a sale. "The emperor brought me here as entertainment for his guests so they can take home their favorite gladiator for good luck to bet on tomorrow's games." He looked at the young lady who was clearly smitten with LEO as she dreamily clutched the figurine to her chest. He winked at her and held out his hand. "Or to simply enjoy as a trophy." She blushed and handed him a coin for her prize.

"Leo?" Julius asked, continuing to study the figurine. "Sorry, but I just arrived in Rome. I'm not familiar with him."

"How can you not *know* about him?" the pretty young lady asked in shock. She was clearly an admirer. "He is both an *eques,* and a *bestiarius,*" she explained, picking up the figurine fighting a lion. "Leonitus is an elite gladiator from romantic Gaul."

Franciscus leaned over the table to get closer to his prospective buyer. "And he is the guest of honor here tonight. Emperor Titus wanted to show him off before the elite people of Rome."

482

Julius's eyes widened, and his heart raced at this news. He gripped the figurine and clenched his jaw in anger. "Where is he?"

Franciscus looked puzzled at his reaction and pointed to the table of gladiators in the back of the room. Raucous laughter accented fists slamming on the table as the men joked and challenged one another to arm wrestle. They were dressed alike in short red tunics and leather belts, with wide leather wrist guards and sandals. The gladiators were slaves to their profession, but tonight they were celebrities, given whatever they desired. Tomorrow they would do the bidding of Rome.

Julius turned to leave the table, but Franciscus reached over to stop him with his hand before he walked away with the unpaid merchandise. "Do you wish to take LEO with you?"

Julius handed the figurine back to Franciscus. "That is an understatement."

The young lady shrugged her shoulders as she locked eyes with the puzzled vendor. She then turned and walked away from the table, glancing to the top of one of the palm trees. Nigel saluted her. She smiled and kept walking to stand behind the crowd of people who gathered near the gladiators, hoping to meet them.

Julius stomped over to the gladiator table and excused his way to the front of the crowd, scanning their faces for his nephew. It took a moment, for Leonitus was now twenty-two years old and no longer a young boy. But then he heard his distinctive laughter and saw the sandy brown hair that Leonitus tossed back as he grabbed the shoulder of a fellow warrior. Julius gripped his fists as his emotions swirled in confusion. He was both angry and happy to see his long lost nephew. Part of him wanted to hug the young man out of sheer exuberance that he was alive and well. But part of him wanted to punch him in the face for the selfish thing he did in abandoning his family to pursue the glory of becoming a gladiator. He didn't know what to say. What could he say, especially as Leonitus was held under the continual gaze of the power elite of Rome?

The young girl stepped up next to Julius, still clutching her statue. "That's him sitting in the middle," she said, pointing to Leonitus.

Julius gritted his teeth. "I know."

"If you want to talk to him, you only need to ask," she told him. "The gladiators are here to do the bidding of Titus's guests. But everyone is too shy or too awestruck to do so yet."

Julius looked down at the young girl who smiled up at him encouragingly. He looked back at Leonitus and swallowed. Julius's palms were sweaty, as he didn't know how his nephew would respond at seeing him. His heart raced but he finally blurted out, "Leonitus, I wish to have a word with you."

The gladiator turned his smiling face in the direction of the voice that called out to him. His face fell as he immediately recognized Julius. "Uncle," he muttered softly in disbelief and shame.

Domitius's ears perked up, and he looked back at Julius and then to Leonitus, watching this exchange. *Julius Antonius?* he thought to himself.

Leonitus slowly stood up from the table, and Julius was taken aback by how tall and muscular he was. His biceps and triceps were massive, as were his legs. He lifted his square chin and walked around from the table, masking his emotions in front of the crowd. He decided to handle this with bold arrogance to deflect any nervousness about the matter. "Uncle! How good to see you!" he exclaimed loudly as he walked over to Julius with outstretched arms. He towered over his uncle and bored into him with his striking hazel eyes.

Julius gave a false smile and locked forearms with Leonitus. "And how *surprising* to see you, Nephew," he uttered through gritted teeth.

He smiled and raised his voice. "Might I have a word with Rome's greatest gladiator?"

"Of course," Leonitus replied, turning to the crowd. "Excuse me for a moment, will you?"

The ladies batted their eyes and smiled, grazing his skin with their fingertips as he walked by. They turned and suppressed screeches and giggles of excitement.

"Walk with me, Nephew," Julius insisted, punctuating each terse word. He shoved him slightly with one hand and pointed to the open door leading to the veranda outside. Together the two walked along the pristine balcony where the flames of torches blew against the gentle evening breeze. Julius looked around to make sure they were out of earshot of the crowd, and then he laid into him.

"Do you realize the pain you caused my mother? How dare you leave without a trace?" Julius began. He spilled out word after word as his anger boiled over. "You abandoned your family and everything we taught you to become a killing machine! A *slave* to Rome? Wasn't it enough that Mama poured her life into you to prevent you from going down this path? She died with a broken heart, wondering what happened to you!" He put his hands on his hips and turned his back on Leonitus, walking a few steps away to regain his composure.

The tall, arrogant Leonitus suddenly felt faint at hearing the news that his grandmother had died. Tears stung his eyes, and he felt like he had been struck in the gut with a blow far more powerful than an opponent in the arena. "Mama died?" He felt sick to his stomach and sat down on a marble bench. He leaned over and put his head into his hands. "I didn't know she would be so sad. I thought all I did was upset her and disappoint her. I thought she'd be glad I was gone."

Julius turned around and frowned, pursing his lips as he saw glimpses of the sweet little boy he once knew showing great emotion over this news. His heart was pricked with pity and grace for his nephew. Julius knew that Leonitus didn't realize what he had done in the immaturity and selfishness of his youth. He also knew that Leonitus had always been lost in his grief and anger. He took in a deep breath and exhaled through his nose. He walked over and sat down next to Leonitus. His voice took on a calmer tone. "I looked everywhere for you. I thought perhaps you had been killed by thugs and thrown into the Rhone River." He paused

484

and hesitated, holding his hand up over the young man's back for a moment. He haltingly placed it on Leonitus. "We both were heartbroken. You are our Leonitus, and nothing you could ever do would make us love you any less."

Leonitus wiped the tears with the back of his hand and turned to gaze at his uncle. "That was before I became a gladiator." He straightened up and wiped his nose. "Now I'm sure you despise me."

Julius exhaled and shook his head. "I might despise what you do, but not who you are."

The young man locked eyes with his uncle and for a moment longed to reach out to him in a huge embrace. Suddenly they heard the laughter from the crowd, and Leonitus was brought back to the reason for the party. He stiffened and lifted his chin. "They are one and the same."

"Excuse me?" came Domitius as he stepped out onto the veranda. "May I have a word?"

Leonitus got to his feet and cleared his throat, erasing any emotion so his adversary wouldn't notice. "Uncle, *you* have a fan here tonight," he exclaimed, holding his hand out to Domitius. "I'll leave you two to get to know one another." He walked away from them, relieved to have an excuse to get away from Julius. He reentered the party and leaned over to kiss the cheek of a noblewoman who lifted her arms for an embrace.

Julius stood as Domitius approached him and wore a puzzled expression. "Do I know you?"

"No, but I know you," Domitius replied with a smile and an outstretched hand. "I am Domitius, son of Eligius. I know of you from Luke's letter. You are the centurion who was with Paul, aren't you?"

Julius was stunned. "How do you know this?" he asked cautiously.

Domitius walked to the marble railing and drew an invisible half fish with his finger. Julius completed the invisible half fish, drawing the secret sign of a follower of Christ. "You are a believer?"

"Yes, and a gladiator. I sold myself to pay for the release of a Jewish believer slave who would have been sent to the arena tomorrow otherwise," Domitius explained. "Leonitus and I are equites, so have had many discussions since I came to the gladiator school. He told me that his uncle taught him to ride horses and handle swords. One conversation led to another, and I figured out that you were the Julius from Luke's letter. While Leonitus confirmed this, he is very hostile to Christianity

485

and will not discuss it with me. I tried to help him with the anger over losing his parents, but he will have none of it."

"You have tried to talk with him about this?" Julius asked urgently with his hand on the gladiator's arm. "If only someone could reach him. I fear for his salvation. He has denied Christ, and he could die in that arena tomorrow."

"I know this full well," Domitius replied with a frown.

A moment of heavy silence hung between them for a moment. "Did Leonitus also tell you who his grandfather was?"

"No, he did not," Domitius replied. "Who was he?"

"Centurion Armandus Antonius. Luke doesn't mention him by name, but he was the centurion at the foot of Jesus' cross," Julius explained.

Domitius's eyes grew wide at this news. "Leonitus is the *grandson* of the centurion who exclaimed, 'Surely this was the Son of God'?" He put a hand to his forehead in shock. "Armandus was his name? This can't be!"

486

"Why, what do you mean?" Julius asked him.

Domitius put his hands to the sides of his face in disbelief. "A centurion by the name of Armandus saved my grandfather when they were shipwrecked at night. That Roman believer sacrificed himself for Eligius who was a slave, and not a believer, but was about to drown."

Julius's heart raced at this revelation. "My father sacrificed himself. YOU are the grandson of Eligius?" His mind raced back to those conversations aboard the ship with Paul and the anger Julius once had over the death of his father. Yet here was the grandson of the man his father had saved.

"Yes, Eligius the elder. My father is Eligius the younger," Domitius explained. "My father became a freedman, and he was a believer like my grandfather, but I rejected the faith and ran off to be a soldier." He stopped in mid-sentence, the revelation hitting him afresh. "Just like Leonitus."

Suddenly the men heard the sound of tambourines and a voice announcing the arrival of Emperor Titus. "Citizens, make way for your Emperor!"

Julius and Domitius looked at one another in stunned silence yet walked back to the open doorway to peer in on the party. Titus entered the room to make his welcomes, and Domitius realized he had to return to the gladiators. "I must go. Pray, my brother!" Domitius exclaimed as he rushed back to join the others.

"Thank you for coming tonight," Titus exclaimed with an outstretched hand holding a silver cup. "It is my joy to provide this evening of celebration as we eagerly await the grand opening of the Flavian Amphitheater!"

The guests erupted in cheers and applause while Titus scanned the room of attendees. The gladiators stood in a row, with their arms behind their backs. His eyes landed on Leonitus. "As you all know, we have a star in our midst." Titus said teasingly, holding out his hands.

The crowds erupted in instant chants of "LEO! LEO! LEO!"

Leonitus lifted his fists in recognition and smiled at the enthusiastic guests. He lowered his fists and bowed humbly as Titus approached him. Titus snapped his fingers, and Franciscus hurried over with a figurine of Leonitus, handing it to the Emperor.

"Not only is Leo good for the games, he's good for the Roman economy," Titus quipped. The people laughed and held up their souvenirs, showing how they had bought one. "I hope each of you will place your bets and cheer for your favorite gladiator tomorrow." He turned to Leonitus. "Tell me, who shall you be facing in the equites match tomorrow?"

Leonitus glanced over and locked eyes with Domitius. He pointed to the gladiator. "I will face Domitius, Sire."

Titus looked over and raised his eyebrows to see the tall, bulky gladiator. Domitius bowed before the emperor. "How intriguing!" Titus exclaimed, turning his gaze from one to the other. He pointed at Leonitus. "Here we have 'lion-like'," Titus said, relaying the meaning of the gladiator's name before turning to point at Domitius. "And here we have 'tame.' I wonder which one will be victorious?" He walked up to look the men in the eye with a sinister expression. "Will the lion be tamed? Or will the tame one be devoured by the lion?"

The crowd once more erupted in chants of "LEO! LEO! LEO!"

Titus smiled. While the crowd cheered, he leaned in to both men and whispered. "Do not disappoint me tomorrow. You two will be the highlight of the games, and I expect you to give me the performance of a lifetime."

Leonitus and Domitius stood with chins lifted high and exclaimed,

487

"Hail, Caesar!"

Titus turned around with open arms to his guests and lifted his cup. "Please, enjoy the evening! I must send the gladiators away now, as they need to be well rested. Tomorrow they will bring you the most spectacular games ever seen in Rome!"

The gladiators all bowed before Titus. Spiculus then led them out of the room. The enthralled ladies continued to reach out and touch the men as they walked by, giggling with adoration.

The people applauded and cheered, "Hail, Caesar! Hail, Caesar! Hail Caesar!" Titus proceeded to walk through the parting crowd to his special couch, as servants buzzed around him to fill his goblet and bring him platters of food. The musicians once more struck up their instruments.

Julius stood in the doorway and locked eyes with Leonitus who turned away defiantly, diverting his eyes from his uncle. Julius then locked eyes with Domitius and they shared a nod and a knowing look of understanding. They would pray for one another, and for Leonitus.

488

Clarie and Nigel exchanged a nod as they watched Julius hurriedly leave the party. Mission accomplished. Julius had come to the party, encountered Leonitus, and made the connection with Domitius. There was little more than they could do from here on out.

"Oh dear," Nigel whispered to himself. "If the lion-like gladiator's heart is not tamed, he could be forever doomed to the dark lion who seeks to devour him."

53

OPENING GAMES

ROME, AUGUST 1, AD 80

Never had the citizens of Rome witnessed what was unfolding before them. It was only 7:00 AM., and the city was electrified with noise and excitement. The streets were packed with people making their way to the entry gates. Fifty thousand ticket holders filed inside, handing their tickets to the ushers and gazing up at the imposing archways that towered over them. Statues placed in every arch gazed out at the eager, bloodthirsty masses.

Vendors called out to customers, offering food, drink, and souvenirs for them to carry to their seats. Franciscus's booth was booming, as everyone wanted a LEO figure. The *Acta Diurna,* or daily notices posted in public places in Rome, advertised that Leonitus would be headlining both the *bestiarii* and *equites* events for special back-to-back performances on opening day. All of Rome was buzzing with this and other exciting offerings running from 8:00 AM until sunset: morning exotic animal matches and hunts, noontime executions, and the afternoon grand finale: the gladiators.

Those of higher Roman status did not have to walk far, as their seats were close to the entrance. The lower classes had to keep climbing sets of stairs until they filed off to their proper station. While the women and slaves walked to the very top of the arena, Rome's senators, knights, dignitaries, and soldiers filled the bottom rows of the arena. The Vestal Virgins were the only women close to the arena floor, and they sat next to the gloriously decorated imperial box. The Emperor would sit under a red awning where the columns were adorned with garlands of fresh flowers. Plush pillows were set on the massive, throne-like gilded chairs for Titus and Domitian, and luxurious couches were provided for their guests. The gleaming white marble seats soon gave way to a sea of white, red, and brown as the arena filled with people. Festive red banners were hung all over the arena, and the red velarium was partially unfurled, as the sun rose higher into a clear blue sky.

No one noticed the small dog and two cats that filed in underfoot as the humans shuffled through the corridors of the amphitheater. Their gaze was on the colorful paint and frescoes that covered every wall, and the sights and sounds of the arena. Nigel rode on Max's back, and he, Liz, and Al ran to the upper level of the arena above the imperial box. When they got to a viewing spot, the humans were actually amused to see the animals there, and petted them as they walked by.

"There be Vespasian's statue," Max pointed out, nodding toward the statue on the opposite side of the arena near the floor.

Liz looked around. *"C'est tragique."* She was heartsick to be in attendance but knew they needed to do as Gillamon instructed. "I am glad dear Kate did not have to witness this, for I do not think her heart could bear it."

"Aye, me lass would have had a hard time," Max agreed with a frown. "I wonder if Clarie be here."

"Perhaps Clarie is below the arena comforting the prisoners who will die today," Nigel suggested sadly.

Al looked around at all the people with food, ready for the entertainment to begin. "Even I don't know how the humans can think aboot eatin' at a time like this." He ducked down next to the railing wall.

"Gillamon asked us to pray," Liz reminded them. She looked out over the unspoiled sand of the arena and knew it wouldn't remain that way. "It is all we can do, no?"

"At least Leo's got his lion helmet," Al bemoaned. "I jest wish he had the full armor o' salvation."

☧

The sounds of blades being sharpened mixed with the loud cheers from the crowds above, as musicians and acrobats filed into the amphitheater to provide the pre-game entertainment. The air was hot and stifling from the smoke of the torches mounted on the walls in the dark corridors below the arena. It was a hive of activity, with hundreds of sweaty humans working behind the scenes to prepare for the coming events. Frightened prisoners awaiting execution huddled together in the filth of their cells. Many wept and moaned. Some sat there in silence, contemplating their fate. Clarie moved among them as one of the faceless slaves minding the doomed victims, offering cups of cold water and whispering prayers of courage and comfort.

Horses neighed from the stalls. They could sense the fear spreading throughout this place, from men and beasts alike. Animal noises of all kinds echoed through the stone passageways from the cages where they were penned. Lions roared, bears growled, tigers snarled, ostriches screeched, and hyenas laughed. The beast master and his servants jabbed and taunted them in an effort to heighten their aggression. The animals had been starved for two days to make them hungry for the kill. These animals would provide the first order of entertainment after the opening bestiarius display.

491

The venatores inspected their belts and made sure their armor adequately covered their torso and upper arms. They looked through the options of helmets and weapons available to them for the wild animal hunts that would follow the animal-to-animal fights.

The gladiators would arrive soon through the tunnel leading from the gladiator school, but they would not enter the arena until after lunch. All, that is, except for the bestiarius. Leonitus was already here.

Leonitus sat on a bench and adusted the strap of his sandal. Spiculus stood over him and watched his finest gladiator prepare himself. He was unusually concerned about the young man. He had a sense of foreboding about the day. "This day will be nothing like you've ever experienced, Leonitus. This venue is unlike anything you've ever seen or heard, and you've never fought both lions and men on the same day."

"I'm up for the challenge, Spiculus." Leonitus stood and replied with a wink and a slap to his trainer's arm. "Don't worry." He adjusted the strap of the leather bands on his arms and legs. He double-checked the knife strapped to his shin and the sword strapped to the back of his belt, and picked up the whip he loved to use. He cracked it a couple of times, smiling at the sound it made. He reached over to pick up his silver helmet, the one that had belonged to his great-grandfather Marcus. "I've got my helmet of salvation, see?" He placed the helmet over his head and smiled at the lanista. He picked up the long spear that was leaning against the wall. "I'll be fine."

Spiculus hesitated a moment and opened his mouth to speak but stopped himself. Domitian had been to see him with a special request but demanded secrecy from the lanista who had leased his gladiators to the Flavians for the opening of their amphitheater. Perhaps the request would not be fulfilled after all. Domitian only wanted to have it in reserve. Spiculus smiled weakly at Leonitus. "Still so sure of yourself, aren't you?"

Leonitus smiled and winked at Spiculus. "Death or glory."

Spiculus nodded. "Death or glory." *Never have those words been so true*, he thought as he watched Leonitus stretch out his muscles to loosen up for his debut in the arena.

☧

492

High up in the rafters around the amphitheater, men appeared and blew into long straight trumpets, signaling the entrance parade for the games. The crowds rose to their feet as the procession entered the arena. Imperial *lictors* walked in bearing the *fasces* that signified the Emperor's power over life and death. They were followed by a small group of musicians and servants carrying images of the gods who would be "witnessing" the games. A scribe walked behind them who would record the outcomes of the events, and, finally, a servant carried palm branches to be given to victors of the matches. Titus had ordered a handful of wooden swords, or *rudes,* to be on hand should he decide to grant any of the gladiators their freedom for well-fought matches. Bestowing such mercy—sparingly—would serve to ingratiate himself to the people.

Suddenly the Emperor appeared from his special entrance to the imperial box and lifted his hands to the roaring cheers of the crowds. "Caesar! Caesar! Caesar!" the people shouted in unison. Titus appeared in rich purple robes, a thick golden neck plate bearing the Roman eagle, and wore a golden laurel crown. Domitian was also dressed in the finery of a Caesar and wore a red robe pinned with a lion medallion. His chair, however, was smaller than Titus's, signifying his subservient position to his brother, the Emperor.

"We've waited a long time for this, Brother," Titus told Domitian.

"It was Father's dream. And you have seen it come to completion," Domitian replied. "All glory and honor goes to you, Brother. With this day, you give Rome back to the people, and, in turn, the people give their allegiance back to you."

Titus nodded, stepped forward, and held up his hands. "Citizens of Rome! Welcome to the inaugural games of the Flavian Amphitheater! May Vespasian and the gods be pleased with the hands that have erected this arena for the people of Rome!" The crowds cheered wildly for a few minutes, and Titus allowed them to revel and build up their excitement. Finally, he held out his hands again and declared, "Let the games begin!" Immediately, white doves were released from cages all around the arena, and flower petals showered the people from the *velarium* above.

"How utterly absurd!" complained Nigel. "Releasing doves of peace and flowers of beauty before the death and carnage of the arena? They must be mad!"

"Welcome ta R-r-rome, Lad," Max reminded him.

493

At the far end of the arena, the massive gates were opened, and light poured into the underground corridor. Spiculus put his hand on Leonitus's shoulder. "You're on. May the gods be with you."

Leonitus took a deep breath and gripped the whip in one hand and the spear in the other. "I will return through this Gate of Life soon." With that he marched up the incline ramp and stepped foot onto the sand for the first time.

The sun immediately reflected off his silver lion helmet, and the crowds went berserk as Leonitus held up both fists to walk around the arena. They immediately began crying his name. "LEO! LEO! LEO! LEO!"

"I can't watch!" Al cried, hiding his eyes. Liz and Nigel sat on the wall, and Max put his paws up on the ledge.

Titus smiled at the response of the crowd, as Leonitus made his way to stand in front of the imperial box. He saluted the emperor, and Titus nodded in approval. Leonitus cracked his whip and suddenly a lion was released into the arena. But the lion was afraid of the noise and shied away from the sound, hovering near the wall.

Leonitus frowned and decided to run toward the lion, screaming. He pulled back the whip and snapped it in front of the lion's face. At first the lion cowered and did not fight back, so Leonitus screamed at the beast and continued to crack his whip.

"LEO! LEO! LEO! LEO!" shouted the crowds.

Leonitus took his spear and jabbed it in the lion's face. Gradually, the lion listened to the people less and focused on the spear and the man more. It held up a paw to bat the spear away. "That a boy!" Leonitus shouted. "FIGHT ME!" He cracked the whip again and sent the lion running toward the center of the arena. He ran after it and began to walk in slow circles around the lion, taunting it. Finally, the lion decided to charge him, and Leonitus threw down the whip and grabbed the spear with both hands. As the lion leaped he plunged the spear into its chest, and the lion roared out in pain, falling on its side.

"KILL! KILL! KILL! KILL!" the crowd now chanted.

Leonitus climbed onto the back of the wounded lion and pulled the sword from the sheath on the back of his belt. "Die, lion," he snarled, plunging the sword into the lion, killing it. He got to his feet and held his arms up, holding the bloodied sword.

494

The people went wild with excitement. "VICTORY! LEO! VICTORY! LEO!"

Titus clapped and held out his hand to Leonitus, who bowed before the Emperor. Leonitus ran to the imperial box and was handed a palm branch. He held it high and ran around the arena, blowing kisses to the ladies and reveling in the glory. He made his way to the Gate of Life while more lions, bears, and ostriches were released from doors all around the arena. It was time for the animals to fight it out.

Liz looked away and jumped down next to Al. "I will not watch this."

"Aye, Leonitus won't be back out until afternoon then," Max agreed, putting his paws back on the floor. "No need ta see all this bloodshed."

"I could not agree more," Nigel said, joining them on the floor. Al still had his eyes covered. "It's okay, old boy. You shan't see anything from behind this small railing wall."

"Good," Al whined, then placing his paws over his ears. "I don't want to hear it either."

☧

Slaves repeatedly entered the arena floor to remove the dead beasts following the animal battles, and then the wild animal hunt with the *venatores.* After they removed the beasts from the arena, they poured out fresh sand to soak up the blood. Next came the execution of prisoners, and the slaves repeated their gruesome task. The victims were removed and taken through the Gate of Death while more sand was poured over the blood. Titus and the elite chose not to stay for the midday entertainment, as it was seen as poor taste by the upper class society to watch the executions. Domitian, however, decided to remain for the executions, feeling that one of the Flavian hosts needed to be present for the inaugural executions. He enjoyed a sumptuous lunch during the event.

"The day is going exceedingly well," Domitian remarked when Titus returned from lunch at the palace. "The crowds were delighted with the executions. Some of the prisoners acted out scenes from mythological plays. I'm sorry you missed it."

Titus nodded. "I'm glad to hear it. But of course, the people eagerly await the main event."

"And it shall be spectacular, I have no doubt," Domitian replied darkly.

495

Titus stepped out again to the front of the imperial box to the cheers of the crowds. "Citizens of Rome, now for the event you have all been waiting for! I give you, the gladiators!"

Immediately the Gate of Life opened, and a parade of gladiators marched into the arena in a procession of pomp and loud music. Servants carried in the weapons that would be used, followed by blacksmiths who would inspect and make sure the weapons were in good order. The gladiators were dressed in an array of ornamental armor purely for show and excitement. Titus had arranged for them to wear silver armor over linen tunics and loincloths trimmed in gold thread. Peacock feathers trailed off their parade helmets, and the crowds roared with excitement to see the gladiators presented in such rich pageantry.

"Where's Leonitus an' Domitius?" Max asked, peering over the railing once more.

Liz and Nigel looked on, while Al cowered next to Max and covered his eyes. "I can't see 'em."

"I believe they shall make their own glorious appearance on horseback," Nigel surmised.

Sure enough, just as the procession of gladiators began exiting to change into their combat armor, two doors were opened on opposite sides of the arena. Out galloped two white horses who were adorned with leather shields over their faces, and riding them were Leonitus and Domitius, wearing golden helmets. Leonitus had chosen two eagle feathers for his helmet, and Domitius had selected two ostrich feathers dyed red for his helmet. A referee walked into the arena followed by an assistant who carried the shields that the *equites* would use once they began to fight on foot.

The crowds roared to life, chanting Leo's name once more.

Titus sat up and leaned forward. "This better be good. Who shall tame who?"

Domitian smiled at his brother. "Who indeed?"

Leonitus reveled in hearing his name. A rush of adrenaline coursed through his veins at the thought of fighting Domitius. Last night after the banquet, he immediately requested of Spiculus that he be kept apart from his opponent. Leonitus had no desire to hear anything Domitius had to say after talking with Julius. He shut out his mind and his heart to everything Julius told him. He needed to stay focused and hard. He needed to remain ruthless to make it through this day.

Domitius took in a deep breath and said a quick prayer. "Give me strength."

Leonitus lowered his lance into position and leaned forward ever so slightly on his horse, putting his legs behind its girth. He squeezed, giving a slight nudge with his heels. He gathered the reins and asked his horse for the gallop. Then he gave the horse its head so there was nothing restraining it as it triple-galloped into a charge. Domitius mirrored his opponent and within moments the *equites* met in the center of the arena. Neither hit their mark, and the two gladiators rode their horses past one another to the far ends of the arena. Meanwhile, musicians playing the *cornu* horn and water organ kept up a steady tempo to keep the crowd stimulated.

Leonitus and Domitius faced off again and charged at one another. This time, Domitius's lance hit Leonitus in the leg, only grazing him but drawing blood. Leonitus turned quickly and came after Domitius, but missed him again. The crowd grew restless seeing their victor struggle. Leonitus scowled and shouted as he charged again. This time he knocked Domitius from his horse with force. The crowd erupted in cheerful applause.

The referee held out his rude to keep Leonitus from charging while

Domitius picked up his shield. The assistant grabbed the reins of his horse to lead it off to the side so a slave could remove it from the arena. Domitius unsheathed his sword, held up his shield and planted his feet into position. The referee lifted the rude, giving Leonitus the signal that the match could continue.

Domitius braced himself as the thunderous hooves of Leonitus's horse came galloping toward him. Leonitus shouted and thrust his lance at Domitius but the gladiator blocked it with his shield and managed to cut Leonitus's other leg with his sword, this time drawing more blood. Leonitus threw his head back and cried out in pain.

The crowd gasped in shock. Titus gripped the arms of his chair in suspense. Domitian smiled.

Leonitus turned and once more charged at Domitius, this time knocking him down as his lance made impact with his shield. While Domitius fell back hard onto the ground, Leonitus dismounted from his horse, grabbed his sword and marched angrily toward him. The referee held out the rude while the assistant rushed over with Leonitus's shield. Domitius got to his feet, trying to catch the breath that was knocked out of him. Blood now covered Leonitus's thighs from the wounds inflicted by Domitius. The referee stepped back so once again the match could resume.

Domitius held up his shield, as he and Leonitus encircled each other to the chants of the masses.

"Leonitus, I will not kill you," Domitius told him.

Leonitus gave a quick laugh and charged his opponent. "Then I will *gladly* kill you!"

The two gladiators met with clanking swords and began an intense sword fight. Leonitus managed to slice across Domitius's forearm, much to the applause of the crowd, but the two kept fighting. After a few minutes more, both gladiators were growing tired, and the referee stepped in to break them up briefly.

Domitian leaned over in Titus's ear. "These two are evenly matched, Brother. Perhaps you should call for *sine missione* to encourage a more rigorous fight."

"Even with the crowd favorite, Leonitus?" Titus asked in surprise. "What about compensation for Spiculus the lanista? Leonitus would be an expensive gladiator to replace."

497

"I've already taken care of that," Domitian replied with a raspy voice. "Leo is undefeated, isn't he? What could be more suspenseful than the thought of an undefeated gladiator dying in his first downfall? It would be an unforgettable launch to these gladiator games in our arena."

Titus nodded at the thought. "Agreed." He stood to his feet and held up his hands. "I declare this match *sine missione*. Resume."

A collective gasp rose from the crowd as people looked at one another in disbelief.

"Wha's that mean?" Max asked.

Nigel and Liz shared a look of worry. "It means without release from sentence of death," Nigel explained. "In other words, no mercy will be given to the defeated gladiator. Whoever falls first will die."

"The emperor has declared *sine missione*. Fight to the death," the referee restated to Leonitus and Domitius before backing away.

Both men filled with fear. One of them would leave here through the Gate of Death. For the first time, Leonitus felt vulnerable. He had never lost a match. Now, even if he had to face defeat, there was no chance for mercy to fight another day. He would die. Leonitus was wounded and knew that Domitius already had an advantage over him.

"Listen to me! You must know something," Domitius pleaded, holding up his shield as Leonitus came after him with a fury.

"SILENCE!" Leonitus shouted, locking swords with Domitius.

The two gladiators fought with intensity as the crowd roared. Domitius suddenly shoved Leonitus and the gladiator fell backwards, his sword bouncing out of his hand. Titus and Domitian stood to their feet. The referee stayed put with his hands clasped in front of him. He would no longer break up the match.

Domitius walked over and put his foot on Leonitus's sword while putting his own sword to Leonitus's throat. "You *will* listen now."

Leonitus lifted his chin back, and fear filled his eyes. He was going to die, and he trembled in fear. Suddenly the crowd started to boo and held their thumbs to their throat, indicating that they wanted Domitius to kill him. Leonitus couldn't believe they would turn on him so quickly in his moment of peril.

Domitius ignored them but kept his sword at Leonitus's throat. "Your grandfather Armandus sacrificed himself in a shipwreck to save the life of my grandfather Eligius because he knew he would die an unbeliever. The centurion at the cross saved a slave because he believed in the Christ. And he believed in the hell of a hopeless eternity apart from him."

The crowd was roaring at a deafening pitch now. "You said you didn't understand how someone could die for another? Your grandfather did, and so do I—because our Savior understood it first."

Suddenly Domitius removed his foot from Leonitus's sword and dropped his arm by his side, letting Leonitus go.

Leonitus's eyes grew wide as he saw the opportunity to escape death. He instinctively grabbed his sword from the sand and jumped to his feet, thrusting it into Domitius's abdomen.

Domitius gasped in pain, gripping Leonitus's arm. He locked eyes with Leonitus, and they shared a look that made time stand still. "The true . . . Gate . . . of Life . . . awaits." He let go of Leonitus and fell back onto the sand.

Leonitus stood there over his body, breathing hard as the referee came over to make sure Domitius was dead. Satisfied, he took Leonitus by the wrist and held up his arm to announce his victory. Titus stood up and applauded, motioning for his servant to deliver a palm branch and the wooden sword of freedom. Domitian remained seated and applauded, but his smile was gone.

Not only had Leonitus escaped death by the sword, he was given his freedom to walk out of this arena forever. He took the palm branch and *rudis* in hand, held them in the air as was expected of him, and walked around the arena in numb disbelief.

Immediately the fickle crowd began chanting his name once more. "LEO! LEO! LEO! LEO!"

But Leonitus didn't hear them. All he heard was the revelation of Domitius's final words ringing in his ears as he walked out of the arena through the Gate of Life.

AND THEN THERE WAS ONE

EPHESUS, AD 94

Prochorus was breathing heavily by the time he reached the simple house perched on the hilltop overlooking the city of Ephesus. The old man briefly stopped to wipe the sweat from his brow and to catch his breath. He looked back down to the valley below and could see the blue water of the harbor. In the distance was the Temple of Artemis. He heard the faint roar of the crowds enjoying the gladiatorial games in the Great Stadium of Ephesus. No doubt men were losing their lives to the wild animals of the arena at this moment. *Oh, my friend, even this place of sanctuary will soon no longer escape the reach of Rome,* he thought sadly.

"John! John! Where are you?" Prochorus called urgently as he entered the humble home. He walked to the garden in the back and saw his friend tending the small grapevine. His little white dog was by his side, wagging her tail. John loved her dearly, for she had been his faithful companion for many years. She never left his side. *There's something special about her. Something unusual,* he thought as he watched her happily grin and wag her tail.

When Mary died, this little dog had comforted John like no one else could. John didn't reveal to Prochorus how long he had actually had 'Chava' as he called her. John surmised that the Master's touch had somehow given this little dog a miraculously long life. She had been with Jesus the very first day John met him, and she stayed with the disciples throughout Jesus' ministry, passion, resurrection, and ascension. She was even in the Upper Room at Pentecost. For some reason, just as John was blessed with Mary, so, too, had he been blessed with this little companion. She was beloved by Mary and brought them much joy in their home, both in Jerusalem and later here in Ephesus. Her little face radiated love, and she had actually helped John to work on his temper, which was always something with which he struggled.

Jesus had called John and his brother, James, the "Sons of Thunder," for they had earned the title for their aggressive, zealous behavior. Incensed at the Samarian village that rejected Jesus' message, John and James asked Jesus if he wanted them to call down fire from heaven to destroy them. When Jesus announced that he would be soon be betrayed, handed over to the Gentiles to be mocked, scourged, and put to death, but rise from the grave, what was the first thing out of the mouths of the Sons of Thunder? "Teacher, we have something we want you to do for us . . . Arrange it so that we will be awarded the highest places of honor in your glory—one of us at your right, the other at your left." Jesus asked them if they could drink the cup that Jesus would drink. "Yes we can!" they had boasted, not knowing what they were saying. How John rued the day he said those arrogant, ignorant words. As he stood at the foot of the cross, he understood why Jesus tried to make the two brothers understand how they didn't know what they were doing.

Now John understood. James, indeed, drank the cup, being the first disciple to die when Herod seized him in Jerusalem. John would never forget that day when Peter ran with him through the streets when they heard that James had been arrested, but how they were powerless to stop his execution. Strangely enough, with the hate-filled murder of each and every apostle, John's temper lessened, and his love grew. He understood more and more the priceless value of the gospel preached by those who died at the hands of the Jews, the Romans, the Greeks, and other pagans. John continually went back to the words Jesus spoke when he hung on the cross. *Forgive them, Father, for they know not what they do.* Those who martyred the apostles didn't know what they were doing, either. They were lost in darkness, and only the light and love of Jesus could reach them. Anger couldn't reach them. Only the love and grace of Christ could work such a miracle, and the blood of the martyrs was producing fruit that would last as they were poured out as a drink offering for a lost world.

So as Jesus worked on John's temper, so, too, did Kate. Whenever John was about to blow up in anger, she would be there staring at him, and he would be reminded of Jesus' command: love one another.

"Then he said, 'I am the vine, and you are the branches. Those who remain in me, and I in them, will bear much fruit; for you can do nothing without me.' Didn't Jesus have a wonderful way of describing things, little Chava?" John asked Kate. She barked happily in reply. He smiled, popped a grape in his mouth, and gave her a gentle pat on the head.

"There you are," Prochorus said. "We've just heard some terrible news. Timothy received a letter this morning."

John frowned. "Have we lost another friend?"

Prochorus nodded his head sadly, and his lip trembled as he spoke with a heavy heart. "Luke. Some pagan Greek priests killed him for preaching in their area."

502

John closed his eyes tightly and leaned his head back as tears stung his eyes. *Not dearest Luke! Not our good doctor!* John's heart felt like it was gripped in a vise as this news sank in. Yet another one of the Master's faithful servants was executed for doing as Jesus commanded him. *Greater love has no one than this: to lay down one's life for one's friends. You are my friends if you do what I command.* Jesus' words continually filled John's mind, especially at times like this. He opened his eyes and looked at the vine, tenderly lifting a bunch of juicy, ripe grapes ready for harvest. *You did not choose me, but I chose you and appointed you so that you might go and bear fruit—fruit that will last—and so that whatever you ask in my name the Father will give you. This is my command: Love each other.*

John turned to face Prochorus and opened his arms to envelop him in a comforting embrace. The two old men hugged and wept over their friend as they stood in this garden. Kate sat below them, also weeping at this news. *Oh, Maker, no! Now sweet Luke is gone!*

Prochorus pulled back and locked eyes with John. "Everyone is gone, except for you, John. You alone remain as one of the founding fathers of the church."

John nodded sadly and let go of his friend. "Every one of them willingly drank the cup they were asked to drink."

"Peter, Philip, Andrew, Thaddeus, Nathaniel, and Simon were crucified; Paul, James, and Matthias were beheaded; Stephen, Barnabas, Jesus' brother, James, and James the Less were stoned. Mark was dragged through the streets of Alexandria, Thomas—speared in India, Matthew—slain with a halberd in Ethiopia," Prochorus recounted. "And now Luke—hanged from an olive tree in Greece."

John sat down on a stone bench. "And then there was one." He hung his head as he looked at the ground in grief.

John had been the one to oversee the churches for these past twenty-five years following Paul's death. Timothy was the pastor of the church in Ephesus, and John traveled around to the churches in Asia Minor, ministering, advising, and guiding them. But now that he was almost ninety years old, many of the church leaders traveled to see him here in this house on the outskirts of Ephesus. Things were less dangerous and complicated up here, away from the watchful eye of the Roman authorities who demanded its citizens to abide by its local standards. They followed the stern laws set forth by the current emperor and last of the Flavians: Domitian.

503

In AD 81, after only two years as Emperor, Titus suddenly died from a mysterious illness. As he lay dying, his brother Domitian demanded that the Praetorian Guard hastily name him as Emperor. He took the title "Augustus" as he became the sole ruler of the Roman Empire. *And then there was one.* Domitian smiled to himself as he assumed total power.

At first the people had great hope that Domitian would be a benevolent ruler like his father and brother before him. He was a skilled leader and an ardent builder for Rome, but he was fanatic about pagan worship. One of the first things he did following his brother's death was to deify him and to build an arch near the Flavian Amphitheater. The Arch of Titus was covered with sculptures depicting the War of the Jews and the fall of Jerusalem. Friezes portrayed the Romans bringing back the booty taken from the temple, including the menorah and treasures that had been paraded through the streets of Rome.

Domitian also discontinued the naval battles at the arena so he could build two levels below the massive amphitheater called the *hypogeum.* This was a complex labyrinth of passages, elevators, and trap doors that allowed the floor of the arena to become a stage of endless surprise and excitement. Lions and other wild beasts could pop out onto the arena floor at any time and elaborate sets could be raised to create an instant new landscape of trees to stage animal hunts. Even elephants could be raised to enter the arena on center stage. Domitian was determined to increase the excitement of the games, and he did not disappoint when it came to death.

His true nature eventually came to light. He was a merciless tyrant who forced his way into the lives of the people in ways unmatched by any of Rome's previous emperors. He decided that it was his sole responsibility to determine the moral code for the people and named himself Perpetual Censor. This gave him the right to redefine the moral code based on what he saw as right or wrong. He could eliminate anyone or any part of Roman society that he determined offensive or unnecessary; if they opposed his ideals, they found their way to the top of his elimination list. At first he secretly arrested and imprisoned those he disliked or mistrusted. But soon he no longer cared about being secretive and publicly arrested, tortured, and murdered scores of people. The people now hated him.

By AD 93, Domitian's wickedness was at an all-time high, when he declared himself *dominus et deus*—lord and god. Other emperors were deified after death, as was his brother Titus, but that was not enough for Domitian. He wanted to be a god while he *lived*. So he constructed temples to himself all over the Roman Empire, including one in Ephesus. No one was safe from the madness of this monster, including John up here in his hilltop home. Domitian was after the ultimate censorship: the silencing of Christians who came from that Jewish upstart, Jesus of Nazareth. And who was now the leader of this movement? John.

"I want you to prepare to take over communications with the churches when the Romans come for me," John told Prochorus, his faithful friend and one of the seven men first chosen to be deacons by Peter and the others in the Jerusalem church.

Prochorus's eyes widened in alarm, and he rushed to John's side, dropping to the ground next to him. "What do you mean?"

John smiled and patted his friend on the shoulder. "It's only a matter of time before I am called to also drink the cup, Prochorus. I cannot expect to escape the fate of my brothers."

504

"But what about Jesus saying you would live?" Prochorus protested. There had long been rumors based on what Jesus told Peter on the beach the morning he restored the disciple that had denied him. When Jesus told Peter that someday he would be led to where he did not want to go, John was standing there on the beach. Peter looked at John and asked Jesus about John's fate. That's when Jesus said, "If I want him to live until I come again, what's that to you? You—follow me." That is how the rumor got out among the brothers that this disciple wouldn't die.

John wagged his wrinkled finger at Prochorus. "That is not what Jesus said, my friend. I must put a stop to this rumor. Regardless, I believe that the Romans will soon come for me."

"Why? What has happened?" Prochorus wanted to know.

Kate also wanted to know and sat there anxiously awaiting an answer. John put his hand down and gently scratched her under the chin.

"I believe I've angered the Roman magistrates," John explained. "I refused their 'offer' to burn incense to the Emperor when I was walking by Domitian's temple on *Kuriakos*, the lord's day."

The blood drained from Prochorus's face. He swallowed hard. All citizens knew *Kuriakos,* which occurred on the first day of each month, as the Emperor's Day. Domitian required all Romans to burn incense to him on this day—*his lord's day.* "If they come for you, John, know this. I will go with you."

The fine smile lines around John's eyes turned upward. "Thank you, my faithful friend."

Aye, an' so will I! Kate barked.

Weeks later Kate heard the sound of horses galloping up the path to John's house early one morning. She jumped up on a chair that sat by the window where she could gaze outside. Her heart fell as she saw two Roman soldiers dismount their horses. One of them carried a set of iron shackles. Kate immediately ran into the room where John slept and furiously barked to wake him.

The Romans be here, John! Wake up!

John lifted his head from the pillow and reached his hand out to Kate. He turned his head to listen and heard someone bang on his front door. "Shh, it's all right, little Chava." The elderly man got up and shuffled his feet, calling out, "I'm coming."

When he opened the door, the two Roman soldiers barged in with no regard for the hour or the intrusion. "What is this about?" John asked.

"Are you John of Ephesus?" one soldier asked, tapping a scroll in his hand.

"Yes, I am. How may I help you?" John replied calmly.

"You're under arrest," the soldier replied, nodding to the other soldier with the iron shackles. "We're taking you to Rome."

The soldier jingled the iron shackles and grabbed John by the wrists to clamp them on. While he secured the chains, the other soldier read off the charges against him. "John of Ephesus, you are hereby charged with high treason, propagating false religion, undermining the state religion of Rome, and refusal to worship the Emperor."

John's face was calm, for as the Roman soldier rattled off the charges against him, all John heard were the words of Jesus:

506

"Peace is what I leave with you; it is my own peace that I give you. I do not give it as the world does. Do not be worried and upset; do not be afraid."

Kate felt helpless as she watched John being carried out of the house. She started barking and followed the men outside, but they simply ignored her. They put John in a cart drawn by one of the horses and mounted their steeds. They galloped off down the path toward the harbor of Ephesus, leaving Kate there alone.

Kate didn't know what to do. *Please, Maker, I can't bear it if ye take John from me! Please spare his life.* She took off running after the soldiers.

ROME, FLAVIAN PALACE, AD 95

Everyone in the imperial court was on edge. Domitian had been on a tirade, wiping out a slew of senators that he suspected of plotting his assassination. Only when he learned that his soldiers had captured and brought the leader of the Christian movement to the palace was he placated. But the plans he had for the elderly rebel were barbaric. Domitian wanted to bring John to his knees, literally, in the throne room.

John stood with his arms still shackled in front of him. His beige tunic was filthy, and his fine, gray hair was a mess. He had not bathed since they left Ephesus for the voyage to Rome, except for the rain that fell on the deck of the ship. While it chilled him, John was thankful for the cleansing water to wipe away the grime from his face. Prochorus had voluntarily accompanied him on the ship when he heard of John's arrest. He was not on trial but would likely suffer John's same fate, depending on the whim of the Emperor.

Suddenly the massive doors to the throne room opened, and Domitian came barging in. He wore a crimson toga and golden crown and stopped in front of John to size him up. He looked the apostle up and down and shook his head. "So you are the leader of all the Christians? Well, let us see if you lead them toward the path that will ensure that they live or die." He smiled darkly and took a seat on his throne. John said nothing but gazed at Domitian with eyes of sad pity. Domitian scowled and squirmed under John's gaze.

"You've heard the charges against you. I would like to hear how you plead on the charge of refusing to worship me," Domitian said, leaning forward with his hands gripping the throne.

507

John did not hesitate but immediately gave Domitian his answer. "I serve the Lord of lords only. I will bow my knee only to Jesus."

Domitian's eyes blazed at John's confident reply. He clapped his hands, and the servants came in rolling two carts. One held a marble stand with incense. One held a massive vat of hot, boiling oil. Domitian smiled and stepped down from the throne. He picked up a long wick and stuck it into the flame by the incense. He walked over to John and held the flame in front of his face. "I shall be merciful and give you one more chance to deny your Jesus and save your life. Take this wick and choose the flame that will determine your fate. Light the incense in worship to me and you will live," he said. Domitian's eyes filled with evil. "Or light the vat of oil where you will be burned alive." Domitian handed John the wick.

John stared deeply into Domitian's eyes and saw the darkness there. *Every man who publicly acknowledges me I shall acknowledge in the presence of my Father in Heaven, but the man who disowns me before men I shall disown before my Father in Heaven.* John recalled Jesus' words and knew that he stood before Domitian as the voice of the Christians, according to this insane man. John had no hesitation about what he would do, for he had chosen the light while Domitian was consumed with darkness. *This is how the judgment works: the light has come into the world, but people love the darkness rather than the light, because their deeds are evil. Those who do evil things hate the light and will not come to the light, because they do not want their evil deeds to be shown up. But those who do what is true come to the light in order that the light may show that what they did was in obedience to God.*

John took the wick and walked over to the vat of oil. He stood watching bubbles surface and pop. Suddenly he remembered Shadrach, Meshach and Abednego, the three young friends of Daniel who were presented a similar option of bowing before the king of Babylon or facing death in a fiery furnace. *King Nebuchadnezzar, we do not need to defend ourselves before you in this matter. If we are thrown into the blazing furnace, the God we serve is able to deliver us from it, and he will deliver us from Your Majesty's hand. But even if he does not, we want you to know, Your Majesty, that we will not serve your gods or worship the image of gold you have set up.* John tossed the wick into the oil and flames shot up into the air.

508

"FOOL!" Domitian screamed. "Throw him in the vat!" he demanded.

Immediately the guards rushed over to grab John. They lifted him up and threw him into the vat of boiling oil, and stood back to witness the horrific fate of the elderly man. Domitian was seething with wicked delight. "This is what happens to those who do not worship me!"

After a moment, the flames extinguished themselves. John surfaced and wiped the oil from his eyes. He held out his hands in front of him in amazement. Nothing harmful was happening! He wiped back his hair with his hands, as if he were taking a bath. He then stood up and stared at Domitian. "Jesus is Lord of all." John confidently climbed over the side of the vat of oil and stood there with his arms outstretched. Oil slowly dripped off him and onto the marble floor surrounding the throne.

Everyone in the throne room gasped in awe of what they were seeing. John was unscathed! Blood drained from Domitian's face, and fear gripped him. He slowly backed away, shaking his head in disbelief. He ran out of the room, screaming, "SEND HIM TO PATMOS!"

55

MIRACULOUS MEETING

I t's been a long time since I've done this, Lass," Kate said, trying to get a solid footing without slipping.

"Once you learn to ride a whale, you never forget," Clarie replied with a chuckle. She had taken the form of a right whale and was gliding gracefully through the turquoise waters of the Aegean Sea.

"Ridin' Craddock across the channel were my first adventure with Max," Kate recalled fondly. "I fell in love with him on that voyage ta France." The Westie gazed at the turquoise blue water as she thought back to that magical day. She had just met Max and Al on the beach in the south of England, as they all were following the fire cloud. They needed to find a way to cross over the channel to France in order to continue following the fire cloud to Noah's Ark. Max had figured out a way that was filled with adventure. He called his old whale friend, Craddock, to carry them across.

The water swirled in ringlets where Clarie's massive fins propelled them forward. "I'm sure Liz would say that love is not only in the air of her beloved France, but it is in the water as well."

Kate smiled happily, turning her nose up to the sunshine and closing her eyes as she recalled her first kiss with Max on the beach where they landed in Normandy, France. Her thoughts then drifted to the hilarious scene of Al's beach landing. He ran as far away from the sea as he could and off into the French countryside where he soon met the love of his life as well. "And in the catnip, too," Kate giggled, remembering Al eating too much of the herb. "I'll never forget the look on poor Al's face after destroyin' Liz's garden."

"Max told me that Al had a lot of pitiful faces that day," Clarie chuckled.

Kate shook her head recalling poor Al. "Aye, I'll never forget how pitiful Al were. Before he ate the catnip on land, he tried ta eat plankton like Craddock an' got a belly full of salt water. That orange cat aboot turned green!"

Clarie laughed, and Kate had to brace herself from the vibrations coming from her whale friend. "Well I'm certain he is glad that you got picked for this particular mission and not him. Al, Max, Liz, and Nigel are finishing up their assignments in Italy and Greece and will see you soon, I promise."

"I can't wait for that reunion." Kate gazed ahead to the island. "It's been a long time ta be parted from me love, but John needs me here."

"Indeed he does, and so does your other contact," Clarie replied. "Let's review everything from the top. I will drop you off on the south side of the island, where you will rendezvous with your new assignment who fishes there daily. Do you remember what he looks like?"

"Aye," Kate replied.

"Good. He will, of course, be curious to see you on the island and will follow you," Clarie continued. "Lead him north to intercept John and Prochorus as they begin looking for shelter. After I drop you off, I'll check on their progress and circle back around to give you the signal that they have landed."

"Alright, Lassie," Kate replied. "John will wonder how I got here."

"There's nothing wrong with making humans wonder about how things happen," Clarie said with a grin. "It keeps them on their toes. Besides, it will set the stage for the miraculous things that will happen here."

Kate looked down into the water and realized they were getting closer to shore. She began to see the sandy bottom and rocks, and knew that Clarie didn't have much more wiggle room with her massive size. "An' it looks like I'll be havin' ta keep on me toes soon as well." She moved closer to Clarie's huge blow hole. "Now ye're sure ye studied how Craddock did this?"

"I promise you, Kate, I must have watched Craddock's delivery scene in the IAMISPHERE hundreds of times," Clarie assured her. "Don't worry. Are you in position?"

Kate stepped over the whale's blowhole and took a deep breath. "Aye, I'm ready."

"Okay, on the count of three, get ready," Clarie instructed her. She took in a huge mouthful of seawater and gurgled out, "One, two, three . . . NOW!"

"WHOOSH!" Clarie suddenly blew the seawater through her blowhole, sending Kate flying through the air and landing close in to shore where the water was shallow. Kate started dog paddling and soon felt the large smooth pebbles lining the shoreline under her feet. She trotted up onto shore and shook from head to tail, sending sea spray flying everywhere. She looked back out to sea and barked at Clarie, who dipped below the water and slapped her tail on the surface in reply.

"No more for you, old man!" The Roman soldier backhanded John on the cheek, causing the elderly man to crumple and fall back onto the ship's deck with a muffled groan. The wooden cup fell out of John's hand and tumbled over to rest at the angry soldier's feet. The Roman picked up the cup and gripped it tightly as he leaned over the prisoner with a snarl on his face. "You and your kind have been nothing but trouble for Rome," he growled. A rogue wave suddenly splashed over the side of the ship, soaking the prisoner and this hardened soldier. The Roman grabbed the railing to steady himself, wiping the sea spray off his face. He looked out to sea and glimpsed the island looming larger on the horizon. A cruel grin grew on the soldier's face, as he looked down at the shivering, wet prisoner. "It's your misfortune you didn't die quickly in Rome. A slow death from hunger and thirst will teach you Christians to defy the Emperor." He kicked the old man in the gut before he stormed away, leaving the prisoner curled up in a ball, gripping his stomach in pain.

Prochorus tightened his manacled fists in anger but waited until the Roman had walked down the deck before he rushed to the old man's side. "John! Are you all right?!" He helped John sit up with his back resting beneath the railing. Their iron shackles clanked together as they moved about.

John winced but put his hand on Prochorus's shoulder. "I'm all right. Just let me catch my breath." He leaned his head back and closed his eyes. The sound of the sea lapping against the hull of the ship had a comforting rhythm to it. He breathed in the salt air and wiped back the stringy gray hair stuck to his face. Prochorus frowned and lowered his head at their hopeless situation.

"If you find the godless world is hating you, remember it got its start hating me. If you lived on the world's terms, the world would love you as one of its own. But since I picked you to live on God's terms and no longer on the world's terms, the world is going to hate you," John muttered softly. "*When* that happens, remember this: Servants don't get better treatment than their masters. If they beat on me, they will certainly beat on you."

Prochorus raised his gaze and looked at John. "Did he . . . did our Lord say that?"

John nodded, and a sad smile appeared at the corners of his mouth. "The night he was arrested." John slowly rubbed his aching stomach and continued quoting Jesus' words from memory. "I've told you these things to prepare you for rough times ahead. They are going to throw you out of the synagogues. There will even come a time when anyone who kills you will think he's doing God a favor. They will do these things because they never really understood the Father. I've told you these things so that when the time comes and they start in on you, you'll be well-warned and ready for them."

A rush of wind blew across the two old men. "How I wish you had written all these things down." Prochorus rubbed his aching upper arms and pulled his knees into his chest. "He wanted to prepare us for times like this, didn't he? Do you think the Roman is right? Will we die of hunger and thirst?"

John reached his wrinkled hand up to the railing and slowly lifted himself to stand. His gaze drifted back toward his beloved Ephesus getting smaller in the distance. His past was slipping away. He turned to see the rocky island getting closer with each passing moment. This was his future. The sea would separate him from all that he loved.

John's body was old, but his mind was as sharp and on fire for truth as it was on that last night with the Master. He took in a deep breath, closed his eyes, and tried to remember the young faces of the eleven

512

others there that night: Peter, James, Andrew, Matthew, Nathaniel, Philip, James the Less, Thaddeus, Thomas, Simon . . . John frowned as the face of Judas entered his mind. He opened his eyes to clear away the betrayer's image. He shook his head in grief and peered into the blue sea below.

Prochorus joined John at the railing. A massive, shadowy figure glided past the ship, deep under the turquoise water, and John started at the mysterious image. It seemed too big to be a shark. He looked back up at the island and could now see men standing on a pier, waiting for them. "I'm the last one left of the original twelve. It matters not how, where, or when I die. I'll join the others when my work on Earth is complete," John said with a broken voice.

"There's a reason you didn't die in Rome," Prochorus affirmed.

The Roman soldiers began shouting at the more heavily guarded prisoners near the front of the ship, getting everyone to stand as they approached the craggy shoreline. It was time for them to disembark. A scuffle began, and the soldiers quickly brought the prisoners under control with whips and clubs. The sound of screams and clanking chains echoed off the cliffs of this desolate place.

513

This volcanic island of exile was reserved for Rome's worst enemies. Murderers, thieves, and other common criminals labeled by Rome as the scum of the earth were doomed to live out their remaining days with hard labor. Political prisoners who had defied or angered the Emperor faced a different fate. John and Prochorus fell into this second group. They were doomed to total abandonment, left to find their own food, water, and shelter. They were given no clothing or medical care. All they had was the clothes on their backs. Regardless of what kind of prisoner you were, escape was impossible, as had been proved time and again by prisoners who risked climbing down the sharp rocks only to be slammed back into them by the strong currents of the angry sea.

"I don't feel much like a Son of Thunder anymore," John lamented, watching the angry Roman soldier making his way back to where they stood, a bloodied whip in his hand. The old man clung to Jesus' words as he was roughly pushed along to the plank that led down to the dock. *I have told you these things, so that in me you may have peace. In this world you will have trouble. But take heart! I have overcome the world.*

The island prison guards immediately began barking orders at the prisoners, separating them into two groups there on the gravelly shore-line. The second group consisted of only John and Prochorus. A grimy, pot-bellied guard with several missing teeth walked along the row of twenty or so hardened criminals, resting a club on his shoulder as he inspected the prisoners. "Listen well, you scum. You now belong to me," he taunted with a sinister smile, getting eye-to-eye with the tough-est-looking prisoner of the lot. "First, you will be scourged. Then you will be worked to the bone every day until I tell you to stop. Soon you will be begging the gods for death." The tough prisoner seemed to melt under the gaze of this guard and hung his head to look at the iron fetters around his feet. The grimy guard was pleased at the prisoner's submis-sive, defeated response.

A group of prison guards surrounded the terrified criminals and led them down a stony path toward their cruel fate. John and Prochorus stood quietly by, wondering what they were supposed to do.

The Roman guard from the ship came over and jingled a ring of keys in the faces of the two elderly men. "Consider yourselves lucky, Chris-tians." He proceeded to roughly unlock the fetters from their wrists, tossing the chains on the ground to be collected by another soldier.

514

John and Prochorus rubbed their sore wrists, and looked up to the barren hillside dotted with caves. The Roman turned and walked back to the ship. Prochorus stepped forward. "Excuse me, Sir, but where are we to live? Where can we find food and water?"

The Roman turned around, and with a mocking tone replied, "Why don't you ask that invisible God of yours? He's all you've got now. Isn't there a tale about how he miraculously made countless loaves of bread and fish just appear out of nowhere?"

The other soldiers laughed, and together they prepared the ship for departure, leaving the two old men standing on the beach. They were exiled, alone, and left to fend for themselves.

As the ship shoved off into deeper water, the Roman soldier laughed and called back to the old men, "Welcome to Patmos!"

Kate felt the sun warm on her back as she trotted along the rocky shoreline. She gazed up at the island landscape and saw how desolate it was here on this island of exile. "Rocks an' rocks an' more rocks. An'

hardly any trees. But a lot of hills an' glens an' heather shrubs. Now this be a strange mystery. This island almost looks like Scotland! Aye, but still it be a lonely place."

Patmos was originally named for the large number of palm trees on the island, but they had long been stripped away from the centuries of inhabitants who mined the land for various uses. Now all that was left was a rocky landscape devoid of the beautiful greenery it once knew. The soil was as depleted as the trees, so not much grew here. But not much needed to grow here. All Rome cared about was an endless supply of rocks for prisoners to labor against for the rest of their days.

Kate scanned the beach and saw a lone figure in the distance sitting on a big boulder, gazing out to sea. As she neared the human she smiled when she saw that he matched the description that Clarie had given her. He appeared to be in his thirties and had a string of fish that he had caught. This was her man.

She went up to the man and barked. He jumped, startled and shocked to see the little white dog. His look of surprise melted into one of delight, and he got off his rock to go meet her on the beach.

"Where in the world did you come from?" he asked. His skin was deeply tanned from years spent in the intense sun on this island, and despite the beauty of his eyes, they were filled with supreme sadness of the years lost to him.

If anyone needs some love, it's this lad. Kate wagged and grinned happily, as the man petted her. He plopped down onto the sand next to her. She put her paws onto his thigh so she could reach his face to give him kisses.

He closed his eyes and basked in the touch of another living being, and one showing him love at that. Happy tears filled his eyes. "I forgot what this feels like," he said with a gentle laugh. He wrapped his arms around the little dog, holding her close to his chest. "Thank you," he uttered in a soft, broken whisper, returning her kiss as he buried his face into her damp fur. He lifted his head and studied her curiously. "You're wet." He looked around to see if he saw another boat anywhere. "Did someone bring you here?"

"Aye, a whale," Kate barked, continuing to wag her tail happily. Suddenly something caught her eye, and she looked out to sea. It was a spray of water— Clarie's signal. *"Time ta go, Lad. Follow me!"* she ran a few yards down the beach, turned around and barked again.

515

"You just got here!" the man protested, getting to his feet. "And you're leaving?"

Kate ran a few more yards down the beach and turned to bark again.

"You want me to follow you, girl?" the man asked, starting to walk toward her.

Why're humans so slow ta pick up on that, I wonder? Kate thought. *"Aye! Come on, Lad!"* she barked again.

The man picked up his fish and started following her down the beach. "Okay, I'm coming."

☧

Prochorus kept his hand on John's elbow. "Watch your step, John. This terrain is very unsteady with all these rocks."

"Then we'll take our time," John answered. He stopped and put his hand up to his forehead to shield his eyes from the sun. He gazed up to the caves he had seen from the harbor and pointed. "We've got to seek shelter up there."

"Shelter and *water*," Prochorus replied in a worried tone. "Although I don't know where we're going to find any."

"We don't, but the Lord does," John declared confidently. "I don't think he saved me from death to bring me here to die of thirst. That doesn't sound like something the Living Water would do."

Prochorus smiled at John's incredible faith. "Thank you for that reminder, my friend." He sighed and looked up at the caves. "Let's press on then."

After John and Prochorus had hiked a while they sat down to catch their breath. They were in dire need of water. Together the men looked around the landscape and saw the harbor below them. They had made it quite a way up and could better make out the unusual shape of the island. "It looks like Patmos has seven mountains across three sections of island," Prochorus noted as he pointed to the landscape.

"Even in such a barren place of exile, God has his imprint of perfection and unity. Seven and three," John replied. As John scanned the landscape he suddenly saw the figure of a man coming up the mountainside from a different path. "Look, Prochorus! Maybe he could help us!"

Prochorus stood up to get a good look at the man. He waved his arms and called out. "Hello! Up here!"

The man stopped in his tracks, just as surprised to see them as they were to see him. He lifted a hand and waved to them.

Prochorus turned to John excitedly. "He's coming! I pray he's a friendly sort." He turned back to follow the man and suddenly noticed the little white dog running ahead of him. As they got closer, Kate barked. Prochorus turned to John with a dumbfounded look. "You won't believe this, John."

Suddenly Kate reached the crest of the hill and ran right over to John, jumping up happily to see him.

"Chava?" John asked, reaching out his arms to pick her up onto his lap. "Is it really you?"

Kate licked John on the face repeatedly, her tail wagging furiously. *"Aye! I've missed ye!"*

Prochorus slowly shook his head in disbelief and held out his hand with his mouth hanging open. "How?"

John leaned his head back and smiled broadly while Kate licked him. "I have no idea. Maybe she stowed away on a ship bringing supplies from Ephesus when she looked for me at the harbor." He hugged her to his chest as the man reached the crest of the hill. "But it looks like she's led this man right to us."

517

"Hello, Sirs," the man said. "Is this your dog?"

"Yes, it is, although we have no idea how she got here on the island," John replied. "Good day to you."

"We've just arrived on Patmos today," Prochorus explained. "But we came directly from Rome. Little Chava here lived with John back in Ephesus."

"How is that possible?" The man wrinkled his brow. "But Rome, you say? Has Domitian sent you here?"

"Yes, we are his political prisoners," John answered.

"More like religious prisoners," Prochorus offered. "John refused to worship that madman."

The man smiled sadly and nodded, sitting down on the rocks next to them. "He sent me here also for not doing his bidding. I've been here for years."

"Then you know this island well? Please, we are in desperate need of water and are trying to find shelter," Prochorus explained. "Can you help us?"

The man lifted a leather flask from his belt and handed it to John. "Here."

"Thank you, my friend," John replied, drinking the fresh water. He closed his eyes in relief and nodded with a smile, handing the flask to Prochorus.

"There's only one spring on the island, and one lake that fills during the winter and spring but dries up in the summer," the man explained. "My cave isn't far from here. I chose to live apart from the other unconfined prisoners on Patmos. Many live down below in the valley, but I found that I could not be around them." He looked up at the sun and saw that it was starting to set. "We better get to my cave where you can stay the night. I can help you find a place tomorrow." He held up his catch. "I have two fish to share."

Prochorus smiled. "Thank you, Friend. We are grateful." He turned to John. "Now if five loaves appear we'll know this is a miracle."

Kate stood there gazing at the three men with her peppy grin. *So far so good,* she thought.

"Come, Chava," John called her as he stood to his feet. He shook his head and smiled at this miracle. "Praise God for his goodness in bringing you to me."

The man looked at John and at the little dog. "Which god?"

"The One I was sent here for worshipping," John replied. "Jesus Christ. Have you heard of him?"

The man's eyes immediately filled with tears. "Yes, but I do not understand him. Nor do I understand his people. I've been haunted by the memory of one of his followers for years on this island." He lifted his hand to wipe the tears from his eyes.

"Perhaps I can help you understand him. Our meeting was no accident," John said, gazing down at Kate with a smile. He put his hand on the man's shoulder. "I believe Jesus himself arranged for us to meet. My name is John," John told him with a smile. That was when John noticed the mark on the man's hand. It was in the shape of a lion. "Tell me, my friend. What is your name?"

The man took the leather flask back from Prochorus, nodded, and locked eyes with John. "My name is Leonitus."

56

CAVE OF REVELATION

The fire snapped, and a rush of sparks rose into the night sky. Leonitus poked the embers with a stick and then tested the fish to see if they were cooked. He had built a fire out in front of his cave that overlooked the island of Patmos. They had watched a spectacular sunset with fiery red clouds against a pink sky. Now stars without number were beginning to appear in the sky.

"I think they are ready," Leonitus said. He lifted the fish from the baking stone and winced as it burned his fingers. "Hot!" He took a knife and cut a piece of fish. He placed it on a thin wooden plate he had made and handed it to John. "For you, John." He placed another piece on another plate. "And for you, Prochorus." He then put a final piece on his last wooden plate, broke off a chunk, and smiled. "And for you, little Chava." Kate wagged her tail.

"Thank you, Leonitus. Allow me to bless our food," John said, not waiting for permission. He closed his eyes as Leonitus was getting ready to put a piece of fish in his mouth.

Leonitus stopped and cleared his throat, putting his fish down. He closed his eyes and bowed his head like John and Prochorus.

"Father, I thank you for your mercy, goodness, and provision. Thank you for safely delivering us to Patmos today, and for allowing us to meet Leonitus through our precious Chava. I thank you for meeting our needs with water, this food, and shelter. But I thank you most for Jesus and his love unto salvation. Bless our new friend, Leonitus, and our time with him," John prayed. "Amen."

Leonitus slowly opened his eyes as John and Prochorus dove in to eating their fish.

"This is delicious, my friend," Prochorus said. "Thank you for sharing your catch with us. John here used to be a fisherman, isn't that so, John?"

"In my youth, yes," John grunted with satisfaction and nodded in agreement. "On one of the last mornings we had with Jesus, he cooked fish just like this for us on the beach," John recalled. He licked his fingers with delight. "Delicious."

Leonitus's eyes grew wide as he chewed. "You actually *knew* this Jesus?"

John smiled and nodded. "I was one of his disciples. He was my best friend, and he loved me. Oh, how he loved me!"

"Jesus actually entrusted his mother Mary to John at the cross. She lived with him until she died in Ephesus," Prochorus added, filling in details that John would not offer himself. "John has been the leader of the churches ever since Paul's death. Have you ever heard of Paul?"

Leonitus closed his eyes and held up his hand. "Wait. You were with Jesus," he said as he opened his eyes. "At the cross?"

John looked intently at the man. "I was."

Leonitus set down his plate, propped his elbows on his knees, and held out his open palms. His eyes welled up and his lips trembled. "So was my grandfather. He was the centurion on duty."

John and Prochorus shot glances of surprise at each other at this revelation. John leaned over and also welled up, whispering softly. *"Surely this was the Son of God.* I'll never forget hearing those words. How miraculous to meet the grandson of the one who said those words, and in such a place as this." John wrinkled his brow. "Do you not believe as did your grandfather?"

Leonitus wiped his eyes with the back of his arm and shook his head in bewilderment. "I don't know what to believe. To answer your question, Prochorus, yes, I've heard of Paul. My father was his lawyer in Rome."

John put his hands to his mouth in stunned silence at this further revelation. "Theophilus?"

"Your father was *Theophilus?* The one to whom Luke addressed his letters?" Prochorus asked in amazement.

520

"Yes. I never read those letters, but the last Christian I knew read them," Leonitus replied, staring into the fire with watery eyes. "I killed him."

John leaned over and put his hand on the man's shaking shoulder as Leonitus began to sob. "What happened to you, dear boy?"

"My grandmother brought my father and Uncle Julius to Rome from Judea when they were boys," Leonitus began. "My grandfather Armandus was to have followed them on to Rome but died in a shipwreck and never arrived. My grandmother did the best she could to raise her sons, but neither of them accepted the new faith that she and my grandfather embraced. My father did not believe in anything spiritual, being an avid intellectual. He didn't show much emotion and love to me when I was little. But then Paul met my uncle on the ship to Rome and introduced him to my father who agreed to take his case. Evidently my uncle and father became believers. My father changed and grew into a loving man. He began telling me about Jesus. He said . . ." Leonitus halted. A tear rolled down his cheek.

521

"Go on," John gently encouraged him.

"He said that Jesus loved me," Leonitus continued, smiling sadly. "I had been exposed to the gods of Rome where we lived, so I thought Jesus was just another god. I didn't understand. Then came the fire that burned down Rome." He stopped, and he clenched his jaw. "Our house was engulfed in flames, and when we tried to escape a lion blocked our path. My parents died, and I sat alone in the courtyard under a fountain while the flames surrounded me. Somehow a friend of my father managed to rescue me and take me to my grandmother."

Clarie, Kate thought, her eyes tearing up to hear Leonitus share his tragic story.

"My grandmother tried to raise me as best she could, among Christians even," Leonitus said with a sad laugh. "But the damage was done. Anger and fear consumed me, and I rebelled against her. She even took us to Gaul, but I fell into the wrong crowd. All I wanted to do was to become a gladiator. I wanted to kill lions." He pulled up his tunic to show the mark on his thigh: LEO. "So I ran away to Rome and joined the gladiator school. I became famous and did what I set out to do. I killed lions . . . and men." He handed the knife to John. It was one carved with his likeness and name.

"I see," John said, studying the knife. "And then?"

Leonitus took a stick and poked the fire to rekindle the flames. "I evidently broke my grandmother's heart. I hated everyone and cared only about myself." He jabbed the logs angrily. "Death or glory," he sneered, shaking his head. "A Christian named Domitius sold himself as a gladiator to pay for the freedom of a Jewish slave. He trained with me and tried to talk to me about Luke's letters, and about Jesus. I didn't want to hear any of it. On opening day of the Flavian Amphitheater, I fought him. Titus called the match as a fight to the death, and although Domitius wounded me and could have killed me on the spot, he told me that he didn't want me to die without knowing Jesus." Leonitus shook his head. "He told me that Jesus was the true Gate of Life that awaited me. He lowered his sword, and I killed him. I received the glory, and he received death. I received my freedom . . ."

"And so did he," John finished his sentence. "Domitius is free in heaven. Oh, dear boy, our brother Domitius wanted you to see the depth of love that he had for you because of Jesus. He wanted to show you what Jesus did for you. And he didn't want you to die apart from grace."

"How could someone love such a despicable person like me enough to *die* for me?" Leonitus protested. "It doesn't make sense!"

John smiled and looked into the fire. "No, it doesn't. Love was never meant to make sense. It is not logical, and it cannot be reasoned with. Your father came to realize this when he finally gave in to the love of Jesus." The wind blew a gentle gust over them, and a memory flashed in John's mind. He stood up to tell the story.

"One night we were sitting around the fire with Jesus, just like we are here. One of the Jewish leaders named Nicodemus came to find Jesus because he, too, didn't understand how Jesus taught about love and grace and mercy," John began. "Nicodemus didn't understand why Jesus taught about being 'born again.' Jesus pointed to the fire and said, 'You know well enough how the wind blows this way and that. You hear it rustling through the trees, but you have no idea where it comes from or where it's headed next. That's the way it is with everyone 'born from above' by the wind of God, the Spirit of God."

John walked over and looked into Leonitus's eyes. Then Jesus said, "'This is how much God loved the world: He gave his Son, his one and only Son. And this is why: so that no one need be destroyed; by believing in him, anyone can have a whole and lasting life.' I'll never forget how Jesus' voice was filled with power and authority."

John stood up straight and held out his hands in front of him. "Jesus gestured with those amazing, healing hands as he spoke. He looked intently at Nicodemus and said, 'God didn't go to all the trouble of sending his Son merely to point an accusing finger, telling the world how bad it was. He came to help, to put the world right again. Anyone who trusts in him is acquitted,' Jesus said with a hopeful tone of good news. Then his face grew serious and he leaned back. 'Anyone who refuses to trust him has long since been under the death sentence without knowing it. And why? Because of that person's failure to believe in the Son of God when introduced to him.' "

The aged disciple put his hands behind his back and lowered his gaze to the fire. "I've seen my share of people refuse Jesus. And they are the most miserable people I've ever known. They are so very lost in their sin, and the door is wide open for the enemy to come in and devour them like a lion. And then, they are lost forever, living an eternity apart from him and with that evil lion."

523

John took a seat again next to Leonitus. "Jesus is indeed the true Gate of Life. And he is also known as the true Lion of the Tribe of Judah. He is good, and he died for you, Leonitus, because he loves you so. Oh, how he loves you." He tapped the lion mark on the back of Leonitus's hand. "Your name means 'lion-like.' The question is, *which* lion do you wish to be like?"

Leonitus looked up at John, moved to his core. "Jesus is a *good* lion? And he died for a sinner like me because of love?" He blinked back fresh tears. "I'm tired of fighting him. I believe what my father and grandmother told me about Jesus. I believe he died and rose again. I believe what Domitius told me and what you've now shared. If he'll forgive me, I wish to be like him. I give my life to the Lion of Judah."

Prochorus got up, and together he and John wrapped their arms around Leonitus's shoulder. "Welcome, Brother. I told John he was saved in Rome for a reason. Perhaps it was just for your sake alone."

Leonitus looked at them in disbelief. "How could that be?"

John smiled. "If he felt you were worth dying for, don't you think he'd go to the ends of the earth to reach you?"

Kate barked, *"Aye!"*

The men laughed at the happy little dog. "See? Even Chava agrees," John said. "My heart is elated that you have laid down your sword for the King."

"Oddly enough, that's what brought me to Patmos, although I didn't realize it," Leonitus shared with them. "After I won my freedom, I was too disturbed by what happened in the arena that day and just lived a life of reckless abandon. I lived off my fame and wealth, doing nothing but enjoying a wretched life. One day Domitian called me to the palace and asked me to head up his new *Ludus Magnus,* the biggest gladiator school ever built. He also wanted me to design his new hypogeum beneath the arena. He wanted me to help him design more exciting ways for men to die, and to train those who would take their lives. I knew I couldn't do it. So I refused him. In a rage he ordered me sent here as a political prisoner, because I was too popular with the people for him to kill me."

"And so you came to Patmos," Prochorus noted, looking at the knife carved with LEO. "How did you bring this knife with you?"

Leonitus smiled. "I smuggled it aboard. I couldn't have lived here without it. It's the only tool I have, but it has helped me survive in this barren place."

"And now you will show us how to survive here as well," John told him, looking up into the darkened night sky now full of bright stars. "Who knew what this day would hold when we arrived on Patmos?"

"Obviously the Lion of Judah knew," Leonitus replied with a knowing grin. "Will you teach me more about him, John?"

"Indeed he did, and indeed I will," John laughed in reply. "And if this is what he ordained for day one, no telling what will happen in the days ahead."

SEVENTEEN MONTHS LATER

"So, the father welcomed the prodigal son with open arms, but it was the *brother* who resented his return?" Leonitus asked as he, John, and Prochorus walked along the beach. They were going to catch some fish for dinner. "That's an incredible story."

"Jesus loved to speak in parables and stories," John noted, patting Leonitus's back. "And he especially had a heart for prodigals."

Leonitus smiled. "Like me."

"Like all of us," John corrected him. "The prophet Isaiah wrote, *All of us, like sheep, have strayed away. We have left God's paths to follow our own. Yet the Lord laid on him the sins of us all.* Isaiah wrote about Jesus seven hundred years before he came."

Leonitus tossed back his sandy brown hair. "Amazing. I've learned so much from you, John."

"Isaiah wrote about Jesus seven hundred years before he came, but I've been telling John that *he* needs to write about Jesus, almost seventy years now after Jesus left," Prochorus said. "John, I've listened to you share your knowledge of Jesus' teachings and character with Leonitus these past months. You need to write this down."

"Matthew, Mark, and Luke already wrote gospel accounts of Jesus' life," John answered, walking along with his hands behind his back as he pondered this request. He yawned and shook his head, feeling tired.

"Yes, but I've heard you tell Leonitus things that Matthew, Mark, and Luke didn't cover," Prochorus relayed. "You've shared the beginnings of Jesus' ministry, and miracles like the wedding feast in Cana where Jesus turned the water to wine, the story of Nicodemus coming to Jesus at night, the woman of Samaria, and the raising of Lazarus from the dead. The world needs to know these stories!"

John scratched his chin as he thought this through. "I never thought about it like that."

"He's right, John," Leonitus insisted. "I think you need to write these things down."

"What in the world would I use for ink?" John asked, laughing.

Leonitus picked up a shell and threw it far into the sea. Kate barked and tried to chase it into the water. He picked up another shell, reared back his hand to throw and halted. "Sepia. *Sepia!* That's where we can find ink." Sepia was a well-known mollusk whose ink was used for writing. "I've got a knife so I can catch them, get the ink, and even carve you a stylus."

"Brilliant, Leonitus! But where will we get parchment?" Prochorus asked.

The three men fell silent, as they considered the fact that parchment was something they did not have at their disposal.

"Well, if the Lord wills it, he'll make a way. Not only do I need

525

parchment, but in order for anyone to read what I write, I think I would need to leave Patmos. At least my writings would need to leave," John said finally, yawning. "For now, I need to rest. I shall leave you to catch fish and enjoy this beautiful Lord's Day. I'll pick some figs and have a fire lit and ready for the fish when you return."

"I like how you Christians . . . I mean *we* Christians . . . took over that title for the Sabbath—the *true* Lord's Day. Today happens to be the Emperor's day, you know," Leonitus reminded them.

Prochorus nodded. "The Lord of Lords conquers every detail as he takes over every heart."

"I never thought I'd say this, but I'd rather be here on Patmos with you two lighting fires to bake fish than back in Rome lighting incense to worship Domitian as lord. What have you two *done* to me?" he joked.

"Paul wrote that anyone who belongs to Christ has become a new person. The old life is gone; a new life has begun!" John replied, holding up his hands in the air. He smiled and turned to walk from the beach back up the path to his cave. "Coming, Chava?"

Kate barked and ran after John to escort him back up the mountain.

John turned to look back at the incredible vista from the entrance of his cave. He could see the beautiful valley and sea below. Every sunrise and sunset proved to be spectacular, especially when tropical clouds built up late in the afternoon, as was just beginning now. Inside, the cave was warm in the winter and cool and dry in the summer. It was divided into three natural rooms with a large stone column in the center, and a low ceiling that the men could reach up and touch. John walked inside and had to pause to let his eyes adjust from the bright sunshine outside. He smiled to hear the sound of Kate's claws clicking as she trotted inside on the stone. "Are you going to take a nap with me, girl?"

Kate wagged her tail and smiled, running over to the corner where John liked to sleep. There was a natural niche in the wall where the elderly man could place his hand to help him up and down from his sleeping spot. Kate turned around a few times and lay down, tucking her feet under her. John smiled and put his hand in the niche, getting down on the cool stone floor next to her. He lay down on his side facing the wall with a grunt. He took a deep breath through his nose and

526

slowly exhaled. He hummed a few bars of a familiar psalm of David as he rested his head. He paused and thought about what his friends asked of him, to write down his recollections and teachings of Jesus. "I am your servant, my Lord. What would you have me do?" With those groggy words on his lips, his heavy eyelids closed. Kate rested her head on her paws and closed her eyes as well. Soon John began to enter a twilight type sleep.

After a few moments, Kate tingled, and her fur rose on end. She opened her eyes and lifted her head. Outside the cave she saw red, orange, yellow, and pink billowing beauty. *The fire cloud!* She stood and walked over to the entrance, mesmerized by what she saw. She could feel the Presence that she had felt many times before. She could feel the Presence of the Maker.

Suddenly John started to restlessly toss and turn. Kate turned back toward him. As she did so, she heard a loud voice behind them, like a trumpet call:

"Write down in a book what you see, and send it to the seven churches—to Ephesus, Smyrna, Pergamum, Thyatira, Sardis, Philadelphia, and Laodicea!"

527

John turned over and sat up abruptly, his face covered in awe and inexplicable wonder. He got up and started walking slowly to the entrance of the cave. Kate turned back to the entrance, and her heart caught in her chest at the supernatural vision. The fire cloud was enveloping the entrance of the cave, and in the center of it was Jesus. Kate fell on her face to see him in a way she had never seen him before. Somehow she was caught up in the vision that John was seeing.

There were seven golden lamp stands, and Jesus stood in the middle of them. He wore a robe that reached to his feet and a gold band around his chest. His hair was white as wool, or as snow, and his eyes blazed like fire; his feet shone like brass that has been refined and polished, and his voice sounded like a roaring waterfall. He held seven stars in his right hand, and a sharp two-edged sword came out of his mouth. His face was as bright as the midday sun.

John fell down at Jesus' feet like a dead man. Jesus leaned over and placed his right hand on the disciple that he loved. "Don't be afraid! I am the first and the last. I am the living one! I was dead, but now I am alive forever and ever. I have authority over death and the world of the dead. Write, then, the things you see, both the things that are now and the things that will happen afterward."

John lifted his gaze and stared into the face of the One who had loved him and had died for him. He had seen him in his resplendent glory on the Mount of Transfiguration, but even that image paled in comparison to what he was seeing now. He was speechless but listened as Jesus continued to instruct him.

"Here is the secret meaning of the seven stars that you see in my right hand, and of the seven golden lampstands," Jesus said. He looked at his right hand holding the stars. "The seven stars are the angels of the seven churches." He pointed to the lampstands around him with his left hand. "And the seven lampstands are the seven churches."

Time stood still as Jesus gave John a revelation of himself, of things that were, and of things that were yet to come.

JOHN'S PEN

EPHESUS, AD 98

The sea kept John away from all that he loved." Kate stared at the infinite horizon of the azure blue sea from John's hilltop house back in Ephesus. "It's hard ta believe we ever even left this place. It were only eighteen months on Patmos, but somehow it all seems like a dream."

"This sea also kept me away fr-r-rom all that I love, too," Max whispered in her ear as he stood behind her. "Bein' back with ye be a dr-r-ream come tr-r-rue for me, Lass."

Kate turned and smiled, nudging Max with her head. "Aye, no wonder John wrote that heaven won't have any sea. No more bein' apart from those we love."

Max kissed her on the head. "Sounds like heaven ta me."

John and Prochorus were gone for a day trip to visit a nearby church, and Leonitus had just left Ephesus to join Julius back in Gaul. While Kate and Max nuzzled and stared out to sea, enjoying their togetherness once more, Al was lying on his belly playing with a coin. Liz and Nigel sat nearby, up on John's desk that was covered with scrolls of the apostle's work.

"Brilliant! I say, John's pen has struck this scroll with pure genius!" Nigel exclaimed, adjusting his spectacles as he studied John's scroll. "He made great use of Plato's philosophy to unlock the Greek mind. Brilliant!"

"Ain't that the writer ye be quotin' all the time, Mousie?" Al asked.

The big orange cat stuck his tongue out to the side as he concentrated. He'd been attempting to send the coin on a 360-degree spin all morning with no success. "Did John quote Plato, too?"

"Indeed Plato is who I enjoy quoting, old boy," Nigel replied, keeping his gaze fixed on the parchment, "but no, John did not quote him."

Liz looked down at Al. "But for his gospel account of Jesus' life, John used Plato's school of thought, shared by all Greeks, to come up with an entirely new way to present who Jesus is. John took a much different approach than Matthew, Mark, and Luke."

Al wrinkled his brow and tried to spin the coin once more. "What were wrong with how the other laddies wrote aboot Jesus?"

"Nothing at all is *wrong,* my good fellow, merely *different,*" Nigel quickly corrected him. "Pay heed as I try to explain what our dear apostle has done here. Right, now that Christianity is seventy years old, it has spread out into the Greek world, and thus needs to be *restated* for a Greek-minded world."

"Ain't that what Jesus wanted?" Al asked, rolling onto his back.

"*Oui,* Albert. The disciples did exactly as Jesus asked," Liz said with a smile. "Despite the cost, they took the gospel to Jerusalem, to Samaria, and to the ends of the earth."

"But what started in Jerusalem and Samaria was communicated from a *Jewish* mindset," Nigel added with a finger raised in the air. "Matthew begins his gospel by presenting the genealogy of Jesus, but genealogy is meaningless to Greeks. As is Matthew's mention that Jesus was the 'Son of David', a king the Greeks have never heard of. And the term Messiah is one that has no relevance to Greeks. *Ergo*, if a Greek reads Matthew's account, they might think they need to rework their thinking to first be Jewish before they can become Christian—they would need to first understand Jewish history and prophecy to appreciate who Jesus is. Do you follow, old boy?"

"Aye, I think so," Al replied, putting the coin over one of his eyes. "What aboot Mark's and Luke's books?"

"Well, like Matthew, those accounts of Jesus focus on the facts of what Jesus did, and John wanted to do more than present the facts again," Liz answered. "He wished to show the meaning and the truth *behind* the facts. Matthew, Mark, and Luke are *historical* gospels. John is a *spiritual* gospel."

"Which brings us back to Plato. You see, Plato and all Greeks are supreme intellectuals," Nigel noted.

"Like me," Al declared with a goofy grin.

Nigel cleared his throat and continued. "They believe in *logos* which means 'word' or 'reason.' They believe in the orderliness that they can see, like the turning of day to night, the changing seasons, and the movement of the stars and planets. They further believe that such order was created by God, or gods as it were. They believe that God gave humans the ability to think, reason, and know. Plato's philosophy was that somewhere there is a perfect pattern of what is good and beautiful, and that anything good or beautiful here on earth is merely an imperfect copy. The great reality, the supreme idea, and the perfect pattern from which all patterns are made *is* God who is not in this world. To the Greeks, the *unseen* world is the real one. The *seen* world is only a shadowy reality. The great problem is how to get that real perfection into this imperfect world of shadows."

"Well, Jesus solved that problem by comin' down here then," Al said matter of factly, rolling back over onto his belly.

"Precisely!" Nigel exclaimed with a clap of his paws. "John has declared that Jesus *is* that perfect reality, come to earth! He is the *Logos,* or the controlling mind of God come to earth in the man of Jesus." He leaned over and read from John's scroll. "So the Word became human and made his home among us."

Liz nodded. "John also gives long lessons after showing the miracles of Jesus. He shows the reader that these miracles were not just wonderful, but they are glimpses into the true reality, which is God. They are not just single events in time, but show what a glorious God continues to do across time!"

Al scratched his chin. "Like feedin' the five thousand?" His eyes widened happily. "Ye mean he'll keep makin' loaves and fishes until we have leftovers?"

Liz giggled. "I know that was your favorite Jesus miracle, *cher* Albert. *Oui,* John means that Jesus is forever the real Bread of Life. And Jesus did not just open the darkened eyes of a blind man once, he is *forever* opening the eyes of a darkened world."

"Here, here. And Jesus did not just raise Lazarus from the dead one time, but he is the Resurrection and the life for *everyone* for *all* time,"

531

Nigel added. "So you see, old boy, the events in Jesus' life were windows into the eternal reality that the Greeks have long looked for."

"Sounds like he'll have a bestseller with that book then," Al said, trying to spin the coin again.

Liz and Nigel scanned the other scrolls on John's desk. Liz put her paws on three small ones. "Nigel, I do believe that in addition to John's gospel, these three small letters would also make good additions to the New Testament."

Nigel scanned the scrolls and nodded in agreement. "I wholeheartedly concur, my dear. John has written several brief letters—yet they are packed with as much genius as anything he has written. And in two of these, he gives mention to the Antichrist, so I believe they are especially important."

"Antichrist? Ye mean Anti-*Jesus?* I don't like the sound o' that at all," Al said with a frown. "Sounds like someone Kate saw when she and John were in that scary cave for John to write his mystery book." He squinted with one eye open and concentrated very hard. He set the coin up right with his paws, stuck out his tongue and tried to spin it again, without success. "I don't get it."

Nigel scurried over to John's most recent work, and rolled it open by running across it with his nose. He stood up and appreciated it with his hands clasped behind his back. "Ah, yes, the mysterious masterpiece from John's pen."

"Revelation," Liz nodded, putting her paw gently on the parchment. She looked outside to Kate and Max. "Perhaps our dear Kate could help lend insight to this puzzling book."

"I say, Kate!" Nigel called with a paw cupped to his mouth. "Could you please grace us with your presence as we discuss John's scroll of Revelation?"

Kate and Max rejoined them in the room. "Aye, wha' do ye need ta know?" Kate asked as she trotted over to the table and looked up at her friends.

Liz and Nigel shared a humorous look. "Everything!" they said in unison.

Max grinned. "Me lass can help us all understand it."

Kate wagged her tail. "I'd be glad ta help if I can. I know I were there when John had his vision, but it still be mysterious ta me. Maybe it would help if I asked ye questions ta see wha' ye know already."

"Splendid suggestion, my dear," Nigel replied, adjusting his spectacles. "Please proceed."

Kate nodded. "John's Revelation has two parts. Do ye know wha' they be?"

Liz scanned the scroll. "I believe that part one involves things which are, and part two involves things yet to come."

"Aye, so part one covers the letters ta seven churches here an' now. Part two be the rest of the book and covers from now until Jesus comes again," Kate affirmed.

"*Ergo,* this book is a revealing or an explanation of things to come in order to help the church chart its course and understand its future destiny," Nigel added. "And although it is filled with mystery, it has many things that we *can* understand. No doubt, some of the mysterious things will be understood with the passage of time."

"Please read the introduction, *mon ami,*" Liz asked Nigel.

"With pleasure," Nigel replied. After adjusting his spectacles, he leaned over to read:

533

This book is the record of the events that Jesus Christ revealed. God gave him this revelation in order to show to his servants what must happen very soon. Christ made these things known to his servant John by sending his angel to him, and John has told all that he has seen. This is his report concerning the message from God and the truth revealed by Jesus Christ. Happy is the one who reads this book, and happy are those who listen to the words of this prophetic message and obey what is written in this book! For the time is near when all these things will happen.

"Aye, so all of it is meant ta bring happy news ta God's people," Kate explained. "Jesus wanted John ta show his followers that he be the King of Kings an' Lord of Lords no matter wha' they go through with all the evil here on earth."

"*Oui,* now that the third persecution of Christians has begun under Emperor Trajan, this book is very timely for the churches," Liz noted with a frown. "But it appears even darker days are ahead."

"As if two per-r-rsecutions weren't enough," growled Max. "Ner-r-ro, then Domitian, now Tr-r-rajan."

"What happened to the good Emperor in between the bad lads?" Al asked.

"The madman Domitian was finally assassinated in AD 96, and Emperor Nerva came to power," Nigel explained. "Nerva released all of Domitian's political prisoners, so that's how John, Prochorus and Leonitus got to leave Patmos and return to Ephesus. The Roman Senate erased the memory of wicked Domitian by declaring *damnatio memotiae*, meaning they destroyed all of his temples, statues, and public displays, and reversed his insane policies. Nero was also rightfully declared *damnatio memoriae*."

"*Oui*, so the Christians had two years of relief from persecution from AD 96-98," Liz added. "While Nerva was a good emperor loved by the people, he adopted Trajan as his son. So when Nerva died of natural causes, Trajan came to power. Sadly, this new emperor has once more begun to persecute Christians."

"Of all the Nerva!" Al bellowed with a frown. "Why'd he have to pick such a bad lad?"

534

"Trajan was a well-respected governor with many legions at his command," Nigel explained. "He shall be a strong ruler for Rome, but he will do great harm to believers."

"So Jesus came ta John with the vision for believers ta know how ta deal with these hard times no matter how many evil rulers come an' go," Kate explained. "But it won't jest be Romans that cause Christians harm."

"Aye, those pagans here in Ephesus killed Timothy last year," Max growled. "All because he told 'em them their idolatry were evil when they were paradin' in the str-r-reet for a festival."

Liz's eyes welled up, and she shook her head sadly. "Our dear Timothy, beaten with clubs. Another martyr, yet one who is with Jesus and reunited with Paul."

Kate nodded sadly. "Read the next part, Mousie."

Nigel nodded and continued to read:

From John to the seven churches in the province of Asia:

Grace and peace be yours from God, who is, who was, and who is to come, and from the seven spirits in front of his throne, and from Jesus Christ, the faithful witness, the first to be raised from death and who is also the ruler of the kings of the world.

He loves us, and by his sacrificial death he has freed us from our sins and made us a kingdom of priests to serve his God and Father. To Jesus Christ be the glory and power forever and ever! Amen.

Look, he is coming on the clouds! Everyone will see him, including those who pierced him. All peoples on earth will mourn over him. So shall it be!

"I am the first and the last," says the Lord God Almighty, who is, who was, and who is to come.

"He's always been aboot clouds, hasn't he?" Max asked. "Fire clouds, exodus clouds, transfiguration clouds, ascension clouds, an' someday comin' back clouds."

"Splendid observance, old boy," Nigel remarked. "Indeed, and Jesus says he is the *Alpha* and the *Omega*, the first and the last."

"And he's everythin' in between, too," Al added. "He's been there through every page o' history, hadn't he? Even when all the human kings come and go, Jesus stays the same. Jest like I always say, he be the great I AM, not the great I WERE." Everyone looked at Al with amazement at his profound insight. "What?"

"Keep readin', please Mousie," Kate requested.

I am John, your brother, and as a follower of Jesus I am your partner in patiently enduring the suffering that comes to those who belong to his Kingdom. I was put on the island of Patmos because I had proclaimed God's word and the truth that Jesus revealed. On the Lord's day the Spirit took control of me, and I heard a loud voice, that sounded like a trumpet, speaking behind me. It said, "Write down what you see, and send the book to the churches in these seven cities: Ephesus, Smyrna, Pergamum, Thyatira, Sardis, Philadelphia, and Laodicea.

"The church is persecuted on the *outside*, but they also are having problems on the *inside*," Liz suggested. "So this book of Revelation is meant to deal with both, no? Believers must unite and make it through these hard times together, with Jesus leading them."

"That's right, Liz," Kate said. "So when John opened up his letter, he said he were their *brother*. He didn't say he were the last of the twelve, or the most important laddie left alive. Do ye know why?"

"I assume he used the term to harken back to Alexander the Great and how he would address his faithful soldiers after they endured battle

535

together," Nigel surmised, lifting a paw in dramatic form. "He would stand with his valiant comrades, put his hand on their shoulders, and say, 'Alexander the Great is proud to be the *brother* of this soldier.' *Adelphos* is the Greek word for brother that he used, just as John has used in this letter."

"So John's sayin' he's a fellow br-r-rother, fightin' the same fight against the same enemy with the same weapons," Max offered. "Sometimes the best thing a leader can do is ta get down in the tr-r-renches with his soldiers so they know he understands wha' they be goin' through."

"Very good!" Kate said happily. "So Jesus came down ta the trenches with all believers, an' John came down ta the trenches with his readers."

Liz smiled. "I wish I could have been there when you saw Jesus, *mon amie.* How wonderful to see him again! John described him just like our Daniel did when he had a similar vision back in Babylon."

"Aye, Liz, it were wonderful. John did see wha' Daniel saw, an' although Jesus looked different, John knew his voice," Kate told them. "How could he ever forget that voice? Now, do ye know why Jesus said ta write ta those seven churches?"

536

"Because seven be the best!" Al exclaimed, continuing to play with his coin.

Liz traced her paw over the seven named churches. "Well, these seven cities are the largest cities in all of Asia Minor, so have the largest churches to influence believers everywhere. Is that why?"

"And, I may add that these seven churches are all connected along the Roman roads," Nigel added. "So circulating the letters shall be easy from these main points."

Kate nodded. "Aye, but there be more. These seven churches make up pieces of a picture of what the whole church looks like. Each church has a different problem, an' over time, the things that these churches struggle with on the inside will be wha' churches will always struggle with until Jesus comes again."

"But Jesus be the same answer ta their problems," Max noted.

"So each of the seven copies of this book of Revelation had the whole letter, with a special message ta each church," Kate explained. "Two churches be good: Smyrna an' Philadelphia. Two churches be very bad: Sardis an' Laodicea. Three churches be part good an' part bad: Ephesus, Pergamum, an' Thyatira. Jesus tells each of them he knows all aboot them an' wha' they be doin', then gives them a word of wha' ta do next, an' wha' they'll get if they overcome their hard times by listenin' ta wha' he says."

"Didn't Jesus call 'em stars?" Al asked, staring at his coin. "Don't stars light up the sky when it's dark?"

Liz blew Al a kiss. *"Magnifique* Albert! That is yet another insight to the meaning of the seven churches. Jesus means for his churches to always be the light in this dark world. And the seven angels or messengers of the seven churches are the pastors of those churches, no?"

"I say, there are quite a number of sevens throughout this mysterious book of Revelation, " Nigel noted, holding up fingers as he rattled them off. "Seven letters to seven churches, seven angels, seven seals and seven trumpets, seven vials, seven candlesticks, seven spirits, a lamb with seven horns and seven eyes, seven lamps, seven thunders, a red dragon with seven heads and seven crowns, a leopard-like beast with seven heads, a scarlet-colored beast with seven heads, seven mountains, seven kings."

"That sure be a lot of sevens in this letter," Max noted, wide-eyed.

"Do ye know why there be a lot of sevens, me love?" Kate asked.

"Because seven be the best!" Al exclaimed again, trying to spin his coin.

Max shook his head at Al. "The Maker likes sevens. Always has. There were seven days of creation, but he r-r-rested on the seventh day."

"C'est bon! The Maker put sevens into everything! Seven days in a week, seven notes in music, seven colors in a rainbow," Liz offered. "Seven means complete."

"Like the seven o' us!" Al exclaimed, pointing around the room. "Except we're missin' two right now."

"So the beginning of the Old Testament begins with the seven days of creation, and it will *end* with a book of sevens about creation's destiny!" Nigel exclaimed. "Brilliant!"

Liz nodded. "So after the first part of Revelation and the seven letters, then comes the second part about what is to come. Nigel, read the heaven scene, *s'il vous plaît.*"

"Certainly," Nigel replied, scanning the scroll. "I say, I can envision some of these words set to exquisite music:

At this point I had another vision and saw an open door in heaven.

And the voice that sounded like a trumpet, which I had heard speaking to me before, said, "Come up here, and I will show you what

537

must happen after this." At once the Spirit took control of me. There in heaven was a throne with someone sitting on it. His face gleamed like such precious stones as jasper and carnelian, and all around the throne there was a rainbow the color of an emerald. In a circle around the throne were twenty-four other thrones, on which were seated twenty-four elders dressed in white and wearing crowns of gold. From the throne came flashes of lightning, rumblings, and peals of thunder. In front of the throne seven lighted torches were burning, which are the seven spirits of God. Also in front of the throne there was what looked like a sea of glass, clear as crystal.

Surrounding the throne on each of its sides, were four living creatures covered with eyes in front and behind. The first one looked like a lion; the second looked like a bull; the third had a face like a human face; and the fourth looked like an eagle in flight. Each one of the four living creatures had six wings, and they were covered with eyes, inside and out. Day and night they never stop singing:

"Holy, holy, holy, is the Lord God Almighty, who was, who is, and who is to come."

The four living creatures sing songs of glory and honor and thanks to the one who sits on the throne, who lives forever and ever. When they do so, the twenty-four elders fall down before the one who sits on the throne, and worship him who lives forever and ever. They throw their crowns down in front of the throne and say,

"Our Lord and God! You are worthy to receive glory, honor, and power. For you created all things, and by your will they were given existence and life.

538

Al wore an unsettled look on his face. "That's a lot o' crazy stuff! Who be those twenty-four lads?"

Nigel tapped his paw on his chin and then held out his hand for an idea. "Perhaps members of the twelve tribes of Israel plus twelve apostles?"

"Crazy, aye, but it were so beautiful!" Kate exclaimed. "I wish ye could've seen it. The MAKER himself, seated in his glory, surrounded by worshipin' an' singin'. Then when the Maker asked if someone could open the scroll that tells wha's ta come, no one could answer. John started ta cry but an elder told him not ta worry. The Lion of Judah could open it by rippin' off the seals! But then Jesus appeared all of a sudden like a lamb instead of a lion. Then a hundred million angels an' every livin' thing fell down an' worshiped him, singin' . . .

Nigel started reading from that point.

> *You are worthy to take the scroll and to break open its seals. For you were killed, and by your sacrificial death you bought for God people from every tribe, language, nation, and race. You have made them a kingdom of priests to serve our God, and they shall rule on earth.*

Al's eyes were huge. "A hundred million angels be up there? How do they all fit then?"

Kate giggled. "Heaven be a big place, Lad! The Maker has lots of angels an' they'll be busy in the things ta come, jest like they've been busy here on earth all along."

> *Worthy is the Lamb that was slain to receive power, and riches, and wisdom, and strength, and honour, and glory, and blessing.*

539

"Truly extraordinary!" Nigel closed his eyes. "I can almost hear the music that goes with these words now."

"Jesus is shown to be the Lion *and* the Lamb," Liz noted. "The lion represents power. The lamb represents sacrifice. Suffering is the secret to Jesus' power. *C'est incredible.*"

"So wha' happened with the scr-r-r-oll?" Max wanted to know. "There's a lot of stuff in there that sounds scary aboot the future."

"Let's jest say that Jesus opened seven seals, an' with each one, it gave a picture of wha' will happen with the kingdoms of the Earth: war, famine, martyrs, plagues, natural disasters, an' the Maker's judgments on it all. Then the visions turned ta the future of the *Church*. A false church with a world empire will rise, while the true Church faithfully presses on until the end of time. There will be a fake Messiah who tries ta act like Jesus an' fools the world. There will be a battle of Satan an' his army against Jesus an' his."

"I know who wins," Al said confidently, not disturbed in the least. "And it ain't that Anti-Jesus."

"I'm glad you know the winner, Al," came Gillamon's familiar voice, with a gentle chuckle. He was standing there in the doorway, Clarie at his side, both in their natural forms. "I see you've been trying to unravel

John's mysterious book of Revelation. Have you figured it all out?"

"Not fully, old boy," Nigel noted. "I wonder if anyone truly can, even John who penned it."

Gillamon nodded. "Indeed, there are mysteries from John's vision that will only be understood with the passage of time."

"But Al grasped the most important thing to know about this book," Clarie suggested, walking over to sit down by Al. "Jesus and his church are victorious in the end, regardless of what happens throughout the ages here on earth."

"That's somethin' ta shout aboot!" Max exclaimed.

"Gillamon, we've been reading all of John's work, and it seems like this book of Revelation would fit perfectly as the ending for the New Testament," Liz suggested. "We were just talking about how the sevens begin with creation and are used in the end of this book of endings."

"All true, Liz. You have reached the final book in your long-standing mission of helping the New Testament come together," Gillamon explained. "I think you'll enjoy seeing how perfectly the Old and New Testaments combine to tell one story, for it is all one story."

"HIS story," Al called out, trying to spin his coin again.

Gillamon smiled. "HIS story indeed."

"This just takes the biscuit!" Nigel declared. "Shall this one story of two testaments have a title?"

"It will be called the Bible," Gillamon answered.

"Gillamon, share the Genesis and Revelation comparison with them. That way they can see how the new book to come will be all one book," Clarie encouraged him. "You're going to love this, everyone!"

"*Oui!* I cannot wait to hear!" Liz exclaimed.

"Very well. What are the first words of Genesis?" Gillamon asked.

"In the beginning, God created the Heavens and the Earth," Nigel replied.

Gillamon nodded. "And at the end of Revelation, John says, 'I saw a New Heaven and a New Earth.' This begins twelve opening and closing comparisons in Genesis and Revelation:

"The gathering together of waters He called the sea . . . and the sea is no more.

"The darkness He called night . . . there shall be no night there.

540

"God made the two great lights (sun and moon) . . . the city has no need of the sun nor the moon.

"In the day you eat thereof, you shall surely die . . . death shall be no more.

"I will greatly multiply your pain . . . neither shall there be pain anymore.

"Cursed is the ground for your sake . . . there shall be no more curse.

"Satan appears as the deceiver of mankind . . . Satan disappears forever.

"They were driven from the Tree of Life . . . the Tree of Life reappears.

"They were driven from God's presence . . . they shall see His face.

"Man's original home was by a river . . . man's eternal home will be beside a river.

"History is one long book," Liz remarked in awe.

"The Bible," Nigel echoed. "Extraordinary."

"I got it!" Al exclaimed, pointing to his coin.

Everyone pointed to see Al's coin spinning in circles while he looked on proudly.

541

"Wha' be that coin ye been messin' with this whole time?" Max scolded. Al's victory announcement came at a very inappropriate time.

Al slapped the coin on the stone floor and held it up. "It's another star coin. Only this time a baby be playin' with seven stars."

"Seven stars?" Liz asked as she jumped down from the table, followed by Nigel. Max, Kate, Clarie, and Gillamon all came over to see the coin. On one side it had a picture of Domitian. On the other it had a picture of a baby sitting on top of a globe, playing with seven stars.

Nigel squinted as he read the inscription. "THE DIVINE CAESAR, SON OF THE EMPEROR DOMITIAN. Domitian minted this coin for his young son who died, after the Emperor made him into a god. That wicked Emperor was obsessed that his family was descended from the god Jupiter. This baby is supposed to be seen as 'baby Jupiter' with the inferred meaning that father Domitian is an even greater god than Jupiter. Madness!"

"Daft emperor! Domitian were no god!" Max growled. "All those R-r-roman gods be fake!"

"*Oui,* and even though Rome destroyed all memory of Domitian from public places, these coins are still in circulation across the empire," Liz explained, studying the coin.

Al furrowed his brow and then smiled broadly. "So the seven churches readin' John's letter will get it easy!"

"Wha' do ye mean, Lad?" Kate asked him.

"Well, don't ye think the people readin' John's letter will know aboot this coin?" Al asked. "They'll hear aboot Jesus holdin' the seven stars in *his* hand, but they'll know that HE be the REAL King God? Not that dead Domitian that tried ta kill them."

"By Jove, he's right!" Nigel exclaimed. "There is imagery in this mysterious letter that will make sense to the believers for what they are facing right now. Extraordinary, the way Jesus gave such a specific image for them!"

"There is imagery in John's letter to the seven churches that will have meaning to them alone, and be lost to future generations of readers," Gillamon explained. "But there is also imagery in Revelation that is lost now on these seven churches but will have meaning to future generations of readers."

542

"How did he do that?" Al asked, scratching his head.

"Because *Jesus* wrote this book of Revelation!" Liz exclaimed. "Gillamon, you told us long ago that a book would come that would be the most important because of *who* would write it. John simply took dictation, no?"

Gillamon nodded. "Correct, Liz. And because Jesus is already in the future, he knows what each generation of readers needs. We are in the third persecution by the Romans, with seven more waves coming from the emperors of Rome. But the Enemy will keep persecuting Christians long after the Romans stop leading the charge, both outside and inside the church. He will never stop until Jesus comes again."

"So what are we to do now?" Nigel wanted to know.

"We shall all come alongside believers for the next seven persecutions, helping them to stay strong and to spread the good news," Gillamon told them. "When the time is right, Rome will fall to the one who truly holds the stars in his hand."

Nigel leaned over and read the end of Revelation. "'Yes indeed! I am coming soon!'

So be it. Come, Lord Jesus!

By this Sign

W hat does it show?" Maxentius implored of the old man, looking at the bowl of sheep guts that the pagan priest used to foretell the future. He was about to base his entire military strategy on the "readings" from this pagan ritual. "Tell me!"

The pagan priest wiped his bloodied hands on a silken cloth and looked up at the arrogant emperor. He then lifted a finger and looked down at the Sibylline Books, oracles of prophecy that the leaders of Rome had consulted for centuries. "We must consult the oracles for a definitive answer."

Maxentius paced around the room, impatient for spiritual guidance. He had declared himself Emperor and seized control of Rome, most of Italy, and Northern Africa six years ago. The empire had been divided ever since the wicked Diocletian had founded a Tetrarchy of four rulers, all with the title of Caesar while he retained senior emperor status. Diocletian and Galerius ruled in the East, and Maximian and Constantius ruled in the West.

Diocletian had instigated The Great Persecution in 303, seeing the growing population of Christians as a direct threat to Rome. Since they refused to honor Jupiter, Diocletian feared that Rome's most powerful god would withdraw his protective favor. He ordered Christians killed on a greater scale and in far worse ways than any emperor before him. He also ordered any copies of Scriptures to be burned and any church buildings destroyed. His bloody reign of terror reached even into his own ranks of Roman soldiers who were forced to sacrifice to Jupiter or face death. Many legionnaires died rather than renounce Christ. Diocletian set the horrific persecution in place and then stepped down to retire and go raise cabbages in his palatial residence in 305. He ordered that Maximian also retire, leaving two emperors over the Roman Empire: Constantius in the West and Galerius in the East.

In the ranks of Diocletian's army was a fine officer by the name of Constantine, who was the son of Constantius. Diocletian acted as if he would groom the young man to step into the role of future emperor, but decidedly let the young man down. Previously estranged from his father, Constantine fled the East following Diocletian's retirement, and went to his father who was in Gaul. Constantius's domain included Gaul, Spain, and Britain. Shortly after Constantine's arrival, father and son traveled to the north of Britain to put down a rebellion of the barbarian Picts beyond Hadrian's Wall. Constantine fought well and earned the respect and loyalty of his father's army. Old and in poor health, Constantius died while they were in York, and the army immediately named Constantine Emperor of the West. However, Galerius declared Severus as the rightful Caesar to take the throne, not Constantine.

But Constantine proved himself and won over the people as well as the army. This did not sit well with Maxentius who was son of the retired Maximian. Jealous that he did not have a throne, Maxentius marched on Rome, which had no sitting ruler, and declared himself Emperor. He promised the people he would cut their taxes and give them free grain. Galerius sent Severus to Rome to take down Maxentius, but in the end Maxentius defeated, imprisoned, and eventually murdered Severus. When Galerius himself came to suppress Maxentius, he also was defeated and soon died. A new Caesar named Licinius assumed power in the East.

By 311 the people of Rome revolted when Maxentius's empty promises were kept only for the wealthy citizens. The poor citizens had to steal what they could to survive, and they now hated Maxentius, who raised, not lowered their taxes. This gave Constantine the opportunity he needed to come against Maxentius. He traveled to Milan to meet with Licinius about consolidating their power, and offered his sister in marriage to seal the deal. They also signed the Edict of Toleration,

544

ending Diocletian's persecution of Christians. While it offered relief to Christians to resume worship, it stopped short of giving Christians full liberty, and it did not restore property that had been taken from them.

While Licinius protected Italy's northern borders from barbarians, Constantine marched south with forty thousand men to lay siege against Rome and defeat Maxentius. Maxentius had been thinking he would stay in Rome with his one hundred thousand men, but today had come to seek out the reading of sheep guts to see if there was a more promising strategy.

"Well?" Maxentius whined. "What does it say, old man?"

The pagan priest had previously recommended that Maxentius stay in Rome and wait out the siege. But as he read the entry in the Sibylline Books for October 28, he raised his eyebrows. "It says, 'On the same day, the enemy of the Romans shall perish.'"

Maxentius's face lit up with excitement. "This must be a sign of victory for *me!* And that is also the date that I seized the throne, so it must be a good omen! HA!" He clapped his hands and stormed out of the room, shouting orders to mobilize his troops and to send word to Constantine to meet him at the Milvian Bridge. Maxentius would meet Constantine on the field of battle, and the arrogant young emperor would most assuredly win by the sign of the oracle.

545

MILVIAN BRIDGE, OUTSIDE OF ROME
OCTOBER 27, AD 312

Constantine walked thoughtfully through the camp, chatting with his soldiers to gauge their confidence in meeting Maxentius in battle. The men knew they were grossly outnumbered so were, of course, nervous. But they trusted their commander more than their emotions.

The sun was beginning its descent as Constantine walked over to the bank of the Tiber River, thinking about what tomorrow could hold. He had made the appropriate offerings to the sun god, Apollo, and prayed for favor, but he had no peace. He gazed up into the sky to the sun and suddenly was mesmerized by a sign.

There above the sun was a trophy of a cross bearing the sign of the Greek letters *chi* and *rho* and the inscription, "Conquer by this sign." Constantine lifted his hand to his eyes so he could study the sign as his men began crowding around him, pointing their fingers to the sign, for they saw it as well.

"What does it mean?" a soldier asked.

Constantine shook his head slowly as he furrowed his brow. "I'm not certain." After a few moments the image in the sky slowly faded and the men went back to preparing their weapons and armory for war. But the image was imprinted on Constantine's mind as he entered his tent to rest for the night.

MILVIAN BRIDGE, OCTOBER 28, AD 312

"Men! Listen up!" Constantine called with a loud voice. It was before dawn, and he had sent messengers to wake the entire army. He carried a shield, and his assistant stood next to him holding a pot of white paint. "The image we saw yesterday was confirmed by the God of the Christians in a dream to me last night. He repeated the message that we saw in the sky above the sun: Conquer by this sign." Constantine reached over and dipped his finger in the paint. He drew the symbol of the *chi*, X, on the shield, topped by the symbol of the *rho*, P. "These are the letters that symbolize the Christ. He has assured me that victory will be ours if we do what he says. You are to make this mark on your shields, for today, we will CONQUER! Are you with me?"

The men rallied and began shouting with enthusiasm, as their hearts soared to see their leader so confident. Immediately they did as instructed until soon, forty thousand soldiers had shields bearing the mysterious *chi rho* sign, the first two Greek letters of Christ's name.

☧

Maxentius knew it was vital to keep Constantine from crossing the Tiber River to reach Rome, so had ordered all the bridges to be partially destroyed for the siege, including the stone Milvian Bridge. The Senate would favor whoever controlled Rome, and Maxentius planned to fight the battle outside the city limits. Because he had disabled the bridge, he ordered a temporary wooden bridge hastily built to carry his troops across the river to wage war.

Maxentius was unprepared for the ferocity of Constantine's men as the battle was immediately upon them. Constantine's army covered the entire length of Maxentius's line, and Constantine ordered his cavalry to charge. Maxentius's cavalry quickly broke, and Constantine immediately sent his shield-bearing infantry against Maxentius's infantry. Maxentius's men were pushed with their backs against the river, and a slaughter began. Many drowned and others then broke ranks to try and escape by swimming across the river or across the wooden bridge. Maxentius himself tried to flee but was pushed into the river. The weight of his armor pulled him under and he drowned.

Constantine won the decisive battle and marched into Rome, victorious. From that moment on, the sign of Christ became not just an emblem for the shields of his armies; it became the emblem for his very life.

☧

In 313, Constantine and Licinius signed the Edict of Milan, granting "to Christians and to all others full liberty of following that religion which each may choose." Christians were finally free to worship in public without fear. For the first time in the history of Christianity, not only did they have Jesus as King, but they had the favor of the Emperor of Rome. Constantine filled his chief offices with Christians, exempted Christian pastors from taxes and military service, built churches, and made Christianity the chosen faith of his court.

547

Following a civil war with Licinius, Constantine was once again victorious using a banner adorned with the *chi rho* sign, and he became the sole emperor of the Roman Empire. Constantine decided he wanted his capital to be in a city untouched by the pagan gods of Rome and one that had not been saturated with the blood of Christians. The aristocracy of Rome still held onto their pagan religion, and Constantine knew he could not administer his rule in such an environment. So, in 324 he moved his capital to Byzantium and founded a new Rome: Constantinople, capital of the new Christian empire. He immediately began building churches and realized that he needed a chief religious advisor. He chose a man from Caesarea named Eusebius who had been imprisoned by Diocletian, and who came highly recommended by a distinguished visitor to Constantine's court—a man with the unusual name of Gillamonus.

Eusebius-

I have thought it expedient to instruct your Prudence to order fifty copies of the Sacred Scriptures, the provision and use of which you know to be the most needful for the instruction of the church, to be written on prepared parchment, in a legible manner, and in a commodious and portable form, by transcribers thoroughly practiced in their art. You have authority also, by virtue of this letter, to use two of the public carriages for their conveyance; by which arrangement, the copies, when fairly written, will most easily be forwarded for my personal inspection. One of the deacons of your church may be entrusted with this service, who, on his arrival here, shall experience my liberality.

God preserve you, beloved brother.

-Flavius Valerius Aurelius Constantinus Augustus

Liz and Nigel looked at one another with jaws gaping after reading this letter from Emperor Constantine.

"Beloved brother? Extraordinary!" Nigel exclaimed. "I dare say, even I wondered if this day would ever come."

"It took three hundred years, but the miracle has finally happened, no?" Liz marveled. "Christian martyrs kept the faith despite the cost, and the gospel survived *ten* persecutions of Rome!"

548

"Jesus himself turned the tide by appearing to Constantine, but the message he gave was one that Christians have known from the start," Nigel answered.

"*Oui!* Victory comes through Jesus alone!" Liz exclaimed.

"And now, my dear, here before us is the moment we've waited for," Nigel added. The little mouse rubbed his paws together and then adjusted his spectacles to glance over Constantine's letter. "He wants fifty copies of the complete Bible!"

"Eusebius has the authority and the privilege to name the books for the New Testament! *C'est magnifique!*" Liz cried happily. "*Mon ami,* it has been a privilege to help these books get written apart from one another. Now to see them finally come together is magical!"

Nigel's whiskers quivered with excitement. "I smile to think of the apostles learning of what has happened with their letters, especially Paul, for he indeed penned the most."

"*Ooh-la-la,* but he has fourteen books!" Liz declared. "That is over half of the New Testament, no?"

"Who would ever have imagined that a Christian killer would end up writing over half of the guidebook for Christians to·use?" Nigel said with a jolly chuckle. "My dear, we serve a most splendid God."

Liz giggled. "I'm glad Clarie told us about her assistance with Jude.

That is the only letter that you and I were not personally there to see."

"Right, but as long as it was one of the Order of the Seven who took part in its writing, I know it will be perfectly suited," Nigel replied.

"There are so many letters written by the apostles and other believers," Liz noted. "How will our dear Eusebius ever cope with the challenge to choose the right ones to include in the New Testament?" She winked at the little mouse.

Nigel smiled and patted her paw. "Since our dear Eusebius must be overwhelmed with the task of determining which books to include, I believe our list will set his mind at ease," he said, pointing to a blank sheet of parchment. "Would you like to do the honors, my dear?"

"Why thank you, Nigel," Liz replied, picking up the pen sitting on Eusebius's desk.

Nigel preened his whiskers excitedly. "Very well, shall we begin?"

Eusebius returned from a time of prayer and sat down at his desk. He tilted his head to see a neatly written list sitting there. He looked but saw no one around other than his petite black cat that was curled up on the desk as usual. "What do we have here?"

Liz just beamed and winked at Nigel who hid in the windowsill. Eusebius picked up the parchment, and stroked Liz softly as he began to read the list:

Matthew
Mark
Luke
John
Acts
Romans
I Corinthians
II Corinthians
Galatians
Ephesians
Philippians
Colossians
I Thessalonians
II Thessalonians

549

I Timothy
II Timothy
Titus
Philemon
Hebrews
James
I Peter
II Peter
I John
II John
III John
Jude
Revelation

"Hmmm. Twenty-seven books," Eusebius said to himself. "Thirty-nine books for the Old Testament and twenty-seven for the new." He smiled and leaned in close to Liz. "What do you think of that, my little black beauty? Does sixty-six sound like a good number?"

"I couldn't have chosen a better list myself, Monsieur," Liz meowed with a coy grin.

"Of course, I'll have to see if this anonymous list is missing any other book choices from my stack of options. And I must do extensive research for the books already universally accepted by the church," Eusebius said, placing his hand on a stack of letters gathered from all over the Christian world. He breathed out with a sigh at the sheer volume of work ahead of him. "This will involve training many scribes to copy so many books into one Bible." He picked up the list and rubbed his chin. "In fact, after the first fifty copies I think we'll need to set up an entire new operation of scribes in Constantinople to copy Bibles to send across the Roman Empire. What a wonderful problem!"

Eusebius took out a fresh sheet of parchment to reply to Constantine with his suggestion of a new center for Bible scribes located in Constantinople.

Nigel saluted Liz from the windowsill and took off on a pigeon. She nodded and stood to stretch. *New Testament written,* she thought to herself. *Mission accomplished.* With that she jumped off the table and sauntered out of the room.

Epilogue:
One Voice

Telemachus wiped the sweat from his brow with the back of his brown robe. "Not much farther, my little ones. We're almost at the end of the Appian Way. Rome is straight up ahead."

Liz and Al trotted along behind the little monk, casting knowing glances at each other. They knew this road well. "I'll never forget the day you ran out on this road to meet me when we arrived with Paul," Liz said, nudging Al affectionately.

"Aye, I had to run and see me love after bein' apart for so long," Al replied. "Do ye think Max and Kate will run out here to greet us then? Maybe they'll bring fish as a welcome gift! Telemachus be clean out o' fish. 'Tis a mystery."

Liz smiled and rolled her eyes at the source of the missing fish. "I do not know, Albert, but I am certain that we will see them soon. Nigel will guide Max and Kate to us when we reach Rome."

A shadow crossed overhead, and Liz looked up to see Nigel waving at them from a pigeon. He had flown ahead to Rome to find Max and Kate while Liz and Al traveled on foot with Telemachus all the way from Constantinople. It had taken them quite a while, for the little monk was slow on his feet, but he was determined to do as the Voice had told him. *"GO TO ROME."*

Telemachus hummed as they walked along, always with a happy tune in his heart. He would stop humming and talk to the animals now and then, as they were the only ones he could talk to as he traveled alone. "I came to Rome once in my youth so I could see the great city. That was after I found Jesus, turning my life around from having been a thief." The little monk frowned at the thought of how he lived before he found Christ. "I wanted to learn as much as I could about the first church, and to see where those early believers sacrificed so much so I could eventually know the Good News. Constantine had recently built St. Peter's Basilica, and that was a sight to see! Supposedly he built it on the very spot where Peter was crucified upside down in Nero's Circus."

"Aye, I were there, Lad," Al meowed. *"Up on Vatican Hill. That were a sad day."*

"Thank the Lord, Constantine outlawed crucifixion," the monk said. He pointed to his left as they neared the entrance to the city. "Now in that direction is the Ostian Way where Paul was taken to be beheaded. Constantine also built a church over that spot as well."

"And, I was there," Liz meowed. *"On the same sad day."*

They heard the throngs of the crowds as they entered Rome. People filled the streets, and soon Telemachus was caught up with them, being pushed along. Liz and Al darted in and around the legs of all the humans.

"What's goin' on?" Al wanted to know.

552

"I hope it is not what I think it is," Liz answered with a frown. "The Games."

"Don't tell me they still be killin' Christians in Flavian's Amphitheater!" Al cried in horror.

"No, Albert, but the gladiatorial games continue, as do the animal hunts," Liz replied sadly. "Although Constantine abolished *damnatio ad ludum* which means human prisoners must fight to the death, the entertainment of gladiators has continued. And the arena is no longer called the Flavian Amphitheater."

"What's it called then?" Al asked.

"Nero's colossal statue still stands outside, so the humans simply started calling the amphitheater the Colosseum," Liz explained.

"Well that's a lot easier to say at least," Al replied. "One good thing, anyway, aboot a bad place."

Telemachus, Liz, and Al came to the magnificent triple Arch of Constantine that the senate erected to celebrate Constantine's victory over Maxentius at the Milvian Bridge. It was covered in sculptures and friezes of the emperor's triumph, expressing how he came to liberate the city.

Liz read the inscription: "*To the Emperor Caesar Flavius Constantinus, the greatest, pious, and blessed Augustus: because he, inspired by the divine, and by the greatness of his mind, has delivered the state from the tyrant and all of his followers at the same time, with his army and just force of arms, the Senate and People of Rome have dedicated this arch, decorated with triumphs.* What a beautiful *arc de triomphe*, no?"

"Aye," Al said as they walked under the arch. When they reached the other side he saw the Colosseum and Nero's statue, now remade into the sun god, *Sol Invictus.* "There be golden boy with his pointy hat then."

Telemachus grunted his displeasure at what was happening. People were filing into the Colosseum. He stopped in front of the giant statue and put his hands on his hips. "I don't believe this, little ones, but I think I have to go in there. I feel a tug in my heart that I'm *meant* to go in there." He sighed. "I don't want to, of course. You best stay out here, and I'll find you later."

With that Telemachus blended in with the crowds filing into the Colosseum.

"Over here, Liz!" Kate shouted from the curb as they passed by.

Liz turned to see Kate and Max sitting together by a statue. It was another statue of Libertas, similar to the one that had belonged to the Roman family of Antonius. "Kate!" She ran over and embraced her dear friend.

Al sauntered over and Max nudged him. "Gr-r-rand ta see ye, lad. How were yer tr-r-rip?"

"Looooooonnnng," Al replied. "Got any fish with ye?"

"Not with me, but ye know they've got some inside," Max replied, nodding in the direction of the Colosseum.

"Oh no, I don't want to go in there!" Al protested, shaking his head. "Bad things happen in there."

"But you must, Al. All of you must," came the statue. The animals looked up. It was Gillamon in the form of Libertas. "You must enter the Colosseum one last time."

Max frowned. "I don't like the sound of this, Gillamon. Wha's goin' ta happen in there?"

"Something very hard, but something very necessary," Gillamon replied. "For the sake of Rome. It cannot fall into the arms of Jesus without this."

The animals looked at one another with puzzled expressions.

"How so, Gillamon?" Kate asked.

"When Constantine became a Christian, he granted freedom of

religion to the people. While he encouraged his subjects to become Christians, it was voluntary. That is how Jesus meant for it to be. He meant for his followers to *choose* him with a change in their hearts and lives. But just a few years ago Emperor Theodosius made Christianity the mandatory state religion of the Roman Empire, and that was a sad day."

"Why?" Al asked, wrinkling his brow. "I thought it were a good thing that everybody would be made Christians."

"*Made* is the key word, I'm afraid," Nigel added as he joined them. "People no longer have the freedom to choose, so the church is filling with pagans, and they are bringing their pagan ideas with them."

"So while the church conquered the Roman Empire, the Roman Empire is in turn conquering the church!" Liz realized much to her dismay. "The military spirit of Rome is turning the church into a *political* organization that looks nothing like the early church."

"Think of the disciples gathered in homes and in upper rooms," Clarie added, joining them in the form of a young man. "Jesus was the main thing, not the structure of who runs the church. Jesus is quickly now taking second place with church priorities."

"Sounds dreadfully like the Pharisees focusing on the law instead of God, all over again," Nigel posed.

"If you thought the persecution of the Romans was horrific, prepare yourselves for what the Maker's own people will do to one another, supposedly in the 'name of Christ,'" Gillamon warned them. "Very dark ages are coming."

"The spir-r-rit of the church be changin' then," Max grumbled. "That evil lion still be tr-r-ryin' ta devour, but now he's hidin' r-r-right *inside* the church ta do it!"

"But this can't be true for all believers!" Kate cried. "There be real Christians still livin' like Jesus asked."

"Of course, Kate, that is true, just like our Telemachus who has obediently followed the Maker's call to Rome," Gillamon replied. A roar came up from the crowd inside the Colosseum. "But you see, Roman society is Christian in *name*, but still such evil continues, like these games of death. If Roman society were Christian in *heart*, these games would have ended long ago. Hearts will change not by force, but by true Christians continuing to do what they've done all along."

"*Oui*, conquer through love by the name of Jesus alone," Liz said softly.

"Come, let's go in together," Clarie told them. "You can sneak in under my cloak."

"I'll be here when you return," Gillamon told them as they walked toward the entrance of the Colosseum.

"I got a bad feelin' aboot this," Max mumbled as they walked under the arch and inside the roaring arena.

☧

Telemachus leaned his hands on the stone railing of the front row of seats, shaking his head in anger and sadness over what he was witnessing. Blood covered the sandy floor of the arena. Two gladiators had already been killed and carried out of the arena to the sounds of cheering masses. The gentle monk was mortified to see the delight on the faces of the people as death was treated so casually. "Father, forgive them. They know not what they do," he murmured, as he shook his head in a soft prayer. He looked up, his cherub-like cheeks flush with emotion. "To destroy precious life is wrong!" he said loudly, slapping his fists on the railing. "It's pure evil! It must stop!"

555

Two gladiators started a fresh match, and the clanking of their swords sent the crowds to their feet. Suddenly the little monk leaned over the barrier and slid over the side, unnoticed by the crowds. But the animals were watching him.

"Wha's he doin'?" Max asked.

"Oh dear, it appears he is entering the arena floor!" Nigel exclaimed.

Al put his paws up to his mouth. "He don't even have a sword!"

Suddenly the crowd also caught sight of Telemachus and a collective, "Ohhhhh!" echoed around the Colosseum. The little monk ran straight up to the gladiators and stepped in between them like one of the referees.

"In the name of Christ, forbear!" the monk shouted. "Please!"

The two gladiators held back their swords and looked at one another in puzzlement at this surprising development. As they stopped fighting, the crowd started booing.

Telemachus got closer, placing his hands on the bloody shoulders of the gladiators. "In the name of Christ, forbear!" he cried again.

The gladiators looked toward the crowds who now started roaring their displeasure at the match stopping because of the little monk. They started pointing their thumbs to their throats.

"No! The people want Telemachus to die!" Liz shouted in horror.

"We've got ta stop them!" Kate cried.

Suddenly one of the gladiators thrust his sword into the little monk's side, followed by the other gladiator.

"NO!" the animals cried in unison while the crowds cheered in approval.

Telemachus's eyes widened and blood trickled from the corner of his mouth, yet he grabbed the shoulder of the second gladiator. He gasped for breath but uttered one more time before he fell, "In . . . the . . . name of Christ . . .forbear."

The little monk fell dead onto the sand and the gladiators held their swords by their sides, not rejoicing but looking lost in the moment. Suddenly a wave of silence fell over the crowd when they realized what had truly happened. The selfless Christian man was pleading with them to stop the bloodshed in the name of Jesus.

556

"The last Christian to shed blood in this arena did so because he didn't have a choice," Clarie told them, a tear rolling down her cheek. "But neither did Telemachus. He had to do what the Maker asked him to do."

Al sniffed and wiped his eyes. "He *had* a choice but chose not to have a choice."

"Look," Nigel told them, pointing to the crowds.

The gladiators dropped their swords onto the bloody sand with a clank. Together the two men gently picked up the body of the little monk and respectfully carried him out of the arena. One by one, the Colosseum began to empty as people silently left their seats and filed out. Soon the Colosseum stood empty and silent as the blood of Telemachus dried in the sun.

☧

The animals gathered back around the Libertas statue after the crowds had left the area. Their hearts were heavy with grief over what they had just witnessed.

"What you don't know is that at this very moment, reports are heading to Emperor Honorius about what Telemachus did here today," Gillamon told them. "In three days he will decree that gladiatorial games will officially end. The last blood spilled in the Colosseum was from one voice shouting loud and clear to stop in the name of Jesus."

Max frowned but nodded with the power of sacrifice to change hearts. "With every dr-r-rop of martyr blood, the soil becomes r-r-rich an' causes a new cr-r-rop of believers ta rise up."

"Telemachus means 'decisive battle,'" Liz added through tear-filled eyes. "The fall of Rome to God has finally happened, but it did not happen with Rome forcing Christianity on the people as its official religion."

Nigel nodded. "It happened with the cry of one voice."

"So it will be throughout time," Clarie offered. "The fall of earthly kingdoms will happen with the cry of one voice."

Gillamon smiled, lighting up the Libertas statue's face. "Do you remember long ago in Jerusalem when I told you that the Maker could sculpt anyone into something new?"

Kate nodded. "Aye. He did it with the disciples. He did it with Saul. He did it with Constantine. An' he even did it with our dear martyred monk, Telemachus."

"Aye, an' now he's done it with the city of R-r-rome," Max added hopefully.

557

A goofy grin appeared on Al's face. "Told ye the Maker would take over the place."

Gillamon laughed softly. "Indeed, Al. Wherever the Maker is welcomed into a given heart or a given land, he'll take over the place."

Al looked up at Gillamon as the Libertas statue with her outstretched hand. He lifted his paw to mimic her. "From the north, the south, the east, and the west even."

Gillamon looked over the flowing robes of the Libertas statue. He thought about the Libertas statue that the Antonius family had taken to France hundreds of years before. The Maker had plans for using that statue in a future mission for the Order of the Seven. Gillamon smiled at Liz, knowing how delighted she would especially be to see the full picture of Libertas unfold. But for now, he would keep that future mission to himself. There were many other assignments for the Order of the Seven to complete before that distant time.

"Even a statue can be made into something new by the right chisel in the Master Sculptor's hand." Gillamon smiled, thinking to the future. "Always remember. One voice can lead a person—or a nation—to embrace the liberty that comes with such a takeover."

A Word from the Author

A biographer has to decide between slowing to a halt here in a bog of conflicting possibilities which can never be resolved, or striding boldly across by a causeway of conjecture. I choose the second course and, without stepping aside to discuss all the alternatives, tell the story as I see it." - John Pollock, *The Apostle: A Life of Paul*

Thank you, Mr. Pollock, for your masterpiece on Paul, and thank you, readers, for allowing me to follow suit in doing the same in my books. Thank you for trusting me to make these stories come alive through the unknown parts of history, telling them as I see them after I've exhausted my research.

At the end of each book I like to give you, my reader, a behind-the-scenes tour of exactly where I strode across causeways of conjecture. It is important for me to lay out the unknowns and the liberties I take as I weave the fiction into the facts. As always, I encourage you to go to the source of truth in God's word to read the actual account of these events. But for now, here are the unknowns and liberties I've taken with *The Fire, the Revelation, and the Fall*:

Paul's letters: I went with Pollock's story that he "pieced together from clues scattered around the New Testament and in secular history." Theories abound as to where Paul wrote certain books, including Philippians. Some say Rome, others say Ephesus. No one knows for certain, so I took the exact scenario painted by Pollock, that Paul was imprisoned in Ephesus and wrote Philippians there.

Roman Road: I found the brilliant Adam and Jesus parallel in Chapter 14, Mapping Out the Roman Road, in the MacArthur Bible Commentary, and their original source was Nelson's Complete Book of Bible Maps & Charts (Nashville: Thomas Nelson Publishers, 1996) 415. © 1993 by Thomas Nelson, Inc.

Roman family of Antonius: This is a fictional family based on real characters, beginning with my centurion Marcus Antonius in *The Prophet, the Shepherd, and the Star*. I made him responsible for carrying out Herod's charge for the slaughter of the innocents in Bethlehem. A powerful plotline presented itself for carrying his family through the next three books, showing the impact of the life of Christ on these Romans. So, his son Armandus became the real centurion at the foot of Jesus' cross in *The Roman, the Twelve, and the King,* as well as the same real centurion that asked Jesus to heal his servant. The centurion Julius and "most excellent Theophilus" are, in fact, mentioned in scripture, but their relationship as brothers is fiction on my part as I made them the sons of Armandus. Julius was the real centurion who escorted Paul to Rome, but I took liberties to make him the soldier that was assigned to Paul in Rome. Luke wrote his Gospel and The Acts of the Apostles to an individual named Theophilus. No one knows exactly who Theophilus was, but given the way Luke addressed him, he was likely a high-ranking Roman official. One commentary presented the possibility that he was Paul's legal counsel in Rome, and that Luke wrote his Gospel and Acts to present Paul and the Christian movement in a positive light for the Romans. As you read Luke's two letters, take notice of the fact that every encounter that Jesus, Paul, or Christians had with the Romans was positive, and it was only the Jews that posed opposition. It is also supposed that Theophilus published Luke's letters and therefore spread his Gospel and the account of Acts throughout the Roman world. Many thanks to my *real* friend, military historian and advisor, Mark Schneider, and his son, Armand, who served as character models for my Romans, Marcus and Armandus.

Paul's nephew who warned Lysias of the plot against Paul's life: We know nothing of him, including whether Paul had ever met him. So it worked well for me to slip Clarie into his sandals.

Peter's years in Rome (and/or "Babylon" from where he writes)**:** Jerome has Peter as pastoring the church in Rome for 25 years. It worked well for me to put him in Rome with Al, and to connect the dots from Cornelius's house, where he met Armandus, all the way to Rome.

John's years before Ephesus and his arrival with Mary there: I put them in Jerusalem where Luke did his research with Mary in the two years of Paul's imprisonment in Caesarea. We know Luke had to have gotten the Christmas story information from Mary, and it was likely during this time, near Caesarea. We know that Mary ended up with John in Ephesus, so I had them depart Jerusalem following Luke's visit.

How Philemon bought Onesimus as his slave: I made up the setting in Ephesus, as I found it incredible that Onesimus is thought to have become the Bishop of Ephesus. I also made up the scene of Paul saving Philemon's life by healing him. In Paul's letter to Philemon, he does remind Philemon that he owes Paul his life. While that may be a metaphoric sentiment, I chose to weave it into the story of getting Philemon and Paul to meet.

Man healed after the Sons of Sceva: Nothing is recorded about the man after the Sons of Sceva tried to release him by using Jesus' name. I just have to believe that Jesus couldn't bear to leave him the way he was.

When Luke rejoined Paul: No one knows exactly. We take clues from Luke's verbiage in Acts when he begins to use "we" in giving the account of Paul's journeys in Acts 20:5. But, since some believe that Luke and Titus were the ones who delivered Paul's second letter to the Corinthians ahead of Paul's arrival, it makes sense to me that Luke stayed there until Paul joined him. I keep Luke with Paul from that point on in the story.

561

Mary's journal: This is a fictional plot line that I developed for *The Prophet, the Shepherd, and the Star*, which I carried through *The Roman, the Twelve, and the King*. There is also no record of Jesus having ever written anything, other than writing in the dirt. And even that was a Jesus secret.

Paul's offense to the Nabatean King in Petra: This is a plausible yet fictional story line that I developed in *The Wind, the Road, and the Way*. Paul, indeed, did something to offend the King of the Nabatean people, and it is plausible that he did so in Petra with his preaching.

Members of the Sanhedrin: Zeeb, Saar, Jarib, and Nahshon are fictional but represent the real players in the story. I wrote them into *The Roman, the Twelve, and the King, The Wind, the Road, and the Way,* and now this book.

Nero's emerald: According to historical accounts, he is said to have used a translucent emerald stone to better see the gladiator games. Assigning Julius to go find it was fiction; however, there is actual graffiti of "JULIUS THE SOLDIER" on a wall in Berenike. I just couldn't resist weaving a thread from my Julius to that Julius.

Fire in Rome: Nero has been blamed for two thousand years for "fiddling while Rome burned." Yes, he was, indeed, insane. Yes, he did want to build his new Golden Palace and needed room to place it somewhere in Rome. Yes, he was away when the fire began and rushed back to Rome and organized relief efforts. Yes, he blamed the Christians as scapegoats so he could deflect the blame. But did Nero actually order the fire? We don't really know, but I decided to keep the traditional blame with Nero to set the stage for the first Christian persecution. And, yes, the fire did break out in the stalls at the Circus Maximus, but fireworks were not involved, so Noah and Bang are off the hook.

Trials before Nero/Paul's death: This is complete fiction on my part, although it is plausible that Paul did stand before Nero himself. What actually happened to Paul after his first imprisonment is uncertain. Piecing together clues from his many letters, several theories have long been debated over what happened during the subsequent four to five years. Some believe Paul traveled to Spain, others to the locations I posed (Crete, Ephesus, Macedonia, re-arrested in Troas), or that he remained in Rome. Since Luke concludes Acts before his trial, we just don't know for certain. We also must rely on church tradition and scant archeological clues about Paul's beheading out on the Ostian Way on June 29, 67.

562

Mamertine Prison: When I visited the Mamertine Prison in Rome, I was awed to stand in the pit where Peter and Paul were kept before their executions. We don't know for sure if they were kept here together, or the timing and details of the events leading to their deaths. We do think that Paul wrote 2 Timothy and that Peter wrote 2 Peter shortly before they died, and likely from prison. I couldn't resist the imagery of seeing them together at the end of their lives and ministries, supporting one another and penning their last words.

Peter's death: Again, this is conjecture based on church tradition, that Peter was crucified upside down on June 29, 67, in Rome in Nero's Circus, which was located where the Vatican stands today.

Paul writing Hebrews: We don't know who wrote Hebrews, but I believe that Paul was the author. *Halley's Bible Commentary* posed the idea of why he did not assign his name to the letter due to his lack of popularity in Jerusalem, and that made sense to me.

Alexander the Great: I relayed historical events about Alexander from the historians Plutarch, Josephus, and Arrian, but the line "Do you want to live forever?" is not historically attributable to him (it comes from the movie, *Alexander*). Daniel's prophecy of Alexander, his visit to Jerusalem, and the scene of him scaling the wall are all true, according to historians.

John's gospel and Revelation: I adore William Barclay's commentaries, and I used almost every bit of his analysis on the writing of John. Many times I find things in Barclay that I do not see anywhere else, such as the Plato connection. I also adore *Halley's Bible Handbook,* which was my lifesaver for explaining Revelation. I took practically every nugget directly from this amazing resource, and I highly recommend that book for in-depth study on any aspect of the Bible. Also, my father, Dr. Paul Mims, preached through Revelation, and I read every one of his awesome sermons to prepare for that chapter. Please visit his website listed in my bibliography for the best sermons out there. I'm so grateful for these brilliant minds that help me to understand biblical truth!

Forming of the New Testament: Constantine ordered fifty copies of the Bible, and Eusebius did, in fact, come up with the same list of twenty-seven books that eventually were confirmed by the church and ratified in AD 397 by the Council of Carthage. Eusebius did extensive research to determine which books to use in his list that had already been generally accepted by the church.

Telemachus: This is a true story, but the details about the little monk's character, personality, and appearance are all mine. We don't know if he was a scribe, but he was called from modern day Turkey to go to Rome, and he did jump down onto the Colosseum floor to cry those words. Two accounts vary the details of his death, one stating that the crowds stoned him to death (but why would the crowds all have stones with them as spectators of the Games?) and the other stating that the gladiators struck him. I went with the last. But the impact he had is the same either way. That was the final gladiatorial match in the Colosseum.

Conflicting historical facts: One of the most frustrating parts of doing research involving events of antiquity is conflicting facts. Whether it may be the biased embellishment of a resentful Tacitus or a vanquished Josephus, or simply the best guess of modern day scholars leading to different figures and hypotheses, the list of conflicting history I've seen in writing this book is endless. For instance, I've seen anywhere from twelve thousand to one hundred thousand Jews were

563

taken as slaves back to Rome after the fall of Jerusalem. Were Christians martyred in the Colosseum or primarily in the circuses of Nero and Domitian? Did Nero set the fire? Were Peter and Paul kept together in the Mamertine Prison? Did John write Revelation on Patmos or back in Ephesus? So be aware that I've submitted the best facts that I've been able to confirm from more than one source, or when only one source was available, to run with what I found. Bottom line is that we know that all of the historical events in this book occurred; we may just not know the specific details of *how* they occurred.

Not enough time: Another challenge with writing this book was the sheer volume of monumental events that occurred at the same time in both biblical and secular history. If I had devoted the time to adequately cover the rise and fall of each Roman emperor, the martyrdom of each disciple, The Jewish War, the building of the Colosseum, the eruption of Mount Vesuvius that destroyed Pompeii, the second major fire of Rome, the persecution of the early church up to Constantine, and the development of the Bible, this book would have been twice as long. I wanted to cover everything in glorious detail, as is "my way," but sadly I could not. So I hope I've at least piqued your interest to go study these many events on your own. In the end, I had to keep the main thing the main thing, and that is the rise of Christianity against a backdrop of impossible opposition.

564

Thank you, dear Reader, for going with me on this incredible journey. You won't want to miss what's coming next with Patrick Henry in *The Voice, the Revolution, and the Jewel.* You've seen how the early Christians lived in biblical times, but the great commission didn't end with the stroke of John's pen in Revelation. The Maker continues to have his special servants throughout HIStory. So get ready, Patriots. It's time to go from Revelation to Revolution. Huzzah!

With Epic Love,

Jenny

BIBLIOGRAPHY

Ancient Megastructures: The Colosseum. National Geographic Channel. 2007. Television.

Arrian, Martin Hammond, John Atkinson, Arrian, and Arrian. *Alexander the Great: The Anabasis and the Indica.* Oxford: Oxford UP, 2013. Print.

Barclay, William. *The Acts of the Apostles.* Louisville: Westminster John Knox, 2003. Print.

Barclay, William. *Barclay's Guide to the New Testament.* Louisville: Westminster John Knox, 2008. Print.

Barclay, William. *The Gospel of John.* Philadelphia: Westminster, 1975. Print.

Bargmann, Dale. *Paul's Missionary Journeys.* Web. 07 Aug. 2014. <http://www.welcometohosanna.com/PAULS_MISSIONARY_JOURNEYS/0.1WhoIsPaul.html>.

"BBC Ancient Rome The Rise and Fall of an Empire." *Constantine.* BBC and Discovery Channel. 2006. Television.

Bible: Good News Translation. New York: American Bible Society, 1992. Print.

"Book Six: Nero." *Suetonius: The Twelve Caesars: Book VI Nero.* Web. 02 July 2014.

Bruce, F. F. *Paul, Apostle of the Heart Set Free.* Carlisle, Cumbria, UK: Paternoster, 2000. Print.

Bruce, F. F. *The New International Commentary on the New Testament.* Grand Rapids: Eerdmans, 1951. Print.

Cairns, Earle Edwin. *Christianity through the Centuries: A History of the Christian Church.* Grand Rapids, MI: Zondervan Publishing House, 1996. Print.

Cavendish, Richard. "Death of the Emperor Claudius." *History Today.* 2004. Web. 15 Feb. 2014.

"Colosseum: A Gladiator's Story." *Documentary.* BBC and Discovery Channel. 14 Mar. 2004. Television.

Dodge, Theodore Ayrault, and Ian M. Cuthbertson. *Alexander.* New York: Barnes and Noble, 2005. Print.

Foxe, John, and William Byron Forbush. *Foxe's Book of Martyrs: A History of the Lives, Sufferings and Triumphant Deaths of the Early Christian and the Protestant Martyrs.* Philadelphia: John C. Winston, 1926. Print.

Gangi, Giuseppe. *Rome, Then and Now: In Overlay.* Roma: G&G Editrice. Print.

Geil, William Edgar. *The Isle That Is Called Patmos.* Philadelphia: A.J. Rowland, 1897. Print.

Grieve, Andrew. *BBC Ancient Rome: The Rise and Fall of an Empire, Episode 3, Rebellion.* BBC and Discovery Channel. 2006. Television.

Halley, Henry Hampton. *Halley's Bible Handbook*. Zondervan Publishing House. Print.

"Heilbrunn Timeline of Art History." *Roman Games: Playing with Animals*. Web. 09 July 2014.

The Holy Bible: New International Version. Grand Rapids, MI: Zondervan Publishing House, 2005. Print.

Holy Bible: New Living Translation. Wheaton, IL: Tyndale House, 1996. Print.

Homer, Robert Fagles, Bernard Knox, and Homer. *The Odyssey*. Print.

"In The Footsteps of St. Paul—Presented by David Suchet." *In the Footsteps of St. Paul*. BBC. 2012. *In The Footsteps of St Paul*. Web. 07 Aug. 2014. <http://www.inthefootstepsofstpaul.co.uk/>.

Jones, Dean. *St. John in Exile*. DJ Productions. Tarzana, CA, 1996. DVD. Live stage one-man play production.

Josephus, Flavius, Paul L. Maier, and Flavius Josephus. *Josephus, the Essential Works: A Condensation of Jewish Antiquities and the Jewish War*. Grand Rapids, MI: Kregel Publications, 1994. Print.

Kent, Homer Austin. *Jerusalem to Rome: Studies in the Book of Acts*. Grand Rapids: Baker Book House, 1972. Print.

Kidd, Elliott. "The Eagle Feather." *"Beast-Hunts" in Roman Amphitheaters: The Impact of the Venationes on Animal Populations in the Ancient Roman World*. University of North Texas. Web. 10 July 2014. <http://eaglefeather.honors.unt.edu/2012/article/32#the-late-republic-pompey-cicero-and-caesar>.

Lewis, E. G. "Sowing the Seeds: ROMAN MERCHANT SHIPS — WAR-HORSES of the ANCIENT WORLD." Web. 15 May 2014.

MacArthur, John. *The MacArthur Bible Commentary: Unleashing God's Truth, One Verse at a Time*. Nashville, TN: Thomas Nelson, 2005. Print.

MacArthur, John. *The MacArthur Study Bible: English Standard Version*. Wheaton, IL: Crossway Bibles, 2010. Print.

Mackinnon, Michael. "Supplying Exotic Animals for the Roman Amphitheatre Games: New Reconstructions Combining Archaeological, Ancient Textual, Historical and Ethnographic Data." *Mouseion* III 6 (2006): 1-25. Mouseion. Web. <http://www.mouseion.com/en/home>.

McGee, J. Vernon. *Thru the Bible: Matthew through Romans*. Vol. IV. Nashville: Thomas Nelson, 1983. Print.

Meyer, F. B., and Lance Wubbels. *The Life of Paul: A Servant of Jesus Christ*. Lynnwood, WA: Emerald, 1995. Print.

Meyer, F.B. *Peter*. S.l.: Harpercollins, 1968. Print.

Mims, Paul. "Sermons." *Sermons on Revelation*. Cornerstone Baptist Church, Cherry Log, GA, 2014. Web. 02 Sept. 2014. <http://www.csbccl.org/csbccl/Sermons.aspx>.

New American Standard Bible. La Habra, CA: Foundation Publications, for the Lockman Foundation, 1971. Print.

Northcote, J. Spencer. *Epitaphs of the Catacombs; Or, Christian Inscriptions in Rome during the First Four Centuries*. London: Longmans, Green, 1878. Print.

Peterson, Eugene H. *The Message*. Colorado Springs, CO: NavPress, 2004. Print.

Phillips, J.P. *The New Testament in Modern English*. Harper Collins, 1962. Print.

Plutarch, John Dryden, and Arthur Hugh Clough. *Plutarch's Lives / the Dryden Translation, Edited with Preface by Arthur Hugh Clough; Introduction by James Atlas*. New York: Modern Library, 2001. Print.

Polhill, John B. *The New American Commentary: ACTS*. Nashville, TN: Broadman, 1992. Print.

Pollock, John Charles. *The Apostle: A Life of Paul*. Wheaton, IL: Victor, 1985. Print.

"Pure History Specials _ Beasts of the Roman Games." *Dailymotion*. Web. 09 July 2014. <http://www.dailymotion.com/video/xsowwz_pure-history-specials-beasts-of-the-roman-games_shortfilms%3E>.

The Real Story: Gladiator. Smithsonian Channel. 2010. Television.

Renner, Rick. *Dressed to Kill: A Biblical Approach to Spiritual Warfare and Armor*. Tulsa, OK: Teach All Nations, 2007. Print.

Renner, Rick. *A Light in Darkness: Seven Messages to the Seven Churches*. Tulsa, OK: Teach All Nations, 2010. Print.

Renner, Rick. *Sparkling Gems from the Greek: 365 Greek Word Studies for Every Day of the Year to Sharpen Your Understanding of God's Word*. Tulsa, OK: Teach All Nations, 2003. Print.

Rodgers, Nigel, and Hazel Dodge. *Roman Empire*. New York: Metro, 2008. Print.

The Roman Colosseum. The History Channel. Television.

"The Roman Colosseum: THE REAL TRUTH." *Unsolved History*. The Discovery Channel. Television.

"Roman Empire & Colosseum." *Roman Colosseum*. Web. 15 Aug. 2014. <http://www.tribunesandtriumphs.org/>.

The Roman Empire Classics. National Geographic Channel. 2011. Television.

"The Seven Wonders of Ancient Rome." *The Seven Wonders of Ancient Rome*. Discovery. Television.

Sidebotham, Steve. "When Rome Ruled Egypt." *When Rome Ruled Egypt*. Discovery. 2008. Television.

Staccioli, Romolo Augusto. *Rome, Past and Present: With Reconstructions of Ancient Monuments*. Rome, Italy: Visions Publications, 1962. Print.

Stott, John R. W. *The Message of Acts: The Spirit, the Church & the World*. Leicester, England: Inter-Varsity, 1994. Print.

Swindoll, Charles R. *Paul: A Man of Grace and Grit*. Nashville: Thomas Nelson, 2009. Print.

When Rome Ruled. National Geographic Channel. 2011. Television.

Zodhiates, Spiros, and Warren Baker. *Hebrew-Greek Key Word Study Bible: Key Insights into God's Word: King James Version, Authorized Version*. Chattanooga, TN: AMG, 2008. Print.

Glossary of Words and Phrases

Liz's French Terms

À bientôt	See you soon
Allons-y!	Let's go!
Bien sûr!	Of course!
Bon	Good
Bonjour	Hello/Good day
Bonne nuit	Good night
Bonsoir	Good evening
C'est ça	That's it!
C'est extraordinaire	This is amazing
C'est incredible	It is incredible
C'est l'amour!	It is love
C'est magnifique	It is magnificient/incredible
C'est tragique	It is tragic
C'est vrai	It is true
Cher/chère	Dear
Déjà vu	This has happened before
Dieu est bon	God is good
Félicitations	Congratulations
Il est ici	He is here
Je comprends	I understand
Je ne comprends pas	I don't understand
Je vous en prie	You are welcome
L'amour	Love
Le Docteur	Doctor
Le Hibou	Owl
Merci	Thank you
Mes amis	My friends
Moi aussi	Me, too

Mon ami/amie	My friend (masc./fem.)
Monsieur	Mister
Oui	Yes
Quel dommage	What a pity
Petit déjeuner	Breakfast
Pour vous	For you
S'il vous plaît	Please
Toi aussi	You, too .

Latin

"Veni, vidi, vici"	I came, I saw, I conquered.

SCRIPTURE INDEX

NOTE FROM THE AUTHOR

I feel an explanation is in order regarding the amount of Scripture that was used in the writing of this novel. Scripture quotes have been woven into the fabric of all my Epic Order of the Seven® and earlier Max & Liz books. But because *The Fire, the Revelation, and the Fall* takes place during the formative years of the New Testament, perhaps readers will find Scripture quotations more noticeable or prominent than in previous books. Please be aware that I do quote Scripture verbatim when a character like Paul is dictating or writing, as I feel it should be verbatim. I've tried to make sure I didn't add to the text when the characters are actually writing their epistles. I do sometimes use many different translations to get the best wording for my reading audience. But this is a novel, and I have characters like Paul thinking and saying words they will later pen, which I believe is how it happened. I'm sure by the time Paul wrote down many things, he had already crystallized thoughts in his mind and in his teachings, part of the inspiration and "God breathed" process. With Scripture being so much a part of this story, I thought it best to provide the following index so readers can know what and where Scripture passages are being quoted.

SCRIPTURES REFERENCED IN
THE FIRE, THE REVELATION, AND THE FALL

Page	Verse	Translation
166	*Acts 23:18–24*	MSG
171	*Acts 23:26–30*	NLT
173-174	*Acts 24:1–22*	MSG
181	*Luke 5:8,10*	NLT
186	*Acts 19:9*	NIV
191	*Luke 19:42–44*	NIV
192	*Luke 21:20–24*	NLT
192-193, 197	*Luke 21:12–29*	NLT
201-203	*Acts 25:8–12*	NIV, MSG
205-208	*Acts 25:23–26:32*	MSG, NLT, GNT, NIV
220-221	*Romans excerpts*	NIV, PHILLIPS
221	*1 Corinthians 13:4–5*	NIV
227	*Acts 27:7–8*	NLT
232	*2 Corinthians 4:7–9*	NIV
234	*Acts 27:24*	NLT
235	*Acts 27:21–26*	PHILLIPS, NIV, NLT
236	*Psalm 107:27–28*	NIV
241	*Acts 27:33–34*	NLT
242	*Luke 23:32–47*	NIV
255	*Philippians 1:21*	NIV
256	*Luke 1:1–4*	NIV
258	*Acts 28:12–13*	PHILLIPS
280-281	*Acts 28:23–28*	NLT
286	*1 Corinthians 13:12*	PHILLIPS
296	*Colossians 1:15*	NLT
296	*2 Corinthians 5:17*	KJV
297-299	*Colossians excerpts*	PHILLIPS, NIV
301-302	*Philemon excerpts*	PHILLIPS
304	*Ephesians 6:24*	NIV
306	*Ephesians excerpts*	MSG

573

ABOUT THE AUTHOR...

Award winning author, speaker and producer Jenny L. Cote developed an early passion for God, history and young people, and beautifully blends these passions together in her two fantasy fiction series, *The Amazing Tales of Max and Liz*® and *Epic Order of the Seven*®. Likened to C. S. Lewis by book reviewers and bloggers, Jenny L. Cote opens up the world of creative writing for students of all ages and reading levels through fun, highly interactive workshops. Jenny has appeared to over thirty thousand students at lower, middle, and high schools and universities in the US and abroad. She is working on two more books covering Patrick Henry and the Revolutionary War, and C. S. Lewis and WWII. Jenny's passion for research has taken her to London (with unprecedented access to the Handel House Museum to write in Handel's composing room), Oxford (to stay in the home of C. S. Lewis, 'the Kilns,' and interview Lewis's secretary, Walter Hooper), Ireland, Paris, Normandy, Rome, Israel, and Egypt. Her books are available online and in stores around the world, as well as in multiple e-book formats (Kindle, Nook, etc.). Jenny holds two marketing degrees from the University of Georgia and Georgia State University. She lives in Roswell, Georgia, with her family. To schedule a talk, book signing, or interview please visit her website at www.epicorderoftheseven.com.

...AND HER BOOKS

The Amazing Tales of Max and Liz® is a two-book prequel series that begins the adventures of brave Scottie dog Max and brilliant French cat Liz through the stories of Noah's Ark and Joseph. Book One: *The Ark, the Reed, and the Fire Cloud* (2009 Readers' Favorite Gold Award for Children's Books) is in pre-production for an animated series and feature film adaptation, DVD school curriculum and VBS program development. Book Two: *The Dreamer, the Schemer, and the Robe* (2010 Readers' Favorite Gold Award for Children's Books) brings Max, Liz, and friends to work behind the scenes in the life of Joseph in the land of Egypt. The Epic Order of the Seven® series picks up where the Max and Liz series left off. Book One: *The Prophet, the Shepherd, and the Star* (2011 Readers' Favorite Gold Award for Christian Historical Fiction) gives Max, Liz, and the gang their most important mission yet: preparing for the birth of the promised Messiah. Their seven-hundred–year mission takes them to the lives of Isaiah, Daniel, and those in the Christmas story. Book Two: *The Roman, the Twelve, and the King* (2012 Readers' Favorite Five Star and Bronze Awards for Christian Historical Fiction) unfolds the childhood, ministry and passion of Jesus Christ with a twist— his story is told within the story of George F. Handel composing Messiah. Book Three: *The Wind, the Road, and the Way* (2014 Readers' Favorite Five Star and Silver Awards for Christian Historical Fiction) begins the two-book saga of the story of Acts, covering the events of Acts 1-18. Watch the miraculous rise of the Church through the fiery trials sent by an Enemy who will stop at nothing to kill anyone who dares to be called Christian.

Please visit:
www.epicorderoftheseven.com
and the **Jenny L. Cote Facebook Page**

ALSO BY JENNY L. COTE

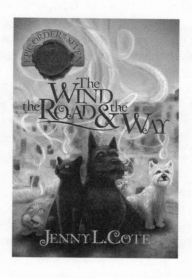

The Wind, the Road, and the Way
Book Three in the *Epic Order of the Seven*® series
Author: Jenny L. Cote
ISBN-13: 978-0899577937

The Wind will change their hearts. The Road will change his direction. The Way will change the world. And the Order of the Seven will change the future for believers while the Enemy seeks their crushing defeat. The events of Acts 1-18 come to life as God's faithful animal team faces a dark, pagan world riddled with false gods, arrange, crucial introductions, assist, with jail-breaks, and plan, risky escapes while overseeing the writing of a New Testament that will inspire and guide believers for centuries to come.

This heart-gripping, action-packed adventure begins a two-book saga that brings to life the events of Acts and the birth of Christianity while showing how each book of the New Testament came to be. *The Fire, the Revelation and the Fall (2015)* completes the events in Acts, with Peter and Paul in Rome, Roman Christian persecution in the arena, and John's Revelation on Patmos. Watch the miraculous rise of the Church through the fiery trials sent by an Enemy who will stop at nothing to kill anyone who dares to be called Christian.

When you buy a book from **AMG Publishers**, **Living Ink Books**, or **God and Country Press**, you are helping to make disciples of Jesus Christ around the world.

How? AMG Publishers and its imprints are ministries of **AMG (*Advancing the Ministries of the Gospel*) International**, a non-denominational evangelical Christian mission organization ministering in over 30 countries around the world. Profits from the sale of AMG Publishers books are poured into the outreaches of AMG International.

AMG International Mission Statement

AMG exists to advance with compassion the command of Christ to evangelize and make disciples around the world through national workers and in partnership with like-minded Christians.

AMG International Vision Statement

We envision a day when everyone on earth will have at least one opportunity to hear and respond to a clear presentation of the Gospel of Jesus Christ and have the opportunity to grow as a disciple of Christ.

To learn more about AMG International and how you can pray for or financially support this ministry, please visit
www.amgmissions.org